All t
Shadowed
Places

By

Marion Shepherd

MAPLE
PUBLISHERS

All the Shadowed Places

Author: Marion Shepherd

Copyright © Marion Shepherd (2021)

The right of Marion Shepherd to be identified as author of this work has been asserted by the author in accordance with section 77 and 78 of the Copyright, Designs and Patents Act 1988.

First Published in 2021

ISBN 978-1-914366-58-1 (Paperback)
   978-1-914366-59-8 (Ebook)

Book cover design and Book layout by:
   White Magic Studios
   www.whitemagicstudios.co.uk

Published by:
   Maple Publishers
   1 Brunel Way,
   Slough,
   SL1 1FQ, UK
   www.maplepublishers.com

A CIP catalogue record for this title is available from the British Library.

For Gail Kainey and Jenny Busby and all those who believed in me, thank you.

CONTENTS

Chapter 1

Eleven-year-old Horacio Woodley ran through the orchard: his heart soared with the joy of being out in the fresh air, revelling in the spring sunshine.

'Hero, Hero, stop,' his sister, Angelica, called as she chased her brother.

'You have to run faster, Angelica,' he called back to her, laughter in his voice as he picked up his pace. 'Like always, I'm going to beat you,' he mocked good-naturedly.

An expression of determination settled over his sister's pink cheeks. Plucking up her skirts and froth of white petticoats higher, Angelica picked up her pace. Hair ribbons coming lose, trailing like banners in her wake as her glossy auburn curls bounced in their freedom. Her feet, encased in high buttoned boots, flew over the rich green grass.

She laughed with as much joy as her brother. Two years younger than, Horacio and shorter by a few inches, Angelica knew she had very little hope of catching him, but that did not stop her from trying.

It was a beautiful Sunday afternoon: quite warm for the beginning of May. The blossom was out in all its glory. White and pink clouds, drawing droning bumblebees.

The children had attended church that morning with their mama and papa. Then they had gone to the vicarage for Sunday school; once these duties had been fulfilled and a hearty luncheon had been eaten, they had been permitted to have some free time before teatime.

The children's destination was the massive oak that flanked the edge of the apple orchard.

Hero reached the tree and sucked in the spring scented air in gulps.

Catching his breath, he turned around just as his sister caught up with him. Hands on hips, face rosy with exertion, Angelica gave her older brother an indignant look. 'You are supposed to be gentlemanly and let the lady win.'

'You know I always like to win, Angel.' He grinned. His hazel eyes flashed with triumph.

Angelica stamped her foot. 'It simply isn't fair; you are better at *everything*.'

'Ha, that's not true, I can't sew for toffee.'

They both laughed then.

'Yes, well, that isn't fair either. I really don't know why I have to be stuck indoors doing needlework, while you are out and about whenever you wish.'

'Well, we have the whole afternoon to run amuck.' Hero gave her a wide grin.

Angelica returned his smile. Then her gaze turned to the boughs of the huge old tree. It was a massive oak that had rested in this spot for hundreds of years, way before the Woodley's owned the land. The upper boughs stretched up into the periwinkle blue sky.

'I will wager you a bag of sweets that I can climb higher than you,' Angelica challenged.

Hero followed her glance. 'A bag of sweets? That's not much of a wager,' he speculated.

Her eyes, so much like her brother's, flashed with determination. Knowing how much her brother enjoyed his desserts and puddings, and didn't put on an ounce of weight, and that wasn't fair either! She upped the stakes. 'And I will give you all my desserts for a week,' she declared.

'And if you win?' he asked with interest.

'Well, I will have the satisfaction of beating you.' She smiled.

'You are on. I accept your wager, sister.'

They grinned at each other in mutual delight.

Hero glanced up at the tree. 'There is one problem I foresee, however. How are you going to make it to the first branch?'

Angelica followed his look. 'Mm, well I might need you to give me a leg up.' A frown creased her forehead.

'Ha, you see, beaten already.'

She shot him a furious look, then looked around for something to aid her. There was nothing she could stand on, and the first branch was at least two feet above her, further than her arms could reach anyway.

Refusing to give in, she walked around the oak and saw what she was looking for: some knots in the trunk she could use as hand and footholds.

With determination, she picked up the skirt of her cotton sprigged dress, including her lacey petticoat.

'Angel, what are you doing?' Her brother peeked around the trunk.

'Eyes closed, Hero,' she demanded.

He stepped away, closing his eyes obediently.

Angelica gathered the skirt of the dress up and tied it in a knot. She was sure that Claire, their governess, would not be pleased with her for creasing her dress so badly, she sighed.

Standing on a protruding root, she lifted her leg, then with the toe of her boot, found a foothold, reaching up, she gripped the next knot in the old trunk.

'If you tell anyone about this, I won't talk to you ever again,' she called as she climbed up to reach the lowest branch.

Hero opened his eyes and saw what his sister was doing. Despite himself, he was impressed.

'Ah, well done, Angel.'

Angelica paused to grin down at him. 'Well, what are you waiting for? Are you joining me or not?' she challenged.

'Yes, yes.'

Two years older than his baby sister, whom he adored, Hero was tall for his age. It only took him a couple of minutes to reach the branch that Angelica had perched on a moment before.

Finally, reaching a broad branch which made a comfortable resting place. Angelica paused in her exertions. Booted feet and legs clad in blue stockings swung in the air as she waited for her brother to catch up with her.

She could see the sunlight shining on his chestnut hair, which was thick and curly like her own.

Hero grunted with exertion as he reached for the next branch, propelling himself upwards.

'So, what do you think?' she asked him as he settled next to her. 'I won.'

Hero gazed upwards taking in the boughs above them. 'Oh, I think there is a way to go yet.'

'That's not fair. I got here first.' She looked mutinous.

'You did, sister, but I can go even higher.'

Before she knew it, he got to his feet, balanced precariously on the bough she was sitting on, then reached up for the next branch.

I'm not having this, Angelica thought with determination, so she followed suit.

The leaves rustled. The branches creaked and groaned as the two of them raced higher. They were like monkeys, swinging from branch to branch.

Gazing upwards, Angelica could see Hero about a foot above her. She let out a puff of air as the loosened bits of leaves and bark, that he was dislodging in his efforts, rained down on her.

Oh, why couldn't I wear britches, they gave Hero a distinct advantage.

Hero, realising that the branches were getting thinner and more brittle now, stopped and looked down.

'I think I've won,' he called with a note of satisfaction in his voice.

Angelica disentangled her hair from a protruding twig, then with further determination, grabbed the next branch and pulled herself up.

'Angel, stop now.' Hero felt a squirm of unease wriggle in his tummy as the branch she had just clasped snapped.

'It's just not fair.' She grunted with effort, reaching for another handhold.

It was at that moment that disaster struck. The branch that she had been standing on groaned, then with a loud crack that sounded like a rifle shot, fell away, leaving the child swinging by her arms.

There was a cacophony as the branch dropped, dislodging smaller branches and leaves as it went.

'Angel, don't move. I'm coming,' Hero shouted, his heart racing with foreboding.

With the agility of one so young, he manoeuvred himself towards his sister.

'Hero, I can't hold on!' fear rippled through her voice.

He moved faster, heart thudding, mouth dry and palms so slippery with sweat they hampered his descent.

He had almost reached her when there was another loud crack, his sister fell. With an awful thud, the sound of which would stay with him for years to come, her young body hit the ground.

The boy crouched, paralysed in the high boughs. Through the leaves, he could see her still figure below: She looked like a broken doll, her arms and legs akimbo - they seemed to be set at such strange angles.

Even from this height, he could see that her eyes were open as if gazing at the sky. There was a trickle of blood steadily flowing from one of her delicate nostrils.

Carried on the gentle spring breeze; white and pink blossoms danced around her.

Chapter 2

Claire Fellows paced the floor of the nursery sitting room impatiently.

Alice, the nursery maid, had set out the tea things on the table by the window, but there was no sign of the children. Claire checked the watch she had pinned to the bodice of her dove-grey dress for the third time. It was unusual for the children to be back late; their tea had been laid out for twenty minutes. Usually, grumbling tummies brought them back in good time.

Walking over to one of the long windows which was barred to half its height, she could see that the bright day was beginning to cloud over. Claire found herself shivering as a fleeting feeling of apprehension touched the nape of her neck. Letting out a breath, she took a few moments to take in the view which was of the walled kitchen gardens and part of the rose gardens.

Since coming to Woodley Hall, Claire had surprised herself when she found she had an extraordinary interest in plants and herbs. She spent as much of her spare time with Jacobs, the groundsman, whenever she could.

Thinking of Mr Jacobs, Claire smiled to herself: he was such a nice man who seemed to have endless patience, as she bombarded him with questions about this plant or that herb. She had been down in that garden this very afternoon, enjoying her spare time while the children were out exploring.

Claire's place in the household was unique: she was governess to Horacio and Angelica, but she was also Emily Woodley's cousin. She and Emily had been close as children. They had kept in contact when they had both married and gone their separate ways.

Sadly, Claire's husband, Joseph Fellows, had died of pneumonia seven years ago: a terrible blow to Claire made worse by the fact that his demise had rendered her homeless.

They had lived above the shop where Joseph had set himself up in a thriving business as a tailor. The business had been successful, so much so that when the shop next door had become vacant, Joseph had bought it. He had spent most of their savings on the project as well as taking out a mortgage to cover the rest of the costs. This being the case when he had died, the event had left Claire with debts she could not repay: she had to sell the business and pay off the debtors, leaving her with very little money and no home.

Upon hearing of the sad news of Joseph's death and her cousin's predicament, Emily had insisted that Claire come to stay at Woodley Hall. She had been welcomed into the family.

Claire found that being with the children helped to heal her grief. She built up an excellent rapport with Hero and Angelica.

Claire was a learned woman, so, when the children got to the age where a governess was required, she suggested to Emily and James that she would like to be considered for the role, even though it was understood that Horacio would be going off to school when he was twelve, but Angelica would still require a governess or perhaps a tutor.

Claire felt it was her way of repaying Emily and James for all their kindness and generosity. They all agreed it was a splendid idea. The children loved her and were delighted with the arrangement too.

There had been objections on Claire's part; when Emily insisted, she was paid for the job she was doing.

'Really, my dear, you have done more than enough for me. I am happy to take up this position pro bono, it would be a delight for me,' Claire had said.

'Well, I have discussed it with James, we are going to give you an allowance, Claire. If you refuse our offering, we shall be most upset indeed.'

In the end, they had come to a satisfactory arrangement.

The children continued to call her Cousin Claire; the staff referred to her as Miss Fellows, a sufficient title for a governess.

Claire had made Woodley Hall her home and had adopted the family as her own.

*

Woodley Hall was a grand house that stood majestically in rolling parkland. It had been a much smaller Elizabethan house called Midcote Hall until it was purchased by Thomas Woodley, great, great grandfather to James.

Thomas, a successful wool merchant, and importer of goods to and from the Netherlands, decided he had had enough of London, the ever-growing city. It reeked with effluence from a sewer system that was grossly inadequate to cope with the rising population. Not to mention the thick fog, which was becoming known as a peasouper, which choked the city and clogged the lungs. He decided that the environment was not conducive to good health for himself or his family.

Thomas was a believer in hard work: he was not a man to sit in an office behind a desk, so was often away travelling across England or abroad. He liked to source his goods face to face, to see and feel the quality of the items he was buying. So, Thomas spent time in Amsterdam, at other times, he travelled the rolling hills, all over the midlands of England, buying wool that was woven at his factory near Gloucester.

As he went about his business, he was also keeping his eyes open for an opportunity. It was during one of these trips that he heard that Midcote Hall and the surrounding land was up for sale.

The estate was nestled in beautiful countryside, on the edge of the Cotswolds. The property encompassed the village of Midcote, which was just over the Oxfordshire border into Gloucestershire.

He went along to the auction and was successful with the bidding; he was delighted with his purchase, even though there was an abundance of wood panelling and small leaded windows, which made the place rather dark, Thomas soon had that in hand, having architects drawing up plans to remodel and extend the house, along with the stables, a model farm and dairy and a mill for grinding homegrown corn. This was a time when successful businessmen liked to show off their wealth. The new house was designed around Doric pillars, frescoes and friezes, mouldings, and neoclassical statues.

It was incredibly ostentatious, but by luck rather than judgement, the house was turned into a lofty and airy family home.

Thomas embraced country life, as did his family. The stables were extensive, and he bred hounds.

The model farm was the talk of all London. Woodley Hall attracted many visitors, ladies in silk embroidered dresses with powdered hair and wide panniers. The men were equally as foppish and flamboyant. Admittedly, the visitors did not see the hard work of farm life, but only the rosy-faced milking maids and shepherdesses with crooks, herding pristinely white fluffy sheep, decked in ribbons through white painted gates, between banks of colourful flowers.

When Thomas became bored with the fickle interest in the model farm, he put his energy into making the estate a successful enterprise. He bought up more land and started growing crops on a rotation basis. He planted apple and pear orchards and made cider and perry. The dairy produced, as well as milk, thick yellow creamy butter and cheeses that were sent in water-cooled containers, via carriage to London.

Thomas was an excellent businessman, where other estates struggled, his own thrived. He paid fair wages, the villagers and local community respected him. Their loyalty to the Woodley family was passed down the generations.

James Woodley, the current squire, was well-liked and respected by all that knew him. Anyone meeting him would describe James as "down to earth", a steady, reliable sort, who inspired confidence in others.

It had taken everyone by surprise when he did not marry. As the years went on, the villagers had concluded that James would remain a bachelor, which was a sad state of affairs: who would there be to inherit the estate? Would this be the end of the Woodley line?

Everyone breathed a sigh of relief when James started courting Emily Armitage, the daughter of one of the landowners on a neighbouring estate.

*

Checking her watch once again, Claire puffed out her cheeks in annoyance, where were Horacio and Angelica? Oh, this really was not good enough.

She strode over to the bell pull, but hesitated, deciding it would be best to go downstairs and find Mr Jacobs. Then she would get him to gather Charlie and Bryant to have them look for the children.

Pausing by the mirror on the wall, she tucked in the stray curls that had escaped the chignon she wore. Then straightened the cream lace collar of her dove grey dress. Her cheeks still looked rosy from being out in the fresh air.

Satisfied with her appearance, she then set off downstairs.

The nursery maid, Alice Fletcher, was seated at the large table enjoying a quick cup of tea while she read a penny dreadful. She closed the periodical when Claire appeared and jumped to her feet.

'Still no sign of them then, Miss Fellows?' Alice asked.

Claire shook her head. 'No, it is most unusual.'

'Aww, I'm sure they won't be far away.' The maid smiled. A short girl with rounded features; her hair was as red as an autumn leaf. She had a plethora of freckles over her nose and cheeks. Alice was twenty but looked no more than fifteen.

'Alice, go and find Mr Jacobs or Mr Bryant, please. Have him send the men to go and look for the children.'

'Yes, Miss. Right you are.' Alice bobbed and left the flag-stoned kitchen.

*

Hero found he could not move; part of him knew he should get down from the tree and run for help, but he just could not do it. He clenched the branch beneath him with hands as white as his face. He couldn't even blink. Despite the warmth of the spring afternoon, icy cold shivers rippled through his body. There was no feeling of time passing; he could have been up in that tree mere minutes or hours.

A voice reached him, someone calling; 'Master Hero, Miss Angelica...' Hero recognised the voice of Bryant, the head groom.

'Here –' he tried to call out, but his throat was dry and thick with choked back tears. 'Here,' Hero called again.

On a neck that was stiff with shock and fear, Hero turned his head and looked across the orchards, spotting the man striding towards him.

Bryant must have noticed the body at the foot of the tree; Hero heard him give a strangled oath as he ran over.

'Oh Lord, oh Lord.' Bryant knelt beside the still figure. Hero watched him checking for a flicker of life, but then quickly assess it was too late. Bryant must have heard a noise from the canopy above him, as he glanced up.

'Master Hero,' he called.

'Here,' came the soft reply.

'What happened, boy?' The man's throat was rough with emotion as he stood up.

Hero shook his head, 'I can't, I can't...', he chanted over and over.

Fearing another accident, Bryant called up to the boy. 'Don't move. I'm going to get help.' Quickly, he shrugged off his jacket and gently covered the young girl's body; then he went running back in the direction of the house. The boy shuffled along the branch closer to the trunk. He wrapped his arms around it, trying desperately to hold on to something substantial. His cheek rested against the warm bark. The tears came then, and his body shuddered with great sobs.

It wasn't long before the group of men appeared.

Through eyes fogged with tears, such was his sense of unreality; Hero watched them approach as if he were in some sort of strange trance; his mind was shutting down, protecting him from the impact of the disaster.

Bryant was accompanied by Charlie, the stable boy (who was also Bryant's nephew), the groundskeeper, Jacobs. Along with Hero's father, James; his two dogs Myrtle and Henry close on his heels.

Even from a distance, Hero could see that his father's expression was grim, his pallor was chalk white. He was a strong, broad, and solid figure in Hero's life, but at that moment, his shoulders were hunched. He walked stiffly like an old man.

Hero longed to descend the tree and run into his father's arms, but he still couldn't move.

'No, no, no.' He heard his father cry out. Rushing over to Angelica's body. James fell to his knees beside her. Carefully he pulled Bryant's jacket away, then with gentle hands, he picked up his precious daughter and held her limp body to his chest.

Chapter 3

Kneeling upon the grass, within the shelter of the boughs of the tree, James Woodley felt his heart splinter: jagged edges sliced through his body. Tears flowed in rivulets down his cheeks as he held Angel close.

'Father,' Hero called to him beseechingly.

James could not look at his son at that moment; instead, he turned to, Bryant, the groom, a long and trusted employee.

'What should I do?' James asked, his voice hollow and bleak.

Bryant put a large hand on the Squire's shoulder in comfort, 'Take her back to the house, Sir.'

In a daze, James nodded. Keeping the body close, he rose to his feet and stumbled back through the orchard towards the house. The subdued dogs were walking behind him.

'I'll go with him,' Seth Jacobs spoke up for the first time.

'Aye, good idea.' Bryant nodded. 'Charlie,' Bryant took charge, 'go and fetch a ladder and we'll get the boy down.'

Charlie nodded and raced off in the direction of the stable yard. It wasn't long before he arrived back with a ladder. Carefully, Bryant leant it against the tree trunk and climbed to where the boy was still perched.

'Come now, Master Horacio,' he coaxed, 'we need to get you down and back to the house.'

'I can't' Hero shook his head vigorously; he was suddenly afraid of what his father might say or do to him. He tightened his hold on the trunk in desperation.

With resignation, Bryant climbed the ladder. Once he had reached the topmost rung, which still didn't quite reach the boy, the groom gave him a sympathetic look. 'What happened, lad?' he asked gently.

'We were racing to see who could climb the highest – I told her not to go any further.' Hero hiccupped with emotion. 'It was an accident,' his words were mumbled through pale lips.

'Aye, I'm sure it was.' The man nodded, kindness and sympathy shone in his dark brown eyes.

That look was too much for Hero. A cold inner voice told him that he did not deserve sympathy; *wasn't all this his fault?*

Letting go of the trunk, he would have fallen if the man hadn't reached out and caught his arm to steady him.

Bryant was a stocky man, with broad shoulders. He had worked with horses all his life; the work was hard. It kept him fit. Despite all that, Bryant did not relish the thought of having to carry the boy down the ladder.

'Right, enough now, down you come,' he said curtly.

Responding to the authority in the man's voice, Hero swung down and set his feet on one of the uppermost rungs of the ladder.

Bryant nodded and started his descent, the boy following.

Hero raised no protest as Bryant set him on his feet at the foot of the tree. 'Come now, lad, let's get you back to the house.'

'I c-c-can't.' The boy shook his head.

The groom placed a hand on his shoulder, then looking him in the eye said, 'whatever the outcome, master Hero, you have to face it like the man your parents want you to be. One that faces adversity, not shy's away from it.'

Hero wiped his tear-stained face with the back of his hand. A nod of the head rewarded the groom.

'Very well.' Hero did his best to straighten his shoulders and get his emotions under control.

'Charlie, leave the ladder, run and fetch Dr Scott.' Bryant instructed the stable lad, who was hovering close by.

'Yes, Mr Bryant.' Charlie nodded and rushed off.

Making their way back to the house, the weight of the world seemed to rest upon the shoulders of man and boy.

What a tragedy this was, Bryant thought. He could not believe what had happened. These two children of the Squire were well-liked, indeed, regarded with fondness by all. This catastrophe would break the master and mistress; they doted on their children.

*

When James walked through the front door of Woodley Hall, Mrs Mason, the housekeeper was leaving the drawing-room where she had set out a tray of tea things for the mistress. Spotting her master with the limp body of his child in his arms, she halted in shock.

The housekeeper knew, of course, that the children were late back for tea. Miss Fellows, the governess, had asked Bryant to go and find them.

Mrs Mason could not take in the scene as the master entered: she only needed to give the child in his arms a glance to see that Angelica was dead – *the sweet child was dead!*

'Oh, my Lord, no.' Her knees almost buckled; she had to lean against the hall table for support.

Mrs Woodley must have heard the woman's exclamation. The drawing-room door opened. Emily stepped into the hall.

'Mrs Mason?' Emily looked to the housekeeper; then her gaze turned to James, who stood as still as a statue just inside the front door. His dark shadow stretched across the tiled floor.

The shock had drained all the colour from his face. His features looked as if they had been chiselled from marble, set in a horrified expression.

'James?' Uncertainly, Emily stepped towards him. Her hand fluttered at her throat as she took in the awful scene – one that would stay with her for years. 'Angelica - Angel...' her steps were hesitant. She wanted, just for a moment, to delay facing this horror she had been presented with.

'I am sorry, my love,' James uttered hollowly.

'No, no.' Emily's eyes flooded with tears; she rushed the last few steps as James fell to his knees onto the cold tiles. Emily knelt beside him. She was sobbing terrible wracking sobs as she took her daughter's pretty face in her gentle hands.

*

When the house came in into view, to Hero it already looked as if there were a shroud of despair hanging over the place: great weighty clouds had gathered threatening rain.

The two dogs were seated at the bottom of the sweep of steps leading up to the elegant front door. Myrtle, a liver and white springer, was whining piteously. Henry, the chocolate brown Labrador, lay with his head on his large paws, a look of puzzlement on his gentle face.

Upon seeing Hero, Henry lifted his head and wagged his tail dubiously.

Hero didn't even see the dogs as he reached the bottom of the steps, his eyes were so misted with misery.

Halting, he looked to the man beside him. He gave the groom a heartbroken look and shook his head.

'I can't, Mr Bryant.' The boy shuddered.

'There now, Master Hero.' The man did his best to soothe him. 'you have to be strong now, there's no hiding from it, the consequences best be faced.'

Hero nodded, together they climbed the steps to the front door which stood wide.

The boy paused on the threshold, the hall was shadowed after the brightness of daylight, but he could make out the figure of his father kneeling on the floor. He could hear his mother weeping.

Looking utterly lost Mrs Mason stood in the middle of the floor, dabbing at her eyes with a handkerchief.

Hero took a step back, reluctant to face what was before him, but Bryant laid a hand on his shoulder and squeezed it gently.

'Come now, lad,' he urged.

The housekeeper spotted them both and rushed over. 'Oh, Mr Bryant, what happened?' She shot a concerned look at the boy, 'What happened, Master Hero, are you hurt?'

'A terrible accident,' Bryant started to explain, 'a fall from a tree.' His words caught Emily's attention. She turned to them both, then with an effort, she got to her feet. She turned her anguished face to her son.

'A fall from a tree?'

'Y-yes, mama.' Hero's gaze dropped to the tiled floor, it was weighted by mortification and guilt.

'You had your sister climbing trees?' her voice was brittle.

Hearing the tone of her voice, Hero shot her a frightened look.

'We were racing,' he found himself trying to explain. 'T-t-then we had a bet as to who could get highest in the tree...' his voice trailed off.

Emily's eyes were huge in her face – shock and horror rippled through her expression.

'How could you,' she hissed at him. The venom in her voice had Hero stepping backwards away from her. 'It's your fault,' his mother's voice was sharp with shock and anger. The boy felt every blow of each word. 'This is all your fault; you've killed your sister.'

'No, mama – no.' Instinctively, he turned back to the robust figure of Bryant to look for comfort.

'It was an accident, your ladyship,' the groom spoke up.

Emily ignored the older man. 'How often have we told you to take care of your sister – how often?' her voice was becoming more and more hysterical now.

Concern for her mistress broke through Mrs Mason's troubled mind. She rushed forward. 'Your ladyship,' she called out.

'STOP,' James' voice echoed about the hall. It was filled with such anguish.

All eyes turned to the Squire as he started to rise to his feet, but it was as if all his strength had left him, he swayed. Suddenly, the terrible pain of heartbreak intensified. It ripped through his chest. He was unsure if he called out or not, but before James knew what was happening, he slumped over.

Even when experiencing intense pain, he kept the body of Angelica close to his chest. The pain increased red hot blades of agony tore through him. His chest tightened as if he had a ton weight compressing it. James found it hard to draw breath. As the pain shot down his arms, he toppled over; his head hit the tiled floor with an awful sound. His body convulsed into a foetal position around that of his daughter's, the world about him faded into darkness.

'Papa, papa.' Hero dashed forward and fell to his knees beside his father and sister – *this couldn't be happening*. It was all too much for the boy; he gave way to great sobs that wracked his body.

*

Dr Scott, the family physician, arrived a few moments after James collapsed.

Walking into the hall, the doctor quickly took in the scene before him. Charlie had told him there had been a terrible accident involving Horacio and Angelica. Still, what on earth was going on here?

Lady Woodley spotted him in the doorway. 'Doctor, it's James, please help him,' she cried, her face as white as a ghost.

He rushed over to James as Bryant carefully lifted Angelica's body out of the way.

Hero, his eyes full of tears, moved away as he watched the doctor's administrations.

It did not take him long to confirm that James was dead. The doctor gave Emily a tragic look as he got to his feet, shaking his head sorrowfully.

Mrs Mason, seeing Emily sway on her feet, rushed forward. She put her arms around her.

'I am sorry, your ladyship, it must have been his heart,' the physician said softly.

'Aww, no,' the housekeeper cried as she did her best to support her mistress who was slumped against her.

All too familiar with the tragedy of death, Dr Scott quickly rallied. 'Mrs Mason, call Miss Fellows and one of the maids to take care of the boy, then take your mistress to her room, I shall be up shortly.'

Grateful to the doctor for taking charge, the housekeeper nodded and guided Emily towards the stairs. Emily did not put up any protest; the severe shock clouded her mind and had rendered her speechless.

Chapter 4

Mrs Mason and Claire put Emily to bed. They were both concerned about her: she was so quiet, complying with their ministrations as if she were a small child. It appeared as if she had shut down completely.

'I will sit with her,' Claire said once Emily was settled under the covers, 'Alice will sit with Horacio,' she concluded.

'Yes, Miss Fellows,' the housekeeper nodded. She glanced at her mistress with an expression full of concern, then left the room.

Claire had been torn, should she stay with Hero, or should she see to her cousin? They both needed her.

As she sat on a chair beside Emily's bed, she felt the impact of the shock of the two deaths suddenly hit her. Closing her eyes, she bowed her head. *How could it happen? How could fate be so unkind?* Shaking herself free of the awful thoughts, Claire knew she dare not examine what had transpired too closely; the awful tragedy would consume her. She had to keep strong for Emily and Hero.

As she had mentioned to Mrs Mason, she had instructed Alice, the nursery maid, to watch over Hero. Alice was a sensible girl, but like everyone else, she was reeling from the impact of what had happened. However, Claire reminded herself that Alice knew her job, the governess felt confident with the trust she had laid at the girl's feet.

She had been so preoccupied with her thoughts that a knock on the door made Claire jump.

'Come in,' she called.

Mrs Mason opened the door, 'It's the doctor, Miss Fellows.' She stood aside to let the man in.

'Thank you, Mrs Mason.' Dr Scott nodded to the woman.

The housekeeper inclined her head in acknowledgement and left.

'How has she been?' The doctor eyed his patient while he asked the question, then paused by the bed. Emily did not move, she lay as if in a trance, staring at the canopy above the bed.

Claire, getting to her feet, shook her head. 'She hasn't said a word, doctor.'

Putting his bag aside, he sat down on the chair that the governess had just vacated. Reaching over, he took Emily's hand in his own. Her skin felt icy to the touch.

'Get one of the maids to make up a fire in here, please,' he ordered as he scrutinised Emily's face carefully.

'Yes, of course, I should have thought.' Claire rushed over to the bell pull.

The doctor glanced at her. 'It is perfectly alright, Miss Fellows, you must be reeling from the shock too.'

'Yes, doctor.' She nodded; a tear dewed on her bottom eyelid.

Turning his attention back to his patient, he said, 'Mrs Woodley, Emily, can you hear me?'

Not even a flicker disturbed her features. Her gentle eyes were large orbs. Her face was almost as white as the lace pillow her head rested on.

The doctor took her pulse, *a little fast*. Getting up, he picked up his leather bag, which he had placed beside the chair and opened it. Taking out a phial of laudanum, he measured five drops into the glass of water beside the bed.

'As I am sure you have already surmised, she is in shock,' he explained to Claire. 'We shall let her sleep for now. A healing sleep,' he concluded as he gently lifted Emily's head and dripped the liquid between her lips. He was pleased when he saw that she swallowed it down.

He left the phial on the bedside table. 'The laudanum will help her sleep for a good few hours. You may give her more if needed. I will be back tomorrow morning to check on her,' he said as he closed his bag. 'I will attend the boy now.'

Claire nodded, then placed her hand on the doctor's arm. 'The bodies?' she asked quietly.

'I had Bryant and Seth lay them out in one of the guest bedrooms. And I have asked Charlie to fetch Mrs Bodkin; she will wash and lay out the bodies and sit with them.'

'Yes, of course.' Claire knew Mrs Bodkin, but had never needed her services: She was the midwife in the village. She also helped to lay out the dead, preparing them for burial after she had done this, she would sit with them overnight, keeping a vigil.

The doctor's eyes were kind when he gave her a sympathetic look. 'Mrs Woodley is lucky to have you here.' Claire nodded dubiously. He patted her hand consolingly. 'You need to let the family solicitor know what has happened. Then have a meeting with Mr Hawkins from Home Farm, he will be able to help with the running of the estate. And Mrs Mason will help you; she's a good woman.'

'Thank you, doctor.' Claire nodded.

When Dr Scott closed the bedroom door, Claire walked back over to the bed and resumed her seat. Emily's eyes were closed now; Claire felt as if her cousin looked *too* still. Reaching out a hand, she clasped the one resting on the coverlet.

'I am here for you, my dear,' she whispered as a fat tear rolled down her cheek. Bowing her head as if in prayer, Claire's mind tried to make sense of the happenings of the day.

Oh Lord, it was too much. Claire shook her head to try and shake off some of her own shock. She knew what loss felt like after losing her beloved Joseph. Claire recognised the same depth of love that James and Emily had shared, a love that was felt so deeply. And, when Claire had been so desperate, they had opened their home, their arms to her: If it hadn't been for the kindness of Emily and James, Claire did not know where she would have ended up.

They were special people, how could fate be so cruel, inflicting this double blow?

*

Emily was aware of movement. People around the bed, hushed voices tinged with worry. But she remained immobile, not wishing to move at all. She did not want to think about what had transpired; if she did not acknowledge what had happened, it would all go away, wouldn't it?

Surely this was a nightmare; she would awaken in a moment feeling foolish.

When the doctor had lifted her head gently and administered the draught, she accepted it without protest, then closed her eyes.

Emily found her mind wandering. To distract herself from the abysmal thoughts of what had happened, she reminisced, going over how she and James Woodley had met.

To ensure that he was kept acquainted with local business affairs, James felt that it was his duty to accept social invites from the other landowners thereabouts. So, when one of his neighbours sent him an invitation to a ball, they were hosting for their two daughters, Emily and Celia Armitage, James had, all be it reluctantly, accepted the invitation. He found, as these things tended to be, that it was a frivolous affair.

Because James was a very eligible bachelor, he was hounded by the bejewelled matrons who desperately wanted *their* daughter to be the one to catch his eye. They flocked about him like beautiful birds of paradise, or prey, whichever way one wanted to look at it.

James was not a man for finery, nor for flaunting one's wealth and privilege. He always found these occasions to be quite torturous; the attentions of the woman cloying.

Before he had even arrived, James had already decided that he would stay only as long as politeness demanded. Then would make his way home to Woodley

Hall and his dogs, Myrtle, a springer-spaniel, and Henry, who was a boisterous Labrador pup.

As he stood awkwardly in the middle of a circle of chattering young ladies, James was unaware that young Emily Armitage was watching him from across the room.

Emily knew who he was, of course, but had never been introduced to him. She had "come out" with her sister Celia the year before, so had never attended the local social events beforehand. The ball, an occasion in which the two young ladies would be paraded under the noses of eligible men. James Woodley being one of the very top names on the list, in the hopes they would be picked as a future bride.

Just like James, Emily hated the frivolity and the attention. When one was put in the position of trying to find a husband (or a wife), it was rather like being a prize exhibit at a horse fair. Emily would not have been at all surprised to find herself being lined up along with the other young women, who were in a similar situation, while the eligible men and their matronly mothers poked and prodded them all. Even going so far as to check their teeth.

Emily knew she had far less chance of finding a suitable husband than her sister: Celia had inherited the beauty in the family. Emily was, she felt in comparison to her sister, rather plain. And as Celia pointed out frequently, "quite bookish".

'You will never find a husband with your nose in a book all the time, Emily,' she had pointed out loftily.

'Maybe I don't want to find one,' Emily had retorted back, which received a very un-ladylike snort from her sister.

'You had better not say such things in mama's earshot,' Celia said, 'she would not be pleased, she would not be pleased at all.'

Emily knew that her sister was correct in her assumption. So, she had no other choice but to accompany the family when they were invited to balls and county social gatherings.

Regarding her marriageable prospects, there was one thing in her favour; their father had settled an extremely generous dowry on both his daughters.

Watching James Woodley as he stood there awkwardly amongst the flounces of lace and frills that surrounded him, Emily could see that he was becoming more uncomfortable by the moment. His face, though tanned, was flushed with the heat. He kept pulling at the silk cravat at his throat. Even from a distance, Emily could tell that his jacket was well cut over his broad shoulders. Still, he looked oddly uncomfortable in these well-cut clothes. He is a man who is used to working out of doors, she thought.

Elizabeth Hartford said something to him; he smiled politely and nodded. However, his eyes had a curious glassy look about them.

Before she knew what she was doing, Emily jumped to her feet and made her way towards the group.

An orchestra had been playing in the other room, and there was a pause until they struck up the next dance. Emily made the most of this interlude; she deftly swept through a gap in the ladies around James. Then she surprised everyone when she took his large hand in her small gloved one and slipped her arm through his.

'Mr Woodley,' she said, 'I believe we have the next dance.'

'Mmm, well, I ....' He looked down at her with a puzzled expression.

'I hope you are not going to disappoint me,' Emily piped up, giving him an expectant smile.

'Of course not, Miss Armitage.' He nodded to the group, a thin smile on his lips. 'Ladies,' he excused himself.

'Well, how rude.' Emily heard Elizabeth say as they walked away.

Emily manoeuvred him out of earshot, quickly changed direction and they both found themselves in the large conservatory overlooking the grand sweep of lawns at the rear of the house.

'I thought you wished to dance, Miss Armitage?' James looked around in bewilderment.

She looked up at him and gave him a mischievous smile. 'I am afraid that was a ruse a on my part,' she declared. 'I decided to rescue you from the matrons and their daughters.' She gestured around the room that was filled with exotic plants and citrus fruit trees. 'I thought that perhaps we could sit and have a little interlude?' She eyed him with interest, wondering what his reaction would be. She was amused when she saw the expression on his face relax. Gesturing to some wrought iron chairs set around a table, she said, 'Come, sit.'

Sitting down on one of the delicate chairs, he gave her a concerned look, 'Are you set on besmirching your reputation, Miss Armitage?'

Giving him a long look, she smiled. 'I am content on finding myself a husband, Mr Woodley, fore there is no avoiding it. I simply will not have my mama insist I marry a preening peacock and move to the city.'

He laughed then, a wonderfully deep mellow laugh, Emily found herself joining in.

'Ahh, Miss Armitage, I do like a person who knows their own mind.'

'I could not agree more, Mr Woodley.' She beamed.

Much to his utter surprise James found himself thoroughly enjoying the rest of the evening. Sitting opposite this charming young woman as they chatted about all manner of things. They were delighted to discover that they both enjoyed reading and had a mutual interest in the countryside.

'I am a man of the land,' James explained, he gestured around the foliage rich room, 'I am not one for grand living like this.'

'Yes, I understand,' Emily responded. 'It does not seem right somehow, that we want for nothing while people starve.'

'So true, Emily, many of the wealthy landowners bring gangs in to harvest their crops while their tenants are desperate for work.'

'Yes, sadly, I have heard of the like; in fact, papa has done just that himself.' As time drew on, James became more entranced by the moment. Miss Armitage, or Emily as she had insisted he call her, was petite, with a charming heart-shaped face that was open and candid. Her eyes, he noticed, were as blue as a hazy summer sky. Her cheekbones were well defined, and when she smiled, dimples appeared at the corners of her prettily shaped mouth. She wore a lavender dress with the minimal of frivolous adornments. The only jewellery she favoured were some pearl-drop earbobs.

James was not a man to notice the subtleties of a lady's attire. Still, the fact that Emily did not need satins, lace, flowers, frills, or bows, made her stand out from the other young ladies. In his eyes, this made her all the more beautiful, interesting, and desirable. There is an endearing freshness about her, James decided.

He was enjoying her company enormously; he was also finding that his respect for her grew by the moment.

'Do you like dogs?' James found himself asking. They could hear the orchestra in the other room and the hum and babble of voices, interposed with laughter now and again. Yet, the two felt as if they were encased in their very own fragrant oasis of earthly wonders as they chatted comfortably.

'I do,' Emily smiled. 'I have a desire to have a King Charles spaniel,' she declared, a dreamy look in her eyes. 'Mama will not have a dog in the house.' 'That is a great shame. I feel that dogs make a house a home,' James declared. 'I have an English Springer called Myrtle, and a chocolate Labrador pup called Henry.'

'Oh, how delightful.'

James felt his face heat up as he found himself saying, 'Perhaps you can come to Woodley Hall and meet them, Emily.'

'I would love to,' she answered with sincerity.

The hour was getting late when James reached across the table and took her hand in his. 'I cannot tell you how much I have enjoyed this evening,' he said, then his eyes dropped, 'I was, um, wondering if you would mind if I called upon you?'

'There is nothing I would like more,' she declared.

His gaze leapt to her smiling face. He matched it with a wide grin of his own.

'You know that I am twelve years your senior,' he cautioned.

'Tut, tut, James Woodley. Don't tell me that you would be bothered by an age gap!'

'Well, no, I just thought ...' his voice trailed off when he saw her expression, he laughed. 'You are jesting with me, my dear.'

'I am,' she said, and giggled.

To the envy of all the young ladies in the close vicinity, James and Emily were married six months later. He bought her a King Charles Cavalier spaniel for a wedding present, Emily was delighted. She called the dog Maddy because she loved her madly.

Her eyes were tightly shut as she lay on her bed, desperately trying to ignore the pain of loss that had settled over her.

Emily sighed. If only she could bottle those feelings – if only – She finally slept.

*

Claire, sitting beside her cousin's bedside, dabbed at her moist eyes with a lace handkerchief. Emily and James were made for each other; they were, *had been*, so happy together – oh lord, this was such a tragedy, Claire wondered what would happen now? The future felt as if it were a dark void full of uncertainty.

Chapter 5

Mrs Mason, Mrs Adams, the Woodley's cook, and Janice, the housemaid, sat in deep, comfortable armchairs around the fire in Mrs Mason's sitting room. 'I just can't believe it.' Ethel Adams shook her head in denial. Her eyes were red from crying.

'It's going to take time for the tragedy to sink in.' Gracie Mason gazed into the fire as if she could read something of the future in those flames.

She had been employed by the Woodley's since she was a young girl. First of all, she had been taken on as a housemaid, like the position that Janice held. When the previous housekeeper, Mrs Watson, was coming up to retirement, she had trained Gracie to take over the position, so it had been a seamless transition.

Gracie knew how lucky she was to work in a position of such high regard. This place was her home, the Woodley's her family.

The loss of Miss Angelica was as impactful as if she were losing one of her very own grandchildren. As for what happened to the master, Oh Lord, the pain in her heart was too much to bear.

Gracie took a sip of the sherry she had poured out for herself and her companions. None of them were big drinkers, but they felt that they needed the comfort and warmth of the fire and the alcohol on this bleak night.

'What do you think will happen now, Mrs Mason?' Janice asked. The maid had an unsettled feeling fluttering in her stomach.

'Well, we will go about our work as normal.' Gracie nodded as if she were confirming the matter to herself. Then she looked at the two other women in turn. 'We must be strong for the mistress and master Horacio. They are going to need good loyal staff and friends about them.' The other two women nodded in agreement. Mrs Mason lifted her glass which was still half-full, 'Now, let us drink up and be off to our beds.'

*

Alice Fletcher sat in a halo of lamplight that made the red curls peeping from her mob cap shine with copper and gold. She was knitting furiously, but her mind was not on the task as she took in the happenings of the day – and what a dark day it had been. Glancing at the bed, she couldn't see master Hero. He was just a shape under the blankets. Alice swallowed down more tears, *aww poor mite.*

The doctor had been and gone, he had offered the boy some laudanum, but Hero had refused it. Dr Scott had nodded, he told Hero that he would call in to see him the following day to check on him, Hero's reply had been a shrug.

Alice felt that the lad should have taken the medicine, but it was not her place to speak up. Glancing at the bed once more, she felt her stomach flip in anxiety; he was too quiet, should she check on him? Then, another thought occurred; perhaps he was asleep? Alice gave a little nod to herself. Aye, that would be it, he was sleeping. She would leave him be, she didn't want to disturb him.

Hero lay on his side in his bed staring at the familiar wall of his bedroom.

The moonlight seeping through gaps in the blue curtains, along with the soft lamplight, touched the row of toy soldiers set on a shelf close to the bed.

They wore colourful uniforms representing the battalions and regiments; he had painted them himself, with the occasional help from his papa. The tiny figures looked devoid of colour now. Their shadows elongated across the wall behind them made them look less like toys and more like menacing imps.

Hero didn't want to think about what had happened that day - he didn't want to think about anything, except the fact that he wished he was dead; that it had been *him*, who had fallen from the tree, not Angelica - that *he* had died and not his dear papa.

The weight of the responsibility for the death of his sister and father rested so heavily on him; Hero felt as if he would drown in the feelings. His lungs were constricted, making it difficult for him to breathe in enough air. His head was pounding with misery; his eyes felt scalding hot as he endeavoured to hold back the tears.

Hero was aware of Alice sitting watching over him. He could hear the clickety-clack of her knitting needles; at first, this had been a comforting sound, but now it raked his nerves and made him grit his teeth. When the rain announced itself with a pitter-patter against the windows, he was relieved. The sound of it helped to break the monotonous noise.

Thoughts bounced around in his head. He longed for the inner voice to stop, to become silent. Closing his eyes tight, he asked God to turn back the time, to change the happenings of this dreadful day. It was a nightmare, wasn't it? It couldn't be real!?

A gentle snore emanating from across the room interrupted the bombardment of the destructive thoughts. Hero, rolling onto his back, sat up quietly and glanced at the plump girl sitting in the corner; her knitting had fallen from her busy fingers. Her chin rested on her chest.

He heard her snore once again, then he pulled back the covers and got out of bed. His feet were bare. He knew the room so well that he was able to avoid the floorboards that creaked. Opening the door carefully, he stepped into the hall then padded across the Chinese carpet, making for the back stairs.

The house was quiet. Hero had no idea what the time was but guessed it must be late as he encountered not a soul on his journey to the back door.

Pulling back the bolts of the heavy door then opening it, he stepped out into the chilly, wet night. Shutting the door as quietly as he could. He then made his way across the yard, heedless of the feel of the icy cold brick path beneath his feet, and the fat raindrops that soon saturated his nightshirt and hair.

Making for the expanse of lawn to the side of the big house, he rushed across the wet grass. Picking up speed, he pumped his arms and legs harder and harder, trying to divest himself of the demons of guilt that had lodged in his mind and heart.

*

Alice came to with a start. She blinked then yawned and rolled her head to ease the stiffness in her neck and shoulders. Her knitting was on the floor. Recovering it, she glanced at the bed. Her heart stuttered with anxiety when she saw the covers turned back and the bed empty.

'Aww, lord.' She jumped to her feet. 'Master Hero,' she called. 'Master Hero, where are you?' Striding across the room, she knocked on the door of the bathing room where the commode was situated. When there was no reply, Alice knocked on the door and called again, 'Master Horacio, are you in there?'

There was a sense of emptiness beyond the door; nevertheless, she knocked once again and opened it. A quick sweep of the room told her what she had already suspected; Hero was not there.

What to do now? She felt perplexed – what was Miss Fellows going to say about this?

She rushed from the room, made her way to the governess' bedroom, knocked on the door and entered. The bed had been turned down but was empty, which confirmed Alice's deduction that Miss Fellows would be sitting with the mistress.

Making her way across the house, she reached the suite of rooms, then knocked on the bedroom door and opened it cautiously.

'Miss Fellows,' she kept her voice low and soft. 'Miss Fellows?' The rustling of silk drew her attention as a shadowed figure walked around the bed where the mistress was sleeping.

'What is it, Alice?' The governess reached the threshold, then ushered the maid out of the room and into the corridor.

'I'm so sorry, Miss Fellows, but its master Hero, he's gone, and I can't find him.'

'You were meant to be watching him, Alice.'

'I know.' Her eyes dropped to the floor in mortification. 'I – I fell asleep,' she confessed.

Claire sighed, 'Yes, I can understand. It has been an exhausting day. I have been fighting sleep off myself.'

Alice looked up, relieved that the governess understood. 'I'm sorry,' she said again.

Claire nodded, her head felt so heavy with tiredness and distress. She looked at the young woman. 'You go and sit with Mrs Woodley,' she decided quickly, 'I will wake Mrs Mason, we shall search the house.'

'Yes, Miss.' Alice nodded.

Claire reached out a hand and took the girls arm, she squeezed gently, 'The doctor gave the mistress some laudanum, so she is sleeping soundly, but do not relax your vigil this time, Alice.'

'No, Miss Fellows.'

Nodding, Claire made her way down the corridor to the back stairs that lead up to the servant's quarters.

*

Hero ran across the wet grass. The heavy rain stung his face and drenched his hair. His nightshirt flapped around his legs, hampering him.

He went down but pulled himself back to his feet, taking no heed to the fact that he was covered in dirt and mud.

Eventually, he reached the treeline and made his way into the coppice wood. The wet weather highlighted the scent of greenery; rich and earthy. The musky smell of fox and badger. The meaty odour of fungi and moss, mixed with the scent of bluebells, which tinged the air with their sweetness.

Suddenly, he came to a halt and bent over, his hands on his thighs as his lungs pumped and his heart thudded. Hot tears, chilled by the rain, flowed down his saturated cheeks.

The intensity of what had happened struck him a deep blow. His legs buckled, he found himself on his knees.

Opening his mouth, he let out a howl of pain and anguish. Wrapping his arms about his middle, he slumped forward and lay in the dirt.

*

Claire woke Mrs Mason, who donned a dressing-gown over her nightwear and slipped her feet into slippers.

Together they did a sweep of the house. Checking on the room where Angelica and James were laid out was the worst thing.

Mrs Bodkin, who was watching over the shrouded bodies, confirmed that she had not seen the boy.

When they reached the kitchens and scullery, they realised that the bolts of the backdoor were undone.

The two women exchanged worried glances.

'I will go and check the stables and rouse Bryant, Mr Jacobs and Charlie,' Claire said decisively.

Mrs Mason nodded. 'I had better go and put some clothes on. It looks as if it is going to be a long night.'

'Yes,' Claire agreed. 'I think we should wake Mrs Adams too. And Janice,' she added.

'Yes, Miss Fellows.' The housekeeper set off down the corridor.

Claire plucked a cloak from the hooks by the door, wrapped it around her, then opened the door and stepped out into the wet night.

Mr Jacobs, Bryant, and Charlie had rooms above the stables.

Claire hurried across the clearing of the stable yard, unlatched the wooden door, and stepped into the stable block. The scent of fresh hay tickled the back of her nose. She heard one of the horses shifting, giving a gentle wicker.

Carefully, she made her way up the dark stairway to the rooms above. Bryant's room was the first one she came to. Knocking loudly on the stout wooden door, she was rewarded by a deep woof, a snuffling coming from the gap on the other side of the door. She heard the bedsprings creaking and Bryant's firm voice telling the dogs to hush.

He must have lit a lamp, as Claire saw a strip of light appear under the door.

Pulling the door open with one hand, Bryant endeavoured to slip his arms into the sleeves of a woollen dressing-gown.

The two dogs greeted Claire. Henry and Myrtle usually slept in the house in James' study, but under the circumstances, Bryant had kept the dogs with him. They had been restless though, sensing the tragedy in the air, they were already pining for their master.

Henry sat down, looking at Claire in expectation, his heavy tail thumped on the floorboards.

'Miss Fellows,' Bryant greeted the governess, the look of concern on her face made his stomach twist in a knot of anxiety; Oh no, what now?

'It's master Horacio,' Claire spoke with some urgency, 'He's gone missing.'

There was no look of surprise on his face, although the grimness of his expression tightened. 'I'll get dressed,' he said, 'You alert Seth and Charlie.'

'Yes.' Claire continued down the corridor. She knocked on the bedroom doors of both the groundskeeper and the stable lad.

They both appeared blurry eyed with sleep. Claire told them quickly what had happened. Before she had finished her explanation, Bryant emerged from his room, the two dogs following close on his heels.

Bryant took charge. 'Get dressed, bring lanterns and some blankets. There's a bit of a squall going on out there.' Then he looked to Claire, 'You go back to the house, Miss, to await our return.'

'But I could help you look.' Claire wrung her hands in agitation.

'Us three and the dogs will find him,' Bryant reassured her. 'He'll be in the woods somewhere,' he added.

'He won't have done anything silly?' Claire didn't know what she was asking, but she feared for the boy: she had a sense of letting him down by not being there when he needed her, but then again, she could not have left Emily either.

'We'll find him, Claire,' Seth spoke up, dropping the formality of title in the tense atmosphere.

Turning to him, Claire gave the groundsman a grim smile. 'Thank you, Seth,' she acknowledged his concern.

'Aye, we will,' Charlie joined in. The stable hand was Bryant's nephew. At nearly fifteen, he was as wiry as his uncle. He stood there in the hallway in this long-johns, his thick brown hair standing up on end.

Bryant eyed the youth. 'Well, go and get dressed then lad.'

'Oh yes' He visibly coloured, stepping back into his room.

Claire would have found it amusing if it weren't for the urgency of the situation.

*

The rain filtered through the boughs above, dripping large drops on the boy as he lay in the foetal position on the woodland ground.

Hero became vaguely aware of hearing someone calling his name. He did not stir, nor call out in response. He just wanted the ground to open up and swallow him. The damp and cold, however, would not allow him to cut off all senses completely, he shivered and shuddered. No matter how hard he tried to clench his jaw, his teeth chattered.

It was Myrtle who found him. The springer danced around where he lay, she barked and then yipped, alerting the others to her discovery. Then she stopped, sniffed at him then nudged his face with her nose. The boy reached out and wrapped his arms around her neck. He inhaled the scent of her; the wet dog smell was comforting in its familiarity.

Mr Jacobs was the first one to appear, lantern held aloft.

'Aww, thank the Lord,' he uttered. 'He's here,' he called out to the others.

Bryant followed the sound of the groundsman's voice; he met Charlie coming from a different direction. They made their way through the woods together.

Both of them heard Myrtle bark again. Henry, who had been with Bryant, dashed forward, the urgency of the situation adding energy to his aged limbs.

Jacobs had managed to get Hero on his feet by the time the others arrived. He had wrapped the boy in a dry blanket that he had carried under his coat.

As Bryant stepped towards them, he too reached under his coat and produced another dry blanket then wrapped that around the shivering boy.

Although his heart went out to the boy, Bryant, feeling that it was best to be direct with the lad in order to get through to him, said, 'Now, am I going to have to carry you back to the house like a girl? Or are you going to walk on your own two feet?'

Hero's eyes darted to the man warily. 'N – n – no,' he mumbled through his chattering teeth. 'I – I will walk.'

The groom gave the boy a nod of approval. They set off back to the house.

The large kitchen of Woodley Hall was a hive of activity by the time the men and Hero returned.

Janice, and the scullery maid, Ida, had built up the range. Mrs Adams had a kettle boiling and pans of hot water steaming on the stove.

Claire had been up to check on Alice and Emily. Alice had informed her that the mistress had not stirred. Claire was now pacing the kitchen floor in agitation and worry as she waited for news of Hero.

When the party returned, she was so relieved to see them.

'Oh, my dear.' Claire embraced the boy.

Hero accepted the gesture, wrapping his arms around her waist.

'Aww, you are getting soaked, Miss Fellows,' Janice remarked.

'It doesn't matter,' her voice was choked with emotion. Stepping back half a step, she clutched Hero's icy cheeks between her long-fingered hands. 'Never do that again,' she said softly, then leant forward and kissed his forehead. 'Right, Janice, please ensure that the bath is topped up with hot water,' Claire said, regaining her sense of authority. 'Mrs Adams, please make some hot chocolate and coffee for everyone.'

'Yes, Miss Fellows.' The cook bustled to the stove. Already, the coffee things had been laid out. Claire had also had the foresight to ensure that the bath in the nursery bathing room was filled and ready for use.

The fire had been built up in his room. Claire helped the boy to bathe as if he were a little child. Horacio did not protest.

With her insistence, he had drunk some of the hot chocolate that Janice had brought up. Without protest this time, he also took the laudanum the doctor had left for him.

Claire sat beside his bed until his eyes had closed. He was breathing regularly and calmly. With a gentle hand, she stroked back his thick, curling hair away from his high forehead. He looked so much like his papa, she thought.

James and Emily had already decided that Horacio would be leaving for school that September. He would be attending Aldersmiths, the same school that the last few generations of Woodley men had been to. The place was situated in the glorious countryside of Kent. She wondered if these plans would still go ahead. It was something she would have to discuss with Emily when the time was right.

Claire hoped that Emily, after this awful tragedy, would still allow him to go to school. If Emily agreed, Claire thought it would be the best for the boy, to give him as normal a life as possible.

Eventually, Claire left the boy to sleep. Pushing tiredness aside herself, she made her way back to Emily's room so she could relieve Alice for a short while.

Chapter 6

When Emily Woodley awoke the following morning, she was greeted by beams of yellow spring sunshine peeping through the gaps in the russet brocade curtains.

Her mouth felt uncomfortably dry, and her head felt heavy. She stretched and did her best to come to. Then the awful tragedy that had occurred the following day hit her with full force.

'No...'

The anguished cry woke Claire, who was napping in one of the wingback chairs. Jumping to her feet, she ran over to her cousin.

Emily grabbed her cousin's proffered hands in desperation. 'Tell me it's not true, tell me it was a nightmare,' she echoed Claire's thoughts.

'I'm so sorry, my dear.' Claire's eyes filled with yet more tears.

'Oh God, no – no.' Emily shook her head in denial. Then she gave Claire a heartbroken look. 'Just for a moment, I had the blessings of forgetfulness.'

'I know, Emily.' The other woman's voice was rough with emotion as she sat down on the bed.

'Hero?' Emily looked at Claire beseechingly. 'How is he?'

Claire pondered on what she should say. 'He blames himself,' she said at last.

Emily's expression turned inward. 'I blamed him. I said some awful things yesterday.'

'It was all said in the shock of the moment.' Claire squeezed her cousin's hands reassuringly. Her skin still felt icy. 'He will understand.'

Emily's bleak expression shifted back to the other woman. 'I'm not sure I can see him.'

'It will take time.' Claire tried a smile; her face muscles felt strangely wooden.

Nodding, Emily pushed back the covers preparing to get out of bed.

'Are you sure you are ready to get up, my dear?' Claire said anxiously as she too stood up.

'There are things to do. Things to arrange.'

'Yes, of course.'

'Please ring for Janice. I shall have a bath.'

'Very well.'

Emily studied her cousin for a moment. 'You look tired, Claire. You sat with me all night, didn't you?'

'For most of it, yes.'

'Go and take some rest, my dear.' Emily's smile was a shadow of its usual brightness. 'I am going to need you over the next few weeks.'

'I shall be here for you. I will do anything I can to help.'

'Thank you.'

Claire found herself enveloped in a tight embrace. Emily was shorter than her cousin by a good few inches. Claire felt as if she were holding a fragile child in her arms.

The two women stayed like that for a long moment, taking comfort from each other's presence, then drew apart.

'Now, go. Get some rest,' Emily urged her.

Claire nodded.

Claire did not go straight to her room but stopped by the nursery to see how Hero was.

She found an agitated Alice waiting for her in the bright sitting room.

The breakfast things had been laid out on the dining table, a bowl of porridge, warm milk, a pot of honey and toast. With one quick sweep of the room, Claire could see that nothing looked as if it had been touched.

'Alice, is everything alright?' she asked warily.

'It's master Hero; I think he has a temperature.'

'Oh, I am not surprised after his jaunt last night. Is he still abed?'

'Yes, Miss.' Alice shadowed her footsteps as Claire walked briskly across the room to the boy's bedroom.

Opening the door, she stepped into a room still dim with shadowed light from the closed curtains. Walking over to the bed, she saw immediately that the boys' cheeks were flushed. He was still asleep, but his breathing crackled. She gently placed her hand on his forehead, which, in comparison to his burning cheeks, was as white as marble. His skin felt clammy.

'The doctor will be coming by this morning. He will check on the boy,' Claire said softly, while she ushered Alice to the door. Back in the sitting room, the governess glanced at the young woman. 'Will you be alright, Alice, while I go and freshen up.'

'Yes, Miss Fellows.'

With a curt nod, Claire left and made her way back to her room. She did indeed feel exhausted but knew she would not sleep. But she would wash and change, and these everyday actions, she hoped, would help her to feel more like herself.

*

When the door opened softly, Mrs Bodkin got to her feet. 'Your ladyship.' The woman acknowledged Emily with a bob of the head as she stepped warily into the shrouded bedroom.

Mrs Bodkin was in her middle-age, lines etched her face. From what could be seen of her hair under her black lace cap, it glowed silver in the dim light. A deliverer of babies and a layer out of the dead: Mrs Bodkin saw life from both ends of the spectrum.

The bodies of Angelica and James lay side by side on the large bed. They were covered in pristine white sheets, and these seemed to glow with an eerie light.

Without prompting, Mrs Bodkin walked to the bed and gently lifted the sheet from one body, then the other.

'They are as prepared as they can be,' she spoke with quiet respect.

Emily approached the bed. She could not say anything: her throat was clogged with such a depth of emotion.

Reaching out a hand, she stroked Angelica's porcelain skin. She looked like and felt like a beautiful doll – *a broken doll.*

'Goodbye, my darling.' Emily spoke so softly, Mrs Bodkin, who stood at a respectable distance, could barely hear her. Emily repeated the action with her husband. Then stepped away from the bed with her head tilted at a dignified angle. Her eyes met those of the older woman. 'Thank you,' she said, her voice held more strength at that moment.

Mrs Bodkin bobbed her head once more as Emily left the room.

*

Although Hero was still battling a fever, Emily had decided that she did not want to delay putting her husband and daughter to rest. She also hoped that after the funerals had taken place, both she and Hero would find it easier to deal with their grief.

It was a beautiful day: the sky was as blue as a forget-me-not. The birds, full of passion and delight at this time of the year, sang merrily, as they perched in the trees that stood testament over the graveyard. The church bell, in contrast, was mournful, a reminder that death was present even on this bright day.

It was no surprise that the funeral was well attended. All the house servants were there, along with Bryant, who was driving the Woodley carriage, and Jacobs and Charlie. The estate workers and the villagers attended as well as people from neighbouring estates, including Emily's parents, her sister Celia and her husband, Arthur Sandford.

The boy stood between his mother and Claire. Horacio gazed at the scene with glassy, feverish eyes.

As soon as the service was completed, the servants made their way back to the Hall to help to lay out the food for the guests who would be attending the wake.

Claire ushered Hero away from the two graves, which were side by side so that Emily could have a private moment.

Robert and Mary Armitage, Emily's parents, walked with Claire and Hero back to their carriages.

'You will have to be the man of the house now, Horacio,' Robert stated abruptly, placing an arm around Hero's shoulders.

The boy wanted to shrug the embrace off. He felt as if his grandfather had just set a heavy yoke about his shoulders. Such was the weight of responsibility and guilt he felt. Hero tried to swallow down the desire to run, to escape this tragic day, these terrible circumstances.

'Yes, Grandpapa,' he answered automatically.

'The boy shall be leaving for school in a few months.' Mary reminded her husband.

'Umm, yes, I suppose you will still need a good education.' Robert pondered.

Claire saw the distress etched on Hero's pale face and spoke up to change the subject, 'Emily has asked me to stay on as her companion,' she informed them as they walked through the lychgate. 'I will do all I can to help.'

'I'm sure you will, my dear.' Mary nodded. 'Emily is lucky to have you to help her.'

When they were out on the lane where the carriages waited, Claire addressed her aunt and uncle; 'I shall wait for Emily. Will you take Hero back to the hall with you, he really isn't well.' she gave Hero a kind look. 'Perhaps you should go back to bed when you get home; you look exhausted.'

'Mmm, I'm not sure that the boy needs mollycoddling,' Robert said gruffly.

'Let him be, Robert,' Mary spoke up firmly, 'you only have to look at the boy to see his quite ill.'

'Humph, well ...' Hero's grandfather huffed.

Claire saw them off and waited with the Woodley carriage for Emily.

'It is a damned shame about your father, Horacio,' Robert said as they settled into the plush interior of the Armitage carriage as it pulled away. 'He was unorthodox in his manner but give him his due he was a hard worker.'

'Yes, he was.' Mary tried valiantly to sniff back her tears, 'and my lovely granddaughter, our darling Angel, I cannot believe she is gone.' Lifting her black lace veil, she dabbed at her red eyes with a lace handkerchief.

Emily's mother was a petite woman with the same heart-shaped face as her daughter. When he looked at her, Hero could see the sorrow etched on her features. It aged her. 'How cruel fate is,' her voice was gruff with grief. Turning away, she gazed out of the window at the high banks full of spring flowers.

'Yes quite.' Robert agreed.

Hero's stomach squirmed as he too gazed out of the window, but he did not see the bright day, everything looked dark and shadowed to him now.

Suddenly, he felt as if he were going to be sick. Everyone blamed him for what happened, didn't they? Even his own Grandmama and Grandpapa.

He tried to breathe normally, but he felt as if his chest was constricted with anxiety: it was a terrible feeling that he was becoming familiar with.

Hero's grandfather, in contrast to his wife, was a large man, with a tendency to portliness. A balding pate made him look older than his sixty-two years. Leaning forward in his seat, he studied Hero with sharp grey eyes.

'If you are half the man your father was, then all will be well and good. You need to be strong for your mama.'

'I will try to be, sir,' Hero answered softly, hoping fervently that his grandfather would shut up.

'Mmm, I am not sure that trying to be, will be good enough, Horacio, all the responsibility will be on your shoulders now.'

Hero swallowed back a retort, then ground his teeth as he nodded. Mary placed a small hand adorned in a black silk glove on her husband's arm. 'I know you are concerned, Robert, but really this is not the time.' She gave Hero a gentle, understanding smile.

Robert patted her hand, then continued nonetheless, 'I am just saying it as it is, Mary, the boy will need to learn and quick smart.'

'I know, Robert, but he will not be alone, he will have you and others to give him guidance.'

'Yes, true enough,' he conceded.

When they arrived back at Woodley Hall as soon as he could, Hero sneaked off. He went to the stables and up to Bryant's room where old Henry and Myrtle had been left until the groom returned.

The dogs greeted the boy.

Henry, who's whiskers looked as if they had greyed even more over the last few days, got up stiffly, nuzzling Hero's hand. Myrtle wagged her tail with more enthusiasm as she came to sit beside the boy on the floor. She leaned into him as he wrapped his arms around them both and cried.

His tears were fuelled by anger, frustration, sadness, and loss - but the weightiest feeling of all was one of guilt.

─···═•◄❮❯►•═···─

Chapter 7

E mily Woodley stood in the graveyard; the other mourners parted around her like the red sea. Gazing down at the two mounds of freshly dug earth, she had placed a perfect cream rose on each of the graves.

She felt strangely detached; there was a numbness around her heart that was icy as hoarfrost. When she turned her mind to it, Emily could not think of a future without James. If she examined her heartbreak to closely, the enormous feeling of loss would engulf her; the only thing she could do was take one moment at a time.

Suddenly, a flapping of wings disturbed the air. A male blackbird, with wings as dark as ebony and a beak as bright as a yellow buttercup, rested on one of the gravestones close to where she stood. The bird eyed her with interest, then hopped down beside her and plucked a fat worm from the freshly turned earth, then flew away with its prize. It was as if the bird were telling her that life goes on regardless.

Feeling the presence of somebody nearby, Emily turned away from the burial site.

Claire stood to one side, waiting patiently for her cousin.

'I'm not sure I can face everyone back at the house,' Emily said, her voice hollow as she made her way over to the other woman.

'I understand, my dear. We just need to get through the day. It will soon be over.'

Emily gave her a searching look. 'Will it?'

The following day, Emily and Hero attended the reading of James' will.

Not being able to face stepping into her late husband's study, Emily insisted that all those mentioned in bequeathments attend the interview in the dining room.

They sat around the large, highly polished walnut table.

Claire was present, along with Robert Armitage, who was there to support his daughter, to explain anything she may not understand. And Mr Hawkins, the home farm manager.

Mr Stokes, the Woodley's family solicitor, sat at the head of the table and gazed at them all over his reading glasses. Before him, set out on the table was James' will.

In contrast to the previous day, the weather was overcast; the rain had been falling steadily all morning. The large room was shadowy. Emily had asked Mrs Mason to light some of the lamps, but even those did not help to disperse the darkness Emily could feel in her heavy heart.

Archibald Stokes was tall, slim to the extreme, so much so, that his clothes seemed to hang on his body. He had an angular face, with sharp features, pinched cheeks and a roman nose. Despite his austere countenance, however, Archibald was a kind man. He had been an advisor to James for many years.

'I am despondent about presiding over this solemn affair.' He gazed about the table with eyes that were as grey as ash. Pressing a long-fingered hand on the paperwork before him, he continued, 'James' will is quite simple; the estate has been left to his son, Horacio,' he looked at the boy who was studying the wood grain of table most intricately. 'Because of his age, the estate will be kept in trust until the boy is eighteen.' As Archibald gazed at her kindly, Emily nodded in understanding. 'I would suggest that a manager for the estate should be sort. In the meantime.' His gaze then turned to Mr Hawkins, 'I know that you will continue with the running of the home farm?'

'Yes, of course.' The manager nodded.

'I have many connections,' Robert Armitage spoke up, 'I can find a trustworthy chap for the job.'

'Thank you, papa,' Emily said softly.

'Yes, very good.' Mr Stokes nodded in agreement. He turned his attention back to Emily, 'As you know, my dear, James has spent nothing of your dowry; in fact, he had me invest some of the money for you. It has paid dividends. You are a wealthy lady in your own right.'

Emily nodded; she felt her eyes sting with tears: what good was money when one had to face such sorrow?

Claire, who was sitting beside her, saw her bleak expression. Reaching out, she took her hand, squeezing it gently. Emily rewarded her with a half-smile.

'Mrs Fellows,' Archibald continued, Claire looked at the man surprised to hear her name mentioned. 'James has bequeathed to you, a sum of five hundred pounds, with thanks for all the service and support you have given the family.'

Claire took in a sharp breath. She shook her head. 'I didn't expect...' her voice trailed away.

'Damn generous,' Robert exclaimed.

It was Emily's turn to comfort Claire; she smiled. 'You deserve it, my dear, I don't know where I would be without you.'

'Thank you,' Claire nodded, then fished in her pocket for a handkerchief to wipe away even more tears.

'There are several small bequeaths,' The man studied a page in front of him. 'One hundred pounds, respectfully, for Mrs Mason, Mr Jacobs, Mr Bryant, and you, Mr Hawkins, for yours and their long and dedicated service to the family.' The solicitor glanced about the table, and everyone nodded. 'The estate has been expertly run,' he continued, 'with a good manager that will continue to be the case.'

'Absolutely,' Robert agreed readily.

'There is one last thing,' Archibald Stokes cleared his throat as all eyes turned to him once more. 'James, of course, made provision for his daughter's future, a generous dowry has been put aside.'

'Yes, of course, he would,' Robert murmured.

Archibald straightened the papers in front of him then looked to Emily, 'Unless there is anything else you wish to do with the money, my dear, it will become part of the estate.'

'Yes, of course,' Emily repeated her father's words, then her forehead creased in a thoughtful frown, 'I wonder, would it be possible to donate the money to some, um, worthwhile cause?'

Archibald looked at her over the top of his glasses. 'We are talking about a considerable sum of money.'

'Mama is correct,' Hero spoke up for the first time, 'my sister's money should be put to some good cause.'

The solicitor glanced at Robert, who nodded his head. 'Very well, I shall leave it to you to decide, and then to let me know where you would like the money to be placed.'

'Thank you, Mr Stokes.' Hero nodded; the man gave him an encouraging smile in return.

As all the business was concluded, Mr Stokes stopped for some coffee, then made his way back to London.

*

The summer was a long one. As if the weather could feel the weight of sorrow upon them, the heat became very oppressive. Several times, dark banks of clouds would collect on the horizon, but came to nothing as the storm did not break.

Emily and Claire took to walking in the garden in the early mornings. It was pleasant at that time, with a hint of freshness in the air.

Henry, who tended to wander around like a lost soul, shadowed their footsteps. Emily felt so sorry for the old boy, James had doted on him, it was obvious the dog mourned the loss of his master.

Maddy, Emily's King Charles Spaniel, had died of old age the year before – Emily still missed her terribly. James had said he would get her another companion dog. Emily had told him several times that she wasn't ready to have another dog. Maddy had been so special, her wedding present from James. Emily found that she mourned the loss of the little dog even more now: it seemed as if all the good things in her life were leaving her. She wondered how much more her heart could suffer without breaking completely.

Her relationship with her son had altered until she barely recognised it for what it had been. Not surprisingly, Horacio had become moody and withdrawn. Emily wanted to comfort her son, but she did not know how to. She knew that Hero was blaming himself for what had happened.

Emily found that when they had some time together, it was unbearably awkward. Emily was far from being a malicious person, and it broke her even more when she realised that she found herself blaming Horacio for what had happened. If he hadn't encouraged Angel to climb that tree, her family would still be intact.

Emily and Claire spent a great deal of time together. They found a mutual comfort in each other: the losses that they had both experienced brought them closer together.

'I have decided to close off all the unused rooms of the house,' Emily commented to Claire one morning as they strolled through the rose garden together. Despite the early hour, they could feel the build-up of the heat, vying with the slight freshness of the dewy morning. They were both dressed in black silk mourning dresses. 'It seems pointless for Mrs Mason to set the maids to cleaning rooms that we do not use often.'

'Yes, I can understand the logic of that,' Claire nodded.

Emily came to a halt beside a bush of deep yellow roses, she leant forward and inhaled the scent of them.

'Hero will soon be gone.' She turned her gaze to her cousin, a frown furrowed her forehead, 'is it wrong for me to feel a sense of relief that he won't be around?'.

Claire took a moment to answer. She gazed out over the landscape thoughtfully. 'What has happened has changed you both,' she said a last.

'I'm not sure...' Emily's voice broke, she took a moment to recover, 'I'm not sure we will ever get back to the way things were.'

'Sadly, that is true,' Claire commented, 'When I lost Joseph, I felt as if my life were over.' She stepped closer to her cousin, 'If it hadn't been for you and James, I don't know what I would have done. I did not want to carry on without him.'

It was Emily's turn to nod in understanding. 'Yes. I can't bear the thought of losing my little boy, but I feel as if he has already retreated from me.'

Claire pulled the other woman into a tight embrace. 'You need to give it time, my dear.'

Emily nodded against her shoulder as the two clung together.

*

Hero had lived in this house, in these grounds, all of his life; after what had happened, however, he felt strangely displaced, as if there was nowhere to call home anymore.

Before the double tragedy, Hero felt apprehensive about leaving for school in September, but that apprehension had been tinged with a feeling of excitement.

Cousin Claire was an excellent teacher with extensive knowledge, but Hero wanted, had needed, more.

His father had attended Aldersmiths, "it is a fine school," he would say, "they strike a good balance between book learning, sports and outdoor pursuits. You will learn all you need to know as an underpinning knowledge, and then, when you are home, Hero, I will teach you how the estate is run." Hero remembered nodding with enthusiasm.

Now, Hero was at a loss as to what to do with himself, so he spent much of his time in Bryant's presence, helping out in the stables. He would do any job allotted to him. He was as capable of cleaning tack and mucking out as anyone. His father had always said; "never ask anyone to do a job you would not do yourself."

The groom, sensing the boy's need for distraction, set him some challenging jobs, Hero set about them and finished them, hoping to be too exhausted at night to stop the tears and the nightmares that haunted him.

Finding it was far too painful to be in his mother's company, he kept his distance and made excuses, so he would not have to sit down with her and Cousin Clare at dinner time or any meal for that matter.

There was no excitement left in him regarding leaving for school. It had been replaced by a desperation to get away from all the sadness.

*

Emily sat behind her escritoire in the drawing-room, her chair placed at an angle facing the room. Claire stood quietly beside her. They both looked very sombre in their black gowns. Emily, always fair, looked as if her skin were chiselled from white marble, the hot, oppressive summer had done nothing to warm her or bring any colour to her cheeks, she felt chilled to the core.

It was the beginning of September, and Hero was due to leave for school the following week.

Emily had asked Mrs Mason to round up the staff as she needed to talk to them.

They were gathered there respectfully, the men with their caps in their hands. The maids looked wary; *what was going on?*

'I have decided to close off the unused rooms in the house,' Emily spoke up. 'All the guest rooms, the large dining room,' she gestured about the room. 'The formal drawing room and the library.' She shifted in her seat. 'I will keep my suite of rooms on the first floor, and Claire will have the rooms next to my own.' Emily looked at Alice Fletcher, who stood there, her lips quivering, *Aww, she knew what was coming, they were letting her go, weren't they?*

'Alice,' Emily gave the young woman a direct look. 'Claire, Miss Fellows, has arranged for you to attend a school in Gloucester. You have, I gather, many of the skills required to become a dressmaker, or possibly a lady's maid. It will be sad to see you go, my dear, but now...' Emily's voice trailed off. Claire stepped in.

'This will be a wonderful experience for you, Alice, the course has been paid for by Lady Woodley. I am sure you will do her proud.'

'Aww, yes, Miss Fellows.' The girl didn't know what to say. She found herself crying and happy all at the same time.

Emily gave her a kind smile, then turned her attention to Bryant. 'We will be letting some of the horses go, Mr Bryant. Miss Fellows and I will keep mounts for ourselves, and we shall keep two carriage horses, and Master Horacio's horse for him to ride when he comes home.'

'Yes, ma'am,' Bryant nodded.

'My father has found homes for the rest.'

'Very good, your ladyship.'

'I know that you and Charlie are good workers, Mr Bryant. I shall ask you to entrust more of the care of the horses to Charlie and for you to help out with groundsman work, helping Mr Jacobs and the new estate manager, Mr Durham, who will be with us next week.'

'Of course, I will help in any way I can, Lady Woodley.' Bryant felt a sense of relief. He had thought he might be turned away from Woodley Hall.

'Thank you, Mr Bryant. I am sure you will.' Emily smiled, then looked to the maids, 'We shall be keeping on Mrs Mason, of course,' she gave the housekeeper a half-smile; Emily had already informed her of the changes that were taking place, so none of them came as a surprise. 'Mrs Adams,' Emily continued, 'Janice and Ada. The rest of you will be taken on as staff working for my parents.'

The maids looked around at each other nervously, they would all be sad to leave Woodley Hall and Midcote itself, but at least they would still have jobs and wouldn't be too far away.

The interview was over. The servants filed out of the room.

'Oh, that was so difficult,' Emily said as she got to her feet.

'I understand, my dear, but as you said, Emily, there is no point keeping a large contingent of staff if you are closing down much of the place.'

'Yes, quite.' Emily looked out of one of the long windows; the hot, dry summer had left the lawns looking more like straw than lush grass. 'Are all the preparations made for Hero's departure?'

'Yes, they are. Alice and I have helped him to pack everything he will need; there are two heavy trunks.'

Emily turned and glanced at her cousin. 'Thank you for everything.'

Claire nodded; her expression was full of kindness. 'You are managing very well, my dear,' she encouraged.

Emily nodded, 'I am doing my best.'

'That is all you can do,' Claire affirmed in sympathy.

Chapter 8

When the knuckles of the taller boy connected with Hero's nose, the group of boys surrounding the fighting pair cheered.

Letting out a 'humph', Hero felt the crunch of bone as a spray of blood gushed from the orifice.

To avoid getting their uniforms splattered with crimson, some of the boys stepped back.

The fight had started when Hero and Alec came across Luther Willard and his cronies picking on the tall, angular figure of Andrew Keene. Keene, who was in the same year as Willard, two years above Alec and Hero, was a self-professed academic. His dream was to become a doctor, following in his father's footsteps. He enjoyed learning which, along with his considerate nature and tall frame marked him out as easy fodder for the bullies.

As soon as he saw what had been going on, Hero, much to Alec's protestations, stepped in.

The bloody nose, which Luther had just meted out, did not stop Hero. He lowered his head and bellowed like a bull as he targeted Luther Willard's midriff.

Willard was a heavier build than Hero, but a lot of his bulk was the result of a fondness for puddings and sweetmeats.

Luther, not expecting such a hard blow, went down as all the air was knocked out of him.

Hero loomed over the prone boy, then kicked him hard in the ribs.

'Watch out, lads, master's on his way over.' Alec Silverman handed Hero a large white handkerchief. Hero swabbed at his nose.

One of the other boys helped Luther to his feet.

'This won't be the last of it,' the older boy snarled at Hero, then his mean gaze swept across Alec and Andrew.

Hero's eyes blazed, 'Looking forward to the next round, Willard.'

'What's going on here?' the master asked, his stern eyes fell on Hero and the bloody handkerchief. 'What happened boy?'

'Nothing, sir, tripped over a tree root and knocked my face against the trunk.'

'Mmm, well it looked to me as if there was a scuffle going on.'

'I can assure you, Mr Browning,' Alec stepped forward with his usual air of confidence, 'Woodley tripped and knocked himself.'

'Mmm,' Mr Browning frowned then looked about the hovering group. His eyes rested on Luther Willard, who was smoothing down his navy-blue jacket as he tried not to think about his tender ribs. 'Is that right, Willard?' the master asked.

'That is correct, sir.' Luther's lips formed a hard smile; he may be the bully of the school, but he was not a snitch.

'Very well.' Browning nodded, 'Now go about your business.' He waved a hand in a general motion, 'And you, Woodley, go and see matron, get that nose seen to.'

'Yes, sir.'

Mr Browning, master of Latin, strode off across the lawn. His black cloak billowing, a swooping bird of prey.

'As I said before, this isn't the end of it, Woodley,' Luther sneered.

Eyeing the stocky boy with dislike, Hero thought scornfully, bloody hell, he's like a bull terrier, he just won't let things go.

Luther Willard had been the bully of the school before Hero had started at Aldersmiths. He was two years older than Hero and Alec. Still, he was one of their dormitory companions: at Aldersmiths, the Mollicy was not to separate older boys from younger ones but to integrate them, with the idea that they would act as mentors to the boys.

The eldest son of a wealthy Bristol merchant, Luthor Willard was a thug and the scourge of the dorms.

Hero had been at Aldersmiths for six weeks. On the first day, he had met Alec Silverman, who occupied the bed next to him. Alec was the only son of a wealthy London family who dealt in jewellery and property.

Not many of the boys boarding at the school were titled or from old money. Many, like Hero, came from a background where the money was earnt by hard work. Hero understood that this was the environment his father wanted for him so that he did not get "above himself".

The majority of the boys at the school felt they had something to prove, so the competition was fierce; no matter the history of the respective families, a hierarchy was always going to be established.

In those first few weeks, Hero was not looking to make friends; in fact, he was quiet and moody, if not downright surly.

Hero did not bend to the dorm rules that Luther had established. It was not that he felt he wanted to rebel. It was because he was still reeling with the shock of the losses at home.

Numb to any bullying, Hero thought it was not worth his time to be intimidated in such a way. He hurt so deeply, nothing else that could be done to him could match that pain.

Hero, almost the same height as Luther, was muscular and fit from all the work that Bryant had assigned him over the summer. He was a handsome boy with a mop of thick brown curls and hazel eyes.

Luther observed that Hero tended to draw people to him without even trying; this made Willard hate Hero all the more. With his good looks and popularity, Luther saw Hero's noncompliance to go against his "rules" as a snub, a form of rebellion.

Fearing that Woodley was out to oust him from his position, Luther looked for whatever situation he could find to pick on Hero, to rile him.

It did not help matters for Hero, that he found himself having bad dreams. Over and over again, he relived the moment when Angel fell to her death. Then sometimes it was his father disappearing into inky blackness. He must have cried out as he had been shaken awake by Alec, who had the bed next to him.

The dreams and crying in the night were weakness' in Woodley's armour. Luther made good use of the ammunition to taunt Hero; 'I hear you scream in your sleep like a girl, Woodley,' Luther had sneered at him. 'words' got around that you killed your sister, then, your father couldn't stand to look at you, so much so, he keeled over.'

As soon as he had met Hero, Alec Silverman noticed the shadows of a damaged life in the other boy's eyes; the self-destructive tendencies, but he also recognised the strength of character, which he possessed; a survival instinct.

Alec was a slim youth, with slicked back, dark hair, and pale features. When anyone glanced at him, they would have thought he was a handsome boy in an effeminate way, but when one looked closer, you could see the steel behind his dark brown eyes and stubbornness of jaw. He knew he was not strong enough to resist Luthor's attention by himself, he needed physical strength, and that was what Hero had in abundance.

Alec, shrewd as he was, a trait inherited from his father, could see great potential in Woodley, he treated Horacio as if he had been a beaten dog, understanding that Hero needed to be coaxed into trusting him.

Alec Silverman came from a family of Georgian Jews, the second generation to be born in England. His grandfather, Alexander, (for whom he was named) had a nose for trouble: he could foresee the economic decline in Russia, could feel the undercurrents of rebellion that were seeping into Georgia. Their lives were dogged by antisemitism and restrictions. So, he gathered up his family and all his worldly goods, which included a plethora of family silver, and emigrated to London.

Publicly, Alexander Silverman renounced the Jewish faith in favour of Christianity. Although, in the privacy of his own home, he kept up the old traditions. Alexander understood the need to make this sacrifice so that he would find acceptance in the business community, by doing this, along with an instinct for sniffing out worthwhile ventures, he quickly made useful connections. It did not take him long to establish a name for himself in the import and export of fine jewellery.

He was one of the first of a mass migration of many of his fellow countrymen; this gave him yet another opportunity. Alexander knew that people needed places to live, so he bought up swathes of property, mostly London slums. Renting out the rooms to immigrants, some Russian and Jewish like himself but many were Irish, fleeing the famine that had ravaged their beloved country.

Hero was not aware of Alec Silverman's attempts to 'pal up,' because they were subtle, a simple kindness done here or there. Gradually, he responded to Silverman's attention with a nod or a reluctant thank you.

'I think you will need to get that nose set.' Andrew Keene gave Hero a concerned look as the three of them strolled across the expanse of lawn back to the school building.

'It's your bloody fault, Keene.' Alec sneered at the taller boy. 'You need to learn how to stand up for yourself.'

'Give it a rest, Alec,' Hero spoke up, his voice clogged from the nosebleed. 'besides, you're a good one to talk.'

'Well, it's true,' Alec bristled, blushing with indignation. He did not like the idea of the friendship that was beginning to form between Hero and Andrew. The notion made him feel vulnerable. 'He should get his nose out of those bloody books.'

'It-its fine, Horacio,' Andrew murmured. They had reached the school building. 'I umm, will leave you to it.' Before anyone could say another word, Andrew reached the sweeping staircase off the spacious tiled hall and took the steps two at a time.

The sickroom comprised of the Matron's room lined with shelves, and a separate ward which housed three cot beds. At that moment in time, no one occupied any of the beds.

Matron, who was a large woman in her fifties, had, in contrast to her thick wiry grey hair that did it's best to escape from her white cap, an abundance of dark hair above her lip.

Hero could not help himself; he gazed at it in fascination as the woman manipulated his nose, none too gently, with large blunt fingers.

'Definitely broken,' she announced.

Ah, Andrew was right. Mmm, no surprise there then, Hero thought, resisting the urge to wince away from the rough fingers.

Washing away the blood, the Matron then rinsed and dried her own hands and sat behind the desk with a ledger open. She recorded the incident and treatment in a surprisingly neat and flowing hand.

Putting the pen down, she gazed at Hero with narrowed eyes; 'I hope you are not going to make a habit of this clumsiness, Woodley.'

'Mm, no Matron, I shall try not to.'

She nodded, 'off you go then,' she dismissed the two boys with a wave of her hand. 'Oh, and don't be surprised if you end up with at least one black eye after that blow.'

'Yes, Matron.'

Alec, leaning up against a wall just outside the sickbay, was waiting for Hero.

When Hero reappeared, Alec placed an arm around the other boys' shoulders. They made their way along one of the wood-panelled corridors back to their dormitory.

Alec spoke up, 'What say you, we make some money from these encounters?'

Hero gave him a sidelong glance, 'What did you have in mind?'

'Well,' Alec paused, Hero halted beside him. 'We both know that Willard isn't going to stop his um, skulduggery...'

'Skulduggery.' Hero wanted to laugh at the term.

Alec raised a quizzical eyebrow, 'how is your bare-knuckle boxing?'

'A boxing match?'

The other boy nodded, pleased that Hero had cottoned on so quickly.

'Yes, we can set it up and take a few bets – what do you say? You could take him, Woodley, you know it.'

Hero found himself saying, 'Yes, of course.'

'I knew you would be up to some sport, Horacio. You can get the better of that yob. Put him in his place once and for all.'

Hero liked the sound of that; he nodded in agreement as he flexed his knuckles, itching to take on the bully.

Fighting or brawling had been an alien concept to Hero until now. He had to admit to himself that fighting Willard had relieved some of his pent-up anger, not to mention the weighty sorrow he carried in his heart every day. During the fights, for a brief moment, he felt that weight lift, as he directed the darkness into the physical act.

As Alec chatted on about arranging the boxing match, Hero's attention wandered to his own thoughts; he had mixed feelings where Alec was concerned: the other boy had been kind to him, shaking him awake at night, saving him from the nightmares. Hero was extremely grateful, but he much preferred the quiet presence of Andrew Keene.

Chapter 9

Bryant opened his sleep heavy eyes and sat up. His room above the stables was dark, but the moonglow still sliced through chinks in the curtains. Damn, it wasn't morning; what had woken him?

Then he heard the soft mewl and whimper from the corner. He realised that something was missing from the sounds of the night - the sound of old Henry snoring: his loud snoring had become such a familiar backdrop to Bryant's sleep, he had long become accustomed to it.

He felt his heart drop as he pushed the bedclothes aside. His bare feet met the surface of the cold wooden floor.

Myrtle, hearing the movement let out another low, sorrowful whine.

Bryant lit the lamp then turned to the two dogs laying on their blankets in the corner of the room. The springer gave Bryant a questioning look, then turned to her companion and licked his face. Henry did not stir even when Myrtle nudged him with her wet nose.

Kneeling, Bryant gave Myrtle a rub behind her ears with one hand as he laid the other on Henry's barrelled chest.

'Ahh, he's gone, Myrtle.' The man felt the prickle of tears form but dashed his workworn hand across his eyes.

Bryant knew that this had been coming, he could see the old boy decline since losing his master. Then Horacio had left for school. The Labrador had been wandering around like a lost soul. Sensing the sadness in her friend, Myrtle shadowed the old dog's every move.

'He's gone,' he said again, 'died in his sleep, the best way to go.' Bryant picked up the corners of the blanket and wrapped up the body of the big dog.

Getting up from his kneeling position, he grabbed his dressing gown from the hook on the back of the door then placed his feet in some slippers.

He knew he wouldn't be able to carry the dog down the stairs and hold the lantern at the same time, so he knocked on Charlie's door. Opening it, he called to the young man, 'Wake yourself, lad, I need your help.'

'What?' Charlie pulled himself from sleep and shrugged off the bedclothes. He shaded his eyes from the light of the lamp that Bryant was holding. 'What's wrong? Is it one of the horses?'

'No, lad, it's old Henry, he's passed.'

'Oh, no.' Charlie shrugged on a jacket over his nightshirt. 'Are you sure?'

'Course, I'm sure, lad, seen enough death in my life.'

Charlie nodded; his mop of untidy hair bobbed. Slipping his feet into his work boots, he followed Bryant. They picked the blanket up that contained the dog, then carefully made their way down the stairs, Myrtle at their heels.

'Best we put him in the work-shed for now,' Bryant said.

'Aye, best place,' Charlie agreed.

'I don't relish telling Lady Woodley what has happened,' the older man felt his voice catch.

'It's been a sad enough time for the family,' Charlie commented as Bryant opened the door to the shed which housed gardening equipment, spare parts for the carriage, the trap and the wagons amongst other bits and pieces.

Gently they laid Henry down on the floor. Both Bryant and Charlie stood together for a long moment, reluctant to leave their friend. Myrtle sat beside Bryant. She too was quiet now.

'Come, girl,' Bryant called at last as he and his nephew made their way out of the building.

As they walked back across the stable yard, Bryant looked to the sky; dawn was still a way off.

Charlie looked at his uncle. 'Anything else you need me for?'

'No, lad, you go back to bed.'

Charlie nodded as he smothered a yawn.

They parted ways on the landing. Myrtle followed Bryant into his room where the lamp was still aglow.

Bryant did not go back to bed; instead, he poured some milk into a pan, lit the spirit stove then placed the pan on it. He sat down on his bed while he waited for the milk to heat up.

Myrtle shuffled over to him, head down, tail between her legs.

'It's alright, lass.' He reached out a large hand and stroked the dog behind her ears. 'You're going to miss your old friend, aren't you,' moving his head closer to the dog, he continued, 'I have to confess, so will I.'

Once the milk started to boil, Bryant turned off the flame, poured most of the milk into a mug, picked up a saucer and drained the rest, 'You'll have to wait a minute, girl, let it cool a while.'

Reaching up to one of the shelves that lined one wall, he picked up a bottle of whiskey. He wasn't a heavy drinker by any stretch of the imagination, but he liked the odd tipple occasionally. This bottle, which was over three-quarters full, had been given to him by the master and mistress last Christmas. Undoing the lid, he splashed a little of the liquid into the milk. After he had put the bottle away, Bryan tested the temperature of the milk in the saucer. He nodded in satisfaction, then put the saucer on the floor for Myrtle. She sniffed it, then drank it up.

Bryant sat down on the bed, making the old springs creak. As soon as the dog had finished the milk, Bryant patted the space on the bed beside him, and the dog jumped up gratefully.

'I'm not making a habit of this, girl,' he said, as he stroked her silky fur, 'so don't get used to it.' Myrtle eyed him with her soft brown eyes, 'Yes, we both need a bit of comforting this night.' He nodded at her, and she sighed.

The following morning, Bryant walked over to the house, he had been up some hours checking on the horses and waiting for the household to stir so he could tell them the news about Henry.

It was the middle of November. The sun was a bright citrus orb in the sky; the colour was sharp and sour. There was no warmth to it. The bricked yard was slick with frost in the unsheltered places.

The groom entered the warmth of the kitchen gratefully. He was relieved to see Miss Fellows there; she was making up a breakfast tray for the mistress.

'Good morning, Mr Bryant.' Claire eyed him as he walked into the kitchen, holding his cap in his hands.

'Good morning, Miss,' he acknowledged her. 'I am afraid that I am here to impart some bad news, Miss Fellows.'

Claire felt her stomach twist uncomfortably, she rested one graceful hand against her chest, as the colour drained from her cheeks.

'What's happened?' she asked in a whisper.

'It's old Henry, ma'am, died in his sleep last night.'

'Oh, no.' Claire dropped her head in sorrow for a moment then looked up. Bryant could see that her eyes were moist with tears. 'I shall tell Lady Woodley.'

'Yes, Miss.' Bryant was relieved that she had taken on the responsibility of letting the mistress know.

Claire nodded as she picked up the breakfast tray and made her way from the kitchen.

When she tapped on the door and entered Emily's room, it was to find her cousin sitting up in bed. The curtains were open; there was a faraway look in her eyes as she stared at the view beyond.

'Did you sleep well, my dear?' Claire asked as she set the tray on one of the polished tables.

'Tolerably,' Emily acknowledged.

Having relieved herself of the tray, Claire went over to the fire, which was still smouldering. She picked up the poker and gave it a prod then picked up the spade of the coal scuttle and added more coal.

By the time she had done this, Emily had risen and donned her robe and slippers. Her long brown hair was a heavy plait that fell down her back. If it weren't for the lines of loss furrowing her face, she would have looked like a young girl. She walked over to the breakfast tray and poured tea out for them both.

Because most of the house was closed off and shrouded in dust sheets, it had become the habit for Emily and Claire to breakfast together in Emily's room every morning.

Having nurtured more life from the fire, Claire walked over to the table where Emily sat nursing a cup of tea in both hands.

Because Claire did not sit straight away, Emily glanced at her and noticed her cousins troubled expression.

Emily must have sensed there was bad news coming, her face tightened with anxiety; her hands began to shake. She set the teacup down with a clatter.

'What is it?' her voice was breathless.

'It's Henry, my dear. Bryant told me this morning that he died in his sleep last night.'

'Oh,' Emily bobbed her head in understanding then turned to gaze out of the window once more. The view was beautiful, a fine autumn day. Wisps of mist stirred across the lawns. The trees beyond were a delight to behold dressed in their finery of purple, gold, russet, pewter, and bronze. 'Ahh,' Emily sighed. 'poor boy.'

'Yes,' Claire sat down and picked up her cup of tea and sipped it gratefully.

'Another part of James gone,' Emily murmured.

Placing her cup down, Claire reached out a hand in comfort, which Emily took and squeezed it gently.

'Yes, my dear.' Claire agreed softly.

After Claire had left her room, taking the breakfast tray down to the kitchen. Emily dressed and pinned up her long brown hair.

When she looked in the mirror these days, the visage gazing back at her was so alien, she hardly recognised herself. Her heart-shaped face had sharpened as her cheekbones had become more prominent. Her skin was terribly pale; becoming drained of colour even more by the harshness of the black she wore. Her ghostly complexion highlighted the purple bruises under her large eyes, which held a flat, deadened look: they are haunted, she thought sadly, as she turned away from her reflection.

*

Emily had Bryant and Charlie bury Henry next to the body of her little spaniel, Maddy. The graves were in the corner of the rose garden and sheltered by a flowering cherry tree, branches bare at this time of the year, but come spring, it was a magnificent sight.

Lost without her master, Hero and her old companion, Henry, Myrtle followed Bryant wherever he went, seeking reassurance.

As the winter drew on, Woodley Hall seemed like a skeleton of its old self. It was as if all the cheer, all the life had been drained from the place.

Emily's mother, Mary, took to visiting her daughter once a week. Although Emily was grateful for her mother's caring administrations, Mary's good intentions only went to highlight the stark reality of her losses.

*

Hero arrived home for Christmas. Claire had written to him to tell him about Henry. Like his mother, he felt the blow: another loss for the family. Myrtle was pleased to see him, however. Again, the boy spent his days in the company of Bryant and Charlie, and the dog joined in happily.

Horacio had a couple of meetings with Mr Durham, the estate manager so that Durham could report and update Hero on the running of the estate. When Hero took the time to listen, it sounded as if the man were doing a fair job.

Having met the new estate manager briefly before he had left for school, Hero had not had time to assess the man. Now he spent more time with him; he realised he did not like him.

Durham was a tall, angular man with an abrupt attitude that Hero found grating. Unfortunately, the man's persona was too similar to that of Hero's grandfather; to the extent that Hero felt as if the man was assessing and judging him.

Acutely aware of the expectations placed upon his shoulders, the thought of having to take over the running of Woodley Hall was daunting, to such an extent that Horacio found himself feeling physically sick with the mere idea of it.

Living back at the Hall was a horrible prospect for Hero, it would mean he would have to face his mother's sadness, and he fancied, accusing looks.

Because they were in mourning, Christmas day was a solemn affair. The family attended church, then Bryant took them over to Ashmore House so that they could spend the day with the Armitage's.

Hero found this stressful, as his grandfather seemed to take delight in reminding him that he was "the man of the house now". Listing all the responsibilities this would entail.

When they first met that morning, his grandfather had shaken Hero's hand. As his beady eyes roamed the boy's face, he took note of the broken nose. He raised a bushy eyebrow at him, 'Been brawling have you, boy?'

'Boxing, grandpapa,' Hero answered.

'Boxing, huh? Mm, I used to enjoy a bit of sparring myself.'

'Really?'

'Yes, a good way of getting rid of any pent-up aggression.'

'Yes,' Hero agreed, did his grandfather understand a bit of what he was going through after all? He wondered.

The time dragged. Hero found himself counting the days before he could leave for school.

The house felt so empty and sad. Christmas without his papa and sister had been heart-wrenching. Seeing his mother's sad face every day made Hero hate himself even more.

When, at last, Bryant took him back to Aldersmiths, Hero felt as if he would be glad to take on the world, anything to relieve himself of this darkness that had settled in his heart and the pit of his stomach.

Chapter 10

Emily and Claire settled into a routine that carried them through the dark winter days.

One morning, when Claire opened her bedroom curtains, she was delighted to notice daffodils and snowdrops under the canopy of trees at the bottom of the lawns.

Spring had always been her favourite time of the year. She decided, after breakfast, she would go out for a nice long walk. She thought to ask her cousin to accompany her.

Out of the corner of her eye, she spotted movement, and saw Mr Jacobs in the rose garden, turning over the soil between each shrub. Because she had been spending so much time with Emily, she hadn't spoken to the man for a while. Seeing him that morning gave her a feeling of warmth and the anticipation of picking up their friendship once more – She smiled to herself, the strength of the feeling surprised her; goodness she was behaving like a schoolgirl.

'It is a beautiful day, my dear.' Claire declared as she cleared the breakfast table in Emily's sitting room. 'As soon as I have taken this down to the kitchen, I am going to set out for a nice long walk, will you accompany me?'

Emily gave her cousin a gentle smile. 'No, dear, I have some embroidery I wish to finish.'

'Are you sure? Some fresh air will do you good.'

'Please don't fuss so, Claire. I am quite capable of spending an hour or so without you watching over me.'

Claire felt her face redden. 'Yes, of course.'

Emily held out a placating hand. 'I did not mean to sound so abrupt, my dear, but you have been hovering over me like a mother hen.'

Claire laughed, and Emily joined in. 'I have been, haven't I.'

Emily nodded and gestured to the window, 'You may bump into Mr Jacobs,' she said, her lips turned up in a knowing smile.

Claire felt her face redden even more. 'I expect I will.'

'You like him, don't you?' Emily asked.

Walking over to the long window and gazing out, Claire answered, 'I do, he is a kind man.'

'There is a great deal to be said about that,' Emily said.

'I wonder why he never married?' Claire pondered, taking in the view.

Emily set aside her embroidery and joined her cousin by the window.

Claire heard her sigh. She glanced at her companion quizzically.

'James told me that he was engaged to a young woman from the village, but she caught pneumonia,' Emily explained, 'sadly she never recovered. Goodness, that was some time ago, before James and I were married.

'Oh,' Claire's hand fluttered to her chest. 'He never mentioned ...' her voice trailed off.

'He is a quiet man all round,' Emily observed. 'In any case, it is not a subject one would discuss often.'

'No,' Claire agreed.

As she took the breakfast tray back to the kitchen, Claire took the time to examine her reaction to Emily's news about Mr Jacobs. He had been intent on marriage, but what an awful thing to happen; Fate was a fickle and cruel mistress at times — plucking happiness away, leaving an empty shell behind.

She and Seth had built a wonderful friendship over the last few months.

It was the companionship she found with him that had kept her fortified. Giving her strength to support Emily. Was it more than friendship? She wondered. Suddenly, doubt set in, if they were becoming closer, then why had he not mentioned what had happened to his fiancé?

Claire donned a light shawl and left the house by the back door. She walked across the stable yard, waving to Charlie as she went.

Making her way to the rose gardens, she breathed in the fresh, scented air.

Spotting the man at the far end of the garden, Claire carried on along the path towards him.

So busy was he, that he did not hear her approach, which gave Claire a moment to admire his physique. He was a few inches taller than herself; he had a broad chest and shoulders. She noticed how the muscles of his arm rippled as he dug in the fork and turned the fertile earth. A robin sat on a branch of one of the rose bushes watching him closely, ready to swoop down and pick up the odd worm. Claire found that these thoughts had tinged her cheeks; she was sure they were nearly as bright as the robin's breast.

'Good morning, Mr Jacobs,' Claire called when she was a few feet away. Jacobs looked up and smiled at her. He has such a pleasant smile, she thought, as she returned his with one of her own. ''Tis a beautiful morning.'

'It certainly is, Miss Fellows.' He stood the garden fork upright in the earth, pulling out a large handkerchief from his brown corduroy trousers, he wiped his hands.

Claire noticed that his jacket, made from hard-wearing tweed, had been hung on one of the rosebushes, his cap sat on top. His hair was dark, which accentuated the liberal streaks of silver running through it. His face, as were his arms, were perpetually tanned and the sun had etched furrows onto the skin of his face which made him look distinguished.

'Her ladyship not with you?' he asked as he stepped onto the gravelled path.

'Not today.'

'I hope you don't think it impertinent of me to ask, how is she?'

'It's not impertinent at all,' Claire reassured him. 'It is wonderful that you care.'

He squinted, his dark brown eyes taking in the beauty of the gardens.

'Aye well, this family has been good to me. It makes me question the Lord's purpose for us when we are presented by so much tragedy in life.' He looked at her; his solemn look turned into a smile. 'Sorry to sound so mournful.'

'Not at all, you have mirrored my very own thoughts just this morning.' He nodded in understanding. 'To answer your question about the mistress,' Claire continued, 'she is taking one day at a time, but it breaks my heart seeing her suffer so,' her voice broke on the last word. She was annoyed with herself as tears pricked behind her eyes. 'Oh dear, I'm sorry. I just seem to be so close to tears all the time these days.'

'It is hardly surprising, Miss Fellows.' His look was candid and gentle. 'You've been doing a grand job keeping everything going.'

Her lips turned up in a hollow smile. 'Thank you for saying so. It just never seems like enough.'

'Aye well, all you can do is your best,'

'That is true.' Her head bobbed in acknowledgement. She glanced at him shyly. 'Your friendship has helped me remain strong, Mr Jacobs,' she glanced down at the gravel. 'I, um, cannot tell you how much it means to me, how much you mean to me.'

When he made no response, her head popped up; she could feel the heat in her cheeks. Oh, how stupid she had been, to blurt her feelings out like a schoolgirl. When she met his gaze, she found that he was studying her closely.

'The mistress is lucky to have you here,' he said.

'Yes, oh, yes.' She found herself giving a nervous laugh.

The man gestured to the rose beds, 'I've finished up here for now, would you care for some company on your stroll?'

'Oh yes, that would be lovely, but are you not busy? I wouldn't want to take you away from your work.'

Leaving the fork where it was, he picked up his jacket and shrugged into it, then popped his cap atop of his wiry hair.

'There is always work to be done,' he said, 'but nothing that can't wait a few minutes or so, especially if it means I can spend some time with a beautiful lady as yourself.'

His words made her flush deepen. 'Oh, mm.'

Jacobs glanced at her: as he did so, Claire noticed that his cheeks reddened under the tan.

'Oh Lord that was very clumsy of me.' His gaze travelled to the coppice woods in the direction they were walking. 'Even when I was a young lad, I never did have the knack of wooing a girl.'

A little laugh escaped her, 'and are you wooing me, Seth?' she asked softly. They had reached the shade of the first trees.

He placed a hand on her arm, bringing her to a halt.

'I enjoy your company, Miss Fellows - Claire,' As he searched for the right words, his gaze wandered over the woods. 'When I see you,' his gaze flickered to her face, there was uncertainty in his eyes. 'Mmm, my heart beats faster with the anticipation of your company.' He sighed as if he were pleased to have confessed his feelings at last.

'Is that a good thing?' she asked carefully. She could not help her heart fluttering with excitement.

Looking at her then, she could see a smile light up his face. 'Oh, aye, it is a good thing, Claire' He took his cap off and ran his long fingers through his hair absently. The gesture made it stand on end comically. Seth studied the leafy ground. 'Something I've been longing to say to you for a while now but never thought I would summon the courage.' He gave a little chuckle as he looked at his companion. 'This was something I never thought I would feel again.'

Claire nodded, 'Yes, Emily told me about your fiancé. I am so sorry.'

He dropped his gaze once more. 'Aye, me too, but these things happen. I was angry for a long time after, mind you. Felt robbed of a future. But James Woodley helped me as did Bryant.' His eyes crinkled in a smile once more. 'They kept me too busy to think, and I was grateful for that. Although the nights were the worse when I had time to dwell.'

'Oh, yes,' Claire nodded in understanding. Together, they continued their stroll. 'I had that when I lost Joseph. I didn't want to face the future.' She made a sweeping gesture, 'coming here helped so much.'

'Aye, it's a good place to be.'

They gave each other a mutual smile.

The conversation between them was easy, natural as they followed the circular path through the trees.

When they came to a glade full of bluebells, Claire stopped and breathed in the sweet scent with pleasure.

'Oh, isn't this wonderful.'

'A glorious display by all accounts,' Seth agreed.

'I will pick some to take back to Emily.'

'I'm sure she will like that.'

Carefully, Claire stepped over the clumps of flowers, so she did not crush any.

When she stepped over a particularly large group of bobbing lilac heads, Seth held out a hand to her. She took it.

His hands were calloused, which was not surprising, but his skin felt warm to the touch. Claire felt a tingling feeling. She wanted to giggle like a young girl. The next thing she knew, she was in Seth's arms. The picked flowers for Emily dropped from her grasp.

Seth gazed down at her, he searched her features, drinking them in with relish.

'May I ask permission to kiss you, Claire?'

She smiled and cupped his cheek in her hand, 'Oh, yes, please do.'

Claire relished the scent of him, earthy, a tang of shaving soap, and fresh air. She adored the feeling of his solid chest against her own. She did not want the kisses to stop, but in the end, he drew back.

He smiled at her, a teasing glint in his eye, 'Well, that was very pleasurable, I must say.'

Grinning back, she said, 'I'm extremely glad you found it so.'

He knelt and picked up the dropped flowers, as he handed them back to her, she noticed a frown creasing his forehead.

'What is it, what's the matter?' She took the flowers from him. Was he regretting the kiss?

'I am more than fond of you, Miss Fellows.' He held her gaze. 'but, in the scheme of things, we are worlds apart.'

'Oh, poppycock,' she found herself saying. Seth raised an eyebrow in surprise. 'Like yourself, I have been a widow for too many years, Seth Jacobs, and after everything that has happened here, I wish to seize happiness where I can, life can be far too short.'

'So, what do you suggest, Claire?' he asked carefully, although a smile hovered on the edge of his lips.

'May I suggest, Seth, that you kiss me again and we can go from there.' Goodness, what on earth had gotten into her? Much to her disappointment, he made no move to do as she bid. She felt her heart stutter and her stomach drop; oh, she had made a mess of this, hadn't she. 'Oh, you must think me such a fool,' she uttered, her voice cracking with emotion. She went to step back from him, but he reached out and took her hand in a firm grip. She glanced up at him once more.

'A little blinkered perhaps, but never a fool,' his voice was filled with kindness, and possibly something else, awe perhaps? 'I have savings,' he continued, a note of gravity weighted his words, 'but no home to offer you, other than a mere room above the stables. And then there is your cousin; the mistress of this estate, what would she think. Or anyone else for that matter if we married?'

'If we married?' Claire's voice was a mere whisper.

His lips turned up in a smile. 'Why, tell me what you were thinking, Claire? That you were going to seduce me and not marry me? I didn't take you for such a wicked woman.'

She saw the merriment in his eyes and gave him an uncertain smile in return. 'You are jesting with me, Seth Jacobs. What exactly are you saying?'

'I am saying, Miss Fellows, that I treasure our time together, and I treasure you. I am delighted that you feel the same, no, not delighted - euphoric; yes, that is the word, euphoric, that you feel something for me.' He gazed over her at the woods beyond, but she knew it was not the scenery he was looking upon but exploring some inner feelings. 'I never thought I would ever feel this way again after losing Margret,' he said at last as he looked at her once more. He smiled tenderly then, 'thank you for opening my heart to love again, Claire.'

'I feel the same after Joseph,' she said in a soft voice.

'Well then, we shall ask the permission of the mistress to marry,' he said with determination, 'when the year of mourning is up, of course. Then, I shall find a place to live in. If you agree, that is?'

'Oh yes,' she found herself saying, 'I do.'

He bent his head then and captured her lips once more.

Chapter 11

O h, my Lord, what just happened? Claire walked back to the house in a daze. Her heart was beating like a hummingbird's wings, and there were butterflies in her belly. She felt – what was it Seth said? He felt *euphoric*. Yes, that was precisely how she felt too.

When she got back to the house, instead of going directly to Emily's sitting room, Claire went to her room, sat down at the dressing table then gazed at the mirror. Her cheeks were flushed, and not just from the fresh air. Tucking a stray curl back behind her ear, she smiled at her reflection. Suddenly, she could see the young woman who had been wooed by Joseph Fellows. Her love for him had been all-consuming and quite passionate. The love she felt for Seth was gentler, although, she did have to admit to herself that her heart had sped up when they had kissed. Claire surprised herself when she let out a girlish giggle.

She placed both hands upon either cheek. 'I'm in love,' she announced to her reflection. But then her expression sobered. What if Emily did not agree to the marriage? What would they do then? Would they both be 'let go' from this place they both called home? "I will find us somewhere to live," Seth had said, but where? Claire jumped to her feet and restlessly paced the pale blue Chinese carpet. *Oh, there was too much to think of, too much to consider.* She knew she would have to hide her happiness from Emily: it simply wasn't fair to feel so happy when they lived in a house so touched by death.

The year of mourning would be up in a few weeks – but as Claire well knew, there was no simple timescale for these things. Emily would still carry those losses, as she would herself; she missed James and Angelica so much, and dear Hero. Perhaps it was too soon – she and Seth didn't have to say anything yet, did they?

Claire flopped down on the edge of her bed. She sighed; her thoughts were in turmoil.

Over luncheon, later that day, Emily pushed her soup bowl aside, barely touched, as she studied her cousin across the table. Claire was intent on staring out of the window.

'You had a pleasant walk this morning, Claire?' she asked.

'Mm, sorry, did you say something?' Claire noticed the enquiring smile on Emily's face and found herself flushing, what could the other woman see in her expression?

'I asked if you had a good walk this morning.'

'Yes, oh yes, thank you.' Claire wiped her lips with her napkin then set it aside, pushing her soup bowl away. 'I picked you some bluebells,' she said, but then her flush deepened when she realised, she had left the blooms in the woods. 'I, um, left them in the kitchen.'

Emily raised her eyebrows, picked up her cup of tea and took a sip. She replaced the cup gently in the saucer.

'Well, I shall be glad to receive them.' Emily continued to eye her companion with interest. I saw you wander off into the woods with Mr Jacobs.'

Claire dropped her gaze so that Emily would not read anything into it.

'Yes, he accompanied me on my stroll.'

'That is nice, my dear.'

'Mm, it was nice.'

'Claire,' Emily's voice was direct, and her cousin glanced at her warily. 'I've known you since we were children, you are more like a sister to me than a cousin.'

'Yes,' Claire nodded in agreement.

Emily leaned across the table as she scanned the other woman's face. 'You have never been able to keep secrets, Claire; it simply isn't in you. Tell me what happened this morning?'

'Seth, Mr Jacobs has asked me to marry him,' she blurted out without thinking.

'Ha, I knew it.' To her cousin's surprise and delight, Emily gave a tinkling laugh.

'You suspected?' Claire was astonished.

'Yes, of course. You always glowed with happiness after spending time with Mr Jacobs. I could see how he would follow your every movement when he was out tending the gardens.'

'Oh gosh, Emily, I have underestimated your gift of observation.'

'Yes, you did.'

Claire jumped to her feet. 'He was, I mean is, going to ask your permission, my dear, and we have no idea of where we shall live...' her voice trailed off.

'Well, of course, I would give you both my permission to marry. And as for where you can live, the Dower house is vacant for now, well, until Hero marries at least. You may live there. Although I shall miss your company terribly.'

Claire realised she was gazing at Emily with her mouth agape. She closed it. 'You would give your permission and let us live in the Dower house?' Claire confirmed, her voice full of disbelief.

Emily smiled, 'Why yes, of course.'

Claire rushed around the table and hugged her cousin tightly. 'Oh, thank you, my dear.' They clung together for a long moment, then Claire pulled away, 'we shall not marry until the year of mourning is up,' she stated. 'I appreciate that, and I do think for the sense of priority, that would be best,' Emily agreed.

'Oh, I cannot tell you how happy this makes me feel.' Claire felt as if she could dance with jubilation. 'Would you mind if I go and find Seth and tell him what you have said?'

Emily smiled at her, 'yes, of course. Off you go.'

After Claire had left the room, Emily sipped her tea which was now tepid, as she replaced the cup on the saucer, she felt the weight of sorrow in her heart. She was always aware of it, every day, every moment, would it ever lift? Did she want it to? That strange notion unsettled her, holding on to the pain of loss would not only damage herself but Horacio too. As Claire had mentioned their year of mourning was almost up, but Emily felt as if it were just yesterday that she lost her beloved husband and daughter. She ached for them.

Then there was Hero; the closeness they had once experienced was drifting away. Emily felt as if she did not recognise her son. She sensed the darkness of death haunting him because she felt it too; they were both alone on ships sailing in the turbulent waters of life.

Getting up from the table, Emily went to the window to look out, she could not see Mr Jacobs, but she was sure that Claire would find him quickly enough. She felt genuinely delighted for her cousin - so glad that Claire could find happiness once more.

*

'Absolutely not!' Robert Armitage's voice thundered, making the three ladies in the room wince.

Claire jumped to her feet in agitation. 'I am not asking for your permission, Uncle Robert. I am telling you that Seth and I will be married in August. I hoped you would give me away.'

'Give you away!' Robert's face was red with anger. 'I cannot believe that you are proposing to marry a mere gardener of all things.'

'He is a well-read man.' Claire defended her beau.

'I have given them my permission to marry,' Emily sat at the tea table with her mother. 'I am happy to offer them the Dower house as a place to live for now.'

'You see,' Robert blustered as he got up from the wingback chair where he had been sitting reading the paper while the ladies had their afternoon tea. 'They haven't even got a place to live.' He threw the paper down on an occasional table.

'We will manage,' Claire uttered softly.

'Oh, Claire, what would your dear mother have said about this.' Mary Armitage spoke up from across the table. She had just been cutting slices of the cook's famous teacake for everyone. Her hand holding the knife, hovered over the cake as she looked at her niece with concern.

'Mother would have been happy for me.' Claire sat back down, but only perched on the edge of her chair.

It was a beautiful June day. The sun streamed through the windows of the drawing-room, where the French-doors had been opened to capture the breeze. The scent of freshly mowed grass could be detected, which made Claire think longingly of Seth's arms.

'Claire deserves this happiness,' Emily spoke up for her cousin. 'Really, it is none of your business, papa. Claire is an independent woman and able to make her own decisions.'

'Ha, able to make her own decisions? Well, I did imbue you both with far more sense. Quite frankly, I am disappointed in both of you.'

'I'm sorry you feel that way, Uncle Robert,' Claire spoke up defensively, 'but it will not change my mind, Seth and I will be married this coming August.'

'Well, we shall have nothing to do with it.' Robert strode over to a sideboard and poured himself a drink from a decanter.

'Robert!' Mary's voice was raised with disapproval.

'Do not moan at me, wife, I need something to steady myself after this catastrophe of a revelation.'

Emily and Claire left Ashmore House soon after, both relieved to be away from the oppressive, disapproving atmosphere.

Claire was driving the one-horse trap, dressed in a driving outfit of pale grey silk, with a light woollen jacket worn over the top. Emily still wore black, although she had added an elegant, cream, lace collar and a cameo brooch to her attire. They both wore hats against the June sun.

'I am sorry, Claire,' Emily broke the silence.

'You have nothing to be sorry about, Emily. I should have known how they would take the news. They may be my aunt and uncle, but they have no right to interfere in my life.'

'No, of course not.'

They were silent once again; the only sounds were the noise of the horse's hoofbeats, the jangling of the harness and tack, and singing of birds in the hedgerows which were filling up with summer flowers.

'I am not going to tell Seth about their objections to our marriage, but I had already told him that I was hoping Uncle Robert would give me away.' She suddenly found her eyes misty with tears which she brushed away with the back of her gloved hand. 'Now, I shall have to make some excuse, particularly if they don't attend the wedding.'

Emily patted her hand. 'I will have a talk with father, to try and change his mind.'

'Thank you.' Claire nodded gratefully.

Seth was surprised the following morning when he found the Mistress' father, Robert Armitage, waiting for him by the bottom of the kitchen gardens.

'Good day, your lordship.' The gardener looked at the older man warily.

'Jacobs.' He acknowledged with a grim expression. 'My daughter and my niece visited us yesterday afternoon.'

'I am aware of that, sir.' Seth removed his cap, mainly for something to do. He guessed this was going to be an awkward interview.

'The story is that you are colluding my niece into marrying you.'

'Colluding?'

'Come now, man, you are taking advantage of a young widow who has no one to stand for her but myself.'

'Lady Woodley has given us permission to marry,' Seth pointed out.

'Ah, she may have done, but she is in no better a position, Jacobs, you must see that. You know that Miss Fellows has received a generous bequeath from the deceased squire?'

Seth gritted his teeth. 'Are you implying, sir, that I am after her money?'

'That is exactly what I am surmising, man.' He gave Seth a steely look, his eyes calculating. 'Tell me exactly what you will be bringing to this union?'

'I have some savings.' Seth felt the colour drain from his cheeks. Oh Lord, would the rest of the world see him as a man of immoral character too – marrying Claire for her money?

Robert saw the doubt enter the groundsman's eyes and he took the advantage, 'You cannot even offer her a place to live, can you?'

'Her ladyship has offered us the Dower House.'

'And what will happen when Master Horacio returns to take over the estate, eh? When he marries, the Dower house will become a home for Emily, leaving you both with no roof over your heads. I know that James paid wages which I consider are far above the average, but it will still be a mean amount for you to keep a woman like Claire, who is used to higher standards. Her five hundred pounds will not last you very long in the real world.'

'We would manage, I love her, and she loves me.'

'Ha, love, what codswallop.' Robert took a step closer; he was shorter than the gardener by a good few inches, but he was still an imposing figure in his riding outfit, whip, and hat. 'I don't believe a word of it. If you do feel something for her, you will not drag her through the mud that society will fling at you both. All doors will be closed to her as soon as you walk her down that aisle, are you willing to destroy her reputation so completely?'

Robert could see that Seth was lost for words. He drove home the advantage once again.

'Ah, I see that you do care about her, Jacobs. Prove to me that you do, leave her well alone. Tell her the engagement is off, that you made a stupid mistake! Even better, leave here, I could let you have a bit of money to set yourself up somewhere else.'

'Are you trying to coerce me with an offer of money, sir?' Seth's tone was outraged, but the doubts that Lord Armitage had fed him, were pulsing through his body with his racing heart. Then, he thought of Claire; his feelings for her, he gathered his strength, his righteousness and love for her. Stepping forward, he looked Lord Armitage in the eye and said, 'You can offer me the stars for all that I care, and I would take none of it. I love Claire, I want a good future for her, for us, and by God, I shall see that happen!'

'And, what of her reputation?' Robert's confidence was waning.

'Aye, well, it takes good muck in which things can be grown, strong and healthy, I have faith in our love for each other.'

'Uncle Robert.'

Both men's heads turned to the direction of the call, to see the topic of their conversation rushing towards them.

Her face pink from the haste, she came to a halt and looked at them enquiringly. 'I just saw Charlie, Uncle Robert; he told me you were here.'

'Yes, umm,' I was just having a chat with Mr Jacobs before I popped in to see Emily.'

'A chat with Seth?' She shot the two men a quizzical look.

'Your uncle is worried about your reputation if you marry me, Claire.' Seth spoke up baldly, Robert shot him a narrow-eyed look.

'Ha, my reputation! Oh, Uncle Robert, do you take me for being so shallow a person that I would worry what others would think of me,' She smiled at Seth, 'of us,' she concluded.

'Well, since your parents are no longer with us, Claire. Mary and I feel responsible for you.'

Claire laughed. 'you make me sound like a young girl; I am thirty-four, and a widow, I have seen enough of life to be mature enough to make my own decisions.' As she concluded the statement, she saw Seth smile with delight and approval; Claire smiled back.

Robert's face flushed with indignation. 'This is not just about you being mature enough to make decisions, niece.' He gestured to Seth, 'should you marry this man, it will be disastrous for your place in society – if you wish to remarry, let me find a suitable husband for you at least.'

This time it was Claire's complexion that reddened with anger. 'How dare you, Uncle Robert. Seth is a good man and a hard worker. We have become friends and closer over the time I have been living here. I would trust him with my life.' While she spoke, she moved closer to her intended. Claire reached out a hand to him which he took. They stood before Robert Armitage as a united front.

'Your life, maybe, but what of your money, Claire?'

'That is enough, Robert,' I think it is time you went on your way.'

'This will spell disaster for you.' He gave his final retort and walked back up the path towards the stables.

Seth looked at her with gentle eyes filled with concern. 'He is correct, my love. Marrying me will do nothing for your place in society.'

'Huh, not you as well, Seth Jacobs.' She turned, so she was looking up at him and poked a finger at his chest. 'I will not have it; do you hear me! Uncle Robert has always been a bit of a bully; I can assure you the only reputation he is concerned about is his own.'

'Perhaps we should give it some more time, Claire, you might change your mind.'

'Oh lord.' She rolled her eyes. 'He's gotten under your skin, hasn't he?' She glanced over the kitchen gardens where vegetables and herbs were being grown. 'We never know how long we have this gift of life,' she said softly. 'I lost Joseph and Emily has lost her husband and daughter.' She gazed into his soft brown eyes then. 'The wedding will go ahead as planned and we shall make the most of our every day together.'

Seth's broad face lit up with a smile. 'Aye, we will that.' He pulled her to him and kissed her soundly.

Chapter 12

'I should have seen this coming.' Claire paced the floor of Emily's sitting room.

Emily sighed and set aside her embroidery work. 'Yes, we both should have.'

Halting in midstride, Claire looked to her cousin. 'I give no store to what society thinks.'

'Ha, that goes for the two of us, then.'

Claire nodded. Walking over to the fireplace, she picked up a pretty Worcester porcelain vase. Absently she turned it in her hands. 'I do not need frivolity. I could not care less if we lived in a stable as long as we are together.'

'It certainly won't come to that, my dear, as I have said, you and Seth are welcome to the Dower House. It is empty. It will be good to have people living there again.'

Replacing the vase, Claire looked at the other woman and smiled.

'Thank you, dearest. It will do for now, but Seth and I will have to think of the future.' Claire blushed suddenly as an unexpected thought occurred to her, 'who knows, I may even have a child.'

'Oh, goodness, yes.' Emily smiled.

*

A few days later, Emily and Claire were seated at the breakfast table in Emily's sitting room, when Mrs Mason knocked on the door.

'There is a letter for you, Miss Fellows.' The housekeeper presented Claire with a silver tray, upon which a vellum envelope sat.

'Is it from Horacio?' Emily asked with interest as she spread some of Mrs Adam's homemade quince jelly on a piece of toast.

'No,' Claire plucked up the letter. 'Thank you, Mrs Mason.'

'Yes, Miss.' The housekeeper left them.

'I don't recognise the writing,' Claire commented as she studied the envelope.

'Well, open it then and discover the identity of the mystery writer,' Emily urged her.

Getting up from the table, Claire retrieved a letter opener from Emily's escritoire. Sitting down once more, she opened the letter and pulled out the single sheet of paper. Scanning the missive, she said, 'Oh, it's from Alice Fletcher.'

'Goodness, that is unexpected.'

Claire nodded as she started to read Alice's words out loud.

"Dear Miss Fellows, I am writing to let you know that I have completed my training with Mrs Bishop, at the Bishop's school for girls. They have been so kind here and

have helped me to seek a position as a lady's maid. I will be starting work in two weeks for a Mrs Tenison of Bath. I hope you don't mind, but I mentioned you as a reference. I just wanted to thank you, and Lady Woodley, from the bottom of my heart, for this opportunity. I still miss you all, but I am looking forward to my new life. It is sad to say, however, that Mrs Bishop is closing her school as she is retiring, and moving to Brighton, so I am one of the last pupils they shall have here.

Yours Sincerely, Alice Fletcher.

'Oh, that is wonderful for Alice,' Emily said as she poured herself another cup of breakfast tea.

Claire folded up the letter, 'Yes, very reassuring, indeed. Although it is a shame about the school closing.'

'Yes. It sounds as if her attendance at the school has helped Alice enormously.' Thoughtfully, Emily sipped her tea.

*

The date was set for Claire and Seth's wedding for the middle of August.

Both Emily and Claire had mentioned the forthcoming event to Hero in their letters. He had written back to Claire, but not his mother, stating how happy he was for her; "Jacobs is a fine fellow, Cousin Claire," he wrote, "I am pleased for you both."

As the days drew nearer to Hero's return, Emily became more and more withdrawn. Claire caught up in the dreamy heights of love, did not notice the change in her cousin.

Due to the extra work that Bryant, Charlie and Seth had taken on, Mr Durham, the estate manager, had suggested that they find an assistant for Seth, so they had taken on a young lad from Midcote, called Stanley; he was eager to learn and a hard worker. Seth found he enjoyed taking the youth under his wing. He found the lads cheeky sense of humour refreshing, particularly after the sad year they had all been through,

*

It was a few days before Hero was due to return, that Dr Scott visited Emily and she asked him to take morning coffee with her.

The July day was beautiful; the windows were open. The scent of summer roses competed with the mellow odour of the coffee in the sitting room.

Emily handed the doctor a cup of the rich brew.

He eyed her with the interest of a physician for a patient.

'You are still looking a little pale, my dear. Are you going out for a walk every day as I suggested?' he asked.

She sighed with resignation, 'yes, doctor.'

Raising a curious eyebrow, he asked, 'Would your melancholy be down, in part, with your parents' disapproval of Miss Fellow's marriage?'

Her gaze was direct as she looked at him. 'Ahh, so you heard about that.'

He nodded. 'Yes, I saw your mother the other day. It seems she is torn.'

'My father has forbidden her to visit us until Claire and I "come to our senses" as he put it.'

'Yes, so I gathered.'

'I shall never marry again, but Claire has found somebody to spend the rest of her life with, God willing. I just want my father to be pleased for her.'

'Yes, of course. It saddens me to hear you have closed your heart to any future possibilities of love, however.'

Giving him a haunted smile, she said, 'James was the love of my life, Dr Scott, no one could ever possess my heart as he did.'

Seeing the depth of her emotions swimming in her eyes, he bowed his head in reverence. 'You were lucky to find that kind of love, my dear,' he said at last.

'Yes,' she answered softly.

Swallowing to clear his throat of the emotion that had risen within him, he said, 'I am concerned about the extra stress this is having upon you, my dear.'

'Please don't fuss doctor.'

He gave her an understanding smile. 'I am sorry, but it is my job to keep an eye on you.'

Returning his smile with a weak one of her own, she said, 'It is also the thought of Hero's return playing on my mind,' she confessed.

He nodded and sat up straighter in the chair. He set his cup aside as he watched the woman intently.

Emily gazed out of the window. Despite the bright day, a dark shadow settled over her features. 'I am not sure how to be with him anymore,' she turned to the doctor. He could see the bleakness of her expression. 'I have noticed that every time he comes home, there is a gulf between us: we no longer have the closeness we used to have. It breaks my heart.'

Dr Scott saw a tear shimmer on her bottom lid. 'It will take time for both of you to heal. To come to terms with what happened.'

Emily nodded, then gazed at her hands which were resting on the polished tabletop. 'I can't help – I can't help blaming him,' she confessed, her voice breaking.

'Mmm, this often happens, we look for things, or people, to blame for these tragedies.'

She turned her gaze upon him. 'It is always there in my head, the shadow of tragedy. When I think of my son, his face is swathed in that darkness, and my heart is cold towards him.' The tear rolled down her cheek. 'I feel helpless. This feeling is so alien; I simply do not know how to change it, doctor.'

'I am a great believer that time heals – time is what you both need.'

Emily nodded, but then confessed, 'I am so frightened that I will never get that feeling back. I feel sick at the thought of seeing him because it opens up all these awful feelings inside me.'

'I do understand, Lady Woodley – Emily. Are you getting enough sleep?'

She shook her head, 'not really, doctor.'

'Before I leave, I will give you a sleeping draught to help.'

'Thank you.' She gestured to the silver pot on the table, 'Would you like more coffee?'

'Thank you,' he nodded.

Once Emily had refilled his cup and sat back down, the doctor said, 'Have you heard about Mr Cormack?' he referred to one of their neighbours on the eastern side of the estate.

'Mr Cormack?' She shook her head.

The doctor took a sip of coffee and placed the cup back on the saucer.

'Sadly, he passed away last week.'

'Oh dear, I am sorry to hear that. I am surprised no one has mentioned it.'

'Well, as you know he was a bit of a recluse,' Dr Scott said, 'there was only old Betty Ward that went in twice a week to do a bit of cooking and cleaning for him. It was she who found him seated in his favourite chair in the library. The cause of death was simply old age.'

'Well, yes, I gathered he was getting on in years. He was a strange man; I remember him chasing the Vicar off when he was trying to bring solace to the man. He called Reverend Thorpe an interfering old woman if I remember rightly.'

'Ha, yes, I remember that too.' The doctor chuckled. 'Surprisingly, he had many books based on philosophy and religion.'

'Really? Well, that is a surprise.'

'Yes, indeed. Sadly, it seems that he has died intestate.'

'Oh, it never really occurred to me before now, but has he any family to inherit?' she pondered.

'The estate has been put into the hands of solicitors, so I gather. They will try to trace any living relatives.'

'If you hear anymore, doctor, please let me know.'

'Yes, of course.'

*

Hero arrived home three weeks later.

Claire and Emily waited at the top of the steps, watching the carriage, which was driven by Bryant and Stan, draw up at the bottom of the steps.

It took a moment, once the vehicle had drawn to a halt, for the occupant to emerge.

Both women could see straightaway that Horacio had grown. His shoulders had filled out. The boyish looks had fallen away, to be replaced by a handsome physique. His broken nose, surprisingly, added to his good looks, giving him a rakish edge. He was hatless, and the summer sun shone on his thick dark curls, bringing out the copper tints.

He gazed up at the two women and smiled, although his blue eyes, which normally shined with merriment, were shadowed.

Emily reached out a hand to grab Claire's arm to steady herself. 'Oh God, he looks so much like James.'

Claire glanced down at her cousin in concern. She too had felt that jolt of recognition seeing this man/boy who now strode up the steps towards them.

'Mama, Cousin Claire,' Hero greeted them.

Even his voice sounds different, Claire thought, it had a deeper tone to it.

'Hero.' So that he did not notice his mother's discomfort, Claire stepped forward, reaching out. Hero took her proffered hands as she kissed him on the cheek. Then she stood back, and her gaze swept him up and down, 'You have grown, my dear.'

'Yes, I suppose I have.' He looked to his mother, 'Mama, how are you?'

'Well, thank you, Hero.' Emily leant up to kiss him on his cheek. He accepted the kiss, and then Claire was the one to take his arm and lead him into the hall.

'Aww, it is good to see you home, Master Horacio.' Mrs Mason stepped forward.

'Thank you, Mrs Mason, good to see you.'

'And you, sir.'

Both Claire and Emily exchanged looks; Mrs Mason's deferential approach underlined the changes that had taken place in the household.

While Bryant and Stan manhandled the two heavy trunks up to Hero's new set of rooms in the west wing of the house, Emily, Claire, and Hero went to the drawing-room, where coffee and sandwiches had been laid out.

Emily had opened up this more formal room as well as the library in preparation for the boy's return.

'How was your trip, dear?' Claire asked as she handed him a cup of coffee.

'It was uneventful.' Hero took the cup and saucer and walked over to the window.

Claire shot Emily a look; her cousin had taken a seat beside the empty grate.

'Good,' Clair acknowledged with a smile. 'And school, are you enjoying Aldersmiths?'

The youth turned away from the window. 'Mmm, as much as one can enjoy school.'

Claire laughed, although the sound was brittle. 'Yes, of course.'

Seeing her discomfort, Hero smiled at last. 'I am glad of your news, Cousin. Jacobs is a good man. Father always admired him.'

'Thank you.' Her smile was genuine.

Hero took a sip of his coffee, then set the cup on the table. 'I must let you know that I had a letter from Grandpapa concerning the matter.'

'You did?' Claire, a look of concern on her face, glanced at Emily, who also braced herself, what was Hero going to reveal?

'What did he say?' Claire asked warily.

'He said that I need to talk some sense into you, Cousin Claire. That as the future squire of this place,' he gestured about the room, 'I should forbid you making such a lowly marriage.'

'Oh, God.' It was Claire's turn to sit down as she felt her knees turn to jelly.

'How dare he!' Emily got up. She walked over to Claire and placed a reassuring hand upon her companion's shoulder. 'I have given them permission to marry, that is the end of it.'

'Absolutely mama, I said as much. I also pointed out that, as I mentioned just now, Jacobs is a respected employee here.' Giving her a reassuring smile, he continued, 'both of you are welcome here: this is your home; the place would not be the same without either of you.'

'Thank you, Horacio.' Claire's voice was thick with emotion.

Emily's expression was still stormy. 'I can't believe he went over my head and wrote to you.'

'I am sorry, mama, but I think he did the correct thing, to seek my counsel as the prospective squire.'

A myriad of emotions flickered across Emily's face; then she dropped her gaze. 'Yes, of course. I understand.'

'Grandpapa also mentioned that you had asked him to give you away, Cousin and that he had refused.'

Claire felt her eyes prick with unshed tears, 'Yes, that is so.'

'Well, I would be happy to do the job if you will allow me?'

Claire's face lit up as she glanced at him. 'Do you mean it, Horacio?'

'Why, yes, of course, I would not have said it if I didn't mean it.'

Claire rushed over to him. He just had time to brace himself before she took him in her arms and hugged him tightly. 'Thank you,' her voice was weighted by emotion and relief.

'Yes, that is exceedingly kind of you, Hero,' Emily commented. As she spoke, she felt a strange pull on her heart. Watching them embrace, how she wished to do the same; take her boy in her arms, but the thought splintered, and she felt the pain ripple through her. When Claire turned back to her, Emily found a smile, nurtured by Claire's happiness.

'Isn't that wonderful, Emily?'

'Yes, my dear, it certainly is.'

Chapter 13

Although Emily tried so hard to behave normally, she felt that Hero's presence in the house had enfolded her in the past: the painful memories that she was trying to set aside became all the more apparent. She knew it would be difficult, of course; everything was still so – so raw. She wondered if she would ever heal from the double loss. And, on top of everything, there was the alienation from her family. She knew very well how obstinate her father could be, he would dig his heels in, and that would be that. She had felt extremely sorry for Claire and annoyed with her father for his rejection of them both.

That very morning, she had received a letter from her sister, Celia, saying she was scandalised that Claire was making such a lowly marriage; she was also angry with Emily, for allowing it to go ahead. With lips pursed in stubbornness, Emily had ripped the missive up.

Then there was Hero; part of her was grateful to him for stepping in to give his cousin away. Emily also had to admit she admired him for standing up to his Grandfather. Goodness, Hero had been at that school for a year; he had grown up so much. Taller than her, but still not quite as tall as Claire. He had filled out. There was an obstinate set to his jaw now.

Hero had mentioned a few times that he had been boxing at school; indeed, his nose, which had been broken, then not set properly, gave him a somewhat rakish look.

Emily wondered what James would have made of it all. He had abhorred violence of any sort.

Emily was grateful to be able to immerse herself into the preparation for Claire's marriage; keeping busy helped her to deal with the bad memories and her awkwardness around her son's presence.

It also helped to distract her from thinking of the future. She didn't know what she would do without Claire's calm presence in the house. The place already felt empty to her – she knew she needed a purpose in life but was at a loss.

*

Hero met up with Mr Durham, the estate manager and Mr Hawkins, who ran home-farm. Everything seemed to be running smoothly on the estate. There were a couple of decisions to be made, but apart from that, Hero had little to do regarding estate business.

As he had done when he had been home previously, he spent much of his time with Bryant and Charlie.

Myrtle, who had been shadowing Bryant's every move after Henry died, was so pleased to see Hero she yipped as she wrapped herself around his legs. When he bent down to make a fuss of her, she jumped up to lick his face with such enthusiasm that he ended up sitting on the cold bricks of the stable yard, Bryant and Charlie laughing loudly at his predicament.

'Seems she's happy to see you, lad,' Bryant called.

'Yes – yes.' Hero could not help but laugh himself. Once he had extricated himself from the dog's enthusiasm, he followed Bryant into the tack room where he and Charlie had been cleaning and oiling the leathers of bridles and saddles.

'We miss the old boy, though,' Bryant commented as Hero brushed off his trousers.

'Yes, poor old Henry. I just wish I had been here to say my goodbyes.'

'Aye, well, it happened quickly, thank goodness. He went in his sleep.'

Hero nodded, 'Yes, Cousin Claire wrote to let me know.'

'So, how are you, master Hero?' Bryant eyed the youth with curiosity as they entered the stables where it was much cooler. He too could not help but notice how much the lad had grown.

'Well enough.' Hero took down a bridle and started cleaning it, once that was done, he started working the oil into the leather.

'Still fighting?' Bryant asked.

'Boxing, yes.' Hero did not look up from his task.

'Had many wins?' Charlie asked with interest.

'One or two, I do well enough,' Hero finally looked up, Bryant could see the pride in his eyes.

'Aye, and what sort of damage do you inflict on the other man?' Bryant set the bridle he had been working on, back on its hook.

Hero shrugged. 'We all have coaching from Master Baxter; he is quite knowledgeable about most sports; in fact, his nickname is Boxer Baxter, 'Hero chuckled. 'He suggested that I continue to spar while I am home, make sure I keep in shape.'

'I'll spar with you, master Hero.' Charlie jumped in with his offer. 'You used to do some boxing, didn't you Uncle Bill?' The youth looked to his uncle inquiringly.

'Aye, when I was a young lad, I did.' Bryant admitted.

'I never knew that.' Hero studied the older man with interest.

'Well, it was a long time ago.' The groom nodded towards Hero's hands. 'Your knuckles are looking a bit red and bruised.'

'Yes, they hurt after a fight.'

'I've got some ointment that will help that, but the best thing is to set up a sack filled with earth. We can hang it from a beam in the storage shed and use it as a punching bag, get those knuckles calloused and used to the punch.

Hero nodded with enthusiasm, 'Yes, thank you, Bryant.'

*

There were three days to go until the wedding. Bryant and Jacobs were sitting together on a bench overlooking the paddocks.

They sat in companionable silence for a while. Seth was smoking a pipe and the aroma of fragrant tobacco mixed with the scent of warm earth. It had been another hot day, and they could feel the stored heat rising from the ground.

'I'm not sure if I'm doing the right thing,' Seth spoke up at last.

Bryant didn't turn his gaze away from the view. 'I know you love her, man, and she loves you, no doubt about that. It was so plain on both your faces during the times you were together; it was comical to behold. I never knew you could blush like a starstruck girl. It was quite a revelation.'

Seth chuckled. 'Ha, I'm glad you found it comical.'

'Oh, I did.' Bryant smiled. 'You don't think you are good enough for her, is that it?'

'Aye, in part, but by marrying me, Claire is ostracising herself from some of her family, I just don't think I can do that to her.'

'They will come around, and besides, the mistress and master Hero are accepting of the union – in fact, everyone on the estate, including me, are happy for you both.'

'Aye, I'm grateful for that.'

'She's a widow, and you lost your Maggie before you could start your lives together; seems to me that you are both deserving of some happiness in life.'

Seth bobbed his head in acknowledgement of his friend's words. 'I don't know about living in the Dower house, though. All the women have been up there for the last few weeks cleaning and sprucing it up; I'm a plain man, not used to finery, and the mistress has insisted we live there rent-free, it doesn't sit well with me.'

Bryant shifted on the seat so that he could look the other man in the eye.

'Aww, listen to yourself, Seth Jacobs, you are one of the luckiest men hereabouts. Be bloody grateful for these blessings, especially after everything that happened last year. And, if the mistress and master Hero won't accept any rent, then that's up to them, don't throw their generosity back in their faces.'

Seth chuckled again, 'Good Lord, that sermon just put me well and truly in my place!'

'Aye, and so it should.' Bryant laughed. 'So, no more whining, man, enjoy your blessings.'

*

It was a beautiful summers day at the beginning of August. The bell of the village church rang joyfully. The church was filling up fast.

Seth, who was dressed in a new set of clothes, kept running his finger around his collar; *crikey, he was not used to being dressed up in such finery.*

'You look very handsome, Mr Jacobs,' Janice, the housemaid had looked him up and down as they waited for Charlie to bring the trap round to take him to the church.

'Thank you, lass.' He flushed. Noticing his discomfort, the young woman laughed.

'He looks very handsome, indeed.' Mrs Mason, who was dressed in her best outfit, as was Janice, bustled into the front hall. She looked the man up and down and nodded in approval as she straightened the cream cravat at his throat, then brushed off the shoulders of his dark brown frockcoat.

'You'll do.' She approved as they heard the wheels of the trap arriving on the gravel at the bottom of the steps.

Seth popped his hat on, he walked down the steps and climbed into the vehicle. He had to admit to himself he was nervous but excited at the same time; *why he felt like a child at Christmas.*

'All ready then, Mr J?' Charlie asked as he set the horse to a trot.

'Aye, lad, I actually think I am.'

Bryant drove Mrs Mason, Janice, and Mrs Adams to the church, then came back to pick up the bride to be, the mistress and master Hero.

Both Emily and Janice had helped to get Claire ready, when she walked down the sweep of stairs to where Emily and Hero were waiting for her, Emily found herself sighing and tears pricked her eyes.

'Oh, my dear, you look so beautiful.' Emily gushed as Claire stepped off the bottom step.

'It is all thanks to you and Janice.' She gave them a thin smile.

'Nonsense, Cousin Claire, you are, and always have been beautiful, and today you are especially stunning.'

Claire glanced at Hero in surprise, 'Why, thank you, my dear.'

He grinned and offered her his arm.

She returned his smile and said, 'Mmm, it appears that you have the nature of a charmer, Horacio.'

'Just saying it as it is.' Hero chuckled.

They walked down the steps together to the waiting carriage.

'May I say, Miss Fellows, you look very fine indeed,' Bryant said as he helped her into the carriage.

'Why, thank you, Mr Bryant. Seems this is a day for compliments.'

'And, so it should be, my dear.' Emily settled herself into the seat opposite her cousin. 'You look beautiful.'

Claire did, indeed, look beautiful in a dress of pale sage-green silk, decorated with embroidered cream and lilac flowers. She wore a half veil made of Honiton lace and carried a bouquet of cream roses and gypsophila.

It didn't take them long to get to the church.

Emily went in first to take her seat, and then Hero walked Claire up the aisle.

Seth was waiting nervously, but as soon as he saw Claire, he forgot his nerves as their eyes met. Claire felt her cheeks blush but kept her eyes on Seth; they both smiled in mutual delight.

As soon as the service was finished, Mrs Mason, Mrs Adams, Janice, and some of the girls from the village, were picked up by Charlie and driven back to the house. They started to lay out the food for the wedding feast on trestle tables which had already been set up on the front lawn of the house.

It was a jolly affair for all. The children from the village ran around on the lawns playing games of tag; their laughter was the most beautiful music on this happy occasion.

Many toasts were drunk, and good wishes given to the couple.

Later on, as the sun began dip in the sky, one of the village lads produced a fiddle, and everyone danced to energetic jigs.

Emily sat quietly, watching the festivities. Despite the happiness of the occasion, she could feel the heaviness of sadness weighted in her chest; James would have been so happy for Claire, it was so sad he wasn't here to witness this special day.

The sound of the children's laughter should have lifted her spirits, but it made her loss all the more poignant.

Despite the hour becoming late, the children still had bags of energy. Emily continued to watch them and wished with all her heart that Angelica was amongst the happy lot.

As the sun began to set, the sky went through a metamorphosis of colour, from rose to peach and apricot. It was at that moment, the liquid gold of the sun glinted off a head of thick curling hair. Emily sucked in a breath, for just a second she thought it was Angelica, her angel still alive, but the thought and feeling passed; of course, it was one of the little girls from the village. Emily dropped her head to gaze at her pale hands resting on her lap.

It was around midnight when Claire and Seth made a discrete departure from the party that was still in full swing.

Although Claire's feet were aching from all the dancing, when Seth suggested they walk to the Dower House, she gladly agreed.

'I simply cannot describe how happy you've made me, Claire.' Seth glanced down at her as they strolled under the canopy of the trees. His eyes were moonstruck with love for this woman.

Returning his smile, Claire said, 'I feel like the luckiest woman in the world.' She wrapped her arm tighter about his own.

'I'm so glad, my dear.'

A soft orb in the sky, the moon cast a glow that tinted the majestic trees with liquid silver. The night was dusty from the day's heat.

The driveway split off; one way led to the entrance to Woodley Hall, the other led downhill to the Dower House.

They turned a corner of the wooded lane, and then the house was in sight. Someone had left a lamp shining in the window to welcome the newlyweds.

The Dower house was a charming place, built of golden Cotswold stone. It was surrounded on three sides by pretty gardens. There were also stables and outbuildings around the back.

Emily had pushed Claire's protests aside when she had told her that she had employed one of the girls from the village, Lily Albright, to help her cousin keep house. 'I have paid her wages for six months,' Emily said in a voice that broke no argument. 'Call it a wedding present if you will.'

'That is far too generous,' Claire protested.

'Tut, you need help, Cousin. You cannot be expected to take on every chore in the house. Besides, I am being selfish,' Emily smiled, 'having some help will free you up for visiting me at the hall.'

Finding that her eyes prickled with emotion, she gave Emily a soft smile.

'You will be alright, won't you?' she asked, her voice full of concern.

Emily nodded, 'of course I will, but please decease from protesting, and accept my gifts with the love in which they are given.'

Claire laughed, 'well, I have no argument for that statement.'

'Good,' Emily nodded in satisfaction.

'Now, you just wait a moment,' Seth declared as Claire reached out to open the front door of the little house.

'Seth?' She glanced at him in surprise as he put one arm around her shoulders and the other under the back of her knees and scooped her off the step. 'What on earth...' She held on to him tightly.

'Mmm, well, I have to carry you over the threshold.' He grunted with effort, 'but it might have been a good idea to have opened the door first!' Claire laughed with delight as Seth fumbled with the catch on the door while ensuring he did not drop her.

With much effort and laughter, he finally got the door open, then carried her across the threshold into the hall.

'Oh, you are a silly man.' Claire swiped him on the shoulder as tears of mirth ran down her cheeks. 'You could have put your back out.'

He gave her a huge grin, 'I've been longing to do that for a long time, Mrs Jacobs, so please indulge me this pleasure.' Before she could say another word, he pulled her into his arms and kissed her soundly.

Chapter 14

As August bowed into September, Hero was more than ready to return to Aldersmiths. He had worked hard sparring with Charlie, under Bryant's supervision. His knuckles were no longer tender but callused and hard. Bryant had to admit that the boy had skill. It had been a pleasure to coach him.

*

Emily felt as if she were going mad as she rattled around in the large house. She could not help but be melancholy, feeling that she had no direction in life anymore.

Considering her son, Emily was grateful that he had school to focus on. She was also very appreciative to Mr Bryant for taking the boy under his wing.

It was the middle of September when Dr Scott dropped by to see Emily. It was purely a social call. Emily was relieved to have a break from the monotony of the long days, so she welcomed the man with alacrity.

Because the weather was still warm, they sat out on the patio overlooking the back lawns that ran down to the paddocks in the distance.

'I saw Mrs Jacobs the other day,' Dr Scott commented as he took a sip of the rich coffee. 'I have to say she is looking radiant.'

'Yes, she is,' Emily agreed as she squinted in the bright light. There were four horses in the paddocks. She smiled when she saw them tossing their heads and frolicking across the yellowing grass. 'I am pleased for her.'

'Does she visit often?' he asked.

Emily glanced at the man; she had caught an undercurrent of concern within the question. 'Oh, she is busy with her married life. I am pleased for her.'

'You must miss her?' The Doctor raised a questioning eyebrow.

'Yes, I do, the house feels so empty.' She looked at him then, 'it is a wonder to me that one person can have such an impact on one's life. That you feel the loss of them so – so deeply when they are not there anymore.' They both knew that Emily was referring to her family losses and not just the fact that her cousin was living elsewhere.

'Yes, my dear, you are quite right, of course.'

Emily continued to gaze off into the distance. 'It has been on my mind for a while now; I recognise that I need a project, Doctor.'

'A project? Have you got something in mind?'

She gave him a direct look. 'Yes, actually, I do.'

'Would you like to share? I have to say you have me intrigued.'

Emily smiled. 'You remember telling me that Mr Collins passed.'

'Yes, of course,' he nodded.

'You also mentioned that there appeared to be no living relatives to inherit the estate.'

'Well, they have been looking into the matter, so I gather.'

'Yes, that is true. I took the liberty of writing to Mr Stokes, the family solicitor, who contacted the solicitors dealing with the Collins estate. He recently let me know that they have found a distant cousin related to Mr Collins.'

'Really, that is interesting,' Dr Scott sat back in the wrought iron garden chair.

'Yes,' Emily nodded. 'There has been correspondence back and forth, the cousin lives in Scotland and has no interest in the estate, other than selling it.'

'Quite frankly, I am not surprised. It has been left to go to rack and ruin.'

Without asking, Emily topped up the doctor's coffee cup and then her own. She set the silver pot aside.

'Did you know that generations of Woodley's have been trying to buy the place for years?' She took a sip of the aromatic brew.

'I have heard the rumours of course; I gather the house and grounds cut a great swathe of land from the Woodley Hall estate.'

'It does. Apparently, it was always something that irked Thomas Woodley. He was dying to get his hands on the land. James had no interest in it, however.'

'So, what are you saying, my dear?' he prompted as he studied her expression with interest.

'I have instructed Mr Stokes to make an offer for the house and lands, on my behalf.'

Dr Scott nearly choked on his coffee. 'You are going to buy the place?'

'I am, Doctor.' Emily gave him a half-smile. 'My offer has been accepted. Mr Stokes is working with the other solicitors. We will shortly be concluding all the necessary paperwork.'

'Good Lord! What does Master Horacio have to say about this?'

'My son has no say in the matter whatsoever. I am using my own dowry money to buy the place. I am going to turn it into a school.'

'A school?' The man looked utterly flabbergasted. Emily gave him a satisfied nod.

'A school,' she confirmed with a wide grin.

Emily went on to tell Dr Scott about the school that Alice Fletcher had been attending, that she had been trained in the accomplishments of a lady's maid and had found a successful position because of it.

'The school, run by a Mrs Bishop, has recently closed as the woman is retiring.' Emily told him. 'She was an advocate for young girls who have truly little chance of finding a good position in life.'

'Good gracious. Are you sure you are doing the right thing, taking on a project of such a scale?'

Emily's gaze turned back to the view before her, although she did not see it as her thoughts turned inwards.

'James left me very well off, Dr Scott. I could continue with this somewhat cossetted life – knowing that one day Horacio will be taking over the estate. I am sure that he will marry, and I would be assigned to the dower house.' Her eyes flickered to his face. 'I have found the prospect of facing such a future quite, mmm, mind-numbing.'

'Goodness, a school?'

'Yes, a school – The Brook School for Impoverished Girls. It has quite a nice ring to it, don't you think?'

'Well, umm, yes.'

'It also means I will not be a burden on my son; we can live separate lives.'

'Well, it seems that you have thought all this through.'

'Oh, I have, Doctor. You are the first person I have told of my plans. Actually, it is mainly down to you that this has come about.'

'Goodness ...' he fumbled for something to say.

Emily smiled at his discomfort. 'I feel that this is a lifeline for me, Dr Scott. After losing Angelica and James, I have felt so distanced from life. It is rather like a large part of my being has followed them to the grave. I don't know who I am anymore. Do you understand?'

Dr Scott cleared his throat and nodded. 'I do indeed, my dear!' He smiled then, an encouraging grin. 'Well then, I feel honoured to be the first person to hear your news, Mrs Woodley.'

When she turned to him, her expression was radiant. 'Thank you.' She nodded with satisfaction. 'I know I shall need help, of course, and my first port of call will be Claire.'

'Oh, I am sure that Mrs Jacobs will give you as much support as possible.'

'Yes, I am lucky to have her in my life.'

'She cares for you greatly. I know she worries about you.'

'I do not need people to worry about me; I simply need practical help.' Emily realised her tone was abrupt. She softened the statement with a smile. 'For the first time in over a year; I feel I have something to live for - something to look forward to.'

The Doctor nodded with approval. 'I can see that, my dear. I am very pleased for you.'

'Thank you, Dr Scott.' Emily's face beamed with purpose.

*

Three days later, the solicitor, Mr Stokes, arrived from London. Emily had a tray of coffee served in James' study.

Mr Collins' cousin's representatives had signed all the relevant papers. Mr Stokes went over all the paperwork with Emily. Then she signed the papers with a flourish of determination.

Mr Stokes presented her with the deeds of Brook House and a ring of keys for the place.

'Congratulations, Lady Woodley, you are now a woman of property in your own right.'

'Thank you, Mr Stokes.' She hugged the keys to her chest.

'You also own the contents of the house. It appears that Mr Collins was something of a collector.'

'Yes, Mr Stokes.' Emily went to stand in front of one of the windows in the study. 'I have to confess that I have been down to the house and peered in through the windows, I can tell there is a great number of, mm, bits and pieces in the place.'

'Oh, there is. I have contacts in the city and can arrange for all the items to be removed.'

'Mmm,' Emily turned back from the window. 'I will let you know if I need to utilise that offer.'

The solicitor bobbed his head in understanding.

Mr Stokes stayed for a further half an hour when they enjoyed some coffee and a piece of Mrs Adam's rich fruit cake. Then the man took his leave and Charlie drove him to the station in the Woodley trap.

When Charlie returned, Emily had him drive her down to Brook House. There was a short driveway to the place which was overgrown. Trees overhung the approach, and even though the day was bright and warm, the place felt dreary.

Mmm, Emily turned her face up to the dappled sunlight. *I will need to get this all cut back.*

The trees thinned, and an expanse of lawn presented itself. The grass was high and resembled a field of golden wheat that had gone amok.

Charlie brought the trap to a halt at the bottom of the steps.

'A bit of a dilapidated place,' the youth observed as he helped Emily down from the vehicle.

She gazed up at the ivy-covered walls and grinned, 'Yes, it is.' She couldn't help the feeling of excitement that rippled through her. 'You can wait here, Charlie. I'm going to have another look around.'

The groom watched her walk up the steps and could hear the jangling of keys as she searched for the correct one that would unlock the front door.

He was curious of course, as was everyone at Woodley Hall. They speculated what the mistress was about, why on earth had she bought this old house that had belonged to the eccentric Mr Collins?

Emily unlocked the door and stepped into the dark hallway. There was a strong, musty smell about the place that tickled the back of her nose. The tiled floor was dusty and streaked with mud in places. An old grandfather clock stood close to the bottom of the stairs; its pendulum hung still. The face was grimy with dust.

Turning left, Emily entered a room, which could only be described as the library; book-filled shelves lined the walls. There were also several piles of books that had been left on the floor and occasional tables.

Heavy burgundy drapes lined the windows, which hadn't been cleaned for years. The ivy growing up the exterior of the house had done it's best to close off these offerings of daylight, so the room was gloomy.

As she wandered around, Emily did not see the heavy furniture or the mottled, grubby walls; she saw bright classrooms, filled with industrious young girls – a step up for them for a better life with good prospects.

*

Upon hearing the news that Emily Woodley's plans had been finalised, Dr Scott called on her a few days later to see how she was getting on.

'I am so happy for you, my dear,' he said after she had outlined her ideas to him.

Once more, they sat on the patio overlooking the lawns, making the most of the fine weather before autumn well and truly settled in.

'Thank you, doctor.' She gave him a grateful smile, then chuckled to herself. 'Ha, I have to say that my family are most disapproving of my ideas; especially my father, who told me that if he had known that I would use my dowry in such a reckless way, he never would have given me the money.' She gave another chuckle. 'He had the audacity to say that he would call in a doctor to assess my sanity.'

'Really!' the Doctor didn't know what to say to that.

When she gave him a direct look, she said, 'Tell me, in your opinion, Dr Scott, have I lost my marbles, as the saying goes?'

He studied her face, thoughtful for a moment. 'Most definitely not, my dear, anything but.'

She nodded, 'that is reassuring, but I do believe where my family is concerned, I have been sent to Coventry.'

He raised his fair eyebrows. 'Ah,' he nodded, 'You don't appear to be to upset.'

The smile she offered him was beaming as she shrugged her shoulders.

'Quite frankly, after everything that has happened, I do not care one jot for my father's antiquated views when it comes to women owning property.'

It was the Doctor's turn to chuckle. 'Well said, my dear Mrs Woodley.' He was delighted to hear her laugh again. She looked years younger. He was pleased for her. 'I gather that Mr Collins' cousin was not interested in clearing the house,' he said after a moment.

'That is true. It is going to take a few weeks to clear everything. I have had several quotes for the work that needs doing. I am happy for Mr Mathews to organise everything.'

'Ah, work for the villagers that is good news.'

'Yes, quite.'

The Doctor shifted in his seat, crossing his legs. 'As you know, I have called in regularly to see Mr Collins.'

'Yes, I know he hasn't been in good health for several years.'

'That is the case. While I was in the house, I had a few chances to peruse the library. I must tell you, some of the books are rare, first additions. They would be classed as collector's items.'

'Really?' She looked at him with interest.

The Doctor nodded. 'I have contacts in the city, my dear. I know a very reputable bookseller who would give you a good and fair price for the additions. Then the proceeds could be put towards the cost of buying all the equipment a school would require.'

'Oh, goodness, yes.' Emily was delighted by the idea. 'Every penny would help.'

'Well then, I shall arrange for him to visit, and we can go from there.'

Chapter 15

'Have you completely lost your mind, Emily!' Celia, her artfully arranged hair finished off with a jaunty hat adorned with peacock feathers. A peacock blue day dress completed the ensemble; all the height of fashion no doubt, thought Emily as she watched her sister flounce around the sitting room, removing her gloves and half cape which she threw on a chair.

Celia's purpose for a visit was to try one last time to talk her sister into some semblance of sanity.

'On the contrary, dear sister, I haven't felt so animated for a long while,' Emily poured out tea for them both, as she did so she endeavoured to remain calm, not to be goaded by her sister.

Celia had arrived out of the blue, in a carriage manned not only by a driver but a footman too; how ostentatious.

When the carriage came to a halt at the bottom of the sweep of steps, the young footman disembarked, then knocked on the front door. He had then enquired of Mrs Mason if the mistress was "at home".

Mrs Mason had closed the door, then sent Janice off in a flurry to find Mrs Woodley.

Luckily, Emily had been present, but this was a rare occurrence these days, as she spent much of her day down at Brook House, supervising the work going on there.

Celia paused in her agitated pacing and gazed down at her sister. 'Quite frankly, I am worried about your decision making, Emily. First, you give Claire approval to marry a mere gardener, and now you have bought a dilapidated house that you say you are going to turn into a poor school for paupers and beggars.'

'Mr Jacobs is the groundsman here, not a gardener,' she corrected Celia, whose expression changed, she looked as if she had just sucked on a segment of sour lemon, her face crumpled in on itself even more, 'And the girls, they may be poor and needy,' Emily continued, 'but they are not beggars, they simply need some help to have a better life.'

'As you know Father and Mother, not to mention Arthur (she referred to her husband), are not at all pleased about any of this.' Celia narrowed her eyes as she inspected her sister. 'Something has happened to you since Angelica and James died.'

'It is called grief, my dear.' Emily stirred her tea vigorously, the silver spoon knocked against the delicate porcelain cup. 'Yes, something has happened to me since losing the two most important people in my life. Everything that has happened has made me realise the fragility of life, and how short it can be.' She looked her sister in the eye. 'The buying of Brook house is a fait accompli. The place is being cleared out. We shall keep some pieces of furniture that may be useful. I have a meeting with an architect and a builder next week.'

'You see, that is exactly what I mean. What on earth has possessed you? Meeting up with tradespeople.' Celia sniffed. 'This is not the behaviour of a respectable lady, come widow. What would James say about all these going's on?' Celia plonked herself down unceremoniously in the chair opposite her sister, the movement sent the feathers decorating her hat bobbing.

It was Emily's turn to narrow her eyes frostily, as she gazed at the other woman, who was dressed in such finery and had every want and need in life pandered to. 'James would be pleased with what I am doing. It is thanks to him investing my dowry wisely that I have the money to fund this undertaking.'

Celia snorted in derision. 'Yes, you are right, but then again, he always was a dreamer.' She tried another tack. 'And your son? What does he have to say about all this? He cannot be pleased, surely.'

'It doesn't affect Horacio, but I have written to him to let him know what is happening and *he is* pleased for me.'

'Oh Lord,' Puffing out her cheeks, Celia sat back in her chair, then her expression shifted once more. 'What will happen to the place if anything happens to you?'

Emily gave her a serene smile, 'Ultimately, I am putting together a board to run the school, they will be the trustees. However, I have already drawn up a will with Mr Stokes; the school shall be bequeathed to Claire and Seth, on the condition they keep it going, which of course they will. So, long after I am gone, the place will be able to continue and flourish.'

Celia took in a sharp breath, 'You are leaving the property to Claire?' Emily nodded and took a sip of her tea. 'How on earth can you trust her? I simply do not understand, Emily. I would question her judgement; after all, look at what she has done in the past. She ran away and married that tailor, who mortgaged his business to the hilt and left her penniless.'

'Claire did not run away as you put it. James and I attended her wedding. Joseph Fellows was a wonderful man, Celia. It was a tragedy what happened. I trust Claire completely. She is more like a sister to me than you ever were.'

Celia's mouth puckered. 'How could you say such a thing?'

'I am simply stating a truth, my dear.'

Emily's sister shot to her feet. 'Well, I – um we, shall have nothing to do with any of this. I feel that you have made some terrible decisions, you are the laughing stock of the local society, and the story is fast spreading like wildfire around town.'

'I am sure that there are many philanthropists in town who would agree with what I am doing.'

'Huh, those misguided fools. There is a hierarchy in this world for a reason; people have their places.'

Emily gave her sister a long look. 'You know, I feel sorry for you, Ceecee (she called her by her childhood name, which Emily knew very well Celia could not stand), with your cossetted and blinkered view on life. Next time you are travelling through London, open your eyes, see what is going on about you; there is a cavernous divide between rich and poor, it is a disgrace.'

Celia turned an unflattering shade of red. Puffing out her cheeks in annoyance, she reached for her cape. 'Well, I can see that I cannot talk any sense into you, so I shall be going. Just don't expect any visits from your family while you are in this- mmm - hysterical frame of mind.'

Emily also got to her feet and walked over to the fireplace where she pulled the bellpull to summon Janice to see her sister out.

When she turned back to the other woman, she said, 'To be quite frank with you: that news is a delight to me, for none of you would be welcome in this house.'

Even though Emily had stood up for herself, she felt emotionally drained after Celia left. She knew that her family would not understand her actions, but that was fine, they didn't need to understand her motives in buying Brook House: This project was not only for herself to find purpose in life, but in memory of James and Angelica, she may have lost her daughter, but she felt she could become a surrogate mother to young girls in need. Claire was delighted with the idea. Emily, however, had not yet informed her cousin that she had bequeathed the school to her.

*

Horacio was stretched out on his bed in his dorm room a letter from his grandfather in his hand.

One of the other boys had received a food parcel from home, so everyone was crowded around him as he handed out sweetmeats, tartlets, and savoury pies; the fare provided at Aldersmiths was nourishing although bland, so this was a pleasant reprise for them.

'Ahh, what's the news from home, Woodley?' Alec Silverman brushed pastry crumbs from the front of his high collared shirt as he took another bite of apple tart. He sat on his bed, which was next to Hero's.

Hero waved the single sheet of paper in the air, 'Oh, another letter from my grandfather strongly outlining his disgust caused by mama's behaviour. He says I should return home immediately and put her to rights. He also suggests that she might benefit from some time in a sanatorium, he feels that the grief over losing my father and sister has unhinged her.'

'Oh Lord, that is a serious accusation.'

Sitting up, Hero swung his legs over the side of the bed and rested his elbows on his knees. He nodded, 'Yes, it is. I, however, am pleased for mama, as she said in her message, the school will give her a purpose in life, she needs that, and quite frankly, I agree.'

'A very gregarious statement, my friend. My Pater would be against my mother being so spirited and independent in her ways.' Alec eyed the other boy, 'Are you sure you shouldn't step in?' He gestured broadly, 'All this won't do your family's reputation any good, I can tell you that for a fact.'

Hero glanced at his friend, 'I see no harm in the project. And yes, perhaps my mother does have a different way of thinking.' Hero placed the letter on his bedside cabinet and got up. He stretched his long body. 'I'm going for a run, fancy tagging along?' He gave Alec an ironic grin, he knew the other boy hated any form of physical pursuit.

Alec shuddered as he popped the last bit of the delicious tart in his mouth. His gaze went to the high window; he could see grey clouds gathering on the horizon. 'No, I shall leave that pleasure to you, Woodley. Don't be long though; it looks like rain; you don't want to be catching a chill before your fight on Saturday.'

Hero gave the other boy a playful poke on the shoulder. 'Now you sound like my mother, Silverman.'

The other boy, laughed and gestured convivially, 'Yes, yes. Just go, run ...'

Hero changed into his gym clothes and made his way out of the building.

There was a chill in the air. It was early October, and the trees were beginning to look splendid in their autumn finery.

He did a few stretches, then set off over the lawns towards the woods that flanked the school land.

When his mother had written to him outlining her project, Hero was more than pleased: the news helped to assuage some of the crippling feelings of guilt he carried with him every day. He recognised his mother's need for a purpose in life, and if buying Brook house and turning it into a school was what she wanted to do, then he would support her all the way. And, as for Alec's comments regarding the family's reputation, Hero did not give a fig for what other people thought.

Reaching the canopy of trees, Hero stepped up the pace from a jog to a sprint. He dashed through the trees as if a huntsman were in pursuit. However, it was his haunting past which stalked him none too stealthily. It didn't matter how fast he ran; he could never escape it. Exercise and boxing helped. He liked to push himself to the point of exhaustion, where he could sleep without the nightmares – sadly, this very rarely happened. He was grateful to Alec; Silverman always had his back, waking him in the night if he were making too much noise.

As he dodged through the undergrowth, he thought about his grandfather's letter. It was unclear to Hero why the man should object so strongly to his mother's plans. They hurt no one, and would, in the long run, help many. Hero decided that, as soon as he had gotten back to the dorms and had a bath, he would write back to his grandfather, confirming that he was supporting his mother's exploits and asking him, very politely, to mind his own bloody business!

*

Claire was walking through the woods, enjoying the bright autumn day. She had just reached the end of the path, where it met the driveway to the big house as a carriage went past. She did not recognise it and wondered who had been to visit Emily.

Turning towards Woodley Hall, Claire reflected how much her life had changed in the last couple of months: Her marriage to Seth had given her so much joy. He was a kind and gentle man; their lovemaking was sweet, tender, and considerate.

She had been surprised when he told her that there had never been another woman in his life since he lost his fiancé, Maggie. 'I knew I could never replace her, and I never felt the inclination,' he had shrugged.

Of course, Joseph had been the only man in Claire's life, so this new relationship was a learning curve for them both, one that was quite delightful.

As was often the case these days, Claire found her mouth turning up in a contented, happy smile. Their life was full and productive.

After the wedding, everyone had been busy helping with the harvesting. Then there was Emily's project: Claire had been astonished to hear about her cousin's plans, but she was delighted by them too, seeing Emily so occupied warmed her heart.

'Other than my schooling, which was undertaken by our governess, I have no idea about education,' Emily told her, 'Would you help, dear cousin?'

'Yes, of course, my dear. It sounds like a wonderful idea. I will do all I can to help.'

Emily had hugged her in delight.

The mistress, and Miss Fellows (well, Mrs Jacobs now), were well-loved and respected by the local community. So, as it turned out when Mrs Mason heard that Claire and Emily were going to sort out all the things that had been left at Brook House and were going to clean the place from top to bottom, their housekeeper took it upon herself to muster help from Janice, Ida, Mrs Adams, and some other women and girls from the village. All of them were willing and happy to help.

Emily and Claire laughed with delight when they found them all waiting at the front of the house, brooms, mops, buckets, and dusters in hand. Their hair swathed in scarves, and aprons on.

For the heavy work, they had recruited Charlie and Stan to help. The two young men were pink-cheeked and smiling shyly, feeling the discomfort from being in such a large group of women who teased them unmercifully, in a good-hearted way.

They all knew it was going to be a big project. It was decided early on to leave the clearing of the library until last. So that the books could be catalogued and sold, it was easier to start in the attics and then make their way downwards.

Many of the items which had been stored in the loft space were ruined by damp. Emily found several places where it looked as if the roof was leaking.

She made notes in a notebook as she went along of all the things that needed doing; checking the roof would be a priority before winter set in, she didn't want all their hard work scuppered by leaks.

Chapter 16

Five years later

Crowds of people, mainly men, encircled the fighting pit in the cellar of the Crown and Garter.

Along with the scent of unwashed bodies, sweat and blood, the atmosphere was heavy with noise, excitement, and expectation,

Horacio Woodley received a hefty blow to the kidneys and huffed with pain. He was also fairly sure one of his ribs was broken. He let the pain wash through him. It was real and raw, almost cleansing. As he fought this man, a Russian sailor that had come into port a few days ago, Hero was fighting his very own demons.

The Russian was the favourite to win this match. He was bullish and muscular, far more so than Hero. He also had the motivation to win the pot, but for Hero, the fight went far deeper. It wasn't so much about winning but surviving; this thought gave him a burst of energy and power that propelled him forward, his head connected with the man's hard stomach. The move took the Russian by surprise; he fell backwards into the crowd.

'Come on, finish im off!' Someone yelled as people hurled Hero's opponent back into the ring.

The Russian roared, he came running at Hero as if he were an enraged bull. Hero, being lighter and faster on his feet, ducked out of the way at the very last minute. He pivoted, punched the man just below his ribs. When the larger man turned to meter out a punch of his own, Hero aimed high, using the man's momentum against him, he caught him on the side of the head, then ducked out of the way as the dazed Russian fell heavily on to the bloodstained sand of the cellar floor.

When the man didn't immediately rise, the crowd roared their approval. The cheering escalated in volume when the referee declared a knockout and Hero the winner.

'Good job, Horacio.' Alec patted his arm dubiously.

As Hero pushed his way through the crowds, hands slapped him on his sweat-soaked back.

'Well done, me lad,' someone exclaimed in his ear.

Somebody passed him a towel, which he used to mop away the sweat. As he did so, he winced when he caught his damaged ribs.

There was going to be a dog fight next. Hero could hear the dogs, who were in cages, barking, howling, and growling nastily. He did not want to wait around for that.

'I've had enough for one night,' he told Alec who was close on his heels.

'Wait to receive your pot and have a drink at least,' Alec tried to persuade him.

'You collect it for me, Alec, I can pick it up later in the week.'

'Why do you always have to be a spoilsport,' Alec said petulantly. 'You are drawing in the crowds now. These people come to cheer you on.'

'You know that popularity does not interest me.'

Alec grabbed his arm, 'Well it should do, we've earned quite a pot tonight.'

'And neither does money,' Hero snapped, pulling himself out of Alec's grip.

Upon retrieving his shirt, jacket, and boots from where he had left them on a stored barrel of beer, Hero got dressed. As he did so, he could hear the sound of the crowd cheering once more, along with the growling and barking of blood-hungry dogs; the sounds sickened him.

'Very well then,' Alec took a step back. 'just remember I'm doing my best to help you exorcise those bad dreams.' Hero gave him a dark look that made Alec regret his words. He raised his hands in resignation. 'Go then. I'll see you later in the week.'

Pulling his jacket on, Hero nodded. He put on his boots as Alec disappeared back to the viewing platform of the fighting ring.

When Hero made his way out of the back of the building, before he reached the door, he could hear a dog squealing either in pain or terror. The sound, which chilled his heart, was coming from the back yard not from the pit. He could also hear jeering, childish voices high with excitement.

Hero opened the door to the yard, the stink of effluent hit him, reminding him that this was where the privy was for the Inn.

The October night was damp, cold enough to chill the sweat on his body, but the chilly air cleared his head.

The yard, which was usually dark, was lit by two lamps set on barrels. The light illuminated a group of several young boys, one of which held a dog, which looked like a terrier, upside down by its back legs. The other boys were taunting the animal with sticks. Hero guessed it was probably a bait dog. It was too small to be a fighting dog.

'What the hell are you doing?'

In unison, the boys turned to look at him.

'None of yer business,' said the youth that held the dog.

'Well, I'm making it my business.' Hero stepped out of the shadows towards the boy, who appeared to be the eldest of the group. 'Put the dog down.'

'Ere, you're the boxer aintcha,' declared one of the group.

Hero saw recognition dawn on the older boy's face when this information sunk in.

'We meant no arm, Mr Woodley,' he said as he lowered his arm, the dog writhed trying to get free. 'We were aving a bit of fun.

The animal's coat was drenched in blood. Hero could see several wounds on the dog. He knew that the smell of blood was intended to rile the pit bulls and mastiffs before they ended up in the ring.

The lads were surprised when Hero took off his coat, 'Give me the dog.'

'Watcha going to do with it?' The boy asked warily.

Hero surprised himself when he said, 'I'm taking it home with me.'

'Eh, yer can't do that,' the boy exclaimed, 'Jolly won't be appy.'

'Bugger Jack Barrett. Give the animal to me; otherwise, I will punch your bloody lights out.' The threat was uttered calmly, which made it all the more intimidating. Within the glow of the lamplight, Hero could see the colour drain from the lad's cheeks.

Meekly the boy handed the struggling dog to Hero, who wrapped the animal in his jacket. 'Now, bugger off all of you, and if Barrett says anything, you can tell him to take the cost of the dog out of my winnings.' With that, Hero strode up the side alley and out into the street.

Wining beseechingly, the dog tried to squirm from his grasp.

'Quiet now,' Hero said softly. 'I have no idea why I'm taking you home with me,' Hero explained to the animal. 'I guess it's because we are both in need of saving in one way or another.'

It was a long walk from the Inn to his lodgings in town, but Hero didn't mind that. He found walking helped to calm him after a fight.

The Crown and Garter was an inn situated in the east end of the city. A notorious place, not somewhere to take a casual stroll alone, especially at night.

Alec's crowd, all rich young bucks out for excitement would have their carriages close. They were also under the protection of Jolly Jack Barrett, rent man for the slums. He had a gang of lads working for him. No one crossed him unless they had a death wish.

Hero did not fear assault in these dark streets that were shrouded in fog drifting up from the Thames. He looked like a ruffian, and he could take care of himself for sure.

The fog curled, draping itself like a lover's caress over every surface, resulting in phantom-like shapes that seemed to loom from nowhere. It also muffled the night-time sounds; dogs were barking and cats fighting. A rowdy song sung bawdily from one of the many inns that the dockworkers frequented.

Suddenly, a shape appeared in Hero's path. It was a woman of undeterminable age.

'Fancy a good time, lovie?' She tried to grab his shirt. Hero sidestepped the woman putting himself out of her reach.

'Not tonight.' As he carried on walking, he could hear the woman hurling several expletives at his retreating back.

The halos of gas-lamps in the fog indicated to Hero that he had arrived in the more affluent part of town.

Wrapped in Hero's coat, the dog had settled down and was quiet in his arms, although he could feel the animals' rapid heartbeat against his chest.

Thinking about his comment to the dog, that they both needed saving, Hero mulled over his current life; he had pretty much been adrift since leaving Aldersmiths the previous year.

Alec had been absorbed into his father's business, but Hero felt as if he had not found his aim in life. Yes, he could have gone back to Woodley Hall and taken over the running of the estate like some antiquated squire, but even now, the place held such bad memories for him. Everywhere he looked the memories of Angelica and his father dogged his steps. He felt suffocated and wasn't able to stay there for more than a few days at a time. Besides,

Mr Durham, the manager, had been doing a good enough job of looking after the place.

The house itself was empty now: his mother had moved into rooms at Brook House. She was absorbed in the running of that school of hers. Hero was pleased for her, glad that she had found something so worthwhile to occupy her days. Cousin Claire helped; she and Seth were still living in the Dower house. They were so happy together it was almost sickening: Hero envied them their love and closeness.

Hero's *home* in town was shared lodgings with another school friend Andrew Keene.

When he had met Andrew at Aldersmiths, the man was training to become a doctor; Hero had given him several opportunities to practise his skills. Ironically, it was usually after Hero had saved Andrew from bullies like Luther Willard.

Andrew was so thankful to Horacio Woodley, being only too pleased to help him after fights or from received boxing wounds: resetting his nose after yet another break, "It'll never be straight, old man." Andrew had exclaimed, "but it gives you a rakish air, and the ladies love that."

'Ahh, you are not the first person to say that.' Hero had laughed.

Andrew was a quiet sort, steady and reliable. He couldn't stand Alec Silverman, but Hero and Andrew had quietly built up their friendship.

"I don't know why you want to live with that bore," Alec had exclaimed after hearing Hero's intention. "You can come and board at Father's house in the city if you are that desperate." Hero had been adamant that he just wanted a bed where he could rest his head, no frills or fancies.

Andrew's place was comfortable enough. The sitting-room was lined with bookshelves and filled with comfortable chairs and a dining table. There were a small scullery and kitchen, but Andrew had a housekeeper that also cooked meals for them. She kept the place reasonably clean and did their washing. The two men rubbed along well, they were both quiet, and probably, Hero would admit, a bit brooding in their ways.

Hero, feeling obligated to do so, still spent a great deal of time with Alec. However, he was beginning to find the relationship claustrophobic.

Alec arranged all of Hero's fights, through the ruffian Jack Barrett. Alec bet on Hero heavily, and almost always won a good pot. He also dragged Hero to dog fights and cockfights. At first, Hero was swept up in the London crowd. He had gone along because it was expected of him. He soon realised that he did not enjoy these vicious blood sports and started making excuses to get out of going. Still, Alec could be persuasive, Hero would inevitably go along with it, but would stay at the back behind the cheering crowds, which consisted of the rough and ready as well as the wealthy toffs out for some entertainment.

The sight of the blood and sounds of the animal's pain, made Hero sick to his stomach. He knew that Alec enjoyed the blood sports, he was always euphoric after a fight, but it disgusted Hero.

'You look as pale as a bloody ghost, man.' When Hero had returned in the early hours of the morning a few weeks ago, Andrew had surveyed his flatmate with a critical eye.

Hero flopped down into one of the armchairs, 'Alec dragged me along to a dog fight, oh lord.' He put his head in his hands as he remembered the awful screams of the animals. The people crowded close to the ring baying for blood, the claustrophobia of hot bodies crowded together, the stink of sweat and blood.

He heard Andrew get up from his chair, then the sound of glassware clinking as he poured out two generous tots of whiskey. Andrew handed one to Hero, which he took with gratitude.

'I don't know why you let Alec Silverman push you around as you do.' Andrew said as he sat back down.

'Oh, I don't know.' Hero, having taken a good slug of the drink, sat back in the chair, he felt utterly drained. 'He helped me a lot at school, you know.

When I had the nightmares.'

'He could see that you were emotionally vulnerable, Horacio, so he integrated himself into your life. He's a narcissist.'

Hero eyed the other man. 'A narcissist, what the hell does that mean?'

Andrew rolled his eyes in exasperation, 'Ahh, says the man that was too busy boxing and running at school to take any notice of the classics.'

'Don't beat about the bush, Andrew, just tell me.'

'Narcissus, the beautiful youth who could not stop staring at his reflection in the water,'

'Mmm,' Hero mused; Ah yes, he knew that Alec could be very preoccupied with himself, he didn't like it one bit if he didn't get his own way.

'Just think about it, Hero. Might be time to start saying "no" to him.'

'Yes, yes.' Hero waved his glass in the air, drained the contents, set the glass down on an occasional table, then got up. 'I'm going to get some sleep,' he announced.

'Good for you,' Andrew turned back to his books, 'alas, I cannot, I've still got study to do.'

'I can't believe you woke me up in the middle of the night to tend to a bloody dog.' Andrew complained as he examined the mutt who was shivering so much Hero thought it was going to collapse any second.

'I just couldn't leave the poor thing to be pulled apart by a pit bull.' Hero told him as he held the dog's snout lest he turned to try and bite the helping hands.

'As far as I can tell,' Andrew said as he straightened up and pushed back his reddish hair off his forehead, 'the wounds are all surface punctures.' He wiped his hands on a towel. 'I will clean them up.' He frowned then.

'What is it?' Hero asked, surprised at the anxiety in his voice.

'Well, if the wounds don't kill him, shock still may do.' He peeled back the dog's lip, 'see the gums they are white; they should be nice and pink.'

'I'm not going to let him die.'

Andrew's expression softened. 'Oh dear,' he said.

'Oh dear, what?' Hero scowled at him.

'You've been bitten,' Andrew said, smiling.

'Punched, but not bitten.'

Andrew patted his shoulder comfortingly. 'Well, are you going to name him?' he asked, then added, 'mind you, he may not make it through the night,' he reminded Hero once again.

Hero wrapped the dog in a blanket and held its quivering body close, 'Wilson,' he said.

'Wilson?' Andrew cocked a quizzical eyebrow.

'That's the name of the street where the Crown and Garter is, Wilson Street.'

'Ahh well, Wilson is as good a name as any.'

The fire was burning low in the grate. Hero stretched out on the overstuffed sofa. The dog, who was still wrapped in the blanket, he held close to his chest.

It didn't take long for Hero to fall soundly asleep.

It was not the pale autumnal light pressing through the cracks of the dark-green velvet curtains that woke Hero the following morning, but the rough tongue that licked his chin that was equally as rough with morning stubble. 'Well, hello.' Hero smiled into the brown eyes which gazed up at him. Responding to his voice, the dog wriggled up his chest and tried to lick Hero's lips. 'Mmm, thank you for the love, mutt, but I have no idea where that tongue of yours has been.'

Sitting up, he unwrapped the blanket, which was still around the dog. The animal jumped down from the sofa, looked at Hero, gave a chuffing noise then ran to the door, which he scratched at with one of his short front paws.

Pulling the discarded blanket about his shoulders, Hero got up. Then winced from the pain in his ribs. Ignoring the discomfort, he went and opened the door. The dog snaked out onto the landing, Hero followed the animal down the stairs then opened the front door, Wilson dashed out into the street, Hero was worried for a moment that the animal would run away. Instead, he watched the dog lift his leg, expel a long stream of urine. Then the dog kicked out his back legs, ran back to Hero, looked up at him and wagged a somewhat stumpy tail. As soon as Hero opened the front door once more, the animal rushed through his legs then back up the stairs.

When he got up, Andrew found Hero seated at the table, tucking into boiled eggs and bread and butter. He had done two extra eggs and had chopped them up for the dog, who had finished them off and was licking the bowl with enthusiasm.

'Well, he's certainly looking better.' Andrew finished tying up the robe he wore over his pyjamas.

'Isn't he just,' Hero smiled, as the dog sat down then looked up at him with anticipation. 'Do you think it will be alright to bath him? He does pong a bit.'

Sitting down at the table, Andrew poured himself a cup of coffee. 'I don't see why not, as long as you are careful. Make sure that he is fully dry before you take him out.'

Hero nodded as he chewed his last piece of bread and butter. 'Thank you, Andrew.' He gestured to the mutt, who was still hopeful for a titbit, 'for what you have done for us both.'

'Ahh, think nothing of it, Horacio.'

Chapter 17

Dorothea Winters (known as Dottie) opened her eyes sleepily, then stretched.

The movement sent the springs of the old bedframe creaking noisily. Evie, her older sister, murmured in her sleep but didn't wake up.

The dull light pressed against the filthy window and through the old sheet that mother had put up as a curtain.

Realising she needed to pee, Dottie got out of bed as carefully as she could, but it didn't make a difference, the springs still protested noisily, the sound made her cringe.

On bare feet, she padded across the chilly room. Shivering, she lifted her nightdress then squatted over the pot that was in the corner of the room beside the washstand.

She wasn't sure what time it was, but it was probably later than they usually woke up. That was when it occurred to Dottie that their mother was absent. It wasn't like her to stay out *all* night: she usually came home in the early hours of the morning.

Making her way back across the shabby room to the bed, Dottie was very tempted to slip back under the covers and cuddle up against her sister once more. But she knew that Mother would not be pleased when she came back and found the girls still sleeping with no work being done. So, she reached over and shook her sister's shoulder.

'Evie, Evie, it's morning, and Mother's not back.'

Her older sister groaned and opened her eyes. 'What time is it, Dot?' she asked through a throat rough with sleep.

'Dunno, it's light, though.'

Rubbing her eyes and stretching, Evie sat up. As Dottie's statement dawned on her, she clarified; 'Mother's not back?' Evie realised that she hadn't needed to get up during the night, to unlock the door to let her mother in, but then again, she usually did it in such an unconscious state, that she may well have forgotten.

'Well, she's not ere,' Dottie stated.

'Here,' Evie corrected her sister automatically as she pushed the bedclothes aside. Swinging her legs over the edge, she sat on the side of the bed. 'She's probably ducked out to get us some breakfast.'

'No, we've still got half a loaf and some dripping from yesterday.'

With a nonchalant air, Evie said, 'Aww, she'll be back soon.'

She got up, then made her way to the pot in the corner and relieved herself. 'Let's get washed and dressed, we can have a bite, and then I can finish off this lot for Mrs Smart,' Evie indicated a pile of clothes that were folded on a chair. All of them had been painstakingly unpicked and remade into serviceable garments. They took them to one of the stallholders down the market, who paid them for their work, then sold the items on, at a good profit, no doubt.

'Alright.' Dottie nodded, pouring water from the chipped ewer into the china bowl. Picking up a washcloth, she rubbed her face vigorously, then washed behind her ears.

After Evie had done the same, she got Dottie to sit in one of the wooden chairs. She undid her plait then brushed out her long fine, honey-coloured tresses. Then she re-plaited it with deft fingers and pinned it up on top of her younger sister's head.

Finished with Dottie's hair, Evie got dressed, then shook out all the bedclothes while Dottie retrieved the tin box from the shelf which contained the leftover bread: they had resorted to storing food this way so that it did not entice the rats that roamed through the cavities in the chipped plaster walls. Placing the loaf on the wooden table, Dottie carefully cut up what was left into three pieces then spread each piece with thick dripping.

The girls sat together at the table that stood under the only window set into the eves. They overlooked the back of the three-story house; the view consisted of the mire that was a back yard, which led to the stinking privy and the roofs and chimneys of more dilapidated London tenements just like the one in which they lived.

Through the cracked glass, the muffled sounds of the city reached them, the rumbling of carts, shouts and cries of starving babes, the thundering of the railway. Dogs barking and church clocks ringing out the quarter-hour.

The two girls had just finished their breakfast when they heard heavy footsteps coming up the creaking stairs.

They didn't think anything of it until someone banged on the door making them both jump.

The two gazed at each other in surprise.

'Who's there?' Evie called.

'It's me, Molly.'

Jumping to her feet, Evie unlocked the door with the rusty key and opened it; the hinges protested as she did so.

Molly Arkwright was one of the women that occupied a room on the ground floor; Mother always referred to Molly and her friend as "ladies of the night", Evie knew of course what that meant, there was no room for delicacies in this place.

The woman stood in the doorway. She was in her nightclothes with a shawl about her thin shoulders. Molly looked tired and dishevelled. The makeup she had worn in the night was smeared across her lips and cheeks. Behind her, on the shadowy landing stood the tall figure of Jack Barrett, the rent man. At the sight of him, Evie felt her heart quiver with unease.

There was a strange look on Molly's face. It made Evie step back from the door. 'What is it?' she found her throat had gone dry, she swallowed hard.

Molly walked into the room while Barrett leaned against the doorjamb nonchalantly. Jack Barrett, was known as Jolly Barrett, not because he had a happy persona, but because of the wicked scar that turned up the left side of his wide mouth into a permanent rictus grin. He was a tall man, with a square jaw and hard features. His eyes were sharp as pieces of flint.

'It's yer mam, lovie,' Molly spoke up, 'she's dead.'

Evie felt as if an icy fist had gripped her. 'What happened?' She managed to ask as hot tears misted her vision.

'Ad a nasty fall, she did,' Jolly spoke up this time, he tapped his nose with his finger, 'saw it appen meself.' His cold eyes roamed the place as if assessing the value of the meagre goods therein, then came to rest on Evie.

'No.' Evie shook her head as ripples of shock ran through her. Her knees buckled. She found herself kneeling on the floor.

'What's he saying, Evie?' Dottie, her face white, looked from Mr Barrett to Molly, then her sister. Without conscious thought, the younger girl had backed herself into a corner.

'Yer not deaf are you, girl?' Barrett's eyes settled on Dottie. 'You eard what Moll said, yer Ma's dead.'

Dottie's wail reached Evie, who got to her feet and rushed to take her sister in her arms.

'Aww, do you ave to be so brutal about it, Jack?' Molly shot him a hard look.

'Best way, in my opinion. Ope you've got the money for a funeral, girl.'

'Not now, Jack,' Molly said, although her voice was quiet and lacked force.

Ignoring Molly, Evie shot the man a tear-filled look. 'We'll find it,' she assured him. 'W-where's the body?'

'I'll get a couple of the men to bring it ere.' He stepped further into the room bringing with him darkness and a chill of dread, 'you've got a few things ere you can sell or pawn,' he picked up a saucepan, it had been well used but was still sturdy. 'That there bedstead for a start,' he waved the pan in the general direction of the bed, 'get a few bob for that, yer will.' Evie nodded as she held the sobbing Dottie to her chest. 'but if yer get stuck, I can lend you a few bob,' he gave her a parody of a smile.

'T-that won't be necessary.'

Jolly's face hardened as, with care, he placed the pan on the wooden table. 'Well, it seems yer sorted then. The body will be ere shortly.' Giving the sisters a long look that Evie found chilled her blood even more. The tall man nodded once then left.

'Don't mind im,' Molly tried to make her words reassuring; they were not: they both knew he could be a brutal man, especially when crossed. 'Now then,' Molly took charge, 'I'll take yer sister down to Margie, she'll look after er, while we, mmm.'

'Yes,' Evie nodded, then pushed her sister away as gently as she could, but Dottie just shook her head and clung to her even harder. 'Go with Molly, Dot,' she coaxed.

'No, don't want to.'

'Go,' Evie managed to inject her voice with some force as Molly took the girls arm to lead her out of the room.

Dottie sagged against the woman as all the fight left her. She let Molly guide her through the door and onto the dark landing.

As soon as she heard them going down the stairs, Evie sank onto one of the chairs and buckled over. Great heaving sobs wracked her body. She didn't know how long she had sat there until the sound of voices and feet on the stairs caught her attention.

She rubbed her sleeve across her eyes as she stood up.

Molly came through the door first. 'Let's strip the blankets off the bed, lovie.'

Evie nodded. Together they pulled off the bedding leaving the stained striped mattress bare.

Two men arrived carrying a makeshift stretcher between them, upon which lay the body of her beloved mother.

Evie didn't recognise the one, but she knew the other man whom she had seen in the company of Jolly, Bill Miller his name was, Evie remembered. A rude and uncouth man; the thought of him handling her mother's body made Evie feel sick.

The two laid the "stretcher" on the floor, then lifted the body onto the bed. Then the two men looked at Evie expectantly.

'You'll need to give em a couple of bob, Evie,' Molly prompted her.

Nodding, Evie took a tin down from the mantle and fished out some coins.

'Course, you could pay us in a different way.' The man who Evie recognised stepped towards her. He was around average height, with a large belly clad under a stained shirt. His eyes, which were the colour of dirty Thames water, looked Evie up and down. He smiled at her, but it was far from being a pleasant smile.

Evie's eyes darted to Molly in panic.

'Leave er be, Bill Miller.'

'Well, now her ma's dead thought she'd take er place.' His gaze did not leave Evie's own as he licked his lips with a pink fleshy tongue.

Molly held her hand out to Evie; the girl dropped the coins into her palm. Then Molly stepped in front of Evie, thrusting the money at Bill, she said, 'Shut yer mouth, leave er be. Ave some respect at least, she's just lost er ma.'

Bill took the coins and handed a couple to the other man. 'Oh, I'll give her some respect, alright.' He chuckled; the other man did the same.

For a moment, Evie thought that they weren't going to leave, then Bill Miller turned and left the room, his crony close behind.

Molly turned to Evie, 'Pay em no heed, girl.' The woman tried a smile, but it didn't reach her eyes. 'Just be extra careful for a few weeks, alright. Don't be caught on yer own if you can elp it that goes for yer sister too.'

'Yes,' Evie's voice was a whisper. She let out a breath that she hadn't been aware of holding.

Glancing at the bed where the body now lay, Molly, said; 'this is going to be hard for you, girl.'

'Mother did the same for Dad. I helped her.' Evie followed the other's gaze as she rolled her sleeves up.

'Aye, I expect you did.'

Together they carefully stripped the clothes away from Nel's icy body. Evie noticed that they were ripped in places, stained with mud and possibly blood, but she didn't want to think too much about it.

Her mother, her once lovely face, which still retained its beauty despite the worries and traumas of life, was bruised. Her lip split, Evie carefully washed the blood away. One of Nel's eyes had been blackened and was swollen shut.

Evie told herself to pretend it was someone else they were attending to. However, it nearly tipped her over the edge of the pit of despair when she saw the bruising around her mother's throat and more on her arms and wrists.

Molly had noticed it too. Their speculative eyes met over the body.

'She wouldn't have done that if she had had a fall,' Evie's voice was soft.

'Aye, well you know how enthusiastic some of the punters can be,' her companion stated.

'I don't actually,' Evie's voice was intoned with bitterness, Molly gave her a long look, then her eyes narrowed.

'Whatever you're thinking, girl, best leave it be. Don't want no accusations flying around. It would only cause more trouble and put you and that sister of yours in more peril. Anyway, you know the peelers won't be interested in another death in this hell hole. And you eard what Jolly said; he will swear he witnessed what appened, that you ma ad a nasty fall.'

'Yes, I know,' Evie's voice was heavy with despair.

Molly gave her a curt nod and continued washing the body.

Evie knew that what the other woman had said was true. It was obvious that her mother had been murdered, but no one would be interested in investigating what happened. She also knew that some of the police were as bad, if not worse, than people like Jolly Barrett and Bill Miller; inevitably money would exchange hands, the police would turn a blind eye and walk away.

When the two had finished dressing Nel's body in her Sunday best, Molly covered her with a sheet.

'Why don't you come down to ours for a bit, Evie? We've got some tea in and a bit of sugar too, I've been told hot sweet tea is good for shock. Then later I can elp you sell or pawn some of these bits.' She gestured about the room. 'A decent funeral is going to be costly.'

The girl nodded, 'We've got some stuff to take to Mrs Smart,' Evie told her.

'Well, that'll be a start then.'

Standing in the middle of the room, her face white, Evie started to tremble as the shock took over.

'Aww, come on, girl.' Molly took her arm and led her out of the room. 'Down the stairs we go,' she coaxed.

Molly, and her friend Margie, were surprisingly kind to the two girls. Margie was a few years older than Molly. She would have been pretty once, but life and her "trade" had taken their toll, but her eyes still had a sparkle of life and humour in them.

Both women fussed about the sisters. Evie found herself sitting on a wooden chair beside a lit fire with the promised cup of tea in her hand. Dottie sat next to her. She was quiet; her eyes glazed as if she had retreated into her mind.

The room on the ground floor was bigger than their own, and not quite so dismal. The fire helped to bring comfort to the place. It looked as if the whoring business was paying well, Evie thought. There was a scent of cheap perfume in the air, which mingled with the musky smell of sweat and lye soap that issued from the few pieces of laundry hanging above the fire on a wooden rail.

'Whatcha going to do now?' Margie asked as she joined Molly, who was seated at the table.

'They need to keep away from Jolly and that letch Bill Miller for a start,' Molly stated abruptly, then went on to tell her friend what had happened that morning.

'Oh Lord, Moll's right.' The older woman took in the girls before her. Evie was a pretty as her ma, if not prettier; despite living in this hell hole, the two girls had lovely skin the colour of cream, with the slightest blush on their cheeks, and lips that looked as sweet as a cherry. And such pretty hair, they had; the older sisters was darker than the younger; who's hair glinted gold in the light from the fire. Aww, the men were going to be swarming around them like the proverbial bees around the honey pot, Margie thought. She also had a strong suspicion that both girls had never lain with a man, which would make them an even more desirable catch.

'What do you mean?' Evie took a sip of the tea, which was hot and overly sweet for her taste.

Margie and Molly exchanged a look, then Molly cleared her throat. 'Yer not a stupid girl, Evie. You know, as well as all the sewing your ma took in, she was also working for Jolly as we do.'

'Yes, I know.'

'Well, the thing is, he's going to be looking for a replacement for your ma,' Molly said.

'A replacement?'

Margie tutted. 'You and your sister will ave to be careful, Jolly will be on the prowl, and you ain't got your ma to protect you now.'

'We'll be alright,' Evie tried to invoke some strength into her voice, but she knew the two women were right; she had already thought as much herself. 'We can keep up with the sewing jobs that should cover the rent.'

Margie nodded, although her expression was bleak. 'You got enough money to give your ma a good send-off?' She asked.

'We may have to sell or pawn a few things. A lot of our savings were spent on Dads funeral.'

'I'm going to help Evie with that later,' Molly explained.

'Good on yer, girl,' Margie approved, 'Yes, you do that, girls. Don't take a penny from Jolly, you are already in his sights, if you borrow money from him, he'll think he owns you.'

Evie felt the ripples of apprehension run icy fingers up and down her spine. Maybe it was time to leave this place? They could get the funeral over and done with then she and Dottie would leave.

She knew she had to keep her sister safe; Dottie had only just turned fourteen. Of course, Evie was aware that girls younger than that had got caught up in the "business". The thought of Dottie in the hands of monsters like Bill Miller made Evie shiver with fear.

No, she told herself as she took another sip of the tea, she mustn't let fear cloud her thoughts, they would take one day at a time for now.

However, Evie was very aware of alarm bells. She knew she had to get them both out of this place. The question was, where could they go?

*

Bill Miller took the couple of bob that the girl had given him straight down to the Crown; he had broken into a sweat lugging that body up two flights of stairs, he needed a drink to wet his whistle. He had earnt it hadn't he?

'Mornin, Bill,' The barmaid greeted him. The pub was quiet at that time of the morning, so Rita was busy cleaning the wooden counter with a cloth that looked as if it would leave more dirt on the surface than was there before. Not that anyone would notice, the patrons were not particular about their surroundings.

Bill inhaled the familiar aroma of the place with relish; sour beer and spirits, underlined with the scent of the tobacco that yellowed the walls and low ceiling, along with the stench of sweat and hard work.

'Mornin, Rita. The usual if you will.'

'Bit early for you, ain't it? She filled a mug with ale that frothed over the rim of the vessel.

'Aye, well I've been lugging a body around.'

'A body?' Her eyebrows raised in interest as she slid the mug over the counter towards him, then leant on the wooden surface, eager to hear more.

Bill took a slug of the drink, wiped away the foam on his lip with the back of a large, grubby hand. 'Aye, it were Nell Winters, you know er, she worked for Jolly and took sewing in, lived in Back Lane.'

'Oh aye, I seen her about, looked a bit too lardy da to be livin around ere. She's got two girls living with er, ain't she?'

'That's the one.' Bill was enjoying being the centre of attention. 'Well, she ad a nasty accident in the night.' He winked conspiratorially.

The barmaid's eyes widened. 'You mean someone done er in?'

'Shhh,' Bill waved a hand in the air, 'not so loud.'

'Yer the only one in ere, Bill,' she pointed out.

Despite Rita's reassurance, he glanced about the room, then leaned forward even more. 'It were one of Jolly's regular customers, got a bit rough.'

Rita nodded, 'Aye, well these things appen.'

'Aye,' Bill finished his drink, then pushed the mug forward, 'fill it up, then.'

Picking up the mug, she filled it to the rim once more and handed it to him. 'So, what about those girls of ers? Bonny they are.'

'Oh Aye, they are that.' Bill wiped his fleshy lips on his sleeve and smiled. 'Don't worry about them; we'll keep an eye on em.' Especially the older one, thought Bill.

Rita nodded again, but saw the look on Bills face, despite herself she felt a ripple of apprehension. Aww, she thought, them poor girls being left alone in a place like this; she feared for them, she did.

Chapter 18

The night before Nel's body had been brought in, Mrs Gill had huddled in a corner on the landing, watching the comings and goings in the house. She had half a bottle of gin in her hand; she took the occasional swig from the bottle.

It was as if the old woman was invisible, or such a common fixture in the place that no one took any notice of her anymore. With her long grey hair that was filthy, matted and lice-ridden, her face pinched, cheeks hollow, no one would be able to tell her age. She had long forgotten to keep count of the years. She had had a husband and children once, but one by one she had lost them all. Like many in these squalid conditions, gin had been her solace after so many tragedies. So, any pennies she managed to beg would be spent on the grog. She was drinking herself to death, but she didn't care, what was there to live for anyway?

Not by any particular choice had she found herself in this house in Little Back Lane. It was as good as, or no worse than any of the squalid dwellings hereabouts. Far better than being out on the streets, particularly at this time of the year. It was late October and getting colder by the day.

On the odd occasion that Jolly had come across her, he'd given her a vicious kick and would tell her to get out: *if she couldn't pay rent, she wasn't welcome to stay here.* She would make herself scarce, hiding away for a few days, then sneak back when the coast was clear.

On this particular cold night, she tried to keep herself warm by pulling her many layers of ragged clothing about her thin shoulders.

The damp frigid air made her chest tighten, making every breath painful. Eh, she knew she wasn't long for this world, one morning she wouldn't wake up that would be that.

The old woman had seen the woman and her two daughters arrive and take the small attic room at the top of the house. She didn't think much about it at the time, but one day she found half a meat pie thrust into her hand. Looking up in surprise she saw it was the mother, Nel Winters her name was, looking down at her.

'Get some food in your belly, Mother,' she had said.

With her eyes shining with surprise and delight, Mrs Gill had watched her climb the stairs; *awe, she had the posture of a lady, that one.* For a brief moment, the old woman wondered where the family had come from, but the thought disintegrated in her muddled mind as she bit into the pie with relish.

That hadn't been the only time that the woman had benefitted from Nel Winters kindness. And her girls; *aww, they were bonny girls, alright.* If her daughters had survived, Mrs Gill would have loved them to be like these two. But she feared for them. This dark place was full of the scum of this earth, the low of the low, predators that would eat those two alive.

Piece by piece, she heard the story about how the unlikely trio had come to this awful slum. It was an age-old story, repeated many a time: the father had been killed in an accident, leaving them to live on a shoestring, the only option was to find cheaper accommodation.

But this woman, Nel, had something about her; if Mrs Gill could have voiced the description to anyone, she would have said it was strength and independence, a determination to live a better life. The trouble with that idea, though, was they drew unwanted attention to themselves.

Everyone knew that Nel and her girls took sewing in, selling items to old Mrs Smart who ran a barrow at the markets. Things had been working fine for them; then the tragedy happened; Jolly Barrett had taken a fancy to Nel Winters. When the family had found it more and more difficult to meet the rent, he took advantage of the situation, manipulating and bullying Nel into giving certain *favours* to him, and then other men, Jolly creaming off the proceeds from the agreement. No one would judge the woman; she did it to keep a roof over her family's heads.

Things had come to a head the night before; however, Mrs Gill had been dozing on the first landing when she heard the raised voices. She opened a blurry eye and saw Nel appear at the top of the stairs a few feet away from where she was sitting, Barrett was right behind her, trying to grab her arm.

'Eh, if you think you ave a choice in this matter, Nellie, me girl, you've got another thing coming!'

'You've already had me out once tonight.' She stepped wearily on to the landing, her once straight back was bent in resignation. 'He hit me. I wouldn't be surprised if I have a black eye tomorrow.'

'Well, it ain't my fault if some of em like it a bit rough.' Jolly crowded her.

She turned on him then. 'A bit rough, huh, that's an understatement.'

This time he did manage to grab her arm. His grip was overly tight, she winced.

Barrett stood over her, using every bit of his greater height to intimidate her. His face set in a rigid façade of anger. 'As I said, you ain't got a choice, now come with me, or by God, a black eye will be the least of your worries.'

'I can't, please no more,' she had pleaded.

Thrusting his face to an inch of hers, Jolly hissed through gritted teeth. 'ow many more times ave I gotta say it, you ain't got a choice. Think of em girls of yours; you want to keep a roof over their eds don'tcha?'

Nel shook her head, 'Not like this. The price is too high; we'll leave in the morning.'

Barrett gave a harsh laugh. 'Well, you think you still ave a choice do yer. Well, let me put you right about that, you do as I say now, or I'll go up em stairs, and I'll grab one of those pretty girls of yours. Maybe the older one, what's er name? Evie? You can go to ell, and she can take yer place on the job.'

'Oh God, no, please, Mr Barrett.' She sagged against him. 'I'll do it,' her voice was barely audible.

'There, that's the spirit. I knew you'd come around to my way of thinking.' He pushed her towards the head of the stairs. She stumbled down them on unsteady legs.

Mrs Gill heard the front door open and close. An ominous quiet settled through the reeking house for a moment, then all the sounds came rushing back; a baby crying, dogs barking, raised voices.

The woman put her hand over her chest and shook her head in denial; *awe, this weren't good, not good at all.* Mrs Gill took a long swig of the gin, gulping it down greedily to help her drown out the fearful thoughts.

It was no surprise to her when the commotion woke her up the following morning, and she heard that Nel Winters was dead.

*

Despite death stepping over their shabby threshold, life continued. With some help from Molly, they organised for the body of their mother to be collected the following day, the funeral being the day after.

Evie was aware that they needed every penny they could get, they had very little in the way of savings as most of their money had gone on giving Dad a good funeral. So, despite all that had happened that afternoon, the two girls made the long journey to the market.

While they were gone, Molly took several things to the pawnshop, for them. The pans, china washbowl and ewer, were amongst them. They weren't worth a great deal, but Molly swapped them for cheaper alternatives and got a few bob into the bargain.

The items of clothing had been carefully packaged in waxed paper tied up with string to keep them clean. Evie and Dottie were taking them to Mrs Smart, who sold things from her barrow at the market. During the week, the market was held in Wentworth Street, on a Sunday, it was set up on Middlesex Street, Petticoat Lane as it tended to be called; It was an old tradition, and the place name had stuck. Neither of the markets were respectable places where the wealthy city dwellers would venture.

It was a fair trek on foot from Poplar, but Evie and Dottie were used to making the journey with their mother. The streets were busy at this time of the day, noisy and ripe with the hustle and bustle.

They took their normal route. There was a short cut which skirted the West India Docks. The two girls had to manoeuvre between delivery carts, workmen and sailors. They caught glimpses of ships; the cargos loaded by stevedores, and the Thames, the banks of oozing mud, which stank of death and rotting fish.

Many of the buildings that were built close to the river were falling into decay. The soot-blackened, pockmarked bricks were crumbling. The cellars flooded by the filthy river water were also undermining the foundations. The buildings tilted, as if in veneration towards the wide stretch of water.

The girls were familiar with the market. It was a busy and lively place, filled with the noise of the stallholders hawking their wares, selling everything from fruit and vegetables to ironmongery and pottery.

Even when their mother had been with them, Evie always disliked visiting the place. There was an underlying feeling of threat in the air. She could feel eyes upon them filled with longing, possibly malice, assessing them carefully. The idea made her feel uneasy, especially so on this emotional day.

Dottie clung onto her sister's hand as they made their way through the crowd to find Mrs Smart.

Walking past an old beggar sitting on the ground and leaning against a wall, Evie could see the stump of his leg protruding from underneath his filthy, ragged clothes.

'Spare some alms for a poor veteran.' Holding a hand out beseechingly he called to them.

Evie found she could not look at the old man, both she and Dottie kept their eyes front as they ventured further into the marketplace.

They spotted the stallholder and made their way over to her.

Mrs Smart was a woman of indeterminable age, although the wiry grey hair that peeped out from under the dark brown knitted hat she wore proved her to be in her middle years, if not older. Dressed in a work-worn skirt and blouse, Mrs Smart was a plump woman with ruddy cheeks and a perpetually runny nose. The boots that peeped out from below the hem of her skirt were of good quality.

She was serving a customer when they approached.

'There you go, dearie, that there jacket will fit your ubbie a treat it will, just what he needs for his Sunday best.'

The woman nodded her thanks then disappeared into the crowds. The older woman turned beady eyes, set in a puffy face, to the sisters.

'I eard what appened to your ma, may God rest er soul.'

'You've already heard?' Evie looked at the market stall holder in astonishment.

'Aye well, word travels fast around ere, you should know that by now.'

'Yes.' Evie bobbed her head as she handed the woman the parcel of clothes.

The old woman undid the string and pulled the paper away. She picked up the first garment, which was a child's waistcoat, which had originally been an old jacket.

'Your ma did fine work; I'll say that much about er.' The woman examined the item closely. 'I'll give you what you are owed today.' She turned her attention to Evie as she placed the waistcoat back on top of the pile of clothing and opened a money bag attached to her belt. 'I presume you are going to carry on with doing a bit of sewing for me?' she asked as she fished out some coins.

'Yes, Mrs Smart.' Evie nodded as she took the payment and placed it carefully in the inside pocket of her coat.

The older woman nodded, but her eyes narrowed, 'course, I won't be able to pay you as much as I did your Ma, you not being as skilled.'

Evie felt her skin prickle with annoyance and Dottie, who was holding on to her arm like a limpet squeezed even tighter.

'Mother taught me well enough, Mrs Smart, I can do fine work too.'

'Ah well, we'll see, shall we. You prove it to me, and we'll go from there.' She picked up a packet that was in a box under her barrow and handed it to Evie. 'There you go, I want these back by Friday.'

'Friday?' Evie felt her heart sink, what with the funeral and everything, it was quite an ask.

Hearing the hesitation in the girl's voice, Mrs Smart said, 'Well, if you ain't sure, give em back, I'll find someone else.'

'It's fine. We'll manage.'

'Good, well see that you do.' She waved a workworn hand, ushering them away.

Evie felt a world of despair settle over her as she turned away. Then she and Dottie started the long walk home.

'She's so horrible, Evie, can't we find someone else to sell to?'

It was the older girls turn to squeeze her sister's arm. 'My instinct is telling me that we'd get the same from anyone around here. Anyway, I think that Mrs Smart has a bit of a monopoly.'

'What does that mean?'

Glancing at her sister, she said, 'it means she's the only one selling clothes like this around here.'

'Oh.' Dottie nodded in understanding.

The crowded market fell behind them as they retraced their steps back to Little Back Lane.

Neither of them noticed the two boys following them through the busy streets.

Chapter 19

The November day was bitter, a damp chill that worked its way into the bones. Jolly Barrett didn't mind the cold too much, although he had the lapels of his wool jacket pulled up to keep his neck warm. He was leaning casually against the wall of one of the warehouses overlooking the docks. It was a busy and vibrant place, with many ships unloading cargos of exotic goods, some of which would come his way to be sold at a healthy profit, he smiled with satisfaction at that thought; this was Jack's domain; he dearly loved the place, slums and all.

He took a long drag from a rolled-up cigarette. The smoke, along with his misted breath, wafted about his head like a halo.

Pinching out his smoke, he popped it in his jacket pocket, waste not want not, he thought. He then fished his silver fob watch, one of his prized possessions, out of his waistcoat pocket and checked the time. He had an appointment with Mr Hill in town in half an hour; better get a move on then.

With a long stride, he made his way to his meeting with an air of expectation. An appointment with Mr Hill meant one thing, there would be some business coming his way.

The offices of the Misters Hill and Barns solicitors were in Sloane Street. Barrett reached the place in good time. It was a high narrow building that seemed to have been shoehorned into place, squeezed between other grander facades.

Opening the door, which had a brass bell attached, the tinkling noise announced his arrival.

The clean-shaven young man sitting at a desk in the rather shabby reception area, looked up as Jolly entered.

'Go straight up, Mr Barrett, Mr Hill is expecting you.'

Jolly nodded his thanks, then climbed the narrow staircase, two flights to the top of the building.

When he reached the office of Mr Hill, Jolly didn't bother knocking; he went straight in, removing his new bowler hat as he entered.

'Ah, Mr Barrett.' A rotund man stood up from behind a heavy wooden desk. 'Just about to have a snifter, do you want one? Chilly old day, what?' 'Aye, it is. Yes, may as well.' Jolly took a seat on one of two chairs in front of the desk.

There was a sound of clinking glasses, the aroma of scotch wafted across the room, mixing with the dusty scent of old carpets and furniture. There was a cheery fire in the small grate, but the chimney needed sweeping, it was smoking, there lay a cloud of smoke which rose and wafted across the ceiling. Despite the impoverished look of this place, Jolly knew full well that a great deal of money passed through their hands every day.

The solicitor handed one of the glasses to Jolly, then returned to the leather chair behind the desk which creaked as he sat down. He took a long slug of the liquor then set the glass down.

With dark eyes set into a soft round face, Hill studied the other man for a moment. 'How are things?'

'All good. We ave another ship full arriving tonight.'

'Good, same procedure as before?'

'Course.'

'Not anticipating any problems then?'

'Nope, the coppers know to keep away, an all my lads will be on duty.'

'Stephen's will be there to help out,' Mr Hill said, referring to the young man that was in the reception area.'

'Course.' Jolly took a sip from his glass and smacked his lips; ah, this was the good stuff. He put the glass down on the leather surface of the desk. 'So, spill the beans, Hill, I ain't got all day. I'm sure you aven't dragged me ere to check on the latest cargo due to arrive.'

The large man leant forward in his chair. 'Mr Silverman has some, um, special guests visiting him at his country home the weekend after next. He would like you to supply some of your delightful ladies to entertain them.'

'That's no problem.' Jolly nodded. 'Is that it?' He felt a sense of disappointment.

'Well, no, Mr Silverman has finally enticed Lord Beeching to accept his invitation.'

Jolly smiled. Interest flickered across his features. 'Bout time, never thought he was going to bite.'

The plump man shrugged his shoulders, 'Well, thanks to you, Mr Silverman was able to offer his Lordship some enticement.'

'So, he wants me to find another girl, then?'

Hill's face infused with colour, whether it was from embarrassment or excitement, Jolly couldn't tell. 'That is correct.'

'The old pervert has been through a number recently, yer know. To find another virgin in Poplar, that ain't an easy task. It's gonna cost.'

'Yes, of course it will.' Hill bristled. 'Well, you know Mr Silverman, he's good for the money,'

Jolly nodded, picked up his glass and drained his drink. 'Anything else?' He set the glass down on the desk.

'No, no, just the usual couple of crates of spirits.' Mr Hill opened a drawer and fished out a vellum envelope. 'There you go, Mr Barrett, this should get the cogs turning.'

The tall man nodded again, reached for the envelope then put it in the inside breast pocket of his jacket, then he stood. 'Delivery day?'

'Make it the Friday afternoon, around 3 pm, for the liquor.'

'Very well, and for the girls?'

'Saturday afternoon.'

'Righto.'

He was already making his way to the door when Mr Hill spoke again. 'And no duplicity where the girl is concerned.'

Jolly turned back. He gave the solicitor a long hard look, which made the fat man squirm in his seat. 'Ave I ever let you or Mr Silverman down?'

'No, no, of course, I know you will come through.'

Jolly popped his hat back on, then with a curt nod, he opened the door and made his way down the stairs.

Bloody man, Hill, thinks e's better than me!

Jolly said nothing to the young man in the reception area when he reached the bottom of the stairs. He made his way out onto the busy street.

But ere's the thing; Jolly Barrett is going up in the world. He ain't being no one's lackey for much longer.

Jack Barrett could have hailed a hackney cab to take him back to Poplar, but he decided to walk back. The walk would give him time to deliberate the requests he had been presented with. Of course, when Mr Hill described what Mr Silverman required, Jolly had immediately thought of Evie Winters and her sister. He would bet his last crown that they were still "untouched"; that mother of theirs guarded them well, up until her demise that is. Now they were vulnerable, and they both knew it. But Jolly had surprised himself: when he thought of the older sister, Evie. He felt a strange stirring inside, something he'd never felt before. Even though she was skin and bone now, she was a pretty piece for sure, with her soft brown eyes and waving hair. No, he decided, it was more than lust or desire; he felt he wanted to protect her. He let out a snort of derision; awe Lord, don't tell me Jolly Barrett is going soft? This ad never appened before, that was for sure.

He was thirty-seven and still a bachelor. He had his choice of the whores who worked for him, that would slake his lust. Some of whom were not working girls, women that had been all too eager to be the one to warm his bed. Despite his scar, he fancied himself to be a good-looking man.

To start with, he had left the Winters sisters and their ma alone so he could assess them: he could tell as soon as he looked at them, they were different, a cut above the trollops in Poplar. Especially the mother: there was some *quality* about her. At first, she appeared to Jolly to be lofty; he felt she was looking down on him. He realised very quickly that she had some learning behind her. This notion made him feel inadequate. There was a need within him to assert his dominance. So, he had entered into a game of cat and mouse to see if he could break her will.

Thanks to his mother, who had sent him to the poor school. Jolly was not completely illiterate. His school attendance had lasted until he was eight.

When he had a fight with another boy and nearly killed him, the school wouldn't take him back, so he had to push forward himself. He could read reasonably well, but arithmetic was easier for him, he could add sums in his head, this gift was useful in the fact he could keep a ledger of all his transactions, no matter what they were. He was becoming a wealthy man on the quiet; to him, wealth meant power. He wasn't having any widow from Bow looking down on him.

Nel's resolve had been surprisingly strong to begin with, despite the extra money it would bring in for her and her daughters, she stood her ground and would not join the group of whores he ran. It was because he threatened her girls, that her resolve broke. She had agreed to take on some of his "clients".

An attractive woman, she had looked after herself and her girls: you wouldn't find any lice on them, no venereal disease. It soon dawned on him that he had made a grave mistake putting her into the whoring business; she was a fine woman and would have made him a good wife. If he were going to go up in the world, he would need a decent wife beside him, one who could read and write and hold her own. Nell would have fit the bill nicely, but he had ruined her.

He only sent her out to some of his more affluent punters; she became very popular. He had let her out far more than he intended as she brought in a good income. Then the worst happened; one of the men had become too rough. These things happened all the time, but Jolly had surprised himself when he had felt a feeling of loss. The man who had strangled her had his throat cut, then ended up with his pockets full of rocks at the bottom of the river.

But all was not lost; there were still Nell's girls; he wasn't going to make the same mistakes with them. It crossed his mind he could have the older one, Evie, who must be around sixteen or seventeen. She had the Mollish that her ma had, plus the fact she would be much easier to handle than her mother ever would have been. Mmm, he thought, maybe it had all worked out for the best after all.

As a safeguard, he had some of his lads follow the girls to make sure they were safe. He had warned all the lads that if they so much as winked at one of the sisters, their life wouldn't be worth living. He had also instructed Molly and Margie, two of his best girls, to keep an eye on the sisters, not to help them too much, but just enough. After all, it would serve his purpose well if they were wanting by the time he came around to offering Evie marriage.

It had been three months since they buried their mother, each week they were struggling more and more. It would soon be time for him to take some action.

Much to his amazement, he found himself visualising a nice house in the suburbs, with a garden and Evie Winters, no, Barrett, it would be, to come home to every night. Ha, he must be getting sentimental in his old age. He chuckled to himself as he dodged a butcher's cart.

Jolly decided to have a word with Hill next time he saw him. There was a nice property in George Avenue, which would soon become empty as the old bloke who rented it was not long for this world, Jack had been impressed with the place, it would do him and any wife just right.

If needs be, he thought, he would take the younger girl in, Jack had a feeling that it would be good leverage with Evie if he offered to look after her sister as well. What more could she have asked for, eh?

But now, after Silverman's orders, Jolly was in a real dilemma: one of the two Winter's girls would fit the bill nicely, so he could take either one to the do that Hill described. The younger one, Dottie, would be the easiest, he also knew that Beeching, the old letch, liked them young.

Evie would still be available to fulfil his ambitions. No, damn it, he couldn't do it. He had been at the beck and call of men like Hill and Silverman all his life. If anything happened to Dottie and Evie got wind of it, she definitely wouldn't marry him. He wanted a compliant woman, not someone he would have to force into marriage. Ah, he knew that Evie didn't think of him as a suitable beau, but he would win her around somehow.

Eh, the quandary irked him, and, as always happened when he felt stressed, it made his scar itch. He scratched at it absently. Jolly worked hard to become the man he was. His father had been a drunken deadbeat — just one of the many thereabouts, who enjoyed taking his frustrations out on his wife and son.

One night, in one of his drunken rages, Jack's father had punched his wife, sending her sprawling across the floor. When Jolly went to his mother's aid, the man had pulled a knife on him. Jack was certain that, given a chance, his father would have cut his throat. The survival instinct kicked in, Jack dodged out of the way, but the blade still caught him in the side of the mouth. Jack had been lucky that it only cut through his cheek and nothing else.

The eleven-year-old Jack was tall and brawny for his age. He fought back and cracked his father's head against the iron grate, killing him outright, no big loss. His ma said nothing about it but helped him bundle the body up and dump it on the mudflats, where the tidal river would pick it up and carry it out to sea. The whole episode had left him feeling so empowered; he felt as if he could take on the world.

It was as the docks came into sight that Jolly had a thought, then berated himself for not thinking of it before. The cargo due in tonight was a human one; refugees fleeing their countries, Russians, Georgians, some Jews. There was bound to be a girl suitable in amongst that lot.

When the immigrants arrived, often having paid a high price for the crossing, they were then expected to part with any other money and valuables they had brought with them, with the mistaken view that they would be housed, and employment would be found for them.

They were taken to the slums and packed into rooms, sometimes as many as three families in one room. Many of them were too weak from the journey to protest, and what would it have achieved anyway? There was nowhere else for them to go.

Through Mr Hill, and then Jack, Silverman paid the captains of the ships, to arrive at the docks at around 2 am a time when it was relatively quiet. Then the "cargo" was unloaded into boats and rowed ashore.

There had been another shipment over a week ago. It was one of those families that now occupied the room across the landing from Evie and Dottie.

*

The moon frosted the clouds and the surface of the water with a silver glow.

The people crowded on the deck of The Lady Charlotte; the ship did not live up to its grand name: it was an old vessel with peeling paint and creaking timbers. The creaking, along with the lapping of the water and the occasional other city sounds were all that could be heard. All the immigrants had been threatened with being thrown overboard if they did not keep quiet.

Suddenly a baby started to cry, the woman holding it pressed the child to her chest.

'Shut that child up, Mrs, or I'll toss it over the side.' One of Jolly's men threatened in a harsh whisper.

The woman could not speak or understand English, but she got the gist of what the man had said, so she held the baby tighter against her breast. The child whimpered then fell silent.

All these people had taken the journey to London with the hope of finding new lives, where they would not be persecuted by antisemitism.

The sailors, as well as Jolly's men, ushered them all down ladders into rowing boats that would take them to shore. As the people climbed into the bobbing rowing boats, their breaths misted in the freezing November air.

Bill Miller was amongst the men on duty. Jolly had ordered him to look out for a "pretty young girl, specifically one on her own." Bill could only guess at the reason behind this request, but he knew it was something bestial, his thoughts were dark with desire.

There were twenty-seven people in all; some were families, others were travelling on their own.

It wasn't long before Bill spotted the ideal candidate to fulfil Jolly's request. A girl, possibly around the age of fourteen or fifteen, perhaps a bit older than Jolly was looking for, but by God, she was a beauty; she had large luminous eyes set in a moon-shaped face that had been sculptured by hunger.

She wore a dark woollen shawl over her head and shoulders, but Bill noticed thick dark curls framing her face. The girl was lovely, alright. She stirred his loins for sure. Bill also noticed that she appeared to be with an older woman, her grandmother possibly. The two of them clung together tightly.

As soon as they were on the dock, the people were all ushered into one of the warehouses. The place was half empty. There were crates, filled with unidentified goods, stacked up along one side; this left an illuminated expanse of floor space. The light did not reach into the far corners, which remained shrouded in weighty darkness.

As the travellers huddled together, they shivered, the place reeked of dampness, and if anything, it felt colder inside the building than it had outside.

Mr Hill's man, Stephens, who spoke Yiddish and Romanian, sat behind a desk entering the names of the new arrivals into a ledger. They were then instructed to hand over whatever they had brought with them to be 'checked'. Some of the immigrant men protested when valuable items were taken away and set to one side.

'You steal.' One man gestured to the silver Minora candle holder and silver tea service that was being unpacked from a small, brown leather, suitcase. These had been the only two items of any worth that he had rescued from their home. A woman, probably his wife, was crying as she held onto his sleeve tightly.

'This is to pay for your lodgings, see.' One of Jolly's men tried to explain as the man became angrier by the moment.

Stephens heard the commotion and quickly rushed over before the episode got out of hand.

'Dos iz deyn tsolung,' he addressed them in Yiddish, gesturing towards the items. 'dem iz far deyn akamadeyshan.' The young man explained earnestly. He put his hand on the other's sleeve to calm him.

The man's face crumpled in dejection and defeat. He nodded his head to indicate that he understood. He moved away with his sobbing wife still clinging to him.

'What did yer say to im?' Jolly's man asked as he put the silver items into a crate.

'I told him that this would be his payment for the accommodation for his family.'

'Yer did, did yer? Well, I ope he doesn't expect to be put up in Buck ouse.' The man gave a harsh laugh.

Chapter 20

S ophia Blum cowered in the dark corner of the large warehouse. She held onto her grandmother's arm to ensure she didn't wonder off, although the old woman sagged against her, frail and exhausted.

Sophia's eyes, usually a luminous grey, were dark with fear as she gazed around the cavernous place.

One of the rough men had told them to wait here. He stood with them as if he were guarding them, but she certainly wasn't going to run; she knew she wouldn't get far, especially with her Grandmother in tow.

Since being evicted from their home, Sophia's grandmother had become more and more muddled. The young woman wondered if it were down to the shock of leaving their home, which was in a small, rural village in the Ural Mountains. They were just two of the many thousands of displaced people fleeing Georgia, Russia, Romania, and Poland.

As tiny as their hamlet was, it was soon evident that the disaster was not going to bypass their village; the shadow of unrest was fast coming their way. The countryside was rife with persecution.

One of the teachers at the village school, Anders Siegel, had been to England and had learned the language. Sophia, who was fifteen, had been one of his most promising pupils and he was very fond of the girl.

Her parents had been killed in a fire five years earlier, leaving her living with her grandmother. He had been hopeful that Sophia would help him at the school as a teacher herself. But, as the clearing of villages got closer and closer, Anders knew it would not be long before their home would be next. He was correct in his thinking, the 'clearing' of their village had started the following year.

Sophia was heartbroken to be leaving her home. Anders was just as upset; there was a deep affection between them bordering on love.

He had arranged that Sophia and her grandmother would join a group heading for England.

'You can put your English to good use, libn,' he used a term of endearment that made her blush.

Her eyes had misted with tears as she looked at him beseechingly. 'Why can't you come with us?'

'I am needed here. There is a great deal of work to be done; I will help other families leave here safely.'

Sophia nodded in understanding as her gaze dropped from his face. Gently he placed his fingers under her chin and tilted her face up to look at him again. Leaning forward, he placed a kiss on her forehead.

'Shalom, libn, stay safe.'

'Shalom, Anders.'

He smiled as she used his first name.

Before he knew what she was about, she went up on her tiptoes and kissed him on his lips. Then, with her face glowing a bright red, she left him to join the group waiting beside a donkey and cart.

The older people and less capable sat in the cart, everyone else went on foot, starting a long journey that would take weeks.

Anders watched them until the group disappeared over the crest of a hill. In his heart, Anders knew he would never see Sophia again. And that none of the evicted people would ever see their homes again.

Set apart from the others; Sophia saw the rest of the group they had arrived with taken away to their new "lodgings", Sophia became more and more panicked.

'I want to go with them.' Sophia found her voice at last.

The fat man gazed at her in astonishment. 'Yer speak English, girl?' Sophia nodded her head. 'Ere, Jack, this little piece speaks English.'

'Does she now?' Sophia watched as a tall man walked over to them. He had a scar on his face which turned his mouth up into a crooked half-smile. When he stopped before her, the girl could not meet his penetrating eyes. She looked down at her feet. 'Well, ain't that just grand.' Reaching out a hand, he lifted her chin with his long fingers, which reminded Sophia of Anders parting gesture. She felt her heart contract and her eyes fill with tears. 'A pretty one at that,' Jolly said with approval.

'Thought she would do the job, Jack.' Bill Miller said.

Sophia's downcast eyes looked up with trepidation. 'What job?' 'We've got some special plans for you girlie.' The man called Bill laughed; the sound was cold and harsh.

'That's enough of that, Bill.' Jolly let go of her chin and indicated the older woman. 'Who's this?'

'This is my Bubulya, um, Grandmother.'

'Aww, Grandmother, ow nice.' Jolly smiled. Much to Sophia's surprise, the tall man put his arm around the older woman's shoulders. 'Come now, Mother, we ave a nice place for you to rest and ave something to eat.'

'She doesn't speak English,' the girl explained.

'Well, that ain't a problem,' Jolly steered them towards the door at the further end of the huge building. 'Sounds like you can pass the message on.'

'Umm, yes.' Sophia translated what Jolly had said. The old woman smiled a gap-toothed smile that emphasised her wrinkled skin.

'Let me introduce myself.' Jolly kept his arm around the shoulders of the old woman as they stepped into the dark street. Bill led the way with a lantern held high. 'I'm Jack Barrett, but you can call me Jolly.'

'Jolly?' Sophia looked up at him.

'Aye, cos of the scar, you get my drift?'

'Yes.' She tried a smile, but she could not get her facial muscles to work. Ever since they had started this journey, Sophia had felt a weighty sense of dread settling upon her. This feeling intensified; she did not trust these two men, especially when they isolated them from the main group of arrivals.

Her trepidation increased as the fat man led the way through streets that were becoming narrower and more rundown.

There was a terrible stench of rotting food, fish, and middens. Sophia thought that she was used to bad smells after having been on that ship for so long, but this was far worse. The stench made her eyes smart.

'Where are you taking us?' Sophia's breath misted in the chill air. 'To a place where there will be a nice fire and somewhere to rest,' Jolly answered.

'I'm not sure ...' Sophia's footsteps faltered.

Jolly shot her a look, 'Well see, ere's the thing, me and Bill can leave you ere, but I promise you, you wouldn't last five minutes in these streets without the protection of Jolly Jack Barrett. So, are you going to be a good girl for the sake of your Grandma at least?'

Sophia managed a nod. They all knew that she had no other choice but to do what they said.

Eventually, they came to a house which was part of a rundown terrace situated down a narrow lane.

'Welcome to Little Back Lane.' Jolly opened the door and ushered them into the hallway. Then he knocked on a door, didn't wait for a reply and opened it. 'You ere, Moll?' he called.

Molly Arkwright was sitting at the small wooden table drinking gin.

There was a fire in the grate, so the room was warm.

'Course I'm ere, Jack, you told me to stay put remember. Lost a good nights pay, I ave.'

'Aww, don't grumble, Moll, you know I'll see you right.'

'Well, just see that you do.' The woman stood up as Bill ushered Sophia and her grandmother into the room. 'So, who have we ere?' She eyed the girl and older woman with interest.

Jolly put a large hand on the girl's shoulder, 'This is Sophia, and this charming lady is her grandma.'

Molly's gaze shot to Jolly's face. 'I thought you said there would only be one of them?'

'Ah, well, things changed.' He gave her a hard look and said pointedly, 'It ain't going to be a problem, is it?'

'No, course not, Jack.' Molly shook her head.

'That's what I thought. Ere we go, ladies, your accommodation.'

Sophia gazed about the room which was lit by an oil lamp and the flickering flames of the fire. It wasn't a large room, but big enough for two beds. Sophia noticed that a curtain could be pulled across the room to separate the beds. There was a shabby dressing-table, filled with bottles and brushes. Along with all the other odours, she could pick out the scent of stale perfume. Clothes hung on hooks on the walls. There was a tin bath leaning against the wall beside a washstand with an ewer and basin. The wooden table and four chairs stood by the small grate which had a range on top. Molly, dressed in a long nightdress with a shawl about her shoulders, put a kettle on the range.

'Now, I've got work to be getting on with,' Jolly said, giving Molly another direct look. 'We all good ere?'

'Yes,' Molly nodded but did not meet his gaze.

'Well, if you need anything Bill will be around to keep an eye on things, won't yer, Bill?'

'Aye.' Bill gave Molly a lewd wink.

'Well, as long as that's all he does,' Molly grumbled. 'Yer knows yer place, don't yer, Bill?'

'No question,' Bill spoke up.

Jolly turned his attention to Sophia and her grandmother, 'Molly ere, is going to look after yer for a bit.'

'How long for?' Sophia found herself asking.

'Well, that ain't for you to ask. You're under my protection now, so you do what you're told.'

Sophia was surprised when Molly came and put an arm about her shoulders. 'She'll be fine, Jack.'

With a curt nod, Jolly and Bill left the room.

Molly ushered the pair to the table and had them sit down, then busied herself making a pot of tea. She placed the teapot and three chipped mugs on the wooden surface, along with a loaf of bread which she cut into thick slices.

Then she quickly buttered them with thick yellow butter.

'Eat.' She indicated the plate. 'Got some real butter in especially, can't let it go to waste.'

'Thank you.' Sophia picked up two pieces and passed one of them to her grandmother. 'Esn, Bubulya.'

Molly picked up her mug of tea. 'She don't speak English?' She nodded at the old woman.

'No,' Sophia confirmed. She was grateful to see her grandmother eating the bread and butter with gusto.

'Where did you learn then?'

The young girl's gaze dropped. 'Our schoolteacher has been to England; he taught me.'

'Mmm, that's lucky.'

'Yes,' Sophia's voice was soft. Meeting Molly's eyes once more, she said, 'You share the room?' she nodded towards the two beds.

'Aye, you'll meet Margie in the early hours. We will share one bed, and you and your Grandma can share the other.'

'Thank you.'

The old woman had finished the bread and butter, so Sophia handed her the mug of tea, then had to steady it as her old hands were shaking.

'Well, you've got good manners.' Molly's head bobbed in acknowledgement. 'Where are you from?'

'We are from Russia, we live, or used to live in the mountains.'

'Mountains, huh, a far cry from this place then.'

'Yes,' Sophia found herself yawning.

After having a few sips of her tea, her grandmother's head was dropping to her chest in tiredness.

'Go on, girl, get yerselves off to bed, you're exhausted.'

'Thank you,' Sophia said again. Then helped her grandmother up. She gently removed her shawl, coat, and boots. Keeping their dresses on, they got under the covers. It didn't take long before they were sound asleep.

Molly pushed her mug of tea away and refilled her glass with gin. Her hand trembled as she brought the glass to her lips; she took a long, fortifying swig of the liquid.

When Jolly had gotten her up the day before, to tell her to be ready to receive a visitor, someone who would be staying with her and Margie for a couple of weeks, Molly was wary.

'What sort of visitor?' she had asked.

He had given her a cold look that had her dropping her gaze. 'You know better than to question me, Moll.'

'Course, Jack.'

So, when he and that letch, Bill Miller, turned up with this pretty girl and her grandmother in tow, Molly had felt her heart contract. The gin in her stomach soured; a pretty young girl could only mean one of two things, he was going to put her on the game, or she was destined for something far worse.

Despite the fire in the grate, Molly sat at the wooden table and shivered with foreboding.

Chapter 21

E arlier that night, Evie's eyes were swimming with tiredness as she tried to focus on the minute stitches, one after the other, that she sewed into the fine linen. Her neck and back ached something cruel, but that was nothing compared to the raw cramping ache of hunger in her belly. Lifting her head, she winced with the pain brought on by stiffness. She moved her neck gingerly to loosen it up.

Gazing at the smoking tallow candle that was almost to the point it would snuff out, she felt that the flickering flame represented her life's worth at that moment. With this thought, she felt a sense of bleakness and hopelessness wash through her.

Carefully, setting aside the needlework, she stood up and stretched her back. Awe, she felt like an old woman.

The cold didn't help either; it gnawed at her bones relentlessly. It was the beginning of November, just three weeks after their mother's funeral, although, to Evie, it felt like an age.

As each day past, she and Dottie were getting into a situation that was becoming more and more desperate. Even with Molly and Margie helping them out occasionally. Every day Evie had to decide whether to buy food, coal, or candles. She also had to consider that she needed to have the rent money when Jolly came calling on a Friday afternoon.

Today, she and Dottie had shared a meat pie at lunchtime. Concern about her sister's health had prompted Evie to ensure that Dottie had a more substantial portion. But again, it meant that there was still no money for coal, so there was no fire to ward off the dampness and chill that had invaded the small room.

Looking out through the grubby window, now devoid of the old sheet that used to hang over it, Evie could see that night had well and truly descended; creeping up on her while she was engrossed in her work.

About an hour previously, she had wrapped Dottie up in both their outdoor coats and had insisted she get under the covers. Glancing over to the shadowed corner of the room, where the old bedstead used to stand, she could see a huddled shape on the ticking mattress which was on the floor.

Above the wailing of the baby from the family who had moved in across the landing, she could hear the rattling in her sister's chest as she breathed. The sound made Evie's stomach clench in fear – Please Lord, don't let Dottie be ill again.

Days after they had buried Nel, Dottie had come down with a fever and nasty cough. Evie had nursed her sister through the worst, while still trying to keep up with the sewing for Mrs Smart. What with that, her mother's death and taking on the responsibility for looking after her sister; protecting them both from the threat that Jolly Jack Barrett had brought to their door, Evie was in a state of utter exhaustion.

Walking about the room to work off some nervous energy, she rubbed her arms to create some warmth. It was no good; she would have to put the candle out. It was her last one; she didn't want to waste it. She would gladly get under the blanket with Dottie and hope for sleep; together, they could keep each other warm.

Evie realised she needed to pee. So, discreetly, she lifted her skirts and squatted over the chamber pot; she would take it to the privy in the morning and empty it, unlike some who would empty the contents out of the window. Evie, put a cloth over the pot to smother the sharp smell of urine; however, that was the least of the bad smells thereabouts, the scent of human detritus hung in the palled air; the smell of boiling tripe, onions, cabbage, dirty clouts, sour gin and beer mingled with the great unwashed. Although Evie was used to the smells by now, she barely noticed the aromas; nonetheless, she dreaded a trip to the outside privy. Eh, she shuddered just thinking about it.

Slipping off her boots, she stripped down to her shift, snuffed out the candle and climbed under the covers. As Evie put her arms around her sister, Dottie sighed in her sleep but did not wake.

Thank God, the baby had finally stopped wailing, but she could still hear the sound of voices through the thin walls, chattering in some gibberish, language she had never heard before.

Evie closed her eyes, as she did so, she felt the familiar tightness in her chest. Tears formed under her eyelids: How could fate be so cruel to them? Losing dad, then Mum died, *no, was murdered!*

This place was poison. Evie didn't know if she could protect Dottie from the evil that was palatable on the air; her fear grew by the day.

If it hadn't been for Dottie becoming ill, she might well have risked leaving here, possibly petitioning the workhouse; they would have been safe there, wouldn't they?

In the darkness, with the weight of dread settling in her heart and belly, Evie allowed herself the luxury of tears, she let out a sob and clutched Dottie closer.

Eventually, she pulled herself together and wiped the tears away with the corner of the rough blanket. Turning her attention to other things, she listened to the myriad of sounds that made up the chorus of the night: Shouting, laughing, crying, even screaming. Dogs were barking, cats fighting and the familiar sound of the church bells chiming on the quarter-hour. And the worst sound of all, the rats scratching in the walls.

Not all the world was like this, she told herself; Mother had told them stories about where she lived as a girl, in Dorset; a place of green fields, like the park only much, much bigger. Evie could barely imagine such a beautiful place. She knew that Mother was learned, Mother had taught her and Dottie how to read, write and sew, although Dottie wasn't the greatest seamstress, so was put to work unpicking seams.

"One day," her mother had said, "I will be making fine clothes for fine ladies. We will live in a lovely house with a garden and have a maid and a cook ..." Evie couldn't imagine that either. Dad had told his wife off for planting unrealistic dreams in the heads of his daughters. "Life is harsh," he had said, Evie was more inclined to believe him, for she lived amid the cruel world that was Poplar – "named after the tree," mother had said, "what could be nicer, eh?", Evie had smiled and nodded, knowing full well that bringing them to this awful place was breaking her mother's heart.

Evie was up before the foggy grey dawn pushed its way through the overcast sky. She got Dottie up, who complained sleepily. Evie got her to pee in the pot, as she did so, she noticed that Dottie's breathing still sounded rough, but she didn't seem to have a fever.

Both girls pulled on their woollen dresses, and Evie picked up the bedding and shook it out. Oh, how she missed the old bedstead.

Pulling on her boots, although not bothering to lace them, Evie then unlocked the door. Picking up the cloth-covered chamber pot, she made her way down the creaking and uneven stairs.

Negotiating the two flights of narrow stairs, she had to step over several people asleep on the landings and even on the stairs themselves. Snoring and mumbled complaints followed her as she brushed passed.

The people resembled bags of rags; all identity stripped away. At least she and Dottie had a room to themselves, Evie thought, but for how much longer? She was getting behind with the rent, particularly as the darker evenings set in, less daylight meant less work done. For some reason, Mr Barrett had been lenient on them. However, Evie didn't trust him one bit. Mr Barrett only did things to suit himself, this sudden turn to benevolence worried her.

When she found herself questioning his generosity, he had said, "It's out of respect for your ma," he had explained, looking at Evie with a strange expression on his face. The look sent ripples of unease down her spine, "I know you'll pay me what you owe, one way or another, soon enough," he had winked at her then.

Reaching the back door, at last, Evie stepped out into the chilly morning and carefully picked her way across the muddy back yard; the ice-covered puddles crunched with every step. The mud was ankle-deep in places, Evie was glad of her stout boots: their boots and their coats were two things she had kept hold of, "no matter what, always make sure you have a good coat and stout boots," She heeded her mother's advice.

The nearer she got to the privy, the more her eyes watered with the awful smell. Should be used to it by now, she told herself harshly.

Gingerly she opened the rotting wooden door and poured the contents of the chamber pot down the dark hole set in the filthy wooden seat.

Then she picked her way back across the yard. She had nearly reached the door when the figure of a man darkened the doorway, blocking her way into the house. Evie's heart jumped into her mouth.

'Well, look who we have ere.' Bill Miller leant against the door jamb and eyed her insolently.

Evie dropped her gaze, wishing that he would leave. 'Good morning, Mr Miller.'

'Ha, see that's what I like about you, Evie Winters. *Mr Miller!*' He chuckled. 'I like a woman who knows her place.'

He looked her up and down appraisingly. 'Oh, and by God, yer turning into a pretty wench.' Much to her horror, he stepped into the yard. Evie took a step backwards as she eyed him warily. 'You ain't got a beau ave you.' It was a statement. 'Not been with a man then?'

Evie felt the heat rise to her cheeks, but she managed to find her voice. 'Keep away from me.'

Bill glanced behind him. 'See, we're all alone, what say you let me make a proper woman of you?'

'No.' Before she knew what she was doing, Evie swung the chamber pot at his head.

She missed as Bill stepped back, issuing a curse. His eyes narrowed dangerously. 'So, you want to play games, eh.' He rushed her then. She dropped the pot into the mud as Bill pushed her up against the dripping brick wall. Then, he grabbed her wrists with both hands and pinned them over her head.

As his hot, reeking breath caressed her cheek, she turned her head away. She tried to kick him, but her long muddy skirts impeded the action.

Holding her wrists with one hand, with the other he fondled her breast under the woollen bodice.

'See, ripe for the taking.' Bill chuckled. Then his hand started to pull up the skirt of her dress.

'Stop, please.' Tears of dread and humiliation ran down her cheeks. Should she scream? Would anyone bother to run to her aid if she did? Screams were commonplace around here, as were atrocities.

When Bill Miller's hard stumpy fingers found the crotch of her drawers, Evie couldn't help herself; she let out a shrill scream.

'What the ell!'

Suddenly, Bill Miller's bulk was gone, Evie found that she was free. Through tear misted eyes, she saw Jack Barrett punch Bill in the face. He put all his weight behind the blow, the man's head snapped back as his nose exploded. The fat man dropped into the filthy mud like a stone.

Jolly's attention turned to Evie, he stepped over and grabbed her arm in a tight grip, then pulled her to him none too gently.

'Did he hurt you, girl?' his voice was rough with emotion.

'No, but he would have.'

The tall man's eyes narrowed as he looked down at her. But Evie knew his anger was not directed at her. Much to Evie's surprise, he reached out and tucked a strand of her long chestnut hair behind her ear.

'I always knew he couldn't keep his pecker in his trousers. You get up them stairs, girl, I'll deal with im.'

Her heart thumping wildly, Evie did what he said. In a rush to get up the stairs, she forgot to take her boots off, a trail of mud and other noxious substances were left in her wake.

When she paused on the first landing she let out a horrified breath. Evie swallowed the bile that had risen in her throat in fright.

Breathlessly, she reached the hollow sanctuary of their room and stepped inside, shutting the door tight.

As soon as the girl had stepped foot back into the house, Jolly turned to the prone man. He kicked him hard in the ribs. Bill groaned and opened his eyes, blinking rapidly. Jolly reached down and grabbed the front of his grubby shirt. He lifted him, drew back his fist and punched him again. After a few more hard blows, the man was dead.

Jolly dragged the body behind the privy. He would get some of the lads to deal with it later.

Dottie, who was sitting at the table patiently awaiting the return of her sister, took in Evie's dishevelled appearance.

'What's the matter, Evie?' anxiety made her voice quaver.

Trying to get the shudders of fright under control, Evie bent over and placed her hands on her thighs. 'I'm fine, just rushed up the stairs too quick.' Feeling as if she were going to be sick, she swallowed rapidly.

'Your boots are muddy.' Dottie pointed out.

'Ah, see I was in such a rush.' She found a smile for her younger sister as she straightened up. 'It'll be easy to sweep up when it dries.'

'I'm hungry.' Dottie exclaimed as Evie pulled off her filthy boots with trembling fingers.

'We both are.' Evie's voice was terse. Well, she had been hungry, but the encounter with Bill Miller had cured her of that at least.

Needing something practical to do, she said, 'Come on, let me do your hair.' Obediently, Dottie came and sat in the other chair, her back to her sister. 'Got to keep the lice at bay.' Evie soothed as she picked up the comb they both used; she combed her sister's long silky locks that rippled down her back.

Leaning back, Dottie sighed, she enjoyed having her hair combed, it reminded her of when mother used to do it. Evie worked on a particularly tricky knot, she knew it must pull on her sister's scalp, but Dottie didn't complain. As soon as she was satisfied, Evie plaited it and pinned it up on top of Dottie's head.

'Now, let's wash that face.' Evie used the washcloth and the cold water she had gathered in their old tin bowl the night before and scrubbed Dottie's face until it was pink. She washed behind her ears, then had her wash her hands. Then Evie did the same, then pinned up her own tresses.

'I'll get this lace repaired on these bloomers; then we can take these bits to Mrs Smart.' Evie sat down at the table on the chair closest to the smudged window. She picked up the work she had discarded the following night.

'Can we get something to eat after, Evie?' Dottie asked as she sat down again.

'Yes, we'll get some bread and dripping,' Evie answered, although food was the last thing on her mind.

Dottie nodded and picked up her work. She was unpicking the seams of an old woollen jacket that was threadbare on the elbows.

Evie tried a few stitches but found her hands were still shaking. She took a breath and started again.

As Evie found herself becoming engrossed in her work, the domestic activity soothed her and calmed her down. So, when there was a loud knock at the door, both she and Dottie jumped.

'Who is it?' Evie found her mouth was dry as she called out.

'Jack Barrett,' came the reply.

The two sisters glanced at each other warily. Evie got up and wiped her sweating palms against her dress.

She opened the door and peered out. 'Yes?'

Jolly pushed open the door and stepped into the room.

'Ere,' he handed Evie the chamber pot that she had left in the yard. 'Thought you might be needing this,' he said with a wry smile. Evie took it from him automatically. 'Now, get yer sister to go down and see Molly,' he said in a voice that broke no argument.

Guessing that this had something to do with Bill Miller, Evie reluctantly did as she was bid. 'Do as he says, Dot, go downstairs.'

Dottie gave them both a curious look that was shadowed by worry then left.

'Bill won't be bothering you again,' Jolly said as he took his hat off and brushed his hand through his thick hair.

His presence made the room feel even smaller as he stood in the middle of the floor.

'Um, thank you.' Evie put the pot down, then wrung her hands nervously.

'I know that you and your sister are struggling.'

'We manage well enough.' Evie found herself saying.

'Aye,' he took in the pokey room, the damp on the walls. Then his gaze rested on the girl once more. 'See, the thing is, I need a wife with a bit of learning behind er.'

'A wife ...?'

'Jack Barrett is going up in the world, and you and that sister of yours could benefit. I'm in the process of buying a nice little ouse in Bow, with a garden an all.'

Evie felt the blood draining from her face as the implications dawned. 'What are you saying exactly?'

'You and me, girl, are going to be married.' He gestured about the room, 'Get you out of this place for a start.'

'Married?' Suddenly feeling faint again, Evie sat down on the chair that Dottie had not long vacated.

'I know that sister of yours ain't well, she can come with us.' Jolly played his trump card. 'I'll even pay for a doctor to see her right.' He tried a smile that made his face look grimmer. 'I'll give you a few days to think about it.' Despite his reassuring tone, he took a step forward so that he was looking down at her. 'I'm sure you'll make the right decision, Evie. Got the rent for Friday, ave yer?'

He didn't wait for an answer. Putting his hat back on, he gave Evie a curt nod of farewell then left.

Evie sat in stunned silence for a long moment. Oh Lord, what was she to do? The thought of being married to Jack Barrett contracted her stomach and sent icy fingers down her spine. The awful trembling took hold of her once again. She wrapped her arms about her torso.

Then she thought of Dottie, her persistent cough. Jack was correct in his assumption; her sister wasn't well.

They were in November, and it was freezing and damp. They had the rest of the winter months looming ahead. She was falling badly behind with the work for Mrs Smart, and therefore the rent.

As she sat there, she hadn't realised that Jolly had left the door open, and an unkempt figure appeared; it was Mrs Gill.

'Offered you marriage as he?' her voice rasped in her dry throat.

Evie looked up at the old woman. 'You heard?'

'Aye, I did. It wasn't im who killed your ma, but he ain't clear of blame all the same.'

'Yes, I know.' Evie shook her head as tears pricked her eyes. Oh, she felt so exhausted, everything was a constant worry that bowed her young shoulders.

'If you says no to im, yer life won't be worth living.' The old woman reminded her, not that she needed reminding. She guessed what the implications would be if she turned down Jolly Barrett. 'The way I see it, you say yes, and you and that sister of yours will be set for life. Or you flee, run now, go to the workhouse.'

'Have you ever been in the workhouse, Mrs Gill?' Evie asked. She felt a bit of reassurance having the old woman's company at that moment, despite the unkempt stink wafting from her.

'Aye,' the woman visibly shuddered. 'Dire place it is, but maybe better for you young uns, safer.' Both of them heard the stairs creaking as Dottie appeared on the landing behind the old woman. 'Ere she be,' Mrs Gill moved away from the threshold so Dot could enter.

Dottie glanced at the woman, then to her sister as she edged her way into the room. 'What's happening?'

Evie stood up and brushed down her woollen skirt. 'Nothing, Dot, everything is fine.'

'Aye,' they heard the old woman mutter as she faded back into the shadows.

'What did she want?' Dottie asked.

'Nothing, just chit chat.'

'And Mr Barrett?'

'Just checking I will have the rent for Friday.'

'And will we?' Dottie asked.

Evie tried an unsuccessful smile. 'Some of it, if not all.'

Choosing to ignore the doubt in Evie's words, Dottie said, 'There are a girl and her grandmother staying with Molly and Margie downstairs.'

'Really?'

Dottie nodded with enthusiasm. 'The girl, Sophia, is nice, but her grandmother doesn't speak English. Sophia told me they had a long journey to get here, all the way from the mountains.' Evie noticed that her sister's face was the most animated it had been for a long time.

Evie smiled, 'Well, I look forward to meeting them.'

'Come down now, Evie, come and meet them.'

'Not now, Dottie, you know we've got work to do, then we need to take it over to Mrs Smart.'

Her sister's expression dropped, but she nodded her head and sat down, then jumped back up and fished in her pocket. 'Here,' she handed Evie a sandwich, 'it's got jam and butter on it, Molly let me have two slices.'

'Thank you,' Evie took the offering, despite her empty stomach, after her meeting with Jolly Barrett, she wasn't sure she could eat it and keep it down. But Dottie was watching her closely, Evie took a bite of the sandwich, chewed then swallowed, although her throat felt restricted with fear, she managed to keep it down, then the hunger took over, she finished off the slice of bread with alacrity.

Chapter 22

Despite the anxiety she was feeling, Evie felt better after eating the bread, butter, and jam. She hadn't eaten anything sweet for so long; the jam had tasted delicious.

After wiping her sticky fingers on her skirt, she and Dottie started their unpicking and sewing.

As she went about this familiar task, a flicker of hope shimmered in her heart: if they could get all this done and down to the market, Mrs Smart would pay them, then she could give the money to Jolly. If she didn't owe him anything, she wouldn't have to marry him, would she? Having a bit of a plan boosted Evie's spirits.

The two girls worked industriously. They were both engrossed in their work that a knock on the door made them both jump.

Exchanging worried looks, Evie called out warily, 'Who is it?'

'Sophia, from downstairs.'

'Oh, she's here, Evie.' Dottie set aside her unpicking and rushed over and opened the door.

223

Setting down her sewing, Evie stood up to welcome the visitor. Sophia was the same height as Dottie; she had a pale face framed by curling dark hair and the most striking grey eyes that Evie had ever seen. They were luminous and quite beautiful.

Dottie grabbed the girl's arm with enthusiasm. 'Sophia, this is my sister, Evie.'

The two girls smiled at each other.

'I hope you do not mind me coming to see you, only that man they call Jolly is speaking to Molly, and they sent me out of the room.'

'That's fine,' Evie answered somewhat distractedly; she wondered what Jack Barrett wanted with Molly?

'You are sewing?' Sophia gestured to the table. 'I sew well. I can help you.'

'Really?' Evie's voice was incredulous with hope. 'We need to get them finished so we can take them to be sold.'

Sophia nodded, 'I understand, my sewing is neat, people tell me.'

'Very good then.' Evie nodded.

Dottie took the unpicking she had been doing and sat on the ticking mattress so that Sophia could have the other chair.

While they sewed, Sophia told them both more about her life and where she had come from.

*

Earlier on that morning, after ensuring that her grandmother had eaten and taken some tea, Sophia put the old woman back to bed. She was sleeping soundly when Jack Barrett had turned up at Molly's door. The first thing the man did was get Sophia to leave the room.

Flashing him a worried look, Sophia then turned to Molly, 'I will go and see Dottie.'

'Aye, good idea, lovie.' Molly nodded.

As soon as Sophia had gone, Jack asked, 'ow are things?'

'Well enough.' For something to do, Molly picked up a poker and prodded the fire.

'They been causing you any trouble?' He nodded towards the bed on the other side of the curtained room. They could both hear the gentle snores of the grandmother.

Molly set the poker aside and straightened up. 'They've been good as gold.'

Jolly nodded. 'Glad to ear it.' He then fished in his pocket and drew out two small vials which he handed to Molly. 'laudanum and opium,' he explained. 'One for the old dear to send her on her way, and the opium for the girl. Thought it might make her more co-operative.'

'Huh, I've eard of the likes of im, he don't want them to co-operate, he wants them to fight back.'

Jolly shrugged, 'You don't ave to give it to er.'

Molly picked up the two small glass bottles. 'I ain't appy about this Jack, yer asking me to commit murder.' Molly's face had drained of colour. 'The old bird ain't got many years left in er.' He smiled crookedly.

Despite the fire, Molly felt goosebumps of apprehension prickle her arms; she nodded, he was probably right.

'Aww, and just to let you know, Bill won't be around anymore. I'm getting young Arthur to ang around, keep an eye on things,' Jolly explained.

'What appened to Bill?'

'Let's just say he made a nuisance of imself with Evie Winters.'

'Oh Lord.' Molly pulled out a chair and sat down heavily, 'I told you many a time e's a right letch, Jack. Is she alright?'

'Aye, she is. And yes, you did tell me. Anyway, he won't be around no more, enough said.'

All the woman could do was nod her head once more.

As soon as Jolly shut the door, Molly got up, grabbed a half-full bottle of gin from the shelf. She didn't bother with a glass. Putting the bottle to her lips, she tipped it up and took a good swallow, then set it down on the table.

Bloody ell, she thought, what is going on? Although Molly was not stupid, as soon as Jack showed up with the girl and her grandmother, Molly knew the two would be used in some dark purpose or other, things she didn't even want to guess at.

Her hand trembled as she picked up the bottle again. She took another good swig.

She wished that Margie was here to talk to, but she had taken lodgings with Rita, the barmaid from the Crown and Garter, explaining that the room in Little Back Lane felt too small for the four of them.

The two bottles on the table caught Molly's eye, getting up, she swooped them up and stuck them behind some crockery on the topmost shelf.

Bloody Jack Barrett, not only was he going to ruin that lovely girl's life. He was going to make her, Molly, into a murderer.

Molly Arkwright had done much in her life that she was not proud of; much of it due to circumstances and the need for survival. It was a hard life on the back streets of London. She had been forced to stoop so low, but she had to take her hat off to Jolly, he had dragged her further into the dark shadows of lawlessness.

*

Evie could hardly believe it when Sophia turned out to be a wonderful seamstress.

'I had to make all my clothes,' she explained to the sisters. 'A man would come to our village, every few months or so, with a cart full of bolts of fabric.' She smiled at the memory. 'It was always so exciting, I like blue, the colour of the mountain sky. I had a striped, blue skirt which I loved; everything apart from a few things that my grandmother and I brought with us has been left behind.'

'That's sad,' Dottie spoke up, looking rapt with everything Sophia said.

'Life is harsh,' Evie remarked, her voice tinged with bitterness.

Sophia nodded, then looked up from her sewing, her gaze took in the sparseness of the room. 'This isn't a good place to live.'

Evie shook her head. 'No, it isn't.'

Sophia set aside her sewing for a moment; she leant forward in her seat. 'Who is this Jolly Barrett, what does he want with us? I have asked Molly; she says that he is going to look after us and give us a good life but, somehow, I do not believe her.'

'Mmm,' Evie was saddened that Molly was lying to the girl, but then again she was under Jack Barrett's thumb, so it was hardly surprising. 'Don't trust Jolly, Sophia.' Evie's voice was vehement. 'If we could, me and Dottie would be out of here quick smart.'

'You have nowhere to go?'

Evie sighed. 'No, only the workhouse.'

'I understand,' Sophia nodded, 'we have nowhere to go either.'

The two girls looked at each other in mutual sympathy.

Later on, Evie was delighted at the progress that they had made that morning, Sophia's help had made all the difference.

Molly had appeared earlier on to check on the girls. When she saw that Sophia was being kept busy, she was happy to let her stay with Evie and Dottie. She also told Sophia that her grandmother was still sleeping, so she didn't have to rush back.

Once all the items were finished, Evie carefully folded them and packaged them up in brown paper, which she tied up carefully with string.

When Dottie expressed a feeling of exhaustion, Sophia offered to go with Evie to take the items to the market.

'I'm not having you stay here on your own, Dottie; you will have to stay with Molly,'

'That's fine,' Dottie agreed, 'it's warmer down there anyway.'

Although, when Sophia told Molly that she wanted to go with Evie, the woman was hesitant to let the girl out of her sight; what if she ran off, or was abducted?

'Please, Miss Molly.' Sophia gave her such a wide-eyed look, Molly agreed.

'You've got time to get there and back before dark, so no dilly-dallying.' She said abruptly.

As soon as the girls had set off, Molly found Arthur, who was keeping an eye on them and told him to follow them closely.

The young lad wiped his hand across his snotty nose. 'You sure Jolly will be appy with this?' he queried her decision.

'Don't think a walk down the market will do em any arm. Now, be off with you, or you'll lose them.'

Arthur nodded and ran after the girls. It wasn't long before he had them in sight. Knowing pretty much the route that the girls would take, he was confident they wouldn't give him the slip.

It was the first time that Sophia had been out during daylight hours since she had arrived in London. Although the place was squalid, her eyes were enormous with interest; taking everything in; the houses, the people, the river, and the docks.

'This place is so big,' she said with awe in her voice. 'The mountains are big where we come from, but to see so many people and vehicles.

'Watch out.' Evie caught the other girl's arm and pulled her out of the way of a coal wagon that was trundling past.

Sophia looked at two children sitting on a blackened step; they were dressed in rags and were stick thin. 'There is so much poverty here.' She shuddered.

'I know,' Evie sighed. 'I don't know any different. I'm scared that me and Dot are going to end up on the streets.'

'You really think that will happen?'

Evie nodded as they turned the corner onto a wider road. 'Even with the sewing, I'm struggling to pay the rent.'

Sophia nodded in sympathy. 'We were poor in many ways where I come from, but we worked the land and traded goods. We had cows, goats, chickens,' suddenly, her voice broke as she felt the tears of homesickness prick her eyes.

Evie tucked the packet of clothes under her arm and took Sophia's elbow, giving it a gentle squeeze. 'I'm sorry.'

The other girl gave her a wry smile, 'It is alright, we shall manage.'

As they continued their journey, Evie gave her companion a sidelong glance. 'Jolly Barrett has asked me to marry him, mm, well asked it not quite right, he has told me he is going to marry me.' She confided.

Sophia halted in her tracks. Her gaze raked Evie's face questioningly. 'Is this what you want?'

Shaking her head vehemently, Evie was annoyed when tears pricked her eyes. 'N-no, I can't bear the thought, but it is probably our only way of getting out of here.'

'And Dottie?' Sophia asked.

Evie hiccupped and wiped her eyes on her sleeve. 'I haven't said anything to her, but that's just the thing, he said she can come too. He even told me he would pay for a doctor for her.'

Sophia nodded. 'Would you be happy with that arrangement?' Evie gave a laughed tinged with bitterness, 'happy? I'm not sure what happiness is anymore.'

Evie told Sophia everything that had happened, the fact that Jolly was partly (or completely) responsible for her mother's death, the attack that morning, and the fact that Jolly had told her that Bill had been "dealt with".

The two girls had just turned into a side street when a gang of around seven lads approached them. Evie didn't think anything of it at first until she found herself confronted by Davey Bowe, a stocky bully around the age of twelve.

'Well, see who we have ere lads.' Davey and the others crowded in on Evie and Sophia making the two girls press together. 'If it ain't miss igh and mighty.' The boy glanced around at his companions. 'Thinks she's better than us, she does. An, who's this?' He eyed Sophia with interest.

'Just leave us be, Davey.' Evie put some force into her voice.

'And whatcha going to do if I don't?' Davey sneered.

'What's she got in the package, Davey?' One of the other lads, who Evie didn't know, pushed forward. He was small and rangy with a snotty nose, which he kept wiping with the back of his hand.

'Let's take a look, shall we lads?' Before Evie understood his intent, Davey plucked the carefully wrapped package from her hand.

'No, please.' She gasped, but the boys were ripping at the waxed paper like vultures around a corpse.

One of the boys grabbed the delicate linen and held the garment up in front of him, earning snickers from the others. 'Aww, look ere lads, ladies' bloomers.'

'Ha, ha, try em on, Albert,' someone called.

Albert stuck his muddy boots through the leg holes, the linen ripped.

231

Evie felt helpless as the boys pulled out the other clothes and started throwing them around.

'Leave them be, leave them be.' Evie was crying now as Sophia clung onto her arm in fright.

Evie didn't know what to do as she saw all their careful work trampled into the muddy ground.

'Whatcha gonna sell now?' Davey grinned at her.

'Come on, Davey, we've ad our fun,' Albert called out, he and some of the others were already moving on.

'Not much point in going down the market now is there.' Davey sneered. Then as a parting comment added, 'Oh yes, and Jolly said he's looking forward to your answer.'

Evie and Sophia stood in the middle of the narrow street; the carefully stitched garments lay about them like the torn banners of a battle lost. Every single one of them was ruined. As she surveyed the carnage, Evie felt as if her legs were going to give way.

'No, Evie,' Sophia exclaimed, her voice was ragged with fright, but she stooped down to pick up a linen shirt. 'Can they be repaired and washed?' Evie shook her head as fat tears flowed down her cheeks. 'We've got no lye soap; we'll never get the stains out.' She sniffed and wiped her cheeks with the corner of her coat.

'That Jolly is obviously behind this,' Sophia said angrily. 'He's backing you into a corner so you will have to say yes to him.'

Before she knew what was happening, Evie doubled over and started to retch. There wasn't much in her stomach to bring up.

'We'll find a way.' Sophia tried to soothe Evie as she rubbed her back.

Eventually, Evie stood up and shook her head. 'I'm not going to let him get the better of me,' her voice was hard. 'We'll carry on to the market, see Mrs Smart and get some more work.'

'Then, I shall come with you and help you, Evie.' Sophia nodded with conviction.

Evie looked at the other girl with gratitude, 'Thank you, Sophia.'

Feeling better now she had a bit of a plan, even though it was probably a weak hope, Evie and Sophia carried on to the market.

Mrs Smart was not pleased when the girls turned up at her barrow where she had her goods on display, empty-handed.

'I ad someone waiting for that shirt.' Her faded blue eyes, surrounded by puffy flesh, were beady as she gazed at the girls. Her cheeks were rosy, not with health but broken veins that spoke of a fondness for the gin. Her nose was reddened and moist at the tip. It was a chilly day, especially for those selling at the market. Mrs Smart wore a thick grey wool shawl around her top half and a thick brown woollen skirt that fell to the top of her sturdy brown boots. A cap atop her head did nothing to keep her wiry grey curls in check; they surrounded her face like coiled springs.

Evie tried to keep her voice steady. 'I'm sorry, Mrs Smart, a gang of lads grabbed the package; all the clothes were ruined.'

'Oh, my Lord.' The woman fanned her face. 'An there's you asking for another job, ow can I trust you now?'

Despite herself, Evie felt anger rising from her chest. 'We've never let you down before,' she stated, there was an edge to her voice. 'Jolly was behind all this; we need more work so that we can pay the rent.'

The woman raised a greying eyebrow at them. 'Eh, Jolly ain't going to appreciate that accusation.'

'It's true,' Sophia spoke up for the first time.

Mrs Smart shot the stranger a quick look, then proceeded to address Evie, her eyes were as hard and cold as ice. 'I can't give yer anything else, can't trust you anymore.' She raised a stubby fingered hand encased in knitted fingerless gloves to forestall Evie's protest.

'That's not fair,' Sophia found herself speaking up for Evie. 'It isn't her fault.'

'An, just who do you think you are, miss?' Mrs Smart eyed the other girl with suspicion.

'My grandmother and I arrived here the other night; we come from the Ural Mountains.'

'Really, now! Well, ain't that grand indeed.'

'Sophia helped us with the last lot.' Evie explained. 'She's fine with a needle. Let us have some more work. We can get them done quick.'

Mrs Smart shook her head. 'I don't know what you've done to upset Jack Barrett.'

'What do you mean?' Evie asked in trepidation.

'Well, he tells me I'm not to give you any more work,' She gave the girl a piercing look, 'says he's got plans for you.'

Evie felt her heart jolt with shock. The man was deliberately ensuring she and Dottie would have nowhere else to go, so she would have no other choice but to take up his offer of marriage.

'Ow much for this, Mrs?' A middle-aged woman stopped at the barrow and picked up a paisley shawl.

As Mrs Smart dealt with her customer, Sophia drew Evie aside. 'What are we going to do?'

Evie shook her head. Once again, she felt hot tears prickling behind her eyes — tears for the unfairness and injustice.

'Well, what you two still anging around ere for!' Mrs Smart addressed the girls that were still lingering beside her barrow.

'Come, Evie.' Sophia put her arm around her shoulders. As the two girls walked away, Evie was very aware of the older woman's beady eyes upon them. Then the market crowd swallowed them up.

'Can't you get some work from someone else?' Sophia asked gently.

Evie shook her head; she looked so dejected. 'No, if Jolly's told Mrs Smart not to let us have any work, then it will be same all over the market.

Sophia could feel her despair. Reaching out, she took the other girl's arm. 'We'll find a way around this.'

Evie gave her a sad look tinged with gratitude. 'That is kind, Sophia, but I can't see any way out of this that doesn't bode well for Dottie and me.' Evie thought of Jolly Barrett and the lengths he was taking to make sure herself and Dottie were indebted to him. Oh Lord, he was an evil man; she could never marry him; she would rather die. Then there was Sophia and her grandmother, what plans did he have for them? Evie shuddered.

Chapter 23

J ack Barrett grabbed Molly's arm in a hard grip. He pulled her against him and pressed his face close to hers.

'What the ell were you thinking of letting them girls go down the Market?'

'I didn't think it would cause any harm, Jack.'

They were in the narrow alley beside the house. Jack let go of her so suddenly it caused her to stumble. Molly reached out a hand and steadied herself by holding on to the wall.

'It were lucky that Arthur was able to let Davey and the others know what was appening.'

'What do you mean?'

Jolly eyed her with a look of such distaste it made her stomach clench with fear. 'I need that Evie Winters in a position that any escape I offer she will jump at the chance.'

'Escape?' Molly's gaze was wary.

She was surprised when Jolly chuckled. 'I'm going to marry the older girl, take her and her sister in.'

'Marry er?' The woman's face blanched as she tried to register the statement; this was the last thing she expected to hear.

'Aye, well, she as some learning behind er, and she's a fine looker. As soon as we get the girl and her Grandmother out the way, the banns will be read in Bow.'

'Oh Lord, Jack.'

The smile he gave her was cold. 'You just ave to keep em all sweet for the time being. An don't let them leave the ouse again, do you ear me?'

Molly dropped her gaze from his. 'Yes.'

'Good girl. Now, I shall be around with some clothes for the Jewish girl, make sure she as a bath and sort out her air.'

Molly nodded.

Shooting out a hand, he grabbed her chin none too gently. Using his superior height to his advantage, he loomed over her once more. She cowered in his shadow. 'I'm counting on yer, Moll, don't let me down.'

Her eyes were watering from the pain of his grip; all she could do was nod once more.

*

When the girls arrived back, Molly could see the despair written all over Evie's pale features.

Sensing her sister's sadness, Dottie ran over to her and put her arms around her. The two sisters hugged tightly for a moment.

'What happened, Evie,' Dottie asked, she studied Evie's expression with concern.

Anxiety coursed through Molly. She was sitting at the table watching the proceedings, as she did so she found herself clenching her fists so tightly, her hands ached. Aww, Lord, she thought, what the ell's appened now!

'A gang of boys destroyed everything,' Evie explained, 'and Mrs Smart wouldn't give us anymore work. She said that Jolly wouldn't allow it.' Boldly, Evie's held Molly's gaze as she recounted the events.

Feeling guilty, Molly was the first one to look away.

'Why, Evie? Why's he doing this?' Dottie asked.

'Best tell her the truth, girl,' Molly called over.

Evie shot the other woman a hard glance, then drew Dottie to an empty chair. The girls sat down, as Molly got up declaring she was going to make some tea.

Evie gave her sister a long look. 'Jack Barrett has asked me to marry him, Dot.'

'What!?' The younger girl shook her head. 'You can't do that, Evie, he's not a nice man.' Evie found herself smiling at her sister's innocent description of the rent collector. 'He says that he is buying a nice house where we can live, and he is going to pay for a doctor to attend you.'

'Huh, oh Lord,' Molly muttered under her breath.

'My cough's a lot better, Evie, I'll be as right as rain when the weather is brighter,' Dottie said earnestly.

Evie reached out a hand and took her sisters. 'That's just it, Dottie, we've got the winter ahead of us, things are only going to get worse.'

'I don't want to live in the same house as Jolly.' A fat tear ran down her pale cheek.

Reaching over, Evie took her sister in her arms and hugged her tight.

'Something will come along,' she whispered into Dottie's ear.

Without ceremony, Molly poured tea for them all and passed the mugs around the table.

'Yer know, yer can't say no to Jolly, dontcha?' Molly's voice was rough. Evie gave the other woman a hard look but nodded. 'See the thing is,' Molly joined them at the table. 'I never thought I would see the day when Jolly Jack Barrett would declare he is going to be married.' She gave the older sister a long look, 'Seems he see's something special in you, Evie. Who knows, yer may be the one to tame im.'

'He is an evil man,' Sophia spoke up.

Molly shot the girl an uneasy look, 'No talk like that around ere, please, the wall's ave ears.' Then she gave Evie an earnest look. 'Yer need to give his offer some real thought, girl: the consequences of you saying no, well.' Molly dropped her gaze to her mug of tea which she held between her hands. After a long moment, she looked up. 'The thing is yer only ave two options; one is to marry the man, and the other is to run. Cos, if you stay around ere, Jolly will see to it you never get another offer of marriage.' Molly's glance darted to Dottie and then back to Evie. 'If you don't capitulate, he will make your lives hell.'

Evie digested what Molly had just told them. She suddenly felt sick to her stomach. Molly had voiced exactly what Evie had been thinking.

A hush fell about the room; the air was thick with the approaching threat. The fire crackled in the grate.

They could hear the noises made by others in the house, and the sound of cartwheels going along the lane. Even Sophia's Grandmother, who could not speak a word of English, could feel the tension, she reached out and held on to Sophia's hand tightly.

Molly was the one to break the silence, she drained her mug and set it on the table. 'Now, after you've finished your tea, go and get yer mattress from upstairs.' She addressed Evie and Dottie, 'you two are going to be sleeping down ere from now on. I'll take the mattress and you two can ave my bed.'

'Is this another order from Jolly?' Bitterness inflected Evie's words.

Molly gave her a hard look. 'Do you want to stay up there,' she raised her eyes to the ceiling, 'in the cold and damp, or come down ere where there's a good fire?'

Evie's expression dropped in defeat, without preamble, she pushed her mug away and got up from the table. 'Come on, Dottie, let's go and fetch our things.'

As soon as the sisters had left the room, Sophia said; 'isn't there anything you can do to stop all this, Miss Molly?'

The older woman shook her head, 'As I said before, that Evie should consider erself lucky.'

'Would you want to marry Jolly?' Sophia asked her, eyeing her with interest.

Molly dropped her gaze. 'Well, he ain't asked me, as he!'

But Molly considered the foreign girl's comment; Ahh, there was a time when she would have jumped at the chance of marrying a man like Jack. If he had asked her and not Evie Winters, she would have said yes. Then she would be safe for the rest of her life. Yes, Evie Winters should feel bloody honoured that she was in Jolly's sights. But, despite these thoughts, the weight of misgivings rested heavily on her shoulders.

*

The next few days passed slowly. Molly kept a close eye on the girls; Evie felt as if she were in some sort of prison. The woman would not let any of them out of her sight.

Evie was also aware that Jolly had one of his boys watching the house. Her heart and stomach seemed to be tied up in knots of anxiety as she thought about the future. She and Dottie, and Sophia and her Grandmother for that matter, needed to get away. But the weather was bleak. The sky was a dark grey tinged with a sulphur-yellow which heralded snow. It was far too risky to try and run with the old lady and Dottie, in her weakened state.

It was towards the end of the week when Jolly showed up again. He had a small valise which he passed to Molly.

'There yer go, Moll. Make sure she is clean. I'm going to get Tommy Dicken to elp you fill the tub.' He glanced about, taking in the girls and old woman who was observing him with interest.

Jolly grinned, which made his scar stretch across his cheek. 'You can all share the water, ladies, make use of the tub, eh?' His suggestion was met with silence as his gaze came to rest on Evie, 'Told yer sister ave yer, of our plans?' He didn't wait for a reply but crouched down in front of Dottie where she was sitting in one of the wooden chairs. 'Me an yer sister's going to be married. I've bought a nice ouse; you'll ave a maid to wait on you like lady muck.' He laughed and stood up. His gaze swept the room once more.

'Now cheer up the lot of yer, yer look like someone has died.' Resting a weighty gaze on Molly, he said, 'make sure everything is sweet for tomorrow.'

The woman nodded. 'Yes, Jack.'

He gave them all a parody of a bow and left.

'What's happening tomorrow?' Evie asked after Jolly had gone. Her breath caught in her throat with dread, did she really want to know?

Molly placed the bag on the table and opened it. 'It is Sophia's big day.' As she tried to smile, her facial muscles felt as if they were carved out of marble and refused to oblige her.

'Big day?' Sophia queried.

'That's right.' Molly pulled out a beautiful white dress decked in ribbons, lace, and bows. Beneath the dress was a black velvet cape lined in red silk. There were a pair of cream kid-leather shoes, stockings, and underwear. Molly examined the items, then replaced them in the case, so there was no chance of them getting dirty. 'See, Jolly as found you a nice man to be your usband, Sophia, a wealthy toff, by all accounts. He will take you and your grandmother in, an you won't ave to worry about a thing.'

'I don't want to be married.' Sophia looked horrified.

Molly's expression hardened. 'You know as well as me; you ain't got a choice in the matter!'

'Then, we shall go.' Sophia turned to her Grandmother, 'mir muzun bakumen avek.' Much to Sophia's agitation, her Grandmother shook her head. 'We must get away from here, grandmother.' There was a catch of urgency in the girl's voice.

Molly shut the case with a bang. 'Jolly has his lads watching this place night and day; you wouldn't get to the end of the street.'

'Then help us, Miss Molly,' Sophia pleaded.

Molly sat down and put her head in her hands. 'I can't elp yer. If I did Jolly would kill me.' She looked up in earnest. 'I didn't want to tell yer this, but he's threatened the old lady if yer don't comply with is intentions.'

'You can't do this, Molly,' Evie spoke up, 'You must help us.'

The woman stood up, tears in her eyes. She pressed her hands down on the table and leant forward. 'I know you ain't dim-witted,' her voice was hard, 'He's a dangerous man, you don't cross Jolly Barrett, never. Now, I don't want to ere another word about this. If you utter one more word about trying to get away, I shall tell Jolly, an he will ave yer locked up somewhere that's a lot worse than this place.'

Dejection settled over them all.

'I'm frightened, Evie.' Dottie tugged at her sister's sleeve.

'I know, Dottie, I know. So am I.'

Evie met Sophia's gaze; her heart faltered when she saw that the other girl's expression was flat and filled with despair.

Sophia knew that her Grandmother was too frail to leave, to undergo yet another journey. Her physical and mental health had deteriorated since they had left their home. And, despite eating the food that she been given, her cheeks still looked sunken. It was as if all the life was draining from her. Her memory had been affected; she always asked where they were. She was tired all the time and slept a lot.

No, Sophia decided, she certainly couldn't leave her grandmother in this place, and she would never survive on the streets. As the realisation dawned that there was no escape for them, Sophia felt her heart tighten in her chest. She would just have to hold onto the hope that Molly was telling the truth, that a wealthy man would indeed take her as a wife and, in turn, would look after them both.

⸺⟨⟩⸺

Chapter 24

Hero dipped his head between the luscious thighs of Lady Vanessa Beeching.

He inhaled the warm, musky scent of her and felt his cock stiffen even more. Oh, she really was a delectable piece of womanhood, he thought with relish.

When his tongue slid into the salty depths of her, it was music to his ears when he heard her moan with pleasure and desire.

'Oh darling ...' she uttered with a sigh, lifting her hips so he could burrow even deeper into her core.

Hero lapped at her juices like a starving puppy until she bucked against him, and he felt her muscles spasm in orgasm.

Raising his head, a broad grin on his face. His chin slick with her nectar when their gazes met.

Her heavily hooded, hazel eyes, that at that moment flashed amber held a note of needfulness and his smile widened. She was insatiable, that was what he loved about her. Oh Lord, he felt as if he were bursting with desire.

Lifting himself on his muscular arms, he positioned himself, then plunged into her sleekness.

Vanessa, more than ready to receive him, met him thrust for thrust.

She wrapped her long legs around him. Her nails raked his back as she pulled him harder against her, encouraging him to plunge deeper and deeper.

The room of the inn was small. There was a fire in the grate which made the place overly warm. The air was ripe with their sexual pleasure.

The firelight glinted and rippled over Hero's broad back, which was glistening with jewels of perspiration. Nessa's fingernails left red wheals on the taut skin. The physical effort and heat plastered his curling brown hair to his head, neck, and shoulders.

'Aah!' He grunted in gratification. It was Vanessa's turn to smile with satisfaction.

Rolling off her onto the bed covered in tangled sheets, he let out a contented breath.

'Oh, that was wonderful as usual, darling.' With a sigh, she rested her head on the pillow next to him. Her flame-red hair, which was darkened by perspiration, was spread out over the pillow.

Hero, hands behind his head, gazed contentedly at the beamed ceiling as if entranced by the knots of wood and cracks in the plaster.

Vanessa turned to her lover. Resting her head on the one hand, she studied his handsome physique. She spread her hand over his broad chest, then ran her long fingers over his flesh, tracing the muscles and his ribs.

'Why do you do it?' She asked, as her fingers lingered on the lemon, lime and plum bruising that had blossomed on the left side of his rib cage. 'It can't be for the money.'

Hero gave her a slanted look and placed his hand on hers, to still her roaming fingers. 'You know it's not.'

Vanessa glanced at him. She wasn't a sentimental woman, but she noticed the depth of sadness that muted his blue eyes, feeling her heart lurch, she gave him a smile that was full of sorrow and tenderness.

'You can't keep on punishing yourself forever,' she said softly.

Hero shifted and placed a finger to her lips. 'Hush,' he said, then bent his head down to kiss her.

His lips curled up in a smile when he heard the groan of desire that issued from the back of her throat. Ahh, she is voracious, he thought with delight as he claimed her once again.

Later, when they both lay there catching their breath and feeling sated, Vanessa noticed the gloom of the early winter twilight pressing against the windows.

'Oh lord, it must be getting late.' Then, without preamble, she swung her legs over the side of the bed and got up.

'Aww, I was just getting comfortable, do you have to be going, Nessa?'

She gave him a smile of appreciation, 'if only I could stay longer.' Leaning over, she kissed his forehead tenderly. Then walked over to the washstand in the corner of the room. She picked up a washcloth, dipped it in the tepid water and started to wipe her body clean. As she did so, she was very aware of Hero watching her every movement.

Lifting a leg, she placed a long delicately boned foot on a chair and put the cloth between her legs. Hearing Hero's intake of breath, she felt a wonderful sense of satisfaction ripple through her.

Feeling Horacio's gaze upon her, Vanessa was tempted to take her time over these ablutions. It was such a shame that she needed to get going, however. After sponging her womanhood, she then ran the cloth over her neck and arms.

Hero, thoroughly enjoying the show, smiled with gratification. Where women were concerned, Vanessa was his first conquest. Alec had dragged him to a brothel in the city when they had both turned seventeen. A birthday celebration, Alec had enthused. It was an interesting evening, one that Hero thoroughly enjoyed, but Vanessa had taught him so much more. Through her, he had learnt how to pleasure a woman in so many different and delightful ways.

She was married with a child and thirteen years his senior, but her body was creamy and curvaceous; stomach muscles still taut, with breasts that were beautifully rounded by motherhood. It was just a shame that they could only meet up like this once in a blue moon; even then, their time together was too brief.

Her ablutions taken care of, Vanessa pulled on her clothes, getting Hero to lace up her impossibly tight corset, over which she wore a blouse of fine cream linen. The rest of her riding habit was dark and sombre. Vanessa loved bright colours, but she did not want to draw too much attention.

Finally, she swept up her glorious mane of auburn hair and tucked it up under her veiled riding hat.

'I have heard that Alexander Silverman is having one of his evenings of entertainment,' she remarked as she checked her reflection in a mottled mirror hanging on the wall.

'Yes.' Hero stretched lazily, 'Alec has insisted I attend, he says I may make some important contacts.'

Raising an ironic eyebrow, she laughed. 'Oh, yes, we all know what kind of connections they will be! Just don't go and pick up anything nasty, Hero.'

He gave her an amused look. 'Why have a whore when I have someone like you to fill my arms and my heart.'

She chuckled, picking up her riding-whip, she poked his chest playfully with it. 'That's what I like to hear.' Leaning forward then, she kissed him on the lips. 'Be good,' she said as she pulled away.

'Oh, always.'

The skirt of her dress made a swishing noise as she walked to the bedroom door. When she turned to him once more, her expression was bleak. 'Please be careful with these bloody boxing matches, Hero, one day some serious damage may be done to you, I couldn't bear that.'

His face was clouded as he sat up, swinging his legs over the side of the rumpled bed. 'It's just a bit of fun, Vanessa, something I'm good at.'

Her eyes lingered on him for a moment longer, then she opened the door and left.

Getting up, Hero stretched once more; he winced as he felt the bruising, a nasty punch to the kidneys. He had almost forgotten the pain when he had been pleasuring Vanessa. Hell, he had almost forgotten everything.

Picking up his clothes, he shrugged into them carefully, trying not to aggravate his injury.

As Hero pulled on his boots, he suddenly wondered if his Grandfather would be attending Silverman's "evening". That's it, he thought, I need to find an excuse to get out of going. He was highly fed up with his Grandfather's constant nagging; "when are you going to grow up and take charge of your life and that estate!" It was always the same tune, every time. Hero had done his best to avoid the man, but unfortunately, they were part of the same social circles.

Picking up his riding hat and gloves, Hero left the warm room behind, took the stairs two at a time and made his way out to the stable yard. He had already paid for the use of the room, so he did not have to trouble the innkeeper.

One of the stable lads appeared with a frantic Wilson under one arm and his horse's reins in the other. The lad put the dog down, and Wilson ran and jumped into Hero's arms.

Hero laughed as Wilson licked his face with rapture. 'Aww, that's enough, mutt, I haven't been gone that long.'

Hade's, Hero's horse looked on with a resigned expression in his big eyes; one indulgence that Hero had allowed himself was the buying of the beautiful hunter. Hades was seventeen hands, with a coat as black as ebony, he was an imposing horse with the temperament of a broody mare. Hero adored him and the dog.

The day was overcast; snow clouds gathered over the Kentish Downs as Hero made his way back to the smoke and bustle of the city.

Hero had thought about renting a house in London, but then he heard that Andrew needed a second person to share his suite of rooms. Andrew had been delighted when Hero suggested that he move in. The arrangement had worked out rather well for them both.

Chapter 25

Stepping out into the fresh air, Vanessa took a deep breath: she needed to steal herself now for the journey home.

One of the stable lads brought out her mare, Violet, then helped Vanessa to mount. She thanked him and fished a shilling out of her pocket and gave it to him.

'Thank you, ma'am.' He pulled the peak of his cap.

Turning her horse with an expert hand, she headed out of the stable yard and then onto the road leading back to the city.

Vanessa knew that her heart would become heavier and heavier, the closer she got to their mansion set on the western edge of the city.

Meeting Hero had been one of her saving graces. She didn't know what she would do without their *liaisons* to look forward to. Vanessa wondered if she loved Horacio Woodley, there was a great affection for him in her heart, which was for sure. He was an excellent lover; especially now that she had taught him so much. Vanessa smiled at that thought.

They had met at a gathering hosted by an old school friend Sarah Frobisher. Hero was there with Alec Silverman, what a contrasting pair they made, Hero, wide of shoulder, and very muscular. A broken nose that only enhanced his handsome, rugged features set under a mop of thick curling hair, which he wore a little too long. And then there was Alec; slim as a blade of grass, with his slicked-back dark hair, a broad forehead, and delicately chiselled physique. They seemed a pair of unlikely friends.

Vanessa had been surprised when she found herself drawn to Hero: at eighteen, he was so much younger than she, but she found him to be quite fascinating. She knew of his tragic history, of course; as did all the London set, a terrible, terrible thing. Perhaps, there had been a part of her that wanted to mother him, to tend and heal his emotional wounds? Whatever it was about him, she could not help herself.

She had made it seem as if he had wooed her, whereas it had been the other way around, she had seduced him. Not that it had taken much effort, in her experience, most young men were guided by their cock. Thankfully, Hero was no exception, but God he was a good lover. What a find he had been.

She praised the day when they had met, it could not have been better timing for her, she had been on such a precipice of despair, Hero did not realise it, but he had saved her. She was living in an intolerable situation under the thumb of a sadistic and evil man. The situation may well have felled any other woman way before that, but Vanessa was a strong woman, although that strength was beginning to fail her, there was only so much time one can live in a state of fear and falsehoods before the cracks start to appear.

Vanessa had been married to Sir George Beeching for twelve years; they had been married when she was seventeen. He was fifteen years her senior. It was a marriage of convenience, not love. Ah, she thought, definitely not love: the only passion she felt for the man was contempt. Whenever she thought about her husband, Vanessa felt a sense of acute anguish and fear.

When they had first been married, George had come to her room often. Vanessa was young and naive then, so when George seemed to delight in hurting her: being exceptionally rough when he was in the throes of desire; she thought that was normal for a man. She quickly came to find that she dreaded the bedroom door opening and his appearance. Having no one in which she felt she could confide in, especially when it was such a dark and delicate subject, Vanessa lived in misery.

It was only when her dear friend, Sarah, had noticed some bruising on her collarbone, did she share her anguish. She had also taken on a mantle of shame because George made her feel dirty and unworthy.

Sarah's face had infused with colour, not with embarrassment but with anger.

'Oh, my dear,' she had said, 'No, it is not like that in all marriages, Jasper treats me so gently, I often wonder if he thinks I will break.'

Vanessa had nodded, tears misting her eyes, but the realisation came to her at that moment, that it was George's depravity and not her actions that were in the wrong.

'Don't fret,' Sarah advised, 'in these marriages, my dear, it is your job to produce an heir. Once that has been accomplished, he will probably leave you alone. Let us just hope that your first child will be a boy.'

She had been so relieved when Sarah turned out to be correct in her assumption: after their son, William was born, George kept his distance. She had breathed a sigh of relief, hoping fervently that this would be the end to the abuse he had dealt her.

Vanessa was not a vain woman, but she knew she attracted attention and envy from other women. She found that she was passed secret notes from many young beaus, pleading with her to indulge in one secret liaison or another; this was amusing. However, there was a part of her that was frightened, she hated that – she understood enough to know that George, even though he had lost interest in her sexually, had left his mark. She remembered one of her Mother's sayings; if you are scared, the only way is to face your demons head-on.

Vanessa felt her duty had been done; George had a son. Now it was her turn to have some fun; why not, she deserved it after all his abuse, didn't she?

The first affair she had entered into had been with a young man she had met at one of Sarah's gatherings. Vanessa had been nervous at first, but he was considerate and tender, he taught her that lovemaking could be so beautiful, then she was delightfully surprised when she found she enjoyed sex.

She used discretion in her dalliances; however, Vanessa was frustrated with herself when she still felt nuggets of fear; what would George do to her if he found out his wife was having an affair?

George was a member of parliament; a scandal would not go down well.

As it turned out though, it was not she Vanessa, who nearly brought about the downfall of the family. Four years ago, an unsettling incident arose which made Vanessa assess her marriage in a new and far darker light.

The hiring of new staff was left to the housekeeper, Mrs Davies, who took on a replacement for a lower housemaid that had left their employ; a young girl called Becky Thomas. Vanessa probably would never have noticed the girl's existence but for what happened shortly after the girl took up the job.

It was not unusual for Vanessa to attend social functions, returning in the early hours of the morning. Sarah had invited her and George to a dinner party, George had decided he did not want to attend another one of Sarah's "frilly frolics" as he called them, which he found incessantly dull. He declared that he was going to his club and may stay there all night. Vanessa had been only too delighted to go without him.

She had arrived home at three in the morning. It had been a delightful evening of good food, good wine, and excellent company; she was in high spirits.

Collins, one of the footmen, had opened the door to her.

'I apologise for keeping you up so late.' Vanessa shrugged out of her delicate wrap and handed it to the man. It was a warm August night, Vanessa was dressed in a pale green silk dress, which set off her creamy skin and flaming hair to perfection.

'That's quite alright, ma'am.' The man nodded formally, then hesitated. 'Mmm,' he looked uncertain then.

'What is it?' Vanessa asked, noticing the look on his face.

'His lordship is home, ma'am.'

Vanessa was a little surprised, but she didn't think too much of the news, George was entitled to change his mind.

'Very well.' Vanessa nodded and made her way up the ornate stairs.

She and George occupied separate suites of rooms, which suited her fine. It was as she was making her way along the corridor, past Georges bedroom that she heard grunting and crying coming from inside.

She stopped still, the blood draining from her face.

'Please no more,' the words were spoken by a female voice. The sobbing increased. It was close to hysteria.

Reaching out a hand, Vanessa turned the brass doorknob then stepped into the room. The sight she saw made her gasp in shock. There was her husband, although he was wearing a black silk robe which flapped open, she could see that he was stark naked underneath. He had a young girl, also devoid of clothing bent over in front of him. His breathing was coming in great gasps as he rammed himself into her.

Vanessa, transfixed by the sight that greeted her, found she couldn't move for a moment — then the next thing she knew, she was screaming with fury and pummelling George on his broad back.

'What the ...' He swivelled around. When he saw it was his wife, he stepped away from the girl; his face was almost purple with rage. 'Get out – GET OUT.' Spittle showered her cheeks.

Vanessa's gaze turned to that of the girl who was still sobbing and was taking great gulps of air. With horror, she saw that her hands had been tied to one of the bedposts. Each ankle was tied to the legs of a chair which the girl was bent over. The position made her vulnerable and unable to defend herself from the onslaught. Vanessa gasped with the shock of the scene, especially when she noticed wheals across the girls back. She had been whipped. Blood was also trickling down her legs.

'George, no.' Vanessa went to help the girl, but her husband caught her arm, holding her in a fierce grip that made her wince in pain.

'Leave now,' he hissed, propelling her towards the door. 'You say anything about this, Vanessa, I shall have you locked away on a count of delusional madness and hysteria, do you understand me?'

She nodded, but her gaze kept wandering back to that of the girl.

He pushed her out into the corridor, then shut the door with a slam, she heard a key turn in the lock.

Vanessa's knees almost gave way; she grabbed the corner of an occasional table for support. She very nearly swooned when she heard the girl scream once more.

What should she do, what should she do? Vanessa paced the corridor. She could hear the animal grunting of her husband, *her husband*; she shuddered at the thought. The terrified crying of the young girl continued.

Placing her hands over her ears, she ran to her room. Shutting the door with a bang, she locked it.

Would he come after her? She wondered; he was in such a rage. Then she realised that she did not care about herself, although she had her son to think of; William, what would happen to him if George acted upon his threat and had her locked up?

Pouring herself a glass of water from a carafe on a sideboard, her hands were shaking so much she nearly dropped the glass, water splashed over her dress, leaving a dark patch on the pale silk.

Vanessa slumped into a chair beside the fireplace.

She spent the rest of the night seated in the chair or pacing the Persian carpet.

Was there anyone she could, or should, tell about what she had discovered? She thought of Sarah, but what good would that do. Vanessa felt helpless.

The next morning, Rose, her maid found her mistress seated beside the empty grate in her bedroom, still clothed in her silk evening dress.

'Ask Mrs Davies to come and see me,' she said before Rose set down the tray with her morning tea.

'Yes, ma'am.' Rose looked apprehensive but bobbed a quick curtsey and hastily left the room.

Vanessa didn't have long to wait before the housekeeper arrived. The woman looked prim and proper in her dark grey dress, cream lace collar and lace cap.

'There was somebody here with his lordship last night, do you know anything about it, Mrs Davies?' Vanessa found herself gripping the arms of the chair so tightly; it was as if it were a lifesaver during a storm. The woman dropped her gaze from that of her mistress' own. 'Answer me,' she hissed, losing her temper.

'No ma'am, just the maids, Mr Collins and I.'

'The maids?' She understood then. The queasiness of dread churned in her stomach. 'Are they all accounted for this morning?'

Mrs Davies gave her a direct look. 'Unfortunately, I have had to let the new girl go. His lordship complained about her this morning. He said that she was, mmm, was not satisfactory.'

'Oh Lord.' Vanessa put her head in her hands. 'Make sure she has a reference please.'

'Of course, ma'am.'

Getting up from her chair, Vanessa opened a drawer of her dressing-table and pulled out some money. 'Here,' she waved the notes at the housekeeper who took it and placed it in a pocket. 'Make sure she gets this. And let me know how she is, please.'

'Yes, ma'am.' The older woman nodded and turned away, but Vanessa called to her before she reached the door.

'In future, Mrs Davies, please ensure that you employ older women or ones that can go home at night.'

'Yes, ma'am.' The housekeeper made to leave, but Vanessa called her back once more.

'Have there been any others?' she asked, her throat was so dry that her voice cracked.

Mrs Davies once again dropped her gaze, contemplating what she should say.

'I take it from your hesitation that this has happened before.' Vanessa prompted.

The woman looked up and held her mistress' gaze for a moment then said, 'I couldn't say, ma'am.'

Vanessa nodded, then dismissed the woman. It was so apparent that this was not an isolated incident. How had she not picked up on this previously?

Getting up, she went to stand by the window that looked out onto a pretty garden. She guessed that Mrs Davies was under strict instructions not to divulge anything of these evil going's on. Vanessa wished then that the housekeeper had told her, perhaps she could have safeguarded the virtue of other young girls, by ensuring that the housekeeper only employ older, and plainer faced women.

Rose helped her dress after she had had a bath.

'Has my husband left for the office?' She asked as Rose finished dressing her hair.

'No ma'am, he is still taking breakfast.'

'Thank you, Rose.' Vanessa got up, 'you may go.' The maid bobbed then left her.

Steeling herself, thinking that facing him now was the best action to take. After all, they lived in the same house. They could not avoid each other forever.

Walking into the breakfast room, Vanessa found that the smell of kedgeree turned her stomach.

George was sitting at the head of the table eating and reading a newspaper. He did not glance up as Vanessa sat down and poured herself a cup of tea.

He took two more mouthfuls, drained his coffee cup then set the paper aside. Then he turned a cold gaze to her. 'I hope you are well this morning, my dear?'

'Yes, quite well.' She nodded. Underneath the white tablecloth, she was bunching up the light cotton of her morning gown in agitation.

'That is good to hear. We do not want a repeat of the hysterics from last night, do we?' She dropped her gaze from his direct one, shaking her head. 'Humph.' He got up then and pulled his gold pocket watch from his waistcoat pocket. 'Time is getting on. I must be going.'

He had to walk past her chair to leave the room. Vanessa felt her skin crawl when he paused beside her. She could feel his heavy gaze upon her. He grasped her shoulder in a hard grip. 'We have an understanding then?'

'Yes, George.'

Much to her relief, he let go and left the room.

Vanessa breathed a sigh of relief.

Since that time, there had been no further incidences concerning the staff, well not as far as she knew.

Making the journey home, ahh, home, more like an empty shell. Vanessa sighed, how she wished that she was free. Free to turn around and go back to the inn, and ask Hero to run away with her, but she knew it was an impossible dream.

Chapter 26

Over the next few days, the temperature fell, especially at night. All the residence of Little Back Lane would awaken to ice-coated windows.

In the room occupied by Molly and the others, they were cosy, however. Jolly ensured they had a good supply of coal. Food was brought in every day by one of Jolly's lads.

'You'll soon be out of this place for good,' Jolly said when he told Evie that an Irish family had occupied their old room.

Evie said nothing, just nodded her head as the feeling of dread settled over her once more.

Despite the warmth and the food, Dottie was not well. Her chest had tightened up again. Her breathing rattled, especially at night. Evie wondered if the stress of everything going on had caused the relapse.

Sophia suggested boiling up a pan of onions and putting them on Dottie's chest, an old and pungent remedy.

'Aww Lord,' moaned Molly, 'Yer stinking the place out.'

'It's no worse than some of the aromas around here,' Evie pointed out, Molly had to agree.

Unfortunately, the remedy made no difference to Dottie's condition.

The following day, Molly was going to accompany Sophia to meet this *mystery man* who was going to marry her. Oh Lord, Molly found that every time she looked at the girl, she felt more and more anxious. The truth of the matter restricted her throat. Guilt was her constant companion; Aww, she was developing a conscience.

Much to their surprise, Jolly told Evie and Dottie that the house he had bought was ready for them to move into. So, they would be leaving Little Back Lane too.

'I'll get Reg to drive you there tomorrow morning. It's a fine ouse,' Jolly said with pride. 'It'll get yer sister out of the damp of this place.' He smiled at them both.

All Evie could manage was a nod in reply. The news had sent ripples of fear down her spine; she was petrified not only for herself and her sister but for Sophia as well: none of what was going on felt right. She had such a powerful instinct to run and take Dottie and Sophia with her.

Jolly was as good as his word; he got the lads to get buckets of water which they warmed on the fire to fill the tin bath. The rent collector also supplied a bar of fragrant soap.

They would have enjoyed the excitement of having a bath if it were not for the shadow of fear that permeated the room, instead it was a sombre affair.

Sophia was the first in the tub. Molly washed her hair for her as it was so thick. 'Aww, this mop is going to take a long time to dry,' Molly commented as she rubbed at her scalp none too gently.

Then she was mortified when Molly insisted that Sophia lay back on the bed to have her pubis shaved.

'Why? I don't understand.' Sophia had tears of humiliation in her eyes as she stared at the ceiling while Molly soaped the area and was using a cutthroat razor. The sensation was so unpleasant and alien, Sophia wanted to curl up and cry.

Evie was also horrified at what Molly was doing to their friend. When she put her objections into words, Molly's expression darkened.

'Aww now, don't yer ave a go at me. I've ad strict instructions from Jolly,' she said with as much patience as she could muster. 'I know it ain't nice, but it's to ensure you don't carry any vermin.'

While Molly was busy shaving Sophia, Evie helped Dottie to bathe. Sophia's grandmother refused all efforts and persuasion to get in the bath. In the end, they gave up trying as the old woman was getting upset.

Molly was the last one to make use of the tub, the water was getting cold by that time, but she didn't complain.

As soon as they were all decent, Molly called one of the lads, who took out the bathtub to empty it.

Early, the following morning, Jolly arrived to take Evie and Dottie to their new home.

There were tears as Evie, then Dottie hugged Sophia tightly – they all knew that they might never see each other again.

Sophia whispered in Evie's ear, 'I will find out where you are and write to you.'.

Evie nodded and hugged Sophia even tighter.

When Jolly ushered the two girls into the lane, Evie saw that there was a trap pulled by one horse waiting for them. Reg Dickens, Tommy's cousin, occupied the driver's seat.

'I shall see you later, ladies.' Jolly grinned, giving them a parody of a bow, which made Evie's skin crawl.

She held Dottie, who was wrapped in her coat and several blankets, close.

It was still dark as they set off, although the sky was turning into an ashy grey as daylight pushed through the clouds.

It was freezing, each breath they took misted in the air.

'Where are we going?' Evie asked the youth. He was tall and rangy, with a shock of ginger hair that bristled about his head. He too was dressed for the weather in an old grey army coat.

'Jolly said I weren't to say nothing to yer,' he said in a voice with a rough timbre.

Evie and Dottie looked at each other; the disquiet mirrored in each of their gazes.

As they drove further into the city, the streets were getting busier; girls off to work at the match factory. Men were going to work at the docks. There were butchers' carts and milk carts. The smell of fresh-baked bread wafted from the bakeries.

The noise and the hustle and bustle were jarring on Evie's nerves. Then a thought occurred to her; if they jumped from the trap, they could disappear in amongst the sea of people. The roads were so busy; they were congested, the lad driving the trap would have to abandon it and pursue them on foot.

'Maybe we should run now?' Evie whispered to Dottie; her voice filled with urgency. 'Do you think you can run?'

'I don't know, Evie,' Dottie whispered back. The apprehension made her chest feel even tighter.

'Oi, watch where yer going!' The driver of a brewery wagon filled with barrels yelled at a young lad that darted in between the vehicles.

Evie gripped her sister's icy hand. 'We've got to try, Dottie, I can't bear the thought of being married to that man, I would rather die.' The trap jerked forward but then stopped again, the road ahead was a bottleneck. It was apparent that it would take a while to get moving once more.

'Alright,' Dottie nodded.

'Now, then Dot.' Evie was sitting on the outside of the seat; Dottie was in the middle between herself and the driver. Luckily, Reg hadn't taken any notice of their conspiring; his attention was focused on driving the trap.

Evie took full advantage of the distraction; she jumped down from the vehicle, not bothering with the step. As soon as she felt the ground under her feet, she spun around and held out her arms to Dottie. Before the driver realised what was happening, Dottie had also jumped from the trap into Evie's arms. Clasping hands tightly, the two dashed along the crowded pavement.

'Ere!' They heard Reg exclaim in annoyance. 'Oi, come back ...'

The sisters held on tightly to each other as they traversed the crowded streets.

Standing on the footplate to get a better view, Reg cursed liberally. The young women had disappeared.

The horse, disturbed by all the tumult, shifted restlessly nearly knocking the youth from his perch.

'Awe, bloody ell.' His face bright with anger, Reg sat back down and tried to decide what to do; should he go back and find Jolly, or look for the girls himself? He would need to find somewhere to leave the trap; he couldn't just abandon it in the street.

Deciding it would be best to go back to Poplar and round up some more of the lads to help search for the sisters. Reg annoyed the other drivers as he turned the horse and trap about in the street to head back the way they had come.

The sisters ran as if they had the devil at their heels. Evie did not want to stop. She wanted to put as much distance between them and Jolly Jack Barrett that she possibly could.

Evie guessed that as soon as Jolly found out that they had made a bid for escape; he would get his lads scouring the streets for them. They needed to find a place to hide.

*

The room felt empty after Evie and Dottie had departed that morning.

Sophia sat down at the table and wept copiously.

'Aww, for gawd sake, pull yer self together,' Molly exclaimed with annoyance, 'anyone would think yer going to a funeral.'

'What about my grandmother?' Sophia looked up at Molly with tear-filled eyes.

'Don'tcha worry yer head about that. One of the lads will sit with her.'

Jolly had instructed Molly to give the old woman the laudanum in a drink, then Bert would keep an eye on her. Once her heart had stopped, he would dispose of the body. Molly was not happy about any of it, but she knew she could not refuse Jolly's request. So, while Sophia was dressing in her new clothes, Molly boiled some milk on the stove and popped a bit of honey in it, then emptied the phial that Jolly had given her into the mug.

'There yer go, she'll be as right as rain.' Molly gave the grandmother the mug of hot milk. The old woman was in bed, and she smiled broadly at Molly as she handed her the cup.

'You'll need to explain to her what's appening,' Molly said to Sophia, as the girl pulled on the stockings she had been given.

'Yes,' she sighed. Sophia was not happy about leaving her grandmother. A feeling of panic began to rise in her. She had a terrible feeling she would never see the old woman again. There was a sense of danger in the air – she there was a tremendous urge to run. 'And, when I am settled in my new life, she can come and live with us?' Sophia gave Molly a pleading look as she searched for reassurance.

'Course.' Molly tried an unconvincing smile of encouragement, then changed the topic to distract the girl; 'Why, don't yer look a picture.' She looked Sophia up and down, 'like a princess.' This time her smile was genuine.

To Sophia, the new clothes felt strange; they were flimsy; a dress made of soft white lawn edged with lace and ribbon. It was short, mid-calf length. Sophia felt as if it were a dress more suitable for a child than a young woman. White stockings, cream kid shoes that wouldn't last five minutes in this place, as soon as she stepped outside, they would be ruined. The area between her legs where Molly had shaved her felt extremely sensitive; it made the girl's cheeks blush in mortification.

In stark contrast, Molly was dressed in a bottle-green tulle dress, decorated with purple lace and ribbons. The outfit was tight about the waste and low in the décollage: she could not have looked more different beside Sophia, who's outfit made Molly's own appear even more garish.

'Ere,' Molly handed Sophia her old boots. 'Best wear these fer now; then you can put yer new shoes on when we get there.'

Sophia nodded, slipped the new shoes off, and put on the boots.

Molly helped her to do her hair. It was naturally thick and curled beautifully.

'No curling irons for you,' Molly commented as she tied ribbons in Sophia's hair.

Soon after that, Jolly arrived. He was early, Molly hadn't been expecting him until late into the afternoon. She could tell straight away that something wasn't right, Jolly's expression was as hard and cold as granite as he walked through the door.

'What's appened?' Molly asked him with concern.

Jolly grabbed her arm and pulled her into the hallway, making her grimace with pain. He kept his voice low, so Sophia could not hear what was being said.

'I should never ave trusted that Reg, as he was driving the trap through town them bloody sisters jumped down and made a run for it.'

Molly's eyes widened with incredulity. 'No!'

Gripping her arm tighter, he said, 'did yer know they were planning to run?'

Molly shook her head vigorously. 'Course not. Whatcha going to do?'

'Find them, of course. The lads are out searching for em.'

'They can't have gone far,' Molly piped up, 'Dottie isn't well, she won't survive nights on the street.'

Jolly nodded, but his eyes narrowed with suspicion, 'if I find out you ad anything to do with this ...' he let his voice trail off as Molly's insides contracted with fear.

'I swear, I never did, Jack.'

Neither of them noticed the bundle of rags in the corner on the first landing, despite the low voices, Mrs Gill had heard Jack's news. She smiled, *good on 'em young uns.*

Oblivious to everything that was happening, Sophia kissed her grandmother's forehead tenderly. She was pleased to see that the woman was sleeping soundly.

'Everything good in there?' Jolly's eyes darted to the doorway to the room.

Molly nodded her head, 'Yes, Jack.'

'Are you ready to leave?' he asked.

'Isn't it a bit early?'

'Only by a couple of hours. I need to get you two over to the Silverman place, Tommy is going to bring the other girls later. I need to be around ere so I can be on hand if there is any news about the runaways.'

'Alright, then.' They went back into the room. 'We are leaving now so get yer cape.' Molly called to Sophia, as she picked up her half-cape that was the colour of crushed plums and draped it over her shoulders.

Obediently, Sophia pulled on the black velvet cloak, then glanced back at her grandmother, who looked peaceful in the bed. The girl also took in the shabby room: this room had been her sanctuary. All of a sudden, she was reluctant to leave the place. She felt as if she were plunging into an icy sea of the unknown.

'Come on then,' Molly called to her. Sophia took one final look around and shut the door.

A short way up the road, there was a carriage which was pulled by two horses waiting for them.

As soon as they were settled in the carriage, Molly produced the pale kid shoes, 'There yer go,' she said handing them to Sophia, who pulled off her boots and slipped her feet into the delicate shoes.

'Aww, you're just like that Cinderella, going to the ball.' Molly laughed in an attempt to lighten the atmosphere.

Chapter 27

Evie and Dottie hadn't gone far before a bad bout of coughing overcame Dottie. She was coughing so much that she started to retch. People passing them in the street glanced at them with distaste, Evie also felt that she read suspicion in their eyes.

'Come here.' Evie pulled her sister down a side street away from the main thoroughfare.

'S-s-sorry, Evie.' Dottie tried to get her cough under control.

'It's alright, love.' Evie hugged her sister close.

Oh Lord, what were they to do, they had no money, no food, no spare clothes, nothing. Suddenly Evie wondered if she had done the right thing running away like this; if they had gone to the house Jolly had bought, perhaps Dottie would have time to recover and once she was better, they could run away then, couldn't they? She also thought about Jolly's offer to pay for a doctor for Dottie. Aww no, they needed to go back. Evie felt tears of helplessness prick her eyes.

As Evie held her sister close, Dottie finally got her coughing fit under control.

'I'm sorry,' she said again, wiping tears from her eyes.

'It's alright, Dottie.' Evie brushed damp tendrils of hair away from her sister's face.

'What are we going to do, Evie?' The girl looked at her with such expectation Evie felt her heart contract.

'I don't know, running away like this, and this cold weather, I'm worried about your health.'

Dottie grasped her sister's arm; her look was one of desperation. 'We can't go back, Evie.' It was as if she had read her sister's mind.

Evie gave her a long look filled with sadness. 'We might have to, Dottie.'

'What about the workhouse? They would take us in there, wouldn't they?'

Evie's gaze looked into the distance as she mulled this thought over. She remembered Mrs Gill telling her about the workhouse. Both options scared Evie – she knew she couldn't spend her life married to Jack Barrett, no matter what he offered, she'd rather die. But she couldn't have her sister's death on her conscience.

It was a bitterly cold morning, but Evie could feel the sweat she had exerted from running, freezing on her body, making her shiver. If the temperature were like this now, what would it be like in the middle of the night without any shelter?

Finally, making a decision, Evie's gaze returned to her sister. 'We are going to the workhouse,' she said with conviction.

The sisters kept to the busy streets, Evie thought there was less chance of being spotted if they were in a crowd.

Neither of them had any idea of where the workhouses were situated. Evie had to take the risk of stopping and asking a girl who was selling bunches of watercress on a street corner.

'Bloody ell, why are yer looking fer a place like that?' She gazed at the two with wide-eyed disbelief.

'We need shelter,' Evie explained, 'mmm, we've only just arrived in London and have nowhere to go.'

'That's a bit bloody daft if yer asks me! Anyways, go up this road till the end, you will get to the Tanner Street work'ouse.'

'Thank you,'

It did not occur to Evie that her ploy of being lost in a crowd, would also mean that anyone in pursuit of them would easily evade detection.

When the sisters had moved on; a young lad went up to the watercress seller and bought a bunch from her.

'What did they want?' He nodded in the direction the two girls had taken.

'What's it to yer?' The girl asked suspicion tinging her voice.

The lad fished in his pocket and waved a shiny sixpence at her, 'It's yours,' he said, 'Only their dear uncle is looking for em.'

'Huh, dear uncle, pull the other one!' She rolled her eyes at him, but still reached out and plucked the coin out of his hand. 'Tanner Street workouse.' He nodded then was gone.

Evie and Dottie were exhausted by the time they reached the place. There was a plaque on the wall that read; "Tanner Street Workhouse, a shelter for the parish poor. Lord have mercy on all thy children."

The building was large, with a formidable redbrick façade.

'What do we do now?' Dottie asked as the two girls paused at the bottom of a wide flight of steps which lead to a heavy double door.

'Knock on the door, I suppose.' Evie took her sister's hand and ascended the steps with a heavy heart.

What neither of them realised was they had come almost full circle; Tanner Street was close to the river and docks – well inside Jolly Jack Barrett's stomping ground.

There was a weighty knocker on the front of the workhouse door. Evie lifted it and let it drop to the brass plate four times. The heavy door muffled the sound of the knocker, which echoed through the hallways.

They waited; Evie was becoming more and more anxious with every moment. When a few minutes had passed, and there was still no answer, she knocked again.

'There must be someone there?' Dottie said, a catch of desperation in her voice.

'Yes,' Evie was just about to knock again when the door was pulled open.

A tall woman, with austere square features, stood in the doorway. She wore a dress the colour of wet slate and a long white apron, cinched at the waist with a black leather belt, from which dangled a chain with a bunch of keys attached. She wore a watch pinned to her bodice. Tendrils of wispy brown hair poked out from under her lace cap.

'What do you want?' Her tone was sharp as her hard gaze drifted over the two girls.

'We are seeking shelter,' Evie explained, 'we have nowhere to go.' 'Ha, isn't that true about the majority in these ere parts. You don't look like paupers to me,' the woman said at last.

Evie realised that the woman was right: after living with Molly, they had eaten well, their hollow cheeks had fleshed out. Their clothes, although well-worn and much repaired, looked in reasonable condition.

Evie's heart raced as she tried to come up with a plausible story; 'We have been evicted from the place where we lived, we have no money for lodgings or food.'

The tall woman, who was the matron of the workhouse, was thoughtful for a moment. It occurred to her that she could sell the girls coats and boots, and anything else they were wearing that was decent. She could also get a pretty penny from the wig maker; both girls had lovely hair that looked clean.

Much to Evie's surprise, the woman stood aside, holding the door open for them.

'You'd best come in then.'

Evie and Dottie looked at each other in relief, then stepped over the threshold.

Tommy Dicken caught up with Jolly just after he had seen Molly and the Jewish girl off. He was on his way to the room he kept in one of the warehouses by the docks.

'I found em, Mr Barrett; they are in the Tanner Street workouse.'

'Oh yes, I know the matron and master there. A mean old bat she is, the master is er usband; he's just as bad. That woman will ave the clothes off em girls backs to sell.'

'What do you want me to do now?' Tommy asked as the two walked up an alleyway. Jack was smoking one of his rollups, the pungent scent of tobacco followed the two figures.

'Go back to Tanner Street, tell Crabtree, that's the matron, to keep em girls there, I'll be along shortly. I ave a bit of business to attend to first.'

With a quick nod, Tommy raced off back the way they had come.

'My name is Mrs Crabtree, and I am the matron here, my husband is the master.' The woman explained to Evie and Dottie as they walked down a large, echoing hall, floored with black and white tiles. The air was still chilly inside the place. An aroma of boiled cabbage and the sharp smell of lye soap hung in the air.

They walked past two young girls who were on their hands and knees scrubbing the floor. They both wore baggy grey dresses, over which they wore aprons that were once white, but were now dull and discoloured from frequent washing. The two both wore mob caps.

As Evie walked past the nearest girl, who looked at her with strangely dull eyes, she noticed from what hair she could see, the girl's head had been shorn so short that it bristled from the girl's scalp. Evie felt stirrings of unease; what had they let themselves in for?

The workhouse was a maze of corridors. Apart from their footsteps that echoed on the tiles and the jangle of keys hanging from the matron's belt, the place seemed strangely quiet, the weight of which seemed to suck the air from the long hallways. The windows were tall. Some looked out over an internal quadrangle. Despite the freezing day, there were people; men, women, and children working out there. They were digging up the ground. It must be a garden, Evie thought.

Mrs Crabtree led the girls to a kitchen. The room was large and lofty. Several large pots were bubbling on the range; the aroma emanating from them did not smell very appealing; boiling cabbage, onions, and tripe perhaps?

A young girl was sitting on a wooden stool peeling potatoes; she didn't look up as they went passed her. Another girl, this one a bit older, stood at a large wooden table kneading dough.

An ample woman sat in a chair close to the range; it looked as if she had nodded off, her double chin rested on her ample bosom, her mouth was open, a dribble of saliva ran down her chin.

'Mrs Tyler,' the matron called out.

The large woman jerked awake. She jumped to her feet. 'What?'

Mrs Crabtree pushed Evie and Dottie forward. 'We have two new ones. Put them to work, will you. I'll come and take their details later.'

'Yes, very well.' The large woman eyed Evie and Dottie with interest.

'Your coats.' The matron held out her hand expectantly.

'Why do you want our coats?' Evie asked, reluctant to hand them over.

The woman gave them an imperious look. 'When you enter the workhouse, any and all possessions you bring in with you, including your clothes and boots, become the property of the parish.'

Evie knew there was no point in arguing, she and Dottie took off their coats and handed them to the matron.

At least it was a few degrees warmer in the kitchen, so that was a small comfort.

Before she left the kitchen, Mrs Crabtree said, 'I haven't asked for your names?'

'Evelyne and Dorothea Winters,' Evie told her, but then immediately thought that it might have been safer to have made up some fictitious names.

The tall woman nodded.

'Mrs Tyler will put you to work. I shall be back later to process you properly. You will be bathed.' She looked them up and down, 'Although you seem a great deal cleaner in comparison to many we get here. Your heads will be shaved to avoid the spread of lice.' Dottie took in a sharp breath, Evie put her arm around her sister's waist in comfort. 'Even though I am allowing you admittance today, out of the goodness of my heart,' they heard Mrs Tyler make a noise that sounded like a grunt of disbelief, the matron ignored the cook and carried on speaking, 'you will still have to petition the board next Friday, they will decide if you can stay on.'

'And if we can't?' Evie asked.

'Then you will be back on the streets.' With that, she nodded curtly, turned on her heel and left.

'You,' Mrs Tyler pointed at Dottie, 'Go an elp Ada with the tatties. And you,' she pointed to Evie with a stubby finger, 'can come and scrape these bones off.'

Rolling up her sleeves, Evie looked into a large metal pot; when she saw the glutinous mess inside, she thought she was going to be sick. She tried to swallow down the feeling.

'Ha, turned a bit green aintcha.' The cook chuckled. 'Welcome to ell,' she said.

*

Sophia would have been excited to see the sights of the city that they were driving through, but she was too frightened. On one level she registered the noise, smells and the general hustle and bustle going on outside. Her companion remained quiet.

'Am I going to be married to a wealthy man?' She couldn't help but look for reassurance.

Molly glanced at the girl with a closed expression. 'Yer going to be looked after. Don't worry yer ead about it.'

It was the same old version of a reply that she had received countless times. Sophia closed her eyes and took a breath. Her hands, resting in her lap trembled. Despite the velvet cloak, she felt cold to the core. Her instincts screamed at her to get away.

Chapter 28

Tommy Dicken used the knocker on the workhouse door, knocking with some vigour.

'What's all the bloody fuss about?' Mrs Crabtree pulled the door open impatiently. It was going to be one of those days she thought with annoyance.

'I ave a message from Jolly Barrett.' Tommy rushed his words. 'The two girls you took in earlier, well they are under Mr Barrett's protection.'

'Oh, Lord.' The tall woman rolled her eyes. 'He's going to put them on the street then?' she asked, although the sisters seemed the most unlikely pair to take up a life of whoredom; but then again desperate measures led to drastic solutions.

The lad shrugged, 'He said ed be round later to pick em up, you just need to make sure they stay put.'

'Very well.' Mrs Crabtree sniffed. There goes the extra bit of money she was going earn off their backs, she thought. However, another thought occurred, if Jack Barrett wanted the girls back so eagerly, perhaps he would pay her a bit of compensation for the inconvenience this had caused her. With that thought, she shut the heavy door and made her way to the refectory where a lunch of thin broth and hard bread was being served.

So they could have something to eat, Evie and Dottie were directed to sit with the inmates of the workhouse.

The two raised curious glances from the other women who took their seats in eerie silence.

There were around thirty women taking lunch in all, Evie noted. They were from a wide age range. All dressed in the dull grey dress and greying pinafores. Everyone wore a cap.

There were several vacant seats as many of the inmates had been sent out on work duty.

As she and Dottie had gone about the chores they had been given during the morning, they had found out that the men, women, and children were segregated; a mother was separated from her children, a husband from his wife; this was a terrible place; Evie was becoming more and more sorry that they had pursued this option.

Mrs Crabtree, a man, who was an orderly, and four other women sat on a raised platform at the head of the hall. The sisters noticed that the fare served to them looked a lot more appetising, ham, potatoes, and cabbage.

Before anyone could commence eating, however, the matron said a prayer. Once the "Amen" had echoed about the hall, Mrs Crabtree said; 'I will remind you all that there is no talking during your meal. You may begin.' She sat down.

In unison, the women picked up their spoons and ate the soupy mixture. Evie noticed that some broke up the hard bread and mixed it with the broth, she and Dottie did the same, which helped to make the concoction a bit more palatable.

Once the meal was over the women were dismissed. Each took their bowls, plates and spoons and placed them in a large wooden tub.

'You two.' The matron picked out Evie and Dottie. 'Go and help with the washing up in the kitchen.'

'I don't like this place,' Dottie whispered as they walked along the tiled corridor.

'I know Dot, but what else can we do?'

*

Sophia noticed from the carriage window that the busy city was being left behind. The countryside was quite lovely, even though heavy clouds gathered on the horizon, it was bitterly cold: snow was on the way.

Eventually, they turned off the road and up a driveway that was flanked by trees. Then there was an expanse of lawn.

Sophia caught a glimpse of a large, grand house. It was like nothing she had ever seen before. *Was she going to be living here then?* Perhaps it wouldn't be so bad. If the man she was going to marry was kind to her, she might well be happy here. She knew she was desperately trying to swallow down the dark fear that squirmed in her belly as she looked for positives; there was hope, wasn't there?

*

Once Evie and Dottie had helped to finish washing all the crockery, Mrs Crabtree arrived in the kitchen.

'You can go and help out in the garden.'

'But it's freezing,' Evie protested, 'we have no coats, and Dottie is not well.'

The tall woman's face darkened, she bent forward. So close was she to Evie, the girl smelt the other's bad breath, the decay of rotting teeth.

The matron said, 'I don't care if she is dying, get yer backsides out there now.'

'I'll be alright, Evie,' Dottie spoke up.

Evie thought to protest once more, but the look on Mrs Crabtree's face robbed her of speech. All she could do was nod.

*

The carriage pulled up in the brick-paved stable yard at the back of the house.

Molly opened the door and jumped down, she turned to Sophia and helped her down the step.

'Come on then.' The older woman linked her arm through Sophia's; they walked up the steps to the backdoor.

Their approach must have been noted as the door opened before they reached it. An austere man, who was short, with a rounded belly, but dressed very smartly ushered them in.

'Ello, Mr Cobb.' Molly gave the man a bright smile, which made his lips narrow in disapproval. 'This 'ere is one of the footmen,' she explained to Sophia as she waved a nonchalant hand at the man.

A footman, yes, Sophia thought as she eyed the man with interest, I have heard of the like.

The kitchen was vast and lofty. Highly polished copper pots and pans hung on the walls. There were jelly moulds and mixing bowls and all sorts of paraphernalia. On the large refectory table were plates of meats and bowls of salads. Loaves of bread, pate's, cheeses, fruit. All of which had been prepared for Mr Silverman's evening of erotic entertainment.

The cook and the maids had been given the evening off; this left three footmen, and the butler to serve the guests.

Looking Sophia up and down with interest, the footman said, 'I will show you up to your room.'

'Aww, a room, ain't that nice!' Molly grinned widely, enjoying the disapproval of the man. Oh lord anyone would think he owned the place.

'I'm scared, Molly,' Sophia uttered in a soft voice as they followed the man up the back stairs, which was the servant's access to the main floors of the house.

'It'll be alright, lovie.' Molly did her best to keep her voice light.

When they walked through a heavy door out onto a long corridor that was carpeted with a Chinese runner. Tables holding beautiful bunches of flowers and elegant ornaments stood sentry along the length. Sophia was rendered speechless; this place was like a palace; she had never seen such luxury.

'Am I going to live here,' Sophia asked in a voice filled with wonder. Her comment drew a sharp look from Mr Cobb, who made a sound of derision.

Molly shot him a hard look in return, shaking her head in warning.

The footmen took them to one of the numerous guest bedrooms. When he ushered the two inside, Sophia was once again awestruck by the opulence of the place.

Chinese carpets in shades of yellow and green lay on the floor. There was a massive four-poster bed with covers and drapes in plush fabrics the colour of gold. The furniture, much of which was French, was polished to a high shine. A large vase of yellow roses stood on a round pedestalled table in the middle of the room. There was a fire in the grate; the room felt comfortably warm.

'You will both remain here until the guests have arrived,' Mr Cobb said haughtily.

'Any chance of a cuppa,' Molly asked as she took her cape off and plonked herself down on one of the French sofas. The footman sniffed in disapproval. 'Go on; you don't want us fainting on his lordship, do yer.' She pushed.

Through narrow lips, the footman said, 'oh very well.'

'And some of 'em little sandwiches and a nice bit of cake ...' Molly called as he walked towards the door. Mr Cobb did not look back this time. He stepped into the hall and closed the door.

Molly heard a key turn in the lock. She was not surprised by this event, but she gave Sophia a glance of concern; she might become hysterical if she knew they were locked in.

Sophia, however, was wandering about the room a look of fascination on her face, she hadn't heard the door being locked.

Watching her, Molly felt her heart contract; the weight of despair washed over her. Quickly she dropped her gaze. She didn't want to think about what would become of the child.

Molly felt a frisson of anger at fate, at Jack Barrett, at life in general for putting her in this awful position. She had long since given up on worrying about her wellbeing, but having the fate of this young girl, who had a heart of gold on her conscience; not to mention feeding her grandmother a lethal dose of laudanum. No, it was too late for old Moll, she was going to ell for sure.

'I cannot believe this place.' Sophia was fingering the yellow and cream curtains draped in swags across the high windows. 'This man must be so important.'

'Aye, he is.' Molly got up and stood beside her companion. They both looked out of the window. From this room, they could see the roofs of the stable blocks, but also the gardens beyond. At this time of the year, the trees had lost most of their autumn cloaks, but it was still an amazing view.

'When will I meet him?' Sophia asked, giving Molly an expectant look.

'Soon.' Molly gave her a half-smile. 'Why don't you take your cloak off, eh?' She helped the girl shrug off the velvet cloak, then draped it over one of the armchairs. She took Sophia's hand and drew her over to the sofa, then bid her sit down. 'I will be going downstairs shortly,' she explained, 'me an the other girls will be mmm, entertaining the guests.'

'Entertaining the guests?' Sophia looked puzzled.

'Well, I ain't going to spell it out for yer.' Molly rolled her eyes. 'There will be someone special coming to meet you.'

'The man I shall marry?' A countless number of emotions washed over Sophia's face, which settled into a look of hope.

Molly dropped her gaze less the girl see the duplicity in her eyes. 'Aye, the thing is, he will expect certain things from you,' she reached out and took Sophia's hand, which was chilled and much to Molly's dismay, trembling. She squeezed it reassuringly then carried on. 'Yer ave to be good,' she said earnestly, 'do everything he tells yer.'

'Everything?' Doubt shadowed her gaze.

'Aye, no matter what.' She squeezed the girl's hand tighter, 'Promise.'

Hesitantly, Sophia nodded.

At that moment, Molly heard a key in the lock, the door opened. Cobbs arrived carrying a tray of tea things, Molly also noted there were some sandwiches and fruit cake.

*

Alexander Silverman got up from his desk and stretched his back. He found that if he sat for too long, it seized up; aww it was not good this getting old business.

He walked over to a sideboard and poured himself a snifter of brandy, took a sip, popped the crystal glass on his desk, then took out a cigar from a humidor. He sniffed it with appreciation. Snipped off the end, then lit a match. He drew on the cigar until the end was a fiery red. The aromatic smoke filled the room. Enjoying a good smoke was one of the advantages of having two houses, one in town, where his wife Miriam was staying, and this place; a beautiful Georgian mansion nestled in the Kentish downs.

Miriam did not like him to smoke, "it makes the air filthy," she would complain. Even when they had guests, she would moan if the men smoked while they took their brandy.

The absence of his wife meant he could enjoy this moment.

Plucking a gold pocket watch out of his waistcoat pocket, he checked the time. Ahh, the hour was getting on. Regretfully, he snuffed out the cigar; he would finish it later. Best to check if everything was in order. He trusted his butler, Mr Franks, to do a good job, but it was always best to keep an eye on the staff.

Alexander opened the study door and went into the library; gaming tables were set up for playing cards. The library led to the billiard room.

Checking the dining room where food was being laid out on buffet tables, Alexander nodded his head in satisfaction; everything was looking good.

'Ahh sir,' Franks appeared, 'Cobbs has just informed me that one of Mr Barrett's, mm, ladies has arrived with the girl.'

'Good, good.' He nodded, but felt his face infuse with blood. 'Where are they?'

'In the yellow guest room, sir.'

'Very well, carry on Franks.'

'Thank you, sir.' The butler, a tall thin man with a balding pate, ducked his head and went about the preparations.

Alexander glanced around the room distractedly; should he go and check on the girl? He wasn't sure what to do.

This desire to bed young girls was not something Alexander felt comfortable about; oh, he knew he should not take the moral high ground on this matter: he liked to bed a lusty whore on occasion; he was looking forward to doing so sometime later that night, but his guest, Sir George Beeching, had tastes that went beyond any yearning that Alexander could imagine. He had found out about them through sources investigated by his lackey, Jack Barrett, who was well connected with the underworld, the dark depths and depravities of the East End of London.

Through Alexander's orders, Barrett had made himself useful to Beeching, finding him young girls to fulfil the man's filthy desires. They were usually from the poorest part of the city, where death happened every day, where these innocent souls would not be missed.

Jack had reported back to Alexander, via Mr Hill, that Beeching had used a couple of the girls so badly, that Jack had no option other than to dispose of their bodies discreetly. This thought made Alexander shudder in horror.

Unfortunately, he needed Beeching to be cooperative in certain business matters, that, if they worked together on, would earn them a grand fortune.

It was all to do with the buying up of prime land in the centre of London. Mainly areas of the East End, where he already owned many tracks of slums and tenements for which Barrett collected the rent, but this was not about homes. Silverman wanted to build new rail-lines under the city that would travel out into the suburbs. Beeching, who was a member of parliament, was on the board of a rival company that was trying to outbid Silverman, but their design was flawed. It would not be as lucrative as the one Alexander had presented.

He had asked Mr Hill to put some figures together; on paper, they looked excellent indeed.

Alexander had approached Beeching at the club where they were both members. He had walked over to the man and sat down in the dark green leather chair opposite him.

Beeching had been reading a paper and drinking coffee, which was dark and rich, Alexander breathed in the aroma with some pleasure.

Beeching had sensed his presence but did not immediately set his paper aside, when he finally did so, he looked at Alexander, cocking an eyebrow at him quizzically.

'What do you want, Silverman? If it is about the contract for the rail line, I do not want to hear another word about it. I am confident that the house will approve of my plans next week.'

'Ah well, Beeching, I just have something for you to consider.' Alexander handed over some papers which outlined future potential profits for his scheme. Beeching glanced at the paperwork, then sat back and studied it in more detail.

'I have not included any of the building plans of the proposed route. I would not want those plans getting into the wrong hands.'

'Mmm, I cannot see how you could reach these figures.'

'They look good don't they, Beeching. Believe me; this can be a reality. Resign from the board and come and join me, we could make a great deal of money.'

Alexander was rewarded with a long look from the other man. George set the papers aside, picked up his coffee, took a sip, then set the cup back on the saucer.

'I will need to see the plans,' he said at last.

Alexander smiled; he too sat back in his chair. 'I am having a get together next Saturday at my house in Surrey. Come along; we can discuss these matters in more detail.' Then he sat forward in his chair. 'The evening will be men only, apart from a few specially selected ladies of the night. I have heard that you have quite specific tastes.' Beeching's gaze flickered with discomfort. A deeper flush brushed his already ruddy cheeks. Alexander tapped his nose with his index finger, 'we all have our little predilections. I have asked my man, whom you are acquainted with, Jack Barrett.' the gasp of shock he heard from the other man was music to his ears, he smiled, 'I have asked him to find you a very special offering, let's call it an enticement. You will have the freedom and privacy to satisfy any, and all needs.'

Beeching cleared his throat and licked his fleshy lips. 'It sounds as if it will be a delightful evening.'

Despite the goosebumps of misgivings that rose on his arms, Alexander said, 'Oh, yes I can assure you of that.'

Chapter 29

Through the kitchen window of the workhouse, Evie could see the dusk settling, an ashen blanket over the city. It was snowing too. It had started while she and Dottie had been outside working on the garden.

Under Mrs Crabtree's instructions, the cook had let Evie and Dot sit by the fire when they came inside. Evie was worried about Dottie; first, the coughing fit she had had earlier, now her breathing rattled in her chest alarmingly. There were beads of perspiration on her brow; she was burning up.

'Well, I ope you realise just how privileged you are aving a place by the fire.' Mrs Tyler, the cook, tutted.

'It is very kind,' Evie said.

'Huh, kind!' The cook sniffed. 'She don't do anything that won't be to er advantage.' She nodded to the door, referring to the actions of the matron.

Yes, Evie thought, she knew something was up. The broth that she had eaten earlier in the day coiled like a slippery snake in her stomach.

The two girls were seated on two low wooden stools, rather like the ones milking maids used. Evie's arm was draped around Dottie's shoulders; her arm tightened with her disquieting thoughts.

Even though the sound was muffled, Evie jumped when she heard the sound of the knocker on the front door.

They heard footsteps and murmured voices that were getting louder. Then the tall figure of Jack Barrett darkened the kitchen doorway.

*

'Why don't you come along?' Hero adjusted his cravat in the mirror above the sideboard.

'No, thank you.' Andrew, who was seated at the dining table, dug into a beef and kidney pie that his housekeeper had left for him. 'Besides, I've ...'

'Yes, I know, you've got study to do.' Hero finished for him.

'We have a cadaver in tomorrow so we can study some real anatomy,' Andrew said with enthusiasm.

'Sounds wonderful,' Hero said blithely. Andrew laughed.

Upon hearing a carriage pull up at the curb outside, Hero glanced out of the first-floor window.

'It appears that my transport has arrived.' He picked up his gloves and pulled them on, then picked up his hat.

'Mmm, have fun, old man.' Andrew waved him off.

When Horacio went down the stairs to the front hall, he wondered once again how Alec had persuaded him to go to his father's bash? Something was becoming more disquieting and cloying about Alec's constant need for attention. Hero was beginning to feel suffocated by his company; to such an extent that he had thought about going home for a while; God, it must be getting bad, he thought, opening the front door to the cold evening. Popping his hat on, he ran down the front steps. The footman, Collins, held open the carriage door for him.

'About time,' Alec said petulantly, as Hero sat down on the leather seat next to him. 'We shall be late, and you know father can't abide bad timekeeping.'

'I apologise,' Hero said automatically. He glanced out of the window as the carriage pulled away. It was freezing, and snow was beginning to fall.

'Here.' Alec handed him a blanket to put over his knees, then passed him a silver hip flask. 'Brandy,' he said.

Hero put the tartan rug over his knees and took a swig of the liquor. It hit the back of his throat; then he could feel the bloom of warmth in his belly.

He had a feeling he was going to need more than one drink to stomach the evening, he did not like the flaunting of wealth for one thing, and for the other, his grandfather was going to be there. He took another slug of the drink, fortifying himself for the evening ahead.

*

As the day darkened, Cobbs, the footman, came in and lit more lamps. He also removed the tea tray, sniffing with disapproval when he saw that the food had hardly been touched.

'Neither of us felt hungry,' Molly spoke up when she saw his look.

'Mmm, I can see.'

'Aww, lighten up, Mr Cobbs didn't we ave a bit of fun last time I was ere.'

His cheeks infused with blood and his lips narrowed. Molly got up from where she was sitting by the fire with Sophia. 'Come on.' She approached him, 'admit it; it was one of the best nights of yer life.'

'Hardly,' he said as he walked towards the door. He really couldn't get out of the room quick enough. He heard Molly laughing at his retreating back.

'You and him?' Sophia asked as Molly paced restlessly around the room. She picked up a bone china figurine of a shepherdess, examined it, then set it down on an occasional table.

'Aye, it earnt me a few extra bob.'

Molly glanced at the clock on the mantel. It was just gone six o'clock, and the afternoon had dragged: Being locked in this room with the girl was driving her mad.

Her emotions were all over the place, part of her wanted to run and take Sophia with her, but she knew they wouldn't survive for long out there; or maybe they would? If she could pull in a few tricks. Make a few bob, and they could get away. Run to another city, one up north, perhaps? She knew that she'd never had the bottle to do it, though, not even to save the girl.

Oh Lord, she thought, she was an accomplice to murder, for the grandmother would surely be dead by now, and one of Jack's lads would have disposed of the body. Then there was Sophia, what would happen to her after tonight - would she still be alive? Molly was acutely aware of the phial of opium she carried in a hidden pocket of her dress, a dose of which she would give Sophia, not enough to knock her out, but enough to make her docile.

Molly felt an acute pain strike her heart; she gasped and doubled over.

'Are you alright, Molly?' Sophia stood up and started towards her companion. There was a look of concern on her face.

Molly waved her hand in the air dismissively. 'I'm fine, lovely, don't fret.'

With a hand clutched to her heart, she looked at the girl and tried to smile. Sophia, backlit by the fire, looked like an angel standing there. Beautiful and innocent. Molly's vision blurred as tears pricked her eyes.

They were both distracted from their thoughts when the door opened.

Molly remembered Mr Silverman from previous visits, so she recognised him straight away. He was a man of middle height. His hair was thick and wavy, dark, but sprinkled with grey. His eyes were also dark but shone with inquisitiveness.

'Ah, good evening to you both.' He strode into the room. His glance brushed over Molly briefly, but then his attention was drawn to Sophia.

The lamplight caught her, actually seemed to caress her, Alexander thought as he took her in. Oh my, she was beautiful, there was something ethereal about her. As he got closer, he could see that her large eyes were of a luminous grey. They regarded him with interest tinged with fear.

'Good evening, my dear.' His wide mouth turned up in a smile.

'Sir.' Sophia found herself bobbing a curtsey which made Alexander's smile broaden.

'Have you everything you need?' Sophia shot a look at Molly, who nodded, then Sophia did the same. 'Good, good. How old are you?' Alexander asked.

'I am sixteen.'

It was Silverman's turn to nod. 'Ahh, good, good.'

'Are you the man I shall marry?' Sophia asked.

His eyes widening in surprise, Silverman said, 'Marry, ah no.' He gave a strangled laugh. Quickly realising that this had been the story they fed the girl, he continued. 'Regretfully not, my dear. You are promised to another.'

'Oh,' Sophia uttered.

All three were distracted by the sound of a carriage arriving in the stable yard below. Then they heard the sound of women chatting and laughing, sounding in high spirits.

'Ahh, my guests are beginning to arrive, please excuse me.' Alexander gave the girl another smile; this time, his expression was one of sadness and regret. As he walked over to the door, he looked at Molly. 'She is very beautiful.'

'Aye, sir, she is.'

'And innocent?'

Molly swallowed and nodded.

With a curt nod, Silverman left.

Once the door had closed behind him, Molly walked over to the window and looked out. Margie would be with the girls, she thought, but the idea of seeing her friend gave Molly no joy at all.

It wasn't long after that that the first guests began to arrive.

*

The carriage pulled to a halt at the bottom of a broad flight of steps. Hero jumped down onto the gravel, followed by Alec.

'Are you going to stay here tonight?' Alec asked him.

Hero shook his head, 'No, I shall go back to the city.'

'Very well, my carriage will be at your disposal.' Alec called out to the driver. 'Collins, you will be needed to take Mr Woodley back to town later.'

'Yes sir.' The coachman raised his whip in a salute of acknowledgement.

As the two young men climbed the steps, the coach pulled away.

'It has its advantages having two homes.' Alec laughed, 'one can take one's pick.'

The door opened as they approached, Cobbs was there to take their coats, hats, and gloves.

'Thank you, Cobbs.' Alec nodded.

'Sir.' The footman bobbed his head.

'Has my grandfather arrived?' Hero asked the man.

'Not as of yet, sir.'

'Well, thank God for that. I can relax for a bit at least.'

'You shouldn't let him affect you in such a way, Hero,' Alec said as they made their way into the drawing-room.

'Too much of a reminder of home,' Hero uttered.

'Well, what have we here?' Alec took in the scene that confronted them. Scantily clad women wandered around. There must have been around twelve of them. Some were topless, wearing only bloomers that left very little to the imagination. Some wore corsets that nipped in the waist and allowed a generous amount of cleavage to spill over the top. Their laughter and chatter reminded Alec of flocks of exotic birds. He nudged his friend in the ribs.

'You see you *will* have fun tonight.' Alec gave Hero a broad grin. He winked, his eyes glittering with lust. 'You may well want me to dismiss Collins after all.'

Hero did not reply as one of the girls approached him with a silver tray upon which were flute glasses filled with champagne.

'A drink, sir,' she said, 'take your pick, you can have anything you want.' She winked at him lewdly.

Plucking a glass off the tray, Hero said, 'A drink will be just fine, thank you.'

'Don't be so dull, Horacio,' Alec complained as he too picked up a glass of champagne.

'You should know by now that I am not impressed by this kind of event.' Hero didn't wait for a reply but walked off towards the billiard-room.

'Aww, don't mind him, my lovely, we can still have fun.' The girl piped up, giving Alec a seductive smile which he returned.

'Oh yes,' he agreed, 'we certainly can.'

*

Evie's initial reaction to Jack Barrett's appearance was one of shock, then of inevitability.

His gaze took her in as he walked towards them. He smiled a smile that wrinkled the scar on his cheek.

'Ad a nice little adventure ave yer.' Barrett's gaze turned to Dottie, who was clinging on to Evie. Her eyes were wide and glassy with fever. Her skin looked sallow, glistening with sweat. Jack gestured to the younger girl, 'Aww, what were you thinking, taking the young un for a tour of the East End?' He laughed, then bent down and picked Dottie up in his arms.

'What are you doing?' Evie stood up in alarm.

'I'm taking yer both ome, what do yer think I'm doing.' Jack Barrett carried Dottie out of the kitchen, along the corridor leading to the front door.

Evie followed in their wake.

Mrs Crabtree appeared, wringing her hands apprehensively.

'I did what you said, Mr Barrett,' she said ingratiatingly, 'Per'aps a little compensation for the trouble and the food these two ave consumed.'

'Aye, I'll see yer right,' he called but did not stop.

The orderly Evie had seen earlier, opened the front door for them. The snow had been falling steadily all afternoon. The white flakes dusted the skyline.

Evie was surprised to see a carriage pulled by one horse waiting at the bottom of the steps. She recognised the carrot top hair of the driver; it was Reg.

The vehicle was old and battered. Jack opened the door then carried Dottie inside and sat her on one of the seats. He pulled a blanket from the corner and popped it around her shoulders.

Getting down, he paused to look at Evie, 'Yer carriage awaits.' He bowed and made a sweeping gesture.

Evie said nothing but got into the carriage and sat down beside her sister. Jolly shut the door. They could feel the shift of the suspension as he jumped up on the front seat beside Reg. Then, with a jolt, the carriage set off.

Chapter 30

E vie noticed that the snowy streets were still busy as the carriage rattled along. They were passing through a more affluent part of town now, a place where the gas lamps had been lit, casting a warm halo of light in the murky darkness. Under any other circumstances, Evie would have found the scene enchanting.

Dottie's head lolled against her shoulder. Her breathing was laboured. When Evie had felt her sister's forehead, she found it was burning hot. She tried to quell the worry she felt: Jolly had said he would pay for a doctor for Dottie, she just hoped he would keep his word.

The carriage turned off the busy thoroughfare, into a quieter part of the city. There were crescents of beautiful Georgian houses and streets of newer houses in neat rows with small gardens at the front.

Eventually, the carriage pulled up outside a house which was on a corner, surrounded by gardens.

There were lights on in a couple of the rooms of the house. From what Evie could see, the place looked pleasant, even pretty.

The carriage shifted, she heard Jolly say something to Reg, then the door opened, he reached in and caught Dottie up in his arms once more.

Jolly pushed open the gate at the front, leaving Evie to follow in his snowy footsteps. He strode up the path, got to the front door opened it, and stepped into a brightly lit hallway.

Even though she was so worried about her sister, Evie still took a moment to take in her surroundings; this place was certainly vastly different from the squalor of Little Back Lane. It smelt clean for a start. The black and white tiles on the floor had been polished to a high shine; they reflected the light from the wall-mounted gas-lamps, making the hallway even brighter.

There was a hat stand and a highly polished hall table, on which stood a vase of winter lilies, the flowery scent wafted from them.

'Ahh, Mr Barrett.' A woman wearing a dress the colour of rain-washed slate appeared from a door right at the far end of the hall.

'Mrs Perkins, this ere's my intended,' he nodded to Evie, 'and er sister, who as you see, is not well.'

'Oh, yes, poor dear.' The woman hurried forward. She was short, with a round, pleasant face. Evie felt reassured by the smile the woman presented to her. 'Up the stairs then,' she waved a hand to hasten Jolly's footsteps to follow her. 'I have a fire going, and the beds have been aired,' she said as she made her way up to the first-floor landing.

Jack carried Dottie up the stairs, then followed Mrs Perkins to one of the bedrooms at the back of the house.

The room was surprisingly pretty with rose-patterned wallpaper and matching curtains. There was a brass bedstead with a flowery patchwork throw draped over it.

'Lay the child down, Mr Barrett,' the woman instructed.

Jolly lay Dottie down on the bed, with surprising care.

'You had better leave now,' Mrs Perkins said. 'We need to get the dear undressed, into nightwear and into that bed.'

'Aye, I'll get Reg to go for the doctor, then I'll wait downstairs.' Jolly left the room and shut the door.

'Help me get her boots off,' the woman said to Evie.

Evie quickly unlaced the left boot as Mrs Perkins worked on the right. After taking her boots off. Between the two they undressed Dottie. Mrs Perkins produced a pretty white nightgown, trimmed with lace; the sight of the garment made Evie think of Sophia and the outfit that Molly had to dress her up in. She wondered how her friend was faring.

'Right, that's it.' Mrs Perkins tucked the sheets and blankets around Dottie. 'She's feverish alright, but I'm sure the doctor will sort her out.'

'I hope so,' Evie said as she hovered next to the bed.

Mrs Perkins picked up Dottie's clothes. 'I'm going to burn these,' she announced, 'they smell something awful; we don't want vermin in the house.' The woman eyed Evie's attire, 'Yours too,' she added.

'We did our best to keep ourselves clean,' Evie said curtly, although she felt a blush sting her cheeks. 'It wasn't easy.'

'Aye, I can imagine. Nonetheless, there are clothes for you in the tallboy and drawers.' Mrs Perkins gave her a long look, 'I don't know any of your history, only that you have had some unfortunate circumstances that Mr Barrett has saved you from.'

Evie gave the woman an astounded look; for some reason, she felt a bout of hysterical laughter bubble in her chest. 'It sounds as if he's a bloody saint; he is far from it.'

The woman's lips pursed primly. 'I will not have language like that in this house.'

Incredulous laughter issued from Evie, she found herself sitting down in a chair upholstered in green velvet. She suddenly felt exhausted, all the stress of running away, Dottie being ill and the worry about Sophia, hit her hard.

Tears welled, she put her head in her hands and wept.

'Now, now.' Mrs Perkins walked over and laid a hand on her shoulder. 'I know that Mr Barrett has a fierce reputation, dear. I'm not blind nor deaf. I hear things. But see, this is the thing, he saved my boy – gave him a job and paid him well. I'm in his debt. I lost my husband last year, and when Mr Barrett decided to buy this place and needed a housekeeper, he offered me the job, it gives me a purpose in life. So, I will not have a bad word said about him.'

Evie looked up at her through her teary eyes. 'He's a murderer and a pimp,' she said, her voice flat.

Mrs Perkins's lips thinned once again. 'I will tell you right now, Miss, you set those thoughts aside, and you accept this opportunity to get out of the gutter. He's chosen you to be his wife; he will look after you and her.' She nodded towards the bed where Dottie lay in a restless sleep. 'There are a great number of evil people in this world,' she continued, 'those that have done far worse than him.' She gestured about the room, 'he's offering you all this, as well as a secure future. Now, are you going to be a good girl, and do as you are told?'

Feeling utterly defeated by the whole situation, Evie nodded.

*

Molly paced the room restlessly while Sophia lay on the bed. The poor child was so exhausted by everything that had happened; she had fallen asleep.

Acutely aware of the vial of opium in her pocket, Molly wondered if she should wake the girl and give her some of the drug.

Cobbs had appeared earlier, bringing in a tray which held a cut-glass decanter of port and two glasses. Molly understood that the items had been brought in for a purpose, to give Sophia a drugged glass of the ruby liquid.

As soon as the footman had gone, Molly had poured herself a generous glass, drinking it in one go, she poured herself another.

Even from the bedroom, Molly could hear men's laughter coming from downstairs. It was punctuated with girlish giggles. Occasionally she heard music playing.

Checking the clock on the mantle, she saw it had gone ten. When would the man appear? She wondered her heart pounding with nervous apprehension.

*

Alexander Silverman laughed heartily along with the group of men who were standing around drinking and smoking cigars and cheroots. He was not happy, however:

Beeching was late, perhaps he wouldn't come? Alexander thought. He resisted the urge to pull out his gold fob watch to check the time once again. Huh, the man may be a lord, but he was uncouth with no manners.

It wasn't long after that moment that he spotted Franks in the grand hall opening the door to admit a guest; much to Alexander's relief George Beeching appeared. The man brushed snow off his shoulders, then took off his gloves, hat, and coat, handing them to Franks.

Alexander quickly made his way over to him.

'Ahh, Silverman.' Beeching did not smile but held his hand out.

'Beeching.' As they shook hands, Alexander said, 'So glad you could make it.'

'Yes, yes. Sorry I'm late, had some business to take care of at the club.'

'I understand.' Alexander smiled, quelling his irritation as they walked into the drawing-room together.

'Oh, I say, you have got a platter of treats on display.' Beeching eyed the half-naked girls; some were wandering around, others sat on men's laps where they were being fondled with great enthusiasm.

Alexander laughed. 'Yes, as I promised we have saved the best titbit for you, George.'

'Oh, yes, I am very eager to meet the girl.'

'You won't be disappointed. Would you like to, mmm, meet her now?'

'I will have a drink first.' George lifted a glass of champagne from a tray carried by one of the footmen.

'Good, just let me know when you are ready to unwrap your gift, and I shall get Franks or Cobbs to show you up.'

'Yes, thank you.'

*

At first, Hero had been on edge waiting for his grandfather to show up, although, after time had passed and he hadn't shown, he had begun to feel hopeful. That hope was dashed; however, when Cobbs informed him that Mr Silverman had received a note from Robert to say he would be late.

His nerves already frayed, Hero swapped the champagne for brandy, he decided to have a couple of snifters, then make use of Alec's offer and get his driver to take him back to town.

Most of the guests knew him; some stopped to talk. Hero was abrupt, not interested in making small talk.

He knew that many of them thought of him as an enigma; he did not appear to be involved in running his estate; instead, he preferred to box. And then, most of his opponents were the rough men of the city and beyond.

To the Ton, it seemed as if Horacio Woodley preferred the company of the great unwashed. Even though many of them had won money betting on him, they still retained their haughty and disapproving demeanours towards him.

Hero spotted George Beeching in the drawing-room, as soon as he saw the man, he ducked back into the billiard-room; What the hell was Vanessa's husband doing here? Hero was under the impression that Silverman and Beeching loathed each other. When they had met up earlier in the week Vanessa hadn't mentioned that George would be attending the evening. If Hero had known, he would have made his excuses. It was one thing worrying about an encounter with his grandfather, but quite another encountering the husband of the woman with whom he was having such a delightful affair.

*

George Beeching quivered with excitement with the thought of his personal entertainment to come. It had better be good too. He still felt furious with Silverman for pushing him into a corner, coming out with this sensitive information about his sexual preferences. He should have known that finding a man like Jack Barrett, who was only too happy to supply him with young girls whenever he required, was too good to be true. But, when Alexander had offered him a 'gift', George had been intrigued. Despite himself, the thought excited him.

He could have tried to find girls himself. There were many walking the shadowy streets in search of gentlemen who had particular needs. But it was risky; there would be no guarantee that they would be "clean". They could carry all manner of disease. And no matter how young they were, or appeared to be, they certainly would not be virgins that was for sure.

These days, George did not delve too deeply into the reasons why he enjoyed and delighted in the corruption of the innocent. Although, he understood enough to know that his first sexual encounter had moulded his desires.

When he had been at school that fateful summer term, ahh, it seemed so awfully long ago now. All the boys in his dorm had been bragging about their sexual conquests.

Never finding it easy to fit in with the other boys, George felt he had some catching up to do.

He had to admit that hearing about all the other boys' pursuits excited and thrilled him. As well as being extremely curious about the other boy's stories, he desperately wanted his own tales to tell.

So, when he went home the following summer, he had decided to look for some sort of *opportunity*. Then, one of the under housemaids had caught his eye. Her name was Biddy Bailey. Members of the Bailey family had been working for the Beeching's for years. George remembered that they were around the same age, as once or twice when they had been younger, they had played together in the gardens.

Biddy had grown into a pretty, fresh-faced girl.

Acutely aware of her, George had contemplated catching her somewhere in the house, but he was concerned that someone might come upon them; at that time, he hadn't been sure what he had in mind; a kiss perhaps? Or something more?

George knew that the maids tended to take it in turns to have an afternoon off. Discretely, he found out when Biddy would be free. And had discovered that she visited her family in the village and usually walked back via the coppice wood; this knowledge had presented George with an ideal opportunity. So, on her afternoon off, he had lain in wait for her.

It had been on a Sunday, late afternoon on a scorching hot July day. The sun was heavy in the sky, ready to burst like an overripe peach, tilting towards the horizon. It was just as it started to set that he first spotted Biddy through the trees. She was wearing a light cotton dress decorated in a daisy print. The lowering sun was behind her, George could see the shape of her legs through the light material. He suddenly wanted to see more of her; his heart had begun to race, his mouth watered as if he were preparing to savour some tasty delight.

Stepping out onto the leafy path in front of her, he made her gasp. She had gazed at him with eyes wide with surprise.

'Oh, master George, it's you. You gave me quite a fright, sir.'

He liked the way she called him sir; it made him feel important. He smiled at her. She returned his smile with a hesitant one of her own.

'It's Biddy Bailey, isn't it?'

She blushed and dropped her gaze. 'Yes, sir.'

'Are you walking back to the house, Biddy?'

When she nodded, he asked, 'Do you mind if I walk with you?'

'Course not, sir.'

They continued walking the grassy path.

'Have you got a beau?' he asked. She gave a little laugh, shaking her head shyly. Twisting around so he could face her. He walked backwards, his hands in the pockets of his light wool jacket. 'I am surprised,' he said, 'a pretty girl like you.'

Her blush deepened. Feeling self-conscious, she still couldn't meet his gaze. 'Aww, you are just being kind.'

'Nonsense.' He stopped walking, which meant she was brought to a halt also. 'You know, I've never kissed a girl.'

'I can't believe that.' She finally looked at him.

'Give me a kiss, and I'll give you a silver sixpence.'

'A silver sixpence?'

He made a show of fishing in the pockets of his jacket. 'Ah, here we go.' He showed her the coin that gleamed in the centre of his grubby palm.

'Oh, I don't know,' she said tentatively, but he could see her eyeing the coin with interest.

He thrust it closer. When she reached out to take the coin, he caught her wrist in a firm grip.

'Ouch, you're hurting me, master George.' Biddy tried to pull away.

'Just a kiss, come on.' Dropping the coin on the leafy ground, he pressed his lips to hers. Putting his arm around her, he pulled her hard against him.

There was nothing that Biddy could do; after all, Master George was far taller and stronger than she was.

Propelling her backwards, he then pinned her up against a tree trunk.

Oh, her lips were so sweet, George wanted more from her but didn't know exactly what? All the chatter in the dorms at school seemed as if it had been a fascinating, exotic language that needed to be interpreted.

He could feel her trembling against him. The feeling of her fragile body excited him. She tried to protest when his fingers started to roam her flesh under her clothes.

George wanted to lay her down on the ground and explore her thoroughly, but he was worried she would scream.

His pulse raced even more when his fumbling fingers found the flesh of her thigh above her stockings. When he delved under her bloomers; he found the place between her legs; it was warm and a little slippery. He could feel his cock stiffen; a heady feeling that he had only experience twice before, both times in the bath, where he had found that rubbing himself caused overwhelming feelings of pleasure.

Biddy was frantic now, wriggling, trying to beat him off. Tears streamed down her cheeks. Her hot tears made him even more determined, eager to make use of the situation.

'Keep still,' he hissed at her, 'or, by God, I'll make sure you and your family lose their jobs up at the house.' Biddy's older sister worked as an upper housemaid; her brother was a stable hand.

His words must have sunk in because she stopped fighting him.

'There,' he grinned, 'that's the spirit. We're only having a bit of fun, you know.'

'Please, master George, don't hurt me.'

He surprised her by grabbing her hand. 'Come with me,' he ordered, pulling her deeper underneath the canopy of the trees. It was slightly cooler there and they were further away from prying eyes.

When they were well away from the path, he stopped, took off his jacket and flung it over a low hung branch. 'Lie down,' he demanded.

'Please, no.'

His expression turned ugly for a moment. 'Remember what I said, do as you are told.' Tears still streaming down her face, she nodded, then lay down on the bed of crisp, dry leaves. 'Good girl.'

When he reached out to lift her dress, he found his hands were shaking in anticipation. Biddy had shut her eyes but remained still as his fingers roamed her thighs. Then she felt his hand snake under her cotton draws once more. Another tear jewelled on her lower lid then slipped down her cheek dampening her hair.

She heard him catch his breath. Then his hands were gone, she dared to feel a sense of relief. Opening her eyes, she could see that he was fumbling with the buttoned front of his trousers.

Biddy was a country girl; she wasn't so naive that she didn't understand what went on between a man and a woman. Horror washed over her, was he going to rape her?

George didn't hide his erect manhood from her; he held it in one hand as the other pulled down her bloomers. His fingers entered her tender womanhood, making her gasp in shock and fright.

While he caressed her with one hand, there was a strange expression on his face as he rubbed himself hard. Then he doubled over. It was his turn to gasp as a milky spume spurted from his cock.

Pulling out his hanky, he wiped himself.

Biddy sighed in relief, but when she went to make herself decent, he said, 'no, we haven't finished yet. I want to see all of you.'

'Aww, no master George.' The girl started to sob once again.

'Shut up,' he hissed, 'or I swear I will smack you.'

Biddy remembered his threat about getting her family sacked. The thought rested on her, heavy and dark. She remembered a story that her older sister had told them. One of her friends had taken a job working for a family in Bath. The son had taken a fancy to one of the maids. He had forced himself on her, and she had gotten pregnant. As soon as the family found out, she was out on her ear.

Biddy realised then that she would have to do everything that young George Beeching wanted.

Later, as the shadows of the trees elongated across the woodland floor, George decided he was hungry for food this time. He got to his feet and brushed himself off.

'You can get dressed now,' he told the girl.

Biddy pulled her clothes on as hastily as she could. Her whole body felt sore and violated from where he had prodded and poked her. She clung on to that sense of relief, however, that he did not stick his manhood in her – that was how babies were made.

After the first instance, George had pleasured himself once more, this time having her on her hands and knees in front of him. He had rubbed himself against her; oh Lord, the feeling of her flesh against him was - he couldn't think of a description strong enough to explain it.

As he adjusted his clothing, and Biddy was fully dressed, they walked back through the woods. George spotted the sixpence shining on the grassy path. Picking it up, handing it to her, he said, 'meet me here at the same time when you have your next Sunday off.'

'I can't,' she wailed, trying desperately to think of an excuse, anything to get out of this situation.

Grabbing her arm, he pulled her close. 'Remember what I said, you will be here, understand?'

Her cheeks flushed, her eyes bleak with despair, she nodded.

Oh, that had been such a pleasant summer, George remembered; what he enjoyed most about the situation was having someone he could manipulate.

He had always felt inadequate in so many ways: his father and mother left his upbringing to a strict nanny, bringing a tutor in when he was five. Then, as soon as they could, they sent him off to boarding school, where he had been overlooked; classed as a below-average student.

The following term, however, he had a plethora of stories to tell the other boys in the dorm.

Once he had finished school, taken over the running of the estate, then became a member of parliament, he felt no real need to marry. He was a busy man, who found his pleasures in whorehouses – only the most expensive, of course. However, the constant nagging from his mother and father had ground him down until he capitulated to an arranged marriage to Vanessa.

Vanessa was young and very beautiful. To begin with, he enjoyed bullying her, forcing her to do degrading things. But he sensed her strength of will. She was not that easy to manipulate. George grew tired of the games, especially after a long day. He found he preferred visiting the brothels, where his needs were met without question. There were still expectations of them both to produce an heir for the Beeching estate, however, so, once she had become pregnant and produced a healthy boy, he had breathed a sigh of relief and left her alone.

George finished his glass of champagne, then called Franks, the butler over.

'I understand there is a room ready for me,' he said.

'Yes, sir. I will get one of the footmen to show you the way.'

'Thank you.' George Beeching nodded and rubbed his hands together in anticipation of the delights to come.

Chapter 31

When the clock struck the eleventh hour, Molly was hopeful that the arrangement had changed, that the man wasn't coming: her gut told her that is was an unrealistic wish. She just wanted the night to be over; if they were kept in this room any longer, she would scream. The inactivity was making her mind race. Then she silently berated herself for feeling that way; she didn't want anything bad to happen to the girl in her charge, but what could she do?

Sophia had woken from her doze on the bed. Still not knowing what time the man would arrive, Molly decided that now was as good a time as any to give the girl the drugged port. Her heart was beating rapidly with anxiety as she handed the glass to Sophia.

Innocently, Sophia finished the drink. 'I have never had port before,' she declared as she put the empty glass down on a table.

'Huh, don't go getting a taste for it.' Molly tried a smile, the muscles of her face felt stiff. The girl must be able to read the duplicity, surely?

They were seated together by the fire. There were several lamps set about the room. The lighting was soft, which made the room feel cosy.

Sophia did not know if it were the warmth of the fire or the lateness of the hour, but she was still feeling tired, her body felt quite languid, her limbs heavy. When she talked, she could hear her words, but it was as if they were not emanating from her mouth. How odd, she thought.

She could not even guess the time when they heard a key turn in the lock. Molly got to her feet as Cobbs appeared, then he stood aside to admit an older man with a thatch of greying hair, a broad, square face softened by bushy sideburns. He was taller than the footman, but not overly so. A taste for good food and wine had given him reddish veined cheeks and a paunch.

Walking in, he scanned the room. When his gaze rested on Sophia, sitting in the firelight. He smiled, showing teeth that were yellowed by tobacco stains.

'Ah, my dear.' He walked toward Sophia, who rose to her feet, albeit a little unsteadily as he approached. 'Oh, how charming you are,' he gushed. Reaching out, he lifted her chin with fleshy fingers so he could study her features more closely. 'and so pretty.'

'Thank you, sir.' When she blushed, his smile widened.

Then his gaze rested upon Molly. 'And, who have we here?'

'Molly, sir.' She did a quick bob, then shot an uncertain glance at Sophia. 'Mm, I will leave you alone to get acquainted.' She went to walk past George Beeching, but his hand on her arm forestalled her.

'Oh no, my dear,' he said, 'I think we would have far more fun together if you stayed.' Before Molly could object,

George turned to the footman, 'You may go,' he dismissed him.

*

Jolly had been as good as his word; he had gotten Reg to go for the doctor. Dr Travis, who must have been in his late sixties, gave Dottie a per-functory examination.

'She is running a high temperature, her chest sounds congested, possibly pneumonia,' he declared. 'If the fever does not break overnight, call me in again tomorrow.'

'Yes, doctor.' Evie nodded as she fidgeted nervously at the foot of the bed.

When the doctor had left, Jolly and Mrs Perkins appeared.

'I'm going to leave you in the capable ands of Mrs P, ere.' Jolly gave Evie a long look. 'Now, are yer going to stay put this time?'

Evie lowered her gaze as a flush flooded her cheeks. 'Yes,' she said softly.

'Well, there you go, Mr Barrett. I'm sure that now they realise how lucky they are to have a benefactor such as yourself, they will be good, won't you?' The woman looked pointedly at Evie, who nodded.

'Aye, well, I shall pop in tomorrow to make sure that everything is alright.' Jack bobbed his head to Evie.

'Yes, of course,' Mrs Perkins agreed.

Jolly gave Evie a brief nod. 'I ope she feels better tomorrow,' he said but didn't wait for a reply, he turned towards the door.

'I'll leave Tommy Dicken with you, Mrs P,' Evie heard him say as they stepped onto the landing. 'he'll elp you bring the coal in and any heavy jobs that need doing.'

'Yes, right you are,' the housekeeper acknowledged.

Sighing in resignation, Evie sat on the chair she had placed next to the bed. Folding her arms on the coverlet, she rested her head on them, as she did so, she could hear Dottie's breathing rattling in her chest. Her sister looked so pale and fragile against the white linen pillowcase.

Evie felt exhausted. She was too tired to ponder the situation they were now in; her only thought was for her sister. 'Please be better tomorrow, Dottie,' she whispered.

*

Molly's hands were shaking so badly she had trouble undoing the delicate buttons of Sophia's white lace dress.

'Strip her, my dear.' The punter had said, his voice was hard as granite now. He sat in a wingback chair in a shadowy part of the room, watching the proceedings with manic delight.

'What's wrong?' Sophia asked; her speech slurred. 'Am I marrying him?' she managed to add.

George gave a laugh that sounded like a giggle. 'Oh, how wonderful.' He clapped his hands.

'Hush now, lovey.' Molly dare not look at the man. She was trembling, not just with nerves but with revulsion. Hatred for these men who preyed on young girls had overwhelmed her. Oh Lord, she thought, what a time to grow a conscience old Moll. If I had a knife on me, I would slash his bloody throat!

The first layer of the pretty lace dress fell to the floor, leaving Sophia standing in the middle of the room dressed in a chemise and bloomers.

Molly shot the man a look. 'All of it,' he instructed, his voice sharp.

'Please, sir, don't do this" Molly entreated. 'You and me, can ave some fun, leave the girl alone.'

George shifted forward in the chair. 'You listen to me, you bitch of a whore, you will do everything that I say, or by God, I will get Barrett to drown you like a stray dog in the river.'

Tears started to run down Molly's cheeks as she untied the first ribbons of the chemise.

*

Evie was surprisingly grateful to Mrs Perkins when the woman brought her a cup of hot milk along with a bowl of water scented with lavender and a washcloth.

Without saying a word, the woman put the items down on a table, went over to a polished wood chest of drawers and pulled out night clothes for Evie.

'Now, you get yourself changed,' the housekeeper said as she handed Evie a white cotton nightdress. 'Give me your clothes, I'll add it to the pile, Tommy can burn them tomorrow.'

Evie was too tired to argue. She nodded as she got up from the chair.

It didn't take her long to shrug out of her clothes. Then she washed herself using the cloth and warm scented water.

'You can have a proper bath tomorrow and wash your hair,' Mrs Perkins commented as she picked up the damp towel and hung it over a wooden towel stand. 'Hopefully, your sister will be well enough to do the same soon.'

'I hope so.'

The woman gave her a kind smile, 'I'm sure she will be. Now, drink your milk then, and get to bed.'

'Thank you, Mrs Perkins,' Evie's voice was heavy with exhaustion. The housekeeper nodded, then left the room, shutting the door quietly behind her.

As the housekeeper made her way along the carpeted hallway, she wondered briefly where the girls had come from originally. The eldest spoke well and had good manners.

Reaching the downstairs hall, she walked through to the kitchen where Ivy, the housemaid, was finishing washing out the pan which the milk had been heated in.

Mrs Perkins put Evie's old clothes in the corner of the scullery, where she had left Dottie's clothes earlier.

'Finish that up, Ivy, then get to bed,' she said as she walked back into the kitchen.

'Yes, Mrs Perkins.' The young girl's voice was heavy with tiredness. It had been a busy day.

*

George Beeching was so inflamed with desire watching the whore undress the virgin girl.

What a contrast the two women made. The older woman, Molly, with her abundance of makeup and gaudy clothes, and the girl with her heart-shaped face, dark curling hair, and pale skin the colour of cream.

He was thoroughly delighted to see that her pubis had been shaved. He guessed she must be around fourteen or fifteen, as she had the rounded breasts of a girl coming into womanhood. Older than he would usually enjoy, but because she was so lovely, with soulful eyes full of trust, he could forgive her age.

George had also noticed her languid movements and realised she must have been drugged, probably with opium, he thought. Ahh, that was a shame, he preferred the girls to be fully aware of what was happening to them. He enjoyed it more when they fought back. But he was entranced and thoroughly aroused by Sophia's beauty and innocence.

Getting up from the chair as the last piece of Sophia's clothing fell to the floor, he said to Molly, 'lay her down on the bed.' He fished in the pocket of his jacket and pulled out some lengths of crimson cord. 'Here,' he handed them to Molly. 'Tie her ankles to the bedposts.'

'No, no!' Molly shook her head in horror. 'Please sir, I will do anything you ask of me.' She plucked at the sleeve of his expensive jacket.

George rounded on her, slapping her hard across the face. 'Do as you are told, woman or I shall knock you into next week.'

Molly shot him a look filled with venom, which the man did not notice as he was concentrating on removing his boots, jacket and trousers.

Her hands were shaking so much, Molly had trouble tying the cords. Seeing the beautiful girl laid out, spread-eagled on the golden coloured counterpane made Molly feel sick. The port she had drunk earlier felt like acid churning in her stomach. Aww, she should have done more; she should never have brought the girl here.

'Now you, get your clothes off.' George instructed Molly as he walked over to the bed and looked down at the vulnerable girl.

'Miss Molly?' Sophia called to her in a voice that was slurred from the drug.

Molly tried to close off her hearing, all her senses, as she stripped out of her clothes. She was used to stripping in front of men; it didn't bother her. She had a thought that if she could entice this man with her own body, he might be distracted, and then persuaded to leave Sophia alone.

'Molly, Molly,' Sophia called from the bed once again. Her head lolled as she searched the room for the woman.

'I'm here, lovie.' Molly walked over to the bed so that Sophia could see her.

'What's happening, is he my husband?'

'Oh, yes, dear girl, I am.' Beeching appeared on the far side of the bed.

He was naked now; Molly could see his cock was fully engorged.

She was already feeling sick; now she felt bile rise in her throat, she tried to swallow it down. The man leaned over and cupped Sophia's cheek with his large hand, then repositioned her face so she could see him. Her eyes were wide, pupils enlarged. 'Bloody shame you had to drug her,' Beeching hissed. 'takes away some of the fun.'

'By fun, you mean raping young girls.' Molly couldn't help herself. 'What's the matter with you, eh, a real woman won't look at you, is that it!'

Oh, she had hit a nerve, his face turned puce with anger. George got up and rounded the bed. Molly, now naked, stood her ground.

'You bloody whore.' He backhanded her with his right hand. The diamond ring he wore on his little finger scratched her cheek; blood oozed from the wound.

Before she had time to gather herself, he slapped her again. This time so hard that her head snapped back.

Molly reeled. As she fell, she caught the back of her head on the corner of one of the bedside tables. The breath escaped her, Molly saw stars as she fell to the floor, then darkness engulfed her.

*

Evie almost felt too tired to drink the milk, but once she took a sip, she gulped it down. In the nightclothes provided, she got into bed next to Dottie and lay close listening to her sister's strained breathing.

Evie intended to stay awake so she could watch over Dottie, but as soon as she put her head down on the pillow, she slept.

*

Sophia's head was reeling. She felt very strange; it was too much effort for her to analyse what was wrong with her.

She was vaguely aware of Molly tying her ankles to the bottom bedposts. There was a feeling of being exposed; Sophia did not like that feeling, but she found she couldn't move.

The man who was supposed to be her husband frightened her. She didn't want to succumb to him. And when she saw him hit Molly, despite the drug in her blood, fear shot through her.

The next thing she knew, she felt a weight on her, someone crushing her chest. The man was atop her, huffing and grunting like some deranged animal. He thrust into her. Tearing at her body. The red pain ebbed and flowed like some raging tide. Sophia wanted him to stop.

*

When Molly came to, her head was reeling, throbbing with pain. She tasted blood in her mouth, her lip and cheek stung. The man had cut it as he slapped her.

She was lying on a plush carpet gazing at the underside of a large bed which was shuddering and creaking. Hearing noises; sobbing and an animal-like grunting. It dawned on her where she was and what was happening; her heart froze in fear.

Carefully, Molly sat up then winced as pain flared. The bloody bastard must have kicked her. Examining herself, she saw that a bruise was already forming on her mid-drift and her left hip.

'Please, no more...'

The utterance made Molly feel as if a bucket of icy water had been thrown over her. Clawing at the bedcover, she pulled herself up onto her knees. She saw the punter; his face was ugly in his perverse passion as he pounded into the girl. Sophia was on her front as he took her from behind.

Molly noticed that the yellow-gold counterpane was stained with blood.

Oh, God. She closed her eyes tight, trying to block out the sight. When she opened them again, she saw Sophia; her head tilted towards her, their eyes met. The haunted look in those eyes galvanised Molly into action.

She found herself frantically crawling across the floor towards the fireplace. The fire was burning low now. Molly had no idea how long she had been unconscious for, but it had been long enough for the swine to have inflicted terrible things on that girl.

Reaching the hearth, she pulled herself to her feet, carefully picked up the shining brass poker from the set of fireirons. Then she staggered towards the man who had his hairy back to her. With both hands, she lifted the poker and bought it down on the back of George Beeching's skull.

Chapter 32

'Oh Lord, oh Lord!' Naked, Molly stood at the foot of the bed. The shock was washing through her; she swayed on her feet. Her hands were trembling violently. Realising that she still held the poker, Molly dropped it onto the expensive carpet. She didn't want to think about the fact that she may have murdered this hateful man!

George Beeching was slumped over the bed, Sophia was trapped, facedown, beneath him. The lamplight glistened across his sweaty back, making him look like a suckling pig.

Molly knew she wouldn't be able to move him by herself; he would be far too heavy. Then she had a thought, using the bedposts to lean her back against, she braced herself, then lifted her leg, intending to kick the pervert out of the way. It took several attempts, but once she had pushed him far enough, gravity did the rest, the man crumpled to the floor.

Molly wasn't sure whether to be relieved or not when she saw a pulse throbbing at his neck – he was still alive, which meant he might soon come round.

Leaning over the prone body, 'Sophia, Sophia,' Molly called to the girl frantically, when she placed a hand on her slim shoulder, Sophia flinched.

Molly could see that her thighs were streaked with blood. Wheals were marking the creamy skin of her back. Molly's heart broke, the man had brutalised her well and truly and she, Molly, had let it happen. 'Lovie, we need to go,' she called again.

At last, the girl groaned then moved. Molly took a relieved breath as she helped the young girl to her feet. Sophia swayed but managed to get her balance. She was still in a stupor due to the opium. Molly was inclined to think that was a good thing at the moment, hopefully, it meant that Sophia had not been entirely aware of what had been done to her. It also meant that she was dopey, her movements were uncoordinated, so Molly had to support her companion.

Scanning the room, Molly quickly retrieved her dress, shrugged it on then hurriedly tied the laces of the bodice. The white, flimsy dress that Sophia had worn to come here would do nothing to keep out a chill. But Molly coaxed her to stand still and, as if she were dressing a young child, pulled the dress over Sophia's head. As she did so, the man on the floor groaned. Molly shot him a worried look. Pulling the dress into place, Molly then collected her boots and Sophia's shoes. Not bothering with the stockings, she slipped the shoes on the girl.

Finally, she grabbed the black velvet cloak with the red silk lining and wrapped it around Sophia's shivering figure.

'Come, we need to go,' she urged. Placing her arm around the girl's shoulders, they stumbled towards the door.

Suddenly, Molly went cold with anxiety; would the door be locked? Relief flooded through her when it opened easily. The two of them stepped over the threshold onto the carpeted landing.

*

Hero had just decided to call it a night, to make a quick exit before his Grandfather arrived when he bumped into Thomas Cranford, one of his father's old acquaintances.

'Horacio, I haven't seen you for a while.' The man was tall and slim; his dark hair was peppered with grey. He had bright blue eyes which shone with intelligence; they were set in a kind face.

'Mr Cranford.' Hero took the extended hand. 'I'm surprised to find you here.'

The man laughed, 'So am I, dear boy.' His gaze followed one of the scantily clad ladies roaming about the room. His expression was one of distaste. 'My company is bidding for a contract to build the new East rail line in the city,' he explained. 'so, I need to circulate and be seen to muster support.'

'Oh yes, I heard about that.' Hero nodded.

'So, how is your mother?' Thomas asked.

Hero felt his cheeks redden in embarrassment. 'She was well last time I saw her,' he said evasively, he didn't want to get into a conversation, especially one regarding his family.

When Hero was finally able to excuse himself without being rude, he decided it would be a good idea to leave through the kitchens: far less chance of bumping into someone else.

He retrieved his coat, hat, and gloves from Cobbs, explained what he was doing and asked the footman to let Alec and Alexander know that he had left.

'Of course, sir.' Cobbs nodded. 'Would you like me to call Master Alec's carriage for you?'

'No, that is quite alright, Cobbs. I shall find it myself.'

'Very well, sir.'

Hero ducked through a heavy baize door that led to the servant's realm. He was passing a flight of stairs when he was nearly knocked off his feet as two women stumbled off the last step.

'Good Lord, what has happened?' Hero took in their dishevelled appearance; they both looked as if they had been in a war zone.

'Aww, sorry, sir.' Molly couldn't meet his gaze. 'We are just leaving,' she said, making to push passed him.

'You have transport?' Hero asked. 'It's snowing out there and will be freezing cold.' He noticed that the younger woman was shivering violently. 'Is she ill?' he commented nodding at Sophia, then asked, 'And you, what has happened to your face?'

'Mmm, yes, sir.' The older woman gave him such a look; he could see the sheer panic in her eyes. 'My face tis nothing.' Molly tried to fob him off.

Something wasn't right here, with a feeling of deep disquiet, Hero suggested, 'Why don't you both come through to the kitchen and tell me what has happened.'

Molly shook her head with vigour. 'We must go now!'

'I know you, don't I?' Hero said as he studied the woman some more: he realised that he had seen her accompanying men to some of his fights. 'You are one of Jolly's girls, aren't you?'

Her eyes widened fearfully as she took in his words. Molly, wondered if she should lie and deny knowing Jack Barrett, but then she recognised Hero, 'Mr Woodley?'

'Yes, that's right.' Just as he nodded, Sophia groaned and slumped forward, Molly lost her hold on the girl. Hero's arms shot out. He caught her before she could hit the floor. As he lifted her off her feet, he noticed the spots of blood on the floor and the streaks down her legs. His eye's met Molly's, 'I think you had better tell me what the bloody hell has happened.'

Molly lifted her hand, stroking the curling hair away from Sophia's hot forehead, she said, 'she's been grievously used, Mr Woodley.'

'By whom?' Hero found himself asking as anger coursed through him. Then a thought occurred, he had seen Vanessa's husband being shown up the stairs by Cobbs. 'Was it George Beeching?' he asked.

Molly shrugged. She gazed up the stairway; the panic was written all over her face. 'Dunno his name, but he was a devil for sure.'

'Where is he? Did he just let you leave in this condition?'

Molly's gaze dropped from his for a second, then lifting her chin, she gave Hero a direct look. 'I clubbed im over the ead.'

Hero didn't quite know what to say to that, this was an unprecedented situation; however, he was appalled by the state of these two women. 'Ahh, I see,' he said, at last, Then the implications of the older woman's statement dawned on him. 'is he, um ...'

'He's alive,' Molly declared, her tone filled with bitterness.

'Right,' Hero's mind worked quickly, he said, 'I was just leaving; I will take you both in my carriage. My roommate is training to be a doctor, and he can attend to you and the girl.'

'Sophia,' Molly said, 'her name is Sophia.'

'Sophia.' Hero nodded.

They walked hastily through the large kitchens to the backdoor. On hooks by the door coats and cloaks were hanging on pegs.

'Grab one of these for yourself,' he instructed Molly.

She nodded gratefully. The shock of what had happened was beginning to sink in even more. Molly had begun to shiver; her teeth were chattering so much, it hurt her jaw to try and keep it under control. Her cheek also ached where the swine had hit her.

Gratefully, Molly picked out a cloak of dark wool then wrapped it around her shoulders.

'Can you support her for a few minutes?' Hero asked, 'I shall need to find the carriage, I will direct it to the bottom of the steps.'

'Yes, thank you, Mr Woodley.' Molly put her arms out as Hero gently placed Sophia back on her feet. She slumped against Molly, but the woman was able to take her weight.

Opening the back door, Hero stepped into the wintery night.

*

When George Beeching started to come too, it took him a while to orientate himself. He realised that he was naked, lying on a plush carpet. There was a musky scent on the air; it was a mixture of sex and blood. Ahh, the girl, he thought as he gingerly sat up. The movement caused his head to throb. When he put a tentative finger to the back of his skull, he felt a tender lump and winced.

Scanning the room as he got to his feet, he found that the girl and the whore had gone. There was a poker lying on the carpet. It occurred to him that the whore might have killed him with that bloody fireiron: She could be had up for attempted murder. But then he thought of the scandal all this would entail.

'Bloody hell!' he spat out the oath. The woman had clubbed him and had run off with the young wench. Stupid fool, he thought, if he didn't catch up with her, Jolly Jack Barrett would. Then, by God, she will pay for what she has done.

Filled with rage, ignoring his throbbing head, he got dressed. Mumbling expletives as he did so.

When he pulled on his tailored jacket, he decided that he would get Barrett to track the women down, then bring them to him. He had unfinished business with them: the girl and the woman would have to pay dearly for this.

Once he had finished dressing, he pulled the bellpull to summon one of the servants.

*

The waiting coachmen were huddled together around a brazier in the stable yard. They were chatting, joking, and laughing amongst themselves.

Hero spotted the man, Collins, who drove the Silverman coach and called him over.

'Master Alec has left you at my disposal.'

'That's right, Mr Woodley,' the man acknowledged.

Hero looked over his shoulder. 'Mmm, I have a couple of female friends accompanying me back to my lodgings, bring the carriage to the bottom of the kitchen steps, if you will.'

'Aye, sir.'

'Oh, and I would ask for discretion. Mm, I have little money with me now, but I will ensure that you will be rewarded for keeping this to yourself.'

Collins nodded. He liked Mr Woodley, who always treated him with respect, not like Master Alec, who Collins considered to be a spoilt brat.

'There is no need, Mr Woodley, I've won handsomely many a time betting on one of your fights.'

Horacio smiled. 'Thank you, Collins.'

Hero retraced his steps; they only had to wait a few moments before the carriage arrived. Together, Molly and Hero helped Sophia down the steps.

As soon as they were in the carriage and it had set off, Molly let out a breath of relief. She knew, however, that she had put herself and Sophia in grave danger. Nowhere would be safe for them, but then again, Sophia may not have survived the night at all if Molly hadn't stepped in; she didn't regret doing so one bit. In fact, Molly wished that she had been stronger. That she had stood up to the old toff once and for all before any harm could be done.

Molly held the girl close. 'It'll be alright now,' she whispered.

'How did this come about?' Hero asked his voice steely.

Molly, her voice rough with emotion and exhaustion said, 'Do I have to go into details, Mr Woodley?'

Hero met her gaze, then shut his eyes for a moment, blocking out the disquieting thoughts. He swallowed and found his throat to be dry.

'No, I can guess,' he said at last. Fishing in his pocket, he pulled out a hip flask and unscrewed the top.

'Here,' he offered it to Molly, 'It's brandy.'

'Thank you.' She took the offered flask and took a good swallow, wincing as the liquor touched the split on her lip. She wiped her chin with the back of her hand; then she offered the drink to Sophia. 'Here, lovie, drink some of this.' But Sophia shook her head.

From the opposite seat, he studied the wounded figure, the light was dim inside the carriage, but the two small oil lamps set in sconces on either side above the doors was just enough for him to tell that the young woman's pupils were enlarged. Her head lolled where it rested on the older woman's shoulder.

'She's been drugged,' he stated an edge to his voice. Molly would not meet his gaze but nodded in reply. 'Do you know what the extent of the damage is?' Horacio asked her.

'N-no sir, but she as been used brutally.'

'Jesus!' Horacio glanced out at the night that pressed against the windows. Was it Vanessa's husband, who had done these unspeakable things? Turning back to the older woman, he said, 'What did he look like?'

'Look like?' Molly bit her split lip, winced, then dabbed at the oozing cut with her finger.

'A simple question.' Hero pushed.

'He was a toff, greying air, side whiskers. Eyes as dark as the devil.' The description wasn't entirely helpful, but Hero's intuition was shouting at him; he knew that Vanessa's husband had done this awful thing.

The journey back to town seemed to take an age. The going was slow in the thick snow. They also had to interrupt the journey once when Sophia declared she was going to be sick.

Molly held the girl while she vomited, then Hero carefully lifted her back inside the carriage. He produced a large, clean white handkerchief so Molly could wipe Sophia's face.

When they finally arrived at Hero's lodgings, Hero called up to Collins to thank him, then helped Sophia down the carriage steps. Her feet did not touch the freezing ground; however, as Hero picked her up and carried her up the steps. Fishing in his pocket for the key, he handed it to Molly so that she could let them in.

Hero carried the girl up the stairs, with Molly close behind.

*

The butler, Franks, handed George Beeching a large whiskey, the man took a good slug of the liquor.

Alexander Silverman hovered close by wringing his hands anxiously.

'The bitch could have killed me!' George exclaimed once again.

'Ahh, well ...' Alexander was saved from answering by a tap on the bedroom door, Cobbs appeared.

'There is no sign of them, sir,' the footman reported.

'Well, they can't have vanished into thin air.' George's face flushed to an even darker shade of puce. 'That whore needs to be hunted down – the bloody woman tried to murder me. I suspect she will go to ground in the bloody slums.'

'Are you sure that would be wise, Beeching?' Alexander spoke up, 'if this story were to get out, think of the scandal.' He had voiced Georges own thoughts.

'Yes, yes, but I want those two bitches found.'

'I am sure that Jack Barrett will see to that.'

'Ah, bloody Barrett.' George slumped into an armchair.

'Let us not forget that he has provided for your, umm, particular needs.'

Waving a hand in the air dismissively, George said, 'Yes, yes, no need to remind me. Fill my glass up will you,' he instructed Franks, who did as he was bid. Taking a long slug of the liquor, he placed the crystal cut glass down on a side table. 'I must see him as soon as possible. I have unfinished business with those two trollops.'

'Yes, of course.' Alexander agreed although he felt a chill run up and down his spine. If only he didn't need to do business with him, the man was a cold-hearted monster.

Alexander knew his reputation was shady, when one had men, like Jack Barrett, working for you one could not help but feel sullied. But business was business. Alexander Silverman was prepared to do whatever it took to ensure his family had the security of wealth now and in the future. He had decided long ago that he would never be put in a place of degradation again.

*

Once Collins, the Silverman's coachman, had dropped off Mr Woodley and the two *ladies*, he decided to stop off at an inn he frequented. He knew that master Alec would be occupied with his entertainment and probably wouldn't want to be taken back to the city until late tomorrow. Collins decided that if any questions were asked about his absence, he would explain that he got caught in the snowstorm when he brought Mr Woodley home. Which wasn't far from the truth as large flakes were falling. It was freezing; visibility was terrible.

*

Hero opened the door to the apartment. When they stepped into the room, Molly spotted a scruffy dog that immediately jumped out of a nice warm basket which was set down by the fire, then came charging across the room to greet his master with great enthusiasm.

'Wait, Wilson. Good boy,' Hero called. The dog promptly sat down and watched the proceedings with intelligent brown eyes, his head cocked with interest.

Hero pushed open the door leading to his bedroom, stepped inside, then very gently laid Sophia on his bed.

'I shall wake Andrew,' Hero said, 'he's a good sort, don't worry.' He addressed Molly, 'He can check her over and then take a look at the marks on your face.'

'Thank you, sir.' Molly tried a weak smile.

Andrew had been in a deep sleep when Hero woke him. He got up rather groggily.

'Splash some water on your face, man, your skills are badly needed.'

'Oh lord,' Andrew rubbed the sleep from his eyes. 'You haven't brought back another stray, have you?'

'No, unfortunately, something much more serious.'

Andrew pulled on his dressing gown and slipped his feet into slippers, then threw some water from the washbowl over his face; the water did the trick of bringing him around.

'She's in my room,' Hero explained as Andrew followed him through the sitting room, then into Hero's bedroom.

Andrew scanned the figure of Sophia, then took in Molly's face. 'Good lord, what on earth has happened?'

'Best you don't know, Andrew,' Hero spoke up.

His friend shot him a wary look. 'Very well.'

'I can explain what has appened,' Molly spoke up.

Andrew nodded. His priority was to check out the young woman/girl laying on the bed. He could see the blood spotting the white dress she was wearing, along with streaks of blood running down her legs.

'The girl's been drugged,' Hero spoke up. 'Opium.' He looked to Molly for confirmation, she nodded.

'This is truly barbaric.' Andrew's already pale face whitened even more. For proprieties sake, Molly stayed in the room, while Andrew checked Sophia over. With every new laceration, every new horror, the man uttered angry words and expletives.

Finally, Andrew stood up and wiped his hands on a towel. 'She will recover from her injuries. Time will be the healer. As for her state of mind,' Andrew shook his head.

All through the examination, Sophia had remained quiet; her head lolled to one side, she gazed at the green fleur-de-lis wallpaper.

Molly dropped her head in sorrow. 'I should never ave took er, I should have done more to keep er safe.' She wailed.

'There is simply no excuse for what has been done to this young woman; however, I would imagine that the men, or man, you work for are ruthless, are they not?' Andrew pointed out.

'Aye, they are.'

'So, I don't suppose you had much choice in this matter.'

Molly shook her head, 'no, neither of us did.'

Andrew gave her a terse nod of acknowledgement. 'Well then, I shall bring some water in, a fresh nightshirt, you can get her cleaned up, and she can rest and sleep. Call me when you are finished, I will check over the cuts on your face.'

'Oh, yer don't ave to worry about me, doctor, I've ad worse done to me.'

A shadow flickered through Andrew's gaze. 'Umm well, there is nothing I can say about that, but I will check you over nonetheless.'

Molly gave him a weak smile. 'Thank you, doctor.'

'Well, I'm not quite there yet.' Andrew's expression lightened, 'but one day soon, I hope.'

Coming from the bedroom, Andrew washed his hands at the kitchen sink. He rolled down the sleeves of his robe as he sat down opposite Hero, who was sitting by the fire. He was nursing a glass of brandy in one hand and stroking Wilson, who was curled up on his lap, with the other.

Leaning forward in his chair, Andrew said, 'Bloody hell, Horacio, what sort of company are you keeping!?' He shook his head. 'I'm not naïve, I know these things happen, but that man, whoever he was, has brutalised that girl so badly, it is unspeakable.'

'I think I know who it was,' Hero said, his soft voice edged with rough emotion.

'Who?'

'Vanessa's husband.'

Andrew sat back in the chair, a look of shock and astonishment washed over his features. 'but he's a member of parliament.'

Hero gave a rough laugh. 'Come on, Andrew; you know the worst of them can be the rich and powerful. The ones that have the money to pay for these kinds of, mmm, services.'

Shaking his head sadly, Andrew said, 'Well, it looks as if you know far more than me about this, old boy.'

Hero nodded his head towards the bedroom door, 'Neither of them will be safe now. Knowing George Beeching and Jack Barrett, at least one of them will want retribution, if not both.'

'Should we get the police involved?' Andrew was thoughtful.

'It won't help, there is corruption amongst them too.'

'Well, what are we going to do with them? They can't stay here.'

'I have an idea,' Hero said thoughtfully. 'When the young girl, Sophia is ready to travel, I'll take them to my mother and Claire.'

'Are you sure that is wise, Horacio? You don't know anything about these women, after all.'

'Well, if my mother and Claire have taught me anything, it is that you cannot judge a book... You only have to look at the number of girls and women they have helped.'

'Yes, yes,' Andrew acknowledged. 'In that case, I feel that it would be a good decision then.'

*

The following morning, Andrew sent a note to say he would not be attending lectures due to illness.

He and Hero sat and ate some breakfast together, then as soon as he heard Molly get up, Andrew knocked on the bedroom door.

'She's still asleep,' Molly whispered.

'Very good,' Andrew acknowledged. However, he still went over to the bed and pressed his palm gently to Sophia's forehead. 'No sign of any fever. That's good.'

'Aye,' Molly agreed.

'Come, sit and have some breakfast, Molly,' Hero called when she appeared in the living room.

'That is most kind, sir, but I should be leaving now.'

'Where are you going to go?' Hero frowned.

Molly shrugged her slim shoulders, 'Only one place I can go, back to Little Back Lane.'

'And what will Jack Barrett do when he sees you?'

'I shall probably take a beating,' her reply was casually spoken.

Hero got up from the table and walked over to the woman. 'I have a strong suspicion that the man who did these things to you, and that girl in there, is a member of parliament. He is a powerful man, with many contacts. Both you and she will be in danger.' Molly shrugged again as if she were resigned to her fate. 'I know somewhere safe where you can both go.'

Hero saw a flash of interest and relief flicker through her expression, and then she dropped her gaze from his. Molly shook her head.

'My fate is sealed. Besides, I deserve every punishment for this. Tis my fault, I knew what was likely to appen, an I took her to that place anyway.'

'Did you have a choice?' Hero asked her.

Molly thought for a moment, 'Not really, but we could have run away.'

'Where to?' Hero pushed.

'Aww, I dunno. Somewhere far from ere.' Then a grave expression shadowed her beaten face. 'She ad a grandmother called er Babula or something like it. Jolly ad me give the old girl a dose of laudanum, just before we left the ouse yesterday.'

'Laudanum!' Andrew spoke up for the first time. 'How much?'

Molly shot him a look, 'Enough to see er into the next life.'

'Oh Lord,' Andrew sat down at the breakfast table once more and put his head in his hands. 'This gets worse by the minute.'

'See, yer arbouring a murderer,' Molly's voice was bitter.

'You killed my Grandmother!' The girl stood in the bedroom doorway holding onto the door jamb for support. She was as white as a ghost.

'Aww lovie, I ad no choice.' Molly rushed over to Sophia.

'No, no, keep away from me.' Tears ran down her face as she waved her hands to keep Molly at a distance. 'I never trusted you. Everything that has happened is your fault.'

Molly found that her own eyes were wet with tears as she halted a foot away from the girl. 'I'm sorry,' she sobbed. 'You're right, tis all my fault. It's alright, lovie, I'm leaving now.' Molly looked at Andrew and Horacio. 'These ere are good men. Mr Woodley and his doctor friend; they will look after you.'

Neither Hero nor Andrew stopped Molly as she gathered up her few possessions.

Before she left, Molly paused by the door, looking back, she said, 'Look after the young un, she's a good girl.' Roughly, she wiped the tears from her eyes. 'I never meant for this to appen. It was out of my ands.'

Hero nodded in understanding, but his face was grim.

'What will happen to her?' Andrew spoke up after Molly had gone.

'I don't know. Maybe she will turn herself in to the police?'

Andrew looked to the stricken figure by the door. 'Now, you need to be back in bed,' he said in a voice that posed no argument.

'My Grandmother,' Sophia sobbed, 'I can't believe she is dead.'

'It is an awful thing,' Andrew said as he put his arm around Sophia's shoulders and guided her gently back to the bed, 'I am so sorry.'

The young girl sat on the edge of the bed. Tears ran down her cheeks. 'I can't believe it,' she uttered, rocking back and fore.

'Hush now,' Andrew sat down next to her, then next thing she was in his arms, trembling like a lost deer.

Eventually, the tears dried up.

'Come now, into bed with you.' Andrew insisted, this time, Sophia complied without objection. 'Is there anything I can get you?'

'Some water, please.'

'Yes, yes, of course.' Andrew quickly poured out a glass of water and was grateful when the girl drained the glass. He studied her carefully, glad to see that her pupils were no longer dilated. 'How are you feeling now?' he asked gently.

'I have pain in my belly and my back stings.'

'Do you remember what happened to you?'

Her face blanched even more, 'Some of it, but I think I was drugged, I felt very woozy.'

Andrew nodded, 'Yes, you are correct. You were, mmm, given some opium.' He felt his anger rise when he thought of the disgraceful tactics that had been used against this girl.

'Opium? There was a woman in our village who was a healer, and she used the poppy seed many times.'

'Yes, it can be used for healing. And, your wounds will heal,' Andrew reassured her. 'I shall leave you to rest now.' Leaving the room, he left the door ajar so he could hear if Sophia called out for anything.

He was surprised to find Hero putting his coat on.

'Going somewhere?'

'Yes,' Hero buttoned his coat and picked up his hat and gloves. 'Are you alright to keep an eye on her?' He nodded towards the bedroom door.

'Yes, of course.'

'Good. I'm going to visit Vanessa Beeching.'

'Are you sure that's a good idea, Horacio, if you come across her husband, what will you do?'

'I'm not entirely sure,' his voice was heavy as he pulled on his gloves. 'but Vanessa needs to know what kind of man she is married to.'

Wilson gave him a heartbroken look when Hero told the dog that he wasn't coming along for the outing.

When he shut the door to the lodgings, a thought swept through Hero's mind like a dark shadow, maybe Vanessa already knew about George's predilections?

Chapter 33

Evie woke up when she heard someone come into the room. For a moment she forgot where she was, but then the feel of expensive sheets reminder her, she was in Jolly's house.

'Good morning.' Mrs Perkins came into view. She placed a tray on a side table. 'Hot chocolate,' she explained. As Evie sat up, the woman walked around the bed and put her hand on Dottie's forehead. 'Mmm,' she placed an ear next to Dottie's chest. 'I think she may have turned a bit of a corner,' she said as she straightened up.

Evie put her hand against Dottie's skin. She didn't think it was as hot either.

'Dottie.' Touching her sister's shoulder, she called. 'Dottie.'

The younger girl groaned, then opened her eyes. 'Evie, where are we?' Her voice was a croak.

'Jolly Barrett's house.'

'Aww no.' She tried to sit up but found she felt extremely weak.

'Shh now, stay still. We are safe. And this lady is Mrs Perkins; she's here to look after us.'

'I've got some hot milk with cinnamon for you, child.' The housekeeper picked up a cup decorated with flowers, then placing her hand behind Dottie's head, she tilted the cup so she could drink.

Dottie took a sip then had some more.

'There, good girl.' Mrs Perkins said with satisfaction.

'Shall I do the fire, Mrs?'

A girl appeared in the doorway. Evie noticed that she was thin, so much so, that her maids uniform hung off her shoulders. Her expression, however, was cheerful and open. She had a scattering of freckles across her nose. Strands of ginger hair peeped out from beneath her mob cap.

'Yes, Ivy,' Mrs Perkins answered. 'This is Ivy Dicken, Tommy's sister.' The housekeeper introduced her. 'She will be helping me to run the house,' she explained.

Evie nodded at the girl in greeting; Ivy gave her and Dottie a curious look as she made her way across the room, coalscuttle in hand.

'Aww, we need a good fire, the snow's thick out there. You should see the garden,' the girl chattered on, 'it's like a fairytale.' She sighed.

'Enough chit chat, Ivy, get on with your work.'

'Yes, Mrs.'

'It's Mrs Perkins, Ivy, remember.'

'Oh yes, Mrs-Umm, Mrs Perkins.'

'Very good.' The older woman nodded with approval. Then she addressed Evie, 'There are clothes in the wardrobe, get yourself washed and dressed. Mr Barrett will be here soon; he will want to talk to you. And you,' she looked at Dottie, 'you stay in bed, we need to get you well again.'

'Evie?' Dottie's voice was edged with anxiety.

Giving her sister a reassuring smile, Evie said, 'It's going to be alright, Dottie, everyone is being kind.' Their gazes held for a long moment, then Dottie nodded.

'Very good,' Mrs Perkins' voice was jovial.

When the housekeeper and the maid had gone, Dottie spoke up once more.

'Are we really safe here, Evie?'

Evie came and sat on the edge of the bed. She stretched out her hand and brushed one of Dottie's curls from her pale forehead. Her hair, which was usually golden brown, was dark and greasy with sweat. A feverish flush reddened her cheeks.

Evie reached out for her sister's hand. 'Oh Lord, Dot, I don't know. If we stay here, Jolly is going to expect me to marry him.' Dottie sucked in a breath. Evie squeezed her fingers gently. 'There isn't anywhere for us to go, besides, you are too poorly to travel.'

'This is all my fault.'

When Evie saw her sister's eyes fill with tears, she leant over and caught her up in a tight embrace. 'Hush now, don't distress yourself, love, you'll make yourself even more poorly.'

When she felt Dottie nod her head, Evie let her go.

'Now, I'm going to get washed and dressed; then we shall have some breakfast. Do you feel like eating anything?' When Dottie nodded, Evie smiled. 'There we go.' She walked over to the large wardrobe and opened it. Inside, there were dresses, skirts, blouses, jackets, and coats. The outfits were beautifully made, in a myriad of soft colours. Evie pulled out a dress which was the colour of purple heather, trimmed with a pretty cream lace collar. Holding the dress up against herself, she glanced at Dottie. 'What do you think?'

'Pretty,' she approved. Dottie's gaze travelled around the room. 'This is a grand house, Evie.'

'Yes, it is,' Evie had to admit that Jolly had found a lovely home, then her heart stuttered, a home or a prison? Goosebumps travelled the length of her arms. Hastily she put the dress down, draping it over the back of a chair.

On further exploration, she found underwear and petticoats, stockings, and other articles of lady's attire in drawers. She also discovered a lovely bathing room leading from the bedroom.

Getting washed then dressed, Evie left Dottie resting in bed, then went down the stairs.

After Evie had left the bedroom, Dottie stared at the canopy above the bed; it was cream silk decorated with roses.

This is all my fault, she thought bitterly, if only I hadn't been ill. Dottie shook her head in despair; she had to get well. She simply had to! So that she and Evie could leave this place. The very thought of her sister being married to Jack Barrett sent shivers of apprehension through her body.

Downstairs, Evie discovered that there was a delightful sitting room, with large windows looking out over the snowy garden. Which, just like Ivy had stated, did indeed look like something out of a fairytale. There was a pretty dining room that opened through to a large kitchen;

it was here that she found Mrs Perkins, Ivy, and Tommy Dicken.

The boy, who Evie guessed to be around fifteen sat at the kitchen table tucking into a plate of bacon, eggs and crusty bread spread with thick butter.

Despite herself, Evie felt her stomach rumble, she blushed, and Tommy laughed. He had a cheeky laugh. Evie noticed that he shared the same freckled complexion and mop of ginger hair as his sister and cousin Reg.

'Yer needs a good feed, yer does,' he commented as he tucked into his food with relish.

'I thought we would have a bite in the kitchen this morning,' Mrs Perkins said as she laid a place for Evie, 'but after that, you should eat in the dining room seeing as you will be the mistress of this house.'

'Oh, I ...' Evie's mouth suddenly went dry, her appetite left her.

The housekeeper scowled at her, 'Don't look so glum, Evie Winters, many a lass would give anything to be in your position.'

'Ain't that the truth,' Tommy waved his fork in the air as he spoke around a piece of bread that he had just popped into his mouth.

'Manners, lad.' Mrs Perkins gave him a light tap around the head. 'Sit, let's eat,' she addressed Evie, 'then you can take a nice, coddled egg up to your sister.'

'Thank you,' Evie sat at the table. Mrs Perkins laid a plate down in front of her; there were two rashers of thick bacon and an egg, the yolk of which was as yellow as a buttercup. Once Evie had taken her first mouthful, she found herself tucking in with relish.

It was a strange atmosphere, Evie could almost imagine that she sat around the table as part of a happy family; Ivy and Tommy were chatty and exuberant, although Mrs Perkins pulled them up if they went on too much. Evie even found herself laughing a couple of times when Tommy recounted some of his adventures.

When she had finished and drained the last dreg from her teacup, Ivy helped her lay a tray for Dottie. Coddled egg, a slice of bread and butter and a cup of tea with milk and sugar.

*

Molly didn't know what to do when she left Mr Woodley's lodgings that morning. It did occur to her to walk straight to that new-fangled Scotland yard and hand herself in for the murder of that poor girl's grandma, and the attempted murder of that old pervert. It didn't matter that she hit him over the head to save Sophia. None of that would be considered; Molly knew she would hang, that was for sure: perhaps that would be the preferable outcome, as she knew that once Jolly got wind of everything that had happened, she would be punished; Ha, punishment would be the least of her worries, she would have her throat cut and be tossed in the river. She found herself shivering with dread.

The streets were already busy as the grey streaks of dawn pierced the heavy clouds. It had finally stopped snowing.

As she walked by, people gave her odd looks; aww, she must look a sight with her hair all over the place, the cuts on her face. Dressed in her bright, gaudy colours. The half cape she wore did nothing to keep out the chill.

There was only one path for her, and that was back to Little Back Lane. She debated with the thought of seeking out Margie, but then she realised that she probably wouldn't be back from the night-time antics yet.

When she finally reached her destination, it was to find her room just as they had left it the day before, minus the old woman.

The bed where they had left her was empty. Of course, the grate was cold; the room felt damp and unlived in.

Molly's heart clenched. She pulled out a wooden chair, sitting down at the table she put her head in her hands and wept.

*

As Hero strode through the busy streets, gloved hands pushed deep into his coat pockets, collar turned up, and hat pulled down, he felt a weight of darkness settle upon his shoulders. This feeling that was so familiar to him now made his skin prickle, his headache and stomach churn.

Andrew had called it a state of melancholia; Hero didn't care what the state was called; all he knew was he had a devil of a time coming out of it.

Sometimes, but not always, the nightmares resurfaced. Hero experienced the death of his sister and father once again, including the crippling weight of guilt. The boxing helped somewhat. Strangely enough, having Wilson around also helped, the little dog was devoted to him, they had saved each other. Seeing Vanessa also helped, she cared for him, possibly even loved him in her way. Hero wasn't sure what he felt for her, was it love, lust, passion? Their liaisons served a need in both of them.

When he reached the Beeching's townhouse, an elegant place built in the last century, he paused at the bottom of the steps.

Part of him wanted to know if Vanessa knew what a monster her husband was. Then a thought rose from the depths of his mind, she was married to that man and had been for years, with no escape, had she been subjected to his depravity? Then again, he had never noticed any marks on her body, and he had certainly taken a great deal of time and pleasure exploring it.

She didn't talk much about her marriage; they had other things on their minds when they met up. The topic of her relationship was set aside and best avoided.

Ahh, he decided, he needed to give himself more time to mull this over. Andrew also had a point, if he ran into George, what would he do?

He had just started walking away from the house when the front door at the top of the steps opened.

'Mr Woodley?'

Hero turned back to see the housekeeper, Mrs Davies, standing in the doorway.

Retracing his steps, he looked up at her. 'I was just passing,' he told her.

'Lady Beeching saw you from the drawing-room window, sir, she asks that you join her for morning coffee.'

'And his Lordship?'

'Has not returned as of yet, sir.'

Hero made a quick decision, then ran up the steps. The housekeeper ushered him into the large, tiled hall, where she waited to take his hat, coat, and gloves which she set aside, then saw him through to the large, sedate room.

'Mr Woodley,' Mrs Davies announced.

'Ahh, Horacio.' Vanessa came to greet him. She looked beautiful as usual in a morning gown of café-au-latte. Her hair was pinned up quite casually. Soft curls caressed her cheeks and slim neck. 'I hope you weren't going to walk past without coming in,' she said as she took his hands.

'Umm, no.'

Vanessa noticed his dark expression. She released his hands. Turning to Mrs Davies, she said, 'bring a fresh pot of coffee and an extra cup.'

'Yes, ma'am.' The housekeeper left.

Hero's gaze scanned the room, 'George's not here?'

'No, he's not returned. Quite frankly, I am surprised to see you this morning, Horacio.' Vanessa took a seat by the fire.

'Something happened last night, Vanessa.' Although she gestured for him to sit, he remained standing.

'What exactly?' she asked, keeping her expression neutral.

'Your husband is a monster.'

Vanessa got to her feet. Her silk dress rustled as she walked across the room. She picked up a carafe from a sideboard, took out the stopper and poured out two generous tots of brandy.

Walking back to her chair, she handed one of the glasses to Hero. He took a sip then took the chair opposite.

'You are telling me something I am well aware of,' she said.

Hero recounted the happenings of the previous night, well the early hours of the morning. He only paused in his recollections when Mrs Davies arrived with the fresh pot of coffee.

The more he told Vanessa, the paler she became.

'He brutalised one of our young maids,' she told him in a voice thick with emotion. Her expression was hazy as she gazed into the past, then she focused on Hero once more. 'He told me he would have me locked up if I mentioned a word of what had been happening.'

'I would never have let that happen,' Hero said vehemently.

'Darling, you wouldn't be able to do anything about it. When one marries, one becomes the chattel of the husband. Then there is William; I have my son to think of.'

'Yes, of course.' Hero drank his coffee which was liberally laced with another tot of brandy.

'I am sorry for the girl,' Vanessa stated. 'I wouldn't want anyone to face a murder charge, but it is a shame in many ways, that this Molly woman was not successful in her attempt.'

'Oh, I don't think she meant to kill him, Vanessa, she did it to save the girl.'

'Ah, who would have thought, eh, honour amongst whores.'

'They are people just like us, trying to survive,' his voice was steely edged.

Vanessa gave him a thin smile. 'That is what I love about you, Horacio, you always see the best in people.'

'I try,' he said, 'but when it comes to people like your husband and Jack Barrett, it is not so easy.'

Vanessa nodded. 'Yes, quite.'

When the Ormolu clock on the mantle chimed nine times, Hero got to his feet. 'I must go; I don't want to encounter George.'

Vanessa also stood. 'Oh, he probably won't be back until noon, but yes, it might be wise that you leave now.'

Doubt flickered in Hero's eyes. 'Perhaps I shouldn't have told you what happened, you will have to come face to face with him ...' his voice trailed off.

Her smile was tinged with sadness. 'Oh, I have had years of practice keeping my utter contempt for him hidden.'

Hero stepped up to her and gathered her in his arms. 'I am so sorry,' he whispered into her soft hair.

Gently, she pulled away. Her eyes glistened with unshed tears. Vanessa placed a tender hand on his cheek. 'I will be fine,' her voice held little conviction.

As soon as she heard the front door close, Vanessa walked over to one of the drawing-room windows and peered out. She watched Hero walk away down the snowy street.

Hot tears ran in rivulets down her face; she bit the side of her cheek to stop herself from crying out. She had tried so hard to turn a blind eye to her husband's exploits; oh, she knew he was still abusing young girls, it was as if it were an addiction to him. When Hero had described the state of the young girl he had rescued, Vanessa felt sick to her stomach. She started pacing the room, her heart racing, there must be something she could do, surely?

*

Molly did her best to pull herself together. She searched the shelves for the bottle of gin she had left there. It was gone, the lad that Jolly had left here to take care of the grandma must have swiped it. Bloody hell, Molly swore. Then did so again when she realised that the tin containing money for food, had been emptied.

Pulling Margie's bed away from the wall, she prised up a loose floorboard. The crevice contained another tin, this time she was lucky; it contained the few bob that she and Margie had saved for a rainy day, or an emergency just like this.

As she rallied herself, Molly realised she had two choices; she waited here to meet her fate. Or to give herself at least half a chance of a future, she would have to run. Molly decided to go for the latter idea; guilt-ridden though it maybe.

Feeling the advent of her doom drawing near, Molly quickly changed into a plain wool dress. Grabbed a carpetbag and shoved all her belongings into it.

Heart pounding, palms sweaty. She donned her thickest coat, then picked up the bag and opened the door.

The tall figure of Jack Barrett blocked her path, he leant forward and grabbed her arm in a tight grip. 'And, where the ell do you think yer going?' he exclaimed, his voice hard.

Chapter 34

When Sophia finally awoke she was disorientated; she looked about the room, where was she?

Then she felt something nudge the hand that lay on the coverlet. She jerked her hand away; her gaze roamed the covers only to be confronted by a pair of brown, soulful eyes.

Wilson whined, wagged his stumpy tail, then nudged her hand once more.

Just for a moment, she had forgotten all the terrible things that had happened. But then she felt her stomach cramp painfully. The whip marks on her back burned. The flood of memories overtook her.

Abruptly, she pulled her hand away from the curious dog, as fat tears formed and rolled down the sides of her face, dampening her dark curls.

When a human form filled the doorway, Sophia's stomach flipped with fear and anxiety. Then she recognised the man who had examined her when she had been brought here.

'Ahh, you are awake,' Andrew Keene said as he walked over to the bed. 'And you,' he directed his comment to the dog, 'should not be in here, especially on the bed.'

Wilson gave the man such a beseeching look that Sophia found the edge of her mouth turned up in a smile once more.

Out of the corner of his eye, Andrew spotted the hesitant smile which filled him with hope: This girl was a survivor.

'Shall I leave him with you?' he asked.

Sophia nodded her head, then said, 'where is the man who brought me here?'

'That was Horacio Woodley,' Andrew explained, 'he is a good sort.'

Sophia nodded again. 'And Miss Molly?' she asked.

'She thought it best to leave, do you remember?'

Taking a moment to recollect, Sophia said, 'Yes, I blamed her for everything.' She wiped her damp face with the back of her hand. 'I know it's not entirely her fault.'

'Yes, well, I feel she may well have done more to put a stop to what happened.' Andrew's voice was bitter.

Gingerly, Sophia sat up. Andrew adjusted her pillows for her.

'We are all victims of circumstance,' she said softly.

'That is very philosophical of you, my dear girl, but what about the fact that she played a part in murdering your grandmother.'

'If it were not for that man, Jolly, none of this would have happened. He has tricked and manipulated my people.'

Andrew indicated the side of the bed, 'do you mind if I sit?'

'No, that is fine.' She studied the doctor as he sat down; he was tall and slim. Hazel-flecked eyes softened his angular features. There was something very reassuring and comforting about him.

Sitting down, Andrew reached out and scratched the dog behind the ears, Wilson chuffed. As the animal's presence seemed to calm Sophia, he said no more about the dog being on the bed.

'I fear that Jack Barrett is only a small cog in a much larger machine. Who are your people?' Andrew changed the subject.

When she got to the part about her, and her grandmother, being taken to Little Back Lane, meeting Molly and Margie, she then told Andrew about Evie and Dottie.

'That evil man is coercing Evie into marrying him. Yesterday morning, goodness was it such a short time ago? He came to collect them.' Her eyes misted with tears once again. 'I am not the only victim in this story.'

Andrew shook his head sadly, 'I don't know what to say, my dear. We must pray that they are safe. I should imagine that if this man, Jack Barrett, whom I have to say I have heard that name before, he arranges fights for Horacio if I am not mistaken, if he intends to marry your friend and to look after her sister, it won't be all bad for them, surely?'

'Mr Woodley knows this man?'

'Yes, sadly he does, as far as I know, the man is a lackey for the Silverman family.' Andrew shifted on the bed, making the springs creak, 'this is a part of Hero's life that

I don't particularly agree with.' Thoughtfully, he looked off into the distance for a moment. 'I am sure that he will tell you his story at some point.'

'I cannot imagine him fighting; he seems so kind.'

'Oh, he has a good heart,' Andrew jumped in, 'He's a good man by all accounts, the fighting, well ...' his voice trailed off. Giving her a gentle smile, he got to his feet. 'Time for you to get some rest now.'

But Sophia surprised him by shaking her head. 'Talking to you takes my mind off what has happened.' Her look was so beseeching that Andrew found himself sitting back down on the bed, his lips turning up in a smile.

*

Jolly pushed his way into the room. Molly retreated trying hard to disguise the horrified look that must be showing on her face.

'Taking a little trip, were we?' Jolly indicated the bag she was carrying.

'I'm taking a few bits to Margie,' Molly said quickly. Her heart was pounding. Her mind raced as she groped for a plausible story.

'Where's the girl?' Jack Barrett put his superior height to good use. He towered over her menacingly.

'She bled out, Jack. That man, a monster he was, used her badly. See what he did to my face.' She swept her hand over her cheek.' She swallowed, then met his frigid gaze. 'Aye, we left, I was going to take er to a doctor, but she collapsed in the street. I ad to leave er, couldn't carry er, could I. She'll be well and truly dead by now if not from blood loss, the exposure to the weather would do it.'

Jack mulled over what Molly had told him. He had been prepared to get some of the lads to go and collect the girl's body this morning from Silverman's place; it was pretty much inevitable to him that she would not survive a night with Beeching. But Molly should never have taken matters into her own hands, Silverman and Beeching were furious. And it had done nothing for his reputation.

'Where did you leave her?'

'We flagged down a milk cart coming into town, the bloke dropped us off, we managed to walk as far as the warehouses, I dunno where exactly, Jack, it were dark.'

Reaching out a long arm, he grabbed her. Pulling her against his body. The grip he had on her arm was like a vice, she winced. 'You've cost me bloody dear, Moll. Yer nearly killed that toff. He's baying for blood, he is.'

Her eyes watering through the pain, she said, 'He would ave killed er, Jack.'

His eyes narrowed. 'Why do you suddenly care so much; she's a stranger to you.'

Molly's gaze dropped from his. 'I know, I don't know what possessed me.' She shrugged. 'She was a good child, I suppose.'

Suddenly, he let go of her; she found herself slumping against the wooden table. His cold eyes raked her face searching for deceit. 'Since when ave you grown a eart, Molly. Yer know in this game there ain't no place for sentimentality.' He leant down so that his face was parallel with hers, Molly could smell the sour scent of his breath. 'Ere's the thing, Moll, me love, this toff wants to see someone punished – it should ave been you an the girl, but seeing as she's dead,' he snorted in derision, 'you are going to ave to take the brunt of it.'

Molly nodded; yes, she would take the brunt of the punishment meted out. She was so intertwined in his deceit. She would trade her life to keep Sophia safe.

'See,' Jolly continued, 'if I find out you've been lying about any of this, your life won't be worth living.'

She looked at him, meeting his gaze with one that was resigned to her fate, she said, 'so either way, it's the end of me, then.'

*

With a little encouragement, Sophia opened up and told Andrew about where she came from. As they chatted the more entranced Andrew became; she had been so strong and resourceful to manage to bring her grandmother, or Bubula as she called her, all this way.

'She was not well,' Sophia told him, 'Her mind wandered, and she would forget things so quickly.'

'Mm, I saw that happen in my paternal grandmother,' Andrew told her.

'I can't believe she's dead.' There was a catch in her voice; Andrew found himself reaching out and placing his hand over hers.

'I am so sorry this has happened to you,' he uttered bleakly. 'You and your grandmother came here looking for a new life and look at what has happened.'

She looked over to the window where the curtains were partially open. Sophia could see the snow-covered roofs of buildings. The sky was full of granite grey clouds.

Thinking of the loss of her parents, she said, 'sad things happen all the time.' She turned her gaze back to his. He has exceedingly kind eyes, she thought, a soft brown, a little like the dogs. With this observation, she found a half-smile touch her lips. Then she frowned. 'You examined me?' A blush was rising in her cheeks.

'Yes.' His answer was said cautiously, this was such a delicate subject.

'I was aware of some of it, but not all,' her voice was soft, 'the damage, I, umm, have pain.'

'There is damage, yes.' Andrew squeezed her hand, 'but you will heal.'

She nodded. 'Mmm, would it be possible to have some water to wash?'

'Yes, of course.' Andrew smiled, delighted that she should make such a request. He had never come across a situation like this before, but he somehow thought that any other young girl would be severely traumatised by what had happened, possibly in hysterics.

Andrew was deeply concerned about his charge, of course, but just talking to her for this short while he could tell that she had the most amazing strength of spirit. And, he had to admit to himself, that he found her to be beautiful; her face was heart-shaped, with an open expression, her lips were inclined to a smile. And those grey eyes of hers, why they were quite mesmerising. He could understand why someone would covet this young woman; with that thought, he felt a hot rage sour his stomach. Andrew was a gentle soul, not a person to be easily moved to anger, but what these people had done to this girl, they should be horse-whipped or worse.

Swallowing down his rage, he said, 'If you are alright to wait for a short while, I can set the bath up in front of the fire for you.'

'Yes, that would be wonderful, thank you, doctor.'

'Andrew,' he said, 'please call me Andrew.'

*

'So, what's going to appen now?' Molly sat at the table. She watched as Jack Barrett paced the room. It didn't take much to go from one side to the other; his stride was long - the room was small.

Stopping to look at her, he said, 'Ere's the thing, I can't leave you ere, I can't trust that you wouldn't try to scarper.'

'I wouldn't, Jack,' she implored.

He put his large hands down flat on the wooden table and leant towards her, 'You can't pull the wool over my eyes, Moll, I know you were making a run for it when I got here.' Her gaze dropped from his, he shook his head. 'I'm going to ave to take yer to one of the warehouses by the river; there's a room where I can keep yer locked up until I ear from Silverman.'

'Alright,' Molly got wearily to her feet, she was ready to accept her fate.

*

Andrew was concerned about how Sophia would manage to take a bath on her own, so he employed the services of their housekeeper, Mrs Gordon, a florid faced, plump woman with a kind heart.

He had to explain a little about what had happened to Sophia, to the housekeeper. The woman was bound to wonder what had been going on when she saw the marks and bruises, marring her body. He explained that Sophia was a friend who needed help. Mrs Gordon adored her two lodgers, Mr Keene and Mr Woodley, lovely lads they were.

If they had a friend in need of help, she would be only too happy to oblige.

Once the bath had been placed in front of the fire in Horacio's bedroom, Mrs Gordon then helped the girl out of her clothes and into the tub.

Mrs Gordon couldn't help but let out a shocked breath when she saw the marks on the girl's body, but she refrained from asking any questions.

The housekeeper aided Sophia in washing her hair, then gently cleansing her body.

Afterwards, Mrs Gordon helped Sophia to dry off, including towelling dry her thick curls. The housekeeper then adorned her in another of Hero's borrowed nightshirts.

'I'll pop out and buy you some clothes,' the woman said when Sophia was back in bed. 'Mr Keene explained that you didn't have time to bring anything with you.'

'Yes,' Sophia nodded, 'I had to escape quickly.'

The woman gave her a long look, her eyes which were an aged blue were still bright with curiosity. 'I don't know who did this to you, lass, but whoever it was, aww, they should be hanged.' She didn't wait for a reply. The woman bustled away, then before she opened the bedroom door, she added, 'I shall make you some chicken soup, dear, help you get your strength back.'

'Thank you,' Sophia nodded, but her eyes misted with tears, her Bubula always made chicken soup if anyone were poorly.

*

When Hero arrived back at the lodgings, he was delighted to find that Sophia was up. Dressed in a plain cream blouse and dark blue skirt, she was sitting at the table taking some soup.

He also noticed that there was some healthy colour in her cheeks, and her thick curls shone glossy in the lamplight.

Wilson had been sitting by her feet; he looked up when Hero walked in, wagged his tail but didn't leave the girl's side.

'Seems like you've been usurped, Horacio,' Andrew laughed when he witnessed the dogs lack of enthusiasm.

'Looks that way,' Hero raised a quizzical eyebrow as he took off his hat and gloves, then hung up his coat.

Sophia set her spoon aside and gave him a wary smile.

'Please don't stop eating on my account.' Hero took a seat. There was a soup tureen set in the middle of the table, along with a fresh loaf of bread. 'Smells good,' Hero inhaled with relish.

'Chicken soup, courtesy of Mrs Gordon,' Andrew explained as he pulled off another piece of bread and used it to mop up the residue of soup in his bowl.

'Good to see you up and about,' Hero addressed the girl, 'how are you feeling?'

She blushed. 'Mmm, alright. I feel better after the bath I had.'

'You had a bath?' Hero looked at Andrew.

'Again, Mrs Gordon was a gem, giving Sophia some help.'

'That's good.' Hero ladled up some soup into a bowl. 'I must tell you,' he glanced at Sophia, 'I went to Little

Back Lane to see if I could find out what happened to your grandmother.'

Sophia glanced up, as she did so she set her soup spoon down it rattled against the bowl. 'What did you find out?'

'I came across a woman who lodges in Little Back Lane, she told me there was a body brought out during the night, but she didn't know if it were a young person or old.'

Tears formed in Sophia's soulful eyes once again. 'That's it then, isn't it?'

'I am so sorry,' Hero said as the two men gave her sympathetic looks.

'Thank you.' Sophia offered him a gentle smile. 'I appreciate everything you have done.'

'You are welcome,' Hero gave her a kind smile in return.

Andrew wanted to know if Hero had spoken to Vanessa, but he didn't want to open up the topic of that conversation in earshot of Sophia.

As Hero tucked into the soup and bread, he told Sophia of his idea of taking her to his mother's.

'I think we should take you sooner rather than later, that's if you are up to travelling?'

'We should give her a couple more days, Horacio,' Andrew spoke up.

'What do you think, Sophia?' Hero pushed.

Her head bowed, she said, 'I, mm, think I would be alright to travel.'

'At least give her another night, man.' There was an edge to Andrew's voice.

'Yes, very well, one more night it is.' Hero agreed reluctantly. His instincts told him that the longer the girl spent in the city, the more danger she was in.

When they had finished lunch, Andrew insisted that Sophia go and lie down to have a rest. She did not argue the point, as quite suddenly she felt utterly exhausted.

Taking her shoes off but keeping her clothes on, Sophia lay atop the covers of Hero's bed, with a blanket over her. The little dog jumped up and snuggled down by her side. She smiled at the dog's devotion. He seemed to understand that she needed that bit of comfort.

Stroking Wilson's wiry coat, Sophia thought of her grandmother; she knew in her heart that the body that had been removed from the slum house was her Bubula; she was dead and gone. Sophia didn't know how she knew, but she did.

During the journey to London, her Bubula had become more and more disorientated. It was as if she had left herself behind in the mountains.

Guiltily, Sophia found that she had to admit to herself that she didn't know how she would have coped with the old woman's fragility. She had planned to find lodgings and some work, but she would not have been able to leave her grandmother alone. Sophia could have done as Evie and Dottie, and taken sewing in. When she thought of her friends, she felt sick to her stomach: where were they? Were they safe? Oh Lord, they were in Jack Barrett's clutches, of course, they weren't safe!

Jack Barrett was the person who was responsible for everything that had happened, Sophia decided. Yes, Molly had been the one to administer the laudanum to her grandmother. And, she had been the person to have drugged her. Accompanied her to that house, then handed her over to that, that *monster*. But Molly *had* tried to save her; did that absolve the whore her from what she had done?

Chapter 35

The room where Jack put Molly was dark and dank. It was in the eaves of one of the large warehouses. The air reeked of rot and decomposition.

There were holes in the roof; small piles of snow lay underneath them.

The air was frigid in this enormous place; Molly shivered violently, not just from the cold, but from the fallout of everything that had transpired over this short length of time.

'One of the lads will be outside the door,' Jolly said as Molly took in her surroundings.

She could see that other prisoners had been locked up in this place in the past: there was a truckle bed in the corner, covered in filthy blankets, a wooden chair, table, and a tin bucket, which she guessed was the privy. On the old, bleached table, half a tallow candle stood on a saucer, so at least she wouldn't be left totally in the dark. That was if someone should bother to light it for her, of course. Aww, this hellhole made the room in the Little Back Lane house feel like a bloody palace in comparison.

Even from this height, they could hear the busy sounds of the docks below.

'With any luck, yer won't be ere for long,' Jack commented as he walked over to the door, he held a large brass key in his hand.

'What do yer think's gonna appen to me, Jack?' she called, her voice desperate.

He paused and turned to look at her. In the dim light, she could not see his expression.

'That's gonna be up to the toffs.'

She nodded her head, then sat on the bed and wrapped her arms around her body.

He fished something out of his pocket, placing it on the table he said, 'Ere, keep the cold out for a bit.'

Molly could see it was a bottle. It looked like a half of gin.

'Eh, you're all eart, Jolly, all eart.'

He did not reply. When he stepped out of the door, closed it, and turned the key in the lock, Molly placed her head in her hands in despair.

'Get one of the other lads to relieve you tomorrow,' Jolly ordered Reg, who was assigned as Molly's jailer.

'I will, Mr Barrett.' The tall lad nodded.

'An, take her a light in when it gets dark.'

'Aye. What about giving er some grub?'

'Yes, yes, that's fine.' Jolly waved his hand nonchalantly as he walked down the narrow corridor.

Molly's "prison" wasn't the only room up there; there were a couple of offices and a storage area, all empty due to the state of the roof. The whole place was in a terrible state of disrepair. It was going to be demolished soon if it didn't fall down before then.

When Jack made his way down the creaking stairs, he mulled over what had happened; his gut was telling him that Molly wasn't being truthful about the Jewish girl's fate. Especially, as he had rounded up some of his boys and had them scour the streets; if the girl were lying dead somewhere on his turf, they would find her body, no one had. But at least Jack could report back to Silverman that Moll was under lock and key, then it was up to them what they wanted to do with her.

It was a bloody shame that he had to lose her, she had been one of his best girl's until Nell Winters turned up that was, but she was losing her looks; no amount of face paint could hide that fact, so maybe this was a good thing? Anyway, she had brought all this down on her head. Jack was sure he would find another girl to fill her shoes soon enough.

Now he had Molly secured; he decided to make a quick visit to his house, *his house*; he liked the sound of that. Check on his intended and her sister.

*

After breakfast, Evie sat with Dottie for a while, then decided to go and explore the house. When she discovered shelves lined with books in the sitting room, she found, despite her dire situation, to be delighted. She wondered if they had come with the house, or if Jolly had purchased them himself: although that thought seemed highly unlikely.

When she and Dottie had eaten a light lunch together, although Dottie barely touched her food, declaring herself too tired to eat, Evie took the tray back to the kitchen.

Then Evie returned to the sitting room and picked a book from the collection on the shelves. It was a copy of Ivanhoe by Walter Scott. She handled the book as if it were the greatest treasure. She, Dottie, and their mother used to read together of an evening. Mother encouraged them both so that they would improve their skills. But it had been such a long time since Evie had had the chance to read a book; aww, this was a real treat.

She took the book upstairs so she could sit and read to Dottie.

'Look what I've found,' Evie waved the book in the air as she walked into the bedroom.

Dottie tried to sit up as a smile wavered on her face. Evie quickly set the book aside so that she could aid her sister.

'I'm alright, Evie, no need to fuss.' Dottie brushed the helping hands away.

Stepping back, Evie retrieved the book, then pulled up a chair. As soon as Dottie looked more comfortable, Evie started to read.

Becoming lost in the story, Evie forgot where she was for a while. When she noticed that Dottie had fallen asleep, she continued reading to herself, making a note of the page number to carry on with the story, when Dottie woke up later on.

The opening and closing of the front door downstairs, along with the sound of voices, brought Evie back to reality with a jolt. She sat up straighter in the chair. Her stomach did a strange flip of apprehension. Setting the book aside, she stood, eyeing the door warily, she knew that Jack Barrett had arrived of course. She tried to swallow down her anxiety, but her throat had gone suddenly dry.

Her gaze darted to the figure in the bed, Dottie was still asleep.

What should she do, she wondered, go downstairs to see him, or wait until she was summoned?

Deciding it was best to take matters into her own hands, Evie strode across the rose-coloured Chinese carpet, opened the door then stepped out onto the landing.

Walking down the staircase, Evie saw melted snow puddled on the tiled hall floor. The invigorating scent of the sharp cold air reached her; she found herself longing to rush to the front door, open it and escape from her fate.

Before she knew it, Evie was flooded by the awful feeling of anxiety, expectation and responsibility that rested, weighty on her slim shoulders. It was the same feeling that she had experienced after her mother had died.

Three steps from the bottom of the staircase, she stood frozen, holding onto the bannisters so tightly her hand hurt.

'Aww, whatcha doing standing there?' Ivy appeared from the kitchen, eyeing her with curiosity.

Evie's nerves jumped. 'I ...' she didn't know what to say.

'Mr Barrett's ere, e's aving a cuppa in the kitchen.' Ivy told her.

Evie found herself nodding, then with her head held high, she completed her journey down the stairs, then made her way to the kitchen at the back of the house.

Jack stood up when Evie walked into the room. Their eyes met; she found that she could not hold his gaze; she was the first to look away.

'Ow's yer sister?' he asked as he sat back down.

'Exhausted,' Evie told him.

'She managed a bit of breakfast,' Mrs Perkins spoke up, she stood at the end of the table kneading a doughy mixture in a large bowl.

'Well, that's a good thing ain't it; shows she's on the mend.'

'Hopefully, yes.' Evie hovered by the door.

'There's a nice fire in the front room,' Mrs Perkins said, 'Why don't you two take advantage, I'll get Ivy to bring a tea tray through.'

'Aye, thank you, Mrs P.' Jack got up from the table.

Without a word, Evie turned and retraced her steps. She walked into the sitting room, Jolly right behind her.

When she entered the room, Evie did not sit but went to stand by one of the windows. The outlook was the snowy garden, which, she had to admit begrudgingly was quite enchanting.

'The banns will be read out starting this Sunday,' Jolly told her. Aware of his close presence, she did not turn around or answer him. When he placed a large hand on her shoulder, she flinched. 'See ere's the thing, you can make this as easy or as ard as you like, but I intend to marry you, Evie Winters, no matter what.'

Swinging around, she looked up at him, meeting his gaze boldly. 'Why me? Surely, you can find someone willing to marry a man like you.'

He made a guttural sound in the back of his throat. Leaning forward, he said; 'Aye, I could that, but see, I've set my eye on you, Missy.' He waved a hand to take in the room. 'See what I'm offering you, a life of comfort. You will want for nothing I can promise you that. And to cap it all, I will look after that sister of yours to boot.'

Evie dropped her gaze. 'I don't want to marry you,' she said softly, 'you understand that don't you?'

'Aye, I do that, you've made it clear. I could turn around and tell you that you have no choice in this, but you do, see. If you don't comply with what I am asking of you, you and yer sister can leave this ouse today.'

Evie shot a glance at him, 'Dottie is too ill.'

Jolly nodded, a brusque bob of the head. 'well then...?' He watched her intently.

Tears misted her eyes. 'Very well, I will marry you,' she said at last.

'There, that's the spirit.' He smiled, the scar on his face making it look more like a grimace. Reaching out a hand, he tucked a curl of hair behind her ear. Evie stood stock still, not realising she was holding her breath. 'I ain't a sentimental man,' Jolly carried on, 'but there is something about you that pulls on my eart.' He gave a harsh laugh. 'Aww, never thought I'd see the day when a girl would smite jolly Jack.' He stepped away from her then, Evie let out a breath of relief. 'You like this house?' Jolly asked.

'Mm, yes, it is pleasant.' A pleasant prison thought Evie.

'You can make any changes yer want, just say the word.'

They were interrupted by Ivy bringing in a tea tray. She set it down on a table beside two chairs near the fire.

'Go about yer business, Ivy, my intended can pour out the tea.' Jolly dismissed the girl, who shot Evie an interested look.

Evie, glad of something practical to do, did as Jack had said. When she handed him a delicate cup and saucer, it looked so out of place in his large, work-worn hands. Even though he was dressed quite smartly, he did not look as if he belonged in this pretty house at all.

When Jack sat down, Evie did the same. She sipped her tea glad of the liquid to ease her dry throat.

'Do you think we need to get Dr Travis in again?' Jolly asked her.

'I'm not sure there is anything more that he can do. I think it will just take time for her to recover.'

'Well, just let Mrs P know, she can send Ivy or Tommy out to fetch him.'

'Thank you.'

They sat in awkward silence. The only sounds were the hiss and crackle of the coal fire.

Eventually, Jolly drained his cup and set it back on the tray. Pulling out a silver fob-watch, he checked the time. 'I ad better be off, got things to do. I will pop back later in the week, see ow things are going.'

'Alright.' Evie did not move from the chair.

She sat there listening to Jack talking to Mrs Perkins. The sound of him gathering his outdoor attire, then, when the front door finally closed, Evie went to set her cup and saucer down, her hands were shaking so much, the china rattled.

*

'You are smitten with her!' Hero eyed his friend with amusement, which increased as Andrew blushed.

'She is incredible, Horacio, her strength and goodness are ...' he was lost for words.

They sat together beside the fire in their sitting room.

More heavy grey clouds had gathered over the city bringing with them an early twilight and more snow. Because of the dark afternoon, the lamps had been lit.

Hero nodded in understanding. 'She needs friends.'

'Yes, she does.' Andrew sat forward in his chair in anticipation. 'You saw Lady Beeching?'

'I did, this isn't the first time Beeching has done something like this.'

Andrew's face hardened, 'I can't believe it.'

'He assaulted one of their housemaids.'

'God, he is an evil man, the lowest of the low. There must be something we can do?'

'I don't know, Andrew. If Vanessa speaks out against her husband, he has threatened to have her locked up.'

'Eh, he is the one that should be locked up. It is an utter disgrace.'

'That is putting it mildly.'

'What with Beeching and that man Jack Barrett out there, it is a wonder that any woman, or man for that matter, is safe.' Andrew gave his friend a long look. 'I can't quite believe that you have allowed yourself to be connected with such people.'

Hero looked up to the ceiling in thought. 'He works for the Silverman's, Alec had him arrange the boxing matches.'

'Well, I hope you are going to sever your ties to them, especially now you can see what they are like.'

'That thought had already crossed my mind, Andrew. When I take Sophia to Brook House, I shall stay at Woodley Hall for a while. It will give me a good opportunity to distance myself.'

'Mmm,' Andrew nodded, 'that may be a good idea. One thing I must tell you, however, is that Sophia mentioned she has two friends who were truly kind to her when she arrived in London. They are sisters, Evie and Dottie Winters; Sophia told me that Jack Barrett is coercing the older girl, Evie, into marrying him.'

'Oh Lord, this gets worse by the moment.' He rubbed at his tired eyes, then met Andrew's gaze, 'Where are they, does she know?'

'No, she only knows that someone took them away in a carriage. That Barrett had found them a house to live in.'

Hero raised his eyebrows in surprise. 'A house? Well, that doesn't sound too bad, perhaps it is a good thing for these girls.'

'Really, Horacio, how can you say that, since when do you agree with young women being forced into marriage, especially with a ruffian like that.'

'Forced marriages, arranged marriages, they happen all the time, Andrew, look at Vanessa's situation for instance.'

Andrew lifted a hand in submission. 'Yes, very well. I get your point. But it will never sit comfortably with me.'

'You are an idealist, my friend.' Hero offered him a grim smile. 'This world, this city, you don't have to dig very deep to discover the dark truths and the filth.'

⋯⋯⋯⋯⋯

Chapter 36

Evie stood at the bedroom window watching the snowflakes falling; some were as large as doves fledgeling feathers. They rested on the glass then melted, leaving rivulets running down the panes.

Dottie was asleep, Evie could still hear her sister's strained breathing.

Closing her eyes wearily, Evie pressed a hand and her forehead to the icy glass. A tightness formed in her chest, she found it hard to draw a breath. Evie understood the anxiety. The feeling had never left her since their mother had died, *been murdered,* she corrected.

This house was going to be her prison, a life with Jolly Barrett as his wife, her nightmare; there was no means of escape. She was trapped. A sob issued forth; her tears matched the tracks of the melting snowflakes on the glass.

*

Through the gaps in the ceiling, Molly could see the day darkening. Heavy snowflakes drifted down and piled on the wooden floor.

Ever since Jolly had left, Molly was seated on the low bed, wrapped in the damp blankets against the chill. She was grateful that she still wore her woollen coat, but it was not enough. Her teeth chattered; her whole body was wracked by shivers that made her bones rattle.

The bottle of gin that Jack had left her was still on the table, untouched. It taunted her, she longed to take a deep swallow, but she knew once she had started, this time she would not stop.

Hearing a key turning in the lock, she looked to the door. The tall, lanky figure of Reg entered.

'Jack told me to light yer candle,' he said as he fished in his pocket for a box of matches. 'And, ere,' he waved something in the air then placed it on the table. 'a bite for yer.'

'M-m-much obliged.' Molly tried a smile without success.

She heard the striking of the match, a halo of light bloomed as Reg set it to the wick.

His features flickered as he looked over to Molly. 'So, whatcha do to end up ere then, Moll?'

'Jack not told you then?'

Shaking his head, he pulled a chair close to the bed and sat down opposite the woman.

'I nearly smashed a toff's ead in.'

She heard the youth draw in a sharp breath. 'What the ell for?'

Molly shrugged. 'You wouldn't understand.'

'Aww, no wonder Jack's pissed, Moll. Given im a lot of grief this as.'

'Huh, given im a lot of grief, ha, look at me locked up in this place.'

'What's he gonna do to yer?' The lad asked.

'That's going to be up to the bugger who ruined a girl's life.'

'The toff?'

'Aye, the toff.' Then something occurred to Molly. 'You picked up the two sisters didn't yer? Evie and Dot Winters from Little Back Lane.'

'Huh, I bloody did. They got me into right ot water they did. Scarpered off the trap I was driving. Took some searching to find em; they were in the work'ouse on Tanner Street.'

'Where are they now?' Molly asked, trying to keep her voice casual.

Reg dropped his gaze. 'Jolly told me not to say anything.'

'Why?'

He shrugged his thin shoulders. 'Ow the ell do I know, but if Jolly don't want me to say nuffink, I shan't.'

Molly nodded; she patted him on his bony knee. 'He's a lucky man to ave such loyalty.'

He looked up. 'Er, thanks.' If the light had been better, Molly would have noticed the blush infuse his cheeks. Reg nodded towards the truckle bed. 'Any chance of a quick one, Moll?'

'Bloody ell, Reg.' She got up and swiped him around the top of his head. 'Bloody cheek you ave, lad.'

'Well, you know, no harm in asking. It'll warm you up some.' He tried again, this time Molly laughed, then winced when she felt the pain from the cut on her cheek. She put her fingers to the wound.

'Did Jack do that?' he asked.

'No, it was the toff.'

Reg stood, then nodded towards the table. 'A slice of meat pie for yer, Moll, eat it before the rats do.'

'You ave it, Reg, I ain't ungry.'

He hesitated, nodded. Picked up the piece of pie and started to eat it as he walked to the door. Stepping back out onto the landing, he closed the door and locked it.

Molly picked up the bottle from the table, unscrewed the lid and took a long swig of the gin.

She had tried her best to save Sophia, which she had done, but not before the monster had inflicted damage upon that poor girl. Molly had seen a lot of violence in her life, directed at her and others. She was still a bit puzzled why she felt such a strong urge to save Sophia; perhaps it was because she could see the goodness in her. The young woman had been unsullied, in the London slums such innocence was rare.

Then there was Evie and Dottie; if Reg had told her where the girls were, she could have escaped, gone back to Mr Woodley, and told him. He might have been able to get them out from under Jolly's clutches.

She sat down heavily on one of the chairs, took another long swig of gin. Her gaze wandered to the ceiling. There were joists not far above her head.

She watched the snow falling through the gaps in the roof; the flakes turned from twilight silver to gold as they caught the light from the candle. It was cold enough in this room to allow them to form small drifts that did not melt.

Taking another drink, Molly put the bottle down, got up, walked over to the bed, and checked the filthy mattress which was made of ticking and filled with straw.

As she knew there would be, there were holes in the fabric, probably where vermin had eaten their way through it. She ripped the fabric into strips then tied the pieces together. She formed a noose at one end. Grabbed a chair then placed it under the joist. Once satisfied with the placement, Molly climbed up and threw the makeshift rope over the beam.

She thought about the toff, the monster and pervert. According to Jack, the man wanted to take his punishment out on her, and Sophia if he got hold of her. Molly wasn't entirely convinced that Jolly had believed her when she told him Sophia was dead; Molly was worried she would not be able to hold on to the duplicity, that she would let something slip that would put Sophia in danger once again.

Taking her fate into her own hands, Molly decided to deny the pervert the pleasure of torturing her. She placed the noose around her neck, then kicked the chair away. The noose tightened; her feet jerked as they hung in mid-air.

Reg had made himself as comfortable as he could in the office on the ground floor of the warehouse. A brazier had been set up, he reached his hands out to the hot coals and rubbed them together. He had to admit to himself that he felt a bit sorry for Molly; she had always treated him well enough. Assaulting a toff, eh! She was going to be in for big trouble over that.

Jolly had been angry with him when he had let the two girls run off; this vigil in this hellhole was part of his punishment.

Reg finished off the other portion of meat pie, then took a long swig from a bottle of beer.

Eh, it was going to be a long night, but at least he had a lamp and some heat; he would check on Molly again in the morning.

*

The following day, Sophia was feeling much better. She still felt sore, but the cramping and bleeding had subsided. The kind Dr Andrew administered some ointment to the wounds on her back, which helped to soothe them.

When Horacio told her, he would take her to stay with his mother the following day, Sophia found herself contending with mixed feelings: she discovered that she was enjoying the company of Andrew Keene.

The "would be" doctor, reminded her a little of Anders. Andrew was intelligent and caring. He had a gentle manner about him that Sophia found comforting.

He had told her that he was delighted with the way she was recovering from her ordeal. 'It would have traumatised anybody going through something like that,' he had said, 'you are quite remarkable, Miss Blum.'

She had gazed into the embers of the fire in the comfortable sitting room. 'I have been through so much, Dr Andrew, yes, I could choose to dwell on misfortune, but life is far too short. Besides, it also means that that awful man still has some influence over me.' She shook her head. 'I'm simply not having that.'

*

Whistling tunelessly, Reg climbed the creaking stairs to the rooms high up in the warehouse. When he reached the landing, he fished in his pocket and drew out the key.

He had spent a restless night in his cubbyhole, had managed to get a bit of sleep with his head resting on his chest, but this had given him a very stiff neck. He stretched his neck first one way then the other as he placed the key in the lock.

Grey light sifted through the numerous gaps in the ceiling. In the dim light, Reg thought that Molly was laying on the bed.

'Wakey, wakey, Molly,' he called to her. As if in answer, the beams creaked drawing Reg's gaze. He saw something, a shadowy figure hanging from one of the joists. Then he spotted the overturned chair.

'Aww, no. Molly.'

He rushed over to the body, grabbed the chair, set it upright, then climbed up. In his other pocket, he always carried a penknife, he grabbed it and started working on the fabric.

Molly's body swung back and forth. Reg didn't need to examine it closely to know she was dead. A chill radiated from the form that was far colder than the winter's day.

*

Later in the day, Andrew and Sophia sat at the dining table playing chess. Hero had gone out to visit the livery stables to see Hades, his hunter, and to ensure that there were a coach and driver available to take himself and Sophia to Gloucestershire the following day. Wilson had decided to accompany his master on his jaunt.

Sophia and Andrew were so engrossed in their game that they didn't hear the ringing of the front doorbell downstairs.

Mrs Gordon, who lived on the lower floor, answered the summons.

'Good afternoon, Mrs Gordon, is Mr Woodley in?'

'Ah, Mr Silverman, I'm not sure, but Mr Keene is at home.'

'Good.' Alec removed his hat as he entered the house. He wore a long black woollen coat with the fur collar turned up. In the other hand, he carried an ebony cane with a silver top.

After he had divested himself of hat, coat and gloves, Mrs Gordon said, 'I'll show you up, sir.'

Alec followed the woman up the stairs. She tapped on the door of the flat, then opened it.

'Mr Alec Silverman to see Mr Woodley,' she announced, standing aside so that Alec could enter.

In his haste to stand up, Andrew knocked over some of the chess pieces. Sophia also stood, she turned to the man by the door. He looked young but older than herself. He was dressed smartly. His dark hair slicked back from a high forehead.

'Ah, Alec.' Andrew strode over to the visitor. 'Didn't expect to see you today.'

'Well, I'm here to see Horacio, where is he?'

'Mm, he's gone to check on his horse at the stables.'

Alec nodded his head, then turned to Sophia. His gaze raked her from head to toe. 'And, who is this?'

Andrew suddenly had a lump of fear in his throat; he swallowed it down.

'This is Sarah, my cousin.' He gestured for the surprised Sophia to step forward. She shot Andrew a curious look as she did so.

'This, my dear, is Alec Silverman, one of Horacio's friends.'

Sophia felt her skin bristle with apprehension as Andrew uttered the stranger's name. Hearing it the second time, she remembered he was connected to the person who owned the big house where she and Molly were taken.

'Ah, I didn't know you had a cousin, Andrew.' Hand outstretched, Alec stepped forward. Sophia had no other option other than to take the offered hand. Alec brought hers to his cold lips and kissed it. 'Very delighted to meet you, Sarah.'

'Mmm, yes and you.'

Sophia felt her stomach drop when the man noticed the bruising on her wrist. His curious eyes flickered to her face as she snatched her hand out of his grip.

Alec gave her a strange look as he straightened. 'Are you visiting for long?' he asked.

'No, she's leaving tomorrow,' Andrew spoke up.

'That is such a shame.' Alec held her gaze, 'it would have been delightful to have gotten to know you better.'

'Are you going to wait for Hero?' Andrew asked.

'Yes, of course.' Alec walked over to one of the armchairs beside the fire and sat down as if he owned the place.

Andrew shot Sophia a troubled look. 'I shall ring for some tea then.' He pulled the bellpull to summon the housekeeper.

'Do come and sit, Sarah.' Alec gestured to the chair opposite. 'Tell me more about yourself.'

'Mm, actually, she was just about to take a nap, weren't you, dear?' Andrew gave Sophia a pointed look, then he turned to Alec, 'She's not been well, she requires rest and recuperation.'

Alec got to his feet once more. 'Oh, I am sorry to hear that.' He gave her a thin smile.

'Yes, I do feel rather tired and have a slight headache.' She put a hand to her forehead.

'All the more reason for you to get some rest then.' Andrew ushered her towards the bedroom.

'She is sleeping in Hero's room?' Alec observed.

'Yes, Hero has very kindly given up his room; he is sleeping on the sofa.'

'Huh, typical, Hero by name and by nature.' Alec retorted, a bitter note to his voice.

'He is a kind man,' Sophia found herself speaking up.

Shooting her a strange look, Alec said, 'He is, to his detriment at times.'

'Yes, well.' Andrew almost pushed Sophia through the door; once she was out of sight, he pulled the door closed.

'What is wrong with her?' Alec sat back down.

'Umm, she is recovering from pneumonia,' Andrew said the first thing that popped into his head.

'Really? It seems rather strange to come to stay in a place where the air is so filthy, when one is trying to recover from an illness such as that.'

'Yes, well, as I said, she is leaving for the country tomorrow.'

'Where does she come from?' Alec asked. 'She is quite intriguing and is extraordinarily beautiful.'

Andrew could feel his face redden as he tried to think up a plausible story. 'Mmm,'

He was saved from answering when Mrs Gordon pushed open the door; she was carrying a tray with two pots and cups and saucers; she had anticipated Andrew's request.

'I've brought up tea and coffee,' she said as she lay the tray down on the table. 'As I know you prefer coffee, Mr Silverman. There is also some of my fruitcake for you.'

'Thank you, Mrs G, you are a star.' Alec smiled.

Puzzled, the housekeeper gazed about the room, 'where is Sophia?' she asked.

'Ahh, you mean Sarah.' Andrew laughed. The laughter held a desperate edge to it. Mrs Gordon shot him a surprised look when Andrew placed his arm around her shoulders and ushered her from the room. Pulling the door closed, he looked over to Alec, who was eyeing him curiously.

'Sophia?'

'Mrs G is getting a bit forgetful in her later years.' Andrew walked over to the table and poured out a cup of coffee. 'Have you tasted her cake, it's rather good.'

*

'Yer bloody idiot,' Jack Barrett raged at Reg. 'Yer should ave kept a closer eye on her.' He paced the room where Molly's body lay on the floor covered by an old blanket.

'Sorry, Jack, I didn't know she'd do something like this, did I!'

Ahh, the lad was right. Jack was just as surprised, shocked actually, that Moll would do such a thing. He had thought she was made of sterner stuff.

'What shall I do with the body?' Reg asked.

'Leave it there for now; I shall ave to get someone to dispose of it.'

'What about the rats?'

'Well, if they ave a field day, there will be less of a body to deal with.' Jolly strode from the room, leaving Reg with his mouth agape in horror.

*

Walking back from the livery stables, Hero spotted the carriage waiting at the curb outside their lodgings. He knew straight away that it was Alec's carriage, and he recognised Collins sitting on the box. Hero's heart sped up as he picked up his pace.

He acknowledged the coachman with a brisk nod of the head. Oh Lord, I should have anticipated this, he thought as he ran up the steps to the front door. Andrew was a terrible liar: he was as honest as the day was long. And, how would Sophia react to meeting another Silverman?

Pulling open the front door, he took the stairs two at a time. Wilson, who was close on his heels, picked up his master's tension.

Hero paused on the landing to compose himself, then opened the door. Sweeping the room in a hurried glance, he spotted Alec seated by the fire, Andrew was pouring out some beverage, coffee by the aroma of it. There was no sign of Sophia.

'Ah, there you are, Horacio.' Alec got up to greet his friend. As he did so, the little dog growled.

'Hush, Wilson,' Hero admonished, the animal sat down obediently as Hero strode across the room to greet his friend. 'Alec, I must say I am surprised to see you, I thought you would be sleeping off the exploits of your night-time antics.'

Alec laughed. 'Well, I had an interesting time that was for sure.'

'I have just introduced Alec to my cousin Sarah,' Andrew spoke up pointedly as he handed the visitor a cup of coffee.

Hero, catching on quickly asked, 'Ahh, yes, where is she?'

'Having a lay down, she needs her rest as you know.'

'It is a shame that she has been ill,' Alec commented, 'If I had known that old Keene here had such an attractive cousin, I would have badgered him to invite her for a visit before now.'

'Yes, well, she's leaving tomorrow,' Hero commented as he poured himself a cup of coffee.

Alec raised an eyebrow, 'yes, so everyone keeps telling me. Are you sure that is wise, the roads out of the city are treacherous at the moment.'

'Well, we shall give it a go.' Hero sat down by the fire. Wilson curled up by his feet.

'We?' Alec asked in surprise as he too sat down.

Hero took a sip of the aromatic brew to compose himself – he realised he had almost slipped up. 'Yes, I'm leaving for home, I will escort Miss Keene part of the way until our journeys divide.'

'Always so thoughtful, Hero.' Alec studied his friend for a long moment, making Hero feel uncomfortable. 'What time did you leave father's gathering?'

'Oh, it must have been between two and three in the morning. Why do you ask?'

Alec shrugged his thin shoulders. 'There was an incident involving one of father's business associates.'

'Really, it must have happened after I had left. What sort of incident?'

'Well, you know that father is biting at the bit to get George Beeching to give him support for the new rail line that will run from the Eastend of town.'

'Yes, I have heard rumours.'

Alec sat forward in his chair with a conspiratorial air. 'Father arranged some enticement to sweeten the deal, but it all went terribly wrong, one of Barrett's whores knocked Beeching for six.'

'Is he alright?' Andrew spoke up from where he was seated on the overstuffed sofa.

'Ha, he's got a hard head,' Alec gestured extravagantly, 'but he is outraged as you can imagine. It seems that good old papa will have to make up some ground.'

'In what way?' Hero asked, trying to keep his voice neutral.

Alec sat back in the chair once again, his eyes narrowed. 'You are close to Beeching's wife, aren't you?'

Hero shifted restlessly in the chair. 'Vanessa and I are friends, yes.'

'Humph, yes, of course, you are. Has she ever mentioned her husband's rather specific, mmm, acquired tastes he has where women are concerned?'

There was an edge to Hero's voice as he answered, 'It is not a subject we discuss, no.'

'Well, the details will shock you, that is for sure.' Alec's gaze was penetrating as he studied Hero. 'Although why he would want to go elsewhere when he has a perfectly beautiful wife at home.' Alec mused as Hero waited for him to elaborate further, but he did not; instead, he drained his coffee cup and set it aside, then got up. 'I really must be going.' He consulted his gold fob watch, then looked at Hero. 'How long will you be at the Hall?'

'I'm not sure.'

'Don't forget you have a match arranged at the Crown in a couple of weeks.'

'Cancel it will you,' Hero said as he too got to his feet.

Alec clenched his jaw as a flush of annoyance coloured his pale cheeks. 'I shall do no such thing. Remember, it is not just your reputation on the line, but mine too. Don't let me down.'

Hero shrugged. 'I am getting rather tired of the fighting. I suggest you start looking for somebody else to sponsor.'

Eyes sparking with anger, jaw clenched even tighter, Alec said, 'After all I have done for you, Horacio, you can't let me down now.'

'I am grateful, Alec, but surely you must have realised that I would be giving up the boxing at some point.'

Alec took a step towards him, Wilson, picking up on the uneasy atmosphere in the room, growled in the back of his throat.

'Oh, shut up you ridiculous mongrel.' Alec drew his foot back as if he were going to kick the dog. Hero's arm shot out; he grabbed Alec's arm in a hard grip.

'You were leaving.' Hero propelled him towards the door.

'Alright, alright.' Alec tried to shrug off his grip. 'I am going.'

Chapter 37

C ollins was sitting on the driver's seat of the carriage waiting for Alec Silverman to appear. Even though he was wearing gloves, his hands felt numb with the cold, he cupped them together and blew on them.

One of the two carriage horses shifted restlessly, the harnesses jingled.

The coach driver spotted Mr Woodley walking up the street along with his little dog. He acknowledged the man, raising the whip and tapping his cap. Horacio nodded in return.

Collins could tell, by the other man's clouded expression, that Mr Woodley did not look pleased to have this particular visitor.

Mr Woodley ran up the steps, his dog at his heels, then disappeared into the tall terrace house.

When he had returned to the Silverman residence in the early hours of the morning, Collins had picked up on the tension issuing from Mr Cobbs and Franks.

From what he had been told, something had happened to Lord Beeching. He had been attacked by one of the *ladies of the night* who had been attending the evening of entertainment. Did it also have something to do with Mr Woodley leaving the party in the company of the two ladies? Collins surmised.

Collins was surprised when the front door opened soon after Mr Woodley had entered, Master Alec appeared. His face was soured with fury. Uh oh, this didn't bode well.

The groom jumped down from his perch to open the door of the carriage for his young master.

'Take me to the club,' Alec demanded as he climbed into the plush vehicle.

'Aye, sir.'

Alec sat back in his seat and peered out of the window moodily. He was not used to anyone saying "no" to him; bloody Horacio Woodley, what the hell was he thinking?

And there was also something very fishy about this cousin of Andrew Keene's.

Alec liked to know what was going on around him (something he had picked up from his father; knowledge held power) When Hero had insisted on moving into lodge with Andrew, Alec had tried to glean more information about the trainee doctor. Although remembering things he had learnt about Keene, when they and been at Aldersmiths together, he was fairly sure that Andrew was an only child, having no aunts or uncles.

His father was some yokel doctor in the back of beyond, somewhere in the west country. And quite frankly there was little else of interest about the man. So, where on earth had this *Cousin* Sarah come from? When he had kissed her hand, Alec had also noticed the bruising on the young woman's wrist; what was that all about?

His thoughts turned back to Hero once more; he was already furious with Horacio, about moving into lodgings with Keene rather than stay at the townhouse with Alec. Now he had to contend with Hero's sudden disinterest in boxing. Of course, that could be down to the influence of Andrew; perhaps he was turning Hero against him. It wasn't just about his reputation, but Alec could feel his friend slipping away from him: slipping away from under his influence. He did not like that one bit.

*

'Goodness, I don't think my heart can take much more drama,' Andrew remarked when Alec had left.

'Yes, quite.' Hero agreed.

They both looked over to the bedroom door as it opened. Sophia appeared her expression wary.

'Silverman,' she said, 'that was the name of the man who owned the house where I was taken?'

'Yes,' Hero nodded, 'that was Alexander Silverman's son, Alec.'

'He is your friend?'

Horacio ran his fingers through his thick wavy hair, his expression grim. 'He was.'

'He saw the bruising on my wrist.' Sophia rubbed at her right wrist as if she were trying to erase the tell-tale signs of the abuse.

'It'll be fine.' Andrew stepped towards her. 'We can feed him some story or other if he asks any questions.'

'I'm not sure he will be that easily deceived,' Hero commented as he poured himself a brandy from a decanter on the sideboard.

As if sensing Sophia's disquiet, Wilson came and sat at her feet. She knelt and stroked the dog's head.

'I think we might be alright for travelling tomorrow,' Hero said. He shot both of his companions an enquiring look. 'That's if you feel up to it, Sophia.'

She nodded tentatively in reply.

'Good.' Hero knocked back the brandy then sat down on one of the chairs by the fire. 'I've hired us a carriage to get to Brook House. I will have Bryant or Charlie come and pick Hades up for me.'

'All sorted then,' Andrew said, sitting down at the table. He glanced at Sophia, 'we had better finish this game then,' he gestured to the chess set. 'Just need to remember where the pieces were that I knocked over.'

'Oh, I'm very sure I was winning.' Sophia found herself jesting, Andrew laughed. The atmosphere in the room lifted.

'Mmm, not sure about that, young lady.' They exchanged a smile. Hero, noticing the exchange rolled his eyes; Oh dear, it looked as if Andrew had fallen for the girl. He studied her for a moment. She was pretty for sure. A head of lustrous dark curls, large grey eyes, fringed with thick lashes. Her complexion was creamy, although there were shadows under her eyes. Her cheekbones were prominent; however, she needed rest and good food.

Hero also worried that she seemed to have gotten over her abuse far too quickly. It was remarkable how she had bounced back, was that possible? He wondered, or was it a result of delayed shock? Of course, Andrew would know more about that. Hero just hoped that neither of them would have their hearts broken.

*

Alexander Silverman sat on the leather chair behind the large desk. His elbows were resting on the surface as he leant forward, his face flushed with anger.

'What do you mean the whore hung herself!?' Alexander glanced at the man with the scar in distaste.

'Aye, one of the boys found er. It was too late to do anything.'

'This isn't on, Barrett. I've got Beeching hectoring me for some sort of revenge for what happened. He's also being awkward, forestalling this deal we were going to come to. Bloody man, can't see a good thing, even when it is blatantly in front of him.'

'I could get one of the lads to take care of im, Mr Silverman, point im in the right direction, if you get my gist.' Barrett spoke up.

'Risky,' Mr Hill interrupted. The large man had vacated his usual seat for Mr Silverman. He was sitting on one of the chairs in front of the desk.

Nonchalantly, Barrett leaned against the wall. His tall and menacing presence made the other two men uncomfortable.

'Everything worth having means taking a risk.' Silverman shrugged his broad shoulders.

'Yer not wrong there,' Jack said.

'If Mr Silverman wants your opinion, he will ask for it,' Mr Hill said acerbically.

Barrett gritted his teeth in anger, then went back to picking at his fingernails with his penknife.

Silverman got up from behind the desk, he walked over to one of the grimy windows and looked out onto the busy street below.

'It's no good; we need to appease the man; otherwise, I shall lose him completely, that will get us nowhere. We need to find him another girl,' he said thoughtfully, turning back to view the room, he gave Jack a long look. 'You must have some other girl that would fit the bill; young, innocent, pretty?' he sighed, 'Although, I have to say that the girl you did provide, Barrett, was incredibly beautiful.'

'I'll have the lads do a scout around,' Jack said.

'Yes, very good, but make sure she is special and innocent,' Silverman said. 'and don't take too long about it, I need a girl found in due haste.'

Understanding that he had been dismissed. Jack nodded, 'Right then.' He headed off.

As he went down the stairs, Jack swallowed down his contempt for the rich fish Silverman, how he wished he could completely be his own man, rich enough to be giving the orders, not taking them.

One day, Jack, just bide yer time, he told himself as he walked through the reception area, then into the street.

Walking away from the office, Jolly pondered the predicament of finding another girl for Beeching. There were no arrivals expected at the docks, at least not for a couple of months, the weather was too bad to make any crossing viable.

He decided to ask Margie if she had any ideas. He would also have to tell her that Molly was dead, he thought, as he joined the throng of people out on the windswept streets.

Jolly found Margie sitting forlornly at the table in the room that she shared with Molly. The fire had smouldered to nothing' The place felt damp and chill. The tall man didn't knock but sauntered in. Margie didn't look up as he entered.

'She's done a runner, aint she.' It wasn't a question. Margie gestured widely about the room. 'All er clothes ave gone. An the bitch took all of our savings with er.'

Jolly eyed the whore, by God, she looked rough. He pondered on what to tell the woman.

Margie was surprised when the rent collector pulled out one of the chairs and sat down opposite her.

'I ope yer not expecting a cuppa.' Margie eyed him with reddened, tired eyes. 'We aint got anything in.'

'Molly's dead, Marg, she hung erself.'

'What?' Margie rubbed at her eyes with a rough-skinned hand. 'Ow?'

'Let's just say that things didn't go to plan for er at the Silverman place.'

Margie shook her head in denial. She couldn't quite believe what she was hearing. Looking Jolly in the eye, she said, 'what the ell appened?

'She clouted a toff over the ead with a poker, then scarpered.'

'Oh, good lord.' As if she could brush off the awful news, Margie bowed her head and rubbed at her face vigorously.

'I found er ere gathering er stuff; she were going to do a runner.'

She eyed him with cold speculation then. 'What did you do with er, Jack?'

Jolly sat back in the chair. 'I ad to take er into hand after all that. Also, the toff was looking for revenge.'

'So, you were going to hand her over to im then.' Her eyes narrowed. 'Moll wouldn't give im the satisfaction, so she took her own life.'

'You've caught on quick, Marg.'

She leant forward in the chair. 'What of the girl, Jack, what appened to her and that grandmother of hers?'

'We dealt with the grandmother. She was reaching the end of er days anyow.' He pushed the chair back; the legs scraped on the floor. Standing up, he said, 'As for the girl, that's another story, Marg. But I ave a job for yer to do. I need a girl, young, pretty, and untouched. Spread the word, will yer.'

Her face blanched of colour, she nodded. She didn't want to think about what had happened to the Jewish girl. She could put two and two together, however. The child was probably dead now; twas no good crying over spilt milk.

Jolly fished in his pocket and threw a leather bag on the table. 'Yer savings, with a little extra for yer trouble.'

'Not like you to be so magnanimous.' Margie reached over and plucked the bag off the wooden surface.

'Aye, well I'm getting married in a month, it's put me in a good mood.' 'Who to?' She asked, but she had already heard the gossip. It was always difficult to keep anything a secret in this place.

'Evie Winters.' He rubbed his hands together as he strolled about the room. 'I've set er and er sister up in a nice ouse in Bow.'

'Well, aint that lovely,' her voice dripped with sarcasm, which Jolly decided to ignore.

'Aye,' he puffed out his chest. 'See the thing is, Jolly Barrett is going up in the world, Marg. An Evie Winters is coming along for the journey.'

*

The following day when Sophia and Hero left for Brook House, Andrew had tried to hide his misgivings; not so much about her health because she was a remarkable young woman who had rallied so well, but because he would be parted from her. He was quite taken by surprise with the depth of feelings he had for her.

Shyly, he had found himself asking if she would mind if he wrote to her. Sophia had smiled and nodded her head.

'That would be delightful,' she had agreed.

Andrew, realising that he had been holding her hands for far longer than was necessary, blushed, then reluctantly let go.

Mrs Gordon had been busy on Sophia's behalf; she had been nominated to buy the girl a good pair of boots, a warm coat, scarf, gloves, and bonnet. Sophia, however, had been distressed when she had learnt that Hero had paid for everything.

'I'm never going to be able to pay you back,' she had entreated.

'I do not expect you to,' Hero had forestalled her, 'besides, Andrew would never forgive me if I let you catch a chill after everything that has happened.'

'Thank you.' She had nodded, 'but I do insist, I will find a way to reimburse you.'

Hero guessed that any argument on his part would be deflected; his reply was a nod of the head.

Mrs Gordon came to see Sophia off. Much to the young girl's surprise, the housekeeper enveloped her in a fierce hug. Sophia felt tears spring to her eyes as they drew apart.

The older woman placed her hands on either side of Sophia's face. 'Now,' she said, 'I am mighty sorry for what has happened to you since you arrived in London.' Her eyes blazed in earnest. 'Those that did this to you, child, will get their comeuppance, you mark my words.'

Sophia brushed a tear aside as the woman let her go. 'Yes,' the reply was choked with emotion.

'You couldn't be in better hands than with Mr Keene and Mr Woodley,' the housekeeper said.

'I know.' They exchanged smiles.

Mrs Gordon had packed a basket of food for them and had provided thick woollen blankets to go over their knees.

The day was grey, the sky heavy with slated clouds, the cover of which had sent the temperature rising. The snow was now slush, mixed with mud, lining the roads and pavements. It looked as if all the colour had been drained from the busy streets which were grimy and dishevelled.

Both Andrew and Mrs Gordon stood on the pavement to wave them off as Sophia, Hero and Wilson boarded the hired carriage.

'How are you feeling?' Hero asked his companion as the carriage driver negotiated the busy streets.

Sophia, sitting opposite with Wilson beside her on the seat, gazed out of the window soaking up all the different things to see. At Hero's question, she turned her attention back to him.

'Well enough, thank you.'

'Andrew is correct, you know. 'Hero smiled, 'you are truly remarkable to have recovered so well.'

Her gaze dropped as she petted the dog with a gloved hand. 'I - I don't know what I shall do if I see that man again.'

The smile slipped from Hero's face; his expression became serious. 'You will be safe at Brook House. The chances of you running into Beeching is extremely remote.'

'Beeching!? Is that the name of my attacker?'

Hero silently reprimanded himself. 'Of course she didn't have a clue who he was, why would she. It was Hero's turn to glance out of the window.

'Yes, that is his name.'

She nodded, but Hero had noticed the shadow of fear that darkened her expression.

The city was left behind as the countryside spread out before them. There were some breaks in the cloud cover; a pale blue sky peeked through here and there.

The trees were bereft of leaves. The fields were more mud than green grass.

The further away from London they travelled, the more Sophia felt her spirits lift. She could understand this place, the passing of the seasons, the natural rhythm of life. The hills rolled gently, not like the peaks of the mountains from whence she came, but she felt that familiarity. It was comforting.

'You see those chimneys there.' Hero pointed out. They had been travelling for a while, stopping off for a short break to stretch their legs just before driving through Oxford.

Sophia followed his direction. 'Oh, yes.'

'That is Woodley Hall. We need to follow this road around then down into the dip, and we shall arrive at Brook House.'

Sensing the fact that their journey was coming to an end, Wilson got to his feet, climbed up onto Sophia's lap, then put his paws up on the narrow windowsill. His stumpy tail wagged so frantically it made Sophia laugh.

'He's glad to be back,' Sophia declared.

'He certainly is.' Hero laughed.

Sophia found that Brook House was a pleasant structure nestled in a crook of land at the bottom of the hill. The brook, which the residence was named after, flowed through the extensive gardens, then disappeared into the dense woodland.

'Oh, it is so pretty,' Sophia said as the carriage drew to a halt.

'Yes, I suppose it is.' Hero lifted the blankets off their knees and folded them, leaving them on the seat.

As soon as the door open, Wilson dived out. He sniffed around frantically, then cocked his leg and peed.

Someone from the house must have seen them arrive as the dark oak door opened. Emily and Claire appeared at the top of the steps.

Mable, Emily's little spaniel, greeted Wilson with a chuffing sound, they danced around each other joyfully.

'Mother, Claire.' Hero handed Sophia down the carriage steps. 'This is Sophia Blum.'

'Welcome, Sophia.' Emily stepped forward and embraced the girl warmly.

Hero had already written to them to tell them some of Sophia's story. Both of the ladies were expecting a traumatised child, not this young woman who held herself with such dignity; they were both pleasantly surprised.

When it was Hero's turn to greet his mother, he was taken aback by how much she had aged. Her hair showed swathes of grey. There were wrinkles around her eyes which he had never noticed before. Her stature seemed smaller. He realised with a jolt that his mother looked fragile. Everything that had happened had taken a toll on her.

'What a sweet dog,' He heard Sophia comment as she and his mother walked up the steps and into the house.

'Hero found her for me, a Christmas present some three years ago.'

'Is mama well?' Hero asked Claire in a soft voice as they followed the two up the steps.

'She insists that she is, Horacio, but I know she has been struggling at times.'

'Has Dr Scott taken a look at her?'

'Oh, yes. Several times, in fact.'

'His findings?'

'Neither of them would say.'

Hero's jaw clenched. He would have to speak to the doctor himself to find out what was going on.

Emily had a small sitting-room which also served as an office, where the old breakfast-room used to be. There was a pleasant aspect looking out over the gardens towards the wood beyond.

Tea was taken along with Mrs Adam's fruit cake. Claire had taken it upon herself to serve everyone.

'Horacio has mentioned you used to help out at the village school where you lived,' Emily commented to Sophia as she sipped her tea.

'Yes, that is correct. If I had stayed on, I would have helped Anders, mmm, Mr Segal to run the school.'

'That is wonderful,' declared Claire as she sat down on one of the sofas. 'I am sure we can put your experience to good use here, while you stay with us.'

'Oh yes,' Sophia nodded with enthusiasm her face brightening. 'I would love that. I also owe so much to Mr Woodley. It would be lovely to give something back.'

'Good, that is settled then.' Claire smiled. 'After you have freshened up, I shall show you around the school.'

Chapter 38

That evening, Emily, Claire, Horacio, and Sophia, were joined by Seth. They had a cosy evening meal around the table in Emily's sitting room at Brook House.

'I usually dine with the girls,' Emily explained. She handed around a china dish of vegetables, they accompanied the fragrant steak and kidney pie Mrs Adams had cooked for them. 'But I thought for your first night here, Sophia, that it would be pleasant to have a family meal.'

'Yes, this is so lovely, thank you.' Sophia smiled gratefully.

As promised, earlier that day, Claire had shown her around the school.

'There are twelve students present at the moment,' Claire had told Sophia, 'but four will be leaving after Christmas: they have all found placements in respectable households,' Claire said proudly, as they wandered around the library. 'Emily is set on expanding. She is hoping to remodel the stables and outbuildings into a school and accommodation for younger girls.'

'Oh, that is marvellous,' Sophia exclaimed as she took in all the shelves filled with books.

Desks had also been set up along with a chalkboard at the head of the room. The room had been brightened, painted the colour of buttercream above the wooden panelling, which had been polished to a high shine as had the parquet floor.

The scent of beeswax Mollish mixed with that of a vase of cream hothouse roses which stood on a small side table. At the other end of the room, a large Chinese rug had been placed on the floor. The rug matched the curtains of soft green and cream, draping the windows. This area was set apart, an area where the girls could come and sit and read quietly. Large, comfortable wingback chairs sat in clusters around small tables.

When she got to the end of the shelving, Sophia turned to her companion. 'I saw much poverty on the streets of London, the children ...' her voice cracked with emotion.

'Yes,' Claire nodded. 'We visit workhouses looking for girls who wish to better themselves, then offer them a place here. Sadly, there are so many; we can only help a few.'

'A few is better than none.'

'Yes,' Claire smiled. 'You are quite right. Tomorrow, you will meet some of the teachers. We help the girls to learn how to read and write. I, myself, teach them how to sew. Emily shares her abilities regarding mathematics.'

'It seems you have so much covered.' Sophia stood by one of the windows, gazing out to the garden which was devoid of much growth at this time of the year, but she could imagine it would be beautiful in the spring and summer.

'Yes, we try.' Claire came to stand beside the girl. 'Mrs Mason, the housekeeper from Woodley Hall, aids the girls with learning how a large household is run. And Janice, who is one of the housemaids from the hall, teaches them the duties of a housemaid and ladies' maid.' Claire laughed, 'it seems we have commandeered all of Horacio's staff. Even Mrs Adams has taken up residence here. She teaches the girls how to cook and how to run a kitchen. She is what I would call a country cook; her fare is simple but delicious. Her pastry melts in the mouth.'

'Will they not be going back to the Hall now Mr Woodley has returned?' Sophia asked.

'Yes, they have already moved back. Apart from Mrs Adams that is; she either sends meals to the hall, or Horacio will eat with us here while he is at home that is. He rarely stays longer than a couple of weeks, which is sad; we all miss him.'

Sophia nodded thoughtfully. 'Yes, you must do.' She wondered why Mr Woodley spent such little time at home.

'So,' Claire interrupted Sophia's introspection, 'What do you think of the place?'

'It is quite splendid.' Sophia glanced at the older woman. 'I would be happy to help out wherever I can.'

Claire smiled with approval. 'I had a feeling you would say that, Sophia. I think that you will fit in well here.'

'Thank you.' Sophia's gaze returned to the garden. 'My friend Evie, and her sister Dottie would love it here also.' Her voice was brittle with emotion. 'Evie's mother was a wonderful seamstress, and she has taught Evie well. She is such a kind person. She looks after her younger sister so caringly.'

'Where are they now?' Claire asked as she sat down in a wingback chair beside the fire. 'I presume they are still in London?'

'Yes,' Sophia answered as she too sat down opposite the older woman. She found herself wringing her hands together in agitation. 'Evie is being forced into marrying a man called Jack Barrett.'

'Jack Barrett? I am sure that I have heard that name.'

Sophia's cheeks took on a reddened hue. How much should she divulge about this man that Mr Woodley was embroiled with? The man who arranged bloodthirsty fights and the downfall of young women, like herself, at the hands of terrible men. She dropped her gaze.

Sophia did not doubt that Mr Woodley had a good heart, but it suddenly occurred to her that he must have a dark side, too. Surely, he would not be caught up with the likes of Jack Barrett otherwise. But then there was Andrew Keene, Sophia felt her heart speed up when she thought of him. He was such a gentle person; he would not befriend someone with an evil streak, would he?

Noticing the young woman's distress, Claire interrupted the flow of Sophia's thoughts.

'This has something to do with what happened to you, doesn't it?' She asked gently.

Sophia would not look at her companion, but she nodded. Claire reached out and squeezed her hand gently.

'I cannot imagine what you have been through,' she said. 'but the nightmare is over now.'

Sophia raised her head then and looked Claire in the eye; her own were swimming with tears.

'For me, yes,' her voice cracked. 'But what of Evie and Dottie. We must do something to help them.'

*

As the thaw settled in, Evie was finding her heart turning to shards of ice. The only way she could handle her situation was to withdraw into herself.

Both she and Jack Barrett had attended services at the small local church to have the banns read. The date of the wedding was set for the middle of January.

She was very aware that they made a strange couple. Jack was so tall, with the awful scar on his cheek. He dressed in clothes that were a little too colourful and flashy to be fitting for a Sunday church service. Evie, in comparison, had taken to wearing dark colours. Her cheeks were pale, her eyes haunted.

The only positive thing that had happened was that Dottie had responded well to the shelter and good food they received. She was gaining strength by the day.

Evie refused to talk about their predicament with her sister; Dottie knew she was unhappy, who wouldn't be under these circumstances. After a while, Dottie cottoned on, so she also avoided the subject. They both went about their day as if this was the most normal situation in the world.

*

'Is she ill?' Hero sat back in his chair. He nursed a glass of good claret. The shimmering candlelight sparkled, ruby in the liquid.

Doctor Scott lay down his knife and fork, wiped his lips with a napkin as he met Horacio's gaze.

The two men were eating dinner in the breakfast room at Woodley Hall. Hero had invited the good doctor to dine with him, mainly to find out what was going on with his mother's health.

Mrs Adams had sent the food over with Bryant, a succulent joint of roast beef served with vegetables and horseradish sauce. Janice served at the table.

Hero felt as if he were rattling around in the large house, but he knew that he had to get used to living here again.

He had decided to open up the library, his father's study, which he had claimed as his own, and the breakfast room, rather than eating in the formal dining room. His old bedroom had been aired, but aside from that, the rest of the house remained shrouded under ghostly dust sheets that gave the place an empty air of neglect. Horacio was so aware of this; he couldn't help remembering when the house was full of love and laughter.

Dr Scott shook his head. 'You need not worry, Horacio, there isn't a physical reason for how she is feeling,' he explained. 'Yes, we have all noticed the change in her. If I were to diagnose anything, it would be a malaise of the heart.' He raised his hand to forestall any question, he explained further. 'It is grief by all accounts.'

Hero took a swig of his drink, then set the glass aside. 'Grief? After all these years?'

The doctor shrugged, 'Some people, like your mama, who feel things so deeply take far longer to recover from these things.'

The younger man nodded his head. 'Don't I know it.'

'Are you still getting the troubling dreams?' Dr Scott asked.

Hero shifted in his chair uncomfortably. 'Not as often as I was. I can understand, I suppose what mother is going through.' He wiped a hand over his face. The Doctor noticed how tired he looked but said nothing. 'At times, what happened that day still feels so – so, vivid - the horror of it all. I still feel responsible,' he confessed. 'It is killing me once again to see mother suffer so. I'm not sure I can stay here.'

Dr Scott sat forward in his chair; a flinty look entered his usually kind eyes. 'You can't keep running away, Horacio, it does no good for either you or your mother.'

'Is that what you think I am doing, running away?'

'Yes, exactly that. And, as for all those boxing matches -' He paused for a moment in thought. 'Don't you think you have punished yourself enough?'

Hero picked up his glass and drained it. Reaching out, he picked up the wine bottle and poured himself another drink. Raising the bottle, he looked at the doctor enquiringly. Dr Scott shook his head.

'Well?' the older man was not going to let Hero off the hook.

'Yes, yes, you are right, of course.' He gestured to the pretty room. 'It's just I don't feel that I belong here anymore – this is no home without Angel and father.'

'Angelica, if she were still here, would probably have been married and living with her husband by now,' the doctor pointed out.

'Yes.' He dropped his gaze. 'I robbed her of all that.'

'Enough, boy,' the doctor injected his voice with reproach. 'It is time for you to stand up and be the man your father wanted you to be. Emily needs you too, more than you know.'

'Now, you sound like Grandfather.'

'Well, I have to admit that I agree with him on these points.'

'Yes, yes, Doctor, I know you are correct.' Hero gave the man an earnest look. 'I fully intend to stay around for a while at least.'

'Well, that is better than nothing.' He picked up his knife and fork and finished off the roast beef on his plate.

Hero called Wilson, who was asleep in a basket by the fire. The dog got up languidly, stretched, then trotted over to his master. Hero gave the little dog some of his beef, which was wolfed down, lips licked in delight.

Dr Scott waved his knife in the air. 'You had better not let Mrs Adams see you feeding her delightful food to the dog.'

'Ahh, she wouldn't mind, she is fond of Wilson.' Hero petted the dog, who sat down and watched him beseechingly hoping for another treat.

*

When he lay in bed that night, Horacio thought about what the doctor had said. Of course, the man was thoroughly correct in his assessment of the situation. Hero knew he was punishing himself, running away from the grief-filled rooms of Woodley Hall. Not to mention facing his mother's sadness which was so evident in her eyes.

As he stared up at the canopy above his bed, he felt his stomach squirm as if he had swallowed live eels. The feeling made him want to retch. Hero was distracted from his thoughts as Wilson, who was laying on the bed next to him, started to yip in his sleep. The little dog's legs twitched as if he were running.

Ahh, at least you still have sweet dreams, boy. Hero stroked the dog's wiry fur. The interaction with the animal calmed him. At last, he found his eyelids drooping in sleep.

*

Sophia could scarcely believe where she had ended up. Brook House and the surrounding countryside was so beautiful. She found Mrs Woodley, who had instructed her to call her Emily, and Claire to be kind and knowledgeable ladies.

The other girls currently attending the school were mainly from the poorer and underprivileged parts of London and Oxford. All of them, for one reason or another, had ended up in the workhouse.

Claire and Emily would visit the establishments and interview some of the girls. A few, despite their dire circumstances, didn't want to leave the cities, the place they called home. But many others recognised that Emily and Claire were offering them a way out of the drudgery: a better life and they were happy to embrace it.

'It takes time for some of the girls to settle in.' Claire told Sophia as they wandered around the slumbering winter garden. 'Coming here, it is like a different world to them, one that they have never seen before.'

'Yes, I understand.' Sophia nodded. Despite the dark-blue woollen coat with it's white fur collar, she shivered. 'One could not be further removed from the city slums.' Her breath misted with the cold as she spoke.

'Very true. We always give newcomers time to find their feet. The changes can be overwhelming, so we ask that the girls who have been here for a while, take the new girls under their wing. Helping them to settle in.'

'Oh yes, that is so wise,' Sophia agreed. 'I remember doing the same such thing when new children started at the village school.'

Claire nodded as she showed Sophia the stables and outbuildings which were going to be converted into a school for younger children.

There was only one stall occupied, which was home to the pony that pulled the trap.

'Charlie, the groom from Woodley Hall, comes down every day to look after Meg here.' Claire stroked the horse's velvety nose. Then produced an apple from her pocket which the pony plucked from her palm with a gentle mouth.

As they walked on, Claire asked, 'How do you find your roommate?'

Sophia was sharing a bedroom on the first floor with a girl called Beth Young. She was down to earth and plainly spoken. With a pleasant, rounded face framed by a mop of thick blonde hair. Despite facing abuse at the hands of her stepfather, her blue eyes still twinkled with good humour.

'She is pleasant,' Sophia said, 'She tells me she has been here for six months.'

'That is correct,' Claire said as they skirted the woods.

'She, mmm, told me that her stepfather did some terrible things to her.'

Claire glanced at her companion. 'Yes, he did.' She shook her head sadly, 'there is so much evil in this world.'

Sophia paused on the brick path, which was slick underfoot. 'She also said that she lost a child when she entered the workhouse.'

Claire nodded. 'Sadly, that is true.'

'Are all the girls here like Beth?' Like me – She wanted to add but didn't.

'Some more broken than others, my dear. Beth is a strong girl; she has settled in very well. She loves cooking, Mrs Adams is delighted with her enthusiasm.' Claire linked her arm through that of the young woman. 'We encourage everyone to look forward rather than back. It is by far the best way.'

*

Horacio had Charlie travel up to London to pick up Hades. Both Hero and Wilson were happy to greet the hunter upon his return at Woodley Hall.

The horse whickered loudly as soon as he saw his master and the little dog.

'He's pleased to see you,' Charlie laughed as he rubbed him down in the stable yard.

'Yes, he is.' Hero smiled as the hunter nuzzled his pocket for treats.

When Hades greeted Wilson, he sniffed at the little dog so deeply that both Hero and Charlie were amazed that Hade's did not inhale the dog completely.

Hero had to admit to himself that he felt more settled with the hunter in the stables. He took to riding out early every morning, reacquainting himself with the estate and occupants.

He reassured Mr Durham that the estate manager's job was still his, that Hero would be working alongside him, at least for the foreseeable future.

There was a part of Hero that was reluctant to let the man go. He was annoyed with himself for admitting that he still required an avenue of escape, and knowing he could leave Durham in charge, was some comfort.

After his evening with Dr Scott, Hero made more effort to spend time with his mother, although he was surprised to find out that this wasn't so easy, she always seemed to be busy during the day with that school of hers.

'Don't come here during the day, my darling,' Emily said as they took afternoon tea in her sitting room, she had a rare afternoon free.

'Why ever not?' He looked at his mother in surprise.

She shook her head and smiled as she sat down by the fire. Mable and Wilson were asleep on the hearthrug.

'You really have no idea of the effect you have on young ladies, Hero.'

He took a sip of his tea. 'What on earth do you mean, mother?'

She cocked an eyebrow at him. 'You have nearly every single one of my girls walking around in a rosy cloud. I do believe they have all fallen in love with you.'

Blushing, Hero laughed. 'What nonsense you come up with, mama.'

Busying herself with cutting a piece of Mrs Adam's Victoria sponge cake, Emily asked. 'Is there anyone special in your life, Horacio?'

'With that question, I presume you mean am I courting?' He took the proffered plate, took a large bite of the buttery cake, then sat back in the chair.

As he brushed crumbs away, he thought about Vanessa for a moment; lord how he missed her. He was also worried about her, being left alone with that monster, Beeching.

Sighing, he replied at last, 'There is no one.'

Perhaps we could have a new year's ball up at the hall. The Jenkin's girl Rosaline is a darling. I think you would like her.'

'I remember, Rosaline; The last time I saw her; she was covered in spots. I think she had measles.'

'It was chickenpox, actually. She has grown into a beauty and has a kind nature.'

Taking a sip of his tea, he placed the cup and saucer down on the side table. 'No, mama, absolutely no matchmaking, promise me.'

All he got in reply was a shrug. Hero rolled his eyes in consternation.

Chapter 39

Margie couldn't quite believe that Jolly was finally getting married. Aww, there would be some broken hearts about the place for sure. There had been several girls who had set their sights on wooing him.

Margie set about her task of finding a young girl for him to present to the toff, who Molly had attacked. As luck would have it, it hadn't taken long to find a suitable girl.

A family around the corner had been thrown out of their lodgings after the father, who had worked at the butcher's, had had a nasty accident. Now, he was unable to work, which meant that his wife and children were struggling.

The family were going to petition the parish to be admitted to the workhouse. Upon hearing this news, Margie forestalled the wife and had offered to give Katie, the eldest girl, a home, and work.

Margie had a good eye for picking girls with the potential to work for Jack: The daughter, who was fourteen, as skinny as they come, with a face full of sores, particularly around her mouth. Matted hair, probably riddled with lice and bitten fingernails, Margie could see beyond these afflictions, however. She knew that she could feed the girl up and have her looking as pretty as a picture in a few weeks.

If the child had been put on the street to work as a prostitute – she would also have been working for Jack, so Margie would have known about it. She was pretty sure the girl was a virgin.

Her mother was only too pleased to hand the child over with the promise from Margie that her daughter would have work and a roof over her head, even if it meant working on the streets. The mother turned a blind eye to the fact she would be a prostitute, which was the lesser of two evils. At least, this way, her eldest girl had a chance for a bit of a life.

'What the ell, Marg!' When he was presented with Margie's offering. Jolly took off his smart bowler hat and ran his fingers through his unruly hair in consternation. 'Yer scraping the bottom of the barrel aintcha.'

The girl, whose name was Katie Arnold, stood to one side. Cheeks, which were now a great deal cleaner, blushed with mortification upon hearing Jolly's harsh words. Her hair, which had been down to her waist in greasy and dirty tendrils, had been cut, so it came to her shoulders.

Margie had bathed her. Then had combed her hair until it shone in coppery waves. She had procured a salve for the girl's sores, so her skin was clearing up nicely.

'Ave faith in me, Jack. When ave I ever let you down?'

'Yes, yes, alright.' He placed his long fingers under the girl's chin then tilted it up so he could see her better. She had dark brown eyes which at that moment, flashed with fear and uncertainty.

Katy had reasonable bone structure and full lips, which held a promise of sensuality. Her body, however, was skinny, her bones jarringly sharp.

Tilting her face one way then the other, he said, 'Aye, I suppose I can see some potential.'

Margie let out a breath in relief. 'Give me a couple of weeks to feed er up, Jack. An for the sores to heal, she'll be a beauty for sure.'

*

Christmas arrived. Emily and Claire had organised a huge Christmas lunch.

All the girls staying at the school helped with the preparations and attended the festive occasion.

Bryant and his wife Louise, along with Charlie, who was still single joined in. Seth was there, as were Hero and Dr Scott, who would have been on his own, as he had never married.

As everybody leant a hand, Mrs Adams, Mrs Mason, and Janice could join in with the celebration.

Sophia found that she enjoyed the day. If she had still lived at home, however, this would have been a day like any other.

Later that night, she lit eight candles for Hanukkah. As she did so, she remembered Anders and her grandmother. Tears dripped down her cheeks as she said prayers for them. Then for Evie and Dottie.

How she wished she could go and find her friends and bring them here. She was sure that Emily and Claire would welcome them. A thought occurred to her; perhaps she could go and find them herself! Although, the idea of placing herself in the vicinity of Jack Barrett once again made her shudder. But she would risk the danger to find her friends.

She could not help but remember that Horacio had associations with Barrett. She resolved to ask him about the man; perhaps he would help her in her quest to find Evie. She knew that Little Back Lane was near the river and the docks in the East End of London. The river was long, and the East End was vast, however. Would she be able to track them down?

Sophia had been delighted when she had received two letters from Andrew Keene – he said he was well and working hard in his training. Sophia wrote back and told him all about the school and the people. She said that she would be thoroughly content if it had not been for missing him, and her disquiet regarding her friends.

When she had found herself explaining how much she missed Andrew, her depth of feeling surprised her and concerned her at the same time. She had only known him for a brief moment. He had seen her during one of the worst time she had ever experienced in her life.

He had treated her with such care and compassion. And, despite everything, he still wished to be her friend, to get to know her better.

Her emotions were in turmoil. There was a logical part of her that understood that some men, once they found out what had happened to her, would see her as *spoilt goods*, they would run for the hills. She had to face the possibility that she may never marry and have children; this thought saddened her deeply.

She had loved Anders and had envisaged a future working alongside him at the school. Living a simple but contented life. With the possibility of them marrying one day; it had been a bright and safe future until the clearings had started and the nightmare of leaving her home began.

Looking back, she saw herself as a naïve young girl; in the last few months, she had had to face adulthood and all the cruel realities of the world.

Her future at present was murky; would she stay at the school and become a spinster? Or would she find love with someone like Andrew?

*

Evie Winters married Jack Barrett on a rain-sodden day in the middle of January. Dottie made an excuse not to attend the service by saying that the damp weather was causing her chest to tighten. She and Evie both knew that the reality was her younger sister could not stand to see Evie giving herself away to that awful man.

Tommy was quite delighted when he was told to stay at the house to keep an eye on Dottie, while Mrs Perkins and Ivy joined Evie and Jack at the church.

Tommy was finding that he was attracted to the girl, Dottie. It seemed like a silly notion to him, but he felt that the room brightened every time she walked in.

The two of them sat in the library sitting room by the fire drinking hot chocolate that Dottie had made. She was reading him a story about a man that had been swallowed by a whale. It was a cosy setting.

Tommy watched the girl. Her head bowed as she read the novel. Her hair, which was held back from her face by a peach-coloured ribbon, was as golden as honey. Soft tendrils escaped, to brush her cheeks, which had rounded out, thanks to the good food and shelter Jack had provided.

It wasn't for the first time that Tommy found himself sending up a prayer of thanks – not that he was a particularly religious person, but he recognised the gifts he had been presented with, not just for him, but for Ivy as well. Mrs Perkins, although strict, was a kindly lady. They had a roof over their heads and good food to eat. Lord, Tommy thought as Dottie turned the page, this was what heaven could be like.

'I wish I could learn to read as you do,' he piped up when Dottie finished another chapter.

She looked at him and smiled. The firelight was reflected in his ginger hair, making him seem like a cheeky angel or imp.

'Didn't you go to school, Tommy?' she asked.

'Na,' he shrugged his shoulders. 'Ad to help Da bring in the money.'

Suddenly Dottie's smile widened. 'I could teach you to read if you like.'

'Really?' He gave her a look filled with hope and longing.

She nodded her head with enthusiasm. 'Yes, why not.'

'Could you teach Ivy too?' he asked.

'If I'm helping one of you, then why not both,' she agreed with alacrity.

With a note of caution, he said, 'Better run it past Mrs P first.'

'I think she would be agreeable as long as I don't keep you from your jobs around the place.'

'Aye, I'd promise her that.'

The two beamed at each other. For the first time in an awfully long time, Dottie felt butterflies of excitement alight in her tummy. She had a purpose now.

Dottie was also growing fond of Tommy, giving him reading lessons meant that she could spend more time with him. In turn, he always found something to make her laugh, to lift her spirits. She was grateful for that, particularly with everything that was happening with Evie; the two of them had been through so much, they had both had to toughen their hearts against the world.

It didn't matter how much her sister tried to hide it from her, Dottie knew how depressed Evie was.

Dottie, on the other hand, was thriving, almost back to full health. Mrs Perkins was kind to them. And she liked Tommy and Ivy. She felt that she was part of a family once again. It saddened her that Evie had been forced down the path of marrying someone like Jack Barrett. Dottie found herself torn; she felt guilty for finding some contentment when her sister was going through hell.

As Ivy could not read or write, Mrs Perkins and the curate of the church witnessed the marriage.

The circumstances Evie found herself in, had instinctively caused her to lock away her heart. Along with her fragile emotions, she simply could not think about what was happening, for if she were to dwell on her situation too deeply; facing the dark future that had been presented to her, she was scared of what she may do.

Standing beside Jolly Jack Barrett at the altar, Evie presented herself as a shell of who she had once been; she had no appetite over the last few weeks, so she had lost weight. The violet bruises under her eyes announced to the world that she had not been sleeping well.

Dressed in a cream dress decorated with dusky pink roses with soft green leaves, she looked enchanting, with a beauty that was fragile, even ethereal.

Mrs Perkins had not said anything to Jack, but despite everything, there was concern about the girl in her charge. Yes, she received wages from Mr Barrett, and he had done a good deed for her, saving her son. The housekeeper owed him loyalty, but she was not a cold-hearted woman.

When Mrs Perkins had accepted the offered role, working for Jack Barrett, little had been said about the circumstances; the story of the two motherless girls, that Jack had taken a shine to the older one. After that, enough had been said to fill in any gaps.

Mrs Perkins had expected them to be troublemakers, to want to bolt with any chance they got. However, noting how close the sisters were, their love for each other was evident every day, she soon came to realise they were good girls.

As the day of the marriage drew near and the housekeeper had witnessed Evie's decline, which saddened her, but she had to keep reminding herself that life could have been a lot harder for these two. She suspected that Dottie, with her fragile health, would not have survived long with a life of poverty. And, if Dottie had died, lord only knew what would have happened to Evie then!

When she had been instructed to prepare the marriage bed, Mrs Perkins could not deny the fact that she felt a leaden weight in her heart regarding the young woman. She sincerely hoped that Jack would be kind to her. Perhaps, if Evie found herself expecting a child soon, that would settle her heart, give her something to focus on apart from her sister; Mrs Perkins took comfort in those thoughts.

*

After the ceremony, the four returned to the house where cold cuts and salads had been laid out for the wedding breakfast.

As soon as they stepped into the front hall, Evie quickly made an excuse to go and check on Dottie.

She found her sister in the bedroom they had once shared; which Dottie would have all to herself now. Evie's heart stuttered with the thought.

'Are you alright, Evie?' Her sister, who had been sitting by the window reading a book, stood up.

Evie's heart stuttered when she saw her sister's concerned face. She tried a smile as she walked over and took Dottie in her arms.

'I shall be fine,' the words were uttered without much conviction. Drawing away, Evie gave her sister a long look.

'I need to face the wedding breakfast, Dot. Come downstairs with me. If you are there, it will help.'

Dottie's shone with understanding. 'Yes, of course.'

Jolly was in a jovial mood as he dug into the food with a hearty appetite, drinking tankards of ale to wash it down.

'You've put on a fine spread Mrs P.' Patting his stomach with satisfaction as he sat back in his chair, which had been placed at the head of the table.

'I'm glad you approve.' The housekeeper beamed, although she had noticed that neither Evie nor Dottie had eaten very much.

'I do indeed.' Looking over at Evie who was seated to his right, he offered her a lopsided grin. 'What think you, Mrs Barrett?'

'Very nice, thank you.' Evie tried an unsuccessful smile. If Jack noticed anything amiss in her reticence, he did not say.

After another half hour had passed, Evie stood, excusing herself from the table so that she could go and get changed. Dottie joined her.

'They are good girls,' Mrs Perkins remarked to Jack as she and Ivy started to clear the table.

'Aye, I've hit on a winner there.' Jolly swallowed down the rest of his ale.

'Mmm –, 'The housekeeper hovered with a tray of used crockery in her hands.

Jolly eyed her, 'Go on, it's obvious you've got something to say, spit it out.'

'Well, I know that it's not my place to say anything, Mr Barrett, but it stands out a mile that neither of those girls has ever been with a man before.'

'I wouldn't ave married er if she were spoilt goods,' he stated bluntly.

Mrs Perkins nodded in understanding. 'I know you've got a kind heart, Mr Barrett,' she decided to appeal to his magnanimous side. 'look at what you did for my boy. I shall be eternally grateful to you.'

He raised a hand to stop her. 'Yer asking me to go easy on the girl, aren't you?' Pleased he had cottoned on, she nodded in relief. 'Ave no fear, Mrs Perkins, I shall treat her as if she were the most fragile creature on this earth.'

Worried that Jack might come looking for her, Evie changed quickly into a navy-blue day dress with trim piping of cream at the collar and cuffs. The dress buttoned up to the neck and was rather austere.

When she arrived back in the dining room, Jack stood up and eyed her.

'Yer look like a school ma'am in that getup.'

Evie found herself flushing. There was an awkward silence.

Jack sat back down. 'Ere,' he held out a large hand to her. Even though his touch made her skin crawl, she felt as if she had no option other than to take it.

She was doubly mortified when he had her sit on his lap. Placing one of his calloused hands against her cheek, he had her turn her head to look at him.

The next thing she knew, his lips were on hers. His breath tasted of sour beer. Evie worried she was going to throw up the little she had eaten, but she managed to weather the intimacy.

'There, that wasn't so bad was it?' he asked as he withdrew. She shook her head, trying desperately not to cry. 'Yer know I saved you from Miller. He would ave raped you; you know that dontcha?'

'Yes,' her voice was soft.

'So, ere's the thing; I'm not an unfeeling man, Evie. You may think me eart is black as a coal pit, and yes, I've ad to do terrible things to survive.' He placed her hand against his cheek, over his scar. 'Me own father did this to me, I ad to grow up quick, I ad to be as ard as nails.'

He looked her in the eye. 'I know yer think I'm responsible for yer ma's death, and yes, I do feel some of the blame. Yer ma was a decent woman; the East End was no place for her or you an Dottie. It's the devil's lair for sure.'

His expression flickered as his thoughts turned to the dark place, then his attention rested upon her once again.

'You may not see me as yer rescuer, but that is what I am, girl, remember that.' He freed her hand; she dropped it into her lap. Jack gave an astonished laugh. 'I ave to say, I never thought I'd find the girl to win me eart, yet ere you are, Mrs Barrett. So, you meet me alfway, alright?'

'Alright.' She nodded. Inside she could feel the portcullis dropping to protect her heart. An icy cold washed through her. 'Alright,' she said again.

*

Jolly left the Bowe house in the early hours of the morning. He pondered his wedding night as he walked through the freezing damp of foggy streets. He had done his best to win Evie over; been gentle with her, well as much as he could be when his passion was inflamed.

Aww, she was a beautiful woman, delicate in many ways, but strong in others. He had hoped that she would respond to him, but she had lain there like a cold fish. He felt in his pocket and pulled out the tin in which he kept his smokes. Pausing for a moment, he set a match to the cigarette and inhaled deeply.

The streets were beginning to awaken, a coal wagon and a milk wagon trundled past him. He continued with a long stride. He supposed he had to put the unresponsiveness down to her inexperience. Lord knew he had slept with several women, all eager to share his bed, and some had the wish of sharing his life, but he had chosen Evie Winters to be his wife. She should be grateful; after all, he was giving her the world, wasn't he?

However, as he crossed the street heading towards the docks, Jolly tried to ignore the feelings of the dissatisfaction of an unreciprocated passion.

*

Evie pretended to be asleep when Jolly got up while it was still dark. She heard the grandfather clock in the hall chime four times. She was aware of him getting dressed then the floorboards creak; the bedroom door opened, then closed.

It was a little while longer before she heard the front door bang shut. She let out a breath, then buried her head in the feather pillow as she wept. Huge, wracking sobs escaped her. She did her best not to make any noise. However, she was so caught up in her misery that she didn't hear the door open. The span of light creeping across the room caught her attention. She thought for an awful moment that Jolly had come back.

'Evie?' The sound of Dottie's soft voice reached her.

Evie sat up. There was nothing she could do to hide the tears from her sister. She used a corner of the sheet to dry her cheeks.

'Oh, Evie.' Dottie ran to her.

Placing the lamp she had been carrying on the bedside table, Dottie took her sister in her arms.

It was too much for Evie, as a dam of tears burst once again.

'Hush now, hush.' Dottie whispered. 'I'm sorry, so sorry.'

Upon hearing these words, Evie drew away, looking Dottie in the eye. 'You have nothing to be sorry for, Dot. None of this is your fault.'

'But it is.' Dottie brushed her tears away with the sleeve of her nightgown.

'No, I'll not have you blaming yourself again. We've spoken about this before, no more blame on your shoulders.'

Dottie nodded, but her eyes were bleak. 'Where's he gone; do you know?'

'No idea.' Evie sat up in the bed. As she did so, she felt the stickiness between her legs. The feeling made her cheeks flamed with mortification.

'Dottie, I need to clean myself up. Pour some water into the washbowl would you, then go down to the kitchen and make a pot of tea for us both. My throat is so dry.'

Dottie hesitated for a moment. 'Alright.' She got up and poured water into the pretty china bowl.

Once her sister had left the room, Evie pulled back the sheets; Oh lord, they were stained with blood – her blood. The discovery sent her stomach reeling; she tried not to retch.

Thinking of Dottie, she got out of bed, then pulled the covers back over the sheets.

Stripping off her nightgown, which was also stained with blood, she threw it on the smouldering fire which took the offering with eager flames.

Quickly, she sponged off the blood and stickiness between her legs as best she could. Pulling on a clean nightgown, she then shrugged into her dressing-gown.

A few moments later, Dottie pushed open the door; she was carrying a small tray upon which was a china tea service.

'Thank you, Dottie, that's wonderful.' Evie took the tray from her and laid it down on a round table by the window.

Evie was grateful when she poured out the tea for them both, to find her hands were steady.

*

Katie Arnold slept in the bed that used to be Molly's in Little Back Lane. She listened to Margie snoring in the other bed behind the curtain. The woman had come back in the early hours of the morning, then fell into bed.

Katie shoved aside the covers and got up. The coal fire needed stoking, so she did that and set a kettle on the iron hob.

Lifting her nightdress, she did a pee in the china pot which needed emptying. Katie sniffed, she bet the old hag would want her to take it out to the privy.

Huh, as time had gone on, Margie had become more and more belligerent and resentful towards her; always scolding her for one thing or another.

It wasn't her fault that she had been staying here longer than expected. Then there were the times when Marge hit the gin; she would become tearful, moaning about her lost friend, Molly. Katie knew the two had shared this room; she had seen them together many a time.

Katie wondered what had happened to the other woman. Mmm, it must have been something awful, judging by some of the mutterings that she could make sense of.

Then there were the visits from Mr Barrett. She had strained her ears to overhear some of their conversations. She quickly gathered that she was being groomed for an important person.

Stripping out of her nightdress, she had a quick wash then pulled on her slip, bloomers, and wool dress, which was a reddish-brown. It was plain, with buttons up the front, but Katie felt as if it were the best dress in the world.

Picking up a brush, she luxuriated in the process of brushing her locks, which, now they were cut shorter, naturally sprang into pretty corkscrew curls.

Regular food had filled out her body. She was still slim, but not overly so. She couldn't help noticing some of the admiring glances she was getting from some of the lads hereabouts, but both Margie and Mr Barrett, had warned her, and them, to keep well away.

Katie made herself a mug of tea, then cut a thick slice of yesterday's bread, spreading it liberally with butter and jam. She sat at the table and chewed her way through her breakfast. Katy knew that her ma would say she had fallen on her feet here; coal in the grate, regular food, being clean, new clothes and boots, what more could she ask for?

Although, in front of Margie and Jack, she acted as if she were dim-witted, she was not as stupid as she made out to be. She knew that there was going to be a high price paid for all this.

Mr Barrett and the woman would not invest so much into her unless they were going to get a decent reward for their trouble; she knew how life here worked.

She had overheard Barrett telling Margie that Beeching, apparently the man she was going to be presented to, had gone away for a few weeks, so everything had to be delayed until he returned.

Margie had sworn; 'Ow the ell am I going to keep an eye on er, Jack. I still need to earn meself a living.'

'I'll leave one of the lads here. They can take it in turns to watch er.'

Mmm, thought Katie, they were expecting her to run, but from what?

---—◆◈◆—---

Chapter 40

Alec Silverman drained the dregs of whisky from his silver hipflask then popped the empty container back into his pocket, as he did so, Alec was jostled by someone pushing past him.

'Watch your bloody step will you,' his voice was slurred.

When he tried to focus on the fight going on in the ring in the cellar of the Crown, he found that he saw double. He rubbed at his eyes ineffectually.

The air that was thick with sweat and smoke stung his eyes and clogged his throat. It was unbearably close in these crowded confines. He desperately wanted to remove the heavy coat he was wearing but knew if he did so, it would be filched for sure.

Alec had bet heavily on the muscular Russian in the ring, but the man was up against an East End docks man, with a thick neck and hard, bald pate, which he put to good use by charging his opponent like a cannonball, catching him in the stomach and knocking all the wind out of him.

The crowd cheered, the noise filled Alec's ears and foggy head with more confusion. His temples started to pound. Suddenly feeling a sense of claustrophobia, Alec turned from the ring and pushed his way through the crowd which jostled him, swearing when he got in the way.

Stepping into the dark street at last, he found it was swathed in thick fog. Taking a deep breath, he then found himself retching, puking up the alcohol he had drunk.

Tears sprang to his eyes. When the fit of vomiting had passed, he stood up and went to take another slug from the flask to clear the awful taste from his mouth, then realised it was empty. Cursing loudly, he shoved the flask back in his pocket, then made his way along the street, holding onto the wall for guidance. He did not see or hear the two figures following him closely.

Morose thoughts rattled around in his head. God, how he missed Horacio: Missing the attention that Hero brought him.

Without Hero in close attendance, Alec knew that he was pretty much ignored; apart from people asking where Mr Woodley was. Why was it, Alec thought, that everywhere he went Hero was well-loved and respected, yet he barely seemed to speak to any of the ruffians. Whereas, they shunned Alec as if he were just another rich toff with money to burn.

I need to find someone else to sponsor, Alec thought, to bring him some kudos, and then sod Horacio Woodley, he could go to hell.

All these thoughts swooped around his mind, a murder of crows dipping and diving with raucous cries, picking at his ego.

Alec didn't know what the time was; all he knew was he has started drinking the previous evening at a gambling club in town, where he had lost significant amounts of money. The losses caused him to drink more heavily than usual, which he had continued to do until he found himself on familiar territory: the fighting ring at the Crown.

His driver, Collins, had tried to dissuade him from going into these notorious streets alone. Still, Alec had insisted, having the carriage and driver wait in the usual place for him, overlooking Waterloo bridge.

As he stumbled along, the swaddling fog wrapped him in an icy grip. It seemed to be getting thicker by the moment. He felt the same sense of claustrophobia he had felt at the Crown wash over him, his heartbeat escalated. Alec suddenly felt vulnerable. He came to realise he had made a grave mistake walking these streets alone.

Not sure if it were instinct that made the hairs rise on the back of his neck, or if he had picked up a sound, distorted by the mist. Alec turned to look back over his shoulder. It was at that moment that a dark shape materialised, then someone hit him over the head.

His vision blurred as he dropped to the filthy ground.

Hands pawed at Alec. He couldn't tell if there were two or three men.

One of them pulled off his coat. His gold fob watch was yanked from its chain. His sapphire and gold cravat pin pulled from his neck. He cried out, hoping that Collins would hear him, when he did so, one of the men swore and kicked him in the ribs. Alec curled up and tried to protect himself. Then he heard one of the men call out, 'Leave im now, someone's coming.'

As Alec's head swam, he heard the sound of running feet.

Despite the cold of the night, Collins felt his eyes, which were heavy with tiredness, closing. He had to keep jerking himself awake. Lord only knew what would happen to the carriage and horses if he let down his guard.

He was bundled up in a greatcoat. He had placed warm blankets over the horses which were beginning to get restless once again.

'Hush now,' he called to them.

Awe, he could curse Master Alec, bloody unfeeling sod he was, he had had Collins and the horses at his beck and call for hours.

Jumping down from the high seat, he walked around to relieve the cramp in his legs. Going over to the horses, he gave them both a rub on their whiskered noses. He fished in his pocket for apples that he had bought earlier from a market stall. It was as he had fed the apple to the second horse that he thought he heard someone cry out.

The larger of the two carriage horses, Stan, nudged his shoulder for more treats.

'Hush now,' he said softly, as he peered into the darkness. Just then a slim dark shape staggered towards him out of the fog.

When Collins realised it was Master Alec, he swore and ran to the young man who cried out as the groom put his arm around him.

Oh lord, he was in a right state. He was filthy and had blood in his hair and running down his neck.

'My ribs,' he uttered, taking in a sharp breath, 'think one's broken.'

'Alright, man, here.' Collins got him to the step of the carriage and had him sit down. 'What happened?'

'Set upon by some bloody ruffians.' Alec put his hand to the back of his head. It came away smeared with blood.

Grabbing Collins lapel, he pulled him close. 'Get me to a bloody doctor, will you. Andrew Keene. Take me to see Andrew.'

'Let's get you inside then,' Collins said, helping the man up the step. Once the door was closed, he grabbed the blankets from the horse's backs, then jumped up onto the driver's seat.

Alec sat back on the carriage seat, a blanket, which smelt like wet horse wrapped around him. His nostrils flared with distaste, but he did not have the energy to fling it aside, besides which he was trembling with shock and cold. Then the disgusting aroma of his own vomit reached him. The blanket was a heavenly scent in comparison. He wanted to gag again, but closed his eyes, breathing through his mouth.

If Horacio had been with him, none of this would have happened, he thought angrily.

The house was in darkness when Collins climbed the steps. When he lifted the brass doorknocker to bang on the door, he felt terrible for disturbing Mr Keene and Mrs Gordon.

Eventually, he saw lamplight filtering through the curtains. Then a moment later Mrs Gordon, dressed in her night attire, opened the front door.

'What on earth...' She took in Collins' worried face.

'Very sorry to disturb you, ma'am.' He nodded towards the carriage, 'but it's Master Alec, he's been attacked. He needs to see the doctor.'

'Oh, good heavens.' The housekeeper placed a hand over her heart in shock. 'You had best bring him in. Can you manage to move him by yourself, Mr Collins?'

'I can,' he affirmed as he ran down the steps.

Mrs Gordon led them up the stairs. Collins had his arm around Alec, who complained bitterly with every movement.

The housekeeper knocked on Andrew's door.

A few moments went by, then Andrew appeared rubbing sleep from his eyes. It was not the first time he had been woken in the night to use his skills to aid another, but he was surprised to be confronted by Alec Silverman, who was in rather a state.

'What's happened?' Andrew asked as Collins led Alec to the sofa.

It was chilly in the room; the fire had burnt low, so Mrs Gordon took it upon herself to add some coal and stoke it into life.

'Have you got any alcohol in this place,' Alec's voice was strained. He looked as white as a sheet. Beads of perspiration stippled his forehead.

'I would say, by the smell of things, you have had enough, man.' Andrew commented.

He gathered swathes of paperwork and letters from the dining table and set them aside, then had Collins remove Alec's ruined clothes, including boots, but keeping his trousers on. Then he bid Collins help the man onto the table so Andrew could examine him properly.

'Bloody hell, can't you be a bit gentler.' The young man complained through gritted teeth.

'You have one broken rib and a nasty bump on the head.' Andrew declared as he stepped back and wiped his hands on a towel.

'Huh, I could have told you that.' Alec went to sit up, but the room began to swim, so he lay back down with a groan.

'Take him into Hero's room.' Andrew directed Collins. 'I will bind the ribs and clean the cut. I will need to keep an eye on him for concussion.'

'Right you are, sir.'

After Collins had set his burden down on Hero's bed, he straightened up with a bit of a groan.

'You look worn out, Collins.' Andrew eyed the man with concern.

His eyes shot to the figure on the bed, 'been a busy night, Mr Keene.'

Andrew reached out and squeezed the other man's shoulder in sympathy. 'Get yourself home; I'll take care of this.'

The groom nodded. 'Thank you, sir, I appreciate that.'

'What,' the voice came from the bed. 'Collins, you need to go and see Barrett, tell him what happened to me. These men need to be caught and taken to account. He needs to track down what has been stolen.' Alec looked at Andrew, 'get a pen and paper, Keene, I need you to write a list of what those hooligans have scarpered with.'

Andrew didn't move; he gave Alec a long look. 'For all you know, Alec, it may as well have been Barrett's men who attacked you.'

With Andrew's words penetrating his pain-filled mind, Alec felt a slither of fear prickle his skin. Surely not?

'No – no.' Alec shook his head, then regretted it. 'I don't believe that. He works for my father. I need a list made and the items found.'

'Yes, very well, we can make a list. Then the enquiries can be looked into tomorrow,' Andrew insisted.

Collins nodded to Andrew gratefully.

'Don't you dare mention a word of this to my father.' Alec called out to the groom's retreating back.

'I will come and check on him tomorrow,' Collins said, then added thoughtfully, 'should I do what he says and not tell Mr Silverman about this?'

Andrew shrugged. 'Probably best not to say anything, although, I would be surprised if Silverman senior doesn't notice the damage done.'

'Aye,' Collins nodded, 'Although, the man is so wrapped up in his business deals, he barely gives the boy any attention.'

'Mmm,'

'Oh, it is a shame,' Mrs Gordon spoke up. 'Poor boy.'

'Hardly poor, Mrs G,' Andrew said.

The woman tutted, 'Well, money doesn't make up for lack of love and care.'

'True.' Andrew acknowledged.

'Stay for a cup of tea at least, Mr Collins.' The woman eyed the groom with concern.

'Thank you, Mrs Gordon, but I need to get the horses fed and watered, they've had a long shift too.'

'Very well, then.' She smiled. She had always liked the groom; noticing how gently he treated the horses in his care when Alec had spent time here with Mr Woodley. She had also taken pity on him, taking out cups of tea and slices of her homemade fruit cake to him. He had always been so grateful.

'I'll come by tomorrow, see if he's well enough to go home,' the groom said.

'I'm not sure he will be, but yes, come by all the same.'

Collins nodded, 'well, I shall bid you good night then.'

'Mmm, not sure if it's going to be a good one.' Andrew sighed as he prepared to see to Alec.

Andrew cleaned Alec up, then bound up his ribs, he found only one broken, the others bruised. Then he cleaned the cut on the back of his head, which needed a couple of stitches.

As Andrew stood up, Alec put a hand to the back of his head.

'You cut my hair.' It was an accusation.

'Yes.' Andrew cleared the equipment away. 'Due to having to stitch you up.'

'I can't go home until it grows back.'

Andrew looked him in the eye. 'You'll just have to wear a hat.'

Alec's eyes narrowed. 'I do not appreciate that statement.'

Much to the other man's further annoyance, Andrew shrugged. 'I shall give you a couple of drops of laudanum to help you to sleep.'

'Fine.' Alec lay back against the pillows. He did not have the energy to hold on to any hostility.

Andrew gave him a glass of water laced with the drug. Alec was soon asleep.

As Andrew washed his hands, he yawned widely. Thank heaven it was Sunday tomorrow – no, he looked at the clock on the mantle, not tomorrow, today.

Andrew wasn't happy having Alec staying here; he sincerely hoped that he would be able to get him out of the way as speedily as possible. Not only that, but he had two long lectures coming up on the Monday which he couldn't afford to miss, this meant that he would be out all day so wouldn't be able to keep an eye on Alec, this thought worried him.

The following morning when Andrew checked on his patient. Miserably, Alec declared that he could barely move. That his head was still throbbing, and he still felt sick.

Andrew rolled his eyes in resignation. It was no good, he would have to keep Alec under this roof so he could monitor him. So, when Collins arrived to pick the young man up and take him back to his London house, Andrew had to tell him that Alec needed to stay put, even if it were just for one more night.

'If you are sure, Dr Keene,' the groom commented out of earshot.

'Unfortunately, I am.' Andrew grimaced, receiving a sympathetic smile from the other man.

'His parents are staying at their country house,' Collins explained, 'so apart from the staff at the London house, there is no one to wonder where he is.'

Andrew nodded. 'But I do want him out of the way sooner rather than later, Collins.'

'Aye sir, I get your drift.'

'Collins,' Alec called from the bedroom.

The two men exchanged commiserating glances as the groom walked into the bedroom.

A fire had been lit in the grate; the room was warm. Alec sat up against the pillows. A bruise on his cheek stood out on his pale skin. Andrew had given him an opiate to dull the pain, so his eyes were heavy.

'I order you to go and see Barrett. I want those ruffians found and punished. And I want my stolen goods back.'

'Yes, Master Alec. I shall take a trip out to the East End, see if I can find Barrett.'

'Yes, good.'

Collins knew that Barrett had lodgings on the first floor of the Crown and Garter, so he walked there on foot, thinking it would be far less conspicuous than driving the carriage or riding a horse.

He was informed by the barmaid, Rita, that Mr Barrett was at home with his wife. His wife! Collins didn't even know the man had gotten married.

When he inquired further, the woman told him he had a house in Bow, but she did not know where it was.

Even with the opiate, Alec was still a belligerent guest: complaining about everything, until Andrew told him, if he carried on anymore, he would frog march him back to his father's London house.

A very disgruntled Alec pursed his lips but said no more.

When Collins arrived back later on in the day and explained that he had not been able to find Barrett, Alec was furious.

'I left a message with the barmaid at the Crown,' Collins told him, 'I'm sure he will be in touch shortly.'

'You're sure, are you!' Alec said scathingly, 'Well, I can rest in peace then.'

Andrew, concerned about having to miss his lectures, was delighted when Mrs Gordon suggested she would keep an eye on their injured guest.

'It's no trouble, Dr Keene.' She reassured him.

'Oh, Mrs G, you an absolute star.' The woman laughed when he wrapped her in a tight hug.

'Aww, get away with you.' She flapped her hands at him; her cheeks flushed in delight.

Although Alec still felt rather groggy after everything that had happened to him, the laudanum was beginning to wear off, so he found himself restless and eager to be up and about.

The housekeeper brought him a coddled egg and bread and butter for breakfast, which he polished off with gusto.

'Good to see you have got a good appetite, Master Silverman.' The housekeeper commented when she fetched the tray.

'I am feeling somewhat better,' he said as he adjusted his position on the bed then winced, 'but his damn broken rib is causing me some grief.'

'Aye, well, it's going to take a while to heal. Now, is there anything else you need?'

'No, no.' He waved her away.

When she returned at lunchtime with a bowl of beef stew with bread and butter, once again he tucked into the offering, while the housekeeper sat with him in case he needed any help.

'I have to say.' Alec looked at the housekeeper with interest, 'I was very pleased to meet Andrew's cousin a couple of months ago.'

'Dr Keene's cousin?' Mrs Gordon looked perplexed.

'Yes, now was it Sarah or Sophia? I cannot remember.'

'Oh, you mean, Sophia.' The woman smiled, then a shadow passed across her features. 'She's not Dr Keene's cousin.'

'Oh, I must have been mistaken.' Alec studied her closely. 'Such a beautiful young woman.'

Mrs Gordon nodded enthusiastically, 'Oh yes, she certainly is, and she has recovered so well from what she went through.'

'What she went through?'

This time the woman blushed. 'I shouldn't say anything about it, but it was so horrible. The poor child being taken advantaged of and being used so terribly.'

'I am so sorry to hear that, Mrs Gordon. She seemed most charming when I met her, although I did notice some bruising on her wrists.'

'Yes.' Tears sprang to her eyes, she fished out a handkerchief from the pocket of her white apron. She sniffed and wiped her eyes. 'I do suppose, however, that if it hadn't have happened, then Dr Keene would never have met her. They write to each other regularly, you know.' She gave a little laugh through her tears, 'I do believe he is quite taken with her, and she with him.'

'Oh how, mmm, fortunate then.'

'Yes, like fate bringing them together.'

'And what happened to her attackers? I hope they have been brought to justice.'

The woman shook her head. 'Mr Woodley and Dr Keene felt that because the man responsible is a member of parliament, nothing would come of any accusations. That it would put Sophia through more agony and possibly put her in further danger.'

'A member of parliament?' Oh, Alec was enjoying this little story that was unravelling. 'How terrible. My father has much influence, Mrs Gordon, perhaps he would see the man responsible brought to justice.'

Suddenly, the woman sat up straighter in her seat, a startled look on her face. She covered her mouth. 'I have just realised something terrible, Master Silverman.'

'What, my dear lady? Tell me; I am sure I can help.'

'Well, you see, the thing is, the man responsible was invited to your father's house. It all happened under your father's roof.'

'No!' Alec said, looking suitably shocked. 'I cannot believe my father would have anything to do with something like this. I must take things in hand and speak to him. He owes this young woman some sort of compensation for what has happened to her.'

'Compensation?' Mrs Gordon's eyes widened with hope, why hadn't her two lodgers thought of this?

'Yes, of course.' Alec smiled as sincerely as he possibly could. 'and of course, her attacker should be brought to account. It doesn't matter who he is. Justice is justice.'

The woman let out a breath. 'If I remember correctly, the man who attacked that lovely girl is called Beecham, or something like that.'

'Beecham, or Beeching?' Alec asked, his heart beating with excitement.

'Yes,' she said, 'Beeching, that's it.'

'Shocking, absolutely shocking.'

'Isn't it.'

'Where is the young woman now, I hope that she is well out of harm's way.'

'Yes, she is. Mr Woodley has taken her to stay with his mother. Sophia is Jewish, you know, driven out of her home, like thousands of others. She came from the Ural Mountains, where she used to help the schoolteacher who ran the small village school. So, considering her experience, it was thought to be the ideal place to take her.'

'Ahh, yes, Horacio has mentioned his mother's school many times. I had an inkling when I met her, Sophia, that she was of our blood. And you say that she has recovered well from what happened?'

'Yes, remarkably so.'

'Good, I am glad.'

A worried look crossed the housekeeper's face. 'I wouldn't want to upset her again, Master Alec, she's been through so much, maybe it is best to leave it be.'

'You leave it with me, Mrs Gordon, I shall sort something out and be the soul of discretion, of course. And, talking of discretion, it might be for the best not to mention any of this to my two friends, when I have made some progress, I will tell them all about it myself.'

She looked doubtful for a moment, then smiled once more, 'very well,' she agreed.

When the housekeeper took the tray away, Alec lay in bed, contemplating this interesting piece of news.

Remembering something that the housekeeper had mentioned, Sophia and Andrew write to each other regularly. He pushed the covers aside, then gingerly got out of bed.

Andrew did his best to concentrate on the lectures, to make copious notes, but his thoughts kept wandering back to Alec Silverman; he did not trust the man one bit. He regretted now putting the burden of care on his housekeeper's shoulders.

He had mentioned his misgivings regarding Alec to Horacio numerous times, but it seemed that these warnings fell on deaf ears.

Perhaps Hero was still blind to Alec's faults!

Andrew was pleased that Hero had gone home for a while, at least he would be out of Alec's sights for the foreseeable future.

Alec found a pile of letters strewn in between notes and bills, which Andrew had cleared from the dining table the previous day. He had left them on the sideboard.

Grabbing the pile of papers, Alec put them on the dining table. Then carefully, he eased himself onto a chair. He had a quick rifle through the correspondence until he found some letters. Yes, they were all from Sophia, the address was Brook House.

Scanning the elegant missives, Alec found them trite, to say the least. He sighed with boredom. Then a paragraph caught his eye.

"Mr Woodley let slip that the name of my attacker is Beeching. Giving him a name shocked me and made it all seem more real. I wondered about asking him for further information, Andrew. But I am unsure what to do. Is he an important man? Am I safe here?"

Alec set the letter aside and smiled. Things were beginning to make sense; he had heard snippets of information here and there; gossip from the staff; there had been an incident during pa's night of entertainment, one of Jolly's whores had knocked Beeching out. A young girl had been involved who was now missing, possibly dead. However, it now seemed as if the girl was very much alive and under Hero's protection.

Upon this discovery, several emotions ran through Alec, a feeling of what? Betrayal perhaps? Woodley was meant to be his friend, but he had been keeping things from him, important things.

Suddenly, a thought dawned on him, Woodley must have been the person who helped them escape, and he had used Alec's personal carriage to do so. Anger flooded through him. He stood up too quickly and grunted as pain blossomed from his damaged ribs. Holding his side, he sat down once again. Jesus, even his own driver, was caught up in this deceit.

Perspiration beaded his brow as Alec took a moment to catch his breath.

His father had always drummed into Alec that information was key; "find out everything you can about people you are close to, who you associate and work with, Alec. Information is ammunition, remember that."

Mmm, was Beeching still looking for the girl? And if so, how much would he pay for some valuable information?

From what Alec could remember of her, she was a rare beauty with those incredible grey eyes of hers. He had a feeling that Beeching would pay well for another encounter with her. But if he weren't interested, perhaps Barrett would find another high paying customer eager to experience the girl's delights?

He glanced at the letters once more, then picked up the one where Sophia had mentioned Beeching's name. He folded it up, then carefully got up from the chair.

Found his trousers, which Mrs Gordon had laundered for him, draped over the back of a chair in Hero's room. He slipped the paper into the pocket, then got back into bed.

Chapter 41

Andrew was heartily surprised and relieved when Alec declared he would feel fine about going home the following day.

'Well, if you are sure.' Andrew cut up a piece of roast chicken that Mrs Gordon had supplied for their evening meal.

'I am grateful for your attendance, Andrew. However, I feel I cannot impose on your hospitality any further.'

Andrew eyed him with an incredulous look: perhaps the bang on the head had imparted some empathy into the man.

'If you are sure,' he found himself repeating. 'Perhaps you would like me to look in on you later in the week, see how you are getting on?'

Alec poured himself a glass of white wine. He raised the glass to Andrew. 'Thank you, Keene. I am incredibly grateful to you. I will send Collins to fetch you if I feel I am in need.'

'Yes, of course.'

The groom had visited earlier in the day, bringing changes of clothes and toiletry items. Alec was now dressed in his nightshirt and dressing-gown and would be able to leave on the morrow wearing his own suit of clothes.

'What will you say if anyone questions you about your injuries?' Andrew asked as he cleared his plate of the last morsel.

'Ahh, a mere accident.' Alec shrugged. 'Oh, I shall think of something.'

*

Vanessa Beeching sat in the austere drawing-room of Beeching Hall. Pellets of rain were being hurled against the glass by a vicious wind, which rattled the window frames.

Although there was a fire blazing in the grate, Vanessa shivered and drew her woollen shawl closer about her shoulders.

She hated this house, the ancestral home of her husbands' family. The drawing-room was in the newer part of the house; it was a long room with high ceilings decorated with mouldings and murals in pastel colours. Every item of furniture was beautifully crafted, much of which was decorated with gold leaf. The place felt more like a museum rather than a home.

She and George had spent Christmas here as they usually did. An insufferable time that Vanessa loathed. Her only joy was having William home. But even this was a delight marred by George and his parents as they endeavoured to pick every shred of confidence from the boy.

Vanessa could sense that her son was not happy at school.

On a rare moment when she and William found themselves alone together, the boy had confessed to his mother that he was being bullied unmercifully.

He had inherited his maternal grandmother's short stature and Vanessa's beauty, well-chiselled cheekbones, auburn hair, pale complexion. A generous and loving heart. However, he did not have the passion and strength of his mother. The resources he needed to stand against the bullies, he was a gentle soul.

All these traits George despised in his son. He had picked on the boy several times over the holiday, telling him he needed to toughen up.

Vanessa understood enough about the situation, to realise that George was intentionally taunting her son to get to her.

Under this roof, George had been courteous towards her, which was all for show. But he still felt the need to attack her with his poisonous arrows whenever he could, her son being his ammunition of choice.

Oh, how she loathed George. She was heartily pleased that they had separate suites of rooms so she could escape now and again.

William left for school at the beginning of January.

When Vanessa saw him off, she could tell he was trying valiantly to keep his tears in check. She had hugged him tight.

'Write to me, darling.' She straightened his collar.

'I will, mama.' He had nodded, but his lip trembled.

'Oh, for God sake, Vanessa, let the boy go.' George stood at the bottom of the steps that led from the portico.

'It's no wonder he is having a hard time at school, the way you mollycoddle him.'

Vanessa stepped away from the boy, who climbed up into the carriage.

'I love you, darling,' she said softly so only he could hear.

'And you, mama.'

The carriage moved forward. Vanessa stepped away. She waved until the pale face of her boy was lost to a curve in the driveway.

In a swirl of forest green silk, Vanessa ran up the steps, ignoring her husband completely.

It was now well into February; under normal circumstances, she and George would have returned to London by now, but Georges' father, Ernest, had been taken ill. The doctor had explained that it was some kind of seizure.

The man could barely speak and had to be fed by a nurse. With all this going on, George felt obliged to stay until the old man turned a corner, although that was looking more and more unlikely as the days went on.

Margot, George's mother, was a tall and stern woman who liked to have her way. Vanessa felt that the woman had no heart, her chest a vacant void of arctic ice. During their stay, she was very aware that the older woman was watching her closely, judging her every move.

Desperate to get out from under these suffocating conditions, Vanessa had asked George several times if she could return to London. Each time he had said no.

Instinct told her that George and his mother were up to something; she just didn't know what. So, she had not been surprised when Margot sought her out when she was in the library reading.

Margot walked over, taking a seat in a wingback chair opposite Vanessa. The two women eyed each other. Vanessa's expression was wary, Margot's filled with obvious distaste.

'George and I have been discussing your health, my dear.' Vanessa felt her skin prickle, but she said nothing. 'He told me that you have been becoming quite, umm, hysterical at times. He is worried about you.'

'I can assure you that the term "hysterical" has been highly exaggerated in this instant, Margot.'

The woman dropped her gaze and sighed as if she regretted what she was going to say next, which of course she didn't.

'Well, it may seem that way to you, Vanessa, but from George's point of view, your behaviour is erratic, to say the least. He is concerned that it will reflect badly on him.'

Vanessa felt a wave of anger, fuelled by injustice flame in her stomach.

'Concerned it will reflect badly on *him* ...' Vanessa let out an incredulous laugh. She sat forward in her chair, giving the woman a scathing look. 'Have you any idea of the terrible things your son has done! He is a rapist of young girls – using them so very badly that they can never go on to lead normal lives.' She swallowed down the tears that threatened to drown her in sorrow. 'In fact, he may well have murdered some of them. Your son deserves to hang, Margot.'

Through her blurred vision, Vanessa noticed that Margot's' coal-dark eyes were hard and assessing.

'Ahh, this is just the kind of delusional behaviour George spoke of. The poisonous lies he said you would spew from your mouth.' She shook her head sadly. 'We feel that it would be a good idea for you to be assessed by a doctor, my dear. We want only the best for you and the family.'

'Oh yes, I am sure you do, Margot. I presume this will be a doctor picked by you and George, one that will have no qualms in proclaiming me to be quite mad.'

'Dr Carpenter is an expert in the field of study, the understanding of hysteria and psychotic behaviour.'

Vanessa jumped to her feet, she strolled across the Persian carpet and gazed out of the window. She did not take in the view of the sweeping parkland. Her heart thumped rapidly in her chest. Her hands felt clammy, as did her forehead. Oh, she needed to be very careful – they were talking her into a trap. George would have no qualms about locking her up; then she would be utterly helpless.

Turning back to face her mother-in-law, she said, 'Very well, I shall see this doctor if it will put your minds at ease.'

A ripple of surprise swept across Margot's features, which she quickly got under control once more. She stood up and brushed out the skirt of her slate-grey day dress.

She nodded, 'Well, I am pleased you have seen sense, my dear.' 'Oh yes,' Vanessa said, 'I see things so clearly now.'

Margot found George sitting in one of the leather button-back chairs in his father's study. Being one of the main rooms from the original Tudor dwelling, it was rather dark. The walls lined in dark oak panelling up to the midway point. The furniture, again all dark wood, had been in the family for years.

There were several oil paintings in heavy gilded frames on the walls; they depicted Beeching ancestors and historical references of the house through different periods of history.

George got to his feet when his mother entered. He set the newspaper he had been reading down on an occasional table where a tray of coffee things had been set. A blazing fire added some warmth to the room.

'She has agreed to see Dr Carpenter,' his mother said as she walked over to one of the heavily leaded windows and looked out at the dreary day.

'Really?' There was a note of surprise in George's voice. 'She knows she hasn't a choice,' he stated thoughtfully.

'Yes, but I am surprised she has capitulated so easily.' His mother turned to look at him. 'Can you foresee difficulties?'

'I'm not sure, Mother, but I think the sooner we get Dr Carpenter here, the better. I shall write to him forthwith.' George walked around the large desk and sat in the chair. He pulled out a sheet of paper and a pen. As he did so, he was aware of his mother's presence behind him.

'You were quite correct in your description regarding the type of accusations she would fire at you.'

He paused for a moment, pen in hand. 'Yes, she has quite a dark imagination, I can tell you.' He gave a small laugh which sounded as if he were choking on something. 'I have put every effort into our marriage, but as you know, mama, Vanessa and I do not get on. She has stored up this spite for many years. I should have taken her into hand much earlier than this.'

'She has always been strong-willed,' his mother observed as she gripped his shoulder tightly.

'Yes.' George held his breath - still, the ink had not touched the paper.

Leaning down so that her mouth was close to his ear, she said softly, 'Assure me, my boy, that her accusations are groundless.'

George tried not to flinch from her touch. He sighed, 'I have already assured you of that, mother. I may have had a little fun with one of the housemaids many years ago. Vanessa seems to have fixated on that; I expect her colourful imagination was fuelled by jealousy. I can assure you that there was no harm done.'

There was a rustle of silk as she stood tall once more, although the grip she had on his shoulder tightened even more.

'Write to Dr Carpenter right away.' Releasing his shoulder, she then left the room, leaving the scent of lavender water in her wake.

George hadn't realised he was holding his breath until the door closed, he let it out with a puff.

He had to allow his trembling hands to still before he could write the missive summoning Dr Carpenter to Beeching Hall.

That evening, Vanessa pleaded a headache to avoid going down to dine with her husband and his mother.

Her mind had been in a turmoil ever since the encounter with Margot in the library.

She paced her bedroom floor as she wrung her hands together in fear and anger. She knew it would not matter what she said to this Dr Carpenter; he would have already been fed these awful lies; that she was delusional.

Any accusations she came up with against her husband would be viewed as inexplicable, fabricated by a mind consumed with anger and hatred. She could sit there and not say a word, but still be condemned - to be incarcerated in an asylum by the statements of her husband and mother-in-law. There was nothing she could do.

She thought of William, her dear child, would she ever see him again? Would they bring him on visits to see his mad mama!

Vanessa shivered, then made a decision, if she were locked up there would be nothing she could do. She would be placed at the mercy of the Beeching's and the doctors. There would be no escape, the only option was to run.

Now filled with purpose, Vanessa strode across the carpeted floor and pulled open her bedroom door.

As she made her way up the stairs that lead to the attics, her heart was racing furiously. She had to get away, and she had to do it that very night.

*

Evie and Jack had been married for four weeks – for Evie, it felt like a lifetime.

Emotionally, she had eradicated herself so completely, that she felt as if she were viewing everything from atop a prison of a turreted tower.

There was a part of her that recognised this pattern of behaviour; she had done the same thing when she had to look after Dottie when their mother had died. It was a survival instinct.

She knew that Jack was getting frustrated with her lack of enthusiasm, but what did he expect? It wasn't as if she said no to him, but she lay under him while he did his business, gritting her teeth and trying desperately not to cry.

Evie held on to the hope that he would get so fed up with her, he would divorce her on some grounds or other.

Mrs Perkins had spoken to her; she didn't know if this was because Jack had mentioned something to the housekeeper, or that the woman had picked up on Evie's state of mind? Probably the latter.

Jolly Jack Barrett was a proud man; Evie was sure that he would not admit to anyone that things were not going well in his marriage.

Jack had let Mrs Perkins know that he would be out all night. When Evie heard this piece of news, she had breathed a sigh of relief. She had managed to get some sleep without worrying that Jack would return at any moment.

Walking down the stairs the following morning, Evie was surprised to hear laughter coming from the library.

When she walked in, she saw Dottie sitting at the table with Ivy and Tommy. The tabletop was littered with books, paper, inkwells, pencils, and pens.

'What on earth is going on here?' She gazed at the trio perplexed. 'And, where is Mrs Perkins?'

'Mrs Perkins has gone out, Evie,' Dottie spoke up. 'She's picking up some new gloves she has had made.'

'Very well,' Evie nodded. 'Explain, please, what are you doing?'

'She's teaching us ow to read n write.' Tommy piped up.

'How,' Dottie corrected him.

Evie glanced at her sister, who was smiling broadly. There was a touch of colour blushing her pale cheeks; she looked happy. *She looked happy!* Evie felt a jolt run through her heart. Dottie's health had improved since they had been here, and now this.

'Does Mrs Perkins know about this?' She asked, gesturing to the contents strewn all over the table.

'Oh yes, Evie.' Dottie spoke up once again. 'I asked her first; she said a bit of reading and writing could get you through life. I'm teaching Ivy how to write her name.'

Dottie picked up a piece of paper where there were a few random lines, however, when Evie looked closer, she could see they were rudimentary attempts at writing.

'Very good, Ivy,' Evie acknowledged,

'Thank you, miss, umm, Mrs Barrett,' she corrected, making Evie wince inside. Ivy beamed, however, as she pushed up her oversized mob cap with ink-stained fingers, luckily the ink was dry.

'An, I've managed my name too.' Tommy said proudly as he pushed a piece of paper towards Evie.

This time she could easily read the name, she nodded and smiled. His enthusiasm lit up his freckled face under his mop of ginger hair.

'Spell it out, Tommy.' Dottie encouraged.

Biting his lip, he pointed to the first letter, 'T', he said. Dottie nodded encouragingly. 'O – M – M – Y'.

'Yes.' Dottie approved.

Just then, they heard the front door open and close.

Evie looked through the open library door into the hall, Mrs Perkins was taking off her rain dampened cloak, she had set a package wrapped in brown paper on the hall table.

Noticing that the package was wrapped in brown paper, gave Evie a jolt; it reminded her of the sewing they used to do for Mrs Smart – Lord; it felt like a lifetime ago.

Unpinning her hat, the housekeeper spotted Evie. 'Is everything alright?' she asked as she placed her hat on a coat-stand.

'You knew about this?' Evie gestured behind her.

'Oh yes.' The woman nodded, then called out. 'Ten more minutes, you two, then I've got work that needs attending to.'

'Yes, Mrs P.' Tommy answered.

Evie followed Mrs Perkins into the kitchen. 'You approve of what they are doing then?' She felt the need for confirmation.

The older woman stopped and gave her a long look.

'I do,' she said. 'I was lucky enough to have a mother that valued learning.'

'Yes,' Evie nodded thoughtfully. 'Ours did too. Although, I am not sure I am happy about my sister forming a bond with those two.'

The housekeeper's face became stony. 'Well, I thought it might help the lass,' Mrs Perkins said as she put the kettle on the range to boil. 'give her a distraction.' Her gaze turned to Evie once more, 'surely you can't object to that?'

Evie dropped her head. No, she thought, she should be happy for Dottie. Although for some reason, this situation made her feel angry. No, she wasn't sure that angry was the right feeling. It was a betrayal. Yes, she felt betrayed.

Mrs Perkins paused once again. She searched Evie's face with a critical eye. 'Does that settle your heart a little at least?'

Evie glanced out of the window. The rain had passed over. It was dry for once, but the clouds were grey, pregnant with the promise of another shower. Oh, how she longed for spring. With that thought something shifted within her – the changing of the seasons would not help her; she would still be trapped in this place.

Dottie was moving on, Evie felt as if she should be thankful for that, but for her, it was just another link in the chain that kept her anchored here. Just then, the sun peeped through a break in the clouds, the ray of brightness left Evie feeling bleaker than ever.

'I'm not sure that it does,' she answered at last.

Chapter 42

The February morning was chilly, damp with mist swirling up from the brook and curling about the trees, embracing the trunks lovingly.

Hero, riding Hades at a gentle pace, inhaled with gusto. The scent of the damp earth filled his nostrils. Ahh, such a relief after the stink of town.

Beneath the trees, the autumn leaves had settled, their colours diminishing into leaf-mulch that would feed regrowth and be insulation for the spring bulbs, which would soon reach their shoots towards a welcoming spring sun.

Catching the scent of badger and fox Wilson was enjoying scampering through the woods, his stumpy tail wagging happily. His antics made Hero smile.

Just then, the little dog came to a halt, sniffed the air, then barked. The dog's attention seemed to be taken by something in a thicket of brambles.

The sound of a twig snapping caused Hero to bring Hades to a halt.

'Who's there?'

When Wilson backed away from the thicket, Hero was amazed to see that his tail was wagging furiously. A slim figure emerged.

To Hero, the figure looked like a young man, but there was something not quite right: The person wore an overly large tweed jacket. A muffler hid the bottom of their face, and a cap pulled low, shaded the eyes.

Although the clothes did not fit well, they looked as if they were well made, as did the riding boots and the leather gloves. Was this some thief trespassing on the estate?

Wilson, however, thought otherwise as he jumped up at the figure, who knelt to make a fuss of him.

'What ...?' Hero jumped down from Hade's back as the person stood straight and pulled off the cap then loosened the muffler.

'Vanessa!' he exclaimed as he took a step towards her.

'Hello, Horacio, darling. I hope you don't mind me coming by for a visit.'

'What the hell have you done to your hair?' he exclaimed with shock.

She reached up and ran her gloved fingers through the untidy stubble. 'I had to chop it off.' She tried a weak smile. 'It's a bit of a story.'

On the evening after the confrontation with Margot, Vanessa used the excuse that she had a headache, so she did not have to go down to dinner.

While her husband and his mother were eating, she had snuck up to the attics and raided the clothes chests for something she could wear as a disguise.

She discovered clothing that must have belonged to George when he was younger. Despite her full figure, everything was over large, but that fact could put that to good use, it would camouflage her curves.

She found everything she needed. The only thing that was missing was a pair of sturdy boots, so she had to wear her riding boots when she left the house.

Vanessa left the attics and returned to the floor below, stopping by the sewing room to pick up a pair of scissors. She could disguise herself as much as possible, but her thick auburn hair would call attention to her.

Back in her room, Vanessa chopped off her locks, as short as she could. Then she threw the tresses on the fire.

Watching her hair going up in flames, Vanessa had a strange sense of everything shifting in her world; this was the end of Vanessa Beeching – she didn't know if she felt scared or liberated by the actions she was taking.

Only taking items that she had inherited from her mother and grandmother. Leaving the rest behind which was all the jewellery that George had given her over the years. One thing to say about him in that respect, he had been generous, but sadly it had been all for show, for impressing their peers.

It was strange she thought, as she packed, that there was a part of her that knew this confrontation was going to happen at some point. The catalyst that would end her marriage was looming closer and closer; however, she had no clue as to the form it would take.

When her dear friend, Sarah, had seen the bruises inflicted by George, she had suggested that Vanessa leave any valuables with her and her husband, Jasper. Which she had agreed would be a wise idea. She had also entrusted her friend to keep a pot of money safe for her, should she ever need to leave George.

When Vanessa made her way stealthily out through the back of the house, she pondered where to go – her initial thought was to run to Sarah, but that would be the first place that George would look. There was only one other place she could go, and that was Woodley Hall.

Hero gathered her in his arms. The scent of damp wool, camphor and mothballs tickled his nose making him want to sneeze, he resisted the urge.

Vanessa was trembling against him – he was used to her trembling with desire, but this was different. Finally, he stepped away, studying her expression with concern.

'What the hell has happened?' He shook his head, perplexed, 'this is something to do with Beeching, isn't it, what has he done to you?'

Reaching up, she pressed a hand against his cheek. 'Partly, yes. God, I know it's early, but I need a tot of brandy.'

'Yes, of course.' Hero gathered himself. Walking over to Hades he mounted, then pulled Vanessa up, who perched behind him, her arms around his waist.

Turning the large hunter, Hero headed back to the hall with Wilson following close behind.

'It might be a good idea not to let people see me,' Vanessa said as they came within sight of the house.

He pressed his hand over her clasped ones in reassurance.

'I am the only one living in the house,' he explained. 'There is only Bryant and Charlie in the stables. Besides, I trust the household to be discreet.'

'Thank you, Horacio.'

Vanessa laid her head against his broad back. She was exhausted, she had had a long trek across the country to get to Woodley Hall. Realising that her disguise would only fool people from a distance, Vanessa kept out of sight as much as possible. If only she could have taken a horse from the stables at Beeching Hall, the journey would have taken no more than three to four hours, as it was it had taken all night.

When they arrived at the stables, Charlie came out to take Hades. He gave a start when he noticed that Mr Woodley was not alone, surveying the visitor with a curious look.

Once he had dismounted and helped Vanessa down, Hero had a word with him, explaining that he had an unexpected visitor and not to mention the fact outside of the immediate staff.

'Aye, Mr Woodley.' Charlie doffed his cap. 'You can count on us.'

Hero led Vanessa up the back steps into the porch leading to the kitchens and servant's hall. They shrugged off their coats, then went through to Hero's study.

'Sorry there's no fire, I shall get one going in a moment,' Hero said as he walked over to a sideboard, he poured out a generous tot of brandy.

'The household is working on a minimum of staff, as my mother has filched them all to work at her school,' he explained. 'Besides, with it being only me rattling around in this place, I do not require a fleet of servants.' He gave Vanessa a boyish grin as he handed her the glass.

'Thank you.' She sipped at the liquid, enjoying the warmth and richness of the liquor. Taking a seat in one of the armchairs, Vanessa watched as Hero started a fire.

Once that task was finished, he walked over to the bellpull to summon Janice.

'I shall have some coffee brought in. Are you hungry?'

As the liquor hit her empty stomach, she nodded. 'Famished.'

When Janice answered the call, Horacio asked her to bring coffee and some breakfast for two.

It didn't take long for her to arrive back with coffee, and a tray laden with boiled eggs, bread and butter and a pot of Mrs Adam's homemade blackberry jam.

Horacio watched Vanessa as she tucked into the food with a hearty appetite, he asked no questions until she sat back with a sigh, nursing a second cup of the rich coffee.

'So, tell me what has happened?'

Vanessa went on to tell him all about Margot's threat to have her locked up.

'Why?' A grim expression chiselled his handsome face into hard lines. 'Why now?'

Vanessa took a sip of the coffee, then placed the cup back on the saucer.

'I have been pondering that exact question.' Her gaze turned to the tall window looking out over the kitchen gardens. 'George has always been scared of me. He abhors my independence and strength of will.' Her gaze turned back to Hero, 'He is also worried that now William is getting older, I will start to spread rumours about the terrible things his father has done.'

'And would you?' Hero asked as his thoughts turned to Sophia.

She leaned forward, elbows on the polished surface of the table. 'Of course I would; he needs to be stopped, Horacio.' Then she sighed. 'While he wields power where William is concerned, I am helpless. I cannot be parted from my boy. It is already bad enough that he has been sent away to a school which he hates.' A tear rolled down her cheek; she wiped it away with the back of her hand.

Leaning forward, Hero held out his hand to her. She took it with a grateful smile.

'Do you remember when I visited you in London?'

'Yes.' Her eyes dropped. 'He had attacked another young girl.'

He squeezed her fingers gently. 'He had. I cannot recall if I told you her name.' Vanessa shook her head as Hero continued. 'Well, her name is Sophia, and to keep her out of further harm's way, I have brought her here. I have to say she has made a remarkable recovery. Currently, she is staying at the school under the protection of Cousin Clare and my mother.'

'She's here?'

'Yes, with her, you have someone who can testify against George. Andrew Keene was the doctor, well trainee doctor, who examined her after the attack. He could also testify.'

Hope flared in her green eyes, then dimmed once more. 'I have to keep William safe, Hero. I don't know what George will do if I start to make trouble for him. He is a vindictive and evil man. I hate that he has hurt this girl, Sophia.' She shook her head sadly. 'Every young girl he's tormented.' Tears pricked her eyes.

Hero got up, walked around the table, then pulled her from her seat. He gathered her in his arms. 'I know, and he shouldn't be allowed to get away with these terrible things.'

Clinging to him, she said, 'yes, perhaps something can be done when I have William safe.'

Pulling away, he kissed her gently on the forehead.

'Ah, very well then our priority is getting William to safety.'

'Yes.'

'He boards at a school outside of Bath if I remember rightly.' Hero confirmed.

'Yes, Millbrook.'

'As his mother, do you have the right to go and visit and remove him from the school?'

Vanessa shook her head, her expression settling into one of sadness. 'Unfortunately not, George made sure that would never happen.' Then she waved a hand towards her hair, 'besides, the way I look now, they would probably think me a beggar or worse.'

'Mmm, yes. Hadn't thought of that,' he acknowledged with a wry smile.

'I do have an idea; however,' Vanessa said, hope lightening her expression.

'Yes, go on.' Horacio encouraged.

She looked at the clock on the marble mantle-piece, the time was quarter to eight in the morning.

'I am a bit of a night owl, therefore a late riser. My maid, Thorpe, won't bring my chocolate in until ten. Much to Margot's annoyance, I breakfast late, then spend the rest of the time in my room or out riding until luncheon.'

'So, no one will notice that you are missing for another couple of hours yet?'

'Yes.'

'The school is about an hour's drive away from here.' Hero surmised.

'I would say so.' Vanessa nodded. 'The headmaster, Mr Cooper, obviously knows of Ernest's condition. So, if a groom arrives with a letter from Lady Beeching to say that Ernest has deteriorated and he has come to take William back to Beeching Hall, would the man agree to let William leave? What do you think?'

'Well, it sounds very plausible, Nessa, I don't see why he wouldn't. I shall summon Bryant and have him get the carriage ready.'

Vanessa reached out a hand to him. 'Thank you, my love.'

Hero, taking it, kissed it, then caught her up in another tight embrace. When he drew away, he looked down into her beautiful face; her cheeks were wet with tears.

Holding her hands close to his chest, he said, 'You know, I think your new hair cut quite suits you.'

Despite everything, Vanessa found herself laughing. 'I know I look awful, but you always say the right thing, Horacio Woodley.'

*

It wasn't until luncheon had been served, and Vanessa had not made an appearance, that George realised that something was amiss.

As the realisation dawned, George felt bile rising in his Throat. The large luncheon he had just consumed, turned sour in his belly.

Summoning Thorpe, Vanessa's lady maid to his study, he questioned her.

The woman, who was well into her forties, had a long face and a stern expression. She had been working for Lady Beeching for five years.

Thorpe had found her ladyship, to be a fair and kind employer. However, her husband left a great deal to be desired; ahh, he was a nasty piece of work by all accounts.

Her dislike of him intensified when he stood over her, his posture was one of intimidation, as she sat in one of the chairs in front of his large desk.

'Where the bloody hell is she?' He asked through gritted teeth.

'As I have already said, sir. When I took her chocolate into her this morning, just after ten of the clock, Lady Beeching was not in her room. Her bed was made, which was strange, but I presumed she had gone out for a ride, as she occasionally does.'

'You say nothing is missing, Thorpe?' Margot asked, she was sitting in one of the straight-backed chairs beside the desk.

'As far as I can tell, ma'am.'

'Your threat has scared her off.' George raged at his mother.

'It was necessary to keep her in check.' She reminded him.

'Huh, I should have known she would do this, I should have had her watched.' George paced the room in agitation.

'Yes, perhaps you should have done.' Margot's voice was icy. 'Thorpe, you can go.' She dismissed the maid.

All the rest of the staff were questioned; no one had seen anything of Vanessa.

None of the horses was missing from the stables either, so if she had run away, she must have left on foot.

A further search was carried out which turned out to be fruitless.

'The bitch has made a run for it.' George seethed.

'Where will she go?' Margot asked.

Turning a face to her that was infused with anger; a thought occurred to him. 'William, she will try to take William.'

With a grim expression and tight lips, Margot said, 'Go, go and find her.

By God, she will be locked up for this before she can do any more damage.'

'Yes, mother.' George rushed to the door.

Chapter 43

'I'm not sure if it is wise for you to come with me.' Hero said as he handed Vanessa up into the carriage. 'I could fetch William for you and bring him here.' His voice was full of concern when he climbed in behind her and took a seat. 'What if George is there already and sees you?'

'He won't look twice at me dressed like this. Don't you agree, I make a fine boy.'

'A handsome one, aye.' Hero couldn't help but smile.

'No, we shall continue with our plan; fetch William from school, then head to Bristol.'

They had decided that it would be a good idea for Vanessa to keep her disguise.

Hero had found her some more gentlemen's garb and had packed it in a small trunk which was strapped to the back of the vehicle.

Before they left, Vanessa had sat at Hero's desk and written the missive to be given to Mr Cooper, the headmaster. She kept the wording simple:

"Unfortunately, Ernest Beeching, Williams grandfather has taken a turn for the worse, William is summoned back to Beeching Hall forthwith."

After they had picked up the boy, Bryant was going to drive them to Bristol where they would pay for passage on the first available ship travelling to America.

Vanessa had asked Hero if they could stop off at Sarah's home to pick up her money, but he had insisted on giving her what ready cash he had.

'I can visit Sarah and Jasper once you are well on your way,' he persisted. 'and pick up your money; I will send it on to you.'

Knowing that her friends would be one of the first places that George would look for her, she felt she had to agree.

'One thing is worrying me, Horacio.' Vanessa gave him a grave look. They sat opposite each other in the carriage. 'I shall be removing my son from his rightful inheritance.' She glanced out of the window at the chill day. 'I'm not sure I can do that.' A tear ran down her cheek. 'I have no right.'

Hero got up and came to sit beside her. He took her gloved hand in his own.

'I, for one, know how much of a burden an inheritance of a large estate can be, Nessa. But perhaps you should ask him what he wants to do, give him a choice.'

Her haunted gaze turned to his. 'But that would mean me explaining why I am running away.'

'Yes, I think you need to be frank with him.'

She nodded thoughtfully. 'How much should I tell him?'

Squeezing her fingers gently, he said, 'that is up to you, my dear.'

Shifting about so that she faced Hero on the carriage seat, the panic had leeched her cheeks of colour.

'What if he elects to stay, Hero. I would never be able to go and leave him, but they would have me locked up for sure, especially after all this.'

'Now, remember what you said to me, if you are locked up in an asylum, you are at their mercy. If you leave now, under your own volition, you will at least be free to do what you wish. You can go to America, and still write to your boy, and when anything happens to Beeching, you can come back.'

'Yes, yes.' She tried a smile: it did nothing to change her grim expression.

Before they reached the doors of *The Millbrook School for Young Gentlemen,* Vanessa and Hero got out of the carriage and waited while Bryant drove up to the front doors to deliver the letter and pick up the boy.

Vanessa did not know how familiar William was with the servants and grooms at Beeching Hall, so she gave the man another note which read; "bring your compass, darling, we can follow our hearts." She had given him a beautiful brass compass as a Christmas present, they had laughed about taking trips together and the possible places that they could visit. She knew that William would recognise that the message was from her. It also gave her a sense of fate; if he agreed to go with her, they would indeed be travelling to the other side of the world.

It seemed to take an age for the carriage to return and pick them up.

Hero and Vanessa kept back from the road, under the treeline out of sight, in case George turned up unexpectedly.

Eventually, they heard the carriage wheels on the drive. Then Bryant pulled to a halt just after leaving the entrance gates to the school. Vanessa and Hero jumped aboard.

William sat on the carriage seat, to Vanessa; he looked so much younger than his twelve years. So young and so vulnerable. His cheeks were white. His eyes looked like large pools. He didn't recognise her until she spoke.

'Oh, my darling.' She rushed over and folded him in her arms.

'Mama, mama, what's going on?'

Bryant drove them about a mile away from the school to give Vanessa a chance to talk to the boy.

'I need to leave, William.' Vanessa's voice was breathless with nerves. 'If I don't your grandmamma and papa will have me locked away. You see, I know things that can hurt your father, dark secrets. Perhaps one day I can tell you more, but not yet.'

'Father has never been kind to you,' the boy said, 'or me for that matter, mama. I know you are unhappy with him.' He surprised her by taking her hand. 'I want you to be happy, mama, more than anything. I would give up any inheritance or fortune for that.'

Vanessa sat there in stunned silence. She did not realise how much her boy had grown up until now. He spoke with depth and insight, perhaps with more understanding of the darkness of the human spirit than she would have liked.

'Are you sure, my darling?' she had to ask.

'Yes, mama, I am sure, where you go, I shall go.'

'It seems that you have your answer, Vanessa,' Hero commented.

She took her child in her arms and hugged him to her tightly. 'Yes.'

*

Andrew was feeling utterly exhausted as he walked through the busy streets back to his lodgings.

The evening was damp and cold. He had spent the day helping out a colleague at his local surgery. The doctor, Stuart Boyde, held a free surgery once a week in one of the poorest parts of the city, the East End.

Word had quickly gotten around: the surgery had become so popular, that Stuart had no other option than to turn people away. Having Andrew help out had been a huge boon, and as he kept telling his friend, there is no better experience in which to learn than to roll your sleeves up and get on with the practicality of medicine.

Finally, opening the front door to his lodgings, Andrew wiped his boots on the mat, as he did so, he inhaled the delicious aroma of steak and kidney pie. His mouth watered in anticipation; his stomach gurgled as he climbed the stairs.

'Ahh, you're back, doctor.' Mrs Gordon called from the hall. 'I shall give you a moment, then bring your tray up.'

'Thank you, Mrs Gordon, you are a star.'

When he walked into the sitting room, he found the table was already laid; a cheery fire crackled in the grate.

This was Mrs G's day for coming in to clean and pick up the laundry. The place looked ordered and welcoming.

As Andrew shrugged out of his coat and hung it up, he saw that all the paperwork that he had left out on the dining table had been sorted into piles, letters, notes, bills.

He blushed in mortification; he really should keep things tidier in here.

When Horacio had been around, Andrew was always respectful of keeping the living-room tidy. All their personal items were kept in their rooms. Andrew had to admit he had become lazy while Hero had been away.

Pulling his shirt sleeves up, he washed his hands and rinsed his face. As he dried off, there was a tap at the door. Striding across the room, he opened it to admit the housekeeper with his dinner tray.

'Smells glorious, Mrs G.' Andrew said in delight. The housekeeper smiled.

'Ahh, not only do you have good food to fill your belly, doctor, you have a letter from Gloucestershire that may go some way to fill your heart.' She gave him a wink, chuckling when he blushed.

'Oh, mm, yes.' He sat down at the table, placing a napkin over his knee, he dug into the pie. 'I shall look forward to reading it after I have eaten.'

She nodded in satisfaction, then left him to eat in peace.

As soon as she had shut the door, Andrew leant over and picked up the letter. He opened it with a paperknife. The message was from Sophia, and his heartbeat quickened with the excitement of hearing from her.

The first thing he noticed was her handwriting, usually so neat, in this letter it appeared to be shaky; there was the odd inkblot too, which was strange.

As he went to fork up another mouthful of food, Andrew scanned the correspondence.

The food did not reach his mouth; however, his heart stuttered as he read the message over again. A chill clutched him. He could not quite believe what he was reading.

"My dear Andrew, I have been in such a quandary - a battle rages inside of me. I find, in all good conscience, I cannot continue with our correspondence. After everything that has happened to me, I am sure that you will understand that I cannot embark on a relationship with any man. Therefore, I have decided to cease my letters and would ask you to do the same. I implore you to abide by my wishes."

She signed the letter; "Sincerely, Sophia Blum."

Andrew's hand shook as he laid his fork down on his plate. Up until this point, he hadn't realised just how much he admired, no "admired" was nowhere near enough to describe his feelings for this remarkable young woman. He had to admit to himself that she had stolen his heart: he loved her. Receiving her letters had been a joy to him, something he looked forward to after a long day.

As he placed the letter down next to his dinner plate, he shook his head in denial. Something had happened to her; he was sure of it.

Jumping to his feet, he rushed into his bedroom to pack a case, by God, he would travel to Gloucestershire and see her; he needed her to look him in the eye and tell him that she no longer cared for him.

Then, another thought occurred to him; perhaps there were some clues or indications that her feelings were changing towards him in her previous correspondence?

He walked back into the living room, picked up the pile of letters from the sideboard, then sat down at the table. He poured himself a glass of red wine that Mrs Gordon had left for him.

Andrew started to read through the letters once again.

The tone of them was light, full of news, descriptions of the people she was getting to know. How much she loved Brook House, Emily, and Claire. The feeling of being useful and working hard. There was one negative thread that Andrew picked up on, Sophia was worried about her friends Evie and Dottie, praying that they were safe and well.

The most recent letter, the one prior to this missive that had dealt the devastating blow, had been received two weeks prior, which Andrew had not realised; he had been so busy that the passing of time had been a bit of a blur.

The letters usually arrived from Sophia every few days. Then this gap had materialised. Something must have happened in the interim, but what?

Something else dawned on Andrew, the letter where she mentioned finding out that her attacker had been Beeching was missing. Andrew jumped to his feet. He shuffled through the letters again, the pile of bills and his lecture notes. When Andrew still could not locate it, he felt a chill ripple of apprehension run through him.

The letter had been misplaced, or someone had taken it; he trusted Mrs Gordon completely, the only other person who had been in his lodgings for any length of time, was Alec Silverman.

Andrew, his jaw clenched uttered several expletives; the bloody sod, Andrew thought, I was right not to trust him. The more Andrew thought about it, the surer he became that Alec was the culprit, he had taken Sophia's letter, the question was for what purpose?

*

It took Alec over a week to feel he had healed enough from his attack to put his plans into action.

While he had been resting in his father's townhouse, he had a visit from the thug, Barrett.

Even in his expensively cut clothes, the man looked so out of place in the smart drawing-room, Alec wanted to laugh, but he kept his dark humour under control.

'Tell me you have found the culprits who attacked me.' Alec sat in an armchair, his feet on a footstool.

The tall man opened his long black coat, fished in an inside pocket, and drew out a small bag.

'There yer go.' He handed it to Alec, who handled it reluctantly as if he thought he would pick up some kind of disease.

Emptying the contents into his lap, Alec discovered that Barrett had indeed recovered his stolen goods.

'Excellent.' He turned his attention back to the ruffian, 'and the men who attacked me?'

'Ave been dealt with.'

Alec nodded, 'good, very good. Have you found a girl for Beeching yet?'

If Barrett was surprised by this question, he didn't show it.

'Aye, Margie is grooming her, a pretty little thing, but strong-willed.'

'I've heard that Beeching isn't in London at the moment,' Alec commented.

'Yes, that's true.'

Alec got up, wincing when the effort caused his ribs to object to the movement. 'Does he know about the girl?'

Barrett frowned, wondering where this conversation was going. 'Not yet.'

'Ahh, good.' Walking over to the bellpull to summon one of the servants to see the man out, he dismissed him. 'You can go, man.'

When Barrett stood his ground, Alec gave him an impatient look, his hand hovering by the pull. 'What is it?'

'Do you know when Mr Woodley will be back in the ring?'

Alec felt his cheeks flush in irritation.

'I am not Woodley's keeper, Barrett. He has made it quite plain to me that he is his own man. I have no idea if he will be back or not.'

Walking over to a sideboard, he picked up a decanter. Alec poured himself a finger of whiskey and knocked it back, then poured another. He did not offer his visitor a drink.

'If you find a suitable contender for me to sponsor, let me know.'

'I'm not sure that will be possible,' Jolly said.

'Why the hell not?' Alec sat back down, placing his glass on a side table.

'You have some outstanding debts, need paying up.'

'Ahh, don't worry about them.' Alec waved his hand nonchalantly in the air, 'just a glitch, my father will cover them.'

'I spoke to Mr Hill yesterday; he says that your father will not bail you out this time.'

'What!' His face infused in anger; Alec forgot his injuries as he jumped to his feet. 'Ahh,' holding his side, he sat down heavily. 'You had no bloody right to talk to anyone about my debts.'

Jolly gave him a smug look. 'I said nothing. It were yer father who passed on the message.'

Picking up the whiskey glass, Alec found that his hands were trembling. He took a sip of the drink as he tried to collect himself.

'Well, no matter,' he said at last, 'I have an, umm, enterprise in the making which will more than cover what I owe.'

'Well, I'm highly delighted to hear that.' Jack gave him a smile which chilled Alec. 'See the thing is,' he indicated the small treasure trove he had given back to Alec, 'I could ave kept them things to sell, they would fetch a fair price to elp pay off some of your debts, especially when your father has said he will not support you. But, out of the kindness of me eart, I decided to return them to you.' The man shrugged, 'Now, I've done you a favour Master Silverman,' he spoke Alec's name with a curl of disdain. 'It would elp no end; if you could persuade Mr Woodley to return to the ring.'

Once one of the servants had seen the hoodlum out, Alec sat back in the armchair endeavouring to calm himself. He was furious, however - angry with Horacio, furious with his father. And Barrett, oh he hated the man with a vengeance – how dare he stand there lording it over everyone, the stupid fool in his well-cut clothes.

The thought that his own father would not help him get out of bother made his stomach churn uncomfortably. He drained his drink, got up and pulled the bellpull to summon the maid.

He knew that Beeching was staying on the family estate in Norfolk as his father was unwell. Alec pondered what to do; he could go to Woodley Hall to see Horacio, to do what Barrett had demanded, get him to come back into the fighting ring. Or, he could seek out Beeching, which had been his original plan.

Yes, he thought in satisfaction, he had a feeling Beeching would pay handsomely to have the girl, Sophia, back in his clutches. Alec remembered what a beauty she was. He just wondered how much he should ask for – how much the man would pay for this little gem of information. Then Alec stopped in his tracks; maybe he should take a trip to Gloucestershire, steal the girl away and take her to Beeching. Alec was quite sure that seeing the girl again would enflame George's ardour. He would pay a high price to have her again, wouldn't he?

When the maid arrived, Alec told her to pack him a trunk with everything he would need for a few days.

*

The hideous odour of vomit woke Katie Arnold from a deep sleep; she was having a wonderful dream too; one where she was rich and lived in a big house, being her own woman, not at someone's beck and call anymore.

Sitting up in bed, she rubbed her eyes. It was cold and damp in the room; the fire had gone out.

She heard Margie groan then her croaky voice, 'You awake?' she called, 'elp me, girl.'

Reluctantly, Katie got out of bed and found the woman sprawled on the floor, vomit and alcohol fumes hit her hard. Katie was used to bad smells, but this made her stomach heave.

Looking to the window, a haze of grey light pushed through the dirty curtain. It must have been early morning.

As she stood there in her nightdress, Margie eyed her, holding out a hand to her. 'Don't just stand there yer little bitch, elp me up.'

Katie leant down. 'I aint yer servant, get yerself up.'

This time, Margie's voice was wheedling. 'Elp me up, lass, there's a good girl.'

Reluctantly, Katie bent down. She grabbed the older woman's arm and pulled her to her feet, where she stood and swayed, then vomited once again.

'Errr, yer dirty old bitch, don't expect me to clean it up.'

'Ere, who are you calling a bitch.'

Margie lashed out at the girl to hit her around the face, but the action was too much, Margie fell heavily. She groaned again and started to weep bitter tears. 'Moll, where are yer, Moll ...'

Katie rolled her eyes. Aww, she had had enough of this. Rinsing her hands and face in yesterday's washing water, she then pulled her clothes on over her nightdress.

Grabbing Margie's old carpet-bag' Katie packed her few possessions, then anything belonging to the old whore worth a penny or two. She also knew where Margie had hidden her pot of money, under one of the floorboards under the bed.

While Margie was still wailing on the floor, Katie moved the bed, levered up the board with an old knife. Fished out the leather bag, which felt reassuringly weighty, she put that in the carpet bag along with the other items. As soon as that was done, she put on her coat, which was a mid-calf length. It wasn't new; it had been bought from Mrs Smart down the market. Katie had been a bit peeved that it was second-hand, but now she was glad: if it had been new, she would have stood out like a sore thumb on these streets.

Shutting the bag, she stepped over the woman as a snore issued from her. Huh, thought Katie, the old cow had fallen asleep. She smiled with satisfaction: it would mean that Margie wouldn't realise that she had scarpered for a while, which would give her a chance to be long gone before any alarm had been raised.

When she stepped into the hall, she didn't head towards the front door; she knew that Jolly had one of his lads watching the house. She made her way through the back, into the muddy yard. The wall surrounding the yard was high, but someone had left a couple of old crates out there. Katie climbed up, threw the bag over the top of the wall. It landed with a thud on the other side, then she pulled herself up, sat on the top for a moment, then dropped to the brick-paved alley below.

She picked up Margie's bag and ran.

*

When Margie eventually opened her eyes, the daylight pressing through the gaps in the curtains was bright. She blinked in the harsh light, then winced as pain shot through her head. Her mouth was bone dry and sour as a crate of rotting lemons.

Gingerly, she sat up. Looking down at herself, she couldn't quite believe the state she had gotten into. Her clothes were covered in dry vomit; eh, it was her good dress and coat too. She had vomit caked on her face and in her hair.

'Katie,' she called as she got to her knees, then used the back of one of the wooden chairs to pull herself up. The room spun for a moment, then settled.

'Katie, where are yer girl?' she called out again.

Checking behind the curtain, the girl's bed was empty. The room was cold too. The little bitch hadn't made up the fire, which was one of the jobs that was expected of her.

Then Margie began to realise that a few bits and pieces were missing. Her heart almost stopped in her chest when she saw that her bed had been moved. Warily, she checked underneath. The floorboard had been levered up.

The space underneath the board was empty.

'No!' Margie fisted her hands as the heat of anger rose into her cheeks. The little bitch had made a run for it, and she had taken all of Margie's stash of savings.

When the implications hit her, Margie sat down heavily on one of the wooden chairs. A shiver ran through her - what the ell would Jolly say when she told him this bit of news. Aww, she would get the full brunt of the blame for this.

Sitting there with her pounding head in her hands, she tried to think of the best course of action, which wasn't easy to do in her alcohol addled brain. If she told Reg to go and fetch Jack, they were likely to start a search for the girl. Margie wondered then what the time was: how long had the girl been gone? Judging by the light pressing at the window, it was late morning. Then, through the other sounds of the house and the busy streets, she heard the tolling of the church clock, twelve chimes – a death knell for Margie.

Oh Lord, she thought, the girl must have been gone for hours. If Reg had seen her go, he would have been in here like a shot to check with Margie what had happened. There had been no sign of him, then again, he might have handed the shift over to one of the other lads.

She groaned. It was all too much. Getting up, Margie found that she was still unsteady on her feet.

Searching the shelves, she came across a half bottle of gin. She un-stoppered it and took a long swig. Then sat back down with the bottle in front of her.

What choices did she have? Aww, her head ached something cruel, making any cohesive thoughts impossible.

Maybe she should make a run for it? Glancing around the room, she realised that anything of any value had gone. Without her savings, she wouldn't get far.

'May that little bitch burn in ell,' She cursed aloud, then took another slug of gin.

Just then, Margie heard the front door of the house open. Then the one to her room. Jolly stood tall in the doorway; he stepped inside.

Chapter 44

Jolly was feeling frustrated when he left the meeting with Alec Silverman. He decided to head to Little Back Lane to check on Margie and Katie.

His sources had informed him that Beeching was still away. Apparently, his father was ill; that meant that Margie would have to look after Katie for a while longer. This concerned Jack, he had noticed a decline in Margie, she always had a fondness for the gin, but it was getting out of hand. She looked old and worn out, and this meant that she wasn't bringing the punters in like she used to either.

Barrett had decided that once the Arnold girl was handed over to Beeching, he would kick Marge out of her lodgings; get a couple of new girls in.

When he came within sight of the docks, dark clouds scudded across the sky. Seagulls called raucously, fighting for titbits left behind on the slick mud exposed by the outgoing tide. Old wrecks of boats thrust ribs of rotting wood towards the dockside; they resembled skeletons of fossilised mammoths.

Pausing to light one of his smokes, Jolly inhaled deeply, then blew out a plume of smoke. As he did so, his thoughts turned to Evie, his wife. Aww, she was a vexing woman, he had tried everything he could think of to make her more amenable.

Jolly shook his head in perplexity as he turned into Little Back Lane: no woman had ever had cause for complaint when Jack took them to bed, they always wanted more, so he couldn't comprehend what was wrong with the woman.

Perhaps she needed a firmer hand, to be taught like a dog to come to heel? Surprisingly, that thought chilled his heart. Jolly did not shirk from violent encounters, a hard fist, sometimes more, was required at times to bring people back in tow. However, his father had been overly zealous where his mother was concerned. Jolly did not want to turn into his father.

No, he decided, he would give Evie time. He was confident she would come around in the end; he was sure of it.

As for her younger sister, Dottie, she was thriving now she had gotten over her illness. Dottie was two years younger than Evie; she still had a childish streak within her which animated her, she laughed easily, was a tonic for the senses. Jolly found himself pondering the thought that he had married the wrong sister.

Spotting one of his lads, Davey Bow, he was eating a meat pie as he sat on an old crate, keeping watch outside the Back Lane house.

'Everything been alright?' Jolly asked him.

Davey swallowed as gravy ran down his chin. 'Oh aye, Mr Barrett, Reg said Margie got back in the early hours, drunk as a skunk she was, but ain't seen either of them after that.'

'Right.' Jolly nodded and then pushed open the front door of the house.

He didn't bother knocking on Margie's door, he opened it and stepped into the room. The first thing that hit him was the stink of vomit. He wrinkled his nose with distaste.

He saw the woman sitting at the table. When he stepped towards her, his boot squelched in the revolting mess on the floor.

'Awe, for Christ sake, Margie, what the ell.' He rubbed the sole of his boot against the bare boards.

Margie took a swig from a bottle as she eyed him with bloodshot eyes; her gaze was fuzzy. 'Ello, Jack.'

Returning his attention to the woman, he was shocked by what he saw; by God, she looked awful. Muck covering her chin. Her skin as white as wax. She had spots of unhealthy colour on her cheeks and the end of her nose, which was dripping snot. Her eyes were haunted, red-rimmed and sunken in her face.

'Bloody ell, Marge, what the ell as happened to you?'

'I ad a bad night, Jack.'

Taking in the room more thoroughly, he asked, 'Where's the girl?'

Margie looked at him; she was trying desperately to stop her hands from shaking. 'She attacked me in the night, did a runner.'

Jolly scowled; his eyes narrowed threateningly. 'How the ell did she manage that, I ad Reg and Danny watchin the place.'

'She must ave went out the back.'

This news was too much for Jolly, he reached out and grabbed her shoulder, pulling her none too gently to her feet.

'You stupid bloody cow, Marge.' He growled at her like a mad dog. 'I give yer one job. One job, an you've let me down!' Shaking his head, his large hands gripped the top of her arms so hard she cried out. Pain also shot through her head, making her feel as if she were going to vomit again.

Suddenly, Jolly let her go. Still unsteady on her feet, she staggered, then Margie fell catching her cheek on the corner of the table. Crying out, she landed heavily.

Jolly stood over her, not bothering to hold out a hand to help her up; instead, he said, 'Get yer stuff together and get out.'

'W-what?' Margie's face crumpled into anguish. She sat on the cold, dusty floor, clutching her cheek. Aww, it felt as if something was broken.

Jolly took a step back; this time avoided the mess on the floor. 'I said I want you out of here.'

'No, no. Please, Jack.' Margie's tear-filled eyes darted to Jack's face. The smouldering rage she saw there frightened her, she hastily looked away. 'Send out a search party, Jack. The boys will find er. I'll make sure she doesn't run off again, even if I ave to tie her to the bed.'

He shook his head, 'Look at the bloody state of you woman, I can't trust you to stay sober.'

'It aint my fault. I miss Moll so much.'

'Yes well, first Molly let me down, now you.'

'I tried, Jack,' she wailed.

'Huh, look at the state of you, Margie, you're done.' He gestured around the room, 'I've been generous letting you ave the best room in the ouse.' He leant down, giving her a look, which froze her heart. 'Yer done ere, get out.'

'W-what do yer mean, Jack?'

Margie eyed him; desperation written all over her face. She tried to grab his trouser leg to pull herself up. Jolly stepped hastily out of her grasp.

'Yer know exactly what I mean, yer old bag. Get out. I've got a line of people who would pay good money for this room.'

Her red-rimmed eyes watered; tears dripped down her cheeks. 'No Jack, please I beg of you, being out on em streets will kill me.'

The tall man's hand shot out. He grabbed her by the scruff of her neck, bodily lifting her to her feet. But she couldn't stand up without support, so Jack dragged her to the door. When he got to the street outside, he dropped her in the dirt.

'Davie,' Jack called. 'Get a mop an bucket, clear up the mess in that room.' He nodded to the house.

'Alright, Mr Barrett.' The lad's gaze darted to Margie, who was on the damp, muddy ground groaning.

'Get on with it.' Jack prompted him.

'Aye.' The young man went to walk past Jack, but Jack grabbed his arm.

He indicated the prone woman. 'You don't let er back into the ouse, yer ear me?'

The lad nodded and dashed inside.

*

When he told George Beeching that his son, William, had already left with a groom who was taking him home to see his grandfather; Mr Cooper, the headmaster of Millbrook School, thought that Beeching was going to have an apoplexy in his office.

'The groom had a letter from Lady Beeching.' The younger man poured his visitor a snifter of brandy.

Thrusting his hand out, George demanded, 'Show me this bloody letter.'

Mr Cooper put the glass down, then shuffled through the paperwork on his desk. Finding the letter, he handed it to Lord Beeching, who grabbed it. Scanning the note as the headmaster hovered nervously.

'This is from my wife, man, not my mother. I gave you strict instructions not to let her visit without my permission. And certainly not to turn up and take the boy.'

'The boy boarded a carriage that was empty; there was no sign of Lady Beeching the younger.' Cooper could feel nervous sweat trickle down his back.

George sat down heavily in a leather wingback chair. Picking up the glass of brandy that the headmaster had put down, he tipped the glass to his lips and drained the contents. He wiped his lips with the back of his hand and put the glass back on the desk none too gently.

'How long ago?'

'Mmm, how long ago, what?'

George gave the man a hard look. 'How long ago did this happen?'

'Before luncheon was served.'

Beeching put his head in his hands, 'Oh God, they could be anywhere by now.' He looked at the headmaster once more, 'Which way did the carriage head?'

The man shook his head. 'After it drove down the drive, I could not see from here whether it turned left or right.'

Getting to his feet, George's face was infused with angry colour.

'This is not the end of the matter, Cooper. By God, I shall ensure that this place is closed down within the year.'

The headmaster gritted his teeth. 'I fear that should this story get about, Lord Beeching,' he parried, 'people will wonder what drove your wife to flee her marriage.'

George's face creased into a manic expression which was beyond anger. Fisting his hands, he stepped towards the headmaster menacingly. Cooper stood his ground.

'How dare you.' George hissed. 'How bloody dare you.'

'I think you had better leave, sir.' Cooper did not step back; instead, he eyed the man coldly.

George shook his head, trying to get his anger under control, then he turned and staggered from the room like a drunkard. As he did so, Cooper let out his breath in relief. He had always found Beeching to be a detestable man, whereas William was a gentle boy – ahh, probably far too gentle for this world – was a joy to teach.

As soon as he spotted George, the carriage driver jumped down and opened the door for him. As George climbed aboard, he instructed his driver to take him to the home of Sarah and Jasper Frobisher.

*

Sarah Frobisher had an open and kind face. A petite woman with a huge heart. She could not abide injustice or violence. Sarah had been saddened when her closest friend, Vanessa, had been involved with this arranged marriage. She detested George, as did Jasper, they both recognised darkness within him; he was a bully of the worst kind.

Her marriage to Jasper had also been "an arrangement", however, they had found in each other many shared interests which brought them together, first as friends, then as lovers.

The couple were very content in their marriage. Sarah had given Jasper two sons and a daughter. A pug named Chisholm completed their family.

On this bleak day in February, Sarah was indulging herself with her favourite pastime, reading. Chisholm lay on the rug beside the fire snoring loudly. Instead of being an annoyance, the sound of his snoring was a comfort to Sarah; she loved the little dog to distraction.

The two boys were away at school, only their daughter, Florence, Florrie, was at home, she was up in the schoolroom with her governess, Miss Howard.

Jasper had ridden over to Home Farm to meet with Mr Thompson, the farm manager.

The house was hushed. Sarah had been so engrossed in her book that she didn't hear the brass bell of the door. The knock on her drawing-room door made her jump.

'A Lord Beeching to see you, ma'am,' one of the footmen announced, 'are you at home, ma'am?'

Before Sarah could say otherwise, George pushed past the young man and strode into the room as if he owned the place.

'Where is she?' His voice was a growl, his face red with anger.

Sarah's gaze darted to meet the shocked one of the footman. Then she swallowed, composing herself. She set her book aside, stood up and brushed out the creases of her lavender day dress.

Chisholm, startled awake, growled.

'Ahh, Lord Beeching.' Sarah stood her ground; she looked over to the hovering footman, 'Arthur, go and tell Lord Frobisher that we have a visitor. And please ask Mrs Marshal to bring in a tray of coffee.'

'Yes, your ladyship.'

She could see that he was reluctant to leave her alone with this mad man. Giving him a reassuring nod of the head, which he returned, then rushed from the room.

'Coffee?! I'm not here on a social visit, Sarah, I've come to find my wife.'

'Vanessa?'

'Yes, of course it's Vanessa, who the bloody hell did you think I was talking about.' Standing far too close for comfort, he used his extra height to intimidate her.

Sarah could smell his sour breath. There was a manic look in his eyes that frightened her.

Chisholm must have sensed her fear, he hauled his round body up on his short legs and growled again.

'I can assure you that Vanessa is not here.' Sarah insisted, endeavouring to keep her voice calm. 'I haven't seen her since you all left for Norfolk. Mmm, how is your father, by the way?'

Her calm attitude must have deflated his anger slightly as he found himself answering her. 'Still the same,' he said.

Sarah offered him a smile, 'Well, no worse then. So that is a good thing, yes?'

'Oh, umm, yes.'

She gestured to one of the chairs. 'Now, why don't you sit and tell me what has happened, George. I will, of course, give you any help I can.'

Suddenly, the bluster went out of him. He sat down heavily in one of the chairs. 'We disagreed. She has gone.'

Sarah sat back down in the chair she had just vacated. Her heart still pounded uncomfortably. She didn't want to think about what this man had put her friend through. Sarah cleared her throat and asked, 'When you say gone, what do you mean?'

He jumped to his feet once more. 'What the hell do you think I mean, woman. Vanessa is ill. She is ill, I tell you. She needs treatment.'

Sarah didn't move, but Chisholm growled again. She stooped down and lifted the dog on to her lap. His presence comforted her.

'She seemed perfectly fine when I last saw her.' Sarah offered.

George rounded on her. 'You and my wife have always been plotting and scheming. How do I know that you are telling me the truth? She could be right here in this house hiding.'

'You are welcome to look, George, I can assure you once again that she is not here.'

Sarah was relieved when there was a tap on the door. One of the maids brought in a tray of coffee things.

'His lordship will be with you shortly, ma'am.' The maid, Lucy, set the tray down on a table. She shot George a look of concern, then asked her mistress, 'shall I serve?'

'No, you may go,' George spoke up, anger making his voice rough.

'Yes, please stay and serve, Lucy.' Sarah was quick to counteract his dismissal.

'Top mine up with a tot of brandy then.' Much to Sarah's relief, George sat back down.

'Yes, sir.' Lucy deliberately took her time to pour out the coffee, to pick up a bottle of brandy from the sideboard and top up his drink. Sarah knew that Arthur had told her not to leave the mistress alone with this crazed man.

The task could only be drawn out for so long, however. Once Lucy had handed Beeching his cup and saucer, she stepped to one side as if she were standing sentinel in the room.

'Oh, for god sake, get out.' George waved a hand to the girl.

'She will do no such thing, George,' Sarah's voice was chilled. 'You have no right to come into my home and take over like this, no right at all.'

Waving a hand in the air, he said, 'yes, yes, of course. I apologise.'

Sarah nodded her head graciously; what on earth was wrong with the man? His behaviour was so erratic? It looked to her as if George was the one that needed *treatment*, not Vanessa – but where was Vanessa? Had she really run away, and if so, why? Sarah shivered with apprehension.

George drained his coffee cup then indicated to the maid to pour him another.

While she was doing so, Sarah was highly relieved to hear voices in the hall; Jasper was home.

Jasper strode into the room. He was a tall man with a swathe of dark hair salted with silver. Older than his wife by eleven years, he still looked full of youth and vitality. Ignoring Beeching, who had risen to his feet, Jasper went straight to Sarah, who placed Chisholm on the floor then stood up. There was such a difference in their heights that she looked like a child next to him.

Taking her hands, which were almost as chilly as his own, he kissed them. As he did so, he scrutinised her expression with concern.

'Are you well, my dear?' he asked.

Sarah nodded. Jasper released her hands but did not move from her side as he turned to face George.

'To what do we owe the honour of this unexpected visit, George?'

'Vanessa has disappeared. I am worried about the state of her health.'

'Well, I am sorry to hear that, but what made you think she would come here?'

George's eyes darted to Sarah. 'She has a good friend in your wife, Jasper, possibly to the level of collusion.'

'Collusion?' Jasper laughed. 'A bit overdramatic don't you think?'

His face darkening in anger once more, George gave Jasper a hard look.

'I am not blind or deaf. I know that my wife and yours have plotted and planned together.' His gaze went to Sarah.

'She has been feeding you lies about me for all these years. I have, mmm, tolerated the situation, but this time it has gone too far.'

'When you say lies,' Sarah spoke up not able to hold back any longer, 'you mean all the abuse you have doled out to her, I have seen the bruises. Then there are the other unspeakable and despicable things that you have done to other young women.'

George's visage reddened even more. Both Jasper and Sarah thought he was going to explode.

Jasper, whose face had drained of colour, turned his attention to his wife. 'What despicable things, Sarah? What has been going on?'

Sarah blushed not in mortification but pent-up anger. As her dear friend had asked her to, Sarah had discussed this matter with no other, but the knowledge was a terrible weight to bear.

'Vanessa begged me not to reveal any of this.' Tears sprang into her eyes, 'but I was the only one she could talk to, well myself and Horacio.'

'Horacio?'

'Woodley?'

The two men spoke as one.

Sarah bowed her head as she bit her lip, oh Lord, she had said too much.

'What the hell has this got to do with Horacio Woodley!' George's voice crawled over her like a thousand wasp stings.

She took a breath and lifted her head. 'Horacio has been a good friend to Vanessa. Married to you, she needed all the friends she could get.'

Jasper put his arm about her shoulders, pulling her closer. Sarah was glad of his presence.

'What has been going on?' he asked her gently.

Sarah indicated George with a wave of her hand. 'During the early years of their marriage, he used Vanessa in the most despicable ways, but not only that, once she was expecting William, he turned his attention to young girls, he is an abuser and rapist.'

'How dare you!' George stormed, stepping towards her threateningly. Chisholm jumped to his feet and started to bark at the man. 'By God, I will sue you for slander or worse.'

Jasper, his face a mask of horror, stepped in front of his wife. 'I do not know what has been going on, Beeching. I trust Sarah completely; she would say none of this unless there were truth behind the allegations.'

Georges' eyes darted around the room wildly. 'Ah well, you see this is the thing, Vanessa is unhinged. I should have taken the matter in hand years ago.'

'That's not true, Jasper,' Sarah spoke up, her voice was brittle with emotion.

George looked the tall man in the eye, shrugged his shoulders while giving a cracked laugh. 'You must understand, Frobisher, how hysterical women can be.'

'I know nothing of the sort, Beeching. I feel that I have gotten to know Vanessa well over the years, and I consider her not only a friend of my wife but mine too. As to everything that has been said this morning, I obviously don't know the details, but one thing I do know, there is very seldom smoke without a fire. Now, I suggest you get out of my house before I punch you into next week.' He took a step towards George, his face rigid with anger.

'Jasper.' Sarah put a hand on his arm.

Beeching, getting the message, turned and staggered towards the door. Before he reached it, however, he turned back.

'If you spread any of these vicious lies about me, Frobisher, I will sue you, do you hear me.'

'Get out!' Jasper thundered. It seemed as if George cowered for just a moment, then turned and left.

Sarah grasped her husband's hand. 'Make sure he is gone.'

'Of course,' Jasper squeezed her hand in return, then strode across the room.

Hearing the front door open and closed, then the sound of a carriage driving over the gravelled drive, Sarah let out a breath of relief.

Oh Lord, that encounter had been terrible. Then there was Vanessa, where was she?

Sarah found that her legs were shaking, she sat down heavily in the fireside chair. Chisholm jumped up and pawed against her legs, she leant over and lifted the dog; he snuggled against her as she buried her face in his fur.

In a few moments, Jasper reappeared. 'It's alright, my love, he's gone.'

'Oh, thank goodness.'

'I think you and I need to talk,' Jasper said as he took the seat opposite her. 'Tell me what on earth has been going on?'

Chapter 45

Horacio, Vanessa, and William reached Bristol in the early hours of the morning.

William had slept most of the way, covered in a wool blanket with his head resting on his mother's lap.

Vanessa, stroking his hair back from his forehead, found she couldn't stop gazing at her son.

Having him here with her calmed her. With him by her side, she knew she had the strength for this undertaking, this journey they were about to embark upon.

Bryant took them to an Inn not far from the docks. Hero then left to buy tickets for them both on the next outbound ship heading towards America.

He was delighted to find that there was a ship sailing within the hour, which was heading to New York. Hero didn't hesitate, he bought the tickets, then rushed back to the Inn.

When Hero had relayed his news, Vanessa found that her hands were shaking. Her mouth was bone dry despite the small ale she had drunk at the inn, whilst waiting in a private room.

'I will miss you, darling.' She gave Hero a longing look, 'if only things could have been different.'

Hero glanced at William, who was busy chatting to Bryant. Seeing that the boy was distracted, Hero reached out and took her hands in his.

'I-,' Hero found that his voice cracked with emotion. He squeezed her hands gently, swallowed, then continued. 'I shall miss you too, my beautiful love.' He gave her an earnest look. 'No looking back now,' he coaxed. 'You and William will be free to make lives for yourselves.' She nodded, but a tear escaped, resting upon her lower lid.

Hero gathered her in his arms and kissed the top of her head. They both heard William and Bryant laugh about something or other. The two pulled apart self-consciously.

There was a chill wind buffeting the docks as William and Vanessa, who was still dressed in her man's garb, boarded the ship that would take them to their new lives.

Hero had given her strict instructions to write and let him know where she finally settled. Then he would arrange to have the money that Sarah had held for her, sent on.

When the ship set sail, Horacio stood on the dock and watched it depart, sailing down the Bristol Channel. He could make out Vanessa's face, which was ghostly pale beneath her tweed cap. Neither of them waved, but Hero did not leave the dockside until the ship was out of sight.

*

'Where to now?' Bryant asked him when they arrived back at the Inn.

'We'll breakfast here, let the horses have a rest, then we shall head to Oxfordshire, I need to see Sara Frobisher, and let her know what has happened.'

'Aye,' Bryant tipped his cap then made his way to the stables to ensure the horses were fed and watered.

Hero suddenly felt exhausted when he sat down in the snug of the Inn. There was a good fire in the grate. The aroma of bacon and baked bread hung in the air making his stomach rumble noisily.

He placed an order for breakfast for both himself and Bryant. As he waited for the food to arrive, Hero's mind turned to Beeching. God, the man was evil to the very core. He hadn't mentioned anything to Vanessa, but Hero had a strong feeling that Beeching would never stop looking for her, that thought concerned him more than he would have liked.

*

When George left the Frobisher's estate, his hands were shaking. His heartbeat drummed in his ears. He felt hot yet cold and clammy at the same time.

He managed to fish his hip flask from his coat pocket, unscrewed the silver top and took a long swig of the liquor.

Oh Lord, everything was getting out of hand. The fact that Vanessa had told Sarah about everything he had done to her and the others made his stomach heave in fear. He feared that he was going to be sick, but he managed to swallow down the bile.

Sarah would tell Jasper everything she knew, but what exactly did she know? How much had Vanessa revealed to her friend?

Beeching decided that he would have to deny everything. Then would fuel the gossip mongers into spreading the word that his wife had succumbed to some sort of hysterical illness or breakdown and was delusional.

In essence, her absence would fuel the gossip if he spread the word that she had been hospitalised for her own good.

Also, as he threatened, he would sue Sarah and Jasper for slander - who would people believe? A member of parliament or a yokel, country squire?

Although, whatever happened, George would be dealing with the fallout. What would all this do to his reputation? A scandal like this could ruin him. Then there was his mother, what was she going to say when he told her that Vanessa had vanished taking the heir to the vast estate with her.

*

Alec Silverman tried extremely hard to disguise his annoyance when he found that George Beeching had left for a couple of days to attend to business.

'He may well return tonight, or more likely tomorrow.' Lady Margot Beeching explained as she sat, back ramrod straight, in a wingback chair close to the fire in the vast drawing-room.

'Well, in that case, I shall book a room at the nearest Inn, then if you could send word to me when he returns. It is a matter of some urgency.' Alec explained, once again.

'So, you have said, Mr Silverman.' Margot gave him a cold look, her lips thin with disapproval.

Alec took umbrage with her attitude. He saw it as a slur towards himself and his family – the Beeching family were old money, many generations of landowners and lords. In contrast, they frowned upon families like his own, immigrants, new money!

Alec's gaze darted to Ernest Beeching, who sat in a wheelchair opposite his wife. A nurse sat on a chair set against the wall, so she was at hand if she was needed. The old man's face looked peculiar as if someone had set a torch to him, and his flesh had melted on one side.

Alec inwardly shuddered when he noticed a dribble of saliva was running down his chin. A limp hand rested in his lap. Alec did not fail to observe, however, that the man's eyes were inquisitive, even though he did not speak, he was following the conversation.

Taking Alec by surprise, Margot got to her feet and rang the bell pull next to the fireplace.

'I shall have one of the maids see you out, Mr Silverman.'

'Oh, um, yes.' Annoyed about being so abruptly dismissed, Alec got to his feet. 'You will send word when George is back then?'

Margot raised an eyebrow, but nodded, 'Yes.'

A maid must have been waiting outside the drawing-room as the door opened almost straight away after the summons.

Alec nodded his goodbyes.

When Collins drove his carriage down the long sweeping driveway, Alec gritted his teeth. How dare they treat him as if he were a nobody!

Several thoughts had occurred to Alec on his long journey to Norfolk; his main objective had been to coerce money from Beeching by promising to bring him the girl,

Sophia. The other idea that he was entertaining, which was becoming more appealing by the moment, was to use the girl, and also the letter he had in his possession, the one that Sophia had written to Andrew Keene, naming George Beeching as her attacker.

It seemed to Alec that his *Lordship* might pay very generously indeed for that little titbit, than he would for the girl, the word "blackmail" popped into his head, Alec Silverman smiled in satisfaction.

*

Evie wanted to cover her ears to block out the sound of voices and laughter that emanated from the other side of the room.

She was seated in the library; from her position, she could see out over the garden that spanned the side of the house.

In her lap, she had a lawn petticoat which had a tear in it. Evie decided she was going to mend it. As she sat there, pushing the needle through the delicate cotton, in the back of her mind was the notion that she did not need to be undertaking this task; she and Dottie had drawers full of underwear; petticoats, bloomers, camisoles, etc. Evie, however, was searching for something - the stability of an everyday task that would ground her in the turbulent world that roared in her head.

With thought, she realised that she should have chosen another room in which to sew. Dottie, Ivy and Tommy were seated at a table at the other end of the room. The "lessons", which Mrs Perkins had agreed to, took place every couple of days when the brother and sister had some free time, turned out to be jolly affairs.

Ivy, being the same age as Dottie, Tommy was two years older; had become firm friends.

Evie had tried her best to warn Dot not to get too close to these people; She must remember that Tommy was no friend of theirs. He was the one who found them the day they had run away and entered the workhouse.

When she had voiced her thoughts, much to Evie's astonishment, Dottie had rounded on her sister.

'I like them, Evie.' She gestured around her pretty bedroom, 'I like it here.' Evie shook her head as tears blurred her vision. 'I know you aren't happy being married to Jack,' Dottie continued, 'but this place is a bloody sight better than where we came from.'

Clenching her fists tightly, Evie felt her nails digging into her palm.

'Don't swear, Dottie.' She found herself uttering ineffectively.

Dottie laughed then. Evie gazed at her sister as if she were viewing a stranger. With the good hearty food Mrs Perkins and Ivy served, her face and body had filled out. Her honey-coloured hair was glossy with good health. She wore it pinned up, which made her look older than her fifteen years. Evie realised with a jolt that Dottie had grown up. Her blue eyes shined as she gave her sister a considered look.

'You need to swallow your pride, Evie. Make things work with Jack.'

Evie blinked at the other girl. She was utterly stunned by what she was hearing. When Dottie cocked her head to one side, Evie's heart quaked, what was coming next? And where had her comrade gone? With Dot by her side, she knew she could get through anything, but it seemed that a great gulf had opened up between them.

'As Mrs Barrett, you have power, Evie.' Dottie pointed out, then turned on her heel and left Evie in a place where the earth tilted beneath her feet.

Back in the present, without realising it, Evie found that she had stuck the needle into her thumb; she withdrew it. Making no effort to stem the flow, she watched, mesmerised as the jewel of blood formed on her pale skin. The blood dripped, blooming like a flower on the white fabric. When Evie heard further laughter coming from the other end of the room once more, the sound grated on her nerves. Evie plunged the needle deep into the pad of her thumb again.

*

It was past midnight. Sophia sat on the window seat in the bedroom she shared with Beth Brownley.

Beth was a robust girl with a perpetual smile that dimpled her cheeks. With a mop of blonde curls and an ample bosom, she looked older than her fifteen years.

She and Sophia got on well; they both had painful pasts that did not dim their enjoyment of life.

Beth had been raped by her stepfather, had managed to *escape,* and was taken in by the workhouse.

Beth had only realised she had been pregnant when she had a miscarriage, very nearly dying from blood loss.

Because she had been in the infirmary on one of Claire's and Emily's visits, they had stopped to chat with her. Intelligence and curiosity brightened her blue eyes. When Emily explained Brook House School to her, she expressed such an interest in cooking. Not just cooking, but the possibility of becoming the head cook in a large household. When they offered her a place at the school, she jumped at the chance.

Sophia heard the grandfather clock from the hall chiming once; one o'clock in the morning. She sighed deeply. The moon hid behind the clouds, the garden below the window was pooled in shadows – some denser than others.

Brook House School was a magical place, a place of healing; but, was it the place itself, or the people? Sophia felt as if she had been enveloped in love here.

Over the few weeks she had spent here, she had pieced together some of the history of Emily and Claire – the fact that Emily had lost her child and her husband on the very same day. How could fate be so cruel? This information also helped her to see Horacio in a different light; they were all shaded with tragedies.

The young woman placed a hand over her stomach. The clouds parted for a moment; the moon silvered a teardrop that left a trail down her pale cheek. She thought and felt as if she had found a home here, but fate had dealt her yet another earth-shattering blow: Sophia strongly suspected that she was with child.

Living in a small village in the mountains, everyone knew everyone else's business. When a woman was expecting, the whole community came together, knitting blankets and warm garments for the child. Sewing layettes, carving cradles, making toys.

The understanding of the cycles of life was accepted without any embarrassment or shaded whispers. It was what it was.

Sophia understood the functions of the body; to put it bluntly, she was aware of lovemaking and fertility. Couples fell in love, or there was an understanding between families that their eldest would become Kiddushin (betrothed) and, at the end of a year, they would marry. If they were lucky, they would be blessed by having many children.

Beth snored, interrupting Sophia's reverie, then mumbled something in her sleep. The young woman turned over, making the bed creak, then sighed.

Suddenly, realising that she was becoming chilled sitting by the window in her nightdress. Sophia got up, grabbed the eiderdown from her bed, she draped it about her shoulders, then sat back down.

It was strange, she pondered, that this outcome had not occurred to her at all.

What that man, Beeching, had done to her had nothing to do with love. His actions were depraved; he was evil to the core. But her body had accepted his seed of life. She shuddered once more, this time with horror rather than cold.

When her time for bleeding had passed, and nothing had happened, she hadn't thought about it very much. There had been many things going on, many changes that she was embracing, so it wasn't surprising that her body mirrored how she felt.

The days went by, however, and there had been no sign of her menses, then Sophia found herself feeling quite unwell, not just in the mornings but into the afternoons too.

She also found that tiredness dogged her. Her breasts felt sensitive; the awful truth began to dawn on her.

The women in her village discussed these things openly, for them, it was not something to be embarrassed by, but something to rejoice in.

Sophia sighed heavily. Once the realisation had dawned, she had written to Andrew Keene.

She found, in all good conscience, that she could not entertain the thought of their deepening relationship: he had been so kind, so understanding. Sophia knew he cared for her, as she did for him. She felt that he was the kind of man that would overlook the fact that her virginity had been taken in such a vile way, but to be presented by this evidence every day would be too much to expect from him.

Writing to him to ask him to cease his correspondence, broke her heart. Then there was Mrs Woodley and Mrs Jacobs, what action would they take if she told them? She was fairly sure that they would not expel her from the school. After all, they understood some of the complexities and issues the girls brought with them. The two women were gentle and understanding. They were giving each girl time to settle here and heal in their own way.

Sophia looked over to the other bed. The moonlight was caressing Beth's blond curls. They had both had similar experiences, but Beth had lost her child – if that had not happened, what would her fate have been?

Pressing a hand against the cold glass, Sophia wondered what to do. Should she present her guardians with this devastating news, or gather her few possessions and leave the place she had come to love?

Chapter 46

When George Beeching left the Frobisher's, he was in such a rage. Collapsing onto the carriage seat, feeling around in his coat pockets for his hip flask. His heart was beating so hard; he feared that a heart attack was imminent.

When he found the flask, he drank the dregs in one go, then longed for another drink.

Jasper was a nobody in the city, but he was a respected man in these rural idles. George did not doubt that Jasper Frobisher could make waves and cause trouble, as could his interfering little bitch of a wife.

George found himself cursing Vanessa for all the trouble she was causing.

He regretted now that he and his mother had delayed taking any action. If they had played their cards differently; not alerted Vanessa to their intentions. They could have gotten her admitted without any fuss. Ahh, he thought, an opportunity missed.

George gazed out of the carriage window, he wondered what his mother would say when he told her that not only Vanessa had gone, but she had taken William with her.

'God curse the bitch!' In a rage, he threw the empty hip flask across the expanse of the carriage.

*

Alec sat in the snug of the coaching inn and wrinkled his nose. Oh Lord, this accommodation was woefully inadequate. He was annoyed that Lady Beeching had not asked him to stay at the house, but then again, would he want to be under the same roof as that old trout? He just hoped it wouldn't be long before Beeching junior was back on home turf.

It was a shame, Alec thought, if he knew where George was, he could have travelled to intercept him. But no, Alec sighed, he would have to stay in this hideous place until the man showed up.

*

Mrs Gordon was worried about her lodger. Poor Dr Keene had not been right for the last few days. She had tried to entice him with all manner of his favourite foods, but his plates were left barely touched.

Her instinct told her that this had something to do with the letter he had received from Sophia, she thought. Goodness, was the girl sick? Had she found another beau?

The housekeeper could not help but notice that the letters from Gloucestershire were becoming less and less frequent.

Now it had been days, nearly a week, since the last one. Dr Keene had not been "right" since. Aww, it was such a pity, it really was.

*

Andrew was beside himself, agitated with worry; his first reaction after receiving Sophia's letter saying she wished to sever all ties with him, had been to pack; make the journey to Gloucestershire and confront her. To find out what had happened to change her feelings towards him.

If she told him directly that she did not care for him anymore, then he would walk away. Doing as she bid him, severing all correspondence with her.

Oh Lord, his heart felt unbearably heavy with these thoughts circling in his head.

Then there was also the issue of the missing letter; Andrew had the feeling that Sophia's withdrawal from him, and the missing letter were connected in some way. And all this had something to do with Alec Silverman.

Andrew felt he needed to seek Hero's advice. Hero knew Alec so well. He would know if the man was capable of such duplicity.

Of course, there was also the possibility that he was overreacting, Andrew pondered. He was a logical man, after all. Matters of the heart did not usually cloud his thoughts.

If only Horacio had been around, Andrew thought. It would have been good to talk to his friend to see if he could shed some light on the situation.

In the end, Andrew decided to immerse himself in his work, to give himself time to consider his position and the action to take.

He also hoped he would receive another letter from Sophia, saying it had all been a mistake, a misunderstanding, then everything would be right with his world once again.

*

Mrs Perkins looked up from the dough she had been kneading, a startled look danced across her face as Evie strode into the kitchen with a curious air of, what? Confidence?

'And, just what do you think you are doing?' The older woman asked.

Evie finished pulling on a pair of leather gloves; they were the colour of crushed raspberries, they matched her long wool coat and hat, decorated with cream silk flowers.

Evie gave the housekeeper a direct look; there was a challenge in her hazel eyes. 'I am going into the city to do some shopping,' she announced.

The two of them did not move for a long moment. Then Mrs Perkins smiled and nodded. 'Aye, a change of scene will do you good.'

'Yes.'

The housekeeper wiped her floury hands on a towel and called to Tommy. 'The lad will go with you, Mrs Barrett. He can hail you a cab and carry your packages.'

Evie thought about refusing to allow the lad to accompany her. She suspected that Jack had instructed that she and Dottie were still to be watched closely. Evie wasn't going to run, however. There was nowhere for her to go.

'Yes, thank you,' she agreed.

The streets of the city were busy. Tommy hailed them a Hansom cab, which Evie occupied while he sat on the seat with the driver.

Evie was now strolling along Oxford Street gazing into shop windows – goodness what a place of treasures it was.

A large shop selling books caught her eye. Instructing Tommy to wait on the street, she pushed open the heavy, windowed doors which made a brass bell chime cheerily. As the door closed, shutting out the busy street, Evie felt a strange sense of peace wash over her.

A man was sitting behind a large counter. He was busy wrapping three books in brown paper. He was elderly, white-haired. The gold framed half spectacles he wore made him look scholarly. He looked up and smiled at her.

Evie returned the smile.

'Good morning, Miss. Are you looking for anything in particular?'

Evie shook her head. 'May I just look, please?'

The man gestured around the shop floor. 'Yes, of course. If you have any questions, do ask. You will see that each section is described by a brass plate positioned at the end of the rows.'

Evie nodded, 'thank you.'

For the first time in months, Evie felt a glimmer of joy lighten her heart. She inhaled the scent of leather bindings, ink, and paper. She fingered the spines of the books as she walked up and down the rows.

In her reticule, she carried some money that Mrs Perkins had given her.

'Your allowance from your husband,' the housekeeper had explained.

Evie had hesitated to take the money but had swallowed her pride. She was entitled to some kind of compensation for the circumstances, wasn't she?

She found a set of popular novels, all bound in burgundy leather, titled in gold lettering.

'I would like these, please,' she said to the man behind the counter.

'Ahh yes, good choice.' He got down from his stool, then plucked the books off the shelf. He set them down on the polished countertop.

With deft fingers, he wrapped the books in brown paper. Evie paid for them.

'Is that your footman waiting for you?' he asked as he nodded towards the window where Tommy stood, dancing from foot to foot with pent up energy.

Taken by surprise by the man's assumption that she had a footman in attendance, Evie blushed but nodded. The owner of the shop carried the parcel for her, then handed it to Tommy.

'Good day, ma'am. Do call in again.'

'Thank you. I will.'

'Watcha got then?' Tommy asked her as they walked up the busy street.

Evie raised her chin imperiously. 'None of your business.'

Tommy shrugged, although he wasn't happy at being dismissed in such a way.

Evie spent some more time wandering the shops. She bought herself a shawl in soft green wool. Then decided to make the most of her freedom to take some tea and cake in a smart tearoom.

Tommy, much to his growing annoyance, had to trail behind her like a lapdog, resentment building with every step.

If Evie had been kind to him, treated him like an equal like her sister did, things would have been different. He wasn't her bloody slave! He thought rebelliously.

After the excursion, when they had been dropped off by a Hansom cab, Tommy could hold back no longer. He dropped her packages on the pavement as he gave her a defiant look.

'What are you doing?' Evie stood there staring at the lad in astonishment, 'pick those up.'

Crossing his arms over his skinny chest stubbornly, he held her gaze. 'I ain't your bloody servant, pick em up yerself.'

Evie, feeling the joy of the outing slip away, stepped over to Tommy and slapped him around the face.

'Remember who you work for,' she hissed through clenched teeth.

There hadn't been much power in the slap, but it had stunned the young man, nonetheless. He put his hand to his cheek as he stepped back from her, not liking what he saw in her expression.

'You may work for Jack,' she continued, her voice bitter, 'I am Mrs Barrett, his wife, do you hear me?'

His usually ruddy face went pale, he realised he had overstepped the mark. 'Yes, right oh.'

'Pick up the packages and bring them in.'

She turned on her heel, pushed the garden gate open and strode up the path. Before she reached the front door, she turned on the lad once more.

'From now on, you will not take any part in the so-called lessons my sister is giving you and your sister. You will make an excuse and keep away from her. If you don't abide by this, I will tell Jack that you tried to kiss me.'

If it were at all possible, the lads face blanched even more. He looked at her with real fear in his eyes. He realised then that he had well and truly underestimated her.

'I won't go near Dottie,' he answered in a small voice.'

'It is Miss Winters to you, remember that!' Evie nodded brusquely, then turned, opened the front door then stepped into the hall. A resentful but contrite Tommy followed her.

*

After seeing Vanessa and William on their way to the other side of the world, Hero had travelled back to Oxfordshire to see Jasper and Sarah.

During the journey, he had taken a seat on the driver's box with Bryant. Chatting to the head groom always made Hero feel better, stronger, and more capable of dealing with challenges.

This time, however, the sadness of losing Vanessa ran surprisingly deep within him. They had not just been lovers they had been friends too. He would miss his companion. They could correspond, of course. There was the possibility that he could go and visit her. However, he had a strong feeling that he would never see her again.

'You alright, Lad?' Bryant gave Hero a sidelong glance.

'Not really, Bryant.' Hero gazed out over the landscape as the vehicle negotiated the narrow, rutted roads. The scenery they drove through was beautiful, yet Hero barely noticed. 'When you know that someone is inherently evil,' he said, 'capable of unspeakable atrocities, even down to taking young, innocent lives, do you turn a blind eye because that person is in a lofty, powerful place?'

Bryant took a few moments to digest this statement.

'What's been done in the past cannot be undone. However, if there is any risk that the person you are speaking of will continue with these evil exploits, someone needs to stop them, bring him or her to justice.'

Hero nodded, 'Yes, you have put my very own thoughts into words.'

Bryant bobbed his capped head. 'If you need any help or support, sir, you know I'm your man through and through.'

Giving him a grim smile, Hero said, 'I know Bryant, and that notion gives me strength.'

They arrived at the Frobisher's estate in the middle of the murky afternoon. A maid admitted Horacio, while Bryant took the carriage and horses around to the stables.

Jasper was the one to greet their guest as Hero was shown into the drawing-room.

'Ahh Woodley,' Jasper strode towards him and took his hand, which he shook with some vigour. 'Let me guess; this unexpected visit has something to do with Beeching and his wife?'

Hero's skin blanched. 'George has been here then?'

'Oh yes,' Jasper guided Horacio to a chair. He could see the young man looked utterly exhausted. 'You will have to excuse the absence of my wife; she has gone to her room to have a rest.'

'Yes, of course.'

'I shall ring for refreshments.'

'Thank you. My groom, Bryant, has taken the horses around to the stables, can you please ensure they are looked after.'

'But of course.' Jasper rang the bell pull.

A maid quickly arrived. Jasper gave her instructions to serve a pot of coffee and sandwiches for Hero and to take the same to the stables for Bryant. She bobbed and left the room.

Looking over to Hero, the older man said, 'I shall pour us both a brandy while we wait, goodness knows I need one. Obviously, we heard some of what has happened from Beeching. He gave us a warped and twisted statement by all accounts. That may just have held a smidgen of the truth, but I am hoping that you can shed more light on the matter, what on earth has been going on?' Horacio did not know Jasper well, but he knew the man had a reputation for being trustworthy. Hero also knew from Vanessa, how much she valued Sarah's friendship. His instinct told him he could trust the couple. So, when he recounted his side of the story to Jasper, Hero left nothing out.

'You are saying that Beeching's latest victim, well as far as we know, is under your mother's care?' Jasper mused.

'She is.' Hero tucked into a plate of ham sandwiches which had been served, along with the tray of coffee. 'We wondered, Vanessa and I if Sophia would bear witness, that Beeching would be held accountable.'

'Have you spoken to the girl about this?' Jasper asked.

Hero shook his head. 'No, everything has come about so suddenly ...'

Jasper nodded thoughtfully, 'I do not know Beeching well. I have encountered him several times in our social circles. I have to say, I have never liked the man, there has always been a feeling of, um, mistrust emanating from him. After he left here earlier today, Sarah told me some of what Vanessa has been through married to that man. You and she were close I gather.' Hero gave the other man a look tinged with defiance. Jasper raised a hand, 'I do not condone adultery, but I do understand that you both needed comfort from each other.'

'Yes, we did.' Hero gazed off into the distance for a moment, 'we have become good friends, who were healing from our individual traumas.'

'Mm, I remember your father, a sad loss, he was a good man. You take after him.'

Hero met his candid gaze. 'Yes, he was. And thank you, that is a great compliment, but one I do not deserve.'

Jasper gave the younger man a sceptical look then got to his feet. 'Now, I suggest you go and have a rest. You will join us for dinner this evening and stay the night.' Jasper's voice broke no argument.

Hero, setting his empty plate aside, also got to his feet. 'I do not want to impose upon your hospitality.'

'Nonsense, Sarah will wish to see you too, which she can do if you stay for dinner. Then you can delay your return journey until tomorrow at least. That will give yourself, your man and the horses, time to rest.'

'Thank you, Jasper. I cannot argue against such an offer.'

'Good, that is settled then.' He nodded in satisfaction.

*

It was two days after Evie's trip into the city when Dottie threw open the door of the bedroom Evie shared with Jack. There was a mutinous look on her lovely face.

Evie was sitting on a pretty window seat, making the most of the hazy spring sunshine. She had been reading one of the books she had bought on her outing. She looked up when Dottie barged in.

'What have you said to Tommy?' Dottie demanded.

Setting her book aside, Evie said, 'What on earth do you mean?'

'I saw him earlier; he told me that you wouldn't allow him to carry on with the lessons I've been giving him.'

'Well then, you have the answer, Dottie, that is exactly what I did say.'

Her face flushed, her eyes watering with angry tears, Dottie almost stamped her foot but resisted the urge. 'Why, Evie? He and Ivy are my friends.'

Getting up, brushing down her sage green day dress, Evie took a step towards her sister. 'They are not your friends, Dottie. They are servants in this house, paid by Jack.'

Dottie looked at her sister with eyes wide with astonishment. 'How can you say that Evie, they have come from the same place we have.'

'That is precisely the reason you should keep your distance from them.'

Dottie shook her head as the tears spilt down her cheeks, 'I can't believe you are saying this, Evie. It's alright for you; you have Jack, I have no one.'

A bitter laugh escaped her. Evie said, 'No, Dottie, Jack has me just where he wants me, but I loathe him. I have to submit to him, allow him to do to me what all married women endure.' She shuddered as she felt her eyes fill with tears. 'I hate the man with a vengeance.'

Dottie's eyes narrowed. 'So, because you are unhappy, you have decided to make me unhappy too!'

'What?' Evie's gaze widened in disbelief, she held out a hand in supplication, 'I'm not trying to make you unhappy, Dorothea, I am trying to protect you.'

Dottie's chin rose as she adopted a stubborn stance. 'Tommy wouldn't do anything to me unless I wanted him too.'

This time, Evie closed the gap between them, 'And, did you want him to?'

'It's none of your business.'

Evie found herself drawing her hand back, the next thing she knew she had slapped Dottie's cheek.

The sisters stood, both gazing at each other in shock.

'Oh, Dottie, I'm sorry.' Evie couldn't quite believe what she had done. First, she had slapped Tommy, and now her sister, what on earth had gotten into her?

Dottie placed a hand over her stinging cheek. She shook her head in denial, then turned on her heel and fled from the room.

Evie did not follow her; instead, she sat back down on the window seat once again. She did not pick up her book due to the hot tears blurring her vision and wetting her cheeks; she would not have been able to read it anyhow.

Why had she told Tommy to keep away from Dottie, was it because she didn't trust him with her sister? He was a young man with needs, after all, Evie thought. When they had lived in Little Back Lane, she knew only too well how a little bit of flirtation could lead to something more, and what the resulting consequences could be.

Tommy had taken a shine to Dottie, and it seemed that his feelings were reciprocated. Evie suddenly felt sick as another thought occurred, was she jealous of Dottie. Jealous of the fact that her sister could choose the person she wanted to fall in love with when that choice had been taken away from Evie forever.

'Oh Lord,' Evie bent her slender neck and let the tears pour from her eyes as she cried great racking sobs.

*

Tommy went about his jobs with a dejected air and a long face.

'What's got into you, Tommy?' Ivy asked him as the two of them sat together at the kitchen table shining up the copper pans for Mrs Perkins.

'It's that bloody Evie Winters; she's warned me to stay away from Dottie.'

'Mrs Barrett,' Ivy reminded him. 'Why's she done that?' Her eyes narrowed, 'what did you do?'

'I aint done nofink, Ivy,' his East End accent more pronounced when he was upset or angry, in this case, it was a bit of both.

'I know yer sweet on er,' Ivy said, rubbing vigorously at a large pan. 'I think she likes you too.' Ivy mused, 'that would explain why Dottie's been a bit off lately.'

'A bit off?' Tommy asked.

Ivy nodded vigorously making her mob cap flap over her thin face. When she pushed it back, she smiled, 'I think she likes you, Tom.'

Hope flashed across his features, 'Yer think?'

'I know you like er, Tommy; it's all over yer face when we sit together doing our lessons.'

Tommy flushed, 'Aye, can't elp it, she's umm.'

'Beautiful?' Ivy offered.

'Aye, that, but she's got a good eart. She's so different from the other girls from ome.'

'Aye, they both are, Tommy. I love Dottie too. She's really elped me with my reading and writing.'

'Well, I'm not so sure you can say that about er sister, Ivy, that Evie is getting stuck up. She slapped me around the face!'

'Aww no!' Ivy's expression darkened, 'I can't believe it.'

'Well, it's the truth!' Tommy said defensively.

She set aside the pan she had been polishing and picked up another. 'What yer going to do about it?'

Tommy stared off into the distance, 'There's nofink I can do.' He sighed.

Ivy gave him a long look, 'yer can ave a word with Mrs Perkins or Jolly.'

Shaking his head, Tommy said, 'probably best leave it alone.'

Ivy shrugged, turning her attention back to polishing the pans.

Chapter 47

Margie couldn't believe that bloody Jack Barrett had chucked her out of her own home, how could he? She'd worked hard for him over the years.

Her footsteps took her to the alleyway behind the Crown. Rita would be at work, Margie knew at some point the woman would take a break, and Margie was hoping her friend would help her.

It was bitterly cold and damp, and she knew that she still reeked of sweat, blood and vomit. Her face was paining her something rotten. Her cheek felt tight and hot with the swelling. Aww, she must look a sight.

Margie sat down behind a crate. She was concerned that Jack or one of his lads would turn up and move her on.

She had lost track of how long she had been waiting when Rita finally appeared.

Margie got to her feet. She could feel the aches and pains in every part of her body, she groaned.

'Oh, my Lord,' Rita exclaimed, 'Marge, you gave me a bloody fright yer did.' Then Rita studied her friend more closely. 'Heavens, what's appened to yer fizzog?'

Margie fingered the swelling with grubby fingers. 'It were Jack – he's turfed me out of the ouse.'

'What? Why?'

'It were that little bitch, Katie Arnold, she's done a runner and robbed me blind.'

'Aww, no.' Rita shook her head, making her brassy curls bounce.

Margie looked at her friend with teary eyes. 'I ain't got a farthing, Rita, can yer lend me a couple of bob?' When Rita hesitated, Margie shook her head. 'Aye, I understand, you ain't got nothing to spare.' She sniffed, wiping her nose on the back of her hand.

'Sorry, Marge. Listen, you wait ere, I'll nip inside and get a small ale and some grub.'

'Ta, appreciated.' Margie felt more like having a bottle of gin rather than an ale, but that would have to do.

The other woman nodded, then re-entered the Inn. Rita was as good as her word; she was soon back with a mug of small ale and a meat pie wrapped in newspaper.

'Ere.' She handed the items to Margie, who popped the pie in her pocket and quickly drained the mug of ale.

'Aww, thank you, lovie.' As she handed the mug back, she smacked her lips.

Then Margie was surprised when Rita shoved her hand down the front of her dress and pulled out a small bag. 'My tips for the day,' she explained as she handed the bag to Margie. 'It's not much, but it might buy yer a bed for the night.'

'Thank you,' the older woman found tears blinding her eyes. 'Yer has been a good friend, Rita.'

'And you,' Rita gave the other woman a half-smile, then her expression changed to one of concern. 'Don't go spending that on the grog, Margie, promise.'

Marge sighed, 'Aye, I promise.'

Rita bobbed her head then added, 'There's a free clinic on Talbot Street. It'll be open tomorrow. Get one of the doctor's to ave a look at that cheek. It looks nasty.'

'Aye, I will.' Marge nodded.

Despite the ripe smells emanating from the other woman, Rita leaned over and hugged her.

'Take care,' she said, then disappeared back inside.

Margie stood there for a few moments gazing up at the sky, which was heavy with the threat of rain.

Making her way along the back alley, Marge checked the coins in the small bag; there was enough there to buy a half bottle of the grog. A small pang of guilt washed through her, but Marge shrugged off the promise she had made to her friend; she needed a proper drink.

*

The atmosphere in the house was heavy with discontent. Dottie refused to speak to Evie after she had warned Tommy to keep his distance.

'What's been going on with you two?' Mrs Perkins asked Evie when she found her sitting in the corner of the parlour reading. 'You could cut the atmosphere with a knife.'

'I told Tommy to keep away from Dottie,' Evie explained, 'they were getting too close.'

'Mmm, well if it is any consolation to you, Mrs Barrett, you did the right thing to step in there.'

'I did!' Evie was astonished that the older woman agreed with her actions. 'But you encouraged the lessons,' she pointed out.

Mrs Perkins said thoughtfully, 'mmm, well I would encourage any child to learn to read and write, so I was all for Tommy and Ivy to do so.' She hesitated then continued, 'They are what circumstances have shaped them to be, but I do believe they can change their lives for the better.'

'Very noble,' Evie's voice was flat as she gazed up at the housekeeper.

*

Margie ate half of the meat pie that Rita had given her. She had to eat carefully due to the pain in her cheek and jaw. Then re-wrapping the other half in the newspaper, she popped it back in her pocket.

After she had done that she then spent all the money she had been given on gin. Aww, Rita would understand, she thought. She needed a few sips of the old "mother's ruin" to get her through the night to come.

Finding a dark corner off one of the many alleyways that were like rabbit warrens, she drank steadily through the night. Nobody noticed her in her dark clothing in amongst the rubbish.

In a drunken haze, Margie eventually managed to nod off.

At first, she wasn't sure what had awoken her. Margie emerged from sleep feeling groggy. Her head ached something rotten, as did the side of her face. Her tongue was stuck to the roof of her mouth.

Suddenly, she was aware of something tugging at her coat. She looked down and saw a large rat trying to get to the other half of the meat pie she had left in her pocket.

'Aww, Lord!' She pulled away from the loathsome creature, just as it found a corner of the newspaper and pulled the small package away.

Realising there could be more of the vermin around, Margie brushed her hands over her filthy coat. Then, unsteadily, she got to her feet, pulling herself up by holding onto the slime-covered bricks of the nearest wall.

By the time she had risen, her head was thumping even more. The next thing she knew, she found herself vomiting up all the drink she had guzzled.

Wiping her mouth on her sleeve, she made her way gingerly up the alley. Despite the haziness of her mind, she remembered what Rita had told her about the free clinic; maybe the doctor could help her, check her over at the very least.

*

Andrew and Stuart worked tirelessly at the clinic. Stuart never failed to remind Andrew that this was the best way to learn about doctoring, placing one's self within the throng of the unwashed masses.

They never knew what sort of condition each patient would present them with, but on the whole, the basis of the issue was usually down to malnutrition and the general poverty.

When Margie arrived at the clinic, the queue was a long one leading out around the corner. Most of the people waiting were women with snotty-nosed children that clung to their skirts, or tiny babies being suckled at the breast.

Despite the dire situation, a couple of women in front of Margie gave her a hard look, inching away from her as they did so. Aww, Gawd, she thought, she must look a state.

Eventually, it was Margie's turn.

The clinic took up the ground floor of one of the narrow houses in a crumbling terrace.

The kitchen and scullery were split by a couple of blankets hanging from a rod in the ceiling. The room that would have been the parlour at the front of the house had been turned into the second examination area.

As she followed the younger doctor through to the parlour room, Margie noticed that there were two crates of oranges standing in a corner.

'What are they for?' She asked, nodding to the fruit.

'We hand them out to the children,' the man explained, 'they are a good source of vitamins.'

'Aww, a good source of vitamins, eh?'

'That's right; please sit.' The doctor pointed to the examination table. Then rinsed his hands in a bowl of water.

'I presume you are here because of that bruise on your cheek?'

'Well, ain't you clever, doc, wouldn't be able to pull the wool over your eyes.'

Andrew shot the woman a look, despite the state of her, she had a twinkle of amusement in her faded eyes.

'Quite.' He smiled ruefully. 'I am Dr Keene. I will examine you.'

Margie winced as Andrew deftly examined her swollen cheek.

'I notice that you have vomited, Mrs umm.'

'Margie, just call me Margie.' She sucked in a breath as he prodded a particularly tender spot.

'Margie?' Andrew took a step back and eyed her with interest. 'Are you a friend of Molly's by any chance?'

'What do you know about our Moll?' She eyed him with suspicion.

Andrew hesitated for a second. 'Well, she helped a friend of mine.'

Margie nodded sadly. 'Aye, she would do that, not that anyone would care.'

'What do you mean?'

Looking him in the eye, Margie said, 'Molly's dead, she hung herself.'

'Oh, Lord!'

'Aye, well, that's what yer get when you defy Jolly Jack.'

Yes, Andrew thought, he could imagine that Jack would not have been pleased that she had attacked an, umm, client. Then helped Sophia to escape.

Turning his attention back to Margie, he indicated her cheek, 'Did he do this to you?'

'He did. Turfed me out of me own ome an all. So, is there anything you can do for me, doc?' She asked.

'Mmm, sorry. I would say that your cheekbone is cracked, but not broken, there isn't anything I can do with it, I'm afraid. But it will heal given time. You've also got a cracked tooth which will cause you problems if it is left, I can pull that for you.'

'Alright,' Margie shrugged.

'Very well,' Andrew nodded and fished in his bag for some pliers. 'Lay back on the table, please.'

'I ope you aint thinking of aving yer way with me, Doc,' Margie cackled.

'I won't, I promise. But this will hurt, I'm afraid.'

'Ahh, just get on with it.' She waved a hand in the air.

It took two attempts to get the whole tooth out as it had cracked in half.

'I hope you don't mind me asking, but do you know of an Evie and Dottie Winters?' Andrew asked as he worked on the second part. 'Ahh, there we go.' He held up the bloody piece triumphantly then dropped it into a bowl. Andrew gave Margie a cup of water, 'Rinse out your mouth. Here spit it into this,' he held the bowl for her.

'Thanks,' Margie did as she was bid then wiped her hand over her lips. 'To answer your question, yes, I know em. The eldest, Evie, is married to Jack Barrett.'

'Yes, I heard. Do you know where they are?'

'He bought er a nice ouse in Bow, but that's as much as I know.'

'Oh, right.' That didn't sound too bad, Andrew thought.

'How do you know about them, anyway?' She eyed the man with interest.

'They are friends of a friend of mine.'

Margie nodded. 'As this got anything to do with the Jewish girl, Sophia?'

'Umm, well, yes.' Andrew was flustered as he put his instruments away. Oh dear, should he have said anything? He looked at the woman then, 'It's just ...' his voice trailed off.

'You don't want Jolly getting is ands on the girl again.'

'Well, yes.'

Margie put a hand to her head. 'Aww, me bonce is splitting. An me cheek urts like ell.'

Andrew eyed the woman with concern. 'You mentioned you had been kicked out of your home, have you anywhere to sleep tonight?'

The woman's already pale face, blanched even more, 'No, doc.'

'Right, take your coat off, I hope you don't think me rude, but it stinks to high heaven.'

'Ah, yes, I know I smell a bit ripe.' She tried to smile but winced. She struggled out of the coat. Andrew handed her a blanket which she wrapped around herself.

'Take a seat over there, when we've finished here, you can come back with me. It would probably be a good idea to keep an eye on you, Margie. I would say you have a concussion; then there's the blood loss.'

'Aye.' She waved a hand at him as she plonked herself down in a chair, 'whatever yer say, doc.'

As Andrew carried on seeing the other patients who were waiting, he heard Margie snoring softly. Mmm, he didn't know what Mrs Gordon would say when he turned up with Margie in tow.

Deciding it would be a good idea to give his landlady fair warning, he wrote a note, then asked the group of people waiting, if one of the older children could run an errand for him.

'Our Fred will do it for you, Doctor.' One of the women volunteered her older son.

'Thank you.' he pressed coins into both their palms. Then handed Fred the note and gave him the address, getting him to repeat it just to make sure.

Chapter 48

After a long afternoon treating patients at the clinic, Andrew, Stuart, and Margie got a hansom cab to take them home.

Stuart was the first to disembark, then Andrew helped Margie, who was still wrapped in her blanket, down the step.

'Aww, I feel like I'm being treated like a queen,' Margie said, looking up at the building, she added, 'is this your gaff then?'

'I rent rooms here.' Andrew explained as he paid the driver of the cab.

Mrs Gordon must have seen them arrive; the front door opened before they reached the top of the steps.

'This is my landlady and housekeeper, Mrs Gordon,' Andrew introduced them. 'Go with her, Margie, she'll help you wash up.'

'I certainly will,' Mrs Gordon eyed the other woman. 'You'll feel better after a bath. I have the tub ready in my scullery by the fire. I've also got a pot of nice hearty stew on the stove.'

Margie didn't quite know what to say, but as the wonderful aroma of cooking wafted over her, she suddenly felt hungry.

'Well, seems like yer thought of everything then.' Margie nodded and followed the woman down the corridor. Mrs Gordon ushered Margie into the scullery where the bath was ready and waiting. Then she helped Margie to undress and get in the tub.

'Aww, I feel like a bloody toff.' Margie sighed in delight as Mrs Gordon washed her tangled hair.

'You will certainly feel better, no doubt about that,' The landlady commented.

Once she had been dried off, Mrs Gordon wrapped Margie in a towel, then had her wait beside the fire, while she looked for some suitable clothes for the woman.

Margie had to admit that she felt better after Mrs Gordon's administrations.

'Aww, Lord, I feel almost human again,' she said, a hesitant smile on her face.

'Aye well, you look a great deal better.' Mrs Gordon gathered Margie's clothing. She held the garments at arm's length, regarding them dubiously. 'I'm not sure I can save these, however.'

Mrs Gordon was a good deal shorter than Marge, she was also plump in body, whereas Margie was shapelier around the bust. The dress she wore dropped to mid-calf, was pulled in about the waist, and tight over the bosom, but Margie was highly delighted with the outfit. Mrs Gordon had cleaned her boots, which were still in a reasonable state, so Margie had slipped them on over a pair of woollen stockings, also donated by this woman.

'I'm grateful to yer, for this.' Margie said as she stood in the middle of the kitchen.

The bubbling pot of stew on the stove smelt delicious. The place felt warm and cosy.

'You are welcome.' Mrs Gordon regarded the other woman with a long, considered look. 'Dr Keene is a kind-hearted man,' she said pointedly, 'I will not tolerate anyone taking advantage of him.'

Margie sighed, 'Oh aye, I get yer gist.'

Mrs Gordon gave her a brisk nod. Then she dished up the stew along with fresh bread, spread with thick creamy butter. Margie helped her carry the dinner items up the stairs to Andrew's rooms.

Having nothing to eat for a couple of days, Margie was famished, tucking into the food with relish. Managing it well, despite the missing tooth and aching jaw.

She was disappointed, however, when Andrew insisted they stick to water to accompany the meal.

As Andrew watched his companion eat, he could not believe the change in her appearance. The bath had washed years away. Her face was still badly bruised, of course, that would take a while to abate. But now her hair was clean and brushed; it curled about her face and shoulders in soft waves. There were remnants of the beauty she had once been.

'Aww, she's a bossy woman your housekeeper.' Margie sat back in the chair and patted her belly. 'but, I've got to give her er due, she's a good cook.'

'Yes, she is.' Andrew smiled, mopping up the last remnants of his stew with a slice of bread.

'So, doc, yer want to know about Evie Winters an er sister? Well, I can tell yer them two girls ave done well for themselves, although you wouldn't think it by the way that Evie is acting; Jack's given er and that sister of hers the world, but from the rumours on the street, she's still digging er eels in, still thinks she's better than us.'

'So, she is married to Jack Barrett?' Andrew clarified.

'Yes, she is.'

'Where are they living, Evie and Dottie?' Andrew asked. 'I presume they are not still living in Little Back Lane.'

'Ha, you would be right there, doc. From what I've gathered, Jolly's bought them a nice ouse in Bow; a set up with a housekeeper and a couple of servants.'

Andrew nodded, feeling his disquiet settle, but he still had concerns.

'You say that Evie is digging her heels in, in what way?'

Margie narrowed her eyes and leaned across the table. 'Let's put it this way, doc. A happily married man, who as his desires satisfied, ain't going to be looking for comfort elsewhere.' She gave a little chuckle and held up her hand as if Andrew would object. 'Oh, I know some that would, course. But I know Jolly was fare taken with that girl, so for im to be looking elsewhere this early on in a marriage, well something aint right.'

'No, I suppose not.' Andrew had to agree. 'Did he force her into marrying him?'

Margie burst out laughing. 'Oh Lord, doctor, ow many people do yer know where their marriage was arranged? Nothing to do with love, for sure.'

Andrew drank some of his water. 'Yes, you are right about that.'

Margie took a sip of her own water; wrinkling her nose in disgust, she set the glass back down. Narrowing her eyes, she gave Andrew a piercing look.

'I may not ave been with it earlier in the day, but I do remember yer asking about our Moll?'

'Yes,' Andrew shook his head sadly. 'I can't believe she would hang herself.'

'Aye, well, she knew she would take all the flack for what appened.'

'Yes, I can imagine.'

'Jolly may not ave put that noose around er neck, but in my eyes, he were the one responsible for er death.'

'I can't argue with you there.'

Later on, when he had given Margie a dose of laudanum to help her sleep, Andrew lay in his bed pondering what they had discussed; so, Evie and Dottie were living in a house in Bow. Evie was married to Jack Barrett, poor woman, Andrew couldn't help feeling. But it sounded as if they had a comfortable life, so, things couldn't be that bad, surely? But then he had to dwell on what Margie had told him about Molly.

Andrew sat up, then swung his legs over the side of the bed. He sat there for a moment, his mind trying to take everything in.

In his bare feet, he padded across the room and went into the living room. He had left the bedroom door to Hero's room ajar, once again it was being used to accommodate another person in need. He could hear snores issuing from the room. Thankful that Margie was resting, he then walked over to the sideboard and poured himself a tot of brandy.

Once he had downed the alcohol, he set the glass aside. At least he could write to Sophia and tell her that her friends were well. This news may entice her to think kindly of him once more. He was still reeling from her rejection and didn't know what to do.

No, perhaps he wouldn't write to her, he would go and visit her to tell her the news in person. He also needed to talk to Hero, to let him know what he had discovered from Margie.

Once again, Andrew found himself wondering why Horacio had continued with his association with Alec Silverman and Jack Barrett!

Then Andrew found the warmth that the brandy had left in his stomach turn to ice. He had a strong suspicion that Alec had taken that letter. No! Andrew decided it wasn't suspicion, he knew it to be true, but why? Then suddenly, he knew: the letter proved that Sophia was still alive. Alec had met her, of course, in this very room, when they had pretended that she was his cousin, Sarah. Seeing the letters, Alec had put two and two together. He knew the "cousin" story was a ruse.

His mind racing, Andrew paced the room. He had never trusted Silverman. He used people to his own end.

So, Andrew summed up; Alec had in his possession a letter that mentioned Beeching in a compromising situation. The letter also proved that Sophia was still alive. What would he do with this information? Andrew wondered, would he take it to Barrett or Beeching?

He suddenly felt clammy all over, and his heart raced with fear. Andrew felt galvanised into action; he had to travel to Brook House as soon as he could. He had to make sure that Sophia was safe.

The following morning, Andrew was up early, not that he had had much in the way of sleep.

He surprised Mrs Gordon by knocking on her door, she answered it, still dressed in her night-time garb.

Quickly, he explained to her that he was travelling to Gloucestershire, that he needed to go and check that everything was well with Sophia.

With a worried expression on her face, she said, 'I have been concerned, Dr Keene that no letters have arrived for a while.'

Andrew flushed and dragged a hand through his already untidy hair.

'Yes, well, she wrote to me and said that she wished to cease our correspondence.'

'Oh dear, did she say why?' the woman asked, then raised a hand. 'No, I do not wish to pry, doctor.'

'Thank you, Mrs Gordon.'

'I will ask, however, has this got anything to do with the compensation?'

Andrew gave her a puzzled look, 'Compensation, what compensation?'

'Well, when young Mr Silverman stayed here, when you were treating him for the wounds he received from that awful attack, he was interested in what had happened to that poor girl. He did say that he would look into the matter. That she should be compensated for what happened under his own father's roof.'

'Oh Lord,' Andrew went quite pale. Suddenly he felt weak. He stepped back and sat down on the bottom stair. Giving the housekeeper a desperate look, he asked, 'did you tell him where she is?'

'I, umm, yes I think I did mention it.' Mrs Gordon's expression fell into a countenance of grave concern.

'Have I done the wrong thing?' she asked, her voice full of agitation.

'It would have been for the best if you had not mentioned it, Mrs Gordon, however, you did not know. It is my fault I should never have left him here alone.'

'Surely he wouldn't hurt the child?' When she saw the look on Andrew's face, she raised a hand to her mouth in shock. 'Oh, I am so sorry, Dr Keene, so sorry. He seemed to genuinely care.'

Andrew gave her a thin smile. 'Alec Silverman can come across as quite the gentleman, but over the years we were at school together, I saw him for what he really is; an unscrupulous man who serves his own interest no matter what the cost. He has used Horacio, although I did warn him, but Hero just couldn't see the situation at all, or perhaps he just didn't *want* to see it.'

The housekeeper shook her head in denial. 'Oh, I am so sorry doctor,' she apologised once more. 'Is there anything I can do to put this right?'

Andrew stood up. Reaching out to take her hands, he said, 'My dear lady, I have done you a disservice. I am laying no fault at your feet, believe me. But there is something you can do for me.'

'Anything, doctor.'

His gaze travelled up the stairs. 'May I leave my current visitor in your charge?'

'Yes, yes, of course.' She nodded.

'Thank you.' He released her hands, turned and bounded up the stairs two at a time.

'Eh, what's going on?' Margie stood in the doorway of Andrew's bedroom and watched him as he packed some belongings in a small bag.

'I have to go away, Margie,' he told her as he packed the final item and closed the bag.

'Away?'

He turned to look at her, then diverted his gaze: she was clothed in one of Mrs Gordon's nightdresses which pulled across her ample bosom. 'Yes, just for a few days.'

'I suppose you want me out then?' She turned away wearily, 'Well it were nice while it lasted.'

'Actually, I have asked Mrs Gordon to look after you.'

She turned back to study his face. 'You have done that?'

'Yes,' he nodded in emphasis. 'She has a spare room downstairs. You can move into that.'

He was surprised to see tears forming in her eyes. 'Thank you, doc. I ain't used to such kindness.'

Giving her a smile of understanding, he nodded once again. 'You are welcome, Margie.'

Stepping up to him, she dipped forward and placed a kiss on his cheek, which was already flushed.

'While you are gone, I shall do me best to find out where the sisters are.'

'You don't have to. We can look into that when I get back.'

'Aye, but I want to elp.' She shrugged. 'least I can do.'

*

It didn't feel like he had been asleep for more than a few moments when he was rudely awakened by the curtains being pulled open. The day was not bright, but the light still made his head pound.

'What the ...' George Beeching sat up in bed.

'Jackson told me you were back.' His mother strode over to the bed and stood there looking down at him. George could not meet her gaze. 'Well, where is she, and where is my grandson?'

'I um,' he cleared his throat as he sat up, resting against the pillows behind him. 'She had already taken William out of school.'

'No!' Margot stormed. 'Where have they gone?'

'I couldn't trace them, mother. We are going to have to employ the help of someone who tracks people down.'

'Well, they must be somewhere. You obviously didn't look hard enough.' She started pacing the floor. 'What did you do after visiting the school?'

'I went to see Sarah and Jasper Frobisher. Vanessa and Sarah went to school together. They are friends.'

'I know that! Yes, I suppose that was a wise move.' Margot paused in her pacing. 'And?'

'They said they hadn't seen her, but of course, they would say that. They have always been in cahoots with Vanessa.'

His mother nodded as she strolled over to one of the long windows and gazed out at the beautiful parkland beyond.

'As you say, we shall have to employ someone to track Vanessa down, we shall have William back, and she... 'Margot turned to look at George, 'she can rot in an asylum. She certainly hasn't done herself any favours by running off like this; in fact, the woman has played right into our hands.'

'Yes, mother. I hadn't thought of it like that, but you are right,' he agreed.

'By the way, you had a visitor call here.'

'A visitor?'

'Yes, that loathsome man, Alec Silverman.'

'What on earth did he want?'

'I am unsure, but he was very insistent on seeing you. I believe he has taken a room at the Inn in the village.'

'He is a good friend of Horacio Woodley,' George pondered. 'It's strange that both of the Frobisher's mentioned Woodley's name.'

'Do you think he has something to do with your wife going missing?'

The man shrugged, 'I very much doubt it, but it is an odd coincidence.'

'Well, get dressed, boy. I shall send a message to the Inn and have Silverman call in here at, say, ten?'

'No,' George thought quickly, 'I shall meet him there.'

Margot raised her chin haughtily. 'Very well. Do get the business, whatever it is, over and done with, George. I do not want the likes of him around here. Then we must send a message to Mr Simmons in London. I am sure he will find someone who can track down your wayward wife and child.'

'Yes, mother.'

George waited until his mother had left the room, then pushed back the covers. Alec Silverman, he thought as he got out of bed, what was he doing here?

*

'Are you alright, Sophia?' Beth asked her roommate in a concerned voice.

She studied the other girl carefully. Sophia was sitting on the edge of her bed; she hadn't made a move to get washed or dressed. Her face was pale. She didn't look good at all.

'Yes, I am quite well. Thank you.' Sophia gave Beth a small unconvincing smile.

It was eight in the morning. Beth was getting dressed ready to go down to breakfast.

Beth finished buttoning her white blouse, there wasn't a uniform as such at Brook school, but all the girls wore white blouses and dark skirts in navy or grey. Their hair was neatly styled into a bun. Depending on what they were doing, they also had crisp white aprons to wear, and mob caps to use when needed.

'Are you coming down for breakfast this morning?' Beth asked, 'Only, you've skipped it for the last few days.'

Sophia nodded, but then what little colour was in her cheeks, drained.

She turned an awful shade of green. Beth had never seen the like.

Hastily, Sophia grabbed the chamber pot and threw up. Luckily neither of them had used it in the night.

'Aww, Sophia, I knew you weren't well.' Beth rubbed the other girls back.

Sophia looked at her companion. 'I'm alright,' she mumbled, but unshed tears shadowed her eyes. 'You carry on.'

Beth held the other girls gaze for a long moment. Sophia was the first to look away.

'I know you told me what happened to you, Sophia,' Beth said, taking the chamber pot from her, she placed it on the floor and popped a cover over it.

Her voice was gentle as she sat beside Sophia on her bed. 'You were attacked by a bastard, just like I was. You know you, um, maybe expecting a child?'

Nodding her head, Sophia could not stop the tears that washed her pale cheeks. 'Yes, I think I am.'

'Aww, poor lovie.' Beth took her friend in her arms and rocked her gently until she stopped sobbing. Sophia plucked a handkerchief from her bedside cabinet, wiped her tears away, then blew her nose.

'I am sorry,' she mumbled.

Beth got off the bed, grabbed Sophia's hands, and knelt in front of her.

'No, no, no,' she shook her head vigorously. 'Listen to me; this is not your fault, Sophia.' She squeezed her chilled hands gently. 'We are going to go downstairs and see Mrs Woodley and Mrs Jacobs and tell them what has happened.'

'I can't.' Another tear dripped over her lid.

'Nonsense, you need help, we shall all help you.'

'I don't want to leave here.'

Beth smiled at her, 'If you end up leaving, I shall come with you. I'm your friend now. I'm not letting that go without a fight.' Sophia found a cautious smile turning up her lips. 'There, see, that's the spirit.' Beth offered her a smile of her own as she got to her feet. 'Now, I shall help you get dressed, and then we'll go and see Mrs Woodley and Mrs Jacobs, and no argument.'

'Very well,' Sophia agreed at last.

Chapter 49

After Andrew had left for Gloucestershire, Mrs Gordon thought it would be best to go about her day as usual.

Andrew had advised Margie to sit and take it easy, but the woman was restless, setting Mrs Gordon's nerves on edge. In the end, the housekeeper gave the other woman some jobs to do. To give her her due she undertook them without complaint. However, for the housekeeper, watching over Margie had been a bit of a chore. It made it a rather a long day, so she was relieved to get to bed that night.

Because Mrs Gordon was an early riser, she never stayed up past nine. On the other hand, due to her years in prostitution, Margie was a night owl and wide awake.

She sat in a chair by the range for a while. Oh, how she longed for a drink to wet her whistle. It would also help to clear her taste buds of the blood that was oozing from the cavity left by her extracted tooth. Remembering the decanter of brandy that the kind doctor kept on the sideboard in his living room, Margie licked her lips.

Spending the day helping Mrs Gordon, Margie had noticed that the keys for the house were kept on a wooden pegboard in a cupboard in the kitchen. Stepping quietly, so she would not awaken her host, she opened the cupboard and reached for the keys.

When she left the apartment, she gently closed the door behind her, then made her way up the stairs. The moonshine through the rose glass window above the front door gave enough illumination that Margie did not need to light a lamp to see her way. There was only one tread that creaked, but the noise was not loud enough to wake anyone.

Upon reaching the doctor's rooms, she unlocked the door and let herself in. It was dark and chilly in the place as there was no fire in the grate.

Margie opened one pair of curtains, found a lamp and some matches, then closed them again. Once she could see what she was doing, she poured herself a hefty tot of brandy, then took herself on a tour of the place.

Aww, there were a good few pieces of silver around, a pair of Georgian candlesticks—a pretty French clock on the mantle. Margie found herself considering what she would get for these bits and bobs if she pawned them? A pretty penny no doubt; she would be able to recoup the savings that the little bitch, Katie Arnold, had robbed her of. There would be enough for her to make a new life for herself. But Dr Keene and Mrs Gordon had helped her, been kind to her, hadn't they; but Margie knew from experience she would soon be out on her ear. She was fending for herself once again.

The more she drank, the more the prospect of a better life appealed to her. Suddenly, she found herself feeling excited about the future. It was a liberating experience; one she had never felt before.

In the room she had slept in the night before, she had noticed a leather valise. She retrieved this from the room; then she went about picking up items that she felt would be worth something.

As she continued to drink, her euphoria switched to a blaze of anger directed at Jolly Barrett. It wasn't her fault that the little cow had run off, Jolly had no right to haul her, Margie, out onto the streets. She had given him years of good service, hadn't she? Brought him in a pretty penny; she deserved a reward.

'Bloody Jack Barrett,' she mumbled to herself as one thing after another went in the bag. Through this process, she was drinking steadily her mind ablaze with the unfairness of life.

None of this was her fault; she deserved some compensation! The more she thought about it, the more fired up she became.

Pouring the last drop of brandy from the decanter, she downed it in one go. Aww, nice stuff that was, smooth and warming, so unlike the harsh taste of cheap gin she usually had to suffer. She shook the decanter against the glass to ensure she had every drop, but her hands were shaking. With the contact, the glass shattered.

'Aww, bugger.' Stepping away from the sideboard. Unsteady on her feet now; she dropped the cut-glass decanter, which also shattered, the pieces joining those of the glass.

Spying yet another glass bottle on the sideboard, which was almost full, she picked it up, opened it and sniffed at it dubiously, the whiskey fumes made her eyes sting, but her mouth watered hungrily.

When the clock on the mantle chimed, as did the bells of numerous church clocks, Margie gave a start. She was very drunk now, but part of her realised she needed to leave before the old biddy woke up.

Shoving the bottle of whiskey into the bag with the other bits. Margie staggered out of the room, then took the perilous journey down the stairs.

Before she made her escape, Margie checked the tins on a shelf in the kitchen, discovering flour, sugar, dried fruit, some oats. When she found the tin with the housekeeping money, Margie smiled in triumph. Emptying the tin of its contents, she stuffed the money in the pocket of the skirt she was wearing.

Margie hadn't changed for bed, so all she had to do was pluck a good coat off the peg, along with a muffler and hat.

Collecting the bag, she left the house, quietly closing the front door.

*

Alec was tucking into a breakfast of cold roast beef and eggs and thick slices of toast with butter and marmalade, washed down by a surprisingly good pot of coffee. Despite the establishment being of a much lower standard of accommodation than he was used to, it was clean. The food they served was also quite tasty.

He supposed some people would call the place quaint, with its low beamed ceilings and horse brasses, but to Alec, he felt the small rooms were claustrophobic, he just hoped that he would not have to stay here for much longer.

He was seated in the snug, where there was a friendly fire going. Alec had procured the room as his own for the duration of his stay. The landlord, Maurice Edwards, was only too eager to meet his customer's demands. The place was an old coaching inn, but since the rail line to London had been finished, his place of business had been struggling to keep going.

When George Beeching turned up on horseback and asked to see Mr Silverman, Maurice found himself nodding and bowing as he showed his lordship through to the snug.

When he heard a tap on the door, Alec got to his feet, wiping sticky marmalade from his fingers on a napkin. He was relieved and delighted to see George Beeching standing in the doorway.

'Well, Silverman, what is all this about?' George took off his hat and gloves and set them down on the table.

'I shall order some more coffee,' Alec said, preparing to call the Inn-keep back.

George raised his hand, 'Not on my account. I do not intend to stay longer than necessary.'

This statement left Alec clenching his jaw in annoyance.

'I have come a long way and have waited a couple of days to see you,' Alec pointed out.

George gave the younger man a sharp look. 'As far as I can recall, I did not invite you.'

Alec took a breath. 'Well, I think you will be glad to see me when I tell you what this is about.'

'Yes, very well.' George pulled out a chair and sat down. Despite himself, he had to admit that he was interested in finding out what this little upstart had to say.

Alec, seeing that he had piqued George's attention, gave the other man a thin smile. 'How is your head?' he asked.

Surprised by the question, he gave Alec a long look, 'Well enough, why do you ask?'

Leaning forward across the table, Alec said, 'I heard that you had an encounter with a whore in more ways than one.' His mouth turned up into a smug smile as he sat back once more. Then he continued, 'When you were a guest under my father's roof, he presented you with a gift; a young and very beautiful, previously untouched girl, Sophia.' Alec watched with satisfaction while a myriad of expressions crossed the older man's face. George tried to hide his interest, but the greed and longing that brightened his eyes were not easily disguised. 'Do you know what became of her?' Alec asked.

'I, umm, thought she was dead.'

Alec gave him a wide smile. 'Oh, she is far from dead. In fact, as far as I gather, she is thriving under the care of Emily Woodley.'

'Horacio Woodley's mother?'

'Yes, that is correct. On the night that you, umm, became acquainted with the girl, you were assaulted by her companion - knocked unconscious.' George found himself nodding. 'Well, they made their escape and Woodley helped them get away.'

George felt the heat from the fire rise through his cheeks; he regretted not removing his coat. 'Bloody Woodley, his name seems to crop up a great deal lately.'

'Yes, well, that is quite another topic. The point is the girl is still alive. I have seen her, and I have to say she is quite mesmerizingly beautiful.'

Licking his lips, George said, 'yes, she was a luscious little piece.' Then he tried to hide his interest once again as he gazed at Alec suspiciously. 'So, why are you telling me all this?'

'Because, I have in my possession a piece of correspondence that says in black and white, that you attacked this young, vulnerable girl, raped her hideously. I was wondering, Lord Beeching how much you would pay to keep this evidence from being bandied about in the city. Along with the girl's testimony, and that of other witnesses; the doctor who treated her wounds, for instance. I would conclude this matter would pretty much destroy your reputation. You would have to retire from the house.'

With a feeling of satisfaction, Alec plucked the last slice of toast from the rack, then buttered it liberally and topped that with marmalade. All the while, he glanced at George as the man digested the news. First of all, his face infused with blood, going almost purple with unexpressed anger, then drained to a greyish white. The man did not look well at all.

Getting up, George shrugged out of his woollen coat, slung it over a chair then gazed out of the small leaded window which looked out over the fields behind the Inn.

'I suppose we are talking about money, Silverman.' George said through tight lips.

'Yes,' Alec said, 'rather a lot of money; five thousand pounds.'

George turned back from the window. The expression on his face was neutral, giving nothing away. 'So, to clarify, I will receive the letter so that I can destroy it, and you will bring me the girl?'

'Yes, that about sums it up. There is just one other little piece of information, which I will divulge to you, as a gesture of good faith.'

Sitting down once more, George said, 'Oh, don't bandy about the bush Silverman, just tell me.'

'You mentioned earlier that Horacio Woodley keeps cropping up in conversations.'

'Yes.'

'He has not exactly made me privy to his liaisons; however, I know for sure that he and your wife are having an affair.'

'Mmm,' sitting back in his seat, the older man studied the ceiling thoughtfully. He knew that Vanessa was having an affair; of course, he did. That was another reason he had agreed with his mother when she suggested they commit Vanessa to the asylum. George hadn't realised though, that the affair had been with the pup Woodley. God, he was years younger than Vanessa, what the hell was she thinking, the bitch.

'Ahh, I can see it is not a complete surprise to you.'

'Not altogether, no.' George admitted.

'If she were my wife, I would have put my foot down.' Alec cocked his head, 'getting too old for you, was she?'

This jibe was too much for George, 'Why you arrogant bastard.' His face flushed the colour of cranberry wine. He pushed himself to his feet, sending the chair toppling backwards. 'By God, I shall see you rot in hell.'

'Hit a nerve, have I?' Alec remained unrepentant, although the violence of the outburst had surprised him. He raised a hand to calm the other man. 'I apologise, it's nothing to do with me where you satisfy your lust.'

'You are damn right it isn't.' George tried to get his racing heart under control. 'Why are you telling me this now?' he asked as he righted the chair and sat back down.

'Because Woodley has betrayed us both; and I, for one, want revenge.'

*

'Oh, my dear girl.' Emily took Sophia in her arms and held her tightly while Claire and Beth stood by.

Sophia found herself crying yet again. Worried about staining Mrs Woodley's dove grey dress, Sophia pulled away, wiping her eyes with a clean handkerchief.

'You have been most kind,' Sophia said softly. 'I will understand if you wish me to leave.'

'Do not distress yourself, my dear, that is not going to happen.' Emily guided distraught young woman to a sofa and had her sit down. Then she looked to Beth. 'You go and carry on with your lessons, Beth,'

The girl shot an enquiring look at Sophia, who nodded.

Surprising everyone, Beth ran forward and placed a kiss on her friend's forehead. 'See you later, Sophia.' She smiled, then left the room.

'You have made a good friend there,' Claire said as she sat down with Emily.

'Yes, everyone has been most kind,' Sophia agreed.

'Now, my dear.' Emily sat forward her face set in an earnest expression. 'Are you sure that you are expecting a child?'

Sophia nodded. 'I understand about having babies,' her eyes dropped modestly. 'The women of my village were open about these things.'

'I think the first thing we have to do, if it is alright with you, Sophia, is to ask Dr Scott to examine you,' Emily said, taking charge.

Sophia thought about this for a moment.

'You may be mistaken,' Claire offered, 'perhaps you have nothing more than a malaise.'

'Yes, I understand that is possible, so yes, seeing the doctor is a good idea.' Mentioning Dr Scott, made Sophia think of Andrew, she felt fresh tears brim, but this time managed to swallow them down.

*

George Beeching sat back in his chair, listening to Alec Silverman outlining the amount of money he was asking for, to keep things quiet.

When he had first found out what Alec had to say, George had felt, just for a moment, as if he were on the edge of a precipice ready to topple into the void. Then it dawned on him, Silverman had made a grave mistake, he had told him exactly where the girl was; ahh, stupid boy.

'Very well.'

'Sorry, pardon?' Alec paused in his oration, giving George a look of surprise.

'I said very well; I shall meet your demands. It will, however, take a few days for me to get the money together. Shall we say, Friday, three in the afternoon? We can meet at Barrett's rooms above the Crown.'

Alec's mind worked furiously. He hadn't expected Beeching to agree so quickly. Would he have time to pick up the girl to hand over by then? Then he thought about Jack Barrett; he would utilise his help, although Alec realised he would have to pay him. 'Umm, yes. That would suit me well enough,' Alec agreed at last.

'Good, good.' George nodded. 'So, just to reiterate, you will give me the correspondence and the girl.'

'Yes,' Alec agreed.

George got to his feet, shrugged on his coat, picked up his hat and gloves, he nodded at Alec, 'Friday then?'

'Yes, Friday.' Alec watched the visitor leave. Then picking up his cup of coffee, which was now lukewarm, he drained the cup. Well, that went much better than he would ever have imagined.

Standing up rather stiffly as his ribs still ailed him, Alec clapped his hands like an excited child. Time to get the next train back to London to set things in motion.

*

When George reached Beeching Hall, he called a footman and ordered the fellow to pack his bags.

Just as he was about to descend the stairs, his mother appeared from the drawing-room.

'Well, what did that snivelling child want?'

His hand resting on the newel post, George said, 'It was just about a bit of business, Mother.'

'Umm, I cannot imagine what sort of business Alec Silverman would be involved in that would entail him to travel up here.'

George sighed. He turned to his mother. 'It was to arrange a meeting with Alexander when I get back to London. We are both involved in the demolition and planning of an expanse of the East End, so we can build the rail line I spoke to you about.'

'Ahh, yes.' She nodded, making her pearl and diamond earbobs sparkle from the sun shining through the long windows. Walking over to her son, she laid a thin hand on his arm.

'I know you have business to attend to, George, but you must find your wife and my grandson.'

'I know, Mother. I am heading back to London this very day to deal with business. I can also see Mr Simmons as you suggested, I am sure he will have someone who could track Vanessa down.'

'Yes, well, I have already written to him to set things in motion.'

George smiled, although inside he was annoyed that his mother had usurped him.

'Yes, very good, mama. Now, if you will excuse me.'

Removing her hand from his arm, she gestured towards the sweeping staircase. 'Yes, of course, go.'

*

Alec, who's bags were already packed, had the driver of the horse and trap he had hired take him to the station.

He was in a splendid mood; on Friday, he would be receiving enough money to pay off his gambling debts and have plenty left over – perhaps he could seek some advice and invest some of it.

The journey to the station took at least an hour. Alec really could not fathom why Beeching could live in the middle of nowhere. Although, he knew the MP had a house in town, then again, when you are a Lord with a vast country estate that has been passed down through generations of Beeching's, one could not choose where that location would be.

For a moment, Alec felt envious of George Beeching: his wealth, his title, and his place in society. After all, Alec's own family were just as wealthy as the Beeching's, possibly more so, but despite that wealth, he could still feel the underlying snobbery with which they were viewed.

Also, there was the situation regarding his inheritance; his father would not let him touch his fortune until he turned twenty-five. Even if his father died before that time, the money and estate would be kept in trust. It simply wasn't fair.

Upon reaching the small country station, Alec found they had timed his journey well. He didn't have to wait long for the next train.

Once aboard, sitting back in the sumptuous first-class compartment, Alec thought of the girl, Sophia? There was something about her that was other-worldly and intriguing. He could see why Beeching was taken with her and wanted her back in his clutches.

Alec sighed as the countryside blurred passed. The Norfolk Broads were beautiful, but he was not interested in the view, his thoughts were elsewhere, musing over the situation he found himself in. Perhaps he should go and pay his friend, Horacio, a visit, take another look at the girl? See why she was so alluring.

With the thought of Horacio Woodley, Alec felt his chest tighten in anger. It was all his fault that he had so many gambling debts, without Woodley to fight for him; Alec was feeling the loss in revenue. Not only that, but Woodley had interfered with everything his father, Alexander, had put in place, ruining the evening for Beeching. The man had been assaulted. And Hero had ensured that the women who had done the deed had escaped. It wasn't a good show, no, not a good show at all.

*

Dr Scott stepped away from Sophia, who was laying on her bed. Emily stood by wringing her hands anxiously.

Adjusting her clothing, Sophia sat up.

'Well, doctor?' she asked.

'Yes, you are correct in your thoughts, Sophia, you are with child.' He walked to the washstand and rinsed his hands, then dried them.

'Oh, Sophia!' Emily came and sat beside the younger girl on the bed. She placed a reassuring hand over Sophia's.

'As for the sickness,' Dr Scott continued, 'I can only recommend ginger tea. Hopefully, it will settle your stomach. It is usually a temporary occurrence, however, so should ease off as time goes on.'

Sophia nodded absently.

'Oh, dear, dear, what shall we do?' Emily uttered a catch in her voice.

'Is it still alright for me to stay here, Mrs Woodley?' Sophia asked in an uncertain voice.

'Yes, of course, my dearest girl.'

Sophia found herself embraced in a reassuring hug which she submitted to entirely.

Dr Scott nodded a farewell, picked up his bag and quietly left the room.

*

Earlier that morning, Mrs Gordon woke up to a fog-shrouded day pressing at the window.

Getting up, she put her feet in her slippers and popped her woollen dressing-gown around her shoulders.

The first thing she did every morning was to stoke the fire in the range and bring it back to life.

Once she had that going, she placed the kettle on the stove to boil.

When that was done, she decided she must go and check on her guest. It was then that she noticed that the key-cupboard was open. Her heart jumped into her throat; oh, perhaps she had forgotten to shut it! With that thought, her nerves settled a little, but when she saw that the spare bed was empty, and the door to her rooms stood wide, she knew that something dreadful had happened.

Upon checking the key-cupboard once again, she noticed that the spare key to Dr Keene's rooms was missing as was the one for the front door.

As fast as she could, she went up the stairs to find his door wide open. A quick check of the place showed the disarray, opened cupboard doors, and drawers. The glass on the floor of the living-room. Then the housekeeper noticed the missing items, the clock, and the candlesticks, amongst other things.

'Oh, no. Oh, dear.' The woman sat down heavily in one of the chairs flanking the cold fireplace. After all the things they had done to help her; the woman had robbed them then run off.

'Oh, what am I going to say to the doctor!' Mrs Gordon stood up abruptly; she needed to call a Bobby. They had been robbed!

*

As drunk as Margie was, she managed to make a quiet exit from the house. The grey light of dawn filtered through a weighted fog. The cold made her jaw throb, especially around the cavity from her pulled tooth, she pulled the muffler around her chin.

The bag she was transporting was heavy now, making it hard to carry. Worried about being spotted, Margie decided to take the items to pawnbrokers in the city, rather than the ones she had used before in the East End.

At least, in the clothes she was wearing, she looked somewhat respectable, even if they didn't fit very well. Then there was the bruising on the side of her face, that didn't look good at all, but she hoped that people would just assume she was fleeing from a violent lover, or husband. She decided that she could put the bruising to good use, a ruse to play on other's sympathy.

Walking in the fresh morning air helped to revive her from her drunken state so that she felt more in possession of her senses.

Margie was sorely disappointed, however, when the first two pawnbrokers she found refused to entertain any business with her.

The second one had looked at her with a suspiciously raised eyebrow.

'These are fine goods, Mrs umm, where did you say you got them from?'

'It's Mrs Gordon,' she used the housekeeper's name out of quick necessity. 'My aunt left them to me, but I'm thinking of travelling.' She placed a hand pointedly against her bruised cheek. 'I need to get away, you see.'

'Travelling, eh?' The man eyed her from head to toe, making Margie feel extremely uncomfortable.

In the end, she snatched the items up, pushed them into the valise and stormed from the shop.

She had more success when she found a place away from the busy streets, down a narrow alley.

The small shop was stocked with all manner of things; false teeth, false legs, stuffed animals, copper pans, spectacles, glass eyes, the list was endless.

When Margie presented the items to the elderly man behind the counter, he looked them over carefully, then named a price.

'Aww, those are good candlesticks, surely you can give me a bit more?'

'Ahh, sadly no.' The man shook his head as he gestured about the shop. 'As you can see, the place is full to bursting.'

Margie was sorely disappointed, but her energy was waning, so she decided to accept the man's offer.

It was mid-afternoon when Margie found herself on Oxford Street. The pavements were busy now, and she followed the flow of the crowds.

Hunger clenched her stomach, so she decided to stop at a tearoom and get something to eat.

Everything about the tearoom was elegant. Margie was shown to a table draped in a pristinely white tablecloth, by a maid who was immaculately dressed.

When she took her seat, Margie glanced around the room. Feeling as if she stood out like the proverbial sore thumb, she noticed that all the women frequenting the place were very smartly dressed. Not only that, but the snatches of conversation she heard was spoken in very posh voices.

Tilting her chin up, Margie told herself she had as much right to be there than anyone.

She ordered sandwiches and a scone with cream and jam, along with a pot of tea.

It was just as she was wiping the sticky jam from her fingers; she looked up. Through the large window overlooking the street, she saw a tall man with tufts of ginger hair poking out from under a cap.

Margie held her breath, well if it isn't Tommy Dicken! He looked older and taller than she remembered. He was spruced up in a good quality set of clothes. It was as she studied the lad, that she noticed he was walking behind a smartly attired lady dressed in green. A jaunty feather decorated her hat. It bobbed as she walked. Margie's eyes fare bulged out of her head when she saw that it was Evie Winters. No, not Winters, she was Mrs Barrett now, Margie corrected herself.

Gulping down the last dregs of the tea, she got up, paid the woman at the counter, then hastily made her way out onto the street.

Luckily, she spotted Tommy. He was standing outside a shop. When Margie drew closer, she could see that it was a smart bookshop.

Finding a niche against a wall, she waited there watching the two. She was just about to think that Evie would never emerge from the shop, when she came out, the shopkeeper opening the door for her, then passing her packages to a disgruntled looking Tommy.

The shopkeeper saluted her as if she were lady muck. Then the two retraced their steps. Again, Tommy was walking a few paces behind as if he were a bloody servant. Then Margie took a breath as she started following them. Huh, that was precisely what Tommy was to Miss high and mighty Mrs Barrett, a bloody servant!

Resentment and anger flared. With renewed vigour, Margie picked up her speed to keep up with them.

There was another stop, this time a tea-room, not the same one that Margie had frequented, but it was just as posh. Again, Tommy was left out on the pavement, a defiant look in his eyes. The lad didn't look happy in his job role, Margie mulled.

Standing there, keeping vigil; Margie could barely believe it. The doctor (she felt guilty for robbing him but pushed the guilt aside) wanted to find Evie and her sister, and there Evie was, just across the street.

Although, Margie realised that she had well and truly burnt her bridges where the doctor and his housekeeper were concerned; after robbing them, there was no going back now.

When Evie emerged from the tearooms, Margie could see her say something to Tommy; then he raised his arm. Margie guessed he was summoning a Hansom cab. Her speculation was on point as a cab pulled up, Tommy helped Evie up the steps then jumped on the back.

Feeling relieved that she had taken the money from the tin in Mrs Gordon's kitchen, Margie hailed a cab for herself, telling the driver to follow the one where Tommy's ginger hair stood out like a beacon.

Chapter 50

Hero left the Frobisher's with fond farewells and promises to keep them up to date with any news from Vanessa.

For the time being, Hero had left the items that Vanessa had entrusted him with, with Sarah and Jasper. They were only an hour's ride away from Woodley Hall. It was no distance to travel, so he could collect them at any time if needs be.

On the journey home, Hero decided to sit on the top box with Bryant.

'You alright, boy?' the older man asked him after they had travelled a distance, with Hero sitting quietly beside him.

He turned in his seat and smiled at his companion. 'Yes, just been a long couple of days.'

'Aye, a bit of drama going on.'

'Yes,' Hero huffed, 'too much. I trust you will keep what has happened to yourself?'

Bryant looked hurt. 'Since when, have I ever betrayed your trust, Master Horacio.'

'I'm sorry, Bryant, yes, I know I can count on you.' Hero gazed out over the rolling countryside. It was quite beautiful. After a misty start to the morning, the day had brightened. There was a feeling of spring in the air.

'It's just that I am feeling, umm, quite lost.'

'You are going to miss your lady friend?'

Hero laughed, 'Oh yes, I shall miss Vanessa, but I am heartily relieved she is out of harms-way now.'

'You love her?' Bryant asked gently.

'I am very fond of her, but I'm not sure if I am capable of love or would even recognise how it would feel.'

'Huh,' Bryant shook his head, 'I thought the same thing, master Hero, then I met Laura, she's a fine woman. She's done a bit to fill my heart, I can tell you.'

Hero smiled, 'I am glad of that, Bryant, you deserve happiness.'

'You are a good man, master Horacio; you deserve happiness too.'

'Aww, now you sound like my mother, man.'

They both laughed.

'Yes, well, love makes a man soften.'

Hero leaned over and poked Bryant's once muscular mid-rift, 'and fat!' he declared.

'Ah well, she's a good cook, no doubt about that, but I bet I can still hold my own in the ring.'

'Well, we shall see about that. I need a sparring partner, get rid of some of this tension.'

'Well, you are on.' Bryant declared as he encouraged the carriage horses forward.

*

When Margie saw the Hansom cab carrying Evie and Tommy stop, she called to her driver so she could get out a few yards away.

Neither of the two glanced in her direction as Tommy, carrying Evie's parcels made his way behind his mistress, up the front path, then entered the pretty house.

Well, will you look at that, Margie scoffed, Jolly's given her a fine place to live. Again, Margie felt the anger and injustice flair. She wondered if Jolly was waiting for his pretty wife to return, would they be playing a parody of happy families?

Across the road from the house, there was a small park where trees had been planted, beneath them shrubs were beginning to bud heralding the onset of spring.

Margie made her way over to the green space. Taking shelter under an evergreen that would afford her a vantage point of the front of the house, she placed the bag at her feet, watched and waited.

*

After saying goodbye to his father, George took the afternoon train back to London. He was extremely relieved to be out from under his parent's scrutiny. He was acutely aware of their accusing and speculative gazes every time he kept company with them.

As soon as he got back to the city, he would go and visit Mr Simmons. Simmons was their family solicitor; they had been dealing with him for years.

He was an efficient, resourceful man, who got the job done regardless. His contacts were numerous. George was confident that Simmons would know the right person to hire to track down Vanessa and William. Once that visit had been attended to, George was going to seek an interview with Jack Barrett.

*

Evie had been delighted with her further purchase of books; she found reading to be a consolation. It provided her with an escape from her troubled world.

After their bitter argument, Dottie was still cold towards her. Evie also felt the discontent emanating from Tommy Dicken. However, Ivy was her usual happy go lucky self and didn't seem to notice any disquiet about the house.

Even though she had upset Dottie, Evie did not regret stepping in to put a halt to the budding relationship.

Tommy, however, didn't know what to do. He had been growing fond of Dottie. He was fairly sure she felt the same way. They had experienced moments when they found themselves exchanging looks, along with somewhat shy smiles.

Even though they both had roots in the roughest part of the city, Tommy felt as if they came from two separate worlds. He had thought that he wasn't good enough for someone like Dottie, who shined with goodness. But he was attracted by that light.

He felt he wanted to protect her, look after her. Aww, he was quite sure what he felt was love. But he had no one to ask about these things. He certainly couldn't say anything to Jack. He had the feeling that he would be out on his ear, back to the East End if he professed his feelings.

Moving to Bow, he had severed many ties with the rougher part of the city. With the teaching that Dottie had been giving him and his sister, the good food, the wages, the smart sets of clothes, Tommy felt as if he were going up in the world; he liked that feeling. However, part of him felt as if he were in limbo. He did not want to go back to the slums. If he wanted to have a life with Dottie, it would probably mean them running away together. He was pretty sure that no one, not even Mrs Perkins, would give them their blessing.

If he left Jolly's employ, he would not have an income. He had not been trained up for any job, so what would he do to support Dottie? That's if she would agree to go with him, of course. Then there was his sister to think of, what would happen to Ivy if he left with Dot, would they take it out on her, throw her out on her ear?

All these frustrating thoughts rattled around in his head. One thing he did recognise; he was angry with Evie Barrett for keeping him and Dottie apart; all his anger was focused on her. It wasn't fair of her to meddle with her sister's friendships.

*

They were a few miles from Woodley Hall when Hero and Bryant encountered a man riding what looked like a bit of an old nag. The man, who looked so uncomfortable on horseback, that both Horacio and Bryant felt sorry for him, did his best to spur the horse on, but it kept stubbornly to its slow pace, determined not to be rushed.

It was when the man turned in the saddle to see who was close behind him, that Hero recognised Andrew.

Bryant, who also recognised the trainee doctor, brought the carriage to a halt.

'Good Lord, man, what are you doing here?' Hero called, jumping down from the vehicle.

Andrew, who looked very red in the face, tried to bring the old horse to a stop, but infuriatingly, it found the energy to dance across the lane. The horse, who could tell that he had an inexperienced rider on his back, was taking full advantage of the situation.

'Whoa, there.' Hero reached for the nag's bridle bringing the animal to a halt. 'There, that's better.' He rubbed the horse's nose. The animal gave a whicker in thanks.

'Oh, Horacio, am I glad to see you.' Andrew slid gratefully from the horse's back.

Noticing his friend's anxiety, Hero gave him a concerned look.

'What's wrong, Andrew, are you ill?'

Andrew shook his head, vigorously. 'No, no, it's nothing like that. It's Sophia, Hero; I fear she is in danger.'

For the rest of the journey home, Bryant tied the hired horse to the back of the carriage. To allow Andrew to explain what had been going on, Hero sat inside the carriage with his friend.

'So, what exactly has been happening, Andrew?'

The taller man shifted restlessly in his seat as if he were going to jump out and run.

'You remember I told you about Alec Silverman coming to me after he had been attacked?'

'Yes, of course, I remember.'

Andrew sat back in the seat, closing his eyes for a moment; he tried to organise his thoughts which had been scattered by the anxiety he felt. Opening his eyes, he looked at his friend.

'Mrs Gordon mentioned that she had told Alec all about Sophia, what happened and where she is now.'

Hero suddenly went cold, he frowned in concern, 'Very well, and?'

Andrew blushed. 'A few weeks ago; I received a letter from Sophia telling me she wished to cease our correspondence. She asked me not to write to her again.'

'I am sorry to hear that, Andrew, I know how well you regarded her.'

Nodding sadly, Andrew continued. 'Yes, well, due to that, I decided to re-read the letters she had sent me, in the hopes of finding a clue as to why she would do that. Then I realised one of the letters was missing: it was the one where she asked me about Beeching and what I knew of him.'

'That was my fault, Andrew, I mentioned the man's name without thought, I am sorry.'

'Mmm well, you know I have never trusted Alec Silverman. When I discovered that there was a letter missing, I questioned Mrs Gordon. She told me how sympathetic Alec had been. Especially so when he found out the attack had happened under his father's roof. He mentioned to Mrs Gordon that he might be able to persuade Silverman senior to pay Sophia some kind of compensation.'

'And that was when she told him where Sophia is.'

'Yes, although he may have already known. I'm not sure when he rifled through my letters.' Giving a huff of dejection, Andrew sat back on the carriage seat. 'This is all my fault I should never have left him alone.'

'You weren't to know what would happen.'

'That's just it, Horacio,' Andrew sat forward angrily, 'I did know he was capable of doing something like this.'

Holding his hands up in supplication, Horacio said, 'What do you think he will do with this information?'

Giving him a long look, Andrew answered. 'What do you think, eh? He's deceitful to the core, whatever he's going to do, it will not be to the benefit of anybody but himself.'

*

Mrs Gordon was friendly with Mr Mason, the man that ran the ironmongers shop down the road from her lodging house. He had done some odd jobs for her now and again. After she had found that Margie had left with several items of silver, and heaven knew what else. She hurried to get dressed, then left the house and made her way to Mr Mason's shop. Then she asked her friend to send his son and errand boy, Jimmy, to find the local bobby Stan Morris.

'I shall go back to the house and wait for him,' she said to Mr Mason, as she left his rather cluttered shop.

When she reached her house and let herself in, she went to the range. The kettle was boiling quite enthusiastically by then; in her haste, she had left it unattended. Oh Lord, Mary Gordon, you may have burnt the house down, she scolded herself, the robbery would have been the least of your worries then.

Constable Morris hadn't been far away: this was his local beat. Everyone thereabouts knew him, so it didn't take Jimmy long to track him down.

Mrs Gordon was heartfully grateful when there was a knock at the door. She ushered the bobby into the kitchen.

'Young Jimmy told me you had been robbed, Mrs Gordon,' he said as she had him sit at the kitchen table while she made them a pot of tea.

'We have, constable, and would you credit it, it was through doing a good deed for someone.'

The man got out his notebook. 'Sit down, Mrs Gordon, tell me exactly what happened. After that, I can take a look around.'

Nodding, she sat opposite him then told him everything she knew about Margie.

'Oh, Dr Keene left the woman in my charge,' she explained, a catch of distress in her voice, 'and this is how the woman repaid his charity.'

'Well.' The constable took a sip of his tea, then set the cup down. 'It sounds as if she is a rough one. You say she attended the clinic that Dr Keene and Dr Boyde run?'

'Yes, that's right; her name is Margie. I didn't hear a second name mentioned.'

The man, who was robust with a round, dimpled face, made a note in his book. 'And, you say that Dr Keene brought her back here because she knew the whereabouts of some friends he was seeking?'

Nodding her confirmation, she said, 'Yes, constable. Evie and Dottie Winters, although Evie has since been married and is now known as Evie Barrett.'

The man looked startled. 'Barrett, you say?'

'Yes, I gather he is regarded as being quite notorious.'

Constable Morris shifted restlessly in the kitchen chair. 'Yes, well, notorious is one word for it. He is a scoundrel, lower than the low. The chances are this Margie is one of his girls.' He blushed, 'Umm, a lady of the night.'

'I understand, constable, I wasn't born yesterday.'

He gave her a wry grin, 'No, of course not,' he acknowledged, 'We've tried to bring him to justice many times, but he is as slippery as an eel.' The man reddened even more as he sat forward in the chair, which creaked under his weight. 'Rumour has it, that he has some of my colleagues in his employ.'

'No!' Mrs Gordon was shocked.

The policeman nodded. 'I'm going to have to tread very carefully indeed, where Jolly Jack Barrett is concerned.'

*

The carriage jolted along the lanes towards Woodley Hall and Brook House. The remaining time of the journey gave Andrew and Hero time to devise a bit of a plan.

'I don't know how Sophia will greet me,' Andrew worried. 'She has made it perfectly clear that she wants nothing more to do with me.'

'It does seem strange,' Hero commented, 'mother and Claire haven't indicated that they have noticed anything amiss with her.'

Andrew gave his friend a long look. 'Do you think they would have talked to you about it if indeed there had been?'

'Mmm, you are right there, Andrew.' Hero leaned over and patted the other man's knee reassuringly. 'The main thing is keeping her out of harm's way. Don't you agree?'

'Yes, of course.'

'Well then, we shall focus on that. Everything else will be sorted out in due course. We have decided our plan of action, and we shall stick to it.'

Chapter 51

Upon hearing the carriage pulling into the yard, an ecstatic Wilson charged out of the stables. The little dog had been sleeping in Hade's stable while Hero had been away.

'Ahh, good to see you back,' Charlie called out to Hero and his uncle, Bryant.

'Tis good to be back, lad.' Bryant jumped down from the driver's seat. 'Get the horses unharnessed, Charlie, then we need a fresh pair hitched up.'

'You going away again so soon?' Charlie looked surprised.

'We are,' Hero answered, 'in fact, we are retracing our steps, Sophia Blum is coming with us.'

'Alright,' Charlie replied without question.

That was when Wilson launched himself at Hero. Hero caught the dog in his arms and laughed as the little dog licked his chin and nose happily.

'Ha, I've missed you too, Wilson.' Eventually, he put the little dog down, but Wilson continued to dance about his master in excitement.

'Andrew and I are walking down to Brook House,' Hero told Charlie. 'As soon as you get fresh horses ready, bring the carriage over will you.'

'Aye, Mr Woodley.' The wiry lad touched a hand to his cap in acknowledgement.

Wilson joined Andrew and Hero as they walked through the woodland, taking a shortcut down into the valley, where Brook House nestled amongst the trees.

The nearer they got to the place; the more nervous Andrew became.

Reaching the school, the two men walked around to the back and entered through the rear door.

'Oh, good heavens, Master Hero and Mr Keene.' Mrs Adams, the cook, bobbed a knee, a big smile on her broad face.

She had a companion with her, rolling out pastry. The girl blushed and smiled at the two men as she considered them with interest. Oh, she had seen Master Woodley several times, he was a handsome one for sure. The other man, who was taller, and quite lean, looked as if he could do with a good feed. He had a kind face, though, with lovely soft brown eyes.

'Umm, could you summon my mother,' Hero asked the cook, 'please, have her meet us in her office.'

'Yes, of course. Beth,' the cook turned to the young woman, 'wash that flour off your hands and do as the master bids.'

'Yes, Mrs Adams.'

When they walked into his mother's office, Hero was met by the scent of rosewater. His mother's favourite perfume, the scent of home.

He stopped in his tracks, however, when he spotted the portrait above the fireplace. It was a painting of himself and Angelica. He had been eight at the time it was painted, his sister six years old.

The painting was an addition to the room he did not expect. Seeing his sister's bright blue eyes shining, looking down at him, Hero felt a blow to his heart.

'Your sister?' Andrew asked as he too looked up at the picture.

'It is. I never thought I would see this painting hung again.'

Andrew placed a sympathetic hand on Hero's shoulder. 'It is an indication that your mother is healing, Hero. A leaf turned ...'

'Horacio.' They both jumped as Emily walked in. 'Oh, it is good to see you, darling.' She walked over to her son and embraced him warmly, then turned to Andrew. 'My dear, good to see you too.'

'Lady Woodley,' Andrew bobbed his head, but was pleasantly surprised when Emily hugged him too, she looked like a young girl beside the tall man.

'Oh, Andrew, please call me Emily, we do not stand on ceremony here. And Wilson,' Emily laughed as she bent down to stroke the dog who was jumping up at her skirts. 'Mable is asleep under the desk in the classroom,' she explained, referring to her spaniel.

Hero interrupted, 'Mother, there is something quite urgent we need to talk to you and Sophia about.'

Emily's smile dropped, concern furrowed her brow, 'Sophia?'

Andrew immediately noticed Emily's worried expression and his heart stuttered.

'There, I knew it! She's ill, isn't she?' He started pacing the floor in agitation. 'I should have known.' He stopped and looked at Emily. 'How bad is it?'

'Oh no, no.' Emily shook her head, but there was a wary expression on her face. 'She's not ill exactly,' she found herself saying. 'It is a sensitive and delicate situation.'

Andrew paused in his pacing, any colour that the fresh air had blushed his cheeks with, slipped away. 'Delicate, sensitive?' As he digested the statement, it took him only a moment to conclude; 'She is expecting a child, isn't she?'

'Oh,' Emily stepped back in distress. 'I shouldn't have said a word.'

This time, Andrew's face infused with colour. He clenched his fists. He was not a man predisposed to anger, but Hero could see it written on his friend's face.

Hero stepped over and put a hand on his arm.

'It's alright, Andrew.'

Pulling out of Hero's grasp, Andrew found himself collapsing into an armchair. 'It is not alright. That beautiful girl will be left with a reminder of what happened to her for the rest of her life.' He put his head into his hands.

'The child is innocent, Andrew.' They all looked around in surprise. Sophia stood in the doorway.

Andrew jumped to his feet and ran over to her. 'Oh, Sophia, my darling, my love.'

Before she could utter another word, he pulled her into his arms and held her tight.

At first, it seemed as if Sophia was going to pull away, but then she surrendered to him. Great aching sobs wracked her body as all the tension went out of her. She had not been expecting such a declaration of love from this man. The outburst had touched her heart deeply, she knew instinctively that Andrew would look after her and the baby.

'Oh Sophia,' Emily went to approach the girl, but Hero shook his head. Then he took his mother's arm and stepped past the couple. Hero closed the door behind them.

'They need to work this out between themselves,' Hero said as they hovered outside the office door.

Emily looked up at her son, 'Ahh, when did you become so wise, my dear?'

'Ha, I'm not sure I would call it wisdom, mother.' He smiled, then said, 'it is good to see the painting up again.'

She squeezed his arm affectionally. 'Yes, isn't it.'

He realised that his mother was looking better. The drawn expression had left her face, which had filled out a bit. Although there were now swathes of grey in her hair, she looked so much younger. Hero wondered briefly, what had prompted this change. Whatever it was, he was highly delighted by it.

Sophia breathed in the scent of him: fresh air, warm wool, a tang of shaving soap. She was amazed to find herself feeling safe in these arms. It was such a relief that Andrew knew the truth. The weight lifted from her heart and shoulders, making her feel deeply emotional and lightheaded for a moment. He knew about the baby, and here he was hugging her tightly. She felt the very essence of him was good to the core.

Eventually, Andrew pulled away and looked down into her tear-filled face. Her eyes looked bigger than usual. The luminosity was a pool of clear water that would drown him in love.

He tried to adopt a stern expression. 'I have to say I am extremely disappointed with you, Miss Blum, and a little angry.'

'Angry?' Worry creased her brow as she studied his expression.

Leaning down, tenderly, he kissed her forehead. 'Yes, that you should think so little of me. That you would push me away so easily; thinking that I would not understand your predicament, that you would not give me the *time* to understand.'

'I – I did not wish to be a burden to anyone. I would not have you feeling sorry for me.'

'Oh, my dear.' He picked up her hand. Her skin felt chilled.

Gently, he walked her over to the fire. They sat together on one of the sofas, he did not release her hand but drew it to his lips. He kissed it so tenderly that Sophia found fresh tears forming in her eyes. When his gaze lifted, he saw her tears. He fished in his pocket for a clean handkerchief and wiped her cheeks as if she were a small child.

'You would never be a burden to me, my love, but the thought of life, a future, without you in it. The notion freezes my heart. Please don't turn away from me again, Sophia.'

She lifted a hand and cupped his cheek. 'But the child?' She placed the other hand over her belly. 'Can you respect my decision that I shall keep this child, no matter what, that when he or she is delivered safely into this world, I shall be a loving mother.'

'Yes, yes, yes!' Andrew dropped to his knees on the Chinese rug.

'You see, those words you have just uttered are the reason I love you so.' He lifted both of Sophia's hands in his own. 'I know we are only just acquainted, Sophia, but I wish to be a part of your child's future, of your future. If you will let me?' He implored her then swallowed nervously. 'I haven't got a great deal to offer you both at present, but once I am qualified, we will have a comfortable life, a loving life together.' Then his expression dropped as he searched her gaze carefully. 'I can give you all the time you need. If you do not wish to be intimate.' He gave her such a worried look; Sophia felt her heart drop. 'But I am presumptuous, perhaps you do not love me or feel anything for me?'

Sophia found herself smiling. 'Oh, Andrew, those words you have just uttered are the reason *why I* love you, too.'

'Really?' Andrew's smile of delight filled the room.

'Oh, yes, really.'

'Marry me then, as soon as possible, marry me?'

'Yes, Andrew.' She found herself being gathered in his arms where he sat on the floor. He held her close and showered her beautiful face with so many kisses she started to giggle. It was the sweetest sound he had ever heard.

'What is going on, Horacio?' Emily asked her son with concern as they waited in the hall.

'It is a long story, mama. When the coast is clear, Andrew and I can explain what has happened.'

Emily gave her son a concerned look. 'This has something to do with what happened to Sophia.'

'Yes, it does. And this news; that she is expecting a child complicates matters somewhat.'

Emily nodded. 'She has been so unwell that we have all been worried about her. I don't believe it was solely down to the dreadful morning sickness she is suffering from. She mentioned to me that she had written to Andrew to sever ties. Sophia is such a special young woman, seeing her misery and not being able to do anything about it nearly broke my heart.'

'I can only imagine, mama.' He took his mother in his arms. They stood there for a long moment.

Eventually, Emily stepped away. 'I am so glad that Andrew is here, that there seems to be a reconciliation.'

'Yes,' Hero said thoughtfully, 'but what we have to say will have an impact on everything.'

The two of them waited in the hall until the office door was thrown open.

Hero saw straightaway that his friend looked so much happier; they both did. Andrew had an arm around Sophia's shoulders. He kept her close as if he didn't wish to let her go.

'We are to be married,' he announced before they had time to step over the threshold and close the office door.

Emily smiled. 'Oh, I am delighted.'

Sophia went to her. They hugged tightly.

'I am heartily pleased for you, Andrew.' Hero grasped his friend's hand and shook it vigorously.

When the excitement died down a little, Hero gave Andrew a pointed look which dampened his friend's enthusiasm, reminding him of the dire circumstances.

'Now, my dear, come and sit down.'

Andrew guided Sophia to a chair beside the fire. He handled her as if she would break at any moment.

Hero smiled to himself. He was pleased to see his friend so happy. That delight was shadowed with concern, however as they divulged the troubling news to the two women.

*

Alec Silverman was highly delighted to be back in the city. He hailed a Hansom cab to take him back to his father's house. As soon as he arrived, he summoned Collins and told the groom to go to the Crown and Garter to leave a message for Jack Barrett.

'Tell him that I shall meet him at the Crown at eight this evening.'

'Yes, master Alec.' Collins was dismissed.

When Collins had gone, Alec once again mulled over a thought that had occurred to him on his journey home; his very own driver had been complicit in these deceitful deeds: he had helped Horacio to get the two women away from his father's house and Beeching.

The realisation that his friend, well once friend, and one of his employees had worked against him and his father, inflamed the anger dwelling inside. It felt like a tight hard knot in his stomach.

He had already decided to sack Collins. To have him leave his employ without a reference, to make sure the man never found decent employment again. He had also toyed with the idea of getting Jack Barrett, or one of his men, to give Collins a good hiding first. And as to Horacio, Alec was yet to decide what he would do about him. The traitorous bastard had to be taught a lesson or two, that was for sure.

When Alec took a long, hot bath, accompanied by two snifters of brandy, he changed his mind about sacking Collins. He would keep the man on for now as he did not want the extra hassle of trying to find a replacement for the groom, especially when he had everything going on with Beeching. He needed to stay focused, at least until he handed Sophia over to the letch, and he had the money in his hands.

There were a few things about this whole situation that gave Alec hope; he could think of several ways to make some profit from all this drama and deceit. All he needed to do was get Barrett on board to help. Alec knew he would have to offer the thug a percentage of the money, but that could not be helped.

When Collins made his way across the city, he could not help but feel an uneasiness, a chill running up his spine; he knew Alec Silverman quite well by now. So much so, that he could recognise the signs that he was up to something.

Alec Silverman had never been an easy person to work for. He was thoughtless and demanding. At least his father had a few scruples, but Alexander Silverman was taking a back seat in the business, giving his son more responsibility.

Picking up snippets of gossip, Collins was aware that Alec had acquired gambling debts, owing money to people across the city. He wondered if his father knew anything about it, he must have had an inkling surely. Yes, he decided, Alexander would know about the debts; he had helped his son out many times, but Collins had the feeling that Alexander was getting sick of digging his son out of these predicaments. The lack of funds would explain why Alec was so secretive and edgy.

When Alec climbed the uneven stairs to the rooms above the Crown and Garter, the rowdy noise from the barroom below followed him as did the scent of unwashed bodies, cheap tobacco and sour beer.

Wishing that he had chosen a different place to meet up, Alec wrinkled his nose with distaste. Being amongst the ruffians and rabble of the East End reminded him of the attack he had sustained. However, meeting anywhere else in the city risked the chance of him and Barrett being seen together, which would no doubt fuel some rumours.

Alec had bought himself a silver-topped cane that concealed a stiletto knife. He needed to protect himself, having the weapon gave him comfort.

Barrett was waiting for him in his 'office'. The room would have been the sitting-room of the innkeeper's residence, but Barrett had made it his own.

Jack was seated behind a large desk, which was exquisitely made, dark mahogany inlaid with lighter wood.

Much to Alec's annoyance, the tall man did not get up when he entered.

'Barrett,' he nodded to him.

'Well, Mr Silverman, what can I do for you? It had better be something important, I ave a ship coming in tonight.'

'Oh, believe me, Barrett, it will be something that will benefit you.' Alec sat on one of the upholstered chairs flanking the desk. 'I have some information for you.'

Jack waved a hand in the air. 'Go on.'

'You remember the girl you found for Beeching, on the night of my father's gathering.'

'Aye.'

'Well, I have found out that she is alive and well.' Alec sat back in the chair, 'in fact she is thriving. Also, Horacio Woodley was the one who helped the two whores escape that night.'

Showing no emotion, Jack regarded the other man coolly. Ahh, he had suspected that Molly had lied to him, but she had received her comeuppance, nothing to do about it now.

'So, what do you propose?' he asked after a moment.

'I have in my possession a letter from the girl, Sophia, naming Beeching as her attacker. While the girl is alive, George is still in danger of being brought to account for what he has done.'

'So, you are planning on blackmailing Beeching?' Jack perceived.

'Yes. I have already taken action to set things in motion. Beeching will pay to receive the girl and the letter. The thing is the girl is currently under the protection of Horacio Woodley's mother in Gloucestershire.'

Jack sat forward in his seat. 'So, you need me to ave a couple of my lads go and abduct er?'

'Yes,' Alec beamed, pleased that Barrett had cottoned on so quickly. 'Ow much are we talking about?'

'Well, I shall give you a finder's fee, of course, and compensate you for your trouble.' Alec named the amount he had in mind. It was twenty per-cent of what Beeching would be handing over. When Jack continued to regard him without betraying any of his thoughts, Alec found his cheeks growing warm.

'Alright,' Jack said at last.

'Good, good.' Alec smiled in relief. 'Beeching is going to be handing the money over on Friday, so we have five days to work out a plan.'

'More than enough time.'

'Yes.' Alec gazed at a collection of bottles on a sideboard, 'I wouldn't mind a shot of that good brandy I can see, to seal the deal.'

'Aye,' Jack got to his feet and splashed some of the warm amber liquid into two glasses, he handed one to Alec.

'Much obliged.' Alec tried to conceal the fact that his hands were shaking as he lifted the glass to his mouth. He took a good swallow.

'Ahh yes, very good.'

Continuing to regard Alec with an icy gaze, Jack raised his glass in a salute.

'There is one other thing,' Alec said as he placed his empty glass on the desk. 'I want Woodley dealt with.'

'When you say dealt with, what did yer ave in mind?'

'Not killed,' Alec shook his head, 'but crippled, in such a way that he will remember his treachery for the rest of his life.'

'That'll cost you extra.' Jolly drained his drink.

'Very well.' Alec had suspected this would be the case. That was why his first offer had been reserved.

It was decided that Jack and two of his lads, Arthur, and Reg, would travel to the Woodley estate, reconnoitre the land, and grab the girl. Jack didn't think it would be a difficult job.

After Alec left The Crown, he had Collins drive him to the club.

As the groom manoeuvred the carriage through the busy streets, he wondered what business Master Silverman had with Barrett? When Alec had boarded the carriage, Collins had noticed that he had a very smug expression on his thin face.

Whatever it was, it was nothing good. Collins felt a cold breath on the back of his neck. Hunkering down in his greatcoat, he urged the horses forward.

The groom decided that he needed to be wary, to keep his eyes and ears open to find out what was going on. He had a strong suspicion it was something to do with Mr Woodley, and him helping those too women on the night of the Silverman do. He needed to find out all he could and warn Mr Woodley if at all possible.

Chapter 52

Earlier in the day, Mrs Gordon and Constable Norris sat at the table in the snug kitchen, while the housekeeper gave the policeman a description of Margie.

She was also able to recount, to the best of her knowledge, the number of items that had been stolen.

'Well, she will be quite easy to spot,' the Constable said thoughtfully, what with the bruising on her cheek.'

'Yes, I thought so too.' The housekeeper poured the man another cup of tea.

'Thank you.' He gave her a smile which dimpled his rounded cheeks. 'I shall just drink this, then I will set about investigating this matter.'

Mrs Gordon nodded. 'You will let me know if you discover anything, won't you?'

'Yes, of course, Mrs Gordon. The first thing I shall do is ask around the pawnshops. Pawning the items she has pinched would be the quickest way of getting rid of them.'

It didn't take the Constable long to track down the stolen items filched from Mrs Gordon and her lodger, Mr

Keene. Enquiries at several pawnbrokers had borne fruit; the items were recovered. None of the shopkeepers were able to shed any light on where Margie was heading.

*

As the daylight waned, Margie used the leather valise as a seat. She watched the house across the road with growing anger brewing inside.

Earlier in the day, Margie had treated herself to a good bottle of gin. She also had the bottle of whiskey beside her but had decided to leave that for later; a good scotch needed to be savoured, a saying of one of her more well-to-do punters.

The more she drank, the more the alcohol-fuelled the flames of anger and resentment festering.

She blamed Jack for Molly's death. Then he had turned on her and kicked her out of her home with nothing! It wasn't right.

Then there was bloody Evie an er sister, living it up in that ouse. It should ave been er and Jack living there; living the life.

There had been a time when she and Jack were close. They were of the same age, brought up together. She knew him before the scar his father had inflicted ruined his handsome face. Even after that, she loved him. She thought he felt something for her, but as he took himself up in the world, Margie found herself being pimped out on the streets.

'Yer my best girl, Margie,' Jack used to say.

Margie put a hand to her cheek, eh, she had been pretty in those days, young and pretty, but look what Jack had done to her!

The street upon which the house stood was reasonably quiet. Delivery carts came and went occasionally. A nanny pushing a huge pram walked by.

Maids were out blackening the step and cleaning the brasses on the doors; this wasn't a particularly posh neighbourhood, but it was a few classes up from Little Back Lane that was for sure.

Night finally settled a damp blanket over the street. Oil lamps were lit then curtains pulled together.

Margie finished the last of the gin and dropped the bottle on the ground. Her stomach clenched in hunger, but she took no notice. It was just as she was opening the bottle of whiskey that she saw Tommy Dicken emerge from the house.

He was dressed in a smart suit of clothes. When he reached the gate, he paused to light a smoke, then stepped out into the street, shutting the wrought iron gate behind him.

Margie watched the young man walk down the road. It occurred to her that he was turning into a younger version of Jack. He also walked like him, a long confident stride.

Margie let out an angry hiss. She opened the bottle of whiskey and tipped the bottle to her lips. However, she was clumsy and spilt some of the liquor down the front of her coat. Swearing colourfully, she tried again, this time she was able to take a long swig.

*

'I am so sorry, my dear.' Andrew squeezed Sophia's hand. 'I should have ensured that your letters were put away safely.' His cheeks reddened, 'your correspondence meant so much to me. I, umm, read the letters several times over.' Oh gosh, thought Andrew, I feel like an inexperienced schoolboy.

Sophia smiled gently as her cheeks flushed, 'I did the same.' Their gazes met, raising smiles between them.

'Oh Lord, look at you two!' Hero rolled his eyes in consternation. 'Have you both forgotten what we are discussing here?' His words brought the two back into Emily's sitting room.

Andrew shook his head. 'No, of course not.' When he glanced at Sophia this time, the worry was etched on his face. 'We must keep focused.' He looked to his friend. 'You know I have never trusted Alec Silverman. I have a bad feeling about all this.'

Emily, looking on from a seat by the fire, asked; 'Do you really think he is capable of pinching this letter and using it for ill intent?'

When Hero and Andrew were explaining what had happened, she felt a dark chill settle over her. She was afraid for her son, his friend, and the dear girl in their midst.

No one could replace Angelica in Emily's heart, but Sophia had gone a long way in aiding Emily's healing process; she could hardly believe that in a few short weeks, she had come to think of Sophia as a daughter. There was something about this young woman that instilled comfort and joy in others.

When she had found out that Sophia was expecting a child, she was so angry and extremely anxious; angry with the man who had done this to this beautiful child, and anxious about how Sophia would manage the situation.

Apart from the sickness, which Dr Scott said was perfectly natural; indeed, Emily could remember it from her own confinement. Sophia had been stoic in her approach, just as she had said earlier, the baby was innocent in all of this.

Emily could see that Sophia had so much love in her heart, more than enough for this child and any other children she would go on to have in the future.

The way Andrew had faced the situation helped Emily to breathe in relief. Her instinct told her that there was great hope for these two. She was delighted that they had decided to marry. But the priority now was keeping Sophia safe from these monsters, George Beeching and Alec Silverman.

James had known the families, although Emily had never met the Beeching's; it was shocking that a Lord and member of parliament could stoop so low, could be so evil. Emily shuddered when she thought about what Sophia, and probably other young girls had been through, at the hands of this devil.

'I don't want to leave here.' Sophia protested when Andrew and Hero outlined their plan.

'We need to keep you safe, Sophia.' Hero explained once more. 'Alec knows where you are. Charlie has brought the carriage around, just put a few items in a valise, and we will take you to Sarah and Jasper. He would never think to look for you there. They are wonderful people. They will look after you, I promise.'

Sophia gave Emily a desperate look. 'Pleases don't make me leave.'

'Darling.' Emily rushed to her and knelt beside her. 'It is not only for your safety but for the other girls too.' She swallowed down her anguish; she didn't want to let the girl out of her sight, although Emily realised it was for the best. And from what she had heard about these villainous men, she was genuinely concerned for her girls.

'Mother is right,' Hero spoke up, grateful to Emily for encouraging Sophia to leave.

'I will come with you to see you settled in,' Andrew added in encouragement.

Sophia mulled over what they had said. She looked at Emily; her argument had had the most impact.

'I am sorry, Mrs Woodley, I was being selfish. I have no wish to put anyone in any danger. I will do as Andrew and Hero say.'

'Good girl.' Emily smiled reassuringly. 'Get Beth to help you pack, lovely. I'll send Charlie up to get your luggage.'

'Very well.' She gave Andrew a shy smile, then left the room.

Darkness had fallen by the time they set off. Hero sat on the driver's seat of the carriage with Charlie. Sophia and Andrew were inside.

Emily, Claire and Beth had stood on the steps of Brook School and waved Sophia off. Beth had gulped down tears; she would miss her friend.

As they negotiated the country roads, Hero found himself filled with anxiety. He hoped that Sarah and Jasper would feel they were able to give Sophia shelter while he and Andrew tried to sort out this mess.

Hero worried about how it was all going to end. No, he decided quickly; it was no good to ponder on an uncertain future; he had to stay focused on what they were accomplishing at that moment.

However, Hero soon found himself dwelling on the fact that he had such an association with someone so dark and untrustworthy as Alec Silverman. But as he looked back at their so-called friendship, Hero realised he had always been aware of Alec's tendency towards bullying tactics and manipulation, especially if he didn't get his way.

Suddenly, a deeper understanding of their relationship dawned on him. Instinctively Hero realised that Alec reflected his self-imposed darkness, which was fed by the guilt he felt every day. Alec had used him, and Hero had complied without objection because he felt he deserved punishment after what had happened to Angelica and his father.

Viewing the portrait of himself and Angelica hanging on the wall above the mantle in his mother's office had given him a shock. When he had looked into his sister's blue eyes, however, he saw love shining from them.

Strangely, at that very moment, he had felt a lightening of his heart, a benediction. His mother had found a way to move on. He knew he had to do the same.

Surprisingly, when he thought of the couple in the carriage, he found himself feeling a pang of jealousy for their happiness - no, the feeling was not one of jealousy or resentment, he decided; Lord knew, he was extremely happy for his friend. Hero realised that Andrew's and Sophia's blossoming relationship had highlighted an emptiness inside of him, which he longed to fill. All of a sudden, Hero found himself missing Vanessa terribly, then with a shock, he understood that it was not *her* that he missed so much, but the companionship and affection they had shared.

Would he ever find anyone to love? To feel that closeness with – indeed, did he think he deserved to have that joy after everything that had happened?

'There is something I must tell you, Sophia,' Andrew said as they settled in the carriage. Sophia had a tartan woollen rug over her knees to keep her warm on the journey.

'What is it?' She found her stomach somersaulting with anxiety; please don't let it be more bad news.

Andrew shifted in his seat so that he was facing her. 'You know I work with Stuart Boyd, running a free clinic in the East End, by the docks.'

She nodded, 'yes, I remember.'

'Well, a couple of days ago, a woman came to the clinic, her name is Margie.'

'Margie, Molly's friend?'

'Yes.' Andrew took her hands in his, 'Molly is dead, I'm afraid.'

'Oh no.' Sophia didn't know how to feel about this news. Molly had been the one to be complicit in her grandmother's death. And then taking her to that house. 'She saved me that night,' Sophia commented at last.

'I know she did, my dear, but I still feel anger towards her, Sophia. She should not have gone ahead with the plan. She should have done something to get you away from the peril you were in.'

'Yes, Andrew, you have just echoed my very thoughts, however, if Molly tried to thwart Jack Barrett, I don't know what he would have done.'

Andrew searched her beautiful face. She looked so innocent, but she was so wise. 'Yes, of course. Every time I attend the clinic, I see the results of violence. Margie was in a bit of a state when she attended the clinic. Apparently, Jack Barrett had assaulted her and evicted her from her lodgings.'

'What did you do, Andrew?'

He gave a wry chuckle, 'Much to Mrs Gordon's dismay, I took her back to my lodgings. We treated her and tidied her up. That is where she is at the moment. I had to leave her under Mrs Gordon's care, so I could come to you to ensure that you are safe.

'Thank you, Andrew.' She gave him a grateful smile.

He picked up her gloved hand and put it to his lips; he did not let it go as he explained further.

'The thing is, she is going to find out where Evie and Dottie are for you. As you surmised, Evie is married to Barrett now. To be fair, it sounds as if she and Dottie are being looked after.'

'I do hope so, Andrew. If Margie finds out where they are, she will tell you?'

'That is the plan.' He nodded.

*

Aww, her head was swimming. She felt chilled sitting amongst the damp undergrowth. Margie rubbed at her face with a dirty hand. Her stomach felt hollow, her mouth dry, breath sour. She swallowed down the acid rising in her throat.

She had watched the house across the street until all the lights had been extinguished, except one, which was upstairs, probably in a bedroom. Once that one had been extinguished, and the house was in darkness, Margie had the notion that the weight of sleep had descended over the place.

After another hour had gone by, marked by the chiming of Bow Bells, Tommy Dicken had still not returned, so she guessed he must have a night off.

This cosy setup, and the knowledge that Evie Winters was living there in luxury, enflamed Margie's anger, maddened her.

She found herself balling her fists and gritting her teeth, making the empty cavity ache; damn Jack Barrett, damn Evie Winters, may they all rot in hell!

She hadn't been aware of getting up and making it across the road until she found herself holding on to the wrought iron gate.

The gate, which wasn't locked, opened with a squeak, Margie stepped on the path leading to the front door. She was still holding the bottle of whisky, she raised it to her lips and took a long swallow, unaware that much of it dripped down her chin, to be soaked up by Mrs Gordon's coat. She left the gate open as she staggered up the path towards the house.

*

Instead of facing the huge bed that she shared, on and off, with Jack, Evie, who was dressed in her nightclothes, was seated in the small library/sitting room. She was curled up on one of the wing-backed chairs; a woollen shawl draped over her shoulders.

This was the only place in the house where she felt comfortable and at peace. It was one of the rooms that Jack rarely stepped in to. Reading was her domain, her escape.

She also hadn't been sleeping well since she and Dottie had exchanged words regarding Tommy. It had been a while ago now, but Dottie still wouldn't speak to her.

Sitting in the library reading took her mind off her loneliness and isolation. She quite often fell asleep in the early hours, waking with a stiff neck after a couple of hours sleep.

She knew that Jack wouldn't be home this night, not that he had mentioned anything to her, but she had overheard him telling Mrs Perkins.

On nights such as these, Evie used to be able to sleep in the bed, but as time went on, she felt as if the bedroom was dominated by *his* presence, by what he did to her.

Evie knew that Jack was getting angrier and angrier and frustrated with her, with her lack of response towards him; what the hell did he think she was going to do? Kowtow to him! He had taken her body, but she was determined he would take no more of her.

Evie started awake, the book she had been reading fell to the floor.

The lamp she had set on a small table next to her, was flickering as if caught in a draft. The fire had gone out completely, Evie shivered with the damp chill which had permeated the room.

Getting to her feet, she felt as stiff as an old woman.

It was just as she bent down to pick up the book that she heard the sound of shattering glass.

Setting the book aside, then picking up the lamp, the noise drew her to the hallway.

Upon opening the door, Evie was aware of several things at once; there was a chilly draft wrapping around her ankles and slippered feet, she shivered. The strong smell of alcohol prickled her senses, and there was a dark shape standing in the doorway of the room opposite.

Catching her breath, Evie stepped into the hall. As she did so, the lamp, she was holding reached out its halo of light and illuminated the countenance of the bulky figure.

'Margie?' Evie cocked her head in enquiry.

'Well, just look atcha. If it aint bloody lady muck.' The woman stepped away from the threshold of the dining-room. Her movements were uncoordinated. She looked as if she were on the deck of a ship caught in a storm.

'Margie, is it you?' Evie couldn't quite comprehend what was happening. 'What are you doing here?'

Margie gave a derisory snort, 'I've come to see yer aint I. To pay me respects.' She cackled. Then lifted the bottle she was holding, putting it to her lips.

Evie stretched out a hand towards her. 'I think you've had enough to drink, Margie, come into the kitchen, I'll make you some tea.'

'I'll give you bloody tea.' Like an enraged madwoman, Margie threw the bottle at Evie.

Shocked, Evie stepped aside, the bottle smashed on the hall tiles. In the same instant, Margie launched herself at Evie.

Her attention taken by the broken bottle; Evie did not see the attack coming.

When Margie collided with her, unable to keep her footing, Evie staggered backwards. The lamp she had been carrying flew from her grasp. The oil and the alcohol greeted each other with greedy relish.

'Yer bitch, yer bitch. This is for poor Moll.' Margie pulled back an arm, ready to punch the younger girl beneath her.

Evie, caught under the weight of the other woman, looked on in horror as the flames found the hem of Margie's coat.

'No, Margie.' Evie tried to issue a warning but was caught a nasty blow which made her head spin, her vision dimmed at the edges.

Even in her drunken and anger fuelled state; Margie realised the danger, she rolled off the prone figure. As she was getting to her feet, the flames consumed the wool of Mrs Gordon's pilfered coat.

'Aww, no, no.' Margie tried to extinguish the flames with her bare hands.

Evie groaned, then realising the danger she was in and the horror before her, she did her best to scramble to her feet.

Filled with panic, Evie called out. 'Margie, Margie.'

Margie had stumbled towards the stairs where she had tried to grab the banister to pull herself up, but the fire had consumed her alcohol-soaked clothes. The flames gripped her so fiercely, the woman was turned into a ball of fire. Margie's awful cries became fainter, then stopped completely as she fell to the floor.

The sight of what was happening; the oily scent of black smoke, burning flesh and wool made Evie want to vomit.

Then the cold hand of frigid fear gripped her once more as she noticed that the flames were making their way up the stairs.

The scene unfolding brought her back to her senses.

'Oh God! Dottie!' Evie screamed her sister's name. 'Dottie ...'

Desperately wanting to run up the stairs, Evie found that the fire had effectively blocked them off, along with the access to the back of the house.

Looking about herself frantically she thought to go out of the front door, which was behind her. But, as well as the deadbolts, it was locked by a key that was kept in the kitchen.

The library door was to her right, the dining-room to the left. The door was open, Evie saw that the flames were being fanned by a draft coming from the room, and the open staircase was acting like a chimney as the flames danced up the stairs like macabre ballerinas.

'Dottie!' Evie shouted as loud as she could. She screwed up her eyes against the heat and smoke.

'Evie, Evie ...' Dottie appeared on the landing above. She looked like a ghost in her white nightdress as wraiths of oily smoke spun around her.

'Dottie, wake Tommy, Ivy and Mrs Perkins.'

'Tommy's not here,' Dottie called. As she inhaled the smoke, it caused her to cough violently.

'Wake the others,' Evie called, 'all of you, go into your room and shut the door, get to the window.'

With relief, she saw Dottie nod then disappear. Evie ran into the dining room, raced across the room. She felt and heard glass breaking under her feet, but she didn't pause to see what it was.

A pane of the window had been smashed. The latch had been opened from the inside, and the window pulled up. That was the place where Margie had entered the house. A small table adorned with pretty ornaments had been overturned, but Evie did not stop to assess the damage. She lifted the skirt of her nightdress and dressing-gown, then climbed out of the window.

She rushed around the side of the house. When she reached Dottie's bedroom window, she looked up, hoping to see her sister's pale face at the glass, she could see nothing.

'Dottie,' she called, but there was no reply. Evie cursed the fact that it was Tommy's night off, she could do with his help right now.

Her heart beating wildly with fear, she opened her mouth and shouted as loud as she could, 'Fire – Fire.'

———◄❨▷——

Chapter 53

Just as the Frobisher's were finishing dinner. Their butler arrived at the table to inform them they had visitors.

Hero apologised profusely for disturbing them.

'Well,' Jasper eyed the trio. 'that is quite alright, Horacio, however, we were not expecting to see you again quite so soon.'

'Ahh, yes.' Hero gave him a thin smile. 'We are sorry to turn up unannounced, but we need your help once again.'

'By the look on your face, it must be for something serious,' Jasper commented.

'It is.'

Sophia hovered behind Andrew, not sure what to do. So, when a very round pug appeared from underneath the table then jumped up at her, she was happy to crouch down and make a fuss of the dog who rolled over to expose his chubby belly, Sophia found herself laughing.

'That is Chisholm, my dear.' Sarah laughed. 'He obviously likes you.'

'Oh, he is delightful.'

'Mmm, delightful is one word for him, spoilt more likely.' Jasper quipped. Then took in the two men once more. 'Shall we retire to my study to talk in private?'

Hero shook his head, 'I think you both need to hear this.'

'Goodness,' Sarah exclaimed, 'You had best come and sit down then.' She ushered them to the table. Indicating to the footman, she said, 'Edward, bring in a tureen of that delicious soup and plates of cold cuts for our visitors.

'Yes, ma'am.' He gave her a formal bow then left.

'That is exceedingly kind of you,' Andrew said. 'We haven't had time for dinner.'

While they were waiting for the food to be brought in, Jasper poured them all a glass of good claret.

'So, what has happened.' Jasper took his seat at the head of the table.

Andrew let Hero take the lead in explaining their situation. He paused as the food was being served, then carried on while they ate.

'Oh gracious,' Sarah uttered, placing a hand over her heart. 'I cannot quite believe what I am hearing. Jasper, you know the Silverman's, don't you?'

'Not well, my dear. I know Alexander Silverman more by reputation. I feel that we should go to him, let him know what his son has been up to.'

'Perhaps,' Hero agreed, 'however, you must remember that Sophia was attacked in his home.

'Good Lord!' Jasper got to his feet and paced the floor of the dining room. 'He is complicit then.'

'Yes, he is,' Andrew agreed bitterly.

'This is a dreadful situation.' Sarah's voice was choked with emotion.

'There is also another consideration,' Andrew spoke up once more. He looked over at Sophia, who nodded her consent. 'Sophia is expecting a child,' he explained.

Sarah glanced at the girl with concern. 'As a result of the attack?' She asked gently.

'Yes,' Sophia nodded.

'Oh, you poor darling.' Sarah reached out to the younger woman, but Sophia shook her head adamantly.

'Shall I explain, Sophia?' Andrew asked her.

'Yes, please.'

Andrew went on to tell the Frobisher's that Sophia had come to terms with the fact that she was expecting a child; that she wanted to keep the baby.

'I have asked Sophia to be my wife,' he said at last, 'she has agreed.' He beamed at his beloved. 'We shall bring the child up as our own.'

'Oh, bravo, my dear.' Sarah dabbed at her tear-filled eyes with a napkin.

'Yes, I concur.' Jasper felt equally moved by the story. He looked at Andrew and Hero in turn, 'so what can we do to help?'

*

Jack Barrett watched on as the queue of people entered the large warehouse. There were old and young, children and babies. They all looked dejected and worn out. Most had fled from the oppression in the north; many had brought treasures with them.

These items were being confiscated by his men, while Mr Stephen's took careful notes describing the items and the person it had belonged to. They were a "down payment" on the shelter and food that would be provided for them, along with the aid to find work – that was the story these displaced people were fed, the reality was vastly different.

The line was getting to the bedraggled last few when Jack heard his name being called.

'Mr Barrett, Mr Barrett!'

Recognising Tommy Dicken, Jack said, 'Hold up, where's the bloody fire?'

When the young man drew close, Jack could see that his face was desolate. Tears washed his cheeks.

'That's it,' he said breathlessly, his voice breaking. 'The fire - the fire's killed em.'

*

Evie sat on the damp grass of the once quaint garden. There were no tears, no hysterics, instead she felt cold, exhausted, and numb.

One of their neighbours, a Mrs Cooper, stood anxiously by the young woman. She had draped a heavy coat over her shoulders.

'Oh, tis such a shame,' the woman shook her head, 'such a shame.'

The grass had been churned up by the horse-drawn fire wagon, as the men had tried to douse the fire.

One of the firemen had climbed a ladder to the room which Evie had indicated. It had been full of smoke. When the man had carried the limp figure of her sister down the ladder, Evie had felt her knees buckle. Her heart broke into a million pieces.

The fireman laid Dottie out gently on the ground before climbing the ladder once more, to check for the others.

Evie had crawled over to Dottie. Shaking her head in denial, Evie begged her to awaken.

'Dottie, don't leave me, Dottie. Please.'

Another of the men had shaken his head.

'She's gone, lass. Here.'

Someone had handed him a sheet. He covered the younger girl's body. He tried to draw Evie away, but she refused, she would not be parted from her sister.

Shivering, Evie held on tightly to Dottie's icy hand. The sheet had shrouded the body. Evie wanted to pull the fabric away but dare not. If she saw Dottie's dear face, everything would feel too real. She didn't know if she could cope with that blow.

The shrouded bodies had been added to, little Ivy and Mrs Perkins. It wasn't the flames that had killed them, one of the firemen had declared, but the thick oily smoke.

One of the men had asked her how the fire had started, Evie shook her head, but he heard her say a name, "Margie". Margie who? He had asked, but he couldn't get Mrs Barrett to say more.

It was strange that when Evie saw the tall figure of Jack Barrett coming around the corner of the house, closely followed by Tommy. She felt relief. A small voice inside her had asked the question, why hadn't she taken the chance to run? They would have thought that she had been killed in the fire. She could have gotten away from this insufferable sham of a marriage. But she had nowhere to go – Jolly Jack, with his scarred face was the only person in the world she had now.

When he walked over to her and lifted her in his arms, she did not object. She clung to him in desperation.

'Awe, she's in a bad way,' Mrs Cooper nodded at Evie, 'reckon she's in shock.'

Jack nodded, 'What happened?' he asked Mrs Cooper.

'I couldn't say, Mr Barrett. My husband heard the screaming. He got out of bed and saw the flames.'

On their way to the house in Bow, Tommy could only tell Jack that when he had arrived back from the Star, a local pub nearby, he found that the house was ablaze. Somebody must have run for the fire-wagon because the men were already there.

Holding his wife in his arms, Jack surveyed the scene. Spirals of smoke rose towards the night sky. There wasn't any sign of flames now.

Quite a crowd had gathered to watch the proceedings, bloody vultures; Jack found himself thinking.

Tommy was on his knees besides Dottie's body. Jack was surprised to see tears running down the youth's cheeks, but then again, he had just lost his sister.

'Come on, Tommy,' Jack called to him. 'I'm taking Evie to the Crown.'

Tommy nodded. Reluctantly, he got up. Wiped his face with the back of his hand, then put his cap back on.

'What about the bodies?' he asked Jack.

'Got to take care of the living first,' Jack answered. 'Once I've got Evie settled, we'll come back to make the arrangements.'

Tommy sniffed noisily, then nodded.

*

Unaware of all the drama taking place in his absence, George Beeching arrived back in London the following day.

Once out of the station, he hailed a Hansom cab. His first stop was to see Simmons, the solicitor, to direct the man to hire an investigator to track down Vanessa and William.

Then he went to his club, where he asked one of the young boys, who ran messages for the members, to find Jack Barrett and arrange a meeting with the man.

As he knocked back a brandy, he was fairly sure he would find that Alec Silverman will have beaten him to it, and already spoken to the thug, Barrett.

It would be interesting to hear what he had said to Barrett, how much he had offered him. Whatever the amount it would be doubled - trebled it if needs be.

He had decided that he would get Barrett to bring him the girl, oh, the very thought of seeing her again made his loins tighten. He would also get the thug to deal with Silverman and Woodley. Silverman, because he dared to blackmail him. And Woodley for his affair with Vanessa and aiding her escape.

Therefore, he was extremely put out and annoyed when the messenger returned and told Beeching that Jack Barrett was busy and unable to see him that day.

'Busy with what?' he asked the boy.

He was surprised when the lad's expression turned to one of relish.

'His whole ouse burnt down, it did. Killed everybody in it.'

'Oh.' George could think of nothing more to say.

*

Evie awoke to dirty daylight filtering through some tatty curtains drawn across two windows.

With no recognition about how she got there, or where she was, Evie found herself in bed. There were the sounds coming from a busy street. These were loud and discordant to her.

The scent of sour beer and frying bacon; both made her stomach heave.

Warily, Evie sat up and found herself dressed in a nightgown that she did not recognise.

As well as the bed, the room was furnished with a wardrobe, chest of drawers, a washstand with a chamber pot underneath. The bed was large, taking up most of the space. Someone had lit a fire in the small grate, but the room still felt damp. A faded rose-patterned wallpaper covered the walls; it was peeling off in places.

When she sat up in bed, the whole nightmare, the fire, Dottie's death, and the deaths of Mrs Perkins and Ivy shook her to the core.

Evie doubled over in pain. The sound that issued from her was that of a wounded animal.

'Aww, you're awake then.' A woman that Evie vaguely recognised entered the room.

Evie shook her head in horror.

When she continued crying, the bed shifted as the woman sat down next to her.

Placing a hand on her shoulder, she said, 'Aye, let it out, lovie.'

Eventually, Evie looked at her. The woman was older than she was. Her eyes were a faded blue that could have been cold, but concern softened them.

Her hair, which was pinned on top of her head in an untidy fashion, allowing for sweat darken tendrils to fall about her face which was pink from assertion. A film of sweat shined her brow. She had once been pretty, but a hard life jaded her beauty.

'I know you, don't I?' Evie uttered, at last, her voice cracked with emotion. Glancing about the room she asked. 'Where am I?'

'I'm Rita.' She indicated the room. 'These are the living quarters above the Crown and Garter.'

'Crown and Garter, the pub?'

'Well, you cotton on quick dontcha.' The woman gave her a wry smile. 'Sorry about yer sister.'

Evie nodded, her head felt heavy, her chest tight. 'They are all dead, aren't they?' she asked at last.

'Ivy and Mrs Perkins.' Rita nodded. 'Aww, poor Tommy, he's beside imself.'

'The house?'

'A burnt down ruin, so I've been told.'

Evie gave a barely perceived nod, 'and Jack?'

'Oh Jack, he's about somewhere. He'll pop in to see yer soon.'

'Does he know about Margie?'

'Margie?' The woman's eyes narrowed. 'What about Margie?'

Evie looked at her in astonishment. She was sure that she told Jack it had been Margie who had caused all this devastation. Noticing the strange expression on her companion's face something stopped her from revealing anything more.

'I saw her the other day; when I went shopping,' Evie said vaguely.

'Did yer now? Well, shopping, ain't that nice.' Rita got up, making the springs of the bed creak once more. 'Well, I've got work to do. You stay in bed and rest.'

'Thank you, but I would rather get up.'

Rita shrugged, 'suit yerself. The doc gave you a draught to make you sleep,' She nodded to a phial on the bedside cupboard. 'So, you might be a bit groggy. You were in a bit of a state when Jack brought you here.'

'When was that?'

'Two days ago.'

'Two days!' Evie couldn't quite believe it.

As Rita went to leave the room, Evie called her back, 'The funerals,' she asked.

'Poor little Ivy and Mrs Perkins have been buried; Jack saw to that. He knew you'd want to be there for your sister's funeral, though.'

'Yes.'

Evie felt the onset of fresh tears. Laying down on the bed in the foetal position, then wept once more.

Rita left her to her grief, gently closing the door behind her.

*

Beeching was beside himself with impatience as he waited to hear from Barrett.

It didn't matter what had happened to the man; business went on regardless – the days were running out; he was due to meet with Alec Silverman on the day after tomorrow. He needed the girl found, and Alec and Horacio Woodley brought to account.

He decided that if he hadn't heard from Barrett by the end of the day, he would go and find the man himself.

*

'Ow are yer feeling?' Jack stood awkwardly beside the bed. His height made the room feel even smaller than it was.

He eyed his wife warily. Evie sat on the bed in her black garb, which Jack had sent Rita out to buy for her, along with some other bits and pieces.

'Like I have just buried my sister,' her voice was a monotone. Then she found the will to look at him. 'Thank you for arranging everything.'

He nodded his head in acknowledgement.

Dottie had been buried in the grounds of the church where she and Jack had married. All through the proceedings, Evie had felt numb, as if she were isolated in a bubble of unreality. Her eyes had ached, but she didn't cry.

Jack had stood beside her as the coffin was laid in the ground.

Unsure how she felt about his presence now, Evie was surprised to find a modicum of comfort having the man beside her at that moment.

Bit by bit, memories of that night came back; the awful spectacle of Margie - her clothes ablaze. The moment when the fireman brought out Dottie's lifeless body, her honey-gold hair reflecting the flames.

Evie remembered being gathered up in strong arms, after that, she remembered nothing up to the point when she had awoken in the room above the Crown.

On the way to the church, the funeral carriage had passed the burnt down ruins.

Jack had taken her gloved hand in his.

'I'll rebuild the place for yer,' he had said.

She nodded but had no reply. Life would never be the same again.

Finding that he felt uncomfortable in her mute presence, Jack shuffled his feet, then strolled over to one of the bedroom windows and looked out. He could just make out the tops of the cranes on the docks from here.

'This aint no place for yer to be,' he said thoughtfully.

'I'm fine.' Evie found herself saying.

He turned and looked at her. 'I'll find a place to rent while the ouse is being rebuilt. You'll need a new ousekeeper.'

'You don't have to worry about that,' Evie said, 'I can take care of myself.'

Giving her a long look, he said, 'Aye, you can.' She wasn't sure if she saw a wry grin on his scarred face. 'You alright to stay ere for a couple more days while I get things sorted?' he asked.

She shrugged again. 'I've got nowhere else to go.'

*

Intending to catch the train back to London the following day, Andrew and Hero had stayed the night with the Frobisher's.

Whereas Horacio was eager to get back to confront Alec, Andrew was more hesitant. He didn't want to leave Sophia, even though he knew she would be in safe hands.

Sophia found Sarah and Jasper to be a lovely couple who made her feel very welcome in their beautiful home.

Chisholm took a liking to the young woman, following her around adoringly, which made everyone laugh.

'You have competition there, my dear,' Jasper said to Sarah wryly.

'So, I can see,' Sarah laughed.

'Yes, Wilson was the same,' Hero eyed Sophia thoughtfully, 'what is it about you that instils such adoration in others.'

Sophia found herself blushing. 'I'm just me,' she shrugged.

The following morning, after they had breakfasted together, Hero waited in the large hall as Andrew and Sophia said their goodbyes in the drawing-room.

'I really don't like leaving you, my love.' Andrew's gaze was full of concern as he held her hands tightly.

'It cannot be helped, Andrew, you need to get back to your studies anyway.' She gave him an encouraging smile.

Releasing her hands, he strode over to one of the tall windows and looked out at the sweeping parkland.

'I'm not sure I will be able to study,' his voice was grave. 'Certainly not until all this horror has been sorted and I know that you are completely safe.'

'I know.' Her silk dress, the colour of purple blackberries brushed across the floor as she came to stand beside Andrew.

'I am frightened,' she said at last, 'but not so much for myself, but you and Horacio.' She placed a hand on his arm and looked up at him anxiously. 'Please don't let him do anything rash, Andrew. He is a lovely man, but I see the need for destruction in his eyes.'

Andrew looked at her in surprise. 'You are very perceptive, Sophia. He has been living with guilt for years; the guilt of which he feels the weight of every day. That's why he boxes, I think it does help him to let go, but it is also a punishment.'

She nodded in understanding, 'I have heard what happened to his sister and father.'

'Yes, a great tragedy.' He placed a hand over hers and squeezed it gently.

'Please take care of yourself and look after Hero.' She looked up into his eyes.

'I will have no fear of that.'

There was a tap on the door; then it opened, Hero appeared.

'Come on you lovebirds; we need to get going if we are to catch the morning train.'

'Yes, yes, I'm coming.' Andrew gave Sophia a reassuring smile, then leant down and kissed her lips gently; he drew away reluctantly. 'I will be back in a couple of days when hopefully, this nasty business will be resolved.'

'Yes.' Placing a hand upon his cheek, he was delighted when she instigated another kiss.

'Oh, for goodness sake.' Horacio rolled his eyes, which made them both laugh.

Sophia and Sarah stood at the top of the sweeping steps beneath the portico, Chisholm at their feet as they waved the two men off.

Charlie was driving the carriage to the station; then he was going to return to keep an eye out for Sophia, to ensure she was kept safe.

'Come, my dear.' Sarah said, putting her arm through Sophia's' 'let's take Chisholm for a walk around the grounds.

'I would like that.' Sophia smiled at her companion, warmly.

Chapter 54

Evie was sitting on a chair which she had placed by the window so she could watch the comings and goings on the street below. She could hear the babble of voices coming from the barroom downstairs as well as the noises from the street.

Much to Evie's surprise, there was a knock at the door then Rita appeared. The woman was carrying four books, and a plate with a meat pie on it. She set the books down on top of the chest of drawers.

'I've brought you a bite.' She handed Evie the plate, then indicated the books. 'Jack thought these would pass the time,' Rita said. She rested her hand on the leather cover of the topmost book. 'I never learnt to read, me. Couldn't see the point in it.'

'Really?'

'Aww, don't look so shocked. When the ell would I get a chance to sit down and read a bloody book.' She waved about the room. 'I work my fingers to the bone in this place.'

'Yes, sorry.'

'Huh, don't be sorry, it ain't a bad life.'

'I'm sure,' Evie found herself saying.

There was a loud bay of laughter from below.

'Well, best get back to it.'

Rita wiped her hands on a stained apron which was covering a red dress that had seen better days.

'Yes, of course.' Evie tried a smile. She found it difficult to compose her rigid features.

Rita nodded, then left the room.

Rita had also brought a pie and a mug of ale up for Jolly, who was sitting behind his desk tallying up the *contributions* taken from the people who had arrived the night before last, the night of the fire.

He looked up as Rita entered. 'There you go, Jack, nice steak and kidney pie for yer.'

'Ow's she doing?' he asked, nodding towards the room next door.

'Quiet.' Rita stood before the desk. 'Aww, she's a bit of a cold fish, aint she.'

Jolly looked up at her, his eyes cold and dangerous. 'Leave it, Rita my marriage aint none of yer business.'

'Right you are.' She backed away face flushed. 'Sorry, Jack.'

When Rita had gone, closing the door behind her, Jack sat back in his chair thoughtfully. Aww, he knew that Rita wasn't far from the truth.

The closest he had felt to Evie Winters was on the night of the fire; when he had picked her up and she had clung to him. He had to admit there was a spark of hope that the fire had changed her, that she would be more open, a willing participant in their marriage. It was not that she had ever said no to him, but she had never shown any inkling of pleasure for being in his company.

He took it as a rejection on her part of course. Part of him wanted to go into the other room and take her several times in that bed, in which he had partaken in many gratifying encounters in the not too recent past. The thoughts made his blood stir.

Jack pushed the meat pie and ale away. He got up and poured himself a brandy. Sitting back down behind the desk, he took a swallow of the drink. He had promised Evie that he would rent her a house and have the ruin rebuilt, anyway she wanted, no matter what the cost.

He suddenly felt a flame of anger spark in his gut. Tossing back the brandy, he banged the glass down on the desk. It didn't matter what he offered her; she would never love him, would never be happy with him; he knew that. It was strange, he mulled, why he felt he needed her love and approval so much? But then, it wasn't so much about her. It was his place in society, where did he belong? Perhaps the burning down of the house was a sign. His kingdom was the East End; this is where he made his life and fortune.

His thoughts were interrupted by the door being pushed open.

'Get yerself gone, Rita,' he called in a harsh voice.

'She's downstairs in the barroom,' George Beeching said as he stepped into the room.

'What the hell are yer doing ere?' Jack eyed the man coldly.

'I sent you several urgent messages, Barrett, the least you could have done is get back to me.'

George removed his hat and gloves, which he placed on the desk. He left his coat on.

'I ain't at yer beck and call, Beeching. I've been busy.'

Jack eyed the other man with a hard gaze. George Beeching's face looked as white and greasy as a tallow candle, although two spots of unhealthy colour bruised his cheeks.

'Has Alec Silverman been to see you?' George asked as, without invitation, he plonked himself in one of the chairs opposite the desk.

'Ahh, I ad a feeling this little visit would be about im.' Jack got up, refilled his glass then poured one for his unexpected visitor. He handed the drink to Beeching, then sat back down.

'The bloody little pipsqueak had the audacity to blackmail me, can you believe it!' Picking up the glass, George knocked back half of the brandy. He looked Jack in the eye. 'He's been here, hasn't he, asking for your help?'

'Oh aye, he has.'

'And ...?'

'I said I would do what he asked.'

Eyes narrowed; George leant forward in his chair. 'What exactly did he ask you to do?'

'He asked me to find the Jewish girl so he could hand her over to you, then he wanted me to deal with Horacio Woodley.'

'Kill him?'

'No, cripple him.'

George flopped back in his chair and gazed at the smoke-darkened ceiling. 'Cripple him, eh? Well, there's a surprise; I thought they were good friends.'

Jolly shrugged. 'Woodley is a better man than most.'

'Umm, well the little bastard is an adulterer, he had an affair with my wife.'

Leaning forward in his chair, Jack said, 'I'd bet me hat that you aint touched her for months, getting too old for you, was she?'

George's face infused with blood as the barb hit home. 'How dare you, Barrett.'

Jolly smiled, making the scar on his face stretch. He held up a hand, 'Ahh, just my little idea of a joke.'

'Well, you can keep your bloody jokes to yourself.'

Still keeping eye contact, he said, 'hit a nerve ave I? I ear that your lady wife has run away.'

George looked at him sharply. 'How the hell did you know about that?'

Jack tapped the side of his nose with a long finger, 'I ave my sources.'

'Ha, yes, of course, you do.'

Sitting back in his chair, which made it creak, Jack said, 'So?'

'So, what?'

'Are you going to tell me what yer doing here, you still ain't said.'

'Whatever Silverman has offered you I will treble it.'

'To do what exactly?'

'I want the girl and Alec Silverman. He has a letter in his possession which could do my career a great deal of harm. Find that, bring it to me so I can destroy it. When I have that, I want Silverman killed, along with his so-called friend, Woodley. Kill them and send them both to the bottom of the river.'

'What will you do with the girl?'

'We have unfished business she and I. I need a place to finish what we started.'

Jack nodded. He continued to eye the other man coldly without saying a word.

'Well?' George shifted in his seat, uncomfortable under Jack's scrutiny.

'I work for Alexander Silverman,' Jack said at last, 'so there's a conflict of interest.'

Beeching let out a bellow of rough laughter. 'Lord man, are you saying you have scruples and loyalties?'

'Mr Silverman pays very well for my services. I wouldn't want to do anything that upsets our arrangement.'

'Alright, I will quadruple the price Alec has offered. I can also be extremely useful to you Barrett. My father is ill, who knows how long he will last. When he's gone, I shall be Lord Beeching, right and proper, inheriting a large estate in Norfolk, and two houses here in the city. With a seat in the house, I shall have influence. If we work together, we can make a fortune what with all the demolition and rebuilding. I have shares in the new rail-line being built. I will give you ten-per cent of these to seal the deal.'

Barrett continued to watch his visitor closely. He did not trust the man one iota. All these *offerings* the man had just laid at his feet sounded too good to be true. He decided to test the water further.

'I want one of the ouses.'

'What?' George looked shocked.

'You eard me, quadruple what Silverman junior is offering, which you aint asked ow much that is, by the way. One of the ouses, the pretty one you ad built across the river. And the shares in the rail-line. I shall sever my business ties with the Silverman's, and work for you instead.'

'I can't let you have one of our city residences, that is a step too far Barrett. In any case, they are still in my father's name.'

Jack nodded he had been expecting as much. If the man had gone on to agree to the deal, it would have made him even more suspicious and wary.

Leaning forward, his elbows on the desk, Jack said, 'So, how much is he blackmailing you for?' He held up a hand. 'Be truthful with me Beeching, because I will find out the truth when I ave the pup in my clutches.'

George flushed. 'Yes, of course. He is blackmailing me for five thousand pounds.'

Alec Silverman had offered him a thousand to undertake the jobs that needed doing. 'Alright, you give me the five grand, plus the shares.'

George picked up the glass, which he noticed was of a good quality lead-crystal. He drained the contents and set it down on the desk. 'Very well, we have a deal,' he agreed.

*

Evie had eaten a small amount of the pie that Rita had brought in for her, but her stomach heaved. She put the rest back on the plate, then washed her hands in the washbowl. The scent of the food made her feel queasy. Picking up the plate, she went over to the door and opened it then stepped onto the landing. There was a chest of drawers standing against a wall. She left the plate there then turned to go back into the bedroom.

As she did so, she realised that the door to Jack's "office" was ajar. what she heard then chilled her blood; *'He asked me to find the Jewish girl so that he could hand her over to you, then he wanted me to deal with Horacio Woodley.'* She recognised Jack's voice.

'Kill him?' She heard an unfamiliar voice answer. A clipped accent, but it was rough with emotion.

'No, cripple him...'

Evie stood there rooted to the spot as the conversation continued.

The Jewish girl? They were talking about Sophia! Where was she? What they were saying didn't sound right at all. Jack was meant to find a rich husband for her, wasn't he? She realised then just how naive they had been. All this had happened just a few months ago, but so much had transpired in between.

Of course, Jack had never found a husband for the Jewish girl, Lord only knew to whom he had handed her over. However, it sounded as if she had slipped away from them, out of their clutches. Evie recognised the name Silverman; she had heard it spoken of a few times in the slums. Jack worked for him. But who was Woodley?

Evie put a hand to her mouth, afraid of being sick. She swallowed down the nausea. Barely breathing, she stood listening at the door.

'Very well, we have a deal,' she heard the man with the posh voice say. *'So, what's the plan then?'* he asked.

Evie was annoyed with herself that she had been so involved with her thoughts, she hadn't heard any of the conversation in between. Now she listened carefully to every word; 'The first thing I'll do is get a message to Silverman,' Jack said, 'I can tell him that I ave some news for him about the business involving you. I'll send one of the lads; they can bring him here.'

'Yes, it sounds like a good plan.' Beeching agreed. 'What of the girl, Alec Silverman, told me she is staying under the care of Woodley's mother. How are we going to get her here?'

Jack scratched his chin. 'If we ave Silverman junior, we could use him as leverage, tell Woodley he needs to bring us the girl; otherwise, we will set the dogs on Alec.'

'Ha, oh, I like the sound of that. In fact, when we have the girl and Woodley, he can be more bait for the dogs.' George said, his eyes shining with relish.

On the landing, Evie hissed in a horrified breath. She felt lightheaded with fear. Reaching out, she pressed her hand to the wall trying desperately not to faint.

'If that's what you want,' Jolly agreed. 'Your money, your entertainment. And the girl, what do you want to be done with her?'

'She can watch the proceedings; then, we shall retire. I want a private room so I can conclude my business with her.'

'That's no problem; you can use one of the bedrooms ere. It ain't a palace, but it will do for the sort of things you ave in mind. Also means we can deal with the bodies in one fell swoop.'

'Yes, very well,' the posh voiced man agreed. 'I want all this done as soon as possible.'

'Alright, bring me a sweetener, a down payment, an I'll get cracking. The lads will track down Alec and Woodley easily enough; then we can send one of my lads with Woodley to pick up the girl.'

'Ah, good. Send a messenger over to the club when you have news.'

'Aye.'

Evie heard movement from the room. She stepped backwards, then silently entered the bedroom. Pushing the door to but didn't shut it entirely because of the sound the latch would make.

Sitting down on the chair by the window once more, she picked up the book she had been reading, only to find her hands were shaking uncontrollably as the impact of what she had just overheard sunk in.

Evie heard the men on the landing, then their voices receding as they went downstairs.

Sitting in the chair, she took some deep breaths. She had to do something! But what?

Standing up abruptly, her first thought was to go to the peelers, step into the station and tell them everything she had heard.

Wringing her hands together in agitation, she looked up at the ceiling. Her vision blurred from unshed tears of frustration. No, she couldn't do that, she knew that there were several policemen who were paid by Jack to turn a blind eye to what went on in the poorer parts of the city.

No! Evie decided she was on her own. Sitting down once again, she tried to organise her frantic thoughts, to put them in order. What did she know? Barrett was sending his thugs out to bring back two men. Then they were going to keep one of them hostage while the other was sent with one of Jack's men to abduct Sophia. If indeed it was Sophia they had been discussing?

Even if that were not the case, Evie intended to do something to help these people.

Evie had a mission: the first thing she needed to do, she decided, was to take a look at the layout of the establishment. Find the cellar where the men would be taken. She had come across the word *reconnoitre*, in one of her books. She knew what it meant; to explore or survey the lay of the land. Soldiers did it before attacking an enemy camp. So, that was what she was going to do.

Evie felt her heartbeat quicken, not with fear but resolve. She opened the door of the bedroom and stepped onto the landing, then went down the stairs.

*

When they reached London, Andrew hailed a cab to take him home, and Horacio summoned one to take him to the Silverman's townhouse, he had a feeling that Alec would be there.

As soon as Andrew stepped through the front door, he was dismayed to find a distraught Mrs Gordon.

'Aww Dr Keene, I'm so glad you are back.'

He felt his stomach plummeting, bracing for bad news. 'Where's Margie?'

The housekeeper quickly explained what had happened. When Andrew heard the story, he was annoyed, not so much with Margie, but himself, he should have realised that she posed a threat, he should never have put Mrs Gordon at risk.

'Luckily, constable Norris has recovered the items, Dr Keene,' she said as they ascended the stairs to his rooms. 'Although the woman can't be traced.' Andrew let himself into his sitting-room. 'I have given the place a good clean for you,' she declared. 'I am so sorry.'

Andrew put a comforting arm around her shoulders. 'Please don't keep apologising, Mrs G, I do not blame you in the least. It is me; I should never have left this responsibility on your shoulders.'

The woman nodded, fished in her apron pocket, brought out a handkerchief and dabbed at her damp eyes.

'What of Sophia, is she safe?' she asked once she pulled herself together.

'It is a bit of a story,' Andrew said, 'Let's make a pot of tea, we can sit down, and I shall tell you what has happened to date.'

'Our dear Sophia is expecting that monster's child?' The housekeeper looked horrified.

Andrew raised his hand. 'Now, we shall have none of that, please. I asked her before I left if I had her permission to tell you all this, she agreed, so please respect her decision. She has shown such strength and resilience.'

'Oh Lord.' The woman nodded. 'I'm sorry Dr Keene, it is just she is such a sweet soul, but I'm worried that having this man's baby will be a reminder to her, of what happened every single day.'

'For some, it would, I am sure. However, Sophia sees this child as an innocent, and so she should. There is some other news I have to tell you.' He couldn't stop the smile that lightened his face. 'As soon as I knew what was happening, I asked Sophia to marry me.' He raised a hand to forestall any response. 'I know many will think this is controversial, but as you know, I hold Sophia in such high regard. We may not have spent much time together, but she has stolen my heart. We will marry as soon as possible. We shall bring the child up together. I will consider he or she like my own.'

'Oh doctor.' the housekeeper wiped at her teary eyes again. 'I am happy for you both.'

He smiled and held up his teacup as if making a toast. 'Thank you, I knew you would be.'

Chapter 55

'You bloody bastard.' Horacio grabbed Alec around the neck and pushed him up against the wall.

Letting out a forced exhalation, Alec's eyes were wide with shock and fear.

'God, I could beat you to a bloody pulp, Alec, what the hell were you thinking, stealing Sophia's letter?'

Alec shook his head. 'N-nothing, there must be a mistake. I didn't take it, I swear. Andrew must have mislaid it.'

Heart pounding, Hero, stepped away. Alec staggered and gasped, the rough treatment had aggravated the pain in his ribs.

'And your cross-examination of Mrs Gordon?' Hero asked, his voice full of scorn.

'Oh, it was hardly that. I was just showing concern.' He straightened his cravat with shaking fingers. 'I meant what I said, father might be willing to give this Sophia person, some compensation for what happened.'

'Like hell, Alec.' His hands fisted at his sides; Shaking with anger, Hero paced the elegant drawing-room of the Silverman's London house.

Pausing in his stride, raising a quizzical eyebrow, Hero asked, 'What exactly were you going to do with this information? Blackmail Beeching?'

Before Alec dropped his gaze, Horacio noticed the shift of slyness, his question had evoked.

'That's it, isn't it!' Hero knocked over a side table in his haste to get to the other man.

'Horacio, please.' Alec lifted his hands as he backed away. 'We could share the money, you and I.'

'Jesus, Alec, I cannot believe what I am hearing. Andrew warned me about your deviousness. I just didn't want to hear it.'

Straightening his dark blue embroidered waistcoat with indignation, Alec said, 'I've been a good friend to you, Horacio. Helping you when you were blubbering like a baby over your sister's death. Keeping the other fellows from bullying you. Encouraging your boxing.'

'Oh yes, all very noble.' Brushing strands of his thick hair back from his forehead, Hero sighed heavily. They both jumped when there was a knock at the door.

Relieved to have a distraction, Alec called to them to enter. The Silverman's butler appeared.

'Another visitor for you, Master Alec.' The man sniffed with distaste. 'One of Mr Barrett's men, he says it is urgent.'

'Oh – um.' Alec shot Hero a wary look.

'Tell them that Mr Silverman will be happy to see him.' Hero spoke up.

The butler shot him a surprised look, then looked to his master for consent. Alec nodded.

*

Rita was surprised to find Evie on the ground floor in the corridor behind the barroom.

'Oh, Jack wouldn't like it if he found you here. Do you need anything, Mrs Barrett?'

Evie smiled. 'I know you said you were busy, Rita, is there anything I can do to help?'

Rita's jaw dropped so far Evie was surprised it didn't hit the floor.

'Umm, no. Jack wouldn't like you wandering around down here,' the woman persisted.

'Oh, I'm sure he won't mind, I can't stay in that room all the time, can I?'

'No, I suppose not.' Rita shrugged.

A man's voice, as rough as sandpaper, called from the bar, 'Rita – Rita, are you goin to serve me or not?'

'Just coming, Ned,' she called back, but she didn't move. She shot Evie an uncertain look. 'Don't be long, then get back up them stairs.'

'I will,' Evie nodded. She was relieved when the woman went through a door leading to the taproom.

Evie found the door to what she presumed must be the cellar. When she opened it, she could see the rough stairs that lead down into murky depths. It looked dark down there. Spotting two lamps set aside on a small table, along with a strip of matches, striking one, she lit a lamp, then stepped over the threshold, following the steps downwards.

The place felt bone-chillingly cold and damp. The floor was earthen, uneven where it had been trodden down over many years. The ceiling was vaulted, with brick columns to give it support.

Evie could detect the limey and slightly putrid scent of the river. She could also hear the constant drip of water too.

Exploring, she walked by crates and barrels, which were lining the walls. Lamp cast high, the shadows bounced and flickered eerily.

Hearing scurrying, she hissed in a breath when a dark shape scampered across the floor, rats! She shivered.

Guessing that they must run under several properties along the street; Evie was surprised by the size of these rooms. They seemed to stretch much further than the pub above.

Walking around one of the pillars, she went through a door and found a room which contained several cages, all of which were empty; they must be for the fighting dogs. The thought made the bile rise in her throat. Her reaction wasn't helped by the odours that permeated the air, the pungent smells of urine, faeces, and blood. On the far wall, she noticed there were chains attached to fixtures in the brickwork.

Backing out of the place, Evie was relieved to be away from it.

She didn't need to go much further before she came across the "arena". Benches had been built, rising in tiers for spectators of various sports, she didn't wish to ponder too much about what they could be. At last, she found an exit that opened up to a back alley - a way out.

*

Tommy Dicken stood in the middle of the posh room fiddling with his cap. He eyed the two men boldly. He knew them both, of course. One was Alec Silverman and the other, the boxer, Mr Woodley.

Tommy had been sent with a message for Mr Silverman that Mr Barrett needed to see him urgently on a business matter. He had also been asked to locate Horacio Woodley and get him to come to the Crown. Hence the surprise of finding both men together. This discovery made his job a great deal easier.

'Compliments of Mr Barrett,' Tommy said, 'He asks for you both to meet him at the Crown, it is an urgent business matter.'

'An urgent business matter, eh?' Horacio eyed Alec, who was looking extremely uncomfortable. 'Well, we had better go and see what Mr Jolly Jack Barrett wants.'

'Umm, I'm not sure.' Alec dropped his gaze.

'It's urgent.' Tommy insisted.

'There, Alec,' Hero said, 'See, it's urgent.'

'Yes, umm – alright.'

'Have we transport?' Hero asked Tommy as he strode across the room to the door.

'Yes, Mr Woodley. An andsom is waiting outside.'

'Good, good. Come on, Alec.'

Tommy cast Horacio a puzzled look. There was something not quite right about this. He had sensed the tension between the two men as soon as he had walked through the door.

Tommy had a nose for trouble, working for Jack in the rough streets of the East End had honed that trait. But there wasn't much he could do about this niggle, so, he accompanied the two gentlemen, saw them into the cab. Then he took up the back step as they set off to the Crown.

*

Robert Fuller had been the butler in the Silverman's London house for eight years. Long enough to see Master Alec grow up. He had never liked Alec, as a boy, he was rude sly and utterly spoilt. Fuller observed these attributes becoming worse as the boy grew into a young man.

Now that his father was spending more time at their country home on the Kentish downs, Alec had taken up residence in the London house. Rather than continue working for the insufferable boy, Fuller was considering finding another position, as was his colleague and friend, the groom, come coachman, Collins.

After Master Alec and Mr Woodley had left in the Hansom with one of Barrett's lads, Fuller stepped out into the stable yard to have a smoke.

'Having a bit of a reprieve, are you?' Collin's appeared from the tack-room.

'One of Jolly Barrett's men turned up,' he rolled his eyes, 'apparently, the business was urgent.'

'Right,' Collins remarked as he joined his friend for a five-minute break. 'And Mr Woodley?'

'He went with them.'

Collins sat on the edge of a brick wall that flanked the steps leading up to the backdoor of the house. 'Well, Woodley is a sensible man, if he's with the lad, then he can't get up to too much mischief.'

'I'm not so sure about that,' Robert remarked, 'before I announced the *visitor*, I could hear raised voices coming from the drawing-room. '

'Mmm.' Collin's gaze took in the yard thoughtfully. 'Wonder what that was about?'

'Aye.' Fuller took a last drag of the cigarette then dropped the butt. 'Well, best get back to it.'

Collins nodded. 'Aye, me too.' He looked at his friend. 'Let me know when the lad gets back, will you.'

Fuller nodded. 'Will do.'

*

Finding out that Margie had robbed them and disappeared upset Andrew.

He was feeling mortified that he had left her here in the first place, but also upset that now there would be no news to relay to Sophia about her friends, Evie, and Dottie Winters.

He wrote a quick note to Sophia to let her know what had happened.

Once that had been posted, Andrew spent a restless few hours waiting for Horacio to return; as bad as the situation was with Alec, Andrew hoped that Hero had resisted the temptation to beat the little sod to a pulp, as much as he deserved it, Andrew did not want Hero getting into trouble.

*

When Evie heard voices coming towards her, she put down the lamp, then hid behind one of the pillars.

'Right,' she heard Jack's voice, 'Tommy's gone to pick up Silverman the younger, then we need to find Woodley.'

'Aye, the ousekeeper didn't know when he would be back.'

Evie recognised the second voice it was Tommy Dicken's cousin, Reg.

'Alright. Well, you get back there, keep an eye on the place. Pick him up as soon as you see im.'

'It's a bloody shame, e's a good fighter e is.'

'Aye well, we are being paid good money for this, so we ave to do as the punter wants. Beeching needs some entertainment, and we're going to give it to im.' Jack laughed, and Reg joined in.

*

Evie hovered behind the pillar, waiting to see what happened next. It was a good job she stayed put as the silhouette of Jack appeared. He walked past her, unaware of her presence. She heard him strike a match, then smelt the cigarette smoke.

Peering out carefully, she saw him sitting on a barrel near the back-entrance door.

She knew she couldn't move. Jack would hear any sound that she made; every noise echoed around the cavern.

Losing track of how long she waited, she kept peeping out. Jack had finished his smoke and snuffed the butt beneath his shoe.

Evie's feet were beginning to ache in her new boots, black ones that Rita had gotten for her.

The chill of the place was seeping through her limbs, she shivered. It was just then that she heard voices coming from the alley.

Hearing a man's voice which she didn't recognise, Evie held her breath as she listened closely.

'What's happened, Barrett, what's the news?'

'Ahh, Mr Silverman *and* Mr Woodley, well there's a nice surprise.' Jack greeted them.

'My God Barrett, I don't know where to start with all this,' Evie heard yet another male voice. 'I have to dissuade you from continuing with this maliciousness.'

'Aye well, sorry, Mr Woodley but the plans have been set in motion.'

'There, see, Horacio, I will cut you in on the money.' The first voice wheedled.

'Well, I ave some news for you, Silverman, I ave been approached by Beeching, e's up the ante. Made me an offer I couldn't refuse.'

'Bloody hell,' the man called Woodley cursed. 'I won't let you continue with this Barrett!'

Evie heard what sounded like a scuffle, a grunt then something heavy hitting the floor.

'Sorry about that, Mr Woodley,' she heard Jack say, 'but Beeching wants revenge for the affair you've had with his wife. It's part of the deal we struck.'

'Good Lord, Horacio!'

'He's fine, not dead yet.' Jack laughed. 'Sorry about this too, Mr Silverman, but Lord Beeching has some business he wants to sort out with you, too.'

'No, Barrett. No!'

Evie risked a peek from behind the pillar; a slight, dark-haired, man was clubbed over the head. He hit the floor with a grunt.

Tommy ran forward to help Jack to lift one of the bodies.

She didn't recognise the man they lifted between them. He wasn't dressed as flamboyantly as his companion, but his clothes were well cut. Obviously, someone from a prosperous family, Evie thought. His thick curling hair fell across his forehead, making him look younger than he probably was.

He was unconscious as the two men carried him past the pillar where she was hiding, then into the room where the dog cages were.

Risking being spotted, she watched as Jack and Tommy emerged, lifted the other unconscious man then took him through to the same room.

Hearing the clanking of metal; Remembering seeing "shackles" attached to the wall, it sounded as if the men were being chained up? Evie shivered again.

Her knees had gone weak. pressing her hands against the damp brickwork for support, Evie felt as if she were going to faint. Gritting her teeth, she managed to get herself under control once more.

'Right, I sent Reg to keep an eye on Woodley's place, so you'd better go an tell im that we ave im, along with Silverman, ere. Once you've done that, go and find Beeching, tell im we've got part of the goods at least.'

'Alright, Jack.' Tommy nodded.

He sauntered past the pillar behind where Evie was hiding. She tried to swallow, but her throat had gone dry from fear.

Just then, Jack emerged, shutting the wooden door behind him, he stepped in the opposite direction that Tommy had taken.

Holding her breath, Evie thought she heard another door close; the one at the top of the stairs maybe?

Stepping out cautiously from behind the pillar, she stood stock-still for a moment, listening carefully. Apart from the drip, drip, drip of the water, there was no other sound.

In a decisive action, Evie picked up the lamp, holding it high, she opened the door and stepped through.

Squinting, she could make out two shadowed forms slumped against the far wall.

When she strode over to them, her heart was pounding so hard in her ears, Evie wondered if she would hear Jack coming if he returned.

Putting the lamp down on the floor, she knelt close to the man she thought was Woodley.

'Hello, hello, Mr Woodley.' She shook his shoulder, he stirred, making the chains clatter against themselves. 'Shush,' Evie squeezed his shoulder in panic. She looked back towards the door, expecting it to open at any moment. 'Don't move,' she hissed at the man. He must have heard her, as he raised his head carefully then looked at her.

'Who are you?' he asked softly.

'Evie,'

'Evie Winters?'

She caught her breath in surprise, 'H-how did you know?'

'S-Sophia.'

Evie felt her stomach clench in fear. 'Sophia, she's in danger.'

'Yes,' Hero went to move his arm. The chains made such a clatter. The noise rang out in the cavernous cellar as if it were a bell in a church steeple.

'Hush.' Evie raised her hand, Hero stilled.

The two men had metal collars around their necks, ones that would be used to tether dogs. Their wrists were tied together with rope, as were their ankles.

Evie puffed out her cheeks in frustration. She would need a key to unlock the collars and a knife to cut their other bonds.

Tears of frustration stung her eyes; she brushed them away angrily.

Oh Lord, Jack Barrett was a dangerous man. The very thought of spending the rest of her life being married to someone so unscrupulous made her feel sick to her stomach.

Suddenly, Evie realised that she didn't need to stay with Jack anymore. One of the reasons she had done so, was for Dottie and the sake of her sister's health, but Dottie was dead. Ever since the fire, Evie had numbed down her emotions even more. She found herself not caring if she lived or died; it would make no difference to anybody.

Taking her quite by surprise, the sense of purpose and resolve gave her strength; Evie decided that she would free these men, then get away.

Viewing their bonds with dismay, she said, 'I need a knife and a key.'

She was surprised when the man called Woodley shook his head.

'No, don't put yourself in danger. Go and find my friend, Andrew Keene; 57 Stratford Road. He's the man I lodge with; he will come and help us.'

'Alright.' Evie nodded. 'Andrew Keene, 57 Stratford Road?' She clarified.

'Yes.' Hero gave her a reassuring smile. 'Thank you.'

'Don't thank me yet.' Evie got to her feet. She looked down at Horacio. 'I will do my best.'

They both nodded, she in resolve and he in encouragement.

Evie dashed from the room. When she reached the far side of the door, she realised that she had left the lamp behind, the place would be pitch dark without it.

About to turn back, she changed her mind, she couldn't leave the two men without any illumination. Besides, she was sure she could find her way back to the stairs.

Reaching out her hands, she felt the wood of a crate beneath her fingers.

Keeping this to the right, she followed the pathway over the uneven floor.

When she reached the stairs, euphoria bolstered her. Climbing hastily, she pushed open the door at the top and bumped into Jack coming the other way.

Evie gasped in shock as Jack reached out and grabbed the top of her arm in a tight grip, he pulled her to him.

'What the ell was yer doing down there?'

'I-um was just exploring.'

He narrowed his eyes. 'This is a dangerous place to go wandering about.'

'S-sorry, Jack.'

He studied her expression carefully; his gaze was full of suspicion.

'What did you see down there, eh? What did you hear?'

'N-nothing.'

'Well see, ere's the deal, I ain't taking any chances.' His grip on her arm tightened. Evie found herself being dragged along the corridor.

'What the ell!' Rita appeared from the door leading to the barroom.

'She's been doing a bit of exploring, she as,' Jack said roughly.

'Bloody ell, I told er to go back to er room, Jack.'

'Aye, well that's where she's going now.'

'Please, Jack, stop.' Evie tried to pull out of his grasp, but she was unsuccessful against his brute strength.

By the time they reached the landing, Evie had tears of frustration running down her cheeks.

'You can't do this, Jack.'

'I can do anything I want. This is my kingdom; I'm in charge ere.'

'Really?' she hissed at him as he pushed her into the bedroom. Realising she had nothing to lose, she rounded on him. 'What you are doing is wrong, let those men go and leave Sophia alone, hasn't she suffered enough.'

Before she knew what was happening, Jolly's hand shot out, hitting her a stinging blow. Evie gasped and staggered. The backs of her knees impacted with the bed. She fell backwards, stunned.

In an instant, Jack was on top of her. He grabbed her wrists and pinned her hands above her head. Evie was reminded of the rough way Bill Miller had treated her.

'Yer little bitch. Aint I been good to yer, giving you everything you wanted? This is what I get.' He stared into her furious eyes, 'been a bit too soft on yer, ain't I. Well, that's going to change. From now on. Yer does what I tell yer, or else.'

'Or else what, Jack? Are you going to rape me? If you expect a response from me, you've got another thing coming.'

'Why yer ...' He pulled back his fist and punched her.

The world exploded into a million stars as Evie found herself dropping into darkness.

Chapter 56

J ack locked the bedroom door, then went back down the stairs. Bloody Evie Winters, the little bitch, what the hell was he going to do with her! After all he had done for her, he expected loyalty at the very least.

He had given her everything, but it wasn't enough for Miss high and mighty. When he reached the back corridor, he decided that after all this business with Beeching was dealt with, he would deal with her too, wring her neck and find himself another wife!

*

'What's happening, Horacio?' Alec asked as he righted himself as best he could. He sat up, back against the wall next to Hero.

'Unsurprisingly, your little arrangement with Barrett has gone very badly wrong.'

'Oh Lord.' Alec winced with the pain from the blow to the head and his healing ribs. 'What are we going to do?'

'Find a way to escape.' Hero replied through thin lips. 'While you were out of it, we had a visit from Mrs Barrett.

It seems she has far more scruples than her husband. I've given her Andrew's address. Hopefully, she can get word to him, and he can summon help.'

'Good, good.' Alec nodded, then regretted doing so.

He lifted his hand, slipped his fingers under the metal "collar" trying to loosen it. The noise reverberated around the room. When he saw a large rat appear within the spotlight of the lamp, Alec screamed like a girl as he tried to push himself further away from the loathsome creature.

'Don't let it near me!' he sobbed.

'Being eaten by rats is probably the least of your problems,' Hero commented dryly.

*

Evie stirred. It took her a few moments to come too properly. She went to sit up but gasped in pain as she did so. Breathing more easily through her mouth, she realised that her nose throbbed painfully. Reaching up a hand, she found it had been bleeding. The blood had dripped down her cheeks into her hair and had stained the bedcover. Unsteady, for a moment, she pushed herself up to her feet then went over to the washstand. Carefully, she used a washcloth to wipe away the dried blood.

Catching a glimpse of her reflection in the mirror above the chest of drawers, she hissed in a sharp breath. Good Lord, she looked like a madwoman. Hair in disarray, face battered and bruised.

Clenching her teeth, she cursed Jolly Jack Barrett. Then remembering the men in the cellar, she swiftly walked over to the door and tried the knob. She wasn't particularly surprised to find it locked, although her heart sank with the discovery. What on earth was she going to do now?

*

George Beeching was delighted to hear from Jack Barrett so quickly.

Tommy, who had delivered the message to the man at his club, accompanied him on the journey to the Crown.

The younger man showed him around the back, Beeching wrinkled his nose as they walked down the damp and odious alleyway, then entered the entrance to the cellar of the inn.

'Bloody awful place,' he commented as he stayed close to Tommy, the lad made no reply.

They found Jack waiting for him in a room lined with cages. Two lamps had been lit. Beeching spotted the two men at the other end of the room.

'Afternoon, your lordship.' Jack, who was seated on an upturned crate, did not get up but saluted the man with a finger to the temple.

'Barrett.' Beeching nodded not taking his eyes off Hero and Alec. He walked over to the two. Alec looked at him with the eyes of a frightened dog. Beeching smiled coldly. 'See, that'll teach you to blackmail me you little mongrel.'

With desperation, Alec looked over to Barrett. 'You work for my father, man. You can't do this, let me go and no more needs to be said.' He looked up at Beeching who was still towering over him. 'We can forget about the money, but I can still give you the girl ...'

There was a sound of the clink of chains as Horacio stirred. 'By God, Alec, you are a lowlife, no better than the rats who run these walls.'

George eyed the other man, 'I hear that the girl is being looked after by your dear mother at that school of hers.'

'Ah, that is where your information is out of date, Beeching,' Hero mocked. 'When I realised that this bastard had stolen one of Andrew's letters, we knew he was up to no good, so we moved her straight away.'

Barrett nodded to Tommy and Reg, who was standing to one side awaiting direction.

Tommy was the one who stepped forward, he grabbed the chain securing Hero and yanked on it, the noise was loud, jarring.

'Where is she, Mr Woodley?' Tommy tried to instil a threat into his voice.

'Tell the lad where she is, Woodley,' Jack called, 'Or we shall have to do some damaged to that andsome face of yours.'

'Ha, Barrett, you know me better than that. Been punched in the fizzog enough times, threats like that don't worry me.'

Jack got to his feet. 'Well, I ain't talking about a boxing match.' He looked at the tall man with the mop of ginger hair. 'Go and get em, Reg.' Jack ordered.

Reg rushed off.

His face white with anxiety, Alec shot a worried glance at Horacio.

They heard them before they were brought into the room, chuffing and growling with excitement.

Reg entered the room with two huge dogs on chain leads. Both had manic eyes, reflecting dark depths by the lamplight. They both looked mad with hunger; both were foaming at the mouth. Judging by their size, Hero guessed they must be Bullmastiffs.

Jack gestured to the two dogs. 'They ain't been in a fight for a while, they're hungry for it. Now, the question is, who's going to be fed to the dogs first?'

*

Andrew paced the living room floor. Where the hell was Hero? He should have been back by now.

When Horacio had gone to confront Alec on his own, Andrew had felt misgivings. He heartily wished he had accompanied him. He also wondered what Hero would do to Alec; Oh dear, he hoped he hadn't killed the little guttersnipe.

Striding over to the windows which overlooked the busy street, Andrew looked out. Darkness had settled over the city. The gas lamps had been lit, but the pavements and roads were still crowded.

Pulling the curtains over the windows, he decided to head to the Silverman house. He had visited it a couple of times with Hero, so he knew where it was.

Pulling on his coat, hat and gloves against the evening chill, Andrew rushed down the stairs. He knocked on Mrs Gordon's door.

When she opened it, Andrew said, 'I'm going to the Silverman's to find Hero.'

'Yes, yes, of course, Dr Keene. I must admit I am worried about him too.'

Andrew swallowed down a feeling of panic. 'If I, umm, don't return by morning call your bobby friend, will you?'

'Goodness.' She placed a hand over her heart. 'What are we talking about, Dr Keene?' The housekeeper asked, her face pale and bleak.

'I'm not sure, dear lady, but I fear that we will have to get the peelers involved at some point, I just hope it won't be too late.'

*

'Oh, this is priceless, Barrett.' George chuckled but kept a wide gap between himself and the salivating dogs.

'Aye, I thought you would approve.' Jack answered looking over to Horacio and Alec. 'So, this is what's going to appen; you, Mr Woodley, are going to go and get the girl and bring her ere.'

'I will do no such thing.' Hero pulled against his bonds.

'Well, this is the thing; you bring er ere, or we feed Master Silverman to the dogs bit by bit.'

'No!' Alec struggled frantically, which made the dogs growl and snap even more. Reg had a job to hold them.

Barrett carried on, 'You get her ere by this time tomorrow or your snivelling friend dies a nasty death.'

'Horacio, please!' Alec tried to grab his arm; Hero pulled away.

'He's no friend of mine, that boat has well and truly sailed.'

'No, Horacio, I beg you. Get the girl, please,' Alec entreated.

Hero turned on him. 'She's worth a thousand of you, Alec. I meant what I said. I don't particularly care one way or another what happens to you.' He looked Barrett in the eye with conviction. 'I don't care what you do to him or me; I won't go.'

'Wait, wait.' Alec sat up straighter, making his chains rattle. 'Andrew! Andrew Keene will know where she is. He is infatuated with the girl.'

'Alec!' Hero hissed, his voice was filled with shock and incredulity. It was this reaction that made Barrett realise that the young brat was telling the truth.

Jack nodded and got up from the barrel. 'Right, Reg, Tommy, go an pay a visit to Keene.' He looked at Alec, what's the address?'

'Don't you dare, Alec.' Hero's voice was heavy with a threat, but Alec ignored him.

'57 Stratford Road.' He gave up the address without hesitation.

'If they don't kill you, Alec, I swear I will,' Horacio threatened through thin lips.

'When you find this Andrew Keene,' Jack said to Tommy and Reg, 'bring im ere so that he can see the hostages. Maybe e will be sensible enough to understand the threat and do the right thing.'

Reg nodded as he put the two dogs into separate cages, pushing the doors closed. Then he and Tommy set off.

'While we wait, I could do with a shot of that good brandy you keep,' Beeching said, wrapping his long coat about himself, it was bloody chilly in these cellars.

Barrett agreed, 'good idea, you wait ere. I'll get Rita to bring us a bottle in.'

'Much obliged, Barrett.'

*

Evie shivered, there was no fire and no coal so that she couldn't light another. However, she knew the shivering, and the chill was more about the shock and fear than the temperature.

Luckily, she had a lamp and matches, so she wasn't in total darkness. But what was she going to do now?

After checking every corner of the room for a way to escape, she had found nothing. Her body riddled with nervous energy; she paced the floor in agitation.

Evie had also considered calling for help from the window or climbing down using a sheet or something like a rope, but it was a long drop. Besides, someone was bound to see her and think it strange. They would probably raise the alarm, which would bring Jack running.

She could still hear a lot of noise from the street outside, and the inn below. She guessed that workers would be dropping by for a pint or two on the way home.

Sitting down on the edge of the bed, Evie, putting her head in her hands, felt the tears of frustration moisten her eyes, but then refused to submit to tears.

The door was locked, the door was locked! She peeked out from under her hands, studying the door. This was an old building, possibly dating back to Tudor or Elizabethan times. Noticing that the door did not sit well in the frame, it had warped over time. Evie felt her heart quicken with hope as she got up, then getting down on her hands and knees, she peered through the keyhole. Straight away, she could see that the key had not been left in the lock.

Standing up once more, she pushed against the door. The latch rattled loosely; if she could wedge something between the door and frame, she could prize it open.

Looking about her desperately, she spotted the fireirons which stood next to a dented coalscuttle. The set consisted of a poker, small shovel, and a brush.

Heartbeat speeding up even more; fuelled by adrenaline, Evie grabbed the poker, ran back to the door, then started to work the metal spike between the frame and the door, the wood of the doorframe splintered. Oh Lord, this could work! Evie doubled her efforts, working feverishly around the latch.

As Jack climbed the stairs from the cellar, he could hear the chatter coming from the barroom. It sounded busy. Sure enough, when he opened the door, he could see that Rita and the other girl who helped her were rushed off their feet.

He decided to grab the bottle of brandy and a couple of glasses from his office upstairs. He fancied a drink, but he didn't particularly want to drink with that insufferable toff, Beeching. However, he recognised that the man could be useful to him, very useful indeed.

Alexander Silverman was taking a back seat where his business was concerned. Jolly knew he would never be able to work closely with Alec. He would end up strangling the boy, he knew it. No, it was time to move on. All these thoughts rattled around in his head as he started up the stairs.

When the doorframe cracked around the brass locking plate, the door opened.

Evie stood there for a moment surprised that her efforts had worked. Pulling the door open further, she stepped out onto the dusty landing. The lamplight from the bedroom spilt out enough from the room to enable her to see what she was doing.

At the top of the stairs, she hesitated. As she did so, a shadowed form appeared, backlit from a lamp in the hallway below.

Stepping back in fright, Evie recognised the shape and the build of the man, it was Jack.

Her heart drummed in her ears. She felt panicked but didn't want to retreat. Jack would see the damage to the door anyway; god only knew what he would do to her then. No, she had to stand her ground or go on the defensive. Realising that she still held the weighty piece of iron in her hand, she didn't stop to allow herself to examine the rash action she was about to take.

As Jack appeared around the corner of the stairwell, Evie lunged down the stairs. She was aware enough to realise that using the poker as a weapon and hitting him would do little damage, he would grab it and her, and that would be that. Instead, Evie held the implement as if it were a lance being used by a knight in a joust. Using her impetus, she barrelled into the man as he appeared around the bend.

Jack, taken by surprise, staggered backwards, hitting his head on the wall behind him. A great bellow of air escaped him. He eyed Evie in astonishment as he slid down the wall.

Evie had used all her weight and force behind the attack, which had been enough to drive the implement into Jolly's torso.

Standing there like a statue, Evie looked down at the prone figure which was sprawled across the stairs.

Was he alive or had she killed him? As blood blossomed around the wound made by the impaling brass poker. Evie began to shake. No! No - she would not give in to tears or fright, not yet.

Using her foot as leverage, she pulled the poker out of his body. It made an awful sucking sound which made Evie want to heave. Fresh blood fountained from the wound. However, the wound was not visible; the man's shirt obscured it, so she could not make out the damage she had done.

In a rush, Evie checked Jack's pockets for a key to the shackles, nothing. Swallowing down her panic, Evie had to step over the prone figure to get to the bottom of the stairs.

When Evie rushed along the corridor, she prayed that Rita would not appear for she would certainly ask questions and raise the alarm – this was Jack's kingdom, no one would let her escape.

Heaving a sigh of relief, she opened the door to the cellar and made her way down into the place that was as icy cold as a crypt.

When she reached the bottom of the flight of steps, Evie staggered. She was annoyed with herself because her legs felt as fragile as that of a new-born deer.

Oh Lord, had she killed Jack – murdered him?! She could hang for this, regardless of all the atrocities that Jolly Jack Barrett had metered out over the years, including having a hand in her mother's death and killing Sophia's grandmother, Evie could still swing for his murder.

The thought of the men in the cellar spurred her on. They would still be in peril from Jolly's men. She needed to free them, help them to escape.

*

Andrew arrived at the Silverman's London home, only to be told by the butler that Alec and Hero had left with one of Barrett's men.

'I am concerned that he has not arrived home, Mr Keene,' the butler, Fuller, voiced his worries as the two men stood together in the grand entrance hall. 'However, knowing master Alec as I do, he may well have gone to the club or a card game.'

'Yes,' Andrew concurred, 'but that doesn't explain why Mr Woodley hasn't returned to his lodgings. I was expecting him back before now.'

'Well, as I say, they both went with Barrett's lackey.'

'Would you mind if I have a word with Collins, Mr Fuller?'

'Of course not, Mr Keene.'

Together they walked through the house, into the kitchens, then out through the back door.

It was dark now, but two oil lamps lit the stable yard. Collin's must have heard them coming as he stepped out of the tack room, wiping his hands on a cloth.

'Mr Keene is concerned about the fact that Master Alec and Mr Woodley have not returned from their, umm, meeting with Barrett,' the butler explained.

'Aye, they have been gone for a while,' Collins agreed.

'I am worried what Horacio might do,' Andrew voiced his concerns. 'There is some nasty business going on which has placed a young woman, possibly others, in danger.'

'This wouldn't have anything to do with the night I gave Mr Woodley and two ladies a lift back to your place, would it?' Collins spoke up.

Andrew nodded, 'yes, I'm afraid it does, but I'm afraid I cannot tell you more.'

'Very well,' Fuller nodded in understanding, 'but what can we do to help?'

'Well,' Andrew pondered, 'if you would accompany me, Collins, to the Crown and Garter. Hopefully, we will find them there.'

Collins scratched his forehead thoughtfully. 'Yes, well, a good place to start. What do you think, Mr Fuller?'

The butler gave them a thin smile. 'Well, I have to say that I would hate to be left in the position of having to explain to Mr Silverman senior that his son has gone missing, and we did nothing about it.'

'Good point,' Collins agreed. 'Give me a few moments to get the carriage out and harness up the horses.'

'Yes,' Andrew let out a breath, relieved that he had some help.

'Is it a good idea to take the carriage and horses into those loathsome streets?' Fuller expressed his concerns. 'Perhaps it would be better to hail a Hansom.'

'He's right,' Andrew spoke up, 'if we walk to the end of the road, we should be able to hail one from there.'

'Aye,' Collins agreed. 'Give me a second then, and I'll get my coat.'

Chapter 57

Feeling incredibly grateful that some lamps had been lit, Evie made her way through the cellar to the room where the two men had been taken.

When she got closer, she heard a voice. She recognised it immediately as the posh man she had heard Jack talking to. Halting, Evie stopped to listen.

'Oh, I am going to be thoroughly delighted to see the two of you get your just desserts for your meddling into my private affairs. You, Woodley, because of your audacity to think that you could have an affair with my wife and get away with it. And you, Silverman, for being so foolish to think you could get away with blackmailing me. Barrett will find the girl and bring her here. She can sit with me and watch as the dogs rip you both apart.'

Evie gasped in horror. She couldn't believe what she was hearing. Then she heard a noise that sounded like a stick being run along iron bars, whatever it was, it made the dogs growl and snarl.

Evie felt her stomach churn in fear.

Something caught her eye; there were a ring of keys hanging on a hook beside the old wooden door. Not giving herself time to think, she snatched the keyring, making the keys jangle together, then she rushed through the door wielding the poker like the sword of a Valkyrie.

Taking in the scene before her, she saw an older man standing by the dog cages. He was smartly dressed, obviously wealthy. Her entrance sent the dogs into a further frenzy of snarling and barking. The man looked at her in surprise.

'What the hell...' Beeching's voice was cut off as the dog closest to him clawed at the door of its cage. Reg had not secured the door properly. The dog managed to push it open, it escaped into the cellar.

Possibly because of George's taunting, the animal turned on him. The man cried out in horror when the dog clamped its massive jaws around his arm. The viciousness of the attack sent him sprawling. His gold-topped cane flew out of his hand.

'Ahhh! Help, help me. For the love of God!' The man and dog wrestled on the floor. The scene was sickening with the sound of ripping flesh and the spurting of a fountain of blood over the floor.

Evie drew in a breath; there was nothing she could do to help the man, so she kept her focus on the two men at the other end of the room.

With the keys in one hand and the bloodied poker in the other, she raced to the far end of the room. She put the poker down, then with shaking hands, she fumbled with the keys.

The noise that the uncaged dog was making riled the other animal. It was pawing at the cage door, biting the bars with its long, powerful teeth.

Spittle flew from the animal's huge jaws as it tried to escape its confines. Beeching was still screaming shrilly; he tried desperately to fight off the attacking dog.

*

When Jack came too, he found himself sprawled on the stairs. Then his memory returned; Evie had attacked him, stabbed him with a poker. Bloody bitch.

Groaning with pain, he clamped a hand over the puncture wound in his stomach.

The effort of trying to sit up sent waves of blackness lapping at his vision. Stars of pain exploded, but he had been through worse than this. Getting up, he held onto the wall, leaving a bloody trail along the faded wallpaper. Getting to the bottom of the staircase, he staggered along the corridor leading to the cellar, where the door stood open.

*

'Thank you for helping us, Evie.' Horacio placed his hand over that of the trembling young woman.

When she nodded in response, he could see that her eyes were wild with fear and shock, he also noticed the blood smeared across her face.

'Are you hurt?' he asked in concern.

'Tis nothing.' She gave him a thin smile. 'Just let me concentrate on finding the key.' She was annoyed with herself that her hands were trembling so badly.

'Here.' Hero took pity on her and plucked the keys from her fingers. He undid Alec's manacle.

Evie picked up the poker and faced the scene in the middle of the room. The older man had stopped screaming now. She hoped that he had fainted, and the dog had not taken out his throat. It was at that moment that she spotted Jolly darkening the doorway. As if he were drunk, he staggered into the room.

Dogs remember people. They remember the ones who are kind and those that are cruel. The huge dog lifted its head; he recognised Jack as someone who had taunted him, that had caused him pain. Then he scented the blood from Jack's wound, the animal launched itself at the rent collector, sending him flying.

'Oh god, oh god...' Alec Silverman was weeping like a child as Hero dragged him forward, helping the girl get past the awful scene. When he reached the door, he pushed them both through, then turned back to help the other men.

'No, you can't go back in there.' Evie placed a hand on his arm.

'I have to,' Hero insisted. 'Where's the poker you were carrying?'

'I dropped it on the floor where you were chained up.'

Hero nodded, then pushed the door open. The scene that met his eyes was one of the most awful tableaus he had ever seen; Jack lay sprawled on the floor his stomach a mass of viscera. The dog, it's muzzle slick with blood, turned to look at Hero.

He could hear the animal panting, lungs working like a pair of bellows.

'Shush now.' Hero held out his hands to the animal as he sidestepped his way to Beeching's body. He heard the man groan; George was still alive.

677

Hero's heart was hammering in his chest as he expected the animal to launch itself at him at any moment.

'Shush now,' Hero said again.

Carefully, he leant down and put his hands under George Beeching's armpits. He started to pull the man towards the door.

'Good lad, good lad.' Hero found himself muttering softly to the dog, as he dragged the cumbersome weight of George Beeching along the floor. They left a bloody trail in their wake.

The dog stood there, head hanging watching Hero from the other side of the room. The other caged dog had also fallen silent.

Hero wasn't sure if it was his calming entreaties, or because the dog was sated after he attacked Barrett, but the animal did not attack again.

When he managed to pull George through the doorway to where the others were waiting, Hero was highly relieved.

Turning to Evie, whose face was as white as chalk.

Hero shook his head. 'Beeching is alive, but there's nothing I can do for Barrett.'

She nodded. Her eyes were glazed from the shock of it all.

'Shut the door, shut the door!' Alec pleaded with Horacio, 'that bloody dog can still get to us.'

'Alright, alright.' Hero pulled the door closed. The dogs were quiet now.

Evie suddenly gasped, then rushed behind a barrel and vomited.

'Are you alright?'

Hero went to follow her, but she waved him away, shaking her head.

'I shall be fine.'

*

Andrew and Collins, who had told him his name was Joe, arrived at the busy tavern. No one showed much interest in them as Andrew grabbed the arm of one of the barmaids.

'Oy!' She tried to pull away.

'Where's Barrett?' Andrew asked her.

'Whatcha want with im?' She glared at him.

'We've come to repay a large debt,' Joe Collins spoke up.

Rita's eyes darted to him, then back to Andrew.

Squeezing her arm, not enough to hurt her; however, Andrew asked again, 'where is he?'

This time her eyes darted to the back of the bar. Andrew let her go, he and Joe pushed their way through the crowd.

'Oy, just a minute.' Rita tried to follow them, but one of the customers caught her arm and ordered another pint.

Andrew and Joe went through the door behind the counter. Both of them noticed the smears of blood on the wallpaper and the drips on the floor. They glanced at each other in concern. Andrew noticed a door at the end of the hallway was open. The two men headed that way. Cautiously, they went down the steps.

No one challenged them as they reached the bottom of the stairs.

'Where are Barrett's men?' Collins spoke up.

Before Andrew could answer, they heard voices echoing about the chamber. Turning a corner, they came across a small group. Andrew recognised Horacio and Alec straightaway. There was also a dark-haired woman with them. She was wiping her mouth with a white handkerchief. She had a bruised face. There was a prone body at her feet; Hero was kneeling beside it.

'Andrew, Collins, thank God.' Hero spotted them and got to his feet. 'It's George Beeching; he has been badly mauled.' Shooting a glance at Evie, he explained quickly, 'Andrew is a trainee doctor.'

She nodded in understanding.

'Mauled?' Andrew rushed over.

'A dog attack,' Evie added. She picked up an oil lamp that had been left close by, raising it so that Andrew could see what he was doing.

One arm of George's coat was in tatters.

'Oh Lord, the bite has gone through to the bone.' Andrew got to his feet as George moaned again. 'We need to get him to the hospital.'

'Yes, of course.' Hero agreed. 'Have you transport?'

'We took a Hansom,' Joe Collins explained.

'I noticed a trolley for moving barrels by the backdoor,' Hero told them, 'we can use that for now.'

'Before we go any further, what the hell's been going on, Horacio? How did Beeching get in this state?' Andrew asked.

'He was attacked by one of Barrett's fighting dogs,' Hero told him.

'Dogs?'

'He was going to feed me to those brutish hounds,' Alec spoke up for the first time.

Both Andrew and Joe glanced at Hero with horror as he filled them in.

'Barrett was going to hold him hostage while I went to pick up Sophia. If I didn't return in twenty-four hours, that would have been it.'

'Good God!' Joe exclaimed.

'Where is Barrett?' Andrew asked, looking around as if the man would pop up at any moment.

'In there.' Hero pointed to the door. 'He's dead.'

'Dead! Horacio, you didn't?'

'He was attacked by one of his dogs.' Evie spoke up once more. Her voice was strangely flat. 'It ripped out his stomach. I – I stabbed him.'

Suddenly, her legs felt as if they could not hold her anymore; she stumbled. Hero caught her before she hit the floor.

'This is Evie Winters,' Hero explained keeping an arm around her. 'well, Barrett, actually. Jack's widow.'

Jack's widow: the words echoed through Evie's shocked mind - Jolly Jack Barrett was dead!

*

When Mrs Gordon responded to a knock at the door, she was concerned to discover two men she did not recognise standing on the top step.

One was tall and lanky, with a mop of ginger hair. The other lad was younger and shorter.

She could tell he was no more than a youth growing into a muscular body.

'Where's Andrew Keene?' the tall one asked.

'He's out at the moment, do you want to leave a message?' When she noticed the two men exchange, what she could only describe as "shifty" looks, she realised she had said the wrong thing.

'Na, think we'll wait till e gets back.' Reg went to push past the old biddy.

Before he could place one of his booted feet over the threshold, both of them were extremely surprised when the old woman plucked a sizeable black umbrella from a wooden stand. She lunged at the two, wielding it as if it were a sword. Both Reg and Tommy stepped back in shock.

'I have a feeling you two are up to no good. You are not welcome here.' She cried, pushing them forward, away from the door.

'Mrs Gordon, is everything alright?' Constable Morris called from the pavement. He was on evening duty and was patrolling the area.

Tommy and Reg spotted the copper. 'We don't want any trouble,' Reg said. They both bounded down the steps and were gone.

'Are you alright, dear lady?' the policemen asked as he ascended the front steps.

'Yes, yes. Thank you, Constable. Although I could do with a nice hot cup of tea, will you join me?'

'Aww, that sounds good, can't stay too long though,' he said as she shut the front door.

*

Through the pipe smoke and people, Rita kept glancing at the door behind the counter through which the men had disappeared. She had an uneasy feeling in the pit of her stomach. What the hell was going on?

'Sally,' she called the woman who was helping her out, 'I'm just going to nip down to the cellar.'

'Alright,' the woman replied as she set down two pints on a wooden table, then wiped her sweat-damp hair off her face.

Stepping out into the corridor, Rita noticed the blood smears on the wall. Her stomach did a strange flip of unease. Then she spotted that the cellar door was open.

'Jack, Jack, you there, Jack?' Rita hesitated at the top of the steps, then went down into the frigid place.

Andrew, Joe, and Hero were just lifting George onto the wooded trolley when they heard the woman call out.

'I'll see to this.' Evie stepped forward before the others could move.

'Rita.' Evie met the woman as she walked around a pile of crates. 'Something awful has happened, one of the dogs has attacked Jack, he's dead, Rita. Dead.'

'Oh, Lord.' The woman placed a hand over her gaping mouth. 'Dead?'

Evie nodded then took the other woman's arm, she steered her back to the bottom of the stairs then paused.

'Listen to me, Rita, as Jack's wife, you do as I say.' She squeezed her arm to drive home the point, Rita nodded, a horrified look still lingered on her face. 'I shall deal with all this. I need you to carry on working, but don't say a word about what has happened just yet, alright?'

'Mmm,' Rita nodded.

'I'm counting on your loyalty to Jack and myself as Mrs Barrett.'

'Yes, alright.'

'Then go.' Evie indicated the stairs. 'And if I hear that you have spread any gossip, I shall feed you to one of the dogs myself.'

'Alright, alright.' Rita's face blanched as she fled back up the stairs.

Evie swallowed hard. She hated threatening anybody; it felt so alien to her. However, there was a sorry mess to sort out; they all needed time to deal with the situation.

'I can't leave you here on your own,' Horacio said as Andrew and Joe wheeled out the trolley. The wheels squeaked on the uneven floor.

'I can't leave.' Evie shook her head stubbornly.

'Very well, then. I shall stay with you.' Hero pushed.

'Seems you two are as obstinate as each other,' Andrew remarked, looking back the way they had come.

'Mmm, it seems so.' Hero found a smile play at the corner of his mouth, although he had no idea why this situation should seem frivolous in any way.

'Really, you don't have to.' Evie protested again.

'Oh, I do; besides, you may need my help dealing with Barrett's lads and the dogs.'

'I can take care of it all myself.' Evie squared her shoulders.

'Oh, I'm sure of that, but I'm staying anyway.' He thought he saw a shadow of a smile touch her eyes before she dropped her gaze.

Once Andrew and Joe had left, Evie and Hero waited for Jack's lads to return.

They knew that they would return empty-handed of course, as ironically, the person they had been seeking had been here for much of the time.

It was agreed that Andrew would take George to the hospital, then Joe would take Alec back to his father's house in Kent, not the one in London. Alec had been a blubbering wreck since the dog attack, and they didn't want to leave him on his own.

Hero had made up his mind that he would tell Alexander Silverman precisely what his son had been up to, then he would walk away and leave the man's father to deal with him. Hero wanted nothing more to do with his so-called friend.

Despite Evie's protests, Hero had re-entered the room where Jack's body was. He had managed to coax the dog back into its cage by using a few pieces of meat pie from the pantry upstairs.

Evie heard the voices before she spotted Reg and Tommy. The two appeared around the corner then stopped dead when they saw Evie standing there, her hands clenched at her sides.

'Mrs Barrett,' as he greeted her, Reg spotted Horacio Woodley standing off to one side. Puzzlement was written all over his face, his eyes darted around the place, probably seeking Jack.

'You.' Evie pointed a finger at Reg, 'didn't secure the door of the dog's cage. The animal attacked Jack; he's dead because of you.'

'What!' Tommy spoke up, his face draining of colour, as did Reg's own.

'You heard me.' Evie nodded towards the door. 'His body is in there on the floor, both of you get in there and sort it out. Take him to the undertaker. I will arrange the funeral. From now on, you take your orders from me.'

'From you?' Reg looked sceptical.

Evie took a step towards him, 'Yes, from me. Or would you rather be out on your ear when I tell everyone Jack's death is your fault.'

'No-no, Mrs Barrett.'

'Good,' Evie nodded her head decisively. Waving a hand in the air expansively, she continued, 'All this business with Beeching and the girl is over, do you hear me?'

'Yes,' the two answered in unison.

'Good,' she nodded again. 'I am going up to the office. Let me know when you have finished.'

'Yes, ma'am.'

Head held high; Evie walked away.

Hero followed her up the cellar steps, then up another flight of stairs to the floor above.

When Evie stepped onto the landing, her quivering legs nearly gave way. Hero reached out and caught her. He guided her into one of the rooms which held a desk and chairs.

'Here, sit.' Noticing the bottles on a sideboard, he poured them both a generous tot of brandy. Taking the seat opposite her, he raised his glass.

'Bravo, Mrs Barrett, you handled them well.' He studied her carefully as she took a sip of her drink. He cocked his head quizzically, 'If I am not mistaken, however, Jack was in a bit of a state before he walked into that room, did you really stab him with the poker?' When Evie nodded,

Horacio raised his eyebrows quizzically. 'I presume this has something to do with the reason that you didn't leave to seek out Andrew?'

'Yes,' she put a hand to her bruised face. 'I bumped into Jack on the way; he locked me in the bedroom next door.'

'He did that to you?' Hero indicated the bruises.

'Yes.'

'How did you get out?'

She met his eye. 'Let's just say that the poker came in very handy indeed.'

Chapter 58

Once George Beeching had been transported to the hospital, Joe and Andrew parted ways. Andrew to stay with his patient and Joe to take a message to Mrs Gordon to let her know that they were all safe. Then he would take Alec home.

Andrew had given Alec a dose of laudanum to calm him down. He slept like a baby in the back of the carriage.

Stuart Boyd assisted Andrew in his examination of George's arm.

'God, that's a terrible mess,' Stuart exclaimed. 'The bite has gone right down to the bone. The bloody animal could have ripped his arm off.'

'Yes,' Andrew agreed as George moaned in pain. 'As it is, we may have to amputate.'

'Ah, there is no doubt, Andrew, we will. The sooner, the better. See how inflamed the edges of the wound are, infection is setting in.'

'We had better get on with it then.' Andrew stepped away from the bed where George lay, his face blanched, sweat trickling down his brow. His deadened eyes followed Andrew's movement.

*

The two sat together in silence for a few moments, although the room was full of the raucous chatter and laughter from the bar below, there was a feeling of being in a secluded bubble.

Hero had found some coal and had managed to light a fire in the small grate. Then he had pulled the chairs closer for some warmth. He had also found a blanket which he had wrapped around Evie's shoulders.

Horacio finished his drink then got up.

'Do you want me to top up your glass?' he asked.

Evie knocked back the dregs, then handed her glass to him. Her hand was shaking as she did so. 'Yes, please.'

Once Hero had completed the task, he sat back down. 'Where is your sister? Dottie, isn't it?' he asked.

'She's dead.'

He sat forward in his chair, reaching out a hand to her. 'Oh, God, I'm sorry. What happened? No-no, you don't have to tell me.'

'She died in a fire,' Evie said softly gazing into the flickering flames in the grate, which was slowly coming to life. She gave a bitter laugh, then looked Hero in the eye. 'We had a visitor, Margie, a friend of Molly's.'

'Margie? Yes, I know of her. Andrew came across her in a clinic he runs with a colleague in the East End. He asked her to find out where you and your sister were so he could let Sophia know. Unfortunately, she repaid Andrew's kindest by robbing from them.'

'Ahh, that must have been where she got the money for the drink.' Evie nodded. 'Well, she tracked us down, alright. The woman was in a terrible state. It was obvious to me that she had been drinking heavily. She said something about Jack killing Molly.'

'Yes, Molly is dead. She hung herself,' Hero told her.

'Mmm, that is sad to know. Well, it doesn't really matter how she died; it all leads back to Jack Barrett.'

'Yes,' Hero agreed as he took a sip of his drink.

Evie continued to gaze into the flames of the fire as the memories flooded back.

'Margie had broken into the house - Jack bought me a house, you know.' She gave a strange brittle laugh. 'He was hoping we could live as a happy family,' a tear ran down her cheek, she did nothing to wipe it away. Hero could see how hard it was for Evie to talk about these things, so he remained quiet as she spoke. 'She tried to attack me. I was holding a lamp. Her clothes must have been covered in liquor; they caught fire.'

'Oh no,' Hero uttered softly.

'I – I couldn't get to the stairs. The front door was locked. I had to get out the way Margie had gotten in.' She gave the man a haunted look. 'I saw Dottie on the upstairs landing. I called to her to find the others and get them into her room.'

'There were other people involved?'

'Yes.' This time Evie wiped the back of her hand over her cheeks. 'Tommy Dicken's sister, Ivy, and Mrs Perkins, the housekeeper. Tommy helped out. Well, he watched us for Jack, in case we decided to run away. It was his night off, so only he and I survived.'

'I am so sorry, Evie.'

'Thank you.' She sighed. 'Dottie and I had been arguing. She and Tommy had formed a bond. I couldn't take the risk of it going any further, so warned Tommy off. Dottie hated me for that.'

'You were protecting your sister.'

'Yes.'

'And the fire, I presume that is why you are living here?'

'Yes.' Shifting in her chair, Evie asked, 'what has happened to Sophia? It was something terrible, wasn't it?'

Hero gazed at the ceiling; how much should he say? 'She has been through a lot like you, but she is safe and well. She never forgot about you and Dottie.'

Evie nodded as fresh tears spilt over and trickled down her cheeks.

The evening wore on; when there was a knock at the door, they both jumped.

'Come in.' Evie called.

Rita arrived holding a tin box with a lock on it. 'The takings for tonight,' she explained. 'Jack always liked to ave em brought up.'

They had been so absorbed in their conversation and thoughts, that neither Hero nor Evie had realised that the place was quiet now, all the customers had headed home.

'Thank you, Rita. Put it on the desk.'

'Umm.' The woman hovered, a worried expression on her face.

'What is it, Rita?'

'Reg and Tommy ave taken Jacks body away and secured the dogs.'

'Good.'

Rita nodded, then said, 'what about this place, an all the other things going on. You going to carry on with everything, Mrs Barrett?'

'The inn will be open as usual, all the other things, well, I shall have to look into matters more thoroughly.'

'Alright.' Rita gave her a hesitant smile then left.

'Are you going to try and keep Jacks, mmm, empire running?'

'I have no idea what I shall do after all this.'

'You are in a dangerous situation, Evie,' Horacio warned her.

'Nothing has changed then.' Her smile was bleak.

They talked late into the night. Hero, at her insistence, told her all about his home and family. What had happened to his father and sister; they recognised in each other the awful guilt they both carried. Although Hero had explained that he felt different somehow, after his recent visit home, something had changed, which helped him to allow things to heal where Angelica was concerned.

'I realised I have been punishing myself for years,' he confessed. 'Angel had such a big heart; I know she would have been angry with me for wallowing in self-pity and guilt.'

'The way you have described her, she sounds like she would have been a remarkable person.'

'Oh, she was.' He smiled. 'She had such a strength of will. She certainly wasn't going to be put off climbing that tree.'

'It wasn't your fault, you know,' Evie said softly, 'what happened to her and your father.'

'As it is with you and Dottie,' he reminded her.

Evie shook her head, 'I should never have married Jack; I should have run away with Dot.'

'Ahh, but you said she was ill, fragile, she would never have survived on the streets.'

'I know.' Evie found herself yawning.

'You need some rest,' Hero observed.

'I'm alright. Tell me more about your mother's school.'

So, Hero chatted on, then when he noticed Evie's head had dropped to her chest. He got up and gently carried her into the bedroom, where he set her down on the bed. Horacio removed her boots, then pulled the blankets over her. He took a seat in the chair. It wasn't long before he found himself asleep too.

*

Andrew assisted Stuart Boyd as the man amputated George's right arm.

All through the proceedings, Andrew had had to set aside his hatred for this despicable man. He wanted nothing more than to walk away and let Beeching die from the infection, but when he had decided to study medicine, he was highly aware of the Hippocratic oath. He was a man of principals: he could never set them aside now. However, both Andrew and Stuart knew there was still a high chance that George would succumb to his wounds and die anyway – it was up to fate now.

Stepping away from the operating table, Stuart wiped his hands. 'That's the best I can do.'

'Yes,' Andrew agreed as two orderlies placed the body on a stretcher to carry him into the ward where a nurse would sit with him.

'Have you sent a message to his family?' Stuart asked as the two men headed towards his office.

'No, but I will see to it. I believe Beeching's wife is away at present, but I will send word to his parents.'

'Good. Good.'

They sat in Stuart's office for a while, then Andrew made his excuses and left the hospital. He was exhausted after all the drama of the day.

*

Two days later, Evie stood at Jack's graveside. Horacio stood with her, but everybody else kept a polite distance.

Both she and Hero were surprised at the turnout. There must have been over a hundred people crowded into the small cemetery. She wondered how many of them were there to mourn Jack or to celebrate his death.

Evie was very aware of the eyes upon her, assessing her. She stood tall in a dress of black silk trimmed in fine lace. She wore a hat atop her pulled up hair. It had a half-veil, so her eyes were obscured. The bruises on her face were changing from grey to purple and olive now.

Curious glances were also cast at the man standing beside her; Mr Woodley had hardly left her side. Most of the people knew him, especially the men who had attended his fights. He demanded quiet respect. Rumour had it that Mrs Barrett had asked Mr Woodley to be her personal protector. Jolly Jack Barrett's death had sent huge ripples through the East End. The vultures were gathering, awaiting an opportunity to swoop in and strip the bones of Jack's "empire".

Reg, Tommy, and Arthur stood a short distance away from the widow. They were all very uneasy, wondering what was going to happen next.

Reg felt responsible for his own boss's death. He should have made sure the dog cage was secure. None of them had mentioned Lord Beeching's part in all this, so mystery shadowed that night.

Gossip was rife of course, but the rumour was, Jack had been mauled by one of his own dogs, and his wife and Mr Woodley had tried to save him. They admired them both for that.

When the funeral was over, everyone went back to the Crown and Garter, where Evie had asked Rita and Sally to put on a "spread".

Evie and Hero kept a distance from the proceedings.

That morning, Evie had received a letter from a Mr Hill, asking to see her urgently regarding Jack's possessions.

'Would you come with me?' Evie found herself asking Horacio, who readily agreed.

Hero wasn't sure why he felt a connection to this woman. Perhaps it was because of their shared losses, or possibly her inner strength of will that radiated from her. He could also recognise the heartbreak that she was trying valiantly not to succumb to. By his personal experiences, he knew it wasn't easy; The way she was handling everything made him admire her more day by day.

Hero had been back to the lodgings so he could pick up some changes of clothes. He had seen Andrew, who told him that it was not looking promising for George Beeching. Although they had amputated his severely damaged arm, Stuart was concerned that gangrene was setting in and George was still clutched in a terrible fever.

'Stuart wondered about a further amputation,' Andrew explained, 'taking it up to the shoulder blade, but neither of us is confident he would survive a second operation.'

'Does his family know?' Horacio asked as he packed some items into a valise.

'Yes, we have sent word. Apparently, Lady Beeching cannot leave her husband's bedside. He has had another seizure, and things don't look promising ...'

'Mmm.' Hero paused in his packing. 'If they both end up dying, the estate will be put in trust for William. And I can let Vanessa know it will be safe for her and the boy to return to England.'

Andrew raised his eyebrows quizzically. 'She will be a widow then, free to marry again after an adequate time of mourning has elapsed.'

'Yes, she will.' Hero gave his friend a wry smile. 'I have no intention of marrying Vanessa. She and I – well, let's just say we needed each other at the time.'

Andrew nodded. 'Yes, I think I understand what you mean.'

'Have you heard from Sophia?' Hero asked as he snapped the valise closed.

'Yes, she is eager to know what is happening. I want to tell her everything that has transpired in person rather than in a letter, but I can't leave Beeching as he is.'

'Andrew, leave Stuart and the nurses to see to that monster. Go and be with Sophia, she needs you.'

'As Evie Barrett needs you?'

'Ha, Mrs Barrett is proving to be a remarkable woman. She is not unlike Vanessa in that respect. Both married to evil men, but each of them has kept their dignity and strength.'

'You admire her?'

'I do indeed.'

*

Taking a hansom cab to the address Mr Hill had given them, Evie and Horacio alighted, then found the rather dilapidated building where the man had his office.

When they walked in, the young man behind the desk stood up to greet them.

'Mrs Barrett?'

'Yes,' Evie nodded. 'We are here to see Mr Hill.'

'Ah, yes.'

When the man peered behind him nervously, Evie and Hero exchanged puzzled glances.

Placing his hands on the desk, he leaned forward. When he turned to Evie, his soft brown eyes shone with a feverish hue behind his wire-rimmed glasses. He had a round, cleanshaven, boyish face. He was the same height as Horacio, but his body was slight, wiry. The jacket he wore over a cotton shirt, seemed to hang off his frame.

'My name is Carl Steffen; they call me Mr Stephens.' He introduced himself, keeping his voice low. 'I need to speak to you rather urgently.'

'About what?' Hero asked.

The man gazed behind him once more as if he expected someone to creep up on him.

'I cannot talk here. There is a tearoom just down the road. I will wait for you there. Please meet me after your interview with Mr Hill.'

Intrigued to find out what he had to say, Evie agreed. 'Very well.'

The young man sighed in relief. 'Thank you. Mr Hill's office is at the top of the second flight of stairs.'

'Thank you.' Evie nodded.

When she went to walk past the man, he reached out and placed a hand gently on her arm. 'Please don't mention our meeting to anyone, especially...' his eyes indicated the ceiling. Evie nodded in understanding.

'What was that all about?' Hero wondered as they ascended the narrow staircase.

'Well, we shall find out shortly.'

They found the office and were bid to enter by Mr Hill.

'Ahh, my dear lady.'

The large man got up and took Evie's hand. He kissed the back of it. Evie tried not to shudder; there was something distasteful about him. She was glad she was wearing her leather gloves, so she did not have to feel his fleshy lips against her skin.

He nodded to Hero, 'Mr Woodley, I am surprised to see you here.' The man indicated two chairs facing the desk. 'Do sit.'

'Mrs Barrett asked me to accompany her,' Hero explained.

'Ahh, very well. Although we have things to discuss which, and I mean no disrespect when I say this, should be kept between ourselves, Mrs Barrett.'

'I trust Mr Woodley.' Evie lifted her chin in defiance. 'He will stay.'

The man shifted in his seat. 'Mmm, very well then.' Mr Hill shuffled some papers. 'Now, after Mr Barrett married you, my dear, he made a new will.'

'A will?' She looked so surprised. Mr Hill gave a little chuckle.

'He wanted to ensure that you, mmm and your sister, God rest her. I am sorry about both your losses by the way.'

'Thank you.' Evie bowed her head in acknowledgement.

'That you and your sister would be cared for in his absence,' he continued.

'Cared for ...' Evie felt the incredulity of what the man was saying settle over her. She had never expected Jack to be the sort of man to leave a will, let alone to ensure that she and Dottie would be *cared for*.

'Yes,' Mr Hill smiled. 'He also mentioned Mrs Perkins, Ivy and Tommy Dicken: he left them small gratuities. However, Tommy will now be the sole beneficiary of that money.'

'Alright,' Evie nodded.

Mr Hill shuffled through the paperwork, finding what he was looking for, he picked up four sheets of paper and handed them to her.

'What are these?' She found her hands were trembling as she took them from his sweaty paw.

'May I?' Horacio held out his hand to her. With relief, she passed the papers to him.

He took a moment to glance at each one. 'Why these are deeds,' he declared.

'Yes,' Mr Hill confirmed.

Hero met Evie's curious gaze. 'These are deeds for a house in Bow. The Crown and Garter pub including two adjacent properties, and a warehouse down by the docks.'

'Mr Barrett was a wise businessman,' Mr Hill said, 'He accrued the properties over the last few years. He saw the potential of the cost of land around the dockyard area. The warehouse is worth nothing as it is; in fact, it is crumbling into ruin. However, the land upon which it stands is very valuable.'

Evie shook her head once more, then she jumped to her feet and ripped the papers out of Hero's hand, she threw them on the desk.

'I want none of this, do you hear me? None.'

'Mrs Barrett, please.' Mr Hill got to his feet.

'Evie.' Hero put a hand on her arm. 'Think about this for a moment. Barrett has left you comfortably off. You will not have to worry about money for the rest of your life.'

She turned on him. 'Blood money, Horacio, tainted with murder, prostitution and god knows what else.'

She was surprised when he reached out and gripped her upper arms, the look he gave her was intense.

'Yes, we all know where it has come from; but you can put it to better use.'

'Better use, how?' She studied his face earnestly.

'Sell the land, Mr Hill says it is valuable. You could put the money towards an enterprise that will help others.'

'As your mother has done with the school you speak of?'

'Well, yes, exactly.'

'Mmm, well the land has been left to you, Mrs Barrett, to do with what you will.' Mr Hill spoke up. 'If you wish to sell it, then I am sure I can find several parties who would be interested, just say the word.'

'Evie, Mrs Barrett, will take some time to think about it,' Hero said, not letting his eyes drop from the woman before him.

Evie closed her eyes for a long moment. When she felt that she had got her emotions under control, she opened them.

'I will do as Mr Woodley suggests. I will think about it and will let you know, Mr Hill.'

'Very well, young lady.' The man nodded and sat back down. He opened the top drawer of his desk. 'Mr Barrett has left you his gold fob watch.' He passed the item across the desktop.

'I don't want it,' Evie shook his head, 'give it to Tommy Dicken if you will.'

Mr Hill could see the determination written on her face, he nodded. 'Very well.' Pulling something else out of the draw. 'He also left you this.' He pushed a thick manila envelope over to her. 'There is five thousand pounds in there.'

'Five thousand pounds?'

The large man chuckled making his generous chin wobble. 'I urged him to open a bank account and place the money in there, but he refused. However, I hope you will have the sense to do so.'

Evie shook her head. 'This is all too much.'

'Evie.' Hero gave her a concerned look, 'we will place the money in a bank, I can help you. You don't have to decide anything now, but at least it will be safely tucked away.'

'Quite right, Mr Woodley,' Mr Hill approved. 'Now, can I offer you a snifter before you go?' he asked.

Abruptly, Evie got to her feet. 'No, thank you, Mr Hill. We shall be going now. I will let you know my decision regarding the land sale.'

'Yes, yes. Very good.'

Hero picked up the envelope containing the money. 'Thank you,' he uttered then followed his companion who was already halfway down the stairs leading to the lower landing.

Chapter 59

When Evie stepped outside onto the pavement, she stood there for a long moment taking deep breaths, enjoying the gentle spring sun that kissed her cheeks.

'Are you alright?' Hero asked as he came to stand beside her.

She nodded, 'Yes, although I can't quite believe what has just transpired.'

'Well, it seems that we underestimated Jack. Whoever would have thought he could be so forward-thinking in his views.'

'He wanted respectability,' Evie said as a Hansom cab rattled past. 'He thought that marrying me, living in that house in Bow would give him all that.'

'Yes.'

She fingered her bruised cheek. It didn't hurt anymore. 'I did not live up to his expectations.'

'Now,' Hero came to stand in front of her, his gaze was earnest. 'You lived way past his expectations, Evie, so far so, you put yourself beyond his reach.'

'Mmm, some would say I isolated myself.' She searched his gentle hazel eyes. 'They would be right, I closed off my heart.'

'Yes, well, I know all about that.' He was the first one to break their gaze. 'Come, let us go and meet this mysterious Mr Stephens, see what he has to say.' Hero presented her with his arm, which she took.

They walked down the street arm in arm as if it were the most natural thing in the world.

The teashop was fragrant with the earthy scent of tea blends and baked goods.

As they entered, they spotted the young man waiting for them. He was seated at a table tucked away at the back. The place was relatively quiet at that time of the day.

Hero informed the waitress that came over to them, that they were meeting a friend. She showed them to the table. Mr Stephens got up to greet them.

Once they were seated, Hero ordered a fresh pot of tea and some toasted teacakes.

'Th-thank you so much for meeting me,' Stephens said, his eyes darting about the room.

'Why are you so nervous, man?' Horacio asked.

The other mans gazed rested first on Evie then Hero. 'You have a reputation for being a fair and good man, Mr Woodley.' Then he addressed Evie, 'Mrs Barrett, I am taking a risk talking to you, but I see goodness in you. And the fact that you are keeping company with this man gives me hope.'

'Hope about what?' Evie asked as she removed her gloves and placed them on the table.

The young man leaned across the table. 'Did you know that your, mmm, husband helped to bring migrants into the country, many of which were Jewish.'

'Yes, I met Sophia Blum and her Grandmother. Sophia became a friend to myself and my sister.'

'Ah yes, there we are.' He smiled. 'She arrived on one of the ships?'

'Yes,' Evie confirmed, 'she told us all about her journey here.'

'Did she say anything about the other passengers?'

Evie shook her head, 'Not really.'

They were interrupted as the waitress brought a tray with their order. She set it down. Hero dismissed her.

'I arrived in this country six years ago,' Mr Stephens told them. 'Because

I could read and write and speak English. I was taken on to help Mr Hill and Mr Barrett. You see, they needed someone to document the items coming into the country.'

'Items?' Hero asked as he buttered a teacake. 'I thought we were talking about the people.'

'Ahh yes, the people and their valuables. You see, in exchange for handing over anything valuable they brought with them, they were told they would be given accommodation and work would be found for them.'

'Mm, don't tell me, they handed the items over but received little help.'

'Yes, Mr Woodley, precisely that.'

'It was all lies,' Evie commented. 'Look what they did to Sophia and her grandmother.'

'I'm not sure what happened there, Mrs Barrett, but what I can tell you, with certainty, is my people received little of the so-called support. They were left in squalor, to fend for themselves. Many do not speak English. I did what I could to help them. You see, I did not relish working for people like Mr Hill, Barrett, and Silverman, but I did understand that by holding a useful position, I could help people.' Mr Stephens shifted nervously in his seat, then continued, 'You see, Mr Barrett had me write down all the goods that came in. He did not know that I kept a separate ledger logging the items, and the people who had owned them.' He gave them both a thin smile, 'I have a talent; God has blessed me with an excellent memory.' He sat back in his chair. 'So, I put this to good use. I hoped that one day I could help to restore at least some of the items to the people they belong to.'

'Very noble, Mr Stephens.' Hero commented, 'but how do we know you are telling the truth, you might be after the items to keep or sell for yourself?'

'Ah, you are a wise man to be cautious, sir. Wise not to trust anyone, especially now that Jack Barrett is dead. He was a notorious man; however, I will say that he instilled loyalty in those who worked for him. He protected his own and rewarded that loyalty.'

'Huh, a villain with morals.' Hero's voice was steely edged.

'Yes,' Mr Stephens gave them a grim smile. 'There will be a number who wish to step into his shoes or will be floundering now he's gone. There was a hierarchy to this villainy.' His gaze rested on Evie. 'You, as Mrs Barrett, will be expected to take up the reins.'

Evie shook her head in bewilderment. 'I can't.'

Her voice broke on these two words, Horacio reached out a hand and took hers in his.

'You don't have to do anything, Evie, but we could use this opportunity to right some wrongs.'

'Yes, listen to Mr Woodley.' Mr Stephens nodded.

She looked towards the large plate-glass window; the street was busy, people walking past, cabs, wagons, and carriages; how she envied them, their seemingly uncomplicated lives. Taking a breath, she turned her gaze to Mr Stephens.

'Where are the valuables?'

The young man gave her an encouraging smile, which lit up his rather serious face. 'They are stored in a locked room situated in the cellar of the Crown and Garter. I believe you are staying there at present?'

'Yes, but I have been down in those cellars.' She shuddered at the memory. 'I found no locked doors; I would have remembered if I had.'

'It is hidden behind a pile of crates, added protection,' Mr Stephens explained.

'And the key to the door?' Hero asked.

'I believe Mr Barrett kept it in his office.'

'We found a few keys but matched them to the locks: front door, back door, cellar door, etc.'

'It has to be there somewhere, probably hidden in a safe or some such.'

'We will check again when we return.' Hero nodded.

'Good, good.' The other man encouraged. He pulled out a piece of paper with his address on it. 'When you find something, send a message to this address. I am in touch with many of the families; they will be delighted to have some of their precious possessions returned to them. But I must stress caution in these matters. There are items of silver and gold and jewellery worth a great amount of money. There will be those who are far less scrupulous searching for them too.'

'Yes, of course.' Hero's voice was grave.

'We must get it out of the inn and back to the rightful owners before someone else decides to claim the items.' Stephen's stressed.

'Well, we had best get moving,' Hero said decisively. 'The sooner we begin searching for this treasure, the better.'

Evie and Hero bid Mr Stephens farewell and made their departure.

When they stepped out onto the street a few moments later, Hero hailed them a Hansom. Neither of them noticed the watchful figure standing across the road.

*

A nurse sat with George Beeching. The man was in a terrible condition: despite the amputation, infection from the dog bites had run amok through his system,

Stuart Boyd approached the bed. He could hear the prone man's ragged breathing as he drew closer.

'How's he been?' he asked the nurse.

'Not good, Dr Boyd. There is no sign of the fever breaking; and when I changed the dressing of the stump, it was oozing pus, it was swollen and angry.'

Stuart placed a hand on George's forehead; he was burning up.

His patient's eyes flickered open. He looked at Stuart, but the doctor had a feeling that he couldn't see him through his tormented gaze.

George groaned. 'I – I,' he tried to speak, but his voice was weak, cracked and dry.

'Hush now, George. Rest, man.' Stuart turned to the nurse. 'I have informed his parents about the situation. However, the father is severely ill himself. He has had another stroke, and the prognosis does not look promising.'

'Oh, Lord.' The nurse placed a hand against her heart in shock. 'Poor man.'

'Yes quite.' But there was an edge to Stuart's voice. 'Keep me informed, will you.'

'Yes, of course, Dr Boyd.'

When he left the ward, Stuart took the long corridor heading to his office.

Stuart was in no doubt that George Beeching was dying; he was burning up with fever. It would have been a miracle if the man survived, so this outcome had not been a surprise. He could not help but feel that George's death would be no loss to humanity.

George Beeching took his last breath that day. Both Andrew and Stuart were present as the nurse covered his face with the sheet.

'You did your best, Doctor,' she said to Stuart.

'Aye, we did. I had better send word to the family,' Stuart commented as he left the room. Andrew walked out into the corridor with him.

Andrew shook his head, 'I have to confess, there is a part of me that is rather glad he is dead.'

Stuart patted his shoulder. 'I know Andrew. I have to say, knowing the awful atrocities he had committed, I feel the same.'

*

When Evie and Hero arrived back at the Crown, Rita was waiting for them.

'This message arrived for you, Mr Woodley.' She handed a piece of paper to Hero.

He unfolded it and scanned the contents.

'What is it?' Evie asked.

'It's from Andrew, asking me to come to the hospital right away.'

'Do you think it is something to do with George Beeching?' she asked.

'Probably. Will you come with me?'

She shook her head. 'No, I will go and search Jack's office for that key.'

A concerned look on his face, Hero said, 'Just be careful. Perhaps we can search for it when I get back.'

She smiled. 'Thank you for your concern. I shall be fine.'

Hero hesitated for a moment. 'Very well, I shall be as quick as I can.'

Once Horacio had left, Evie removed her gloves and hat.

The barroom was quiet, with only a couple of customers. Evie knew it would soon become busy again when all the workers finished their shifts.

Rita was wiping the top of the bar but was giving Evie furtive looks.

'Everything alright, Rita?' Evie asked.

'Oh, aye.' The woman nodded, sending her brassy curls bouncing.

'Very well then, I shall be upstairs if you need me.'

'Alright.'

As she left the room going through the door behind the bar. She was aware of Rita watching her every move.

Making her way up the creaking staircase, Evie pondered on the happenings of the day. She was still dumbstruck that Jack had left her property and money. The five thousand pounds was tucked away in her reticule. She would have to open a bank account and pay the money in. It would be safer than keeping it at the Crown.

The realisation suddenly hit her that she was a free woman. Not only free but a woman of means too! She did not need to stay in this ungodly place. She could sell the land, and property and travel if she wished to. Or do as Horacio suggested, put the money to good use.

Evie remembered him telling her that his mother was hoping to extend her school, maybe she could help with that? It also dawned on her that this would be the perfect way to keep a connection alive with Horacio Woodley. He had been such a strength to her, she didn't know how she would have coped without his quiet, yet strong presence.

She was just wondering why Horacio would go out of his way to help her as she stepped into Jack's office and saw the chaos in the room. Evie gasped. Someone had rifled through all the desk drawers. There were papers and ledgers strewn across the floor. One of the drawers that would contain pens and ink had been pulled out. When she looked more closely, she could see a cavity, a secret drawer.

It only took her a moment to put the pieces together; the key to the locked room had been kept here, someone had found it, but who?

She turned around and dashed from the room. Running down the stairs, she went along the corridor and opened the door that led down to the cellars.

The frigid air welcomed her, she shivered. After the spring sunshine, the cellar felt colder and even more unwelcoming.

Pausing at the top of the steps, she listened carefully; all appeared to be quiet down there.

Evie hated the place and did not relish going down into the depths alone. Swallowing down her misgivings, Evie was just about to step down the first stair, when she heard a floorboard creak behind her. Before she could turn around, someone pushed her hard from behind.

The world spun as she tumbled down the stairs. The air was knocked out of her. She cracked her head against something hard. A darkness that was blacker than the cellar itself claimed her.

*

'Sorry I had to get you to come all this way,' Andrew apologised to Hero.

'That's alright, Andrew.' Hero kept pace with his friend as they walked along the hospital corridor. 'I knew there was a good chance that Beeching would die from those wounds. They were horrendous. But even so, I still can't quite fathom he is dead.'

'Yes. You know I would not usually think ill of the dead, but that monster is no loss to the world.'

'Yes,' Hero agreed.

'The body will be sent to Norfolk. We have also had word that his father is seriously ill. There is a strong possibility of a double funeral.'

Horacio nodded a grave look on his face. Andrew shot him a sidelong glance, 'what will this mean for Vanessa?' He asked.

'Well, William is the heir, so the estate will probably be held in trust for him. Vanessa will no longer have to tolerate Georges abominable and suffocating presence.'

'The news will be a relief to her.' Andrew observed.

'It will, although she will still have to deal with George's mother, Margot. She can be a bit of a harridan by all accounts.'

'I hope that Beeching left Vanessa the means to live an independent life.' Andrew commented thoughtfully.

'Well, we shall see. I will write to her as soon as possible to let her know what has happened.'

'Yes, do. Although it might be a good idea to wait a couple of days, to see what happens to Lord Beeching senior.' Andrew advised.

'Ahh yes, good idea.'

They paused by a double door opening into one of the wards.

'What about Sophia, will you write to her or tell her in person what has happened?' Hero asked.

'I will travel down to the Frobisher's' at the weekend and tell her then. I can accompany her back to Brook House. Now that Beeching and Barrett are dead. She is no longer at risk.'

'Well, that is a relief,' Hero commented, 'I am sure mother will be pleased to have her back under her wing.'

Andrew chuckled, 'I am sure. Why don't you and Evie accompany me? It would be wonderful to reunite the two friends. I am sure they will find comfort from each other.'

'Yes, that is an excellent idea. Talking about Evie, would you believe Jack Barrett left her some property and a substantial amount of money.'

Andrew's eyebrows shot up in surprise. 'Really? Goodness, who would have thought it.'

Hero gave his friend an enigmatic look. 'Yes. We also found out today that there is a hidden treasure trove in the cellars of the Crown.'

'Good gracious, what will happen next!'

'Yes, quite.'

*

Carefully, Evie came too. She was lying on something lumpy, in a place that felt cold and damp. She went to move but found that her head thumped with pain. Evie would have gasped, but there was something in her mouth: a piece of rough cloth, a gag.

Her eyes shot open. There was a roof high above her: she wasn't in the cellar at the Crown then. Evie could see lighter patches of the sky that was folding into darkness through holes in the roof.

When she went to move, more cautiously this time, she found her wrists and ankles were tied together with rope.

A noise made her turn her head. There was a pool of lamplight in a far corner.

Evie heard something else; a match being struck? Suddenly a light flared nearby. A face loomed close by, then was gone when the match went out. All she could see after that was the glow of the cigarette, a firefly in the darkness.

The scent of tobacco wafted over her. Her stomach clenched with fear. It was her husband; Jolly Jack Barrett was alive.

Chapter 60

When Horacio left the hospital, twilight had well and truly set in. The darkling bloomed. The lamplighters were out in force.

The streets were busy with people on their way home after a long day. Hero would have hailed a cab, but the roads were clogged with traffic, so he decided to walk back to the Crown.

As he got closer to the river and the docks, he could see the mist swirling up from the dark water. It was an eerie sight, the ghosts of the drowned looking for retribution. He shivered, pulling the collar of his coat up to keep his neck warm.

Past the last bridge, into the East End, there was a marked difference to the streets. No gas lamps had been lit here. Dockworkers trudged home, heads bowed, backs bent. Snotty nosed children still ran about the streets or sat on cold front steps.

His hands deep in his pockets, Hero bowed his head as he dodged the people.

As the streets narrowed, the crowds became lighter.

A movement in front of him made Horacio glance up. A man was walking towards him.

Hero was not quite sure what alerted him to an approaching threat. Maybe it was his ingrained fighting instinct? He pulled his hands out of his pockets. The man walking towards him was heavily built with a bullish neck.

Hero didn't recognise him.

A narrow alley branched off to the left. As Hero and the bullish man reached the adjacent entrance, another man stepped out in front of Hero.

Horacio was ready for trouble.

In one lithe step, he dodged out of the way. Pivoted on light feet and landed a punch. The thickset man cried out and bludgeoned into his companion.

'Aww, he's broke my nose.' The man moaned as blood gushed.

'Ere.' The other man rushed Hero. There was something metal glinting in his hand, a knife?

Hero danced out of the way. The man's momentum took him sprawling into the mud.

It was apparent to Hero that these men were thugs, not fighters, using brawn to take people down.

Taking advantage of the situation. Hero ran at the larger man. Punched him just under the ribs, sending him bending double as blood splashed from his broken nose. Another punch had him doubling over once more. One more punch felled him like a massive tree. He collapsed with a grunt.

Again, Hero's quick instincts saved him from the lighter man's knife thrust. He dodged and twisted. One arm went around the man's neck, and the other grabbed the hand holding the knife. Hero used their momentum to slam the attacker into the crumbling brick wall.

Horacio was pleased to hear the knife fall to the pavement with a clatter.

'Who are you?' he questioned the man as he held him tight against the wall.

'Don't care what yer do; I aint saying nuffink.'

Before he knew what was happening, Hero spun him around to face him. The man was slightly taller than Hero, but Horacio put that to good use; he used all his energy to shove the man against the wall once more, knocking the wind out of him. Then he jammed his bent arm up and under. Pressing hard against the man's exposed throat.

'Tell me what is going on, or by God, I swear I shall put an end to you right here.' The man's breathing gurgled in his throat as Hero pressed harder. Then he tried another tack. 'Do you know who I am?' He was rewarded with a nod of the head. 'You know then that I am a boxer?' The man gave another nod. 'I have done a great deal of damage with these hands of mine,' Hero said, pressing harder.

'Tommy Dicken ...' the words were barely audible. Hero let the man go. He slumped forward onto his knees, gasping for air. His companion was close by groaning in pain.

'Tommy Dicken? What about him?' Hero persisted.

'He hired us to take care of you.'

'When you say take care of me, you mean to kill me?'

'Aye, that's the plan.' The man looked up at Hero, tears running down his face, he was still holding his damaged throat. 'e wants you an the woman out of the way.'

Horacio felt oily coils of fear curl in his belly. 'What woman?' he asked, although he was fairly sure he knew who it would be.

'Er, yer know.'

'Evie Barrett?'

The man nodded once more.

Hero stepped forward. The man looked up at him in fear as Hero landed a blow with so much force the man slumped unconscious.

Hero bent down and picked up the knife. It had a sharpened edge with a bone handle.

Looking over to the other man, who was still writhing on the muddy ground, Hero asked, 'where is Evie Barrett?'

Eyes bulging, the prone man shook his head.

Knife in hand, Hero, squatted down next to the man.

'Tell me where Evie Barrett is? Otherwise, my face is the last thing you will see in this life.'

'I dunno, honest, Mr Woodley. We were told to take care of you while the woman was being picked up.'

'Picked up? Picked up from where?'

'T-the Crown.'

Hero nodded, 'How long ago?'

'Dunno,' the man answered again.

Hero searched the other's eyes. Evie might still be at the Crown or had already been abducted. He grabbed the man's grubby shirt collar and pulled his head up.

'If anything happens to Mrs Barrett, I shall personally track you down and put an end to your miserable life.' He kept his voice soft, which made the statement all the more menacing. 'You know how Jack Barrett died? His own dogs mauled him.'

'Aye, aye.' He nodded vigorously, then groaned as the movement sent the pain erupting once more.

'Well, if I see you again, I shall personally feed you to those vicious animals. Do you get my drift?'

'Aye.'

'Good.' Hero pulled back his arm, landing another punch that sent the man into oblivion, as he had with his companion.

Horacio got up from his crouch and started to run in the direction of the Crown and Garter.

*

Oh Lord, Evie Barrett thought as she lay on the lumpy bed, gagged, with wrists and ankles trussed up. Jolly Jack Barrett had come back to haunt her. Will she ever be rid of him?

The cigarette still flared a short distance away.

As her eyes adjusted to the semidarkness, Evie was able to make out a seated figure. Sensing that someone was watching her, she longed to rid herself of the gag so she could speak; ask some questions at least.

When she heard the wooden legs of a chair scrape against the floor, Evie watched the figure, and she could make out movement.

The cigarette was dropped and snuffed out with a booted foot. Then the person picked up the chair and moved closer to the rickety bed.

*

Instead of entering the Inn through the crowded barroom, Horacio went down the side alley to the back of the building. In case anyone was on the lookout, he carefully approached the back door that led to the cellars.

Seeing that there was no one on sentry duty, Hero breathed a sigh of relief; he may have been a fighting man, but he did not enjoy inflicting injury or pain on another being outside of the ring. He had left those two thugs unconscious in the street. There was always a possibility that they would have their pockets searched and throats cut by the scavengers of the streets, but he couldn't think about any of that now.

The door to the cellar was unlocked. He opened it and stepped inside the dank cavern.

There were a couple of lamps and a matchbook standing on one of the beer barrels. Hero struck a match and lit the lamp. He knew it was risky, drawing attention to himself; however, the cellars were pitch dark. There was no other lamps lit. Besides, relying on his instincts once more, he had a feeling that the place was empty.

As he made his way through the multiple rooms, he came across several crates which had been moved to block the walkway. He could see an open door and an empty room. Ahh, this must have been the place where Jack kept his pilfered treasure.'

There was no sign of Reg, Tommy, or any of Jack's lackeys.

Hero paused for a moment. He needed to check if Evie was here, but something told him he was too late.

Reaching the bottom of the cellar steps, he put the lamp down, ran up them, then opened the door to the back corridor.

He checked upstairs first of all. He saw the chaos in Jack's office. Coming to the same conclusion as Evie had done earlier. Whoever had done this, they had found the key to the door in the cellar.

There was no sign of Evie, although she had been here. Hero spotted her hat, gloves, and reticule on a chair by the darkening window.

*

The man, for she was sure it was a man, came towards her. Evie was very aware of her heartbeat drumming fast, echoing in her chest. The brightness of the lamp silhouetted the person.

He moved closer to her, set the chair down, then sat beside the bed. His features were still in silhouette.

Evie blinked at him helplessly.

Leaning forward, the man reached out and pulled the gag from her mouth.

'Welcome, Mrs Barrett to yer fine palace, with wonderful views of the river.'

'Tommy?' her voice was brittle with dryness, she swallowed. 'Tommy.'

'Aye.' He sat back in the chair, pulled out a tin, got out another smoke and lit it. This time, Evie could make out his grim features. He took a long drag then blew the smoke out of his mouth.

'What do you want, Tommy?' Evie struggled to sit up, but with her wrists and ankles tied; it was awkward for her to move.

'What do I want? Well, see, the thing is, I was onto a good thing in the ouse with Mrs P, our Ivy and Dottie, but yer had to open yer gob and tell me to keep away from Dot, who was the best person in the world. I loved er, yer know.'

'I'm sure you did. I'm sorry, Tommy.'

'Aye well, it's a bit late now.'

'The fire wasn't my fault, Margie showed up; she had been drinking. She tried to attack me. I dropped the lamp ...' Closing her eyes tightly to stop the tears, Evie's voice trailed away. The thing was, she did feel responsible for Dottie's death and the other three. 'Alright,' her voice was soft. 'What do you want, Tommy?' she asked at last.

'I've got everything I want. See, I know you an Mr Woodley went to visit Mr Hill and ad a word with that Mr Stephens. I knew he would tell yer about the treasures hidden in the cellar of the Crown. So, me and Reg decided to take matters into our own ands. Reg is my cousin yer know, only family I've got left now.'

'So, you have taken the silver and gold that belong to the Jewish families?'

'Yes. Me an Reg, are going to sail to America to make a new life for ourselves.'

'That's a good thing, Tommy.' Evie found herself encouraging him as she vied for time. 'But the goods belong to other people.'

'Ha, course they do, do yer think I'm gonna worry about that!'

'No, I suppose not. But listen, Jack left me some money. Mr Hill gave it to me today; five thousand pounds. I'll give it to you and Reg, in return for the things you found in the cellar.'

'Where is the money?' he asked.

'I put it in my reticule which I left upstairs at the Crown.'

'Well, thanks very much, *Mrs Barrett*.' I'm sure that'll come in nice n andy. An, now you've told me where it is, well what's ter stop me taking that as well?'

'Oh Lord, Tommy.' Evie shook her head. 'Please just let me go, you can have the money, then you and Reg can go on your journey. I would wish you well.'

'Yer would wish me well. Huh, well, that's rich indeed. Yer certainly didn't wish me well when I ad me eart set on yer sister, did yer.'

Evie felt anger flare. 'And do you really think that Jack would have given you *his* blessing? You have to remember Dottie was his sister-in-law, would he have wanted someone like you marrying her?'

'Ah, yer bitch.' Before Evie knew what was happening, he slapped her hard around the face which knocked her back onto the lumpy mattress. All the pins holding her hair had come loose, her long locks trailed over her eyes.

He leant over, picked up a handful of her hair, then used it to pull her towards him, Evie gasped in pain.

'This is what's gonna appen,' Evie could smell his sour breath against her stinging cheek. 'I sent a couple of the lads to pick up Woodley. You an he were meant to be at the Crown together so we could ave took you both then. 'It were me who pushed yer down the stairs, by the way.' He chuckled. 'Could ave broke yer neck, but as luck would ave it ...' pulling her hair again, which made her eyes water even more, he continued. 'So, ere we are.' Leaning closer he said, 'I'm just waiting for Mr Woodley to get ere, then you an im are going for a nice swim in the river.'

'Why Horacio?' Evie asked, 'what has he done to you?'

'He's been elping you. You've ad im running around after yer like a bloody lap dog. He should ave been dead, im an that pup Silverman. So, we are just finishing up with Jack's final orders.'

*

Once Horacio had searched the upstairs of the Crown, he ran down the stairs and into the barroom.

It was busy and noisy. Both Rita and Sally were running around like headless chickens, but that didn't stop Hero from grabbing Rita's arm in a strong grip.

'Ere!' She gave him a startled look and tried to pull away.

'Where is she?' Hero hissed through gritted teeth.

'What? Dunno what yer talking about.' Rita shook her head.

'Ere, Rita, I'm dying of thirst.' One of the men called to her.

'Can't yer see I'm rushed off me feet.'

Hero didn't let go, but searched her expression as he said again, 'where have they taken Evie, Rita?'

'Who? What do yer mean?' She looked genuinely puzzled. Hero had a strong suspicion that she was telling the truth; she didn't know what had happened to Evie.

'Damn it.' Abruptly, he let go of her arm and pushed through the crowd, then found himself standing outside on the street as the fog swirled around his feet.

*

'Well, Jack would be so proud of you, Tommy, assaulting his wife, his widow,' Evie said sharply. 'And, what of Dottie, you said you loved her, yet you are going to kill her sister.'

'STOP-stop...' Tommy let go of her hair and sat back in the chair.

'Dottie was my world,' Evie persisted, 'Yes, we had fallen out, but we always forgave each other. Think about it; how would *she* feel about this situation.'

'Err, yer a bitch.'

Tommy placed his hands over his ears to shut out her words. Then dropped them once more. He leant towards her. Before Evie knew what was happening, he pulled the gag back over her mouth. 'Yer messing with me mind.' He got up and kicked the rickety chair, it clattered across the floor and bumped into the table where the lamp stood.

The glass broke as the lamp hit the floor. The oil splashed across the floorboards; greedy flames leapt up in pursuit.

'Now, see whatcha done.' Tommy rushed over and started to stomp on the flames to put them out, but they grabbed at the bottom of his trousers, hellish fingers seeking purchase. The next thing, one of his trouser legs was aflame.

'Ahh,' he danced around like a marionette.

Evie sat on the bed. Her tear-filled eyes were full of horror. She shook her head frantically as memories of the fire at the house came back to her. She could see Margie go up in flames. She could see Dottie at the top of the stairs.

Oh Lord, she thought, it's poetic justice, I escaped the first time, now I shall die here.

Part of her felt relieved that it would all be over, no worries about the future, but then an image of Horacio Woodley popped into her mind – Hero would save her.

*

Hero didn't know where to go, where to look. He walked back and forward in front of the Crown; his aching fists clenched at his sides. Think, think, Horacio, where would they take her? Where?

Realising that he had to act, Hero started to walk in the direction of the river.

The warehouses loomed against the skyline – Ahh, the warehouses! Jack had left one of them to Evie. His heart sped up, as did his feet as he made his way to the dark, rippling water.

*

Tommy took off his jacket and tried desperately to douse the flames with the fabric. He managed to smother the flames that licked his trouser legs, but the ones fed by the lamp oil delighted in dancing across the floor.

There were hessian sacks stored in the lofty space. Old bones of unwanted furniture and goodness knew what else. The hungry fire consumed these offerings with relish.

Oh, God! Her movements hampered by her restraints; Evie still managed to roll herself off the bed.

Tommy turned to look at her. His features were macabre in the flickering flames.

He took a step towards where she was lying; it was at that moment that the floor gave way beneath him.

Evie closed her eyes in horror as she heard the scream of the falling man.

*

It was like a maze, these back streets. Hero, his heart pounding pushed past dark figures. His search was not being helped by the swirling fog which had ridden the back of the incoming tides.

As he squelched through foul-smelling waste, Hero decided that as long as he kept going towards the river, he would come across the warehouses eventually.

He was just jogging down yet another narrow lane when someone emerged in front of him. It was as if the figure had walked through the brick wall. The image made the hairs on his skin stand up on end. He shivered.

'You looking for Nel's girl?' the voice, which was a harsh croak, was equally as disquieting as the grim figure.

Hero discerned it was a woman wearing filthy rags. In the darkness, her face was moon white, cheekbones and eye sockets seemed hollow, demon-like.

When a skeletal hand appeared and reached towards him, Hero couldn't help but step back.

'I mean yer no arm, mister.' She cackled at his obvious disquiet. She shuffled closer. The scent of her was riper than the effluent in the streets. 'Yer looking fer Nell's girl,' she repeated.

'Evie Winters!' His heart rate increased with excitement this time.

'Aye, the older sister, bonnie lass.'

'Yes, yes, she's missing, do you know where she is?'

'Aye, they always forget Mrs Gill, they do.' She pointed to her eyes. 'I see's everything, I do.'

'I'm sure you do,' Hero nodded, 'Have you seen her tonight? She is in danger. I must find her.'

'Aye, the two carrot tops took er.' She pointed to the end of the alley. 'Follow me, and I'll show yer.'

She walked as if her feet were hobbled. Hero tried not to complain at the slow pace. He only hoped this was not a fool's errand following this old crone. She could well be leading him into some sort of trap.

*

Reg and Tommy had stored the three crates full of items of gold and silver, along with other valuable goods in one of the ground-floor rooms of the warehouse.

This was the same place where Molly had been kept prisoner. Reg hated being here, especially on his own. He fancied he could hear the beams creaking with the weight of a hanging body.

He was seated next to the brazier which wasn't doing much to dispel the damp chill.

Tommy was upstairs with the woman. Reg wasn't happy about this. He wanted to take the goods and go, get away. But Tommy had insisted on retribution. Blaming Evie Barrett and Horacio Woodley for Jack's death.

Strangely, Tommy focusing on the woman and Woodley meant that Reg didn't have to face his guilt; after all, he was the one who hadn't secured the door on the dog's cage, Bloody hell!

When he and Tommy had been searching for the key to the room down in the cellar of the Crown, Reg had found Jack's silver hip flask. He had filled it up with liquor. Unscrewing the top; he took a deep swig. Wiping his lips with the back of his hand, he felt the brandy hit his stomach. As the warmth flared within, Reg nearly jumped out of his skin when he heard a loud groan and crack, as the floor to the attic rooms gave way.

⸻⬦⟨⟩⬦⸻

Chapter 61

Horacio was full of misgivings as he followed the old crone through a maze of narrow streets.

She turned back to him once in a while to check he was still following her. Sometimes she would pluck at his sleeve with her thin bony fingers. He wanted to pull away but resisted the urge.

'There.'

Mrs Gill paused at the end of an alley. Hero could see a mammoth building in front of him; a monster rising from the fog. He looked to where she was pointing. His heart almost stopped when he saw flames sprouting from the roof.

'Evie is in there?' He looked to the old woman for an answer, but she had gone. Looking around frantically, he couldn't see her anywhere.

'Mrs Gill,' he called, but all he could hear was the lapping water of the river and the strangely distant noises of the city at night. It was as if she had morphed into the swirling fog and vanished.

When he heard the noise of timbers cracking and falling in on themselves, which sent sparks into the night sky from the warehouse roof, Hero ran the rest of the way, trying to find an entrance to the place.

Eventually, he found a pair of stout doors with a chain and padlock, then noticed a smaller door near the corner of the building. He was just about to try the handle when the door was flung open. Reg nearly knocked Hero over as he ran out of the building.

'What the hell is going on, man?' Hero grabbed the arm of the taller man.

'He's in there, he is!'

'Who-who's in there? Is Evie Winters in there?'

'Aye, and our Tommy, think e's dead. God, he's dead alright.'

'Tommy's dead?'

Reg nodded his head vigorously, his expression bleak. 'The ceiling gave way; the building's on its last legs.'

'Where is Evie, mmm, Mrs Barrett?'

'Up in the attic where Molly swung.'

Before Hero had a chance to ask him more, Reg fled, his long legs flying over the slippery ground.

It was as if the building was lamenting its demise. The timbers popped, cracked, and moaned.

As he entered the building, Horacio was quite sure that no fire wagons would take the risk of entering these streets to save this place, which was falling down anyway. Hero knew the only person who could save Evie, was himself.

*

Andrew felt exhausted when he arrived back at his lodgings. He was extremely grateful to Mrs Gordon when he found that she had placed the copper tub by a roaring fire in the sitting room.

'It'll be a bit cool now, Dr Keene,' she said, 'I'll top it up with some kettles of hot water for you.'

'You are a star, Mrs G,' he said as he took off his coat and scarf.

As she lifted one of two large copper kettles from the range, she poured the water into the tub, then did the same with the other kettle.

She tested the water, 'Ahh, it's warm but not boiling.'

'That's fine. To be honest, after the day I have had, I would be happy with bathing in the arctic ice.'

'How is your patient?' She asked.

'Well, I may as well tell you, George Beeching died of an infection caused by the dog bites.'

'Aye,' she nodded. 'Well good riddance, that's all I can say.'

'I can't help but agree with you there.'

She looked him in the eye. 'So, when are you going to tell that dear girl the news?'

'I shall travel to Oxfordshire this weekend. I can tell Sophia what has happened. And if she is agreeable, I will escort her back to Brook House.'

'Oh yes, that's a good plan. She will be delighted to see you, no doubt.'

'Well, I'm glad you approve.' Andrew smiled.

'Oh, I do indeed, Dr Keene. Now, I'll leave you to have your bath. When you have finished, give me a shout. I have a nice steak and kidney pie for your dinner.'

'Oh, thank you, you really are a gem.'

Picking up the two large kettles, Mrs Gordon went back downstairs.

Andrew wasted no time, he got undressed and eased his long frame into the tub, as he did so, water splashed over the edge, but the landlady had put towels on the floor just for this purpose.

The water was pleasantly warm. Andrew laid back and sighed. God, what a couple of days it had been! He couldn't quite believe what had happened to George Beeching. The man had got his comeuppance that was for sure.

He then thought about Sophia; he couldn't wait to see her at the weekend. He wondered how she would take the news regarding the death of her attacker. She had such a kind heart and beautiful soul. He knew she would not wish ill on anybody, not even the man who had abused her so gravely.

He wondered if they would talk about the wedding. From their previous conversations, they had both agreed they would like to marry sooner rather than later. It wasn't just about giving the baby the best start in life; it was the genuine love they had for each other: if anybody had told him that he would be afflicted by that old adage "love at first sight", he would have scoffed and laughed it off. But it was the fact, that despite her awful circumstance, Sophia had been able to open her heart to him. For him, it was something close to miraculous.

As he washed his neck and the cricks out of his shoulders, he felt a fluttering of delight and anticipation in his stomach. He would soon be a married man.

*

When Hero ventured further into the building, he found the rubble from the floor above. He saw Tommy Dicken's body draped over a beam. The fire danced along the beam and licked at the man's prone body.

As hungry flames, flickering amber, orange and blue, cavorted long the wood. Hero wondered if the beams had been treated with pitch to preserve them from the elements, and that was why the fire was spreading so quickly.

Hero felt as if it would be only a matter of moments before the place went up completely.

He wished to god that he had asked Reg where Evie was being held. But then remembered Reg's statement; Evie was up in the attic where Molly had swung!

From the debris surrounding Tommy's body, Horacio could tell that they were beams. As the flames gathered momentum, he saw that the oily, black smoke was being drawn upwards – Evie was up there somewhere, he had to find her and fast.

Discovering a set of stairs, he made his way upwards. The stairs were made of wood, but luckily, they had been set into the outer brick wall on one side, which was as well, as the railing was in dire need of repair.

Thinking it was the best course of action, Hero kept close to the brick wall, trying each step as he did so, worried that it would give way when it received his weight.

*

Evie lay helpless on the dirty floor beside the old bedframe. She watched the flames dripping from the beams into the ragged hole in the flooring. It was as if Tommy had fallen through the gates into some sort of hell.

Over in one corner, the hessian sacks had caught fire. It raged there feeding hungrily on the fodder; the flames were tall and menacing.

Smoke curled up through the holes in the ceiling. The acrid smell of it caught the back of her throat and made her eyes water.

When more debris fell into the jagged hole, Evie started to wriggle on her belly towards the door.

*

Hero reached the landing above without mishap. He peered into several small rooms until he reached one at the end of the hallway. All these rooms were under the rafters of the huge roof. Hero wondered if the foundations would stand up to the fire: how many more cave-ins would there be?

He opened the last door and stepped through. In the flickering flames, he saw Evie straight away. She was on the floor, and she was moving! Hero felt incredibly grateful for that fact.

Evie spotted him. Her expression was one of desperation and fear.

When he got closer, he realised she was bound and gagged. Cautiously, he took a step towards her as more of the flooring broke away and fell into the pit.

'Jesus!' Hero found himself swearing.

Taking a deep breath to still his nerves, he ran to Evie. Pulling the gag out of her mouth, he gave her what he hoped was a reassuring smile.

'It's alright. I'm here.'

'Horacio.' The name was muttered so softly; he wasn't sure if he had heard it at all.

He fished in his pocket, locating the knife he had retrieved from his attacker earlier in the evening. At the time he wasn't sure why he had picked up the weapon, now Hero felt thoroughly grateful that he had done so. He started to cut away the rope tying her wrists together.

The fire crackled and hissed as if it were an audience booing down a parody of some stage show.

'Can you walk?' He asked her as he finished undoing the tether at her ankles. She nodded.

Bending down, he helped her to her feet, then popped an arm around her waist as he ushered her to the open door.

They both heard further sounds of destruction when they reached the top of the flight of steps.

'It's alright, it's alright ...' Hero kept murmuring the re-assurance, for his benefit as well as hers.

When they reached the bottom of the stairs, they heard an almighty crash as more of the building fell in upon itself.

'This way.' Hero grabbed Evie's hand. They bolted towards the open door.

Stepping outside into the foggy, damp air, Hero turned Evie towards him so he could see her face. He brushed tendrils of her long hair out of her eyes and off her face.

'Are you alright?' his voice was filled with concern.

'Yes, I think so. Tommy Dicken pushed me down the stairs at the Crown.'

'Good Lord, you could have broken your neck!'

She suddenly found herself being drawn into a tight embrace, which she relished as she clung to his reassuring strength. Then images of Jack popped into her head, particularly the one when she thought that Tommy had been Jack's ghost. She shivered.

Hero pulled away. He slipped out of his long coat and wrapped it around her shoulders.

'Thank you.' She gave him a small smile.

Looking back at the warehouse where the smoke and flames caressed the foggy night, Hero said, 'Let's get you back to the Crown, we'll pick up a few things, then I shall take you to Andrew so he can check you over.'

'You really don't have to.'

'Oh, but I think I do, for my peace of mind at least.'

When they negotiated the streets back to the Inn, they found that word had gotten out about the fire. People were running towards the spectacle. They jostled Hero and Evie as they went by.

The pair of them made it to the Crown. The bar was almost empty even though it was still early in the evening. Hero guessed that the drinkers had been tempted away from their pints to see the fire.

'What the ell's going on?' Rita asked. 'And what the ells appened to you?' The barmaid took in their bedraggled appearance.

'There is a fire down by the docks,' Hero explained quickly.

'Aye, words got about.' She narrowed her eyes. 'Don't tell me that you two were involved?'

'In a manner of speaking, yes.' That was all he was going to say on the matter.

Rita rolled her eyes, then took in Evie's appearance. 'An, look at the state of you, seems like trouble follows you around, don't it?'

'Seems that way.' Evie gave her a wry smile.

'We are going to pick up some bits and pieces; then I am taking Mrs Barrett to see a doctor.'

'Alright.' Rita nodded.

When they were in the rear corridor of the Inn, Evie said, 'The items that belong to the immigrants will be pilfered if people find them in the warehouse.'

'I doubt anyone will go near the place until the fire has gone out.' Hero replied as they descended the stairs. 'We can sort it all out in the morning. The main thing is to make sure you are alright.'

Evie paused on the landing and looked at the man standing beside her.

'Thank you,' she said softly, 'you saved my life.'

'Ahh well.' Hero smiled, 'quid pro quo as they say.'

*

Andrew was just sitting down to tuck into the steak and kidney pie that Mrs Gordon had made when he heard a commotion in the hall downstairs.

His hair still damp from his bath; he sighed as he put down his knife and fork. Visitors at this time in the evening usually meant trouble or someone in need of his services; he may only be a trainee doctor, but that didn't stop people seeking out his help.

He walked out onto the landing, then looked down the stairwell. It was Hero with his arm around Evie Winters, no Barrett, he corrected himself.

They both looked bedraggled, Evie was as white as a sheet.

'What on earth has happened?' Andrew took Evie's other arm as they stepped onto the landing.

'It's a long story,' Hero muttered. 'Evie was pushed down the cellar stairs of the Crown. You need to check her over, Andrew.'

'Yes, yes.' He indicated that they go through to Hero's bedroom.

As they lay Evie gently down on the bed, Andrew said, 'Well, I have to say life is never boring when you are around, Miss Winters.'

'It certainly seems that way.' She favoured him with a thin smile. 'You are not the first person to make that kind of comment this evening, Andrew, but I could do without all the drama.'

Andrew gave Evie an examination while Hero waited in the sitting room.

'You have a nasty bump on the back of your head,' Andrew told her, 'a bruised shoulder and ribs, but you haven't broken anything, thank goodness. I shall give you a draught to help you sleep. You will probably feel very sore when you wake, however.'

'Thank you, Andrew, you are most kind.' Evie smiled although she felt absolutely exhausted.

He nodded, returning her smile. He then fetched a vial of laudanum from his bag, measured out five drops into a glass of water, then helped Evie to drink.

He tucked in the sheets and blankets, then left her to rest.

Walking into the sitting room, Andrew looked over to where Hero was standing by the fire.

'What the hell's been going on this time!'

'Sit down Andrew; it's a bit of a story that involves a ghostly old woman.'

'What?' He raised his eyes in speculation. 'Well, this calls for a brandy by the sound of it.'

'I don't know about one. I think we may need two or three.'

Chapter 62

After the awful fire that burnt down the warehouse, Evie, with Horacio Woodley's help and that of Mr Stephens, hired men to go through the rubble and clear it. While doing so, the men kept a look out for the crates of valuable goods. They were all amazed when they found the crates intact. Some of them had been scorched, but miraculously the valuables inside had not been damaged.

Rumour had spread that Jack Barrett's ghost haunted the warehouse. Neither Hero nor Evie did anything to quell the gossip: if it meant that people would not go near the ruins, all well and good.

Thanks to Mr Stephen's thorough documentation, they were able to return a number of the heirlooms to their rightful owners.

There were a few pieces left over, however, so these were kept in storage with the hope that they would be claimed at some point; if not, they would be sold. Evie and Mr Stephens decided that the money would go towards helping further immigrant families arriving in London.

Through Hero's solicitor, Mr Stokes, the warehouse land, the land upon which the house had once stood and the Crown and Garter pub, were sold, making Evie into a wealthy woman in her own right.

However, Evie found that there was something distasteful about this situation she found herself in. Thanks to Jack, she could live an independent life; however, she felt that the money was contaminated.

As they sorted out the legal work, Evie found that she didn't have to think about the future too closely, but there were times when it snuck up on her; she felt as if it were a gaping, dark void; where would she go now? What would she do?

While Horacio and Evie sorted out all the formalities and paperwork required for the sale of the land and buildings, Andrew travelled to the Frobisher's' to tell Sophia, Sarah, and Jasper the news about George.

They were all deeply shocked by what had happened – it was quite a story; Barrett had abducted Hero and Alec on behalf of Beeching.

And then there was the dog attack, but not only that, there was the attack on Evie, being pushed down the stairs of the Crown, then being taken to the warehouse, which had burnt down in a fire.

'Are they both well?' Sophia asked, her voice weighted with concern. They were sitting in Sarah's comfortable drawing-room. Chisholm, Sarah's pug, sat at Sophia's feet.

Andrew, who was sitting next to her on the chintz sofa, took Sophia's hand and gave it a gentle squeeze. 'Yes, my love, thank goodness they are.'

'Well,' Sarah exclaimed, 'it sounds as if dearest Hero lived up to his name.'

'Yes,' Jasper agreed, 'I have to say, I wasn't expecting such a horrific tail!'

'Yes,' Andrew nodded, 'and it could have been a great deal worse.'

Sarah and Jasper insisted that Andrew have dinner with them and stay the night, then the following day he and Sophia would travel back to Brook House.

'I really can't believe what has happened, Andrew.' Sophia said as they strolled arm in arm around the beautiful gardens that afternoon. Daffodils were nodding their heads under the trees and in the flowerbeds that flanked the path.

'I know, my love.' Thoughtfully, Andrew gazed out over the rolling hills. 'I think it will take us all some time to get over this.'

She nodded. 'I am still trying to comprehend that dear Dottie is dead.'

He squeezed her arm gently. 'It is a tragedy, indeed.'

Sophia paused beside a pretty fountain decorated with frolicking nymphs. She looked up into Andrew's eyes.

'Evie will be alright after all this, won't she?'

Andrew picked up both her hands and held them against his chest.

'You know Evie is strong, Sophia. With all the love and care she will receive from you, Emily, and Claire, she will have the time and the environment in which to heal.'

'Yes, not to mention Hero.' Sophia smiled.

'Ahh yes, Horacio. I do believe he is quite besotted with the courageous Evelyne.'

Sophia gently pulled one of her hands out of his grip. She reached up and cupped his cheek. Andrew smiled and leant into the caress.

'It is difficult to imagine sometimes,' Sophia said softly, 'that all the horror that has befallen us, has led us to a place of love.'

'How true.'

Sophia stepped into his embrace, the next thing they were kissing deeply, until Andrew pulled away, his face flushed with pleasure.

Sophia studied his kind features. Her face blushed with delight, and she said, 'Do you think we can get married sooner rather than later?'

'Well, yes, of course, if that is what you would like.' Andrew smiled.

Sophia nodded. 'Yes, that is exactly what I would like. Can we be married in May, do you think? It is such a lovely month, spring folding into summer.'

'Ahh, that is poetic.' He took her arm once again as they carried on with their stroll. 'Yes, May can be a delightful month for sure,' Andrew said thoughtfully. 'Mmm, I don't see why not. We can have the banns read and then be married. But it won't give us time to plan anything elaborate.'

She tightened the hold on his arm. 'I don't want anything elaborate I have everything I want right here.'

Andrew paused once more to gaze down at her. 'You know, you never fail to delight and surprise me.'

Sophia's smile was melancholy. 'I have realised that things are not really important, but people are, especially the ones you love.'

'Yes, well said.' He kissed her gently on the forehead.

Placing a hand over her belly, which was beginning to curve gently, her expression was thoughtful.

'Traditionally, it is not a custom in Judaism to have godparents. However, I have no related family here.' She found her eyes misting with tears, 'My grandmother was the last.'

'I know.' Andrew squeezed her hand gently.

Sophia gave him a small smile. 'I love Evie as a sister, as I did Dottie,' she continued, 'I trust Mr Woodley, Horacio. I have given the matter much thought; I would dearly like to ask Evie and Hero to be godparents to this little one. Do you think they will agree, especially under the circumstances, how the child was conceived?'

Andrew drew her to an elaborately decorated cast-iron bench. They both sat down.

Turning to her, he said, 'My dearest, Evie and Hero love you. You have been and are so brave. As you have said, the child is an innocent being deserving of love. They understand that. I am sure they will both be delighted if you ask them to be godparents.'

She smiled, then sniffed. Andrew drew out his handkerchief and wiped her tears away.

'And you are happy about this also?' she asked as she got her emotions under control.

'Yes, I am. I think it is a fine idea.' Andrew Beamed with delight.

The following morning, they said their goodbyes to Jasper, Sarah, and Chisholm, then made the journey back to Brook House.

Sophia and Andrew were greeted with open arms by Emily and Claire. They were full of questions and concerns, so once more, Andrew had to recount the awful things that had happened in London.

They were closeted in Emily's sitting room, come office, as he explained everything.

Claire had been pouring out tea for them all.

'Gosh, I can't quite believe this!' She paused in her task to take in the horror of the situation.

'This is a dreadful story,' Emily agreed. 'but it doesn't sound as if there is anyone to bring to justice now?'

'No,' Andrew agreed, 'only Reg, and no one knows where he is.'

'So, the fire that burnt down Evie's home, then the fire at the warehouse, were not connected?' Emily reflected.

'Well, yes and no.' Andrew explained, 'It was one of Jack Barrett's, umm, ladies of the night, Margie, who was responsible for the fire at the house.' He hesitated as he gazed out of the window thoughtfully. It was a pretty garden, lawns and flowerbeds running down towards the coppice wood that flanked the land between Woodley Hall and the school. 'I don't think I realised just what a terrible state Margie's mind was in. I was able to see to her physical wounds, but not the emotional ones. Then I left her alone with Mrs Gordon.' He shook his head in regret.

'You weren't to know what she would do, Andrew.' Sophia spoke up. 'Evie explained that Margie must have been drinking heavily.'

Andrew nodded. 'Yes, I know, and much of the alcohol she consumed was from my sideboard.' He rubbed a hand across his face. 'In hindsight, I should have left her in the care of Stuart, at the hospital. After all, the poor woman was in a terrible state, grieving for her friend, then being forcibly removed from her home.'

Handing him a cup of tea, Claire said, 'You weren't to know what she would do, Andrew. And don't forget you were worried about Sophia's safety.'

The man gave her a wry smile and nodded his thanks as he accepted the hot brew. He took a sip of his drink.

Emily shook her head in disbelief. 'Goodness, it is beyond imaginings that Evie was caught up in two dreadful fires.'

'Yes. Evie is lucky to be alive, lucky that Hero saved her,' Andrew agreed.

'Yes,' Emily placed a hand over her heart. 'I don't know what I would have done if I had lost Horacio, especially now that I feel we are both moving on with our lives.'

'Yes quite.' Andrew concurred. Then changed the subject to something far cheerier. 'Now, there is something that myself and Sophia wish to tell you.' He set his cup and saucer aside and picked up Sophia's hand. 'We have decided to be married in May, and we hope that you will attend the wedding?'

'Goodness,' Emily got to her feet, she reached over and took Sophia in a tight embrace. 'We shall be delighted.'

'Oh yes,' Claire declared, 'we would never have forgiven the two of you if you had eloped.'

Seeing that she was jesting, Andrew laughed. 'I don't think Sophia would have forgiven me either if I swooped her away, not giving you both a chance to attend the wedding.'

'I certainly would not,' Sophia laughed.

*

Once the Crown had been sold, Evie had moved into Mrs Gordon's spare room. She found it comforting having Horacio, Andrew, and the housekeeper close by.

Evie wasn't sure if it were the past that haunted her slumber or the thought of an empty future, but she kept having terrible dreams where she would be caught in a fire. She would see people writhing in the flames: the faces changed, Jack, Margie, Dottie, Tommy; she saw them all in these nightmares. Occasionally, there were huge dogs with great slobbering jaws jumping out of the fiery inferno to attack her.

On one particular night, the nightmares had been so bad that Evie's screams had woken the whole household. She came to with a start to see Mrs Gordon, Hero, and Andrew, who had recently returned from Gloucestershire, in her room. Their expressions were full of concern.

'I'm sorry,' she mumbled, tears dripping down her distraught face.

'It's alright, Evie.' Hero sat down on the edge of the bed and took her in his arms, where she shuddered against him continuing to weep.

Once she had calmed down, Andrew gave her some laudanum to help her sleep.

When she was resting soundly, Mrs Gordon went back to bed and Hero and Andrew went back upstairs.

'How long will she have these dreams for, Andrew?' Hero asked as they walked into their living room.

'Ahh, it's impossible to say, my friend.' Andrew poured them both a brandy and sat down beside the empty grate. 'In fact, with the experiences you have had, you know more about this than I do.'

Horacio nodded thoughtfully. 'You know it's strange,' he said as he took the armchair opposite, 'I haven't had any bad dreams for a while now, not since the last time I went home. Something has changed. I feel a sense of inner peace.'

'That's good, Hero. It sounds as if you are well and truly on the road to healing.'

'Yes.' Hero smiled as he considered his friend's words, then his expression changed to one of concern. 'What can I do to help Evie?'

'You really do care for her, don't you?' Andrew eyed his friend as he took a sip of his brandy.

'Ha, yes, I do.'

'Why, you're blushing like a love-sick girl.' Andrew chuckled.

Hero joined in.

'You know, I think it was the moment she walked into that hellish room with that poker, she looked like a Valkyrie, her expression was so fierce. She was so brave taking on Jack Barrett, and then freeing myself and Alec; when that bloody beast of a dog could have easily mauled her.'

'Yes, well, it's not surprising that she is having these bad dreams after all that.'

Hero nodded in agreement. 'I think I will ask her to come and stay at Woodley Hall for a while, give her some time to decide what she wants to do. She can also see Sophia while she is there.'

'That is an excellent idea. Sophia can't wait to see her friend. And, as you know, she was devastated to hear about Dottie's death.'

'Yes, well perhaps they can be a comfort for each other.'

When Hero suggested that Evie come and stay at Woodley Hall, she was reluctant at first, but the thought of seeing Sophia swayed her.

'If your mother and cousin are agreeable, I shall stay at Brook House,' Evie declared. 'I would not want to damage your reputation.'

Evie was surprised when Hero burst out laughing. 'As if I give a fig about my reputation, Evie,' he declared.

She found herself smiling warily at his humour. She remembered their long night at the Crown after everything had happened; Hero had not mentioned having a woman in his life, apart from Vanessa Beeching. He hadn't gone into much detail of course, but she had the feeling they had been lovers. The thought of that and the other realisation that he may have a suitor that he had not told her about, made her heart flip most peculiarly; she realised with a jolt that she was jealous. Evie felt a flush of heat blush her cheeks.

'I would like to see your home and meet your mother and your cousin,' she continued, hoping he had not picked up on her embarrassment. 'So, I shall come for a visit as you suggest, but I will stay at an inn or the school.'

'Very well, then.' Hero rolled his eyes but smiled good-naturedly.

Evie, remembering Hero's comment about putting the money she had inherited to good use; had made a contribution to Stuart Boyd to help him set up the free clinic in the East End permanently.

Although she hadn't seen the place, she had also decided to put some money aside to donate to Brook House School, to help with the planned extension that Hero had told her so much about.

While Evie Winters and Horacio Woodley had been tying up all the legal paperwork that involved Jolly Jack Barrett's will, they took some time to scout the streets around Little Back Lane and the docks.

Horacio had told her the story about Mrs Gill, the old woman who had led him to the warehouse that was ablaze. They both wanted to thank her, and hopefully help her out of her dire circumstances.

'I might never have found you if it wasn't for her,' he had explained to Evie.

At first, everyone they had asked about the old Lady told them that they hadn't seen her for months, they all presumed she was dead.

'Aye, she kicked the bucket she did.' Another old crone told them, 'they found er body in the river.'

'When was this?' Horacio asked, a tingle of superstition prickling his scalp.

'Ow the ell do you expect me to remember that!' She had eyed the handsome man with a look of expectation. Hero fished some coins from a money bag and passed them over. 'Aww, it was last winter sometime,' the woman continued as her bony hand closed around the coins.

Evie and Hero exchanged glances; both of them felt goosebumps rise on their skin.

'I don't believe in ghosts,' Horacio said, injecting his voice with what he hoped was strength.

'Neither do I,' Evie answered, however, she shuddered thinking of Mrs Gill and the ghostly image she thought had been Jack but was in fact Tommy Dicken. 'I think we shall have to come to terms with the idea that we shall never find out for sure what happened.'

'Yes,' Hero agreed.

*

Once they had boarded the train and started their journey west, Hero felt this was as good a time as any to explain about Sophia and the baby.

'Evie, there is something I must tell you regarding Sophia.'

Evie pulled her interest away from the passing countryside. She gave Hero a worried look.

'What is it, is something wrong?' She felt her whole body stiffen, ready to receive more bad news.

Hero shook his head, 'No, there is nothing wrong exactly.'

'Well, what is it then?' she found herself snapping at him then immediately regretted it.

Understanding her agitation, Hero was not fazed.

'Both Andrew and Sophia have agreed that I should prepare you, rather than it being a shock.'

She twisted around in her seat so that she was facing him. 'Oh, for goodness sake, Horacio, spit it out.'

Hero lifted a hand. 'Yes, give me a moment. I am getting to the point, which is, I have to say, a delicate subject.'

She reached out a hand to him. Her voice softened; she regretted her irritation. 'Tell me please; you are scaring me.'

Taking her offered hand, he squeezed it gently.

'You know, of course, that Sophia was, mmm.'

'Raped.' Evie offered the word with bitterness, as her stomach flipped with anxiety.

Feeling his cheeks redden, Hero closed his eyes for a moment.

'Yes,' his voice was heavy with emotion. Then he opened his eyes, giving his companion a direct look, he continued. 'I feel the only way to tell you this, is to come straight out with it; Sophia is expecting a child.'

Evie's eyes widened in shock. She pulled her hand out of his grip and covered her face.

'Oh no, oh no.' She shook her head in denial.

'Evie, Evie ...' Hero gently took her hand once more. 'Listen to me, please. Sophia understands that, although the child was conceived in horror, the child is innocent of any wrongdoing. She has accepted this news. She seems quite delighted with it.'

Evie looked at him, her eyes misted with tears. 'Happy about it ...?' Hero nodded. 'There is something else,'

'Oh, Lord.' A tear ran down her cheek.

Hero decided it was best just to carry on with his news. 'As you know, Andrew was the one who attended to Sophia's wounds on that awful night.'

'Yes,' Evie nodded.

'Well, despite everything that had happened, they formed a strong bond. And, when Andrew heard about the baby, he asked Sophia to marry him.'

'Really? Andrew and Sophia are getting married?'

He smiled, 'yes, they are. Sophia thought it would be best if I told you about all this before you are reunited. The pregnancy,' Hero blushed once more, none of this was a subject he was comfortable with, 'is beginning to show.'

Evie let out a strange sound. Hero was unsure if it were a sob or a laugh. She shook her head as she gazed out of the window once more. The countryside went by in a blur.

'I knew she had a big heart.' Her voice was so soft that Hero could barely hear her words. 'but this.'

Placing a hand on her shoulder, he said, 'you need to respect her decision, Evie.'

When she turned back to him, his heart plummeted, her expression was so bleak.

'I'm scared, Horacio, that I will view this child as a constant reminder of what we have all been through.'

'I have to admit that both Andrew and I felt the same way, Evie. We were worried for Sophia that she would feel this way too. However, she is strong and determined. We must all respect her wishes. Actually, I am delighted for Andrew; I have never seen him look so happy. He is quite besotted with her.' As I am with you, he wanted to add but didn't.

'Very well.' Evie swallowed. 'I love Sophia as a sister,' her voice caught, 'and I will love the child as an aunt would.'

'Yes, I believe you will.' He gave her a smile of encouragement.

Chapter 63

Charlie met Hero and Evie at the station, then drove the carriage back to Brook House.

'It is beautiful here,' Evie stated in a soft voice as she took in the scenery and the quaint villages they drove through.

'Yes, it is.' Hero smiled. 'One of my ancestors, Thomas Woodley, found the Hall and fell in love with the place. Especially, the countryside.'

Evie nodded. 'My mother came from Dorset, where she met my father. He lost his job so we moved to London so he could find work. My mother did her best to try and settle there, but we all knew her heart was calling for these green hills.'

'Yes, I can understand that. London has been my temporary home. I have to admit there was a time when I couldn't face coming back to Woodley Hall to live, too many bad memories.'

Evie turned away from the window of the carriage and studied her companion closely. 'That must have been hard for you, Horacio.'

'Bloody hard.' He brushed a hand across his face. 'It seemed as if every corner of the place held awful memories.'

'But you are coming home to live this time,' she pointed out. 'So, what has changed?'

Hero was thoughtful for a moment. 'Last time I came back, mama had placed a portrait on the wall of her office. It was a picture painted not long before the accident and Father's death. We both look so happy in it. Huh,' he made a strange noise, 'this may seem odd; indeed, I can't explain it myself. But when I saw Angelica gazing down at me. It was as if she were in the room, right there with me. I felt a lifting of my heart. The guilt I had been holding on to all these years seemed to drain away.'

Evie reached out a hand to him. 'Oh Hero, that is incredible.'

He smiled, 'yes, it is. I never thought I would be settled in myself enough to face coming back to live at the Hall permanently.'

'And now you are.'

'Yes, I do believe I am.'

*

Sophia was delighted to be back at Brook House. To be reunited with Beth, Emily, and Claire. Not to mention Wilson, who had been missing his master terribly, so was thrilled to see one of his friends.

When Sophia received word from Andrew that Evie had concluded her business in London, and she would soon be travelling to Brook House, Sophia felt excited about seeing her friend again; however, a flutter of apprehension quickly replaced that feeling.

She knew that Evie had been through her own type of hell. Both Horacio and Andrew had mentioned that her friend had bad dreams. Sophia realised that she, herself, had been on the edge of a precipice of despair after she had been raped. Andrew, and her determination, had helped to pull her back from that dark place. Sophia just hoped that she, Andrew and Horacio could do the same for Evie.

When the carriage pulled up at the bottom of the steps leading up to the front door of Brook House, the door was opened before Hero and Evie had a chance to get down from the carriage.

Janice stood at the top of the sweep of steps, then Wilson appeared. He nearly knocked the maid flying as he barrelled down the steps, barking in delight.

Hero held out his arms to the animal. The dog jumped into his embrace, then desperately tried to lick Hero's face.

Evie, a hand fluttering over her heart, laughed. 'Gracious, what a greeting.'

'Yes,' Hero laughed too. 'This, my dear Evie, is Wilson.'

'Oh, goodness, you're here.' Emily came down the steps. She was dressed neatly in a dark blue skirt and a simple cream blouse with a touch of lace at the collar. Her straight chestnut hair had been pulled back into a chignon. Her steps were shadowed by another dog who ran over to Evie with its fronded tail wagging furiously. Evie knelt and stroked the dog's glossy head with a gloved hand.

From the library window, Sophia watched Hero and Evie arriving. She found that she barely recognised her friend: Evie was dressed smartly in a black skirt and closely fitting, tailored jacket. Her hair was pinned atop her head. She wore a small hat which was unadorned of feathers and ribbons, but sat at, what only Sophia could describe as a jaunty angle. Evie's back was straight. She looked very elegant.

With a jolt, Sophia noticed how much older and thinner her friend appeared. Evie's complexion was pale. Her cheekbones were a little too sharply defined. However, when she smiled down at the dog at her feet, she looked like the Evie that Sophia remembered.

Sophia turned away from the window and made her way into the front hall, where she waited for Hero and Evie.

'I am so pleased that you have decided to come and stay here, Evie.' Sophia heard Emily saying as they stepped into the wood-panelled hallway.

'Thank you for agreeing to have me here.' Evie offered Emily a smile, then saw Sophia step into the Hall, Emily hesitated.

The two young women hovered on the parquet floor and gazed at each other, oblivious of the dogs, Hero, Emily, and Janice.

'Oh, Sophia.' Evie rushed to her friend and gathered her in her arms.

'Evie, Evie, Evie.' Sophia hugged her so tightly Evie could barely breathe.

Evie managed to draw away, her face wet with tears. She glanced down at Sophia's belly. 'The baby ...?' there was an edge of caution in her voice.

'Is well.' Sophia smiled.

Evie nodded, then the two fell into another embrace.

'Come, Horacio.' Emily called to her son. 'Come and have some tea with me while we leave these two to get reacquainted.

'I am so terribly sorry about Dottie, Evie.' Sophia said as the two of them walked around the pretty gardens of Brook House. Evie was pleased to stretch her legs after the journey.

Evie nodded, 'Yes, thank you, Sophia. I knew you would be upset about the news.'

'Oh Evie, I can't believe what you have been through.'

Evie paused and took in Sophia's face: she looked very well, Evie thought. Her cheeks were rounded in her heart-shaped face. Her luminous grey eyes sparkled. Her hair was glossy with good health.

'Or you, my dear friend.' She offered Sophia a small smile. 'Although you look the picture of health now.'

Sophia nodded as she took her friend's arm. 'I am well,' she agreed. 'Please do not misunderstand me,' she shuddered, 'that awful night ...' she was interrupted when a blackbird flew down from a treetop, plucked a juicy worm from the grass and hopped into the shrubbery.

'I can't imagine.' Evie squeezed her arm.

'Molly drugged me,' Sophia continued. 'I can't remember much of it, although the following day, I suffered much pain.'

Evie felt a tear rolling down her cheek; she wiped it away. 'I'm sorry,' she murmured.

Throwing her a glance, Sophia said, 'there is no need for you to be sorry, my dear. It was one of the worst things, yes, but strangely what happened has brought me to a wonderful place.'

Evie's smile was wider this time. 'Horacio told me that you and Andrew are to be married.'

Sophia nodded, 'yes, we are.'

Stopping once more, Evie studied her friend's expression. 'Are you sure this is the right thing for you, Sophia? You could find someone to adopt your child, could you not?'

Sophia pulled away from her friend; she gazed out over the brook and the trees beyond. 'That thought did enter my mind,' she pondered, 'but I found that I could not entertain the idea. Then Andrew found out what was happening, and we talked...' She turned her gaze back to Evie. 'I never would have thought it possible, Evie, that one could come to love another person in such a short time. That is how I feel about Andrew.'

Nodding, Evie said, 'Yes, actually I do believe that. You became like a sister to me and Dottie, Sophia.' Suddenly she felt tears brim in her eyes. 'We thought we would never see you again.'

'Oh, my dear.' Sophia rushed over and took the other woman in her arms once more.

Evie was surprised and embarrassed to find herself crying great sobs against her friend's shoulder.

'They have been a while,' Horacio commented as he paced the floor of his mother's office.

'They have a great deal of catching up to do,' Emily commented as she sat back in a chintz upholstered chair and sipped her tea.

Hero glanced at his mother as he pushed his thick hair from his face, 'Yes, yes, of course.'

'You care very much about this Evie person.' His mother eyed him with undisguised interest.

'Yes, well we've been through a lot together.' He sat down in one of the armchairs and crossed his legs.

'Yes, you all have.' She observed.

Restlessly Horacio leant forward, elbows on his knees. His expression was earnest.

'Oh, you should have seen her, mother, she was so brave to help us. Especially up against the likes of Jack Barrett and his cronies.'

'Mmm, well, you know I didn't approve of the company you were keeping, Horacio, but I knew you needed to work through your demons, so I kept my worries to myself.'

'I'm sorry to have worried you, mama. But if it were not for my connections to these people, I would not have been able to help Sophia or Evie.'

Before Emily could comment, the door opened. The two women entered the room.

Hero jumped to his feet. Then when he saw Evie's red eyes, he rushed over to her.

'Are you well, Evie?' his voice was full of concern.

'Yes, it is no matter, Hero. Just an emotional reunion.'

'Of course.' He ushered her to a chair, guiding her gently as if she were an invalid.

Sophia and Emily exchanged glances. Lips raised in knowing smiles.

*

Beth had politely moved out of Sophia's room so that Evie could be close to her friend. Making the most of each other's company before the wedding and Sophia's move to London.

Andrew and Sophia had decided that she would move into his lodgings after the wedding. Mrs Gordon had been delighted to hear this news. Immediately, she had set to, having Horacio's old room turned into a nursery. Both Andrew and Sophia were delighted by Mrs Gordon's enthusiasm.

Sophia ensured that Evie was involved with the planning of the wedding; not that there was much to do, as Emily and Claire had taken over much of the work, insisting that Sophia and Andrew would have a sumptuous wedding breakfast.

The girls attending the school had picked up on the excitement and were like a flock of twittering birds, chatting and giggling about the forthcoming event.

Evie found herself helping with the making of Sophia's dress. It was beautiful, pale grey silk which matched the young woman's eyes—decorated in soft pink and pale green flowers and leaves.

Evie continued to wear black as she was mourning Dottie, although Sophia had persuaded Evie to wear a dress a few shades darker than her own, trimmed in a dove grey. Sophia had also voiced her distress that she and Andrew would be getting married while Evie was still in mourning, but Evie had reassured them that she was happy for them to do so. She stressed most adamantly that they should be married before the baby was born.

'Dottie would have been so happy for you, Sophia.' Evie announced as they sat together, embroidering the flowers around the hem of the dress.

'Yes,' Sophia nodded, her smile was a sad one. 'I do believe she would.'

The days flew by so quickly that Evie didn't have time to dwell on her situation overly much, and she was relieved about that.

*

Sophia and Andrew were married on a bright and sunny spring morning. The bells of the village church rang joyfully.

Sarah and Jasper had been invited, as had Mrs Gordon, who was absolutely delighted to be asked. She had a beaming smile on her face all day.

The girls from the school, along with the staff from Woodley Hall and many of the locals, filled the church.

Evie, who was sitting between Horacio and Emily felt very emotional. She could not help but think how much Dottie would have loved this event. It also occurred to her how different this was to her marriage to Jack Barrett.

She was delighted for Sophia and Andrew: everyone could see that they were deeply in love. But she would miss her friend terribly when she moved to the city. Especially so, during the night.

Since Evie had arrived at Brook House, the two had shared a bedroom. Evie was ashamed somehow to admit that she was still having nightmares about the fires, what she had done to Jack, and the dogs attacking Jack and George Beeching.

Many a night, she had awoken with tear-streaked cheeks and her heart pounding in her chest. Sophia would take her in her arms. Rocking Evie gently, Sophia would croon to her as if she was a small child. Evie felt guilty of depriving her friend of sleep, especially in her condition.

Evie had wondered about moving out of the bedroom, but Sophia had insisted she stay put.

After the wedding breakfast, which everyone had a hand in preparing, Andrew and Sophia, along with Mrs

Gordon, left for London, Charlie driving the Woodley carriage to the station for them.

'Are you well, Evie?' Horacio asked her. He had been looking for her since Sophia and Andrew had left. He discovered her seated on a wrought-iron bench looking out over the woods. The brook chuckled only a few feet away.

He sat down next to her.

'I am well.' She gave him an unconvincing smile.

'Sophia told me that you still have bad dreams.'

'Huh,' Evie jumped to her feet in a rustle of grey silk. 'She really shouldn't have mentioned it.'

Getting to his feet once more. 'She was - ' He shrugged his shoulders, 'is, worried about you, Evie.' He studied her face. She looked pale with dark smudges under her eyes.

Evie nodded. 'That is kind of her, but she need not be.'

Coming to stand beside her at the edge of the water, Hero said, 'I understand from Claire, that Beth will be moving back into your room, and there are two new girls due to arrive next week. Why don't you come and stay at the Hall?' *Let me take care of you;* he wanted to add.

'I'm not sure what I shall do now Sophia has left.' Evie gazed out over the trees. 'Or where I shall go.' She gave a small laugh, 'at least I don't have to worry about money, thanks to Jack Barrett.'

'You're not thinking of leaving, are you?' Hero was surprised at how much that statement had affected him.

Turning haunted eyes upon him, she answered, 'I'm not sure,' her voice was vague. She gestured casually. 'This is a beautiful place, and your mother and Claire, well, everyone really, have been so lovely to me, but I'm not sure that I belong here.'

It suddenly occurred to Horacio that Evie was feeling just as directionless as he had felt until he had come home. He felt more settled in himself now. He was working with Mr Durham, the estate manager, forming plans for the place in the future. James Woodley, Hero's father, had established a good business, and Horacio wanted to keep his legacy alive and expand it.

'You are helping to teach the girls sewing at the school, so I hear.'

'Yes, yes.' Evie found a smile that lightened her expression. 'I must admit I do enjoy that.'

Hero nodded as hope flared. 'Well, that is good. You see, you do have a purpose.'

She sighed as she bowed her head. 'I fear there is something wrong with me, Hero.' When she looked at him once more, her eyes were bleak. 'I feel – I feel broken.'

'Oh, my dear girl.' He stepped forward and gathered her up in his arms.

⸻◆⸻

Chapter 64

Evie felt even more unsettled after Sophia had left for London. Realising then, that she had leant on her friend's support emotionally, because Sophia recognised what she had been through. Surprisingly, Evie felt the same way about Horacio Woodley.

He too, had tasted the evil of those dark streets of London. It seemed to her that both Sophia and Hero could leave the darkness behind. She was not so sure that she was strong enough to do it too.

After three consecutive nights where nightmares had awoken her, and poor Beth had been hovering at the end of the bed not knowing what to do to help; Evie decided that she could not stay at Brook House any longer.

'Horacio has suggested that I go to stay at Woodley Hall,' Evie said to Emily the following morning after a particularly bad night. 'I feel that might be for the best.' Her cheeks burning in embarrassment or mortification. 'I don't want to keep disturbing Beth when I have these bad dreams.'

'Oh, my dear.' Emily got up from her desk. Walking around it to where Evie stood. Emily took the young woman's arm and guided her to one of the armchairs that looked out over the garden. Aware of the bad dreams that Evie was having; her heart went out to her.

'I can still work here?' Evie asked.

'Yes, of course, you can.' Emily sat down, as did Evie. The older woman gave her a concerned look. 'Perhaps we should get Dr Scott to attend to you.'

Evie shook her head. 'No, I do realise that I am the only one who can fight these demons.'

Thinking of the dark times she went through after losing James and Angelica, Emily found her eyes prickling with tears for this young woman.

'You must remember, Evie, that you have the support of all of us here.'

'Yes, thank you.' Evie found a grateful smile for her companion. 'Do you think it would be alright to accept Horacio's offer? If I do so, it will probably cause gossip hereabouts.'

Emily gave a little chuckle, which reminded Evie of when Hero laughed at her previous misgivings.

'Oh, my dearest, this family has never stuck to what people perceive as convention. When James and I married, my family were not pleased. Then when Claire married Seth, well that just added to the mix.' She gave Evie a long look. 'Horacio cares for you, you know.'

Glancing down at her hands which were resting in her lap, Evie nodded. 'As I do, him. I don't know what I would have done without his support.'

'Yes.' Emily reached out and picked up one of Evie's hands, her skin felt chilled. 'Go and stay at the Hall for a while, my dear. Give yourself time to work out what you wish to do for the future. There is no rush to make any decisions.'

'Thank you.' Evie's smile was one of relief.

*

Horacio was thoroughly delighted when Evie told him she would like to take up his offer to stay at Woodley Hall. He understood the reason why she had made the choice; so, he kept his feelings of elation in check.

He recognised Evie's strength of character; therefore, he could also see how close she was to breaking point emotionally.

It was strange he pondered, how she could deal with so much, but then, when she was in a place of safety, the demons had arisen in force. He resolved to help her as much as he possibly could.

At first, Evie was overwhelmed by the size of Woodley Hall. She didn't just have a bedroom, but a dressing room, bathing room and a sitting room of her very own. The room that she, Dottie, and her mother, had shared at Little Back Lane was tiny in comparison.

It also felt alien to her to have Janice and another maid, called Ruby, waiting on her. Yes, she had had Mrs Perkins as a housekeeper and Ivy as a maid when she was married to Jack, but they had been quite informal – more like a family. When she thought about them, she was surprised to feel a tug on her heart. She would never have thought she would miss anybody from that life, except for Dottie, of course.

As well as her suite of rooms, there was also a huge library at the Hall. Evie could not help the excitement she felt as Hero showed her around the place.

'This is bigger than the bookstore in London,' she exclaimed as she wandered around the large room.

'Yes, it is rather spectacular,' Hero smiled, relieved to see the shadow lift from Evie's expression, even if it were only momentarily.

Hero encouraged Evie to come out with him so that he could show her around the countryside and the Woodley estate; the two of them took long walks through the woods and hills together, with Wilson running beside them or running off chasing rabbits. Occasionally, they took Mable, Emily's spaniel with them.

It surprised Evie, and scared her just a little bit, how much Hero's company comforted her; maybe it was their shared losses and the guilt they recognised in each other that brought them closer together, but every time she saw him, Evie could not deny that she felt a stirring in her heart. It was almost painful: she had worked so hard to set her feelings aside, to turn off her emotions; to cage her heart within protective walls, she was finding it difficult, and quite frightening, to allow herself to open up to these people, especially Hero.

The fear overwhelmed her at times, so she would go off on her own, allowing the beauty of the spring sunshine and the verdant countryside to soothe her.

*

Vanessa Beeching sat at a table at a popular café that overlooked Central Park.

Ever since she and William had arrived in New York, she could not get over the energy that abounded: there were people everywhere one looked.

The building work and construction in the city were ceaseless. The energy was one of hustle and bustle. She loved the vibrancy of the place.

William had settled into his new school. Vanessa was surprised to find herself feeling content in her life. Although, she knew she would have to find some sort of work, something that would support herself and William for the future.

This notion made her take a long hard look at herself, what skills did she have? She had lived such a sheltered life, first at home, then with George. She had never needed to consider working until now.

Vanessa had just drained her coffee cup when she saw a familiar figure coming towards her. The man was Bernard Warren, a friend and colleague of Mr Stokes, the Woodley family solicitor. They met up once a fortnight to exchange news.

Even though she had been careful, changing their names; she was now Valerie Brown, and William's new name was Robert.

These meetings made her anxious, She was always worried about what she would hear from England; would George find out where she and William were?

'Good afternoon, Mrs Brown.' Bernard lifted his hat in a gesture of greeting.

'Good afternoon, Mr Warren. Do sit. I shall order us some more of this excellent coffee.'

'Ahh, for that, I would be much obliged.' Taking off his hat and laying it on the table, he sat down opposite her. Waited until she had dismissed the waitress, then slid an envelope over the red and white checked tablecloth.

Vanessa recognised Hero's handwriting. Her stomach somersaulted in anticipation.

She opened the envelope with a butter knife, pulling out the single piece of paper inside.

"Dearest V," Hero had written, in his untidy scrawl. *"I hope this finds you and William well. Do not stress, my dear, but I must inform you of two grave pieces of news; your husband, George Beeching, is dead, and your father-in-law Ernest Beeching has also passed away. It is finally safe for you and William to return to England.*

With the very kindest of regards,

Horacio Woodley."

'Good news?' Mr Warren asked as he tried to decipher her expression.

'Of a sort.' Vanessa found her hands were shaking as she folded up the letter and put it in her reticule.

As the waitress appeared and placed a tray down on the table, a flock of doves rose into the air from the park opposite. Vanessa watched the birds fly up into the splendid clear blue sky. She smiled to see their beautiful white wings catch the sunlight.

Vanessa poured out coffee for herself and her guest.

'Mr Warren, I wonder if I could trouble you to book passages back to England for myself and William.'

He raised an eyebrow, noticing that she had used her son's real name. Ahh, something major had occurred, but it was not his place to ask questions.

'Of course, dear lady. When are you proposing to leave?'

'As soon as possible.' She sipped her beverage.

'And will you be returning to our fair city?' he asked. He admired this woman and was hoping for more time to get to know her.

'I think not.' She set her cup aside, then rose to her feet. Mr Warren followed suit. 'Let me know when you have the tickets.'

'Of course, Mrs Brown.'

She reached out a hand to him, 'It's Lady Beeching, actually.'

He nodded his head, his lips curling into a half-smile. He took her hand and brought it to his lips.

'Your ladyship,' he acknowledged. He hadn't known what was in the missive. However, he understood enough about their circumstances to realise any danger she and her son had faced was now over.

With a brief nod, she picked up her lace gloves then slipped them on. She made an elegant figure in her smart outfit of taupe silk.

When she walked along the pavement away from him, the brightness of the sun set her hair aflame.

Ahh, he was going to miss these meetings, Mr Warren thought with regret as he drained his coffee cup.

*

It was a Saturday morning, Evie and Hero sat at the table in the sun brightened breakfast room at Woodley Hall.

Evie was buttering a slice of toast. She was just about to spoon up some of Mrs Adam's delightful gooseberry jam when Janice walked in with the post. The maid presented it to Hero on a silver tray along with a letter opener.

'Your post, sir.'

Evie hid a bemused smile; she found these traditions to be so formal and outdated.

'Thank you, Janice.' Hero scooped the envelopes from the tray. 'You may go.' He dismissed the maid.

'Ahh, there's one for you, Evie.' Hero glanced at the envelope, 'Looks like Sophia's writing.' He handed the letter to her.

'Of course it's from Sophia,' Evie smiled, 'who else would be writing to me.'

'Ha, yes.' Hero laughed.

Sophia wrote to Evie every week without fail. Evie very much looked forward to hearing from her; she was well and had settled into her life with Andrew quickly. Evie was delighted that her friend was so happy.

'Ahh,'

Evie looked up. 'Not bad news, I hope?'

He shook his head, 'No, it's from Vanessa, she and William are on their way home.'

Her stomach gave a curious little skip, Evie frowned as she studied her companion. 'Well, you must be pleased to hear that?'

'Yes,' he looked at her with a beaming smile. 'I am, indeed.'

Suddenly losing her appetite, Evie pushed her plate away.

'If you will excuse me.' Popping Sophia's letter in the pocket of her dark blue skirt, she got to her feet.

'Yes, of course.' Hero was distracted by Vanessa's letter and didn't notice Evie's shadowed expression as she left the room.

'I'm leaving for London, mama,' Hero told his mother later in the day. 'Vanessa Beeching is on her way back from New York. I feel I must be there to greet her when she gets back and update her, let her know what has transpired during her absence.'

'Do you really need to go, Horacio?' His mother studied him. She was sitting behind the desk in her office at Brook House. 'Can't you leave all that to Mr Stokes or the Beeching solicitor?'

'Vanessa is coming home as the trustee of her son's inheritance, and the only family she has, apart from William, is Margot Beeching. You know what she is like, mama, a cold fish to say the very least.' He started pacing the floor. 'You know she hates Vanessa. Why, she was complicit with George's plans to lock Vanessa up, she had a lucky escape.'

'Mmm, yes, that was an utter disgrace. I know there is no love lost between them; however, they must learn to get on, for William's sake.'

'Yes, that is true.' Hero gazed out of the window overlooking the pretty gardens. The roses were coming into bloom.

'What about Evie?' Emily asked.

Hero turned back to look at his mother, 'I think she will cope without me for a day or two.'

'Is she still getting bad dreams, do you know?' Emily's voice was full of concern.

'I don't think so. Indeed, Evie is looking brighter in herself.'

Emily nodded, 'Yes, now you mention it, when I have seen her taking lessons, she does look well.'

Hero shrugged, 'There, you see, nothing to worry about.' He strolled around the desk, kissed his mother on the forehead and left her so that he could ride back on Hades to the Hall.

*

Evie could not quite understand why it was, that this house felt so much bigger and emptier with Horacio away. Without his presence, she felt strangely adrift; it seemed like the heart had gone out of the place.

Sitting on the window seat of her bedroom, she looked out over the moonlit gardens below. It looked as if all the colour had been drained from the land; it was monochrome and hard-edged.

Restlessly, she got up and paced her bedroom floor. She wore her long white nightdress. When she caught sight of herself in her dressing-table mirror, she looked ghostly. An entity that belonged to another time. An alien in this gracious house. The thought unsettled her even more.

Picking up her robe, she slipped it on, then made her way downstairs to the library.

Scouring the shelves, she picked out two books. Making herself comfortable beside the empty fireplace, she drew a lamp close and opened the first book.

It wasn't long, however, when she realised that not even the story of Uncle Toms Cabin, by the American author, Harriet Beecher Stowe could hold her interest.

Glancing at the French clock on the mantle, she saw that it was nearly one o'clock in the morning. She wondered what Hero was doing; was he out with Vanessa Beeching? Or perhaps they were in bed together, making love right at this moment. Evie felt a sharp pain in her chest. It made her want to double over. She shook her head as tears moistened her eyes.

'You are so ridiculous, Evie Winters!' she admonished herself, as she set the two books down on a side table. You are in love with Horacio Woodley - you have to admit it to yourself! She wiped the tears from her eyes. She knew that he and Vanessa had been lovers, that Hero felt affection for this older woman, but did he love her?

Her husband was dead. She was a widow; Evie snorted, as she was herself, of course. Vanessa was a widow and free to marry again once her time of mourning had elapsed. And let's face it, Evie thought bitterly, this woman is far more suited to being a mistress of a grand house like Woodley Hall! She was born to it.

Despite herself, Evie found herself trying to imagine being mistress of this place – the idea was simply beyond her.

Suddenly, she made up her mind that she had to leave. It would be far too painful to see Horacio every day; to see him married to Vanessa or another woman from a wealthy family! Someone who would naturally want her gone from under this roof.

Feeling anxious and claustrophobic in this huge house, Evie gasped as if in pain.

The following morning, Evie sought out Emily, who was taking an English class.

Noticing how grave her expression looked, Emily handed over the class to one of the older girls and took Evie through to her office.

'What on earth is the matter, Evie?' She ushered her to sit, but the younger woman remained standing.

'I have decided to leave, Mrs Woodley.'

'Leave?' Emily sat down on the chair behind her desk. 'What on earth for, I thought you were happy here, Evie.'

'In many ways, I am.' She tried a smile of reassurance which didn't quite work. 'Ever since everything from my previous life has been concluded, I have been feeling directionless.'

'Well, yes. I can understand that.' Emily nodded thoughtfully. 'But you have a purpose here, Evie. I was hoping you would stay on as a teacher at Brook House.'

Evie bobbed her head, she walked over to the window and looked out; it was such a pretty garden which was beginning to fill with summer blooms.

'That is kind of you,' she acknowledged.

'Evie.' Emily got up and came to stand beside her. She was shorter than the younger woman by at least half a foot. 'This has something to do with Horacio, doesn't it?' Shooting the other woman a look of surprise, Evie felt her cheeks begin to burn. 'He admires you greatly, you know,' Emily said before Evie could form a reply.

'As I do him.'

'Then why leave?'

Her expression when she turned to Emily was distraught.

'But that is the problem, don't you see. I cannot live here while he marries another woman, possibly this Vanessa Beeching, he loves her.'

'It *was* more like an infatuation,' Emily spoke up. 'Of course, I heard from the gossips that the two of them were having an affair. I disapproved, but there was little I could say.'

'But she is back now, and free to marry,' Evie pointed out. 'That changes everything does it not?'

It was Emily's turn to take in the view. 'We've been through so much together, Horacio and I,' she said thoughtfully. 'I knew he had withdrawn into himself because he felt guilty about what happened to Angelica and his papa. It didn't matter how many times I reassured him. It made no difference. He is sensitive and kind-hearted; he always has been.'

'Yes,' Evie replied softly, 'I can believe that.'

Emily nodded. 'I have seen such a change in him recently; he's turned a corner.' She gave a little laugh, 'we both have.' Gazing at her companion, Emily continued. 'This change I see in Hero has a great deal to do with you, Evie.'

'Me!' She gave Emily a look of disbelief.

'Yes, you.'

The young woman shook her head. 'I am just one of the people he has *saved*.'

'Ha, yes, Hero living up to his name.' Emily took Evie's hand in her own. 'Yes, that may have been a part of it, to begin with, my dear, but I really do feel that his affection for you has bloomed beyond a simple desire to help and support you.' Emily smiled. 'When dear Sophia and Andrew got married, Hero could barely take his eyes off you. I saw love in those eyes.'

Evie's heart skipped a beat. She wanted to believe the words she was hearing, but she shook her head vigorously.

'No!' Evie pulled her hand away. Her expression bleak. 'I-I can't.'

'Can't what, Evie?' Emily's voice was full of concern.

'I feel so empty inside. I'm not sure I have the capacity within me to love Horacio back; to love anyone for that matter.'

'Of course you have, Evie.' Emily stood her ground. 'Why did you come to see me today?'

Evie shot her companion a surprised look. 'You know why, Mrs Woodley, I can't live here, and watch Horacio marry another woman.'

'Ha, yes exactly, my dear. And why do you think that should be, Evie?' Emily pushed. 'Why does it hurt you so much to think that way? You've already said how much you admire my son.' Emily watched as a myriad of expressions clouded the younger woman's face.

'Yes, yes. I ...' Evie's voice petered out.

'You love him?' Emily encouraged gently.

'Oh, Lord.' Evie sat down in one of the armchairs. She let out a breath, 'Yes – yes, I love him.'

Chapter 65

Vanessa Beeching had arrived back in London after a long voyage across the Atlantic.

Both George and his father had already been buried, so she had not attended either funeral. She was rather relieved about that; she was pleased she did not need to go through the sham of being the grieving widow.

The journey had given her time to think. She knew that she would still have to face another threat in the form of her mother-in-law, Margot.

If it were not for William and his rightful inheritance, Vanessa mused, she would never return to England. She would have left Margot to take over the house, title, and grounds, to let her do with them what she will. However, due to everything that had transpired, Vanessa needed to face the woman, to ensure that William would be able to claim his inheritance when he came of age.

When Vanessa and William arrived back in the city, they took up residence in the London house.

It wasn't long before Margot got wind of the news that her daughter-in-law and grandson were back in the country. As soon as she heard, Margot travelled down from the estate in Norfolk.

Vanessa had to steel herself when Margot and her retinue of servants turned up. She was grateful that Horacio had insisted he stay to support her during the encounter.

Margot, looking elegant in a black silk day dress, walked into the drawing-room with an air of confidence and belonging.

'So, you have finally shown your face.' She looked Vanessa up and down. A sneer shadowed her expression. Then she turned to Horacio. 'And what is *he* doing here?'

'Horacio is here to support me.' Vanessa stood by the empty fireplace.

The June day was pleasantly warm, the sun slanted through the tall Georgian windows.

'Ha, to support you, or climb between those wanton thighs,' Margot scoffed. Vanessa's face blanched, but she said nothing. Waving a gloved hand in her general direction, the older woman took a seat. 'Ah, you think we didn't know about your affair ...'

'I am so pleased to hear that you are so well informed, Lady Beeching,' Hero spoke up, 'you will ultimately know then, just what a monster your son really was.'

Margot shot Hero a dark look. He was satisfied, however, to see a mixture of fear and uncertainty flickering in her eyes.

'I don't know what you mean.'

'Well then, let me spell it out for you.' Hero sat down and crossed his legs, Vanessa also sat down, but she was perched on the edge of her seat as anxiety sped up her heart. 'When Vanessa had to escape the threat of being locked away in an asylum, I had my solicitor, Mr Stokes, hire a man to track down victims of your son's abuse.' It was Margot's turn to go as white as a sheet. 'As luck would have it,' Hero continued, 'we found several women who had been grievously used by him. And that included a woman who was in your employ when George was a mere thirteen years of age. Then we found two young maids who worked in this very house. They have all made statements, Margot. Of course, George cannot be brought to justice now, but I do think that fate took a hand in that.' Hero gave her a hard smile. 'If you make life difficult for either Vanessa or William, these statements will become public knowledge.'

'But that will ruin the Beeching reputation.' Margot shot Vanessa a hard look.

'Yes, to an extent,' Vanessa spoke up. 'William and I, are the innocent victims in this, Margot, we are ready to weather the storm, are you?'

The woman dropped her head. She couldn't look her daughter-in-law in the eye any longer. Oh Lord, she had known that there was something wrong with George, she hadn't wanted to face it. Margot lifted her head and pulled back her shoulders.

'Very well, what do you wish me to do?'

'William and I will stay here in London. I have already sent word to the staff in Norfolk; they will close up the big house. When you travel back, you can take up residence in the Dower House.'

For a moment, both Vanessa and Hero thought that the older woman would dig her heels in; however, it only took a moment before Margot nodded in agreement. 'If that is your wish.'

Oh, it is.' Vanessa gave the woman a cold smile.

'That went better than expected,' Hero commented once Margot had left.

It had been agreed that Margot would not stay at the house, but would take a suite at a London hotel, then travel back to Norfolk the following day.

'Oh, I am trembling.' Vanessa took a seat in one of the armchairs.

'In relief, I hope?' Hero eyed her with concern, then went over to the sideboard and poured them both a healthy tot of brandy.

'Thank you,' Vanessa smiled at him gratefully as she took the proffered glass, she took a sip, nodded then set the glass down. 'Yes, relief in many ways, but also sadness, Horacio.' She wrung her hands together in anxiety. 'It really shouldn't be like this. Will has been cheated of a father, grandfather and now a grandmother.'

Hero was distressed to see tears in her eyes. Sitting down beside her, he gently picked up her hands. They were chilly, so he rubbed them together to illicit some warmth. 'You have me,' Hero found himself saying. 'I will always be a friend to you.'

She pulled her hands away, giving him a melancholy smile. 'Ahh, you are so sweet, Horacio. But I don't know what Evie Winters will think if we continue our, umm, friendship.'

Sweeping his dark hair from his forehead, he stood up. 'What does all this have to do with Evie?'

'Oh darling, Hero, I don't think you have realised that you have sung her many praises to me; how strong she is, and how brave she is … etc.' Vanessa laughed. 'What with that and the way your face lights up when you speak of her. It is literally written all over your face, my dear, you love this young woman.'

Hero puffed out his cheeks in resignation. He flopped back in the armchair. 'Oh Lord, is it that obvious?'

'Yes, my dear, it is.'

After his talk with Vanessa regarding his feelings for Evie, Hero suddenly felt an urgent need to get back to Woodley Hall – he needed to tell Evie how he felt about her.

Uncertainty oiled his belly with nervous energy, and when he had been presented with his supper at the hotel where he was staying, Hero found he couldn't eat a morsel of it. To calm his nerves, He drank half a bottle of good claret, then wished he hadn't. Deciding it was no good, He made up his mind to travel back to Gloucestershire the following day.

*

After seeing Emily that morning, then teaching two lessons after luncheon. Evie walked back to Woodley Hall through the woods.

She felt exhausted, but it wasn't from physical activity; this was emotional tiredness – she felt drained, especially when she considered the revelation that Emily Woodley had presented her with; she loved Horacio Woodley, she loved Horacio Woodley – this awareness should make her heart feel glad, should it not? Evie mulled, as she bent her head to walk under a low bough.

Wilson, who had been decidedly dejected since Hero had left for London, went running past her. He was chasing invisible rabbits. His enthusiasm for the game made Evie's lips turn up into a smile.

The early summer sun dipped in the sky, blushing the clouds with apricot and peach. Oh, this was a wonderful place, Evie thought, Dottie would have loved it here, and so would their mother.

Not particularly eager to get back to the Hall, Evie found her booted feet taking a path that was unfamiliar to her. Before she knew it, the woods opened up.

She found herself on the fence line to the orchards. The sun's warmth and June showers were helping to ripen the fruit on the trees; they would be ready for picking come September or October, so she gathered from Seth, Claire's husband, who was the groundsman here.

Her heart skipped a beat when she saw the huge oak tree flanking the woods from the orchard. Oh Lord, this was where it had happened, wasn't it? The place of Horacio's nightmares. Evie's steps were unsure, yet she felt a pull, a need to explore the place, and its ghosts.

She halted on the shadow line where the huge branches spread above her. Evie closed her eyes for a moment. No breeze disturbed the boughs. The only sounds she could hear were the buzzing of insects and Wilson barking at something a way off.

She took some steady breaths, but then jumped when she felt a hand touch her shoulder. Evie spun around, expecting someone to be standing behind her. A puzzled look creased her brow when she found she was alone. At that moment, Wilson appeared, as he did so, the leaves above her ruffled as if a wind had sprung up. Wilson came to stand next to her, but his head was thrust forward, his nose twitching in curiosity. When his stumpy tail started to wag, he took a few hesitant paces forward.

'What is it, Wilson?' Evie found her throat was dry as she watched the little dog. She swallowed as the breeze increased, a spiral of dry leaves beneath the tree danced. Wilson wagged his tail harder and yipped at the strange manifestation. Evie, her skin prickling, stepped back. Just as rapidly as it had started, the strange phenomenon died away; everything was still once more.

Not realising she had been holding her breath, Evie let out a sob of pure emotion. Despite herself, she felt her eyes prick with tears; Oh God, not again. Wiping the back of her hand over her eyes in frustration, she was heartfully sick of crying.

Get a grip, Evie; she admonished herself. Yet, she found she could not stop her eyes misting as her heart contracted painfully in her chest.

Through her blurred vision, something on the bark of the tree caught her attention, she stepped under the boughs and saw the initials H.W and A.W carved there; Hero Woodley and Angelica Woodley.

Tracing the letters with her fingers, she felt that strange prickling feeling happening once more. Looking upwards, she could see the canopy of trees above her. As the sun rested on the horizon, it set the leaves aflame. Suddenly, finding her legs had become weak, she slid her back down the trunk of the tree. She sat amongst the gnarled roots and gazed out over the woods.

Evie wasn't sure how long she had been seated there, but the sun had gone down. The sky was the dark blue of a summer night.

Wilson, realising that Evie wasn't going to return to the Hall just yet, sighed and settled down beside her. Evie rubbed his ears distractedly, the little dog accepted this fuss as consolation, although he had been looking forward to his supper.

When the dog's head popped up, his tail started to wag, Evie looked out over the orchard. A shadowy form on a horse was coming towards her.

Wilson took off like a rocket, yipping happily.

Evie's breath caught in her throat when she realised it was Horacio. He was back.

Getting to her feet, she brushed down the skirts of her black dress, then tucked some stray curls behind her ears.

'Evie,' Horacio called, he brought Hades to a halt as the little dog danced around them. Then he dismounted, leaving Hades and Wilson to greet each other.

Hero's glance took in the tree, then came to rest on Evie's face, pale in the dappled, soft shadows.

'I've been looking for you. Mother told me you had left Brook House for the day, so I expected to find you at the Hall when you weren't there – I, umm, thought you had left.'

'No, I haven't left, as you can see.' She offered him a thin smile.

'Yes, so I see.' He gave her an uncertain smile in return. 'And I am extremely thankful for that.'

'How did your business with Vanessa Beeching go?' She asked as she stepped out from under the tree.

'Well enough.' Hero pushed back his unruly hair from his forehead. As she approached him, he could see that she had been crying.

'Evie, are you well?' He closed the gap between them, lifting a hand he pressed it to her cheek. She gazed at him with large eyes; her expression was unfathomable.

'Mother told me you were thinking of leaving, please don't say it's true. I umm, don't think I could bear it if I lost you.'

Closing her eyes, Evie revelled in his touch. She brought her hand up and covered his.

'I'm scared, Horacio,' she said softly. She didn't move; neither did he.

'What of, my love?'

Opening her eyes, Evie studied him closely.

'I have lost everyone I have ever loved, Horacio, I told you once I was broken, do you remember?'

'Yes, of course, I remember, it broke my heart to hear you say that.'

Evie nodded. 'It may take some time before I can open my heart completely to you.'

'Oh, Evie.' He gathered her up in his arms. She stiffened for a moment, and Hero thought she was going to pull away, then he sighed in relief as he felt her relax against him. 'I love you so much, Evie Winters,' he said, 'with all my heart.

She drew back a little and gazed up at him. 'Do you mean that?'

'Oh yes, oh yes, of course, I mean it.' He shrugged his shoulders. 'I'm a terrible liar.' He offered her a smile.

She smiled up at him, searching his expression. Ahh, she knew he loved her. In that very moment, she felt her heart open up, petals of a delicate flower opening to receive the joy of the sun.

'And I do believe that I love you back, Horacio Woodley. It is a strange feeling after everything that has happened, but I think I could get used to it.'

Hero and Evie didn't have to announce to the world that they loved each other; people began to notice the intimate smiles. The tenderness between them - that when they walked together, they held hands.

It felt as if the whole estate and everyone at Brook House were waiting for an announcement, although they realised that Evie was still in mourning for her sister. No one judged the two; they were simply happy to see Horacio Woodley smiling again.

Neither Hero nor Evie felt as if they needed to rush things. Both of them were happy to allow their relationship to blossom naturally.

They enjoyed being in each other's company, and that was enough for the time being.

*

Horacio wasn't sure if Evie had noticed the significance of the date that was fast approaching. She hadn't said anything to him, and he felt he did not want to bring up the subject. Evie was doing so well; she seemed happy. He didn't want anything to jeopardise that feeling of wellbeing, but there was no getting away from the fact that it had been nearly a year since Dottie's death.

'I wonder if you would accompany me on a trip to London?' Evie asked him as they sat and ate supper in the small dining room of the Hall that evening.

He lay down his knife and fork and gave her a long look.

'You wish to visit Dottie's grave?' he speculated.

'Yes, I do.' She nodded. Picking up a tumbler of water, she took a sip. 'I would like to lay some flowers on the grave.'

'Yes, of course. Shall we visit Andrew and Sophia while we are in town?'

'That would be wonderful. We won't be forgiven if we don't.'

'Ah, yes, quite true.' Hero laughed, pleased to see that she was still in good humour.

Horacio stood a respectable distance away while Evie placed a bouquet of pink roses on Dottie's grave.

She stood there in the cemetery for a long moment. Hero wondered what was going through her mind.

Evie made an elegant figure in her navy blue travelling outfit. The blouse she wore under the fitted jacket had a froth of white lace at the neck. Emily had presented Evie with a beautiful sapphire brooch which James had given her; Evie wore the brooch on the silk lapel of her jacket. It was the first time that Hero had seen her wearing something feminine and pretty.

Evie looked up, seeking his gaze where he stood leaning against the wall. Her eyes sparkled with tears, but she smiled and nodded.

Hero strode over to her and took her arm. Together they left the small graveyard and walked under the lychgate into the street.

After hailing a cab, they headed to Horacio's former lodging house.

Evie and Sophia sat on a tartan rug near the fireplace, playing with the baby, who, at the age of five months, was sitting up and taking an interest in the world.

Sophia had given birth to a daughter who they had decided to name Rebecca Doretha, Rebecca for Sophia's grandmother, and Doretha for Dottie. She was a beautiful baby with a head full of soft dark curls and eyes as large and luminous as her mother's.

While the two women were distracted by the baby, Andrew took the opportunity to talk to his friend.

'Evie is looking well,' he remarked as he sat back on one of the dining chairs while tucking into a slice of Mrs Gordon's fruit cake.

'She is, Andrew, thank God.'

'So, have you asked her yet?' Andrew gave his friend an amused glance as Hero blushed.

Taking a sip of his tea, he then remarked. 'I want to, desperately, but I never know when it will be a good time.'

'Oh, she's so clever!' Sophia enthused as Rebecca knocked down some wooden bricks that Evie had stacked up for her. The baby chuckled in delight, and the women laughed.

Andrew brushed some cake crumbs from his shirt. 'After today Evie will be out of mourning.'

'I know.'

'So, when you get back to Gloucestershire, there is nothing to stop you.'

'Only nerves, my friend.' Hero gave him a rueful smile.

'Nervous that she will say no?'

'Yes, or worse, I could frighten her off, then she runs away.'

'Horacio Woodley, you must be blind, man, she adores you, every time she looks at you, she glows.'

Hero shot him a questioning glance, 'Really?'

Andrew rolled his eyes, 'Yes, really.'

*

Two days later, when Evie and Horacio had arrived back at Woodley Hall, they settled back into their routine.

Evie was teaching a class at the school and Hero had a meeting with Mr Durham, the estate manager.

After the meeting had ended, Hero found himself feeling restless, so he decided to ride Hades up into the hills with Wilson joyfully running behind.

Reaching a high peak which had a wonderful view of the Cotswolds, Hero brought Hades to a halt. He dismounted and left the animal to graze and Wilson to run after rabbits which he had no chance of catching.

Hero walked the grassy hillock, back and fore. 'Evie Winters, I love you, will you marry me?' 'Evie, you know I love you, I, umm, can't imagine life without you ...' He swept his unruly hair back from his forehead. Oh Lord, he really should have asked Andrew for some tips. But then again, for Sophia and Andrew, it had been a mutual decision between them, and Sophia's delicate condition had complicated the circumstances.

He sat down on the mossy hillock and plucked a daisy from the grass. Hero smiled to himself, he could remember Angelica pulling daisy petals and reciting the rhyme; "He loves me, he loves me not ..."

Feeling utterly foolish, Hero found himself plucking the flower petals. When he ended on "she loves me..." he smiled with resolve. Called to Hades, mounted then called Wilson, Hero did not head back to the Hall, but Brook School.

The tall windows were open, sunshine, along with the fresh country air, made the room bright.

Evie, who was taking a handwriting and reading class, walked up and down the rows of desks. She had ten pupils in her class, ageing from eleven to fourteen.

All the girls were diligently copying down letters in copperplate script.

'That's excellent, Annie.' Evie nodded her head with approval.

The girl looked up at her, the praise of achievement shone in her eyes.

'Thank you, Miss Evie.'

Evie returned her smile, just as she did so, a commotion outside caught their attention.

'What the...' Evie stepped over to one of the windows to see Hero bring Hades to a halt on the lawn outside, a panting Wilson dancing around the horse's hooves.

Evie watched quite mesmerised as he dismounted. Hero was wearing tight riding breeches and a white shirt under his unbuttoned jacket. His hair was untidy; his face was flushed with fresh air and exertion.

'What's Mr Woodley doing, Miss?' Annie asked. All the girls had assembled by the windows.

'Umm, I'm not sure.' Evie swallowed as Hero, who did not glance at the windows, strode with an air of determination across the lawn.

They heard the front door open. All eyes, including Evie's, looked to the classroom door. Sure enough, it opened.

Hero did not hesitate in the doorway but walked between the desks. His gaze was upon Evie, who stood stock still, a ray of sunlight caressing her beautiful face.

Nervously, the girls looked at each other, someone giggled.

'What on earth is going on, Horacio?' Emily appeared in the doorway. She had seen him arrive from her office window.

Hero said nothing, but when he reached Evie, he leant over and took one of her hands in his.

'Evie Winters – Evie, I love you so much it hurts. God, please put me out of my misery, say you will marry me, please.'

The whole room seemed to retreat until it was only the two of them standing in the sunlight. The girls and Emily held their breath.

Evie studied Hero's handsome face as if she were drinking it in for the first time.

Her lips turning up into a smile, she said, 'Yes – Oh, yes, Horacio Woodley, I will marry you.'

They both laughed as the room erupted in girlish giggles and cheers.

'Come now; the class is over for today.'

Emily, a huge grin on her face, ushered the girls out of the room. As Evie stepped into Hero's arms, Emily shut the classroom door behind her.

Epilogue

The Indian summer was over; there had been a frost during the night, a prelude to winter. The trees looked magnificent in their cloaks of autumn colours.

The small village church was crowded; everyone wanted to see Mr Woodley marry the young woman who had captured his heart.

Evie looked beautiful as she walked up the aisle. She was dressed in a silk dress, the colour of soft heather. Her thick, curling hair was pinned atop her head, making her look taller. She walked with dignified grace. Her bouquet was one of late summer roses, supplied by Seth Jacobs. The church had also been decorated with roses and ivy.

Sophia was there with Andrew by her side. Sophia held baby Rebecca up so she could see what was going on. The baby blew spittle bubbles and giggled happily, making those close by smile widely.

Sophia and Andrew had travelled up from London, along with Mrs Gordon, who had been thoroughly delighted to have been invited. She sat beside Sophia.

Having no children or grandchildren of her own, she had adopted baby Rebecca, caring for her and loving her as only a proud grandma could.

Walking up the aisle alone, Evie felt so many emotions that nothing made sense to her, so she focused on Hero's steady gaze. Her eyes locked with his, their smiles a perfect match. He looked so handsome dressed in his finery, but her smile widened when his hair flopped over his forehead. Ahh, he always had a dishevelled air to him, and that was just one small aspect of this man that she loved.

Hero watched Evie walking towards him; He felt that glow in his heart that only seemed to manifest when she was close to him; a feeling of deep love. He knew that they were kindred souls, meant to be together. They had both been badly hurt early in life, but they were healing each other.

Wilson, sitting next to Hero, wagged his tail joyfully to see Evie. Everyone laughed when the little dog ran to meet her and jumped up at her skirts, expecting fuss. Evie bent down and stroked his head. Then Bryant stepped forward and scooped the little dog up. He received a lick on his chin for his efforts.

Evie's heart was fluttering in her chest. Overawed by her emotions; she had been glad of Wilson's comical interjection.

Wishing that her mother and Dottie could have been here to see her married. Just as she entertained that thought, the sun shone through the stained-glass window with such brightness; it made Evie blink.

The autumnal sun was infused with such benevolence, that Evie felt her nerves lift, and her smile broaden; the manifestation reminded her of what had happened the day that she had visited the old oak tree.

Hero beamed at his bride to be. He had never seen her look more beautiful. Holding out his hand to her, Evie took it, as she did so, she felt a great sense of the *rightness* of the moment. Happiness washed through her.

Hero too felt the pull on his heart; they had been drawn together by their mutual losses.

As they stood together at the altar of the pretty village church, they both felt bathed with feelings of love and finally, belonging.

⸻◆⸻